A Time to Love

'I'll get you a drink,' said Grant, who looked more in need of one than she was. Several people stopped him on his way to the long refectory table and there were women among them who seemed, to Sophie, to know him well. She leaned against the window-frame feeling rather peculiar, the thought having just occurred to her that perhaps *he* was her destiny, and not Clement. But, oh, she did love Clement! Why could it not be Clement who spoke such words to her and looked at her with such ill-disguised yearning? Grant was like her; he wore his heart on his sleeve. He wanted a love affair with her, or perhaps she had got it all wrong? She was not sure enough of herself, sure enough of being able to distinguish flirtation from passion. Was there a difference in this strange new world where people did not behave as they did in novels? A little voice inside her was saying, 'He can be your Experience. He will look after you. You are young – take what is offered you, whatever it is. Don't be a coward, let him be your lover, don't think ahead, any further . . .'

JUNE BARRACLOUGH

A Time to Love

Mandarin

To Margaret

(13.3.31–17.6.87)

who had a happy life.

A Mandarin Paperback

A TIME TO LOVE

First published in Great Britain 1989
by Methuen London
This edition published 1990
by Mandarin Paperbacks
Michelin House, 81 Fulham Road, London SW3 6RB

Mandarin is an imprint of the Octopus Publishing Group

Copyright © June Barraclough 1989

A CIP catalogue record for this book
is available from the British Library
ISBN 0 7493 0301 8

Excerpt from L.A. Strong's 'The Bride'
reproduced by kind permission of
the Peters, Fraser and Dunlop Group Ltd.

Excerpt from John Masefield's 'Roadways'
reproduced by kind permission of
The Society of Authors as the literary
representative of the Estate of
John Masefield.

Printed and bound in Great Britain
by Cox & Wyman Ltd, Reading

Contents

one

BEGINNINGS

Quant'è bella giovinezza
Che si fugge tuttavia!
Chi vuol esser lieto, sia:
Di doman non c'è certezza.

How beautiful is youth,
And yet it flies away!
Who wishes to be happy,
Let him be happy now:
For tomorrow nothing is sure.

Lorenzo de Medici

1
London 1910
Sophie and Edith

The girl was wearing a red tam o'shanter and that was the first thing he noticed about her. It was pearled with drops of rainwater and had not protected her hair from the rain either. He saw, when she turned to order her cup of tea and plate of toast from the waitress, that the hair was thick and plaited in a double knot at the nape. The mackintosh she wore was wet but she draped it casually over the back of a vacant chair and attacked the toast, when it came, with great appetite.

He was the only other occupant of the table – most of the other tables were full; that was why she had chosen his. They were both trying not to look at each other, in the way that English people avoid glances from strangers by sliding their eyes sideways or looking at a distant spot. He had been reading, preparatory to going out into the rain again, for he had entered the ABC only to avoid the rain, not from hunger. He had tilted his chair backwards and was holding his book some distance away from him. Under cover of his book he looked at the girl, and liked what he saw. She was still trying not to look at him after the first colliding glance. Having despatched the toast she began on the tea and then, with a casual air, managed to focus on the title of his book. That interested her. But when he put down the book she quickly looked away, down into her cup, though not before she had seen a handsome, masculine face, probably belonging to a man in his late thirties. He returned to the book but looked, under cover of his reading, sideways at her. She had taken out a small notebook from the large bag which she had placed on the floor by her side and was poring over a page of figures, frowning a little.

She was thinking how she would love another piece of toast, but that would mean only an apple for supper. She was determined on spending as little as possible in London, needing all her money for the rent of her room, not far away, in the nearby YWCA hostel for working girls. Then she closed the notebook, rooted in the large bag once more and brought out her reading matter, which she opened by her half-empty teacup. The man was now trying to see what his table companion was reading. He had recognized the mustard-covered linen of a series of books he himself had published, before he could see the title, which was *The Stories of Chekhov*.

The girl read on, lost in the book, remembering only to finish the tea. Then she looked up, in a daze, put the book down and sighed involuntarily.

He was curious about her. She looked a nice young woman, with a pretty face over which pleasure and melancholy had played as she read. He wanted to say something, but knew it was not done. But she had just caught sight of the title of his own book as he pocketed it, preparatory to leaving, and she gave a little start. He was reading poetry.

The girl was thinking, dare she ask the man for information? He looked respectable and kind. She fished in her bag again and brought out a crumpled piece of paper which she spread out on the table. She frowned again. It seemed to contain a map or diagram. The man was an adept at reading upside down writing and saw that the name of one of his rivals was printed at the top of the paper.

Sophia Rose Ridsdale was just about to pluck up her courage and ask him if he could direct her to Paternoster Row, which seemed miles away from where she was at present, when he said on an impulse:

'Excuse me, but can I help you?' It sounded foolish as he said it.

The girl looked up, startled, and he said: 'At your service.'

But he was a *gentleman*, she thought, though gentlemen did not usually go to the ABC teashops, except in emergencies.

'You are reading one of my books,' he explained. But Chekhov was dead, she thought confusedly, when he went

4

on, 'I published it. Publishers have the habit of laying claim to their authors, you see.'

'Then perhaps you could tell me how to get to Messrs Selwyn and Blount? I've walked miles, I'm sure, and am nearly back where I started.' She did not want to say she was lost, because she was not really, but felt a little lost.

She had a pleasant voice, he noted with approval, with a tinge of a provincial accent. 'You are taking them a manuscript?' he enquired, enjoying teasing her.

It was Sophie's turn to deny his assumption. 'No, I am looking for work. Somebody at the YWCA told me that publishers take on temporary clerks sometimes, so I was going to try them. It will be the sixth place I have tried,' she said, rather mournfully.

'Oh dear – you will wear out your boot leather.' He looked at her more closely, summing her up correctly as intelligent as well as pretty. 'Grant Miller,' he said with a bow and took out a card from his waistcoat pocket. 'Perhaps I can help?' he said again, handing her his card across the table.

Sophie, with visions of the White Slave Traffic, wondered whether he was going to whisk her away, but Chekhov decided the matter. The man's smile and voice were reassuring, too.

'I may be able to help with work,' he said. 'If you could call tomorrow at 3a Gower Place; it's not far from here, off Bedford Square. Give the card to the lady downstairs and tell her to send you up to me.' He rose to go.

Why not? How exciting! Sophie's heart gave a jump. Perhaps this was what they meant by the Hand of Fate?

Grant Miller was thinking, what a damned quixotic thing to do. But there was, in fact, a vacancy for a general factotum at his office.

'Well, thank you,' she said, rather awkwardly, staring at him. She went on: 'I was going to be a teacher, you see. I trained to teach at home.' She paused as he looked at her again. Well, if she were going to be a teacher she would at least be able to spell. 'It's meant to be the best profession for working girls,' she continued, 'but I didn't really want to teach.'

He wanted to ask, do your parents know you are in London? but did not, asking instead, 'Is your father a schoolmaster, then?'

5

'Oh no, Dad is a farmer.'

'Well, come along and see if we can find something for you. At any rate, I approve of your reading matter.' He bowed again then and she half-rose. Should she shake him by the hand? He saw her confusion and ended it by giving a little dismissive flick of his palm, turning it upwards so she saw the thick gold ring on his finger.

'Thank you,' she said.

He stood up and, after another smile, went out, thinking of her eyes and wishing he had a daughter instead of a stepson. He was a fool, though he had done nothing to be ashamed of.

Sophie sat on for a moment – it would not do to follow on his heels. What was life without a risk or two, she thought. Chance meetings, atmospheres – a little like the story she had been reading.

She had looked so bedraggled, but gallant, he was thinking, so serious and young. And readers of the Russians should be encouraged, especially if their fathers were farmers and they did not want to be teachers. How old was she, he wondered – twenty, or less? He pushed his umbrella up to the sky and smiled to himself.

The next morning, when she turned up at his office, he had not forgotten her. This time she was not wet from the rain, but was still wearing the red hat.

And mercifully, Sophie Ridsdale could both spell and punctuate and so was taken on in the office of Miller and Penn, Publishers of London, WC1, in the year nineteen hundred and ten.

Edith Broughton looked round her newly-acquired room with some perplexity. Her trunk was still standing where Mrs Macalister's odd job man had placed it, after much puffing and bending and with an expression that said quite plainly: 'She will not tip me enough for all my trouble.'

Edith had given him sixpence which seemed to her reasonable at the time. Later, she thought perhaps it should have been a shilling and then he would have pushed it to the window embrasure for her. But she had wanted him gone, had wanted to savour the first delicious moments of solitude after the bustle of the sooty journey and the cab and the London

6

streets. So he had gone, suggestively rubbing the sixpence on a corduroy thigh.

The room was high up in a tall Bloomsbury house let off into 'flats' and rooms, and Edith had already sent on a few pieces of furniture and a box of books from Yorkshire. They were waiting for her now and she decided to get the room shipshape even before she baptized the new kettle on the small gas-ring which Mrs Macalister had exhibited a few moments before, along with the tiny gas-fire and the washstand with piped cold water. The attic storey was only partially furnished: the house was a superior lodging house, in fact.

Edith drew a long breath and then half pushed, half pulled the now empty trunk until it sat under the dormer and could be covered to make a window seat. Then she sat on it experimentally and looked at her room from the new direction. Rather, there were two rooms, one leading out from the other, and she had not yet had time to explore the second. Mr Kenworthy had found the place for her when asked by Edith's father. He had reported favourably on it and all Edith had to do was settle herself in.

There was a little bed on her left provided by Mrs Macalister, next to it the white-panelled outer door. Facing her was another small door leading into the other room which had obviously been used as a bed-sitting room when the two previous tenants were each paying half of what Edith had agreed to pay – ten shillings a week – more than she could really afford, though she had some savings.

The room she was sitting in had been offered as bedroom, kitchen and washing room and she had intended to use the connecting room as her sitting room. Somehow, though, she was beginning to feel at home in this first room and wondered whether she really needed another. There was a table opposite her which would do for reading. Next to it the room turned its corner and there were the washstand, the gas-fire, gas-ring and a low chair.

She sighed and rose and went through the half-open door to the second room where stood still another bed and a chest of drawers of a rather sulky brown. So she was, in fact, paying enough rent for two people. No wonder it was expensive by Leeds standards. Edith filled the chest of drawers with the rest of the contents of her trunk – scarves and underwear and gloves, and hung up her two afternoon dresses, her coat and skirt and hat in the wardrobe she found in the further room. Then she dived back into the drawer again and brought out a gauzy 'Liberty' wrap and returned to her kitchen-cum-bedroom to place it thoughtfully over the trunk. Yes, that would do. Decidedly the room needed a little cheering up; perhaps she would be able to buy a print or two and add a bookcase, but for the present it would do. Edith did not care over much about her surroundings but made sporadic attempts to look respectable.

Where should she sleep? There was no gas-fire in the opposite room, she found on further inspection, and it would be cold in winter. What a luxury it would be to undress in the warmth; not as good as the bedroom fire at home, but better than nothing. She decided, for the present, to use the second room for eating and reading. Her mother would probably have said it would make a nice little parlour for entertaining women friends. Since, as yet, she had no friends, the idea was only of academic interest. It was a problem: she did not need two rooms and she did need the money she earned. Mr Kenworthy had obviously thought Father would be paying her an allowance to add to her earnings at Miller and Penn's. He did not know Edith wanted to live on her wages. Her savings were for the proverbial rainy day, and that had not yet arrived. She glanced out of the window at the sky. It was now growing dark but there was a subdued glow when she tiptoed up to unfasten the hasp and look out over the trees and other tall buildings in the distance. London, all waiting down there below her. Unknown and perhaps unknowable.

She decided to make herself a cup of tea, filled the kettle at the basin and then found the meter was fed by a penny in the slot. Fortunately she had some change and by the time the kettle was boiled and the screw of tea watered in its pot, provided by Mrs M, she had walked round her domain once more, flung a cushion on the bed, hung up her dressing-gown and washed her grimy hands. Everything was unpacked and in its place and ready for the morrow when she would present herself, the new lady typewriter from the north, to undertake what she hoped would be interesting new work.

Mother would think it rather sordid, she thought, looking round the little room as she sipped her tea but that did not worry her. Edith had little interest in luxury or even comfort, perhaps because she had had a good deal of the latter at home and was temperamentally averse to the former. Father was a brick, encouraging her to fly away. She knew he would miss her. Her mother would not miss her so long as her brother Edward lived at home, for Edith had not been a very adequate companion for her conventional mother in the matter of gentle talk of hats and ribbons and the price of meat.

It was time for bed. Tomorrow, whatever it might bring, could wait. Edith, who appeared to many people to pass her life in a brown study, got herself in her own methodical way to bed, reserving deeper thoughts for the moments before sleep.

Half past eight the next morning and an autumn sun and pale blue sky heralding clear weather saw Edith out in Gower Street on her way to her first day at Miller and Penn's. She had breakfasted on an apple and another cup of tea and was in good spirits. The street was busy with girls hurrying, like herself, to offices. Horses and carts and drays, a few hansoms and occasionally an omnibus, rumbled along the cobbled road. In her portfolio was the letter of introduction from Kenworthy, in case they had forgotten about her. She walked along slowly, for she did not like to hurry, and they had said nine o'clock. Her spectacles were perched on the end of her nose, otherwise the street was a blur. She might easily have been on her way to the British Museum where, even now, the frequenters of the Reading Room were assembling in the courtyard. She gave them a glance as she passed and made her way round to the square. She saw in front of her a girl in a large red tam o'shanter running along before she, too, turned into the square. Edith pushed her spectacles firmly back on to the bridge of her nose and followed the tam o'shanter round the corner and across a road off the square. The tall house, number 3a, had an open door that led into a dark entrance hall. A woman sitting in a small cage on the right was busy with a telephone, and a staircase led upwards and downwards from the hall.

Edith approached her. 'Excuse me. I'm expected this morning by Mr Miller. I'm a new typewriter, er, Miss Broughton,' she said rather hesitantly.

'Take your coat downstairs,' replied the woman, pointing to the nether stairs. 'Mr Miller's up on the second floor. Don't worry – I'll tell him you're here.'

Edith went down the stairs and found herself in a cellar-like space where a row of hooks, already bearing various mantles and umbrellas and hats, confronted her. There was a large pierglass opposite and she caught sight of herself as she took her coat and hat off and wondered whether to go straight up. Then, behind her, she glimpsed the red tam o'shanter on a hook and turned to see the girl whom she had followed shaking her hair and thrusting pins into it. The girl smiled and then disappeared through a door Edith had not noticed, and behind which she heard laughter and glimpsed a large table piled with parcels as the door swung to. The post room, she thought. Perhaps the girl was a clerk.

Edith ascended once more to the ground floor and then walked slowly up two more flights. The door opposite the stairs was shut but bore the legend 'Grant Miller'. Good. Now she must wait a little to get her breath before knocking. Just as she was about to, the door opened and a young man with brown, centre-parted hair edged out. He took no notice of her, so she waited for the door to close and then knocked. It burst open once more and Edith was confronted by a tall man, dressed in tweeds.

'Excuse me, I'm expected at nine,' she managed to say.

He looked enquiringly, then said, 'Go on in and wait for me. Miss Broughton, is it? Have a good journey? I'll be back in half an hour. Look, sit here and type me up this letter. Theo's away, or late. There's all you need. Back soon.' He thrust a paper in her hands.

There was a smell of pipe tobacco which hung in the brown velvet curtains over the window. Edith sat down without more ado, tried the machine, found some paper and carbon – surely he would need a copy – and was soon busy. When she had finished deciphering his hand, which sloped forwards and was of an angular and crabbed variety, she dared to look round the room. There were two chairs; if one were Mr Miller's, the

10

other must be that of his personal secretary. So she would not be sitting here for long. There must be another room meant for her. She got up and looked out of the window and was looking out of it when the man returned. He was humming an air she did not recognize and when he sat down and gestured to the letter, she handed it to him, saying, 'I took a copy – I hope that's all right?'

'Well, Miss Broughton,' he said after perusing it, 'welcome to the firm. I may call on your services today; we're very busy downstairs. Meanwhile, have a look round and meet 'em all. Oh, by the way, did you find somewhere to live? Some diggings? Kenworthy said he was going to look for you; good fellow, old Kenworthy, isn't he? And you were with Ransome, were you then?'

Edith answered the questions in the order they came. 'I have a small flat, Mr Miller, just off Gower Street. Professor Ransome has retired now from Leeds.' She spoke composedly.

'Ah, then you may be of use. I've just taken on a girl from your part of the world, younger than you I'd think. She's being a dogsbody, but I think she'll carry on here, and the child has nowhere to live. Do you know of anywhere?' This seemed rather unusual for an employer.

'Well,' Edith was thinking she had two rooms and only needed one, 'I could ask my landlady – it's partly furnished –'

'Good,' he said. 'Do that, will you? It's a Miss Ridsdale, only been with us a fortnight. She's in the post room.'

Edith went down to the cloakroom, wondering how she, only twenty-four hours away from Yorkshire, should be finding accommodation for someone in a city she did not know. Later, she discovered it was typical of Miller, who was kind to his employees, and yet expected instant solutions to problems.

She knocked at the door in the basement she had seen open earlier, opposite the large pierglass, and it was opened by a boy not much older than fifteen who had a pencil behind his ear and a general air of perkiness. The girl was sitting at the table, inexpertly tying up a parcel.

'Are you Miss Ridsdale?' Edith asked.

The girl looked up, startled. 'Yes – do they want me?'

11

'No, no. I've only arrived this morning, I saw you come in. It's Mr Miller; he asked me if I knew anywhere you might find a room . . .'

She was wondering if she could bear to share her eyrie with anyone else and trying to distinguish the features of the young woman.

'I'm sorry,' she said, 'I should have introduced myself. I'm Edith Broughton and I only arrived yesterday.'

'I'm Sophie,' said the girl. 'Would you know of a place? I'm in the YWCA and it's dreary. I *could* afford five shillings a week; I don't earn a very princely sum here.'

Suddenly Edith decided.

'Let us get to know one another, and then perhaps I might help,' she said shyly.

'Then a cup of tea is indicated,' said Sophie and got up. 'Willy, do fill the spirit kettle and go out for some buns. You can have one if you do.' No one else seemed to be around for the moment. 'Mrs Smeaton is usually in charge here, but she had to look after her husband who is an invalid,' chattered Sophie. 'And I got a job here just by chance. You wouldn't believe it! I met Mr Miller in a teashop. I'd run away from school . . .'

'From school?' echoed Edith.

'Oh, I hope I don't look young enough to be a pupil. I was – I mean, I trained to be a teacher, but I couldn't stand it. I came to a job three weeks ago in Croydon and I just decided I couldn't stay. It's all right – I'm not really untrustworthy. It wasn't *my* idea in the first place!'

Edith sat down and Sophie rapidly began to retail the story of her life up to that moment.

Sophia Rose Ridsdale was twenty and came from a village in the North Riding, had been to the Leeds City Training College for elementary teachers for two years. She had not wanted to stay in Yorkshire, where her parents had a small farm, had been left a little sum of money by her Uncle John and had departed, ostensibly to Croydon, but, in fact, determined to seek her fortune in the Metropolis. She had not seen herself as a fledgling teacher at Thirksay Village School 'for the education of the poor in the principles of the Church of England' and did not like the rector. She *had* thought of working for the Women's League for Suffrage, but they had no money to pay anyone, relying on voluntary work; she had tried to find a post reading newspapers to blind people, but there were none, so she had decided to try publishers' offices. Then she had chatted in the ABC in Bloomsbury with a pleasant man who had offered her a job, out of the blue, in his office; a lowly one, but a *job*. He had turned out to be Mr Grant Miller and Edith knew the rest.

Willy came in with the kettle and the combined ministrations of Edith and Sophie succeeded in getting it alight.

'Do you need help with those parcels? Mr Miller just told me to go around and meet everyone – it seems very free and easy here.'

'Oh, it is, but we work very hard when there's a crisis,' said Sophie, who seemed very much at home in the place. 'There'll be another one soon – Theo Carmichael is away, too.'

'Yes, I think he asked me to do some of her work. I must go and see him now, I suppose.'

'I'll show you round when I've got all this ready for Willy to take to the Totters GPO,' replied Sophie. 'Have a cup of tea, Edith. I say, you do come from the north, don't you?'

Edith had been a little astounded by Sophie's tale. Sophie seemed respectable and the mention of the Women's League for Suffrage had intrigued her. 'I come from Leeds myself,' she replied as they sat eyeing each other and sipping the tea, to which Sophie had added a slice of lemon which she appeared to keep in her rather capacious handbag.

'Perhaps we have seen each other before in Leeds?' mused Sophie.

'I think we may have,' admitted Edith, though she was not at all sure. 'Do your parents know where you are?' she asked, thinking that Sophie was not yet twenty-one.

'Oh, yes they know I'm in London. I haven't told them yet I'm not intending to teach. Once I find a room – I still have some of Uncle John's money – I shall write and tell them about – all this,' she gestured round the dusty room.

'Perhaps we could meet in the break for luncheon?' suggested Edith.

'I'll take you to the ABC,' said Sophie, smiling.

'Miss Broughton?' said a voice, and an elderly man was holding the door open and peering vaguely inside.

'Yes.' Edith got up.

'Mr Miller said to show you round and then he says come up to his office – he's got some work for you.'

'I'll try to meet you outside at one,' said Edith quietly and followed the man out.

Sophie Ridsdale went on with her parcel-packing, addressing the labels in a clear, upright hand with a few flourishes. She did hope that she had not appeared too impetuous to the new young lady. She had liked her. Perhaps her luck was still turning and she would find a decent lodging.

'My trunk's still at the station,' she said to Willy, who was pasting the labels on the parcels. 'I wasn't going to let them think I'd stay long at the hostel. It's a lovely trunk with my initials, "SRR". Do you think it'll be safe there?'

'Shouldn't worry, miss,' said Willy, which was what he usually said. He found this Sophie a strange young lady, a bit like one of them actresses his brother had been to see at the Music Hall.

Edith was able to escape from a large pile of correspondence at one o'clock and Sophie was waiting for her in the hall. They went off together and ate a penny pie each and drank a halfpenny cup of coffee in the new ABC with its marble topped tables and steamy atmosphere.

'Isn't it exciting!' said Sophie, her eyes shining. 'Just think – I'm in London and there are my sister and brothers still in the village thinking about harvest and rabbit catching. It doesn't seem possible it's the same world, does it, Edith?'

They had decided to dispense with the formality of surnames and Edith found she was enjoying Sophie Ridsdale's company more than she had enjoyed anything for a long time.

Thus it was that she decided quickly to offer Sophie the other room next to hers and to share the rent with her if Mrs Macalister would agree. Perhaps if they offered eleven shillings together, she would.

So a green trunk was rescued from King's Cross station and came to repose in the inner room at the top of the old Georgian house. With it came its owner, 'SRR', Sophia Rose Ridsdale, and a new life began for the two young women.

Edith had offered to pay six shillings if Sophie could pay five and with this arrangement Mrs Macalister was placated. Edith felt it was unlike herself to decide anything so quickly and Sophie urged her to give her a month's 'probation' to see if they got on well together, being a little uneasy, in spite of her good luck, that somehow Edith would find her annoying, or would wish, in the end, to be alone.

'I like being alone, myself,' said Sophie on their first evening together after the day's labours at Miller and Penn's, 'and everyone has a different routine.'

Edith smiled. 'I haven't had time yet to devise a "routine",' she replied. 'I've got my room and you've got yours. If you want to be by yourself we need only meet for meals.'

'Oh, I didn't mean that I would mind *your* being there,' said Sophie quickly. 'Only that you don't know me and people always say that women never get on together, particularly if they share a kitchen.'

'Well, it's not much of a kitchen, is it?' asked Edith, surveying the gas-ring. 'I wish you had your own basin. You could fill a ewer every night and take it into your room, then you could wash in peace, morning or evening.'

'Yes, I will,' said Sophie quickly, thinking that perhaps Edith was shy of her ablutions.

'There's a bath with a geyser we can have once a week,' went on Edith. 'So I suppose we can remain quite clean!'

Those first few weeks seemed to pass quickly and they both found it a comfort to have someone to talk to occasionally, yet neither abused the solitude of the other. They discovered, much to their amusement, that they shared the same birthday, November 20th, although Edith was two years older than her new friend.

Most of their talk was of their reading, with occasional attempts at discussing love and men and life in general. Edith came from a slightly higher social class than Sophie, and Sophie was aware of it. When Edith said: 'Oh, Father is a manufacturer – I expect publishers think that is sordid,' Sophie smiled.

'Would you rather come from a poor farm?' she enquired.

She soon began to stop worrying about intruding in Edith's life for, as their acquaintance deepened, both young

15

women found that they seemed to complement each other. Their strongest link was that they both came from the north.

They were a good pair when seen together, each gaining by contrast with the other. Sophie, with her dark brown hair, favoured red and navy blue – the red tam o'shanter was her favourite possession. She wore her hair long in a 'Cadogan' in the fashion of a girl a little younger than herself, with the result that she could be taken for a girl of seventeen. The reason for this youthful style was Sophie's constitutional inability to dress her hair tidily, and her impatience with fashion. She had a large mouth with a full lower lip and a snub nose and determined chin. Her figure was also youthful: slight, almost thin, with slender ankles and wrists and long, tapering hands. She had about her a certain élan and vividness which implied nervous energy and quickness of apprehension.

The contrast with Edith's fair tallness was extreme. Edith dressed usually in brown and wore her yellow scarf as a cravat in unique concession to a brighter colour. Her green eyes and pale gold hair and the milky tones of her complexion brought out Sophie's gipsy sallowness when they were seen together. It was to be expected that Edith would be slow of speech, and quiet and gentle in her delivery, and that she would ponder before venturing an opinion, although her opinions, when expressed, were often surprisingly forthright. Sophie, on the other hand, talked long and loud and was often mortified by her own garrulousness and the impatience and vehemence she betrayed. If Sophie began to wish she were more like Edith, Edith had not given the matter any thought, not because she had a high regard for herself, but because of an inability to see herself as others saw her character. There were depths in Edith which Sophie sensed. Neither did the whole of Sophie's true nature appear on her bright surface. She was less in harmony with herself than was Edith, whose thoughts tended to the abstract and to a realization that the mystery embedded in personality was not a matter that could be conveyed in words. So she did not try to convey them.

Gradually they came to appreciate each other and Edith envied her friend's ready sympathies and antipathies and began to search her own heart. Sophie admired and envied Edith's calm, and her sensibility, and hoped to grow up like her. Edith

16

was grown up and yet in many ways seemed childlike, a grave child, with that naïveté underneath which was paradoxically more apparent on the surface with Sophie. Sophie's deepest feelings had been focused on many objects of romance – people and places and books – leading to similar states of mind as those that had been her first reactions, as a child, to beauty as she saw it in the rolling green landscape of the Vale of York.

Even Sophie did not try at first to explain all her feelings to Edith so her friend did not know of the immense nostalgia which Sophie brought out of that childhood, and believed Sophie to exist in the present moment, to be a new 'London' person who had thankfully cast aside the shackles of her upbringing. And Sophie did not know, either, that Edith's deepest feelings had, so far, been centred on the moors and desolation of the Pennine Valleys which she never spoke about. But both young women continued to feel drawn together because of a shared Yorkshire past – perhaps they did not need to speak of the details of those past lives.

They did speak of their parents and each heard the other's descriptions of Mother and Father with incredulity. Edith could not imagine a father who was not powerful, in control, and successful, nor a mother who was not of secondary importance in the scheme of things. And Sophie tried to conceive of a father who was not gentle and dreamy or a mother who was not brave, assertive and full of the power of the will. 'Mother has no imagination, so she has no doubts,' she said once to Edith as they sipped their bedtime cocoa together. A London moon was shining through the dormer windows as it had on Edith's first night there, and for a moment the world was far away.

Edith looked at her meditatively. She wanted to ask Sophie whether she loved her father better but was timid about asking about such a personal thing. Sophie went on, answering the unspoken question.

'I admire my mother more, of course, but I like my father better.' Maybe, now, Edith would confess some personal prejudice in family matters.

'Mama and I have little to say to each other, but Papa is a very strong person. I suppose I took him for granted, thinking he was just what a Papa should be.' She was then silent, a little amazed that she had put that into words.

'I'd have liked a strong and successful father – it is what society expects, Edith – yet I think I prefer men like my dad. I don't like men to be always telling us women what to do.' replied Sophie.

Sophie had become an ardent 'suffragist'. 'Of course,' she added after a pause, 'it is easier to be what society wants us to be; in thrall to some man, I suppose – father or husband or even a brother. What is your brother like, Edie?'

'Edward?' Edith was again silent, thinking it over. 'I think he is not like Papa – he has never stood out in my mind. Mama and he are very thick.'

'And do you mind that?'

'Why, no. Women usually prefer their sons, don't they? Or is that again the result of your "society"?' She was amused.

'Mother finds Harry and Jerome a bit of a trial, I think. They are so noisy and undisciplined. Alice and I were, of course, never allowed to be like that. Mother may be the "man" in our family but she still sticks to the idea that girls should be obedient, I suppose because she had to be herself. Her parents were very strict with her.'

'Papa works so hard. Don't you think the *men* have a hard time of it?' said Edith.

'Everyone has a hard time of it at home; my mother works just as hard as Dad. Not in the fields, of course, though some women do, but running the house with all the baking and cleaning – ugh! I couldn't live like that. I'd much rather be a man. Have *you* ever wanted to be a man, Edith?'

'Never,' replied Edith, laughing. 'I can't imagine you as a man, Sophie, but I can see you married to one.'

'Oh, Edith – can you? What sort of man would want to marry me? Mother thinks I'll never be married; she can't believe I'd ever be fit for marriage. And I can't either. *You'd* be a gracious wife, though. I can see you in a hostess gown, shimmering away, with lots of little children and a dear, successful husband, something in the City, or a lawyer perhaps, while I toil away in the office till I'm old and grey.'

Edith smiled. 'You are silly, child, I don't see that at all.'

Sophie wanted to ask why, but forebore. There were some things even Sophie could not yet ask of her friend. She yawned.

'I must go to bed, for if I can't sleep at least I can rest. I wish I could sleep like you, Edie.'

Edith loved sleep and enjoyed her dreams which, though not frequent in her recollection, were pleasant.

'Oh, the delicious darkness,' sighed Sophie as they bade each other goodnight and each went to her separate narrow bed under the eaves. Sophie was prey to recurrent nightmares and often cried aloud in them, but Edith was such a good sound sleeper that she was never woken by the sounds from the next room.

The young women had both been working extremely hard at Miller and Penn's. The day began there for them both at a quarter to nine when Sophie would take in the day's post and sort it out. Together with Willy she would sit at her table in the basement and wait for further orders. Miller himself was to find her one day sweeping round the wooden floor and polishing the dusty windows. He gaped for a moment but said nothing. The next day Sophie found that the basement had been attacked by the scrubbing brush wielded by Mrs Acaster, the drudge, who should have cleaned it long before.

Edith, on the other hand, was before her typewriting machine in a first floor office room at nine o'clock, waiting for Mr Miller and Mr Edwards to come in with their letters. They did this in a spasmodic manner so that sometimes she had nothing to do, and at others both men expected twenty letters ready in two hours. The office, which took in all storeys except the top one of the dignified old house, was the proverbial hive of activity. They were chronically understaffed and eventually one of the editors, a Mr Edwards, sensing that Edith might write rather well, asked her to compose some blurbs for his new series of gothic mysteries sold under the name *Moon Murders*.

Garnett Edwards was an untidy Welshman with peculiar sexual habits (a penchant for the page-boys of the nearby Bloomsbury hotels) and a total disregard for cleanliness. Most of the staff at Miller's avoided him, but he was indispensible to Miller on account of his flair for the saleable, and the profits he thereby brought to the firm. But Edwards's best days were over, though his 'ninetyish' figure, with its dirty brocade waistcoat, the beard lost in the depths of his cravat, was still a force to be reckoned with. Edith disliked his moist, rather over-red little lips but admired his mind.

His ideas were good, but he was tiring in the writing of his own pseudonymous novels which had been such a success three or four years before. His principal pseudonym, known to all at number 3a, was Bevis Constantine, under which he also edited his 'Moon' series. Edith recognized his talents as she was often called upon to type for him when other business could wait, and could not resist, even so, half-consciously improving his syntax which was erratic.

He came in one day waving a recently completed typescript at her and making sounds expressive of disapprobation. Usually he ignored the girls and women on the staff, but he did not seem to mind Edith who spoke to him impersonally and was not afraid of him. This time, however, he was angry.

'You altered my paragraph on the "wailing wonder of the deep",' he accused her, standing near the typewriter, his rancid breath billowing over to her.

She replied levelly, 'I thought you had written mammals by mistake when you were describing the sharks.'

'Well, then, I must have meant whales, monsters of the deep, the ones which spout.'

'I thought,' said Edith, 'that you wanted the sharks because they were man-eating. I'm not sure, but I don't think whales, on the whole, eat men.'

'You mean I can't have it both ways? Well, then, omit the mammals,' he said grudgingly.

'But then, Mr Edwards, we can't have the whales as well because you want them later when you describe the spouts of water in the moonlight over the ocean.'

'What do you think then, young woman?' he asked, peering over his half-moon spectacles which were an incongruous addition to his large, pocked face.

'I think,' said Edith composedly, 'that you must have the whales *here* and leave the sharks to another story, or perhaps later when you describe Cornwall.'

Edwards walked to the window and seemed to be considering things in general; his temper had evaporated.

'I'm sick of these stories,' he then muttered. 'I want to get on with my Nineties book. You ought to write, Miss – er – '

'Broughton,' said Edith quickly.

'Finish this off for me,' he ordered her.

Thus it was that Edith first became part of Bevis Constantine. No one else knew, not even Sophie at first, for Edith was almost ashamed of her facility for writing rubbish, though she could not help writing it well. It seemed that she only had to shut her eyes and begin to invent and the most incongruous stories, filled with monsters and corpses and drowning maidens and weird battles and epic descriptions, would rise in her consciousness. Once she had despatched them in prose they bothered her no longer. Garnett was uneasy, but relieved. His series bored him and he wished the damned public had not taken to the pseudonymous Moon series with such gusto. But he left it to her. The most he would ever admit a woman to be was 'capable', and this Edith most certainly was. He did not enquire whether it was quite fair on her. She was lucky to be of use. It was not 'real' writing, she thought; not what she wanted to write, but what she could write, though where the ideas came from was a mystery. So far, her 'real' writing, apart from many notebooks neatly filled with thoughts for poems, had been confined to an article on Norse mythology she had written for the Leeds professor, which to her amazement, he had had printed.

Many poets and journalists and aspiring novelists flitted in and out of the office and, as time went on, it sometimes fell to Sophie to conduct them to Grant Miller's inner sanctum, where a large pile of unsolicited and mostly to be rejected manuscripts teetered on a dusty table which Mrs Acaster avoided. Now and again Grant would put aside one of these efforts for further consideration and Garnett and Miss Carmichael would go through them again and sometimes send them to one of their 'readers'. Unlike many publishers, Miller preferred to see them first, before sending them out. He was astute at not missing anything of value, though it was seldom that a genuine 'discovery' was made.

One day, two or three weeks after Edith had had her conversation on sea monsters with Garnett Edwards, Sophie was in Grant's office waiting to take down some letters for Willy to post. The boy was not allowed in the inner sanctum upstairs, but confined to the basement. Grant had not come in and Theodora Carmichael was briskly writing at her window seat. She was a tall, dark girl who, it was said, had been to one of the Oxford colleges for women. Sophie envied her, for Miss Carmichael was paid a good deal more than Sophie felt *she* would ever earn, and it was rumoured that Theo, who had no office training, had been taken on because of some distant cousinship to the publisher. Her manner to the junior staff was brusque but not unkind. For her part, Theo had noticed the new clerk and wondered about her. She seemed to be a friend of Miss Broughton, the new lady typewriter, who was such an improvement on that girl from Kilburn who had got married. Miss Carmichael did not approve of marriage in general, although she had had hopes (soon squashed) of finding a masculine soulmate at Miller's. This Sophie was a pretty girl, she thought, and seemed to have had an education of sorts. But what was *she* doing here when so many women friends of her own were existing at home without work? Perhaps she was ambitious to rise above her clerking and parcel-wrapping and letter-sorting, an ambition Theodora could not deny her. But, still, it was not usual.

'You ought to learn to type,' she said in a curt way to Sophie who was waiting for instructions.

'Yes,' said Sophie doubtfully.

'Women do not stay long in offices,' went on Theo and saw an angry blush creep over Sophie's face. 'You are lucky to have found work,' she went on.

'I thought that as I *read* a lot,' began Sophie and broke off as Mr Miller arrived.

Theodora continued to look interrogatively at her.

Grant advanced on the sorted pile on his desk and murmured: 'Any good?' to his amanuensis.

'I thought – this,' replied Miss Carmichael, ignoring Sophie now.

Grant took up the slim bundle she held out to him and, noticing Sophie still lurking in the corner of the room, said breezily: 'I heard you saying you read a lot.' He looked round at her. 'Come here. We could do with a fresh and unspoilt opinion.' Theodora glowered.

'You were reading when you were in the ABC,' he said.

'Yes, I have always read a good deal.'

22

'And what *are* your tastes? Poetry? Prose? Belles lettres? Adventure stories? I know you read Chekhov!'

'Everything,' replied Sophie simply. 'At least, I read all I can lay my hands on, but I don't like everything I read. I prefer novels and poetry – Thomas Hardy,' she added.

'Not many Hardys here,' said Miller. 'Take it, though. Go on, take it home and read it and write me a report.'

Sophie looked overjoyed and muttered thanks.

'Don't thank me, young woman, I shall want a proper report. Fetch me Mr Edwards on your way down.'

Sophie escaped, with the bundle clutched against her bosom, and could not resist dropping in on Edith who was sitting typing away industriously.

'Edith, he's asked me to read this,' she burst out. 'Mr Miller – Miss Carmichael looked daggers. He wants a fresh opinion, "A fresh, young opinion",' she repeated, laughing.

'Is he going to pay you, dear?' asked Edith, stretching her arms behind her back and yawning.

'Oh, I shouldn't think so. It is an honour, isn't it?'

'What is it then?'

Sophie looked for the first time at the manuscript she held in her hand. '*Poems of the Plough and the Harvest* by Clement Bartholomew,' she read. 'One off the slush pile. Mr Miller wants a report. I told him I did read verse!'

'Perhaps you will discover a genius,' said Edith, bending to her work once more, and Sophie danced away to put the papers in her satchel which held an apple, a book of the poems of Meredith and a purse with sixpence in it for her lunchtime pie or bun.

She and Edith still spent their free hour together in the ABC or, on a fine day, they bought bread and cheese and ate their luncheon, such as it was, in one of the many Bloomsbury squares.

That very afternoon, as though the day had not held enough wonders, there arrived to see Mr Miller a youngish couple whom Edith heard called 'Frank' and 'Kitty' as Miller greeted them on the stairs. Edith always left her door open, as she did not like the sensation of being enclosed and was by this means always able to hear the comings and goings. Sophie had retreated to her basement warren and was busy crossing off items from a catalogue of books which were to be taken to the stock rooms in North London, so did not hear the couple arriving.

One of Miller's acolytes, a young man whom everyone called Toby, called in to see Sophie shortly afterwards. He was reputed to be the financial brain behind Miller and Penn's operations and was always the first to spread gossip. Miller's was unusual in that, although the staff was small and the place often chaotic, they were, on the whole, younger than they had been in Grant's father's time, when they had operated from a small house in John Street, and this made the ambience free and easy to an extent unheard of in staider firms.

Toby poked his nose round the basement door and said, 'He's taking on Frank Laurence, on Garnett's recommendation. He will *do*, Miss Ridsdale! He will do! I say, is that a kettle I see? Can you brew a teapot on your primus? I'm exhausted.'

Sophie sighed and wished she could say that Mr Toby was quite capable of making a cup of tea for himself. But that was what she was there to do, as she well knew. 'Ships and shoes and sealing wax,' she muttered.

'Oh good,' said Toby, and deposited his feet on the table. 'They've got the best china out up there,' he motioned. 'No talk yet of royalties, so I'm not needed. Nothing so sordid. But Frank Laurence is a cracker and we've got him from Lane's. Have you read him?'

For the second time that day the humble teacher from Thirksay was being asked her opinion, but she was this time unable to give it for she had never heard of Frank Laurence.

'He's here with Kitty Moray; you know, *Tales from an Austrian Resort*.'

She had heard of them and asked whether Mr Laurence also wrote short stories.

'I'll say not. He's a novelist *á la* Gissing, out to shock the bourgeoisie, but popular. I say, this is a good cup of tea!'

'Thank you,' said Sophie primly.

'Who is brewing tea for your great ones, then?'

'It'll have to be Miss Carmichael,' said Toby. 'She thinks she's above such things. But you know, Grant's a radical man in more ways than one and if you work for him you find yourself doing all manner of odd jobs. Saves on the cash, as I well know. His father used to employ six more staff just to do the dogsbody

24

jobs, but this Mr Miller's got more sense.' His eye caught the bundle of manuscripts which Sophie had been asked to read. 'Conscripted you, too, has he? I hope you write legibly, he's a stickler for his reports to be written in copperplate if you can't type 'em.'

For the second time Sophie felt useless. Why could her Uncle John not have sent her to learn to be a secretary instead of an elementary school teacher?

'I expect your friend, Miss Broughton – she's awfully jolly, isn't she? – she'd type 'em for you.'

'Perhaps he won't like what I write?' ventured Sophie.

'I'll give you a word of advice. Pay attention to your spelling and grammar and startle him with something novel and he'll give you more. When I first came down from 'Varsity I used to read for him, till they found I couldn't spell but had a head for figures. So they got an accountant on the cheap to begin with. I'm not complaining. Must fly!'

Off he went and Sophie looked again at the manuscripts; she determined not to open them until she had got back to her little room, could not think clearly in all the bustle of the office, and wondered how Edith managed it. She was thinking about 'Clement Bartholomew'. It sounded rather a romantic name and she was trying to picture his unknown face when she heard the door slam above, on the ground floor, and rushed to the window to see if she could catch sight of the literary couple leaving. She got a good view of their feet as they walked away: two pairs of boots, one masculine and well-polished and the other a high pair of button boots under a black skirt, rather shorter in length than was customary. She must read this Francis Laurence. The world was opening up.

Clement Bartholomew seemed to come from the West Country as far as Sophie could tell from his verse. She was immediately bowled over by it and sat, chin in hand, by their mutual gas-fire, dreaming over the wad of papers, whilst Edith wrote a letter home. The poems told of rural places and rural occupations, but there was a wealth of sensuous imagery and a passion for the description of the particular; of the shiny machines as well as harvests, hay-making, flowers, woodlands, manual toil, spring skies, winter trees. She saw the 'hoary rime wrapped around

25

each twig like furry fingers' and the 'skies of icy cream tinged with blue'. What a wonderful person he must be, this poet who wrote so well of the sorts of places and objects she knew herself. He brought tears to her eyes, half mourning her own country past, for in essentials it was of England he wrote, and that England was the North Riding just as much as the West Country. There was a poem about a cathedral which must have been Exeter, and yet it brought back York Minster to her so that she felt she was under its high arched traceries, leaning in the golden light that entered its long windows. He spoke of pink rambler roses and she saw the ones at home once more, the ones her Aunt Rose had been named after, they said, and therefore her own roses, for she was called Rose after that aunt. His words brought back the moon silvering the harvest fields, with the stooks all ready to be carted away the next day, and the trembling hare in the same moonlight.

She wondered what she could say of the verses. If she liked them, doubtless others would. Mr Miller probably thought she had the lowest common denominator of literate taste inside her. Oh yes, she liked them. Occasionally, though, there was a hardness, a refusal to be loving, when he described the landowners and the tithes and the unremitting toil. It reminded her of the forbidden 'Tess' which she had managed to read in Leeds. His language was quirky too, salty. It made you see the familiar (and *how* familiar) again and with new eyes. She thought he did not just accept the 'beautiful', but strove to particularize it. Although he sympathized with the poor, he saw them as part of nature and as objects also for verse. This did not assort with his rebellious verses about them. There were two people at war in his work. Had he, too, been brought up on a farm? Was he still there, perhaps, sending his verses down with the milk train? He could not still live in the country, surely, unless he had a sophistication acquired from reading. She wondered how old he was. Why could girls not write like this? Of course, they could not write about the ale-house, because girls did not go into ale-houses, unless they were drabs. And they could not write thinly veiled allusions to love under the haystacks because women could not be scandalous. Why not? What did the girl accompanying the poet on his moonlit walks feel? What did *she* feel when she was lying in the straw beside the poet? Perhaps

26

the language here would be censored. It was a little strong for public taste, although Miller's were in the vanguard.

Edith had gone out to post her letter. The girls were finding they got on together very well, sitting together sometimes but, as often, each retiring separately into her room.

Sophie stirred, rose, and sought pencil and paper to try to assemble her thoughts in a manner appropriate to a publisher's Reader. Had Mr Miller read these poems, she wondered? She went into her own little room to find a book and when Edith tapped at the door to ask whether she would like a bedtime mug of cocoa, she was feverishly writing. There was so much to say and how could she say it all? What was the language of criticism? She must convince her employer that these were unusual poems and so she must quote. But what else could you say, except that they were good? She crumpled up her first attempts and decided to be bold.

'Is this all right, Edith? What do you think?' she asked.

'"These are wonderful poems. Mr Bartholomew shows great skill in varying his language to hit the reader over the head each time with the aptness of it, to the *feelings* he has rather than the *thoughts* about his native country and the individuals who populate it." It's a bit like John Clare – the book you found on the barrow.'

'What *is* his theme, then?' asked Edith.

'Oh, you must read the verse. He writes of everything he knows: the life of the poor, the seasons of the year, agricultural machinery, the birds, the winds, the work – '

'But what does he wish to say about it, other than describe it?' pursued Edith.

'Oh, well, he is angry, I think, about the conditions of rural England.'

'It is revolutionary, then?'

'No, no. Most of the poems are descriptions of things he loves.'

'But if he loves them he will not want them changed?'

'I think that is true, too, yet . . .' Sophie was silent. She was really talking about herself. How could you love a thing which was the product of inequality and injustice and depended on a social system which must go? Yet she did, and perhaps the answer was that the truth and beauty and cruelty, too, of the

27

countryside depended upon nature rather than human nature. Still, it was a puzzle. Which she continued to think about after she had handed Mr Miller her reactions to the verse, written as Toby had suggested in as neat a hand as she could manage. He did not say anything about it for a week or so and then, one day, when she was taking instructions from Theo Carmichael about some parcels that had gone astray, he came into the office and said, with his back to her, just as she was about to go, 'Come up to my office at six, Miss Ridsdale, will you?'

Sophie's heart was immediately beating in high and irregular fashion. He was going to give her the sack; he must be. He had looked rather grim, she was sure. Even the two or three male clerks whom she passed on the stairs on her way to the downstairs office seemed, she thought, to be looking at her with pity and scorn. She tried to get a hold on herself in the basement in front of the big mirror before going back into the post room. Staring at herself she saw eyes as big as gig-lamps. Putting her hands on her hips she tried to breathe slowly and deeply, but it did not seem to do any good. When she went up to his office at six o'clock, having told Edith not to wait for her, she was feeling just a little better.

Edith had said, 'Perhaps he wants to talk about your "crit". He wouldn't ask you to stay behind just to dismiss you, Sophie.'

She knocked firmly at his door just as Theo Carmichael was coming out of the room. Sophie always felt purposefully ignored by Theo, but advanced into the room nevertheless. Mr Miller was behind his desk and there was a fire burning in the grate. Stacks of books teetered on every available surface and on the floor, too, but they were neatly arranged and she could not help looking around at them, oblivious for a moment of her employer.

'Come in and take a seat, Miss Ridsdale,' he said, lighting an elegant pipe and leaning back in his chair. 'So you think you are qualified to write of rural life?' he began.

Sophie was so relieved that he had not begun by handing her her wages with a curt 'You will finish tomorrow', that she was emboldened to speak quickly. 'Are you thinking of Mr Bartholomew's verse, sir?' she asked.

'Indeed,' replied Mr Miller. 'I read your little piece. Too much enthusiasm, if I may say so, but you have succeeded in making me want to read the poems, which I have done. Although not *quite* as keen to publish them as you would seem to be, I admit they have merit.'

Sophie felt rather excited.

'But you haven't answered my question. You told me, when we first met over that cup of tea, that your father was a farmer. I wondered how much actual experience you have of the topics Bartholomew is concerned with. Did you go rabbit catching, ratting, hay-making with your brothers?' He looked down at his desk. 'You write that the poet is in two minds about his rural life,' he turned over her paper, which she could now see before him, marking the pages of a book he was reading. '"Must rural poetry come from a sense of inequity and injustice?" Well, must it? Can it? You must answer your own questions, you know, if you are going to be of any use as a Reader.'

'I am in two minds myself,' replied Sophie. 'Farmers are not ones to write of the beauties of nature – they haven't time. The labouring girls do all the things you've just described, and I don't know whether they notice the moonlight or hear the sound of the beck. I did, because I was not expected to help very much. They wanted me to be educated – at least, Mother and Uncle John did.'

'And now you are, indeed, "educated"?' pursued Miller, looking at her with a direct, rather uncompromising gaze so that she wanted to shift her own from his.

'Oh, I can't call myself educated, except that I know now what hard lives most people lead, especially the women. I feel guilty when I think of my luck – getting away and working here,' she said ingenuously. 'But women have a bad time of it, on the whole.'

'Aha,' said Grant Miller. 'You are a Feminist, I see?'

'I go to suffrage meetings, so do many girls I know, but we are not getting very far with repairing the injustices.'

She stopped, thinking, now I've shown I'm neither a lady nor a person to be trusted. But Grant only laughed. 'There are some men who would agree with you – perhaps *we* might call ourselves Feminists? – but I was puzzled by the obvious liking you have for the old forms and ways of

29

life, too. The contradiction you find in our poet maybe comes from yourself.'

'Yes, I suppose it does,' she answered. Would he say anything about the way she wrote, rather than the content? She had taken such pains with the piece but had been unsure of the form required.

'You write with a certain directness – that is all we require in our Readers – and you are very young,' he added. 'The people who buy our list will all, one day, come from your generation. All good publishers look ahead, otherwise there would be no progress and we'd lose our markets as our purchasers died off!'

'I know nothing of markets,' said Sophie.

'But you know what you like?' he asked.

'I know what I feel. But I wouldn't elevate it to a general rule. Perhaps I am typical, so might be useful,' she said, humbly.

'I'll give you another book,' he said in reply, and scrabbled about a table at his side, finally handing her a less slim volume than the verse of Clement Bartholomew. 'Fiction, this time. Compare it with Wells, will you? That is, if you've read any Wells. Take it home now. All settled and satisfactory now with your diggings, I hope?'

'Oh yes! I'm sharing with Miss Broughton, thank you, Mr Miller.'

'I want a report before next Monday,' he said. 'Off you go.'

Sophie managed to fumble with the door-knob without dropping the book and departed in high excitement.

'Typical? No!' thought Grant Miller when she had gone.

Both Sophie and Edith worried a good deal about their clothes, which always seemed to be dirty, in need of mending, and inadequate. Edith had always been dressed by her mother's dressmaker, and Sophie had a young aunt who was clever with her needle, but they were both aware, when they looked around the West End, that their 'fashionable' clothes were not very fashionable in London. They would 'do' of course, for the office, but Sophie longed for a dress of Liberty design, for velvets, boas, crisp white cravats, a fur collar and a costume with frogging. Tonight, as she made her way down Gower Street in the light from the gas lamps, for it was already dark and winter seemed to have set in, she shivered a little and planned the purchase of a long-handled umbrella and a bunch of artificial violets at a little shop she had seen open late, in the direction of Holborn. Edith, she thought, might worry if she were late back and would want to know the news from the Miller front. She would forego a shopping visit until Saturday afternoon.

Although Sophie would have worried if Edith were delayed arriving home, being a prey to alarms and undue anxiety, Edith had no such worries about her flatmate. Only when she heard Sophie's step on the stairs that led to their eyrie did she lift her head from a book and think about boiling some water for their eggs and tea. There were some crumpets, too, which they could toast at the gas-fire. How nice it would be to have a roaring log or coal-fire, but she brushed the thought of home away. The gas-fire was a luxury and they managed well on it; no skivvy like that kept by Mrs Macalister must climb four flights of stairs with a coal-scuttle. When Sophie burst in, Edith was sitting with her feet up on a stool and a long toasting fork in her hand. She had taken off her boots and pulled her skirts up over her long legs in their black stockings. Sophie took off her coat and came back from her own room, shaking her sleeves out.

Edith deliberately asked her nothing about the inter-view with Miller, for she could tell from Sophie's face that it had gone well and waited for Sophie to spill it all out.

Sophie took the fork from Edith and Edith fetched some water for their boiled eggs. This 'tea', usually at about six or half past, was the high spot of their day and could be indulged in within twenty minutes of leaving work, since they lived so near to the office.

'I bought two oranges,' Sophie said.

'Good,' said Edith.

Sophie then lapsed into thought and, not till she saw Edith looking at her rather speculatively, did she give a start and jump up.

'Leave the kettle to me – he thinks I'll do,' she got out in one breath.

Edith laughed. 'So he is persuaded of your Clement Bartholomew's merits?'

'Oh, I expect he'll get other advice, but he seemed to think I was more or less on the right lines. He's given me a novel and asks me to compare it with Wells. I've only read the new one, *Tono Bungay*. What else should I read? Fancy his thinking girls actually *read* Wells. It'll be Shaw next.'

Edith took the book and looked at it curiously. Sophie had not even had time to do more than glance at it.

'It's by that Francis Laurence; you know, he came in the other week.'

'Oh, I remember. I saw his feet,' replied Sophie. 'Let me have a look.'

Edith handed the book back to her and took one of her own.

'It must be an earlier book – we took his latest,' she said.

'Come and eat at my table, it's not fair, you having all the mess of the eggs and toast,' said Sophie. She went into her own room and laid a table-runner and two plates and cups and saucers. Edith brought her book in too and soon they were both munching toast dipped in egg, and scooping out oranges, reading the while.

Mr Clement Bartholomew, an as yet unpublished poet, was not milking cows or regarding the winter moon. Or, at least, he was not doing the latter in his home county of Wiltshire, but was, at that moment, eating a splendid meal in Soho on the strength of two articles accepted by *Country Life*, and the advance on one of them. He was not alone, but accompanied by two male friends, Austin and Seb, who were also aspirants to London's literary and artistic Bohemia, all scraping a living in their own ways; Seb in a shared studio in Chelsea and Austin with Clement, in a basement in World's End. It was rare for the evening to see them in Soho; usually, bread and cheese and beer from the pub had to suffice. Austin was distinguished from the other two by his height and a languid grace about his movements, but all three were thin, wore their hair floppily over their faces and had discarded the stiff collars that were *de rigueur*. Clement still kept his West Country vowels and had a certain farouche shyness arising from his awareness of his lowly origins, and a determination, nevertheless, not to give the impression he had risen above them. Austin had no problems over his accent or his social manner, being of late down from

Cambridge. Seb's hands were still streaked with paint and he was taking the opportunity to drink wine, which he could not usually afford. Clement had just had a letter from Miller and Penn's about his verse, but he held out no high hopes of being recognized for what he was. Pastoralism was in vogue in poetry it was true, but he did not see himself as a writer on country matters; more as an experimenter in form, who would also tell the nation things it did not yet know about the people who fed the fashionable world, the Hodges and Padges as he put it, of the neglected countryside. With his 'betters', Clement was acidly sarcastic and bitterly critical of London high-handedness, at the same time as determined to show it he was master. The friends were discussing the fashionable theories of death and re-generation. Clement had been bowled over by his reading of Dostoyevsky and Austin was arguing for Tolstoy. All were agreeing that English writers could not go on in the old ways, that some revolution was round the corner that would sweep away the old world for good, in religion, in politics and in art.

'We're miles behind the continent, our thinkers only scratch the surface. No one knows anything here about religion or philosophy. They're all stuck in the nursery tea syndrome of their class,' said Austin, who looked a good representative of that essential Englishness himself.

'Or writing popular novels,' said Seb.

'That's the women,' said Clement.

'Ah, women,' said Seb, sighing.

'You know,' said Austin, 'when I was in Montparnasse last year I was astounded, all as poor as church mice, but the food! Dear chaps, you have not tasted food – '

'Yes, quite,' said Seb. 'What do you know of England, who only England know?'

'Oh, I don't know,' said Clement, moving the pepperpot sideways and frowning. 'I'm content with England; I'd rather write for *Country Life* than one of your fashionable Frenchified revues. I'm only a peasant, and the people aren't going to be influenced by all that continental stuff.'

'The people aren't going to be influenced by anything,' said Seb, draining another glass and looking surprised at it now, empty, in his hand.

33

'All the up and coming novelists I see Grant Miller taking on are very English,' remarked Austin. 'All telling their romantic stories as though Oscar had never been.'

'What else was *he* but romantic?' asked Seb. 'Come on, fellows. Back to the studio, if your legs will take you. There's some "opal hush" to be brewed by the nice beaded ladies.'

'We've spent a fortune here,' said Clement gloomily as they paid their bills and each forked out one shilling and sixpence for their admittedly copious *table d'hôte*.

'Back to cheese and pickled onions tomorrow.'

Austin was still declaiming on the sights and sounds and smells of Paris when they made their way out through Soho and across Westminster to Pimlico and then along the river to their haunts in Chelsea.

By the time they arrived, an hour later, in the Kings Road, they were arguing about Kipling again, and Shaw, whose play was on at the Court Theatre for the price of a shilling. They passed a coffee-stall and each brought a penny cup, then Clement left the other two there and went to his basement where, like most young men, he lived in some squalor. This did not worry him or impede the flow of his thoughts. He was not tipsy enough to feel either drowsy or lively and sat down with a book and a pen and paper. There was no heating in the room so he wrapped himself in a rug when the warmth of the meal and the walk had worn off and read steadily till two in the morning. He then went to bed and did not hear Austin come in, being deep in a dream of home, of walking through a ferny copse with the sky eggshell blue through the lace of branches. He was surprised to find it winter when he awoke to contemplate another day of tramping round publishers and magazines with his work, before he remembered Miller and Penn had 'called him in'.

There was a letter from his mother in the box in the ground floor hall and he stuffed it into his pocket and wished that missives from Wiltshire did not always make him feel guilty.

Clement Bartholomew was extremely ambitious, proud of his rural background at the same time as wishing to escape it, self-consciously aware of the lives of all the obscure Judes who were scattered the length and breadth of England, but aware, too, that the technical skills which had led to his apprenticeship at sixteen as a designer of engines in Swindon, could lead to a better life than that of a poet. But he wanted to write, could not help himself writing, and found poetry in machines and in all man's inventions, as well as in trees and streams and harvests. He had come to feel that human scientific and engineering inventions were, by extension, also part of a 'natural' world, but was uneasy that they were changing beyond recall the world he had loved. Yet they would also change English society with its stupidities of hereditary wealth and power.

Clement hated Society, yet also could not help resenting that he was not one of those who led it and wielded power from within its magic circle. His motives were not, therefore, pure and he knew it, and despised himself. Machines and new inventions would surely distribute powers more equitably, so he was for them; but a natural pessimism led him to think that man would always make a mess of things; and so he would bury himself again in that country world he had known and lived from boyhood. Compromise was needed and Clement was not a compromiser. He had little money, only a few savings from living at home, when he had walked daily into Swindon and back to make economies. So far, he had not needed more than he earned but, having at last abandoned a promising career on the strength of a few poems accepted in West Country newspapers in order to try his fortune in London as a professional writer, he was miserably aware of his poverty. His friends, Austin and Seb, had private incomes. So far, for Clement, London society had meant only a meeting with a Fabian group, but *they* included a few novelists and poets who had found him 'interesting'. One or two characters of literary Bohemia who lived in a hand-to-mouth fashion had persuaded him to come out of his shell and had not seemed to find his ideas unusual. The articles he had sold on a changing countryside were a turning point, he felt.

Miller and Penn had had some of his verse for weeks. He had despaired of hearing from them, and now it seemed they might be interested. He had not sent all his poems on machinery to them, judging that his interests would be better served by appearing a rural and unsophisticated writer. He left Chelsea for Bloomsbury on a yellow Camden Town omnibus, his mother's letter in his pocket, and feeling that he was thousands of miles away from home.

Sophie Ridsdale was busy when he reached the imposing portals off Bedford Square, so did not see him arrive. It was Edith who saw him first, when he was taken upstairs to wait outside Miller's sanctum. Theo Carmichael was still busy in the office but came out soon afterwards and glanced at the young man, who had been given a seat in the outer room. Edith thought he looked round him like a hare in a meadow, almost sniffing the air, and warily regarding each table and chair as though there might be a trap laid for him under it.

'Mr Miller will not be long,' said Theodora, and swept out.

Edith went on with her typing and Clement looked covertly at her as possibly the most interesting of the natural phenomena to be observed here. He thought that with her long neck, she looked like a swan, a golden-haired swan. Then he glanced at his shoes and wondered how long it might be before they needed repair. He was a dab hand at shoe and boot repairs for he liked working with his hands.

Edith saw only a blur sitting on the chair. She never saw people very clearly and had had the impression that he was taller than he turned out to be when he stood up again to be greeted by Grant Miller at the open door of his office.

'Sophie's protégé,' thought Edith. She hoped, for Sophie's sake, that they were going to take him on to their list. The door had just closed when Sophie arrived with some invoices. She was out of breath. Edith looked up and smiled.

'Mr Clement Bartholomew is in the office with Mr Miller.'

'I know, I just heard. I wanted to see what he looked like!' She giggled slightly and had a rather nervous and excited air. She tiptoed to the door.

'Sophie!'

'Can't hear anything!' She tiptoed back and sat down on an empty chair next to her friend.

'Theo'll be coming up again,' said Edith mildly.

'Perhaps they are saying nothing, just communing with his genius,' Sophie went on. Her light tone did not deceive Edith. 'He's so good,' sighed Sophie. 'I do wish I could meet him!'

'You can certainly see him when he comes out, or downstairs in the hall.'

'What does he look like? You saw him, Edith.'

'I'm sorry,' confessed Edith, 'you know I'm short-sighted.'

'Oh – Edith! Then I shall lurk on the stairs,' said Sophie a moment later, and disappeared.

Clement Bartholomew was, meanwhile, sitting rather awkwardly, leaning forward on a cane chair known as the 'Authors' Special', with one hand in a pocket, facing Miller at his desk. Miller stood up from behind his desk and sat down again in a chair opposite Clem, perhaps trying to make his visitor feel more at ease. In this he did not succeed, for Clement felt an interrogation was getting closer, and looked out of the window, waiting for the older man to begin.

Miller was a man sufficiently cynical to be a shrewd judge of character. Even so, he liked what he saw of the young man who was obviously not out to please or ingratiate himself. Still, it was the young man's writings that were his concern, not his manner, and he intended a little gentle criticism before moving round to conditional acceptance – conditional on a good deal of cutting and sorting out of theme. He looked steadily at the poet and registered the curly hair, the long-lashed blue eyes and the thin hands which belied the rest of the body, which was not slender. About twenty-six was his unspoken calculation.

Clement looked up at Grant Miller and saw a tall man, casually dressed in tweeds and Liberty tie and soft collar. An assured manner, too, of course. Certainly he must be assured, representative as he was of the class which settled the fate of people like himself. For a moment, Clement hated him. Then he made an effort to stop the hate. He was here to get accepted on another's terms; the publisher could pick and choose. But Miller seemed a little hesitant about beginning discussion and first offered Clement a cigar, before cutting his own. Clement felt at another disadvantage. He had, as a matter of fact, never smoked a cigar before, but was damned if the fellow's upper-class airs were going to put him off.

He plunged in. 'I've never smoked a cigar before,' he said.

'Then I shall cut yours for you and you can watch me. Not that I should be encouraging my authors in vices,' replied Grant, smiling.

His authors! thought Clement. Then he cleared his throat, felt suddenly light in spirit. Grant's tones were genial and

Clement had thought at first, 'All the better to reject me with,' but now he looked enquiringly at him and took a puff at the cigar. However, Grant could be wary as well as genial.

'Although, in fact, I've had good reports from my Readers . . .' he began.

Clement looked steadily at him and waited for the end of the concessive.

'And although, on the other hand, I am convinced myself you have something to say . . .' another concessive: what could the fellow be up to? Clement swallowed.

'I think the work needs a bit of tidying up.'

'You want to publish me?' Clement got out, suddenly afraid that 'one of our authors' meant only 'one of our visitors'.

'Yes, we do. All our Readers agree, and so do I, if you will agree to a cut now and then, and also – ' he paused, 'I have another young fellow on my books here – perhaps you may have heard of him or met him around – his name's Frank Laurence, a novelist really, I suppose, but he brought in some verse which would assort well with yours, if you would agree to a mutual volume.'

Clement tried to look as though he were unaffected by all this, but succeeded only in looking lofty. 'Oh?'

'We thought, a short run to test the water. Do you know Frank Laurence?'

'No. I mean, I've heard of him. I've never met him.'

'You shall meet,' said Grant. 'He comes from Derbyshire, not near your neck of the woods. I've given him one or two of your poems.' He handed a bundle of papers to Clement. 'And here are some of his. You're invited to a small gathering on Doughty Street on Thursday at six, I was to tell you.' He went on, having got that item out of the way, 'We thought one slim volume with you both, in two parts, not mixed up. *Two Young Poets of Rural England* – something like that. If you were agreeable to choosing what we all thought were your best – '

Clement wondered who was to do the choosing. Miller went on, 'We could bring it out in the spring. Frank has a novel with us for Christmas. I've marked the ones we want from you both. Miss Carmichael will type them up as we'd like them. Think it over and write to me, will you? And don't forget Thursday, it's

38

Kitty Moray who's giving the party, I imagine. You know her work, I'm sure?'

Clement thought that was it and was rising to go, having said so far nothing sensible, but Grant gestured him down again.

'I thought you should leave out the commentary and collect the seasonal pieces together. You might do some "changing countryside" pieces later if this goes well. But we want the owls and the stoat and the trout fishing and the harvest. I fish myself – liked that one!'

Clement saw the publisher's long, lean figure sitting in some preserve where trout were tickled for the benefit of the haute bourgeoisie and looked fierce.

'And the harvest – our Miss Ridsdale liked that particularly.'

Clement was frowning now and Miller darted an amused glance at him.

'Think it over. Try it chronologically through the year. You'll see we've cut about a third. Once you've got an audience we might take the others.'

Clement wondered who this Miss Ridsdale was, but said: 'I've published in *Country Life*, though my feelings are for the future.' He thought that sounded rather pompous, so added, clutching his cigar, which had gone out, and stabbing it at the window, 'I mean, the poems you like are my most conventional ones. Things have changed since *The Return of the Native*.'

Grant Miller smiled. 'I know.' he said. 'Laurence would agree with you. But you can't expect the public to see it that way unless they've seen first that you feel for the romance they like to find in your rural spots.'

Clement thought, well, he has to sell the books, I can't blame him, and I do want to get into print. He cleared his throat. 'About payment?' he said, trying to sound more like a hirer of threshing machines to an unwilling farmer.

'Twenty-five pounds down and the royalties over a thou,' said Miller quickly.

Twenty-five pounds! That was a fortune to Clement Bartholomew and justified, for the moment, any assault on his artistic integrity.

'That for me or for the two of us – Mr Laurence as well?'

'For you. We wouldn't take you on if we didn't think we could make money from you,' said Grant. 'Part of it

39

will ride on the back of Laurence, but he doesn't mind that if you don't.'

Did he mind? Clement thought not. If his stuff were better than this Frank Laurence's, the critics would see it and if it were not, which he doubted, he would be carried on the back of the better-known man. Generous it was of *him*, he supposed.

'Frank is a good-hearted chap,' said Miller, 'In spite of his rebarbative appearance.'

Good, thought Clement, perhaps we'll get on. He must say something, intimate some thanks. 'I'll have a look at them straight away and go on Thursday,' he said. 'It's very gratifying, Mr Miller. All I want is recognition, but I'll have to see the other chap first.'

'Of course,' said Miller. He stood, and the interview seemed to be at an end. 'Could you tell Miss Broughton to fetch in the correspondence as you go out?' he said.

Clement rose and turned as he opened the door, 'I'm very pleased,' he said, and meant it.

Theo did not come into the office until about ten minutes after Clement had gone, so Grant Miller had plenty of time to digest his last visitor. He thought he understood him, but then Grant often did think he had understood people. As far as awareness of social embarrassments were concerned, he probably did. His own grandfather had been a printer made good and, until the end of the last century, the family had never had money. What Grant's own father had had was style, which still counted for something in the world of publishers and journalists, till recently a tight coterie. Grant himself had been sent to a public school where his good looks and sharp brain had preserved him from the wrath of masters and the bullying of boys.

He thought he recognized in the young Clement just a little of the critical quality which he himself hid under an urbane and kind exterior. Not that he was not also kind inside, but he had his blind spots and one of them was an inability to see that his own success irked others. He sensed in Clement Bartholomew a sarcasm deriving from insecurity, an insecurity which took Grant back twenty years to his own youth. For Grant Miller possessed a will of iron. When necessary he would drive himself along and when he fought he would fight to the end.

He saw that in Clement, and that Clement's life was likely to be a tougher battle than his own. He himself had hedged his bets and come to some arrangement with society. After several affairs before the age of thirty, he had married a widow with an only son and installed them and himself in his father's old home on the borders of Surrey and Kent. It was here that the trout fishing took place.

A smile crept over Miller's face: there was something in the young man who, in spite of his powers of observation and his political stance, was yet a pure 'poet' and one whom he must publish.

Grant was not often given to introspection and so did not wonder what his visitor had made of *him*, beyond registering that he was probably regarded as a member of the idle rich. It was usually easy to draw the fangs of such a man – too damnably easy. It was abstractions that Clement was interested in, that was it. Clement was a believer in getting at the Truth, not settling for an amused and amiable experience of the contingencies of life as it was lived. Except that he was young, so the contingencies were inescapable and usually had to do with not enough money, not enough sex and not enough work, or too much work of an uncongenial kind. Clement would be a strong hater, destructive even. Was he, Grant, any better? He shook his head, lit a pipe and went back to Toby's accounts, but he was restless and decided to go home early. He needed to think about the rest of his Spring List.

For his part, Clement went down the stairs with a calm and measured tread. They wanted to publish him! What would they want to take? He must go to the nearest café and think about it. Life was opening up. He was so full of a surge of achievement that he did not notice the young, dark girl who was standing in the shadows of the hall as he went out into the autumn sunshine and made his way to the coffee-shop on Bedford Row. He could afford a cup of coffee today.

He did notice both Edith Broughton and Sophie Ridsdale the next Thursday at the gathering on Doughty Street of a dozen to twenty young men and women.

Sophie and Edith had certainly known nothing of the invitation to Kitty Moray's till the day before, when Grant recollected that Laurence had asked whether he knew any intelligent young ladies who were not too formally mannered, who perhaps worked for him and who would come to help Kitty give her party. Did he mean to help with the refreshments? Grant asked amusedly. No, no it was just that they were very informal these days and he had noticed those girls round the office and Kitty had been saying how there was a gulf fixed between people of their sort and the workers of the world. . . .

So Grant had passed on the message and Theodora had sniffed and said she did not go to parties whose hosts she did not know. She knew Mr Laurence, of course, in a way, but it was not 'done' in her circles to mix business and pleasure. So Grant had asked Edith if she would like to meet one or two of his authors and take Miss Ridsdale with her. Sophie was, of course, overjoyed, could not believe her luck. This was more like it! This was what she had left home for. And why should the staff not meet their authors anyway?

They both thanked Mr Miller and went, after great agonizing on Sophie's part – less, on Edith's – about appropriate garb. They need not have worried.

It did not seem so unusual to Edith and Sophie that 'working girls' should be invited to writers' parties. When they arrived they saw two other girls, who had apparently had some connection with Frank Laurence's former publishers, already hanging up their coats in the narrow entrance hall of the flat at number 37, Doughty Street. For this was decidedly mixed company and Sophie, for one, felt she had reached her spiritual home when they climbed the staircase and heard a pleasing bubble-like sound of conversation punctuated by high, bird-like laughter. The two girls who had preceded them were introduced as Horatia and Chloë and seemed not to be on their *first* visit. The room was a double one with high ceilings and an ornamental grate. Somebody, somewhere, must have some money, thought Sophie, as their hostess, Kitty Moray, she of the skirt and elegant black boots, came up to them with a feline grace.

'Grant Miller said he would send you,' she said in a musical voice. 'Do mingle, won't you. There's tea and some wine and some cake.' Then she was gone and they saw her

42

talking to a man who lay sprawled in a large armchair at the other side of the room.

Edith felt as though a pane of glass was separating her from the other occupants of the room as she received a beaker in her hand from a young man with a hawk-like nose and floppy hair. Sophie took in the furnishings and leaned against the window embrasure, occasionally sipping a glass of wine. Besides Horatia and Chloë and Edith and herself, she saw the man who must be Frank Laurence. He had red hair, she saw now, and a fierce expression, and was talking in a corner to another man whose name she did not know. Toby came up to her and she tried not to look surprised. She had not thought *he* would come to a party of Bohemians.

'Do you know Austin Speight and Sebastian Harman and Cora Benson?' he asked, settling himself by her.

'No,' answered Sophie. 'I don't know anyone but Edith and you – and I've seen Mr Laurence and his wife at the office.'

'She's not his wife,' whispered Toby.

'Oh?' Well, of course, she would not be his wife, Sophie supposed. She looked at the room again with its deep armchairs pushed to the corners and the screen in front of the marble fireplace, the cushions on the floor, the scarves of brightly coloured material draping the pictures and the patterned rugs, and then turned to look at the walls where several charcoal sketches were pinned. There was a light in the corner from two candle-sticks and two more were on the hearth and above it. In the air was a sweetish smell of some perfume as though incense had been offered. Oh, it was a lovely room, full of lovely people, she thought as the wine began to circulate through her veins. She turned to say something to Edith, for Toby had been joined by the man he called Sebastian, but Edith was now in a corner near the door, standing by herself. Until a man who had just come in joined her, and Sophie saw, with a lurch of her heart, that it was Clement Bartholomew. But then he was being steered to Frank Laurence's corner and Edith had moved up to the fire and was looking into it.

There were just too many people to have to sit down as one did in a sitting room at home, and just too few to make standing unpleasant. A gruff, middle-aged lady with hair like a bird's nest was standing in another corner and, yes, she *was* smoking a cigar! Gracious Heavens! Sophie decided to concentrate on meeting as many people as possible and moved to join tall Horatia and small Chloë, who were dressed in material similar to some of the hanging scarves of purple and mauve and pink silk. She wondered if they were students from the Slade; they looked delightful.

'Isn't it jolly?' said Toby's voice behind her again. 'Meet Seb. Seb, this is Miss Ridsdale – Sophie. We were up at 'Varsity together, Seb and I.' Sebastian smiled and flicked back his long locks. 'Seb is a painter,' explained Toby.

'Yes,' said Sophie. 'I can see that. He has paint on his shirt.'

'Oh dear,' said Seb. 'I cannot look respectable. Clem said I must look respectable – respectable company, he said.'

'Did you say Clem?' asked Sophie.

'Yes, Clem Bartholomew. Do you know him?'

'I've read him,' said Sophie. 'And I want to meet him. He's just come in, hasn't he?'

'Yes, he's over there, talking to that beautiful woman in green,' replied Sebastian, indicating Edith.

'That's Edith Broughton. We both work at Miller's,' said Sophie. Seb was easy to talk to. He was very polite, in spite of looking like a fallen angel. 'When Mr Bartholomew comes over here I should like to meet him,' she went on, feeling very daring and hoping she was not drunk. 'I read his verse, you see, for Mr Miller.'

'Did you, now? Good stuff, isn't it? Do you write?'

'I used to when I was a child,' said Sophie, 'but I'd rather not do what I can't do well, so I just read nowadays.'

'Clem has come to talk over his new book with Laurence. Look, he's going over to him now. He says they – you – want to bring out twin volumes; his poems and Laurences's.'

'I didn't know Frank Laurence was a *poet*; I thought he wrote stories,' said Sophie.

'He writes poems too. I thought everyone in this room but me would be a writer. We painter chaps keep close together too, but Austin – he writes philosophy – introduced me to Clem. I was at school with Austin.'

At school with one and at 'Varsity with the other, thought Sophie. 'You didn't know Clement – Mr Bartholomew – before, then?'

44

'I wasn't at school with him and he wasn't at Oxford, lucky beggar,' said Seb. 'Come and meet Austin.'

Austin was now sitting on the floor between Chloë and Horatia, and patted a chair behind him for Sophie. She wondered what the two young women did. Could they be writers too? Then Edith was by her side again, whispering, 'You must meet your poet – I've already talked to him.'

'Yes, I know, I saw you,' said Sophie. 'But he's busy talking to Mr Laurence.'

Several other people had now joined the party. They all seemed to know each other. Would she and Edith ever belong like that? Seb was asking if she had ever been painted, because he would like to paint her and Edith. He had already, it seemed, painted Chloë and did not want to paint Horatia. Indeed, Horatia was rather horselike in appearance when you looked at her in profile, Sophie thought.

Oh, she *must* talk to Clement Bartholomew and tell him how she had loved his poems. But he and Frank Laurence were still in earnest conclave at the end of the room.

'I expect the men will go on to a coffee-house, or a pub,' yawned Chloë. 'Excuse me, I didn't get to bed till three this morning.' She had a slight drawl but Sophie, who had a good ear, thought she detected the vowels of South London underneath the drawl.

Five men and five women were now left and a table was drawn into the middle with a coffee urn and a Chinese teapot displayed on a vivid cloth. Their hostess, who had disappeared for some time, was pouring. Sophie went up to the table and caught Clement Bartholomew's eye just as he was getting up from his seat near Laurence. He was not tall, no, he was not, but she saw his dark blue eyes and the slim hands that held a glass.

'We are only here on sufferance,' murmured Horatia's voice in her ear. 'They all come to pay court to Kitty.'

Why, never again might she be in the same room as the poet! Something must be done. He came up to the table then, and she handed him a cup that had been filled with coffee. When in doubt, give a man something to eat or drink.

'Do you want coffee?' she said brightly.

Oh, thank you,' he said, surprised.

'I read your poems – at the office – I told Mr Miller how good they were!' she said in a voice that seemed to her to tremble. 'You *are* Mr Bartholomew, aren't you? I was talking to your friend, the artist.'

'Oh, Seb,' he murmured, taking the cup and looking at her. 'You work at Miller's, then?' he asked, after a silence which Sophie employed in stirring her coffee.

'Yes. I believe you met my friend Edith – over there. We both work at Miller's, but Edith has a proper job – I'm just a general factotum.'

'Are you Miss Ridsdale?' he asked. 'Miller said Miss Ridsdale had liked my poems – you must be a Reader then?'

'Yes, I am. I mean, I'm Sophie Ridsdale, but I'm not really a Reader, or only one with a little "r". Mr Miller believes in testing public reactions to his list, so he asks the lowest common denominator of the reading public for their views.' She smiled, rather liking that phrase of her own invention.

'How do you get a job like yours?' asked Clem then, with genuine interest. Girls were generally teachers or peasants in his experience, but the girls here seemed both original and clever, though he had a suspicion that some of them were not what his mother would have called ladies.

'I got mine through meeting my employer in a teashop,' replied Sophie truthfully.

'Oh, I say,' said Seb, who had come up, this time with Edith. 'Is that true?'

'Quite true,' said Sophie. 'But we work hard, don't we, Edith?' Edith smiled and Clement looked at her swan-like neck. Edith, it was true, looked a lady. 'Edith, of course, has worked in a university,' pursued Sophie.

Edith was silent.

'It's awfully jolly here, isn't it?' said Clement, trying the words on for size. How were you expected to talk to these women?

Then Kitty Moray came up holding a beautiful Persian cat. 'A-ha,' said Sebastian. 'I should like to paint that.'

'You must paint Kitty, then,' said a voice, and Frank Laurence was there, cutting a loaf of bread with tidy, dextrous movements.

Sophie thought, yes, he should paint her against the Chinese screen, holding a fan, with the cat at her feet. There was something extraordinarily self-contained about Miss or Mrs Moray. She looked inscrutable. Not in the way Edith was, but more aware of the fact of her inscrutability.

Edith was thinking how lively Sophie was. These were her sort of people. She fitted in here. She herself, did not. I would like to go back and write a Bevis Constantine story, she thought. She looked round. They had said Garnett Edwards would be coming, but she had not seen him. At that very moment the door was flung open and a hearty 'halloa, there' preceded the sight of Garnett himself, followed by a young man with a high collar and mincing gait.

'Garnett, darling,' said Horatia and bestowed two kisses on his venerable cheek. No one said anything to the young man, but he did not seem to mind, moving to the pierglass over the far wall and contemplating himself in it.

'Yes, I saw your friend Edith on Monday,' Clement was saying to Sophie.

'Where's Carmichael?' asked Edwards. 'Too Bohemian for her tastes, eh?'

'Probably at the suffragette meeting,' said Toby.

'Suffragist,' said Sophie, and they all looked at her.

'Indeed, why not?' said Kitty, stroking the cat. 'Come and sit round the table everyone. The men are not to be allowed off to the pub. We women require entertainment.'

'I say,' said Seb. 'Are you a suffra-what's-it, then, yourself?'

'I'm a suffragist,' said Sophie.

'So are we all, dear,' said the young man who had accompanied Garnett.

Their host, meanwhile, had been out and come back with a large loaf, a pot of butter and jar of jam. 'Home-made,' said Kitty. 'Frank baked the bread downstairs this afternoon. The jam was sent from the country. Eat.'

Sophie thought she had never been so happy, sitting round the table with all these new friends and able to feast her eyes, discreetly, upon Clement Bartholomew. She had certainly felt something for him before she had ever met him, but that evening, like a sudden burst of sunlight on a green landscape, she was sure she had fallen in love.

Sophie said nothing of her feelings for Clement Bartholomew

to anyone, even to Edith, for she was at that stage at the beginning – the burgeoning – of an infatuation, when it is enough to be alone with thoughts and daydreams. She was not even especially desirous of seeing him; it was enough to know he existed. She knew that the feelings were all on her side, for she was not vain enough to think he had noticed her particularly, or would even remember her. She thought, I have all my life to make him love me – or, at least, make him let me love him. She looked forward, rather, to the hour or so in bed alone when she could think about him and construct fantastic futures. Being quite a good actress when her own feelings were involved, she was able to make cool enquiries at work about the 'Poems' and their future fate. Would Clement, as she thought of him, agree to join forces with Frank Laurence to make a double or twin volume for Mr Miller? She had observed the talk between Clement and the novelist at the party in Doughty Street and correctly surmised that they had not met before. Edith could help here, of course, as she was more apprised of the Miller plans and took the publisher's correspondence down for him.

'It seems they've not yet agreed,' she had said to Sophie one day a week or two after they had been launched in Bohemia, or what Sophie liked to think must bear some relation to it.

Sophie wondered whether Miller would soon allude to her 'discovery', but was at first disappointed. Miller was a busy man. He had not forgotten though, and came down to the basement one day at the beginning of December.

Sophie was quick to seize the occasion of his unusual presence in the basement office. He seemed to be looking at her with an enigmatic expression and she hoped he was going to give her more 'reading' to do, though anything but Clement Bartholomew's verse would be a disappointment, she felt. (She had not enjoyed the poetic novel, which had seemed rather old-fashioned.)

'Your judgment has been approved,' he said, turning to face her and leaning against the table as he waited for Willy to bring him a parcel from the sorting office which had been delayed. He must mean Clement's poems.

She must show initiative by reacting immediately to this, so she said, 'If I could be useful, I hoped you might give

48

me some more reading to do. I'm afraid my report on La Gallichan's novel was not very enthusiastic.'

Miller, who had been looking at the way her hair was looped over the back of her neck and thinking again how attractive she was, took some time to reply. When he did he said, 'Oh, that was all right – fine – I saw your point. You shall have some more poetry – there's nothing much at present, though. Going away for the holiday, are you, Miss Ridsdale?'

As a matter of fact Christmas had been looming in Sophie's thoughts; whether to go north for the short holiday was a problem. The railway ticket, even third-class, would cost a lot of money and she thought that a present for the family and a long letter might just do instead. They always appreciated her writing to them and the excuse of lack of funds would be acceptable. Anyway, she wanted to go the next suffragist meeting which was just before the holiday and to be held in a large hall in High Holborn, not far away from the flat. 'I don't think so,' she replied. 'It seems a lot to pay for just three days. I shall wait till the summer when it's much nicer on the farm.'

She had a very easy manner, he thought; she was polite but friendly, did not seem aware of her charm. Or was her lack of coyness just another of these female ploys? No, he did not think so. 'Good, you must get some fresh air,' he murmured.

'I want to go to the NUWSS meeting,' said Sophie, 'that would be a nice Christmas present.' He must surely know that the initials stood for National Union for Women's Suffrage Societies.

'So you think Asquith will change his mind?'

'No, but we must go on trying,' she said.

He marvelled that a child – he thought of her as almost a child – from some wild farm, with only the education appropriate for an elementary school teacher, should interest herself in such matters. In this he under-estimated her. Sophie had been formed far more by her reading than her 'education' or her parents.

'I support the Women *Writers* Suffrage League, myself,' he said after a pause. 'Have you read their pamphlets?' Then Willy knocked at the door, and Mrs Smeaton, who did not at all approve of what she called Miller's 'familiarity' with his staff, particularly his female staff, came in and looked crossly at Sophie, who was lounging against the large post-table with every appearance of enjoying herself. But there was nothing she could say and Grant Miller departed upstairs without waiting for an answer.

At the very first meeting of the NUWSS she had attended, a sparsely-attended gathering in the hall of an ethical church, Sophie had observed the presence of Theo Carmichael, and smiled. Theo had smiled, rather frostily, back. It was hard, Sophie had thought; hard to be accepted by women like Theo. She knew that she was lucky to find herself at Miller's; Theo probably thought she did not deserve to be there, but the work was not beyond her capabilities and women ought to stick together. If *she* had been Miss Carmichael she would have welcomed a little nobody and striven to make her feel welcome in the big world. And anyway, what were they all doing worrying about suffrage, if not to help other women a lot less lucky than themselves, even a lot less lucky than she herself? But the barriers of the few years which separate twenty and twenty-eight were not as potent as the barriers of class. Was this what the socialists meant by Changing the World? Must one be a revolutionary to change the minds of other women, even of a Miss Carmichael, who obviously did not think that poor women were as worthy as rich ones?

Sophie, who thought the daughters of professional men must all be rich, thought Theo Carmichael was rich. She did not know that, at Oxford, Theo Carmichael had noted for herself the gulf which separated the professional middle classes from the real aristocracy. Sophie registered the thought once again as she packed up the parcels of books that she must read more to understand this curious English society. She vowed to improve both her knowledge and her thinking, for she was all at sea when she encountered in real life the sort of people she had, till then, only read about. Mr Miller was a mystery; Miss Carmichael was a mystery. Reading was pleasurable but it made you think you knew more than you did. How would Clement have appeared in a book, for example? Or Kitty Moray? Were they as self-conscious as she was? Why could you understand someone like Thomas Hardy and yet not understand the tone of voice of your employer, or of a fashionable novelist? Perhaps

Hardy, too, had felt lost in the London world. She was sure that Clement did. But if you were a genius, people could begin to see things in a new way, your way. She was *not* a genius, and so she must learn. Life on a farm, with the job of a teacher as the best you were likely to be offered, was no preparation for London life. Edith did not seem to worry about how to act and feel and be. She just was. Perhaps Edith was a genius, too. Edith was a reader – but of seventeenth-century poets of whom Sophie had never heard, and of eighteenth-century novelists.

Edith was, in fact, quite concerned about Sophie's worries over the way society worked, and guessed they had more to do with her friend's personal position in life than with any general philosophy. It was true that Sophie was a passionate Feminist with no equivocations. 'It's just a relief to believe in something,' Sophie had said to her once. 'Most things you begin to grow sceptical about, but not that.' Edith, too, had made a shrewd guess about Sophie's feelings for the young man, Clement, for Edith noticed more than she ever let on. She might be short-sighted and have an air of abstraction, but she was fond of Sophie.

Clement Bartholomew had been quite embarrassing as far as the amount of attention he had paid *her* on the admittedly few occasions of their meeting was concerned. She saw he was intelligent, but he had no idea of her true thoughts. She had nothing to offer a man like that. So Edith had determined to advance Sophie's cause when she could, if there was ever an opportunity. Meanwhile, she was busy enough, redrafting a botched Bevis Constantine tale which would occupy all her spare time before she paid a visit north at Christmas to her parents.

It did not seem to worry Sophie that she would be alone over the Christmas break. 'I'm looking forward to it,' she said ingenuously. 'I don't mean I don't like living with you, Edith – I do – but I'm always happy alone and I can read and go for walks.' Privately, she was a little afraid of Christmas, afraid that, if she went home, her mother would somehow prevent her returning to London. She must give her parents just a little longer to realize she was not going to teach and by the summer she would feel more secure and also, perhaps, take Edith with her on a visit to Thirksay. They would approve of Edith, she was sure, even if she were to puzzle them.

51

Before Edith left, there came the big meeting of the suffragists to which Sophie had been looking forward. As well as the 'ethical' meeting, she had been to one small tea meeting already in a queer private house in Hampstead where she had been puzzled by the mixture of wealth and radicalism and felt shy and silly. On the evening before Edith finally departed from King's Cross for her stay in Yorkshire, Sophie, her mind full of these matters, stopped on her way home from work to buy some mimosa from a flowerseller. The price was so extortionate that she could have bought quite a bit of her rail fare with it. She was, however, immune to such considerations. Beauty was as important as justice. When she arrived at the attic flat she found Edith in the throes of packing.

'It's only three days,' said Edith, thinking of Sophie alone. 'Will you eat enough? Won't you be dreadfully dull all by yourself? You could come with me, you know.'

'*You* wouldn't be dull by yourself, Edie,' replied Sophie, arranging the spray of blurry yellow flowers in a jam jar and sniffing the blossom.

Edith got up and dusted her skirt. 'I bought you a little pudding,' she said, going to the table and displaying a small bowl covered by a cloth. 'All you have to do is steam it in a saucepan over the gas. Mind you put plenty of water in, though.'

'Thank you, Edith. My present to you is a book. Don't open it till Christmas Day – promise?' She had searched the barrows on the Farringdon Road for something which would accord with Edith's taste and found a little book which looked extremely old and appeared to be by the same author as the *Centuries* which Edith so loved. 'And I shall do my well-known recipe of haddock,' she added. This was Sophie's principal contribution to the culinary art and consisted of pouring boiling water over a piece of fish which was then left to stand till it was cooked. It was delicious, especially if you could affort a pat of butter.

Edith smiled. 'You must go to your meeting. Have some scrambled egg with me first, though.' Edith liked cooking and was good at it. 'Who is to address your meeting? I thought Theo Carmichael said something about an alteration.'

'She didn't think to tell *me*,' replied Sophie. 'But I heard her say something to Mrs Phillips. It's to be Cora Benson.'

'But wasn't she at the party in Doughty Street?' asked Edith.

'Yes, she was the woman who smoked a cigar and left before Mr Edwards came in with his friends. Rather exotic, isn't she, for the NUWSS? Oh, Edith, I do wish there were more girls like me there. There's no one really young or ordinary. I feel like their grand daughter. If they're to succeed it'll take years and years and they'll need someone to carry on the good work when they're dead, won't they?'

The struggle had been going on for so long, she thought, as though they were all on a sort of moving platform which only seemed to move because of an optical illusion, since the background never changed. 'Perhaps we ought to be more extreme,' she mused, picking up a stray stocking that had escaped Edith's suitcase. 'But I can't see it would do any good in the end. Something is bound to happen, isn't it? We must win in the end. It's all so unfair.'

'Well, you have your life to lead even in an imperfect world,' said Edith comfortably.

Sophie felt she ought, perhaps, to be more of a rebel. It seemed she could make only puny gestures towards the only 'cause' she could believe in, but she knew she was not made of the stuff of martyrs. In the end, guiltily, she would dream of Clement Batholomew rather than the vote. Yet – and here, as usual, she balanced out her thoughts – if things did not change for women in general, relations between men and women, even in particulars, even in love (in which she believed), would be different, imperfect, flawed. She struggled to voice her confusion; was there a link between personal, spontaneous visitations of feeling and the 'facts', which said that even these sacred feelings arose only from a combination of time and place and person, with nothing 'eternal' about them? That, she could not bear to believe and so, in the end, she was silent, struggling with herself. It made you feel you were not in control of your own destiny, like Tess or Sue in the Hardy novels. Not that that would bother Edith. She sometimes wished she could see inside Edith's head where, she was sure, thoughts were marshalled very clearly. Edith went her own way and that did not include future attendance at suffragist meetings.

'I wish I were like you,' Sophie mused as they ate their toast. 'I feel I ought to do things, but in the end I believe in this sort of timeless 'truth' thing. That's why I can't really belong anywhere.'

'Perhaps because you've had such a struggle to get *here*, Sophie, I mean to come to London and not teach and everything.'

'Yes, but *they* say that you don't change things through individuals, but through political movements. And even the little I've done so far is only a manifestation of the world 'March of Progress'. I don't feel that; I'm sure there have been plenty of other girls who thought as I do; they're not just part of the March of History, are they?'

'You should stick with art,' said Edith, laughing.

'Give me poetry any day, I agree. Still, I must go and do my bit. I suppose it's because I feel guilty.'

But when she arrived at the meeting, which was not far away, she did not feel guilty, but rather angry. Why should they need to come out on a cold winter's night? Why should such dreadful things go on in the world whose fate was decided by rich and powerful men? Sophie was thinking more of the slavery of life for ordinary women – and some men, too, she supposed, – than of having a vote. Who were these people who represented you, anyway? Another lot of bankers and rich landowners and, even if they were not, why didn't more men, even from the working-classes, make an effort to try to decide their own destiny?

Outside the hall was bleak and Sophie was one of the first arrivals. She looked curiously at the other women when they arrived in twos or threes or descended from cabs with their chaperones. Didn't they all come from the very class which oppressed everyone, including women? They all looked the same, except for a handful of older women who were dressed in black. There should be someone like Kitty there to cheer everybody up. But the cause was serious. No room for frivolity. That was what men liked: frivolity. Good, meek girls with proper attitudes towards themselves, allowed to be frivolous for a few years before marriage. She wondered if Clement was a Feminist and decided not. Mr Miller was. Perhaps his wife was a sober-hatted lady with principles? She would think about it later and concentrate on observing it all so she would at least have something to tell Edith.

Mrs Fawcett was announced to be indisposed when the meeting finally began. There was a little platform at the far end of the hall with chairs for four people, three of them occupied, and the seats in the hall were quite well filled with ladies wearing large hats. A lady on the platform got up and said, 'Our slogans tonight will be "Votes for Women! Freedom or Slavery! Open the Franchise! Persuasion will Reform!"'

Sophie had brought along with her a copy of the *Women's Suffrage Journal* which she did not, in fact, find very stirring. She liked the sound of another journal but had not been able to find a copy, and anyway, buying papers like this cost money she could ill afford. She wished Miss Carmichael, whom she had glimpsed at the front of the hall with a woman friend, would lend her some more to read. *The Women's Dreadnought* sounded so much better, but perhaps it advocated violent means?

She tried to concentrate on what was being said but the women's voices were rather feeble and those sitting at the back found it difficult to hear. She should be bolder and sit at the front. It was Cora Benson who was speaking now. She recognized her from Doughty Street.

The woman took a glass of water and a long drink from it and suddenly they were all electrified by her loud, gruff voice: 'They say, our socialist brothers, that they will not vote for our cause because, if women do get the vote, being naturally conservative, they will return representatives of the forces of reaction to Parliament. I say, one: it is against natural justice to leave matters as they are. Two: how do they know how we will vote? Three: are we to believe even our socialist and Fabian brothers just because they are men?'

She was persuasive, yet Sophie felt (but would not have confessed to anyone) that the whole point was somehow lost in the rhetoric. Even if, or when, everything was sorted out – the poverty and the injustices and the lack of freedom – what, then, did you live for? And did it make a difference what you lived for if you were female? Was their cause really the same as that of the male manual worker? Why, most of *them* were the worst oppressors of women, in their own homes! Not her dad, no, he was not an oppressor – more a victim. But she had the uncomfortable feeling that it would be easier to be a revolutionary if you were a man, and that was really what Cora

55

Benson had been saying, wasn't it, only the other way round? She did not truly belong either, to these nice, quietly behaved, sensible, rational people. They all looked as though they had comfortable homes and kindly parents, or were kindly parents themselves. Why did she not feel at home here? And on the other hand, was it all worth it? And if it were, shouldn't it be carried to extremes?

'After the questions there will be a charge of twopence for a cup of tea,' announced another middle-aged woman called Cicely Emery. 'At the back, on the tables,' she added.

Sophie saw that some working women were waiting with a large teapot and cups and saucers. Was she not really a believer in the suffrage? But of course she was! It was all so unfair and horrible that women suffered, like that marvellous woman, Mary Wollstonecraft – Shelley's mother-in-law. Shelley, her great hero. Atheist. Feminist. Poet. But was he really a Feminist? Could a man ever be one? She remembered that poor Mary Shelley had kept having infants who died. But would Shelley, or his mother-in-law, have fitted in here? Were they the same sort of people? Where could a Clement, with his own rebellions and devotion to England and his poetry, fit in? She waited till a few people had got up and gone to the back of the hall to be served with a drink of tea and then got up herself. How many thousands of meetings would have to be held before the world changed? She was in a brown study when a voice at her shoulder said: 'Did you agree?'

She turned and it was Grant Miller. 'Oh, Mr Miller, I didn't know you came to these things! Of course I agreed – didn't you?'

'Been a supporter for years, not that it's made much difference. Thought we might make a book of some of these speeches with a commentary. Have you seen Miss Carmichael?'

'She didn't see me, she's at the front.' Sophie was suddenly rather shy. Mr Miller seemed different out of his offices; nearer, larger.

He regarded her steadily. 'Come, let me get you a cup of tea. How are you going to get back? It's really not done to walk the streets of London alone, you know.'

'That's why I'm here,' replied Sophie. 'So it *will* be "done".'

'That's not what they're worried about – will votes for women change the social code?'

'I never had to worry about things like that. I mean, we were closely supervised at the college, but only rich girls have chaperones. I'd rather be a working girl.'

She looked so small and vulnerable that his heart contracted. It was not true that he had come to listen out of loyalty or conviction or to pass the time of day with Theo Carmichael. He had come because, quite simply, he was enchanted by this young employee of his, and knew he should not be, and must not be. But there it was; meeting a girl in an ABC teashop and taking her to work for you was unorthodox, but not actually against the rules. Did he want to do anything against the rules? He rather thought he might. But she was not a little milliner or a society hostess. He sighed. He was too late to go back to Chimneys tonight. Sophie had no idea of his inchoate feelings, he knew, and she ought never to know.

Sophie was thinking he was rather nice, and he was very kind. And after all, he had given her the readings to do and given her a job. But what would a man like him want with her? He was unapproachable to her in any real sense. She liked him, but he was old and came from a different world. It simply did not occur to her that he might like her personally. She was always afraid of being too presumptuous, knowing that her natural manner might appear so, and so, that evening, she was quiet and listened to him, and smiled, and thought about Clement Bartholomew.

2

Thirksay

'Most roads lead men homeward
My road leads me forth'

John Masefield: *Roadways*

By the first day of the New Year, Edith was back in London.
She had added a day or two of unpaid leave to the Christmas
holiday to make her trip worthwhile. Whilst in Yorkshire she had
one day taken a tram and gone out, alone, from the furthest stop,
on a long walk to visit her aunt in a more countrified part of the
Riding. There were great tracts of real country between all the
towns and cities, for once out on the hills they soon gave way to
moors. The visit had been pleasant – more than pleasant, it had
seemed to ask her what she was doing in London, far away from
her roots in the little smoky valleys and the bare hills. And she
had enjoyed the solitude. But the north had also been freezing
and she had returned to London with a cold. Sophie ministered
to her with cinnamon and lemon and insisted she spent a Sunday
in bed. Edith lay back and listened to Sophie extolling the virtues
of independence. Sophie had had a wonderful time, she said,
reading and walking and visiting parts of the capital where she
had never been. So many people, buildings, shops, parks . . .

Sophie did not know that on her peregrinations to Chelsea,
hoping for a sight of Clement, after Christmas, she had been
seen by her employer who had first noticed her tam o'shanter
bobbing up and down by the river. Grant Miller had not exactly
followed her: he had business in Chelsea and it had happened
that, as he had stood waiting to cross the road by Cheyne Walk
and was looking over towards the river, the red blob had come
into view with the small figure of Sophie underneath it. He had
realized who it was, and watched her for a time, and then crossed

58

the road, keeping his distance behind her. Then Sophie stopped and leaned on the river-walk parapet and he had stopped too and hoped she had not seen him.

It was a day when he had escaped from his family celebrations. He thought he had graced his wife's Christmas table in Surrey for long enough, and had also managed a 'talk' with his stepson, Fabian, who was at an ungrateful age. He had been annoyed with himself, for wherever he went at Chimneys, in the large house which had been designed for his father in the Nineties with its 'medieval' look (but, fortunately, far from medieval plumbing), and in its long gardens which stretched into meadows with a stream at the bottom, he had kept seeing Sophie Ridsdale's face and hearing her voice. He wished he could have given her a Christmas box, but he knew it was forbidden. He had contented himself with thinking that there would be many gatherings and parties in the coming months of the New Year when his staff could easily be invited. Perhaps at the Blands in Eltham, perhaps in Hampstead. But he was disturbed. He had tried to pretend nothing was happening to him that had not happened before – he well knew the symptoms of frustrated desire and wished they would go away – but the sight of Sophie walking along had affected him deeply. He would have loved to have a daughter like her, he thought again, but perhaps it was a good thing he had not, if these were the feelings she aroused in him. He had forcibly turned himself in another direction that day in Chelsea and occupied himself with calls of a professional and business nature, one to a lady in Fulham whom he had known for several years.

Sophie, of course, knew none of this and would have been amazed and incredulous if she had. She had been trying to find a way of introducing Clement Bartholomew's name into a conversation with Edith, when Edith said, 'That letter you brought back from the office for me – did you know it was a New Year card from Mr Bartholomew?' Edith was a little worried that she had been chosen to be the recipient of Clement Bartholomew's good wishes and had a feeling it should have been sent to Sophie. She thought she had better mention the card, as Sophie was sure to find out. Edith had no particular interest in Clement, had indeed preferred Sebastian, his artist friend.

'Perhaps he'll invite you to a New Year party,' said Sophie, wistfully.

'I wouldn't go without you,' replied Edith firmly.

Sophie went on wishing that she knew Clement better. It was so difficult to come across him, whilst it was easy to see Toby or even Austin, whom she often glimpsed in the street when she was on her way to work.

As it happened, they both saw the young man before he could invite either of them to anything. He and Frank Laurence came into the office in the second week of January to discuss their projected volume with the publisher. By then it had snowed and was bitterly cold, and Edith was still suffering from whatever she had picked up in Yorkshire. The days were dragging, now that Christmas was over, and life seemed nothing but work. Both the women were looking forward to the spring, when at least the gas meter would stop being so greedy and they could shed some of their heavy winter clothes. Their long skirts dragged in the slush and had to be dried and then brushed on arriving home. In the time she could spare from thinking about Clement, Sophie talked a good deal about the summer holidays. She was determined to take Edith home to the Vale of York.

'We could go walking and help with the harvest, or hay-making if we went earlier; it would do us both good. And Mother and Dad would take one look at you and know I was all right in London. They'll never forgive me, of course, but I shall go to see them when I've saved a bit. You will come, Edith, won't you?'

Edith was quite agreeable. They got on so well together and seemed to have shared their lives for longer than four or five months. She was surprised that neither of Sophie's parents had made any attempt to come to see their errant child in London. Her own parents were going to Scotland in the summer.

Sophie went on thinking about Clement. Why should the person with whom you were sure you had an affinity be so elusive?

When she saw him on the day he came to the office with Frank Laurence she was again disappointed. The men were coming out from Grant Miller's office with the publisher, who was accompanying them to a lunch on Charlotte Street. Although Clement did look at Edith (who was busy and had

60

not looked up) he did not see Sophie, who was peeping out from a door downstairs. She thought there was perhaps an 'atmosphere' around the three of them, as though there had been, not exactly an argument, but a little constraint. After that day Sophie made a great effort not to think too much about the poet; she knew the signs of infatuation in herself. Yet hope still rose in her when she had forgotten to try to forget him. One day she *would* be able to get closer to him, she was sure; probably through Kitty Moray. As well as hope, she kept herself going on anger. That was for the days when she thought about the position of women and thought she ought to become more militant, more committed. London, however exciting, was a man's city. Women who ventured out alone were always prey to male attention, a not always agreeable attention, and that stirred some deep anger in her. In the meantime, there was always work to do.

For Edith there was extra toil for Garnett Edwards, which she did in her own time. She was able, at last, to visit the British Museum where she slipped into the Reading Room with a sensation a little like that she had on the Yorkshire moors – of having come home, being expected. At that time Sophie pretended there was too much going on in life for her to have time for delving further than the novels and poetry she read. Edith, on the other hand, refused politely to go to any suffragist meetings with Sophie; smaller ones than the first, in strange little halls. Sophie still did not feel really at home at these meetings, even though Theo Carmichael, who was often present, once unbent a little and discussed with her the prospects for the future of womankind.

Then, one March day, Frank Laurence came into number 3a alone. Usually he was with Kitty – Sophie had often seen them walking by. They made a charming pair, Kitty-and-Frank; Sophie thought it was wonderful to see them as a pair and yet know they were obviously well-suited and happy together without benefit of clergy. How *she* would like to be one of a pair, to find her good companion, friend and lover all in one. She thought she 'saw through' Kitty but it did not stop her idolizing her a little.

Frank Laurence, though, could be a little intimidating. That afternoon he looked quite grim. It was foggy outside and the clatter of cabs and carts on the cobblestones which surged continually around their ears, even in the office, and the shouts of street vendors, were dampened down.

In spite of being promoted by Grant to answer simple requests, make up parcels for booksellers and despatch messages to authors who lived in the country, Sophie was a little bored and wished she could read something further for her employer, who seemed to have been avoiding her in the last weeks. She hoped he was not regretting having taken her on. She had not been lazy and knew she had done her best to help everyone, since all manner of odd jobs fell to her.

Frank passed her in the hall as she was climbing up to a room on the ground floor from her basement cell, with a bundle of letters to give to Toby for checking, and some invoices for filing. 'Is Mr Miller in?' he asked in his direct, no nonsense, you-know-who-I-am voice.

'Yes, I think so, Mr Laurence. I should go up to the ante room. Have you an appointment?'

'No, I have not. I shall beard the lion in his den. Where have you been? We've seen no one – been very dull since Christmas. You must come round again and see Kitty.'

'Are we bringing out your book with Mr Bartholomew then?' she asked. 'How is it going?'

'That's what I want to see him about. Clement is still agreeable to Miller's suggestions, but I'm not; I've had second thoughts.'

'Oh, I thought it was all settled?'

Sophie had made it her business to try to find out exactly what was going on with the projected joint book of verse, but that Frank Laurence might be having misgivings filled her with alarm.

'I thought – I mean, Mr Miller told me some time ago it was all going swimmingly. He thought it was a good idea; he said how generous of you it was to share that book with Mr Bartholomew – '

'Yes, but you see, I'm not a poet and Clement is. I mean a real poet, not a scribbler. He doesn't want to write verse for Philistines – our concerns are different.'

'It seemed a good idea at first,' he went on, not noticing that Sophie had looked startled at the description of his wares (honesty was one of Laurence's strong points). 'What I am trying to say, Miss Ridsdale, and I wish you could get it into the head of that employer of yours, is that Bartholomew is a writer they'll still be talking about in a hundred years. As for me, I am an entertainer, y'see, who can't keep proselytizing.' He looked suddenly glum, younger. Perhaps he needed Kitty Moray to keep him going, she thought.

'I'm a splendid critic, of course,' he went on, 'so I know Clement must have a volume to himself. Say something, will you?'

'I'm only an assistant here, not even a Reader, just an office – ' (she nearly said 'nobody', but it sounded self-pitying), 'worker,' she finished.

'But you know Miller, I'm sure. He always gets intelligent girls to work for him. Tell him I'm here to plead for Clem.'

What could she do but accede to his request, though it was none of her business? She would do anything for the beautiful Clement, but asked herself why he could not come and plead his cause for himself? He would perhaps be frightened to lose the possibility of publication.

'I've been asked not to speak for him,' said Frank Laurence. 'But I *shall*. You don't know what sort of a writer he is; he mustn't get cluttered up with double volumes.'

'Surely your name would help him?' said Sophie. They were still down in the hall, speaking almost like conspirators under the graceful wrought-iron staircase which wound round above them.

'No, no, it's better to start as an "original". You don't think I care about my poetry sales? Why, verse only brings in enough to feed the cat, if that. And Kitty and I manage on our hack work. No; Miller must do a book for Clement alone – I know what I'm talking about.'

'I read the poems, too. It was I who told Miller how good he was.'

'I thought you were only the office girl,' he said teasingly, looking less fierce.

'Well, I am. But Mr Miller likes to test out his products on those who might buy them, or would buy them if they had any money.'

63

'I'd better go up,' said Frank Laurence. 'Tell you what – you must come round again to Doughty Street. What about tomorrow evening?'

'Oh, thank you. Will Mr Bartholomew be there?' she asked, trying not to sound too interested.

'I'll ask him, to meet an admirer! Clem knows only *Belles dames sans merci*, or milliners – he ought to meet a young lady or two.'

'We have met already, when I came before.' She was going to say, 'May I bring my friend Edith?' but it sounded like a child's tea-party, and anyway, she wanted Clement to herself.

Telling Edith that evening, she could not know that Frank Laurence had thought, 'What a pretty little filly,' and described her to his friend, Kitty, that afternoon.

'Oh yes, she was here before, when Clement came before Christmas. I told her then to come again with that tall, beautiful young woman who also slaves for Miller,' Kitty had said, then, 'I'm glad he promised to think it over again.'

So when Sophie braved the Miller den the next morning and said she thought perhaps Mr Bartholomew ought to have a book to himself – greatly daring and even frightened at her temerity – Grant had already thought it over.

'Laurence told you to ask me, did he?'

'I know it's not my business,' said Sophie, 'but he did seem awfully upset.'

Grant, who had his own reasons for not being cross with Sophie, only smiled and offered her another book to read for him, this time an allegory of female rights by a Mrs Humphrey Addiscombe. She accepted it gratefully and fled.

'Clement has agreed to a smaller print run and Miller will do him by himself,' said Kitty Moray when Sophie was ushered into the Doughty Street chambers that evening.

'I'm so glad.' Sophie was looking around the large, airy room, once more drinking in the cushions and the flung scarves and the piles of books and the bowls of pot pourri. No one else seemed to be in evidence.

'Frank will be in later. You must sit down and tell me all about yourself,' said Kitty. She was interested in girls like Sophie and could bend the full force of her charm upon them. They were also useful for 'copy'.

Sophie felt the charm and was not thrown by it. Kitty Moray was how a woman *should* be. She was shown to a deep armchair near the fire and Kitty sat on the other side of the fireplace contemplating her.

'Tell me,' she said again, 'how you come to be working at Miller's – we don't stand on ceremony here.' The Persian cat came up and rubbed against Sophie's skirts.

'Mr Miller met me in a teashop,' Sophie began, and Kitty burst out laughing. 'I know, it is rather peculiar, isn't it? But I was in London, where I'd come to teach, and I couldn't bear it and decided I'd rather do anything but.'

'Anything?' asked Kitty Moray, thinking of the twenty-year-old *she* had once been, but with a nice little income from her father in Australia.

'Anything to earn enough to eat and not go back home.'

'Ah, *ma chérie*,' said Kitty, rather affectedly. 'So he rescued you, did he?'

'Gave me a job,' replied Sophie. 'Edith had one already – she is a trained person. I was fit only for teaching farm children their tables.'

'But that could be quite interesting, I think,' mused Kitty. 'You could write about it. No one writes about the work women do. Frank likes to think he is *au fait* with women's lives, but I tell him it's not so. And you live on your wages?' she asked.

'Of course,' said Sophie, 'and I have so many people to talk to and so much to do and see. London is wonderful. I've never seen so many rich people. I suppose it's as if all the rich people at home – in the castles and halls – were multiplied by a thousand or two and all crammed in the same place. I didn't understand before about the class system, you see,' she said. 'Now I think it will all change; it must, mustn't it? And especially if we get the vote.'

'The ruling-classes will never change, my dear,' answered Kitty. 'We take what we can from them, from those who read and are interested in art and music.' She went out and returned with a Chinese lacquered tray on which was a teapot and two shallow cups. 'You are very impressionable, little one,' she murmured as she poured out, and added a squeeze of lemon from two thin slices on a green plate. 'Money is necessary, I know that. You'll find it matters more than you think. They say the world is about to change and I hope it does. But until it does, we have to keep our heads and drive as hard a bargain as we can, we writers.'

Sophie was flattered. 'I can't write,' she said. 'Edith can, but has little time for it.' She wanted to ask: 'How do *you* make your living and live in this pleasant flat?' Instead, she said, 'To earn your living from your pen – that's rare, isn't it?'

'Oh, if you can call it a living,' answered Kitty, carelessly.

Sophie thought it was a better living than her parents had ever made. Perhaps Francis Laurence wrote what he did just to survive.

'Frank has the talent to make money from a nice mixture of originality and what the public will stand,' said Kitty, guessing her thoughts. 'People like Clement and his friends will be taken up, if they're lucky, by Miller and his cronies; indeed, he – they – will have to be "taken up" if they are going to survive. It's never been easy; you only have to read about Dr Johnson and poor old Keats and Hazlitt. Greatness usually arrives after death.'

Sophie shuddered. 'What about Mr Wells and Mr Bennett? They must make a lot of money, and think of Dickens and Thackeray. Surely it's not impossible?'

'And think of the hundreds and thousands who don't,' said Kitty. 'Ah, here is Frank, and he's brought Clement, I see,' she said, as voices were heard on the stairs.

Sophie was thinking, isn't there another meaning to the word 'rich'? Rich in friends and books and talk, having the sort of life you want, have always wanted, like Kitty's life and Mr Miller's? Was it just knowing the right people, going to the right places, speaking other languages, travelling, having taste – was that all it was? But people who wrote and painted and were different came sometimes from 'ordinary' families. Clement, for example, and Thomas Hardy, people said.

When Clement came in, her preoccupations seemed petty. Clement *was* from the people, the respectable poor; Clement *would* have a different life because he was gifted and original. All those intellectual nabobs would see it; he would be famous, she knew he would. What could she ever do to help him? He was above her and beyond her.

It was hopeless: Clement did not look at her as she wanted him to. All she wanted was to look at him, and then for him to notice her and for them to be friends, if nothing else. But

66

he and Kitty were talking of other things than love. She liked Clement for that, for his ability to see through sham and fashion. She was content to sit and be silent and vowed she would read and read to try to catch up with these people who yet seemed to have some secret she wanted to share. It could not, then, be true that you needed only money to live in a civilized way, like her host and hostess. Did Clement perhaps even see through *them*? He looked sceptical.

'Miller is a middle-class Fabian,' stated Clement. 'He's made his peace with Society, which tolerates him just as they tolerate you, Frank; you write what they can feel proud of themselves for reading.'

Frank Laurence smiled. He did not seem to mind being semi-insulted by his new friend. His was a strange character: irascible and overbearing from time to time, but not with those whom he considered to be his equals in ability or promise.

Sophie understood only a little of what they were discussing. To her, a comfortable, professional home was as high as she had realized existed. But on evenings like this she began to understand the standards to which her friends aspired and they were not those of the middle-classes. Clement was different from Kitty and Frank and all the others, she thought that evening, for he really knew what the life of ordinary folk was like and despised those who lived on private incomes, or pretended to. He was shy and so, in his shyness and penury, would have to be accepted by people, some of whom might have no inkling of his own genius, but had money. He seemed to know a good deal about things other than poetry; he could hold his own in conversation, knew about painting and music and new ideas from other parts of Europe and Russia. How did he come to know all this? It was clear he had not spent all his time in Wiltshire studying trees and badgers and old pathways.

She felt protective towards him, as though he were like her; ignorant of the world of money and fashion, except through reading, and underestimated. She said nothing to anyone of these conclusions about Clement, not even to Edith. It was a new thing for her, not to talk about the object of her feelings. And Clement himself seemed unaware that he had such an earnest listener, who took a burning interest in his work and his mind.

Later, she thought she was in love, if that was the right word, with his unconscious, or his soul; with the unwilled part of him. He was finally elusive, though she might bend all the force of her own not inconsiderable willpower and charm to a consideration of catching his interest. Was she clever or original enough for him? Why, in any case, should a man one fell in love with, a man one could become crazy about, ever reciprocate? It seemed, anyway, that this was not going to happen. When she tried to appear aloof she succeeded only in appearing haughty. How did women go about snaring a man? She did not quite put that question to Edith in the next month or so, managed only to ask more generalized questions about relationships with the opposite sex. But Edith could not help, except to say, 'I suppose these things happen or they don't. And sometimes they may happen at the same time to the same two people. Or not.'

'How sad,' was all Sophie could reply. It had not escaped her notice that Clement always asked after Edith when she saw him at Kitty Moray's, where she had taken to dropping in occasionally; and finally she asked Edith to accompany her one Saturday afternoon to Doughty Street, after work. Sophie could not help feeling annoyed about his indifference towards her and obvious preference for Edith, though it was rather stupid of her to feel that, to say the least. She did not blame him for liking Edith better than her – she, too, preferred Edith to herself! Edith was, she felt, a superior character; but superior characters should not be hankered after by Clem Bartholomew.

Kitty had invited her friends to meet and walk a little in London in the direction of certain bookshops where they were to hand in prospectuses of the new review, *Counterpoint*, which she and Frank were to edit. Subscriptions were being sought to impress any backer before the quarterly went into its first printing. After solicitation of bookshops, the company was to repair to a Bloomsbury hotel for tea. It sounded a reasonable way of spending a Saturday afternoon to Sophie. Edith was a little tired of *The Serpent of the Sea*, which she was amending for Garnett Edwards, and agreed to come along. But when they arrived at Doughty Street it was to find Kitty alone.

'Frank is lunching with Austin; I said I'd do the rounds with you,' she said.

An April sun was out in the streets and Sophie could not help noticing how heads turned to look at Kitty as she walked along in her high boots, with an artist's bag on her shoulder and a gauzy blue scarf anchored with a bunch of violets and wound round her long neck.

They were to walk to Mecklenburgh Square and then to Lambs Conduit Street and into that part of Holborn next to the City where there were many printshops and bookshops.

'It is a pity Clement could not come,' said Sophie to Edith as they walked behind Kitty, rather like bridesmaids.

Kitty heard her and turned. 'He will meet us at the Hotel Russell on the way back,' she said.

Sophie's heart gave a sick little lurch. But she was pleased.

In the ensuing tramp round the dark shops and the strange back streets with their organ-grinders and flowersellers and the occasional group of urchins skipping in the middle of narrow alleys, she forgot Clement and gave herself up to observing. London was so vast. She was still a visitor. When would she feel herself as much a denizen as Kitty? Edith bought a book of etchings of birds printed a hundred years before, whilst Kitty thrust their hand-stencilled sheets into the hands of bookshop owners and held out to them her list of signatures. They mostly seemed amused to see the three women, but a few promised they would take a copy or two. Lawyers' clerks were much in evidence in the district and old gentlemen who had spent their Saturdays for the last fifty years in these shops and others like them. The daffodils on the barrows reminded Sophie of home, where they grew wild. The petals were a pale, creamy colour, with yolk yellow crowns and she could smell their scent in the distance. What had Clement said about daffodils in that poem where he spoke of the 'furry rime like gloves'? She rubbed her fingers together in her gloves, thinking of it.

When they finally arrived, around five o'clock, in the Gothic pile of the hotel, and were ushered into a large room at the back, its scattered tables covered in gleaming white linen, awaiting parties of tea drinkers, Sophie clutched her purse, wondering how she was going to afford such a sumptuous place. Edith did not seem worried. And there was Clement, already seated at a table and reading a book!

'You are all my guests today,' said Kitty, removing her gloves and gesturing grandly at the seats. Clement stood up, more as if he had learned that this was the thing to do than out of any spontaneous politeness.

The tea, when it came, was delightful, and the crumpets even more so. Sophie was quiet. Edith was her usual peaceable self, smiling and eating her crumpets absentmindedly.

'It doesn't look as though Frank is coming,' said Kitty, looking at her watch. 'The wretch! He's probably gone off with Austin to discuss the meaning of the word "good" and whether to say something is "yellow" is like saying it is "good".' Edith looked interested, but said nothing.

Sophie asked Kitty more questions about her proposed venture.

'Perhaps you will write something for us, Miss Broughton?' said Kitty. 'Sophie tells me you write. We have reports from St Petersburg and Paris, notes from the English countryside from Clement here and some of my stories and Frank's criticism.'

Edith looked surprised. What was Sophie getting her into now?

'We need a piece on English legends and the decline of the folk tale,' said Kitty decisively.

Clement was staring at Edith as she protested. 'The Norse legends are still a force up in Yorkshire, of course,' he said.

'It would need a great amount of reading – there must be many experts you could call upon for English folk lore,' replied Edith quietly.

'But not many who would write for what *we* can pay,' said Kitty.

'Don't you want to get into print, Miss Broughton?' asked Clement.

'Well, I will see. There's a lot of material, but it would need working up, and I have so little time.'

'You are a working woman, I know,' said Kitty, kindly.

Sophie was surprised that Edith was even contemplating an acceptance. What a lot she did not know about her friend!

'You *are* E. Broughton who wrote in *Materia Norsica*?' asked Kitty, after a pause. 'Frank reads all sorts of strange publications!'

Edith blushed. 'Oh, yes, but that was last year when I had more time, at home. When I'd finished working for Professor Muir there always seemed to be time. Here, we are always in a rush.'

'You are not a London person,' said Clement suddenly. 'I don't think *I* am either,' he added, and then looked down at his buttery fingers.

'None of us is that,' said Kitty, gathering her gloves and preparing to pay. 'Artists belong anywhere,' she said grandly, 'but are not appreciated unless they can move among their own kind.'

Edith looked at her quizzically, but said nothing.

'You know, Kitty Moray is rather absurd, isn't she?' said Edith that night to Sophie when they had returned to their attic eyrie and were sitting mending their stockings. Sophie looked up in surprise. It was unusual for Edith to pass judgment on anything or anyone.

'I'm sorry, Edith, if I told her you wrote. It was because, somehow, she assumed I did and I wanted to get it straight. And you *do* write, Edith – I didn't know you had published.'

'It was nothing, just a little piece of research I did in the library at the university. How on earth could Frank have come to read it?'

'I thought it was rather rude of Kitty to assume you would write for nothing,' pursued Sophie.

'Was it? Yes, I suppose so. Yet, think of all the work I do for Garnett!'

'What *do* you do for Garnett, Edith? He does keep you busy! I hope he'll pay you.'

'He said I should receive a sum at the end of the year for helping with the new editions of his *Monsters of the Deep* and *Serpents of the Sea*. I like writing for him. Do you think I should ask for more? It seemed part of the contract at Miller's.'

'Does Mr Miller know you do all this extra work for Mr Edwards, then?'

'I don't know. I thought he must, but perhaps he doesn't. Isn't life difficult?' Edith smiled then.

'Do something for Kitty, even if it's an honorary sort of writing. It would get you known.'

71

'I don't particularly want to be "known",' said Edith. 'Particularly not as an author in the Moon series!' How could she explain, even to Sophie, that she wrote to feel she existed, but that to bring her writings to the public view was quite different, another thing entirely from a scholarly monograph. No one must ever know how much she wrote for Garnett. It would be almost indecent, a form of exhibitionism for the 'public' to see her as the author of monsters that arose from her own subconscious.

'Sometimes, Edith, you look so far away. Clement kept looking at you. He obviously thinks you are a Mystery. I wish *I* could look like that.' It was true she did envy Edith a little, but she could never be jealous of her.

'No you don't, Sophie. You are always in contact with people; you're not shy like me,' said Edith, unable to realize she was in any way enviable.

'Oh, in some ways I don't think you're shy at all, Edith,' said Sophie. 'Only with people who don't really matter. You don't care to make an impression, that's all.'

'We shall have to entertain them, but how can we up here? We can't let Kitty go on paying for teas, or she will think perhaps that is sufficient payment for anything she can get you to write,' Sophie went on.

'Yes, it is a problem,' said Edith. 'It is hard being a "furnished woman", isn't it?'

'Better than being a daughter at home,' replied Sophie.

Through such conversations and accommodations the two women got to know each other better, and if Sophie was sad that 'her' poet seemed more interested in her friend that in herself, she said nothing. Edith did not appear to notice and was vaguely polite to him.

In the event, Clement and Frank went off on a walking tour when Clement's book was at last with the printers. Kitty went to Paris to meet some French women writers and Edith and Sophie talked more of their summer holiday which slowly came into view as spring arrived and then summer and the rooms grew lighter and the Autumn List was finalized at Miller's. Sophie was given more work to do, sorting out many old letters which had lain in cupboards since Grant Miller's father had started the firm, and Grant would watch her with an expression that Theo Carmichael privately thought of as wistful, and rather disgusting.

Sophie had been helping on the trade counter where the men came daily from London bookshops to ask for the firm's books demanded by their customers. She helped fill the enormous sacks they brought with them and marvelled that anyone could carry such burdens. In the same room on the ground floor at the back of the 'house', worked Mrs Smeaton and two elderly male clerks. Mrs Smeaton made up the invoices and Willy came up to help pack smaller parcels of books for 'abroad'. Toby's two assistants worked on the top floor above Mr Miller's office, filling in ledgers and recording mysterious calculations. At the top of the house, on the floor above them, was a room of stock, piles of books that had still not been sorted out and sent to North London where the new 'succursale' had been established to cope with the overflow of volumes. The general impression was of brisk trade and reasonable profits.

After the book by Mrs Humphrey Addiscombe, Grant had given Sophie no more to read and she was shy of asking him. She had not liked the book by the married lady, allegory or no. It exalted men and she had found it too conventional. The lady was supposed to write in a 'daring' way, but there had been, she thought, too much attention to social chit-chat and a knowing sort of insider speech which Sophie half envied, half despised. She had said as much to Mr Miller. So she read steadily on in her own way and the days, weeks, months, passed quickly.

The time had almost arrived when she was to spend her two weeks in Thirksay, joined by Edith. Mrs Ridsdale had written long letters to her daughter, by turns agitated and hectoring, but seemed to Sophie to have calmed down a little after Sophie's descriptions of her work in Bloomsbury and the news of a small rise in salary which she had unexpectedly been offered. She had wondered whether it was for her 'reading', but Grant had said nothing. Sophie guessed she had allayed her parents' suspicions about her way of life, which, though blameless, was an unusual enough course for a daughter of the village to have chosen. She felt half-sick, half-excited, to be going back, glad that Edith would accompany her, and a little frightened that, after that, she might never get away again. London now felt like home, though her night dreams were never of London, but of the green meadows and red and white cottages of her childhood village.

Sophie had felt that, this year, she must make an effort to get on with her mother and not be seen to be leaving in a hurry. Perhaps the next year she would go with Edith to Leeds. In the meantime, as the holidays approached and London became stuffier and more and more tiring, the two young women lay on their beds in the evening, reading. For Sophie, Ramal's *Poems of Childhood* and the new *Poetry Review* and Hardy's *Dynasts* and her ever beloved Housman, made a counterpoint to her busy days at the office, whilst Edith was deep in her notes on some curious legends which she had been allowed to read in the British Museum, where Kitty Moray had introduced her to the dispenser of Readers' tickets.

The day finally came when, their bags packed, they set out early one Saturday morning to make the long journey north to York where they would take a local train and then be met by Sophie's father. Mrs Macalister had even graciously waved them goodbye. They had had to pay forward rent to be assured of their rooms on return and Sophie half suspected Mrs Macalister would lease their top floor to visitors in their absence. They had tidied away all evidence of their occupancy for what their landlady called 'summer cleaning' and each taken a suitcase of belongings with them. Sophie had taken books, should she need to be reminded there was another world beyond Thirksay.

The day dawned warm and became warmer as the train from King's Cross sped them back north. 'What a summer!' everyone said, making conversation on the train to the two young ladies in their second-class carriage.

Sophie had insisted on travelling in style; the journey was part of the holiday, after all. 'Don't you wish you were going to France?' she had asked, wistfully, as the fields of Lincolnshire came slowly chugging by.

'No,' replied Edith. 'I'm sure your farm will be more interesting than stuffy old Paris.'

Sophie was silent, for Edith had been Abroad whilst she had only dreamt of it. Kitty Moray had written rapturous post-cards from Paris and seemed to want to stay there, in spite of the planned publication in the autumn of the long awaited *Counterpoint*.

Edith was thinking of her writing and of the reality of the places they passed which had stayed throughout history, and wondering whether this England they were seeing bore any resemblence to its medieval, and even older, self. She wished she knew more, was always aware of the gaps in her knowledge. Her work at Miller's was almost a soporific. She had typed away, thinking of other things, always careful to check her work. Even when writing for Edwards, although for periods her whole mind would be engaged in some technical descriptive problem, she was aware that other ideas were pushing for recognition. She did not have a hunger for novels as Sophie did. Fiction, especially her own attempts at it, was a froth on the surface of the life of the mind, a second-order activity. She wanted something more substantial. Thoughts, which came to her from some depth she did not know she had visited, were more important, but it was difficult to make anything coherent from them. She needed the discipline of research, needed time to think round a subject, not be for ever darting here and there like Sophie.

But she smiled at her friend who had been her usually loquacious self as far as Grantham, but who was now silent. She hoped Mr Ridsdale would be there to meet them in a gig at the nearest railway station to Thirksay as he had promised, for Sophie's case was heavy. She, herself, had brought only her notebooks, a little volume entitled *Tales of the Riding* and her usual clothes and brushes. What a nuisance travelling was! In her reticule she had put a pack of sandwiches and a Thermos. The sandwiches were finished and the tea drunk by the time the Minster hove on to the horizon like a great ship on the flat plain. Pilgrims must have seen it like that, she thought. Sophie exclaimed and pointed and they smiled at each other before reaching down their cases to change trains in York.

'Why do people wear so much?' grumbled Sophie. 'It's so hot – you need only a camisole, no stockings or shoes. We could paddle in the brook and catch minnows, I suppose.'

A little girl in a sun-bonnet and a boy in his best sailor suit also seemed to be waiting for the local train with their mother. The mother was agitated over smuts from the train that had landed on her son's pristine collar.

'It must be dreadful travelling with children,' whispered Sophie. 'Dad will be there with the gig at Market Sowerby. I do hope the train won't be late.'

It *was* a little late, but was a welcome change after the hot platform. They lowered the window down on its thick leather belt.

'Don't you wish you were going east to the sea? We are going the wrong way for that,' sighed Sophie.

Edith thought Sophie was never quite satisfied, always wished she were somewhere else, but she saw that her friend was nervous.

'I do hope you'll like it,' Sophie kept saying.

'I'm sure I shall love it,' was Edith's repeated rejoinder.

The train was going through a wooded area and when they came through it she saw low hills on the horizon on their right.

'Further north, behind those hills, are the moors,' said Sophie. 'Then Whitby and the sea.'

'I've never been to Whitby. Father knows some old ladies who live near Bridlington – sort of aunts of his.'

'Oh Bridlington's a bit tame,' replied Sophie. 'Whitby's lovely. Perhaps we could go on a day trip there from home.'

'Once you get home you won't want to travel again,' said Edith sensibly.

'No, perhaps not. My uncles and father have to go to market every week and I like going with them. But we can go on long walks round the village and sit in the orchard.'

'Should we offer to help with the farm work or the harvest?' asked Edith.

'Oh, no, except perhaps collecting eggs or picking green-gages. The village women still do a bit of gleaning, but the reaper-binder doesn't leave much over. When I was little, father always made me give my gleaning away. Sometimes the hay harvest is very late, but by now they'll have brought the haywain home. I used to ride on the top!' She was silent, thinking of it. Then she added, 'Dad used to pretend we were really helping him when we were little.

'He sounds a nice man, your father.'

'Yes, he is, but farming never really suited him. My uncles have always been active. Father sees more to the managing now, since the farm's grown. Mother even wants Dad to send Harry and Jerome to school in York. I don't know if they could afford it. My sister works in the post office – did I tell you?' Sophie spoke rapidly, filling Edith in on domestic details and, as the neared the market town, Edith learned more of the background of her friend's first eighteen years that in all the ten months of their acquaintance. She was eager to meet Sophie's family, feeling she knew them quite well already.

The little train finally slowed down to a narrow platform and the name 'Market Sowerby' in metal letters came into view. They tugged once more at their suitcases and Edith pushed a few hairpins vaguely back into her bun. Then the train stopped with a hiss of steam. The lady with the children was soon on the platform, pointing to the guard's van and directing a porter, and Edith and Sophie descended, too. Sophie looked up and down the platform, but no one seemed to be there.

A porter came up and said to Sophie: 'Your dad's waiting outside t'station with t'gig. He said to put your bags on my trolley, like. Nothing in the guard's van, then?' He seemed to be well acquainted with her. 'How's London, then?' he enquired as they walked alongside him. Without waiting for a reply he went on, 'Never been meself. Eh, it's not a patch on York, I'll be bound!'

The air was still and warm and over the fence of the station yard there was a field of meadowsweet. Elderflowers drooped their heavy musk in pools of scent over the railings further on. They passed through a little booking office which seemed untenanted, but a voice said, 'Afternoon, George,' from behind the ticket counter with its arched glass opening. The lady and the children seemed to have been swallowed up somewhere and all that was in evidence in the sudden glare of sunlight beyond the outer door, was a pony and cart with a man standing by, holding the pony's reins. He threw them over into the cart and came towards them. Edith saw that he looked very like Sophie, but his eyes were of a lighter hazel than hers.

'Dad!' She ran up and hugged him.

'Where's your luggage, then, is this all? Afternoon, George,' he nodded at the porter.

'Aye, Mr Ridsdale. Train was nobbut five minutes late.' The porter pocketed the offered shilling and stowed their cases in the trap, a low, cumbersome, dusty affair with two seats facing forwards and two backwards.

'Dad, this is Edith Broughton.'

Thomas Ridsdale shook Edith's hand a little awkwardly. 'Well, we'd best be off. Your mother's been rushing around all morning, baking and all. You'll be hungry. What time did you leave, then?' They told him as they shook out their skirts and then wrapped them round and climbed into the gig, not before Sophie had patted the pony's face and said 'Hullo, Silver. Remember me?'

Edith could not see Sophie's father at all clearly, as he stood for a moment before climbing on to the driver's seat, but she sensed a benign presence. Of course, she was predisposed in his favour, partly because she preferred to like people until they proved themselves dislikeable, and partly because Sophie loved him. She thought about Sophie's family and wondered what to expect from the rest of them as they were trotted slowly through winding lanes edged with trees and meadows, past signposts with outlandish Viking and Anglian names on their outstretched arms: Crayke and Alne and Flawith and Thwaite and Thirksay.

Sophie's farm was named Church Farm and had been developed from a smallholding when some land was sold off, the century before, by a titled landowner, Lord Dawne. Sophie had said that generations of agricultural labourers had made up her family, with an admixture of yeomen, and a schoolmaster from York in the middle of the last century.

They passed the schoolhouse, small and slate-roofed, on the main street of the village which culminated in a square-towered church with a large graveyard that had no boundaries at the back and led to a meadow and a further stile. Then they were down another lane leading off the street past the post office at the corner, and now the overhanging beech trees cast shade and made a triumphal arch for the pony as she sedately but wearily trotted the last few hundred yards home.

Church Farm was a mellow, red-brick built farmhouse, with large swathes of honeysuckle over its porch which was glassed-in at the front. Behind, were the farm buildings proper, where the pony took them and came to a full stop with a sniff and toss. They were all still for a moment. Then, 'Mother'll be waiting at the front. Go round, will you, and I'll fetch your stuff in,' suggested Mr Ridsdale.

They got down and the only sound was that of some hens behind a fence in the yard and the liquid, trickling music of a stream.

'All the farm-hands are out in the fields, Dad says, and Harry and Jerome are staying with Aunt Phoebe,' said Sophie.

Edith followed her to the front of the house and there, now in the porch, was Sophie's mother, a tall, surprisingly well-dressed woman with a careful smile of welcome for her daughter's friend. She had a loud, firm voice and great surface liveliness of manner, yet she did not clasp Sophie to her with any great appearance of affection. Perhaps Sophie had not yet been forgiven for deserting her well-planned future, for later, when Mrs Ridsdale, presiding over a plenteous ham 'tea' in the gleaming parlour, said, 'Your Uncle John can't come on Tuesday,' Edith thought it was with a certain grimness.

Many questions were asked of poor Edith, who began to realize why Sophie had been so insistent her holiday be passed by them *both* at Thirksay. It was evident that Mrs Ridsdale would have dearly loved to get her daughter alone and subject her to an inquisition, but politeness prevented her from doing this in front of her daughter's friend. Instead, she pumped Edith. Edith managed to give a creditable picture of their joint working life, omitting the momentous meeting in the teashop and any mention of young poets. Sophie was impressed. Edith appeared so well-bred and gentle and seemed to convey that her own parents were pleased to have her in London, which quite mollified Sophie's mother.

'But will it *lead* anywhere?' she asked finally when they had got to the plum cake stage and the sun was lower in the sky. Mr Ridsdale had gone off to the cows, summoned by a farm-hand. 'We thought she was so lucky to train as a teacher,' continued Sophie's mother a little belligerently, adding, 'she got first prize in composition and history all through school and the college gave her a good reference. We were so upset when we heard she wasn't taking the post in Croydon. I don't know what her Uncle John thinks.'

'But, Mother,' interrupted Sophie. 'I shall soon be earning as much as Bessy Thwaites in the schoolhouse.'

'Your father should have gone down to London with you,' replied her mother firmly and, turning to Edith, 'He couldn't be spared in the autumn. I wanted to go myself and settle her in.'

'Dad didn't say anything. I think he's glad I've found work I like,' said Sophie.

'Oh, well, he always spoiled you. There's one thing to be said; you can always find a post in a school when you've tired of gadding about, publishing books. Though good posts don't grow on trees.'

For the moment the topic was left. Edith knew it would return. They helped the farmer's wife clear the table and went up to the long landing that ran the whole length of the farmhouse and from which, various bedroom doors led off.

Edith's room was fresh and clean with a white ewer with pink roses round its rim, a patchwork quilt and a smell of beeswax. After the rather dusty rooms at Mrs Macalister's it was welcome and she sat at the window. It looked out over a flower garden at the back. A girl came down the path and into the house, and she heard 'Alice!'

'Hello, our Rose!'

So, her friend was called Rose by her sister, though she had not noticed the mother call her anything. Sophie seemed closer to her father, as Edith had expected. Edith put her clothes away dreamily and went down to the parlour. Sophie was waiting by a door that led into the back of the house down a passage tiled brick red with a wooden door and latch.

'Do *you* call that a sneck?' asked Edith, pointing to the latch.

'Yes – do you? Oh, Edith I'm so glad *y*ou're here. I'm sure Mother thinks you're a most suitable friend for me; do you mind?' Sophie whispered. 'Come and walk in the garden. They're all out thistle cutting and Alice wants to meet you.'

'Yes, I heard her come in. It's a lovely room you've given me. Ought I to ask your mother if she needs help with anything?'

'No. Mother's gone for a little walk, now it's a bit cooler. She wants to tell Dad what she thinks should be done with the oak field.' Sophie chattered on, partly to cover the nervousness she felt at admitting Edith to her childhood home. Edith thought the Ridsdales were all very friendly, and naturally they would be concerned for their eldest daughter, alone in London, having thrown up what they must have considered a promising career.

They went out through the front porch with its glassed-in, pointed gable. There was a strong smell of geraniums and phlox and Edith breathed it in with pleasure. The sun was still warm and there was the sound of the brook in the distance and of voices from the fields which came right up to the bottom of the farmhouse garden, over a little wall.

'Mother wanted you to sit in the parlour,' said Sophie. 'But I told her you wanted to see round the farm – not that there's much to see. I believe father hasn't much left now in the cornfields. He's been growing rhubarb and concentrating on selling milk to the village. Uncle Joe has most of the big fields now.'

They walked down the garden and then over a stile and round back to the farmyard on the other side of the house. There were some red-tiled barns and a pump, and by an outhouse, a duck pond, on which several brownish ducks were circling slowly. Also a tall, stiff-necked gander.

'You must eat some nettle salad; have you ever eaten nettles? I'll make you some,' said Sophie.

Then they were walking into the orchard beyond the pond where Sophie proudly displayed some ripening greengages. 'We're famous for these,' she said. Edith was silent, taking in all the details one by one and adjusting her spectacles which were making her nose ache. 'They'll be clover cutting tomorrow and next week,' Sophie went on. 'Such are the excitements of rural life.'

'It's simply lovely,' said Edith with unaccustomed enthusiasm, so that Sophie stopped and looked at her.

'You really like it, Edith?'

'It's beautiful. But I feel I should be doing something to help. Do they work all the time, your parents? Are they never idle?'

'Yes, there's no leisure on a farm. I'm no good at farm-work and, of course, Mother never intended me for it. Harry and Jerome aren't too keen either, I suppose seeing Father and Mother always so busy. Educated beyond their station, they are,' said Sophie. Then she fell silent as they walked round, back to the other side of the house.

'Are there woods?' asked Edith.

'Oh yes, and mushrooms and a magic tree.'

In a field near the house Edith could just make out what looked like a cricket pitch.

'The boys from the village all come to play cricket here – the rector is Captain – it's like a religion, cricket. I used to play when I was little; I liked to pretend I was a boy.'

'But women *do* play cricket, at least, they did at my school,' said Edith.

'After they've finished harvesting all the fields they'll have a supper, probably at uncle's, and the children will all play here; every year it's the same. But we could perhaps get away on bicycles if you wanted to see more. You haven't seen the village yet either – '

A girl was sitting on the stile as they came round to the top of the fallow field on their way back to the house.

'Alice, come and meet Edith,' shouted Sophie. 'She's shy,' she added. 'She thinks you're a great, grand lady.' Edith laughed and they went up to the girl who jumped rather awkwardly off the stile. She had a long, brown skirt and a blue ribbon in her hair and did not resemble her sister in any shape or form.

Alice shook Edith's hand and appeared dumb. 'I hear you work in the post office,' ventured Edith, trying hard.

'Yes, Alice is one of the world's workers,' her sister replied for her.

But Alice then said, with a little spirit, 'Give over, our Rose! It was quiet today – I wouldn't mind a bit more excitement.'

'Edith knows me as Sophie,' said Sophie grandly.

'But Rose is a lovely name,' said Edith.

They were back in the garden now and the air was a little cooler.

'Our Rose always called me Mary,' said Alice. 'So I call her her second name.'

'I don't call you Mary now, though.'

'That's my name, too,' said Edith.

'Oh, is it? Rose, will you ask her – you know . . .'

'Oh, Alice, ask her yourself!'

But Alice blushed and, after an awkward little bow, said she must go in and help Mother.

'What does she want?' asked Edith.

'Oh, she's got one of those Confession and Autograph books – they're all the rage in the village. It was the first thing she said when she came in from work: will you ask your friend to write in my book?' Sophie laughed.

'Oh, I see. Yes, of course I will.'

It had not escaped Edith that Sophie was a little ashamed of her sister's provincial manners.

The three girls were later given a cheese and curd tart supper in a small room off the main kitchen and Edith hoped that Mrs Ridsdale was not going to put herself out too much for her. Edith saw there were York hams hanging beyond, in the outer kitchen, when she firmly entered the inner kitchen and offered to help with the dishes. Mrs Ridsdale was surprised, but offered no resistance. If she was also surprised at Edith's competence with the tea-towel, she said nothing.

A helper, Mrs Elsie Wainman, was left to clear the kitchen before she went round the back to finish off the last milking. After the supper, Edith was ceremoniously taken into the parlour with Alice and a piano was presented to her, an object of red silk pleats and stool to match. It was obvious that all these diversionary tactics were seized upon by Sophie to avoid what her mother obviously wanted; a long chat about Sophie's life in London.

When the farmer's wife finally did come into the parlour, apron-less, Sophie managed to get Edith to talk once again about their mutual work and life, and Edith could not help but make a further good impression with her quiet manner and gentle politeness. 'It is so kind of you to have me here,' she was beginning, but Mrs Ridsdale swept on.

'Sophie will have to look after you. Will you go to church tomorrow, daughter?'

Sophie thought discretion was the better part of valour and, anyway, it would be better to get the villagers and their questions over, so she agreed that she and Edith would accompany Alice.

Then Mrs Ridsdale asked Edith to play the piano. Sophie hoped that Edith would. It would help, to listen to some music, and perhaps her father would come in then. Dusk was falling and the air of the parlour was faintly spiced with the fragrance of the stocks under the open window. There were shouts of goodnight and the lowing of animals, and then a door was bolted.

'Dad has to get up at four,' said Alice.

'Oh, he'll come in a moment. I do wish the boys were back; we need their help,' grumbled Mrs Ridsdale.

Indeed, Edith was aware, when Sophie's father came in and perched himself on the Windsor chair, that this was not his usual way of spending an hour's leisure on Saturday evening.

'Edith is going to play,' announced Sophie.

Edith moved to the piano, for she was not in the least shy about her accomplishments, though she only admitted to a few people what they were. Still, she had promised Sophie, and then she must excuse herself and go up to bed. So she sat down with no preliminary hesitations and smiled at Sophie and immediately began a Chopin valse. She played well, without music, for the memory was in her fingers. Those hours of practice at the Leeds Girls' High School had paid dividends and the Ridsdales were much impressed. Sophie, in particular, was proud of Edith and muttered a thank you on the stairs as they made their way, finally, up to bed.

In the morning Edith got up early, not wanting to miss anything of the holiday that stretched ahead. She was fascinated by the farm and the village and Sophie's parents, so unlike anything or anybody she knew. She did not want to disturb the family when, soon after dawn, she went down into the garden that was still dew-laden, with that scent of summer you may travel a continent to smell and find all the time at home, and which you remember for ever. It was very slightly misty, the sort of mist that presages a hot day. The sky was cloudless and the faint pink was merging now with a pale summer blue.

She need not have worried about disturbing anyone, for Mr Ridsdale was already there talking to a labourer in the courtyard of the farm. Edith heard a faint mooing from the cowsheds, so supposed the milking was in process of completion. She wished there were something useful she could do for Sophie's mother, but shrank from appearing too soon in the morning. She had always liked the early morning best, feeling full of energy and yet peaceful. She had slept well, with the lavender scent of the linen sheets in her nostrils, but had wakened to the sound of birdsong before dawn.

Edith wandered to the orchard, sure that no one had seen her. The gander was curled up on the plashy grass, but rose when he saw her. They stood looking at each other for a moment, sizing each other up, and then Edith moved tactfully away. She was eager to see the rest of the village, but decided she had better go in, if she could escape Mrs Ridsdale, who she was sure would immediately set about baking if she espied her guest.

She managed to whisk up the stairs, and met Sophie yawning on the landing.

'Goodness, Edith, where have you been? I've only just woken up and that was only because Father called me.'

'I went out for a little walk – the sky was so inviting,' replied Edith, smiling. 'But don't tell your mother. I don't want her to keep feeling she's got to feed me.'

'Oh, Mother'll be in the kitchen anyway. The men have a good breakfast of bacon and eggs every morning.'

'Has your sister gone to work already?' enquired Edith as they went down the stairs together.

'Alice starts at half past eight. But have you forgotten it's Sunday?'

'Yes, I had,' admitted Edith, 'but the men are working today?'

'Oh, yes. If there's work to do they do it, Lord's day or not.'

'Are you going to church, as your mother suggested?'

'I'll go to please her and get the village gawpers over with. Will you come with me? You don't have to.'

'I like the music,' admitted Edith, 'but I don't take Communion.'

'I didn't think you did. Like me, you're an agnostic, aren't you? Not that I was ever confirmed; I was baptized Chapel.' Sophie dropped her voice as her mother came round the corner from the kitchen. 'Here, Mother, let me. We'll just have a bite and then be off to St Wilfred's,' she said hurriedly.

Mrs Ridsdale smiled at Edith and stated there was porridge already laid out in the kitchen if they did not mind eating there.

Edith began to feel one of the family and yet quite protective of the usually independent Sophie when the latter was being alternately ordered around or taken for granted by her mother.

That first morning they went to church without any older members of the clan. Sophie seemed concentrated on the service and apparently unaware of the nudges and glances that were directed at them. At the end of Matins, when the congregation filed out slowly into the summer morning, whose balm was now warmer and seemed to drip like honey gold on the tombstones and the porch, Sophie gave a few dazzling smiles to several selected parishoners and spoke to one or two of them, introducing Edith as her friend from London. Edith took it all in good part. Greetings were exchanged, health enquired about; old ladies smiled and younger women, with armfuls of toddlers, nodded their heads at Sophie. When, finally, they were out of the churchyard and through the lych gate, Sophie gave a brief sigh.

'Thank God that's over,' she said irreverently. 'Now they'll be able to tell Mother they saw me and that I'm still alive and undamaged. They all mean well, I know, but they're so nosey! They want to know everything about me – always did. It gets on my nerves. Still, Mother can go on holding her head high. Let's forget them now. I've done my duty. Come on Edith, we can sit in the bower and have a glass of lemonade; it's home-made with lemons and sugar – you've never tasted anything so delicious.'

And sit in the arbour at the side of the house they did, at the scrubbed wooden table, before a large pitcher of lemonade with floating lemon peel and a bowl of sugar. The table stood against a red-brick wall covered in honeysuckle, which Sophie buried her face in. They sat with their hands in the sun and their faces in shade under two large straw hats provided by Sophie's mother 'to avoid sunstroke and freckles'. Alice soon joined them and Edith felt at peace and almost drowsy with content.

As they sipped their cool, sharp drink in thick country glasses, the sun seemed to enter Sophie, too, so that she smiled and seemed to forget her annoyance. She waved to an old lady who had suddenly materialized through the hedge, carrying a gosling in her arms against a pinafore of black satin. 'It's Aunt Rose-Ann – she's nearly ninety,' whispered Sophie. 'She takes a gosling everywhere, but never seems to mind when he's fattened up for Christmas.'

The gosling must be the gander's progeny, thought Edith. 'Perhaps it's just that she likes the idea of an always renewable goose,' she said.

Alice looked at her curiously. She was walking out that afternoon with young Ben Tollerton from another farm and was impatient to get her dinner over. 'I'll be off to help Mother,' she said, after waving at her great aunt, who then came up and released the gosling with a pat. He promptly sat down.

'Your mother's asked me in for your Sunday meal,' said the old lady, after Edith had been introduced. 'Aye, it's a grand day to see you back, Sophia Rose. Did she tell you she were called after me?' she asked Edith.

'Yes. I think both your names are beautiful,' said Edith, making an effort.

The old lady was pleased. 'I live in yon' cottage,' she said, and pointed behind her to where a chimney could be seen poking through greenery. 'Me and the gosling,' she said and almost cackled. She had gnarled hands and wore a cap which might have graced an eighteenth-century painting. Edith was enchanted and looked forward to hearing some salty speech. 'You wouldn't think I were born in eighteen twenty-two, would you?' asked the old woman, as she made her way slowly up the path with her stick.

'My goodness!' said Edith.

'All the rest have gone long ago – all the rest – my mother and my sisters and brothers, all from consumption. But I was spared. Outlived his old lordship, I have.' She paused a moment by the ramblers and her eyes seemed to grow misty. 'I never married, young lady,' she said. 'That's why I'm still here, you know.'

'That's right, Aunt Rose-Ann,' murmured Sophie.

Aunt Rose-Ann clutched Edith by the sleeve. Her eyes were now bright and she seemed fully rational. 'Never marry, my dear,' she said. 'Take my advice. Isn't she lovely?' she said, turning to Sophie, who smiled.

'Yes, Aunt; Edith is very beautiful, I think.'

Edith took all this in her stride and did not seem to mind the old lady's eccentricities.

'*You* must wed, Great Niece,' went on the old woman. 'I hear you're making a life in London. I never went myself but my sister did. Soon came back, though.'

'Will the goose stay there?' asked Sophie, pointing to the bird, who seemed comatose.

'Oh, aye, he'l' wait on me. Now where's that dinner?' answered the surprising old lady.

'She's what they call a character,' whispered Sophie to Edith as they went in.

Mrs Ridsdale had not much time for this survival from pre-Victorian days and answered her questions in monosyllables, too busy carving and handing round the roast beef and roast potatoes. Edith was surprised. She had never seen a woman carve the joint. Sophie's family was rather unusual. As well as the girls and Mr and Mrs Ridsdale and the aunt, two women were also eating with them and the conversation was all of the farm and the coming week's work. Edith learned that the oat fields were late, but they hoped to continue with the thistle cutting and clover cutting in the next day or two.

Mr Ridsdale concentrated on talking to Edith and she found plenty of questions to ask him. 'It's hard, country life,' he said.

'I think I would like it,' said Edith.

'Nay,' he answered. 'You'd get no time for your books, lass. It's nowt but work. I know – I used to be a reader once.' He looked guiltily into his glass of beer, but his eyes smiled at her over the brim. Edith thought once more that he was very nice and that Sophie was his true daughter.

It was after they had walked Aunt Rose-Ann back to her cottage, after the meal, and were on their way back, complete with gosling, that Sophie said, 'My Uncle John, he's her son.'

'But I thought she – she never married?'

'She didn't. It was a bye blow, they said the local squire's. Anyway, it was nearly seventy years ago – she won't say.'

'And your uncle?'

'He's not my uncle really. I suppose he's my father's cousin. Oh, he went to Hartlepool and made good in business; that's where I got the money to go to Leeds. He took a fancy to me.'

'Does he never come home to see his mother, then?'

'Not often. She's proud of him, though, still calls him John Boy.'

'You ought to ask Alice to ask your Aunt Rose-Ann

to write in her Confessions Book,' said Edith, laughing. 'What extraordinary lives people have.' She thinks *you* should marry, anyway.'

'Just what you told me yourself, Edith. There must be some deficiency in me; people always think I should be married. Perhaps you can see why the very idea fills me with a sort of horror. And anyway, I wouldn't want to keep house. Look at Mother, never sits down – '

'I think we ought to offer to help with the clearing of that delicious lunch.'

'Dinner, you mean. No, she's got Elsie and Clara to help today. And she'd rather we were out of the house, I think, when she does put her feet up. I thought we might go for a walk to the village and then sit and read in the garden. What would you like, Edith?'

'It's nice just to be here, so different from Roundhay.'

They were standing looking over the orchard pond now, but the big gander was nowhere to be seen.

'Yes, I expect one day I *shall* miss it all, but you'd go away if you were me, wouldn't you?'

'Don't forget, I went away myself. But that was father's doing really.'

'My father misses me, I think,' said Sophie.

They walked among the apple trees whose fruit was still small and unripe. An elder, like a green hood with a lace ruffle, had settled itself in one of the hollows of an old trunk. Probably the seed had been put there by a bird. They could hear nothing but a distant shout and the bark of a dog, with the occasional moan of a stock-dove.

'Summer is the best time here,' said Sophie. 'In winter it can be very cold. We have to go to Sowerby for coal to light the big fires and sometimes in August to stock up, but this summer is marvellous, isn't it? I can't remember it ever being warmer.'

'What do they usually do at Christmas? Do all your other relatives come for a dinner?'

'Oh, they have a monster ham tea. You saw the hams in the outer kitchen, and oatcakes and apple pies. They preserve the fruit in the attic with grease. It's cosy in winter with the lamps lit, I suppose, but there's always some emergency on a farm. You can never relax.'

'Yet you don't seem at all like a farmer's daughter, Sophie. Don't you take any interest in animals and grain and growing things?'

Sophie looked surprised. 'Not really. The boys are supposed to. I used to help make the butter, but Mother doesn't bother me much with that now. *Didn't* bother me,' she corrected herself, remembering that she no longer lived in Thirksay.

'I'd like it,' declared Edith. 'I like growing things and baking and that sort of hard work – it's silly, isn't it? You wouldn't think it to look at me, would you? Must be my ancestry coming out.'

'But you want to be a writer, Edith. How can you have a life like that and have any time to write or think?'

'I don't know. I suppose it's not possible. I'm being "romantic," I suppose.'

'Tell me what *you* do when you're at home, Edith. How do "burghers of Leeds" spend their time?'

'Well, it's less feudal than Thirksay,' began Edith. 'I mean, I noticed here what a hierarchy the village is, with your Lord What's-his-name at the Hall. I don't suppose he's seen around very much? *My* father never goes to church, so we haven't that pressure either, and the servants aren't very much in evidence.'

'Do you have many – I mean, servants? That sounds more feudal to me!'

'No. Just a cook and she can't cook, and a housemaid and a parlourmaid and a boy for the carriage and the odd jobs, and a woman who cleans and washes up. We're not grand. Father would rather not have any, I suppose, but you know men; they like their things cleaned and polished and washed for them. Mother's more of a decoration; she must get bored. I was bored, you know; tea at the tennis club, and expected to join in amateur dramatics. There's a musical society, quite good really, and lots of people garden and do photography or collect stamps or play croquet, and call on each other to gossip, and read silly novels.'

'Don't you miss any of that in London, then?'

'Oh no, gracious me! No, I preferred to read books from the library or go on long walks or out on the tandem with father.'

'He must miss you, then.'

'He's always busy with his work. We're not gentry, you know, Sophie, we're "in trade".'

'But he's got plenty of money,' pursued Sophie, seeing her friend in rather a new light.

'He finds the English middle-classes stifling,' replied Edith. 'Like your father, he's not ordinary.'

'But having enough money must make a difference?'

'Yes, I know. Mother seems to spend enough, and he gave me an allowance, but when I came to London I said I wanted to manage on what I could earn. I've got money in the bank, but I haven't touched it except to go home; railway fares and that sort of thing, and an occasional book.'

'But having it must make you feel different? I mean, you could live more splendidly if you wanted, Edith.'

'Yes, I suppose so, Edith sighed. 'You mean silk slippers, fancy clothes and ribbons, tennis racquets and a phonograph, a typewriter and a bicycle. But they're not important, Sophie.'

'I don't suppose many people in the village have seen a typewriter or really fashionable clothes, except on the young ladies at the Hall. Bicycles, yes, I think they're the best thing ever to have been invented, though the villagers really prefer horses, I think. All the money goes on the reaper and binder and hiring the threshing machine and on coal to keep warm and oil for the lamps. Perhaps one day they'll bring gas as far as Thirksay, but I can't believe it.'

'I want to leave something when we go, for your folk,' said Edith, 'but it's difficult. What if I bought a cricket bat for your brothers and then your mother wouldn't feel offended?'

'They're coming home soon. They're always saving for cricket bats and balls so I'm sure that would be lovely. But you're our guest, Edith. Mother hates to feel she's rather poor and is very insulted if I try to give her anything. Hurt pride, you know. A cricket bat would be nice.'

'Then I shall buy one when we go to market. When is your market day?'

'It's Friday in Sowerby and Wednesday in Northallerton, but we don't go there very much. Only for things we can't buy in Sowerby.'

'And I brought a little cloth with me. I'll give her that,' added Edith.

The two were then silent, lying on their backs looking at the moving skies. They were to have many such conversations during the week, but they took place in a haze of well-being and only occasionally were more serious matters touched upon, like the character of Clement Bartholomew, or the feelings both of them brought to the future from their different childhoods.

The kitchen at Church Farm was really the heart of the place. There were two kitchens, in fact: one was where the family ate at a large wooden table, laid in honour of Edith with a lacy cloth, starched so much that its points were stiff under the legs of the eaters. It had a large corner cupboard containing preserves, honey and greengage jam and bottled fruit, and a special stand for the oil lamp. An open dresser stood against another wall with pots and cups and plates, all carefully washed after every meal and with a cupboard underneath with the best china and the meat plates and the silver spoons handed down from generation to generation. At meals in the evening the lamp was ceremoniously placed in the middle of the table and an enormous brown teapot made its appearance. Coffee was never drunk, but Edith did not miss it. There was the dark, brewed tea and a plethora of home-made buns and cakes and pies and potted meats, and the bread from the village baker which arrived twice a day and was made from the wheat grown by a neighbouring farmer. Oats were the staple diet, even more than bread, porridge with thick cream – again in Edith's honour – and pats of butter from their own dairy.

The other kitchen, the back kitchen, was next to the old dairy and was filled with the smell of cheese seeping through muslin, and of buttermilk, always regarded as a sure pick-me-up for invalids. The great range was there, too, where the cooking of meat took place and there was another deal table for baking and rolling out pastry. Edith had never eaten so much pastry in her life and was sure she would return to London with unrecognizable girth. What with that and the pork brawn and the bacon and the porridge and the thick bread, they ate well, if plainly. Fruit was not plentiful until the apples and plums should make their appearance at the end of the month. There was a neglected herb garden, too, which Sophie said her grandmother had used a lot, but which her mother had no time for.

They went on a tour of the farm, of course, to see the two pigs, kept for the family's needs, and the ten cows and the turkeys and the dozen or so hens and the rooster, whose sharp but mournful cry continued to wake Edith every morning. And she saw the oats nearly ready for harvesting and the field of clover and the hay field, which had not long ago been mown and raked, and the field of rhubarb of which Mr Ridsdale had great hopes. The smell of the farm was a good mixture of cow dung and growing grass, of milk and summer. Edith was even given a special pot of honey by Aunt Rose-Ann, whose speciality it still was. She was a bee-keeper and had a small swarm at the bottom of her garden in a hive; she had a dovecote, too.

'Harry and Jerome are back tomorrow – I hope they've behaved themselves in Hartlepool,' said Mrs Ridsdale one day in the middle of the first week. They were staying with her brother and his wife. 'So long as they've not turned the place upside down. William lets them run wild up there but they'll have to help a bit when they get home.'

Harry, Edith learned, was fifteen and wanted to be a sailor, and Jerome had been a delicate child and, being the youngest (he was thirteen), had been spoilt. Mrs Ridsdale continually harped upon their education, though her husband was silent. 'If *you're* not going to teach, Sophie, perhaps Jerome will. He had quite a good report from the Central School.' Apparently they both went to school in Sowerby, to a higher grade establishment. 'Harry is so lazy, Edith,' said Sophie's mother. 'What do you do with a boy who won't work?'

'Harry works at what he likes, Mother,' said Sophie, but her mother frowned and dropped the subject. Fortunately, the subject was not brought up again whilst Edith was staying at Thirksay, except once, when Mrs Ridsdale asked Edith whether her father took apprentices. Edith promised she would do what she could and would ask her father.

'He'll run away to sea,' Sophie said. 'He's Mother's favourite and he'll do what he wants. Soon he'll be too old to be told what to do and Father won't try to speak to him. Boys never seem to feel guilty.'

However, nothing very terrible seemed to be in evidence in Harry's character when he arrived back with his brother the next day. He seemed quite an ordinary boy, if rather a tease to his younger sibling. They departed to the fields almost as soon as they had arrived.

Edith got up every morning to the smell of polish and pastry and summer air lingering in the house. Added to it, now, was the scent of clover, which lingered from the cutting in the field. Sophie went out gathering wild flowers and the boys went bathing in the brook, which was dammed up beyond the village, making a deep pool. The sun went on shining and the rain did not come and it was decided to cut the cornfield on the Thursday. Several other small farmers had got together to share the reaper-binder and there was much argument about whose stockyard should host the threshing that autumn and winter. The greengages ripened on their trees in the orchard and Edith wrote that green was her favourite colour in Alice's book. The green, with its pale greyish bloom, blending into a touch of gold, was the colour she meant.

'They'll do for the agricultural show in Easingwold,' pronounced Thomas Ridsdale. 'Even earlier than we thought. We may have to pick them and put them in cold storage.'

He was proud of his fruit and chatted with Edith, at first shyly, and then with increasing ease. He was always busy, but had an air of melancholy that assorted strangely with his sunburnt face and hazel eyes. Edith decided she would be a gleaner, too, on Thursday, when some corn was to be cut, and Sophie provided two sun-bonnets of a style that delighted Edith, for they were long with a frill round the neck and looked like an item of clothing that had once been worn all year round, long ago.

Harry, a tall youth, with no resemblance to either of his parents, was at first a little shy of Edith, too, but she spoke to him in such a direct and uncomplicated way that he was won over and pronounced he would like to take her picture, along with his sisters', with the new camera which was the pride of his life. He seemed a serious enthusiast, quite unlike the whooping boy who was to run after the rabbits and 'beat' them into the centre of the fields to be slaughtered later.

They began to cut one cornfield on the Thursday. The reaper-binder chuntered round the field, slicing the ripe barley and then forming it into sheaves. Great clouds of midges settled everywhere and were occasionally swatted by the farm-workers. The sheaves were to be carted immediately by a pair of large horses to the barley barn. The farm was small – only about one hundred acres – but the land was rich. The eight-acre field was almost cleared. There were still oat fields to be harvested, of course.

Sophie, as she stood watching at the edge of this field, seeing the smaller and smaller circle of uncut barley, felt slightly sick. Edith noticed and asked if they could begin their back-breaking task of gleaning, along with some of the village women, who had brought large straw baskets made of the same material as their hats, which were like coal sacks. Not that the reaper-binder left much; it was more of a custom than a necessity now.

'Not until the animals have been flushed out,' replied Sophie. 'That's the tradition. The boys come later with their guns. I hope there isn't a hare in the middle. They're such beautiful animals.' Then she remembered a poem of Clem's about the same subject and it suddenly made her feel a little better. At least someone else noticed such things and sympathized.

'You needn't watch,' said Edith.

'I make myself, every year. It's nothing, I suppose, only that the outcome is obvious.' But the men had gone over to the hedge for a rest and a mug of beer, so the small circle of waving barley was left alone.

Suddenly, whilst no one was looking, and whilst the horses were busy cropping at the edge of the field, there was a sharp, zig-zag rush and there streaked across the field from the dark gold centre a long, lean, leaping thing. It reached the shelter of the hedge before anyone had realized what it was.

'The boys weren't here,' shouted Sophie. 'He's got away! He's got away!' She jumped up and down, shading her face with her hand.

'There's still plenty rabbits in there,' said Mr Ridsdale, 'even if the owd hare made a dash for it.' He looked at his daughter and put a hand on her shoulder. 'Sophie always minded that part,' he said to Edith. 'I've told her, why come and watch? But she will come.'

'I was praying for him,' said Sophie, 'and he did it, the hare, he got away!'

The boys and men had gone off now to the farm, for their shotguns.

'A daft lass,' said her father fondly. 'But there you are; we can't all be alike.'

Edith knew the hare was not just a hare to her friend, but almost a symbol of her own escape. The air was now very heavy and the men feared rain, so the horses were detailed to hurry up and return as quickly as possible to collect the rest of the sheaves. Reinforcements, in the form of cold water, were waiting for the women, who did not drink beer.

'Where will he have gone, the hare?' asked Edith, curiously.

'Far away,' replied Sophie softly. 'And he wasn't old. He was young.'

They followed the stooping women then, stopping to pick the fallen barley beards, putting them in the bags which Sophie had brought. It was hot work and an hour was enough for Sophie. But Edith worked on, enjoying the rhythm of the task, the freckles on her face standing out from the effort. Sophie went up to her and it was almost as if Edith was somewhere else; she had to speak twice to her before her friend heard her. At last, though, she straightened up and groaned. 'How do they do it so quickly? We're nothing but townies, Sophie. Look how much more some of them have picked!'

'You did far better than I did,' said Sophie. 'Come back for some bread and cheese and a rest and we can come along again in the evening. They'll probably want to begin on the other field. I'm not waiting for the boys and their guns this time,' she added. She coughed in the tickly dust of the shorn field. Harry was seen at the end of the field then, with a shotgun, and seeing the girls, he waved and emitted a sort of yodelling sound.

'Ugh!' said Sophie.

Edith did not want to wait for the men and lads with the guns either; though she was not squeamish, she did not enjoy sport for sport's sake and particularly when the result was a foregone conclusion. Anyway, the oat fields were not yet harvested and would be finished only the next week. The rain had held off, so there was now no hurry. She would go out and help again the next day. The women were still in the fields, bending to their task, when she slipped away with Sophie.

'We don't own enough land now to have a *real* harvest supper,' Sophie was explaining. 'When all the great uncles' harvest was gathered in – it took several weeks sometimes – they would all celebrate together, with everyone who had worked on the farm during the year. Hay harvest is even harder work, though, I think. And potatoes are dreadful – back-breaking.'

'It's not like it was,' Sophie's mother was saying that evening as they ate a supper of beef stew and baked custard. 'It used to be the only time they got a square meal, some of them. I can remember two hundred people sharing a moonlight feast, with singing in the barn and beer, when they brought the harvest home. That's when I was a child.'

'Things are bound to change,' Sophie's father put in. 'With the reaper-binders and threshing machines, they've already changed. One day, perhaps, the workers will get a just reward and not lease their land from the manor house or the estate, by way of ourselves.'

His wife looked at him swiftly as if to say, 'Don't start on politics: we have a visitor whose father has made money.'

'Dad believes in a better world,' said Sophie affectionately.

'Well, I shan't see it, but it will come,' he said. 'Farming's not where it'll start, though; nothing so conservative as your farm-worker.'

'Do you wish you'd left and gone to the town to work then, Dad?'

Mrs Ridsdale frowned again and gave Sophie a warning glance this time, but Mr Ridsdale only smiled.

'Dad is a sort of Socialist,' Sophie said to Edith when they went on their walk round the farm before bed. The night air was warm and there were midges whining around and a moon rising beyond the trees round the pond. 'He believes in the possibility of a better system,' she went on as Edith said nothing. 'Things must change. To have all the wealth in the hands of those who *don't* earn it, it stands to reason that's not right. The land should be freehold. It's funny, you would think Mother would be a far better revolutionary than Dad – she's got more fighting spirit. But she so loves respectability and is afraid she'd lose the respect of her "betters".'

'You're rather hard on her,' said Edith.

'I know. Perhaps Mother and I are too alike. We see through each other.'

Edith had noticed that Mrs Ridsdale had an appetite for admiration, whether it was for her apple pies or her hard work. This appetite usually went with a high opinion of oneself, or perhaps a need to think highly of oneself, since no one else did. She did not suppose that the daily work of a farmer's wife had much in it of praise for what was done well; rather, there would be censure if it were not. Edith wondered idly, as they strolled round the orchard in the dusk, whether Sophie, too, needed praise; she had not noticed it. Or maybe it was that Sophie would one day need it if she were not happy. Perhaps her mother had been a happy girl and then been disappointed? But which came first, the capacity to be disappointed or the mistake of asking too much? Circumstances altered cases. It was just that she glimpsed a similar willpower and self-dramatization in both women, or guessed it in the case of the mother. Sophie had said, months ago when they first met and were discussing their parents, that she was a strong woman, Edith remembered. How much was she putting into the mother's character that Sophie had said was there?

'They used to sing a lot together,' said Sophie, 'but when there were money troubles, they stopped. Father liked to sing with her. I think he loves her, you know. Mother can ride a bicycle, too – Harry taught her – and she can run faster than any of us. She's very brave. I'm not like that. She needed a strong man, a daredevil, I think. Father is too quiet for her, too easily pliant to her will.'

'How can we know anyone? Especially our parents?' Edith remarked after a silence, when they were sitting on an upturned tree trunk.

'Don't you think there are some people happy by nature, though?' Sophie persisted. 'Like Dad. He's a happy person, sure things will improve. Mother doesn't believe in progress; I think she's rather cynical. You'd think she would welcome a less respectable daughter than Alice. But she's always worrying about what other folk will think.'

'I suppose you have to, in a little place like this.'

'Yet she's quite simple in other ways. I'm sure I know far more about real wickedness than she does.'

'I wouldn't be too sure. That's why she wants you to have a "respectable" career.'

'But why always make me feel *guilty*?' cried Sophie. 'I hate prejudices. Perhaps, one day, if Dad's Utopia comes about, people themselves will be different. Do you think so?'

'I think people have always been much the same, except they haven't always had much opportunity to be themselves. Look at my mother, she doesn't worry about larger issues – leaves them to Father. She's conventional too, more so than Father. Father's the one who wants to improve the world; he's a bit like your father in that.'

'The other day she said, "I don't want any girl of mine using papier poudre", to poor Alice, who had only been trying to take the shine out of her nose when she met her young man. How ridiculous! Not that *I'm* interested in powdering my nose. But I ask you, Edith, what harm is there in it?'

'I think it's respectability you don't like, Sophie,' said Edith sensibly.

'I suppose not. So I'm a real revolutionary?'

'You want to have a civilized life.'

'Don't we all? It's hard to believe in Kitty and Frank when I'm here. It makes me think I shall never get away and find them again. They make me feel I can be myself. Partly because they are quite rich, and they do what they want.'

'I thought no woman did what she wanted in this benighted society,' said Edith, poking a little fun.

'Now, Edith, you know it's a question, not just of sex, but of power. Yet I must confess,' she said, after Edith had said nothing, 'that I'd like to belong to a wider sort of world, really belong. Not always feel an outsider. There is so much to love, isn't there, in the world?' She thought: I should try to love my mother, but it is beyond me at present.'

'Are women always outsiders, then? They can't be, if you think Kitty has the ideal life.'

'Oh, I don't know. It's a muddle in my mind. Do I want to be a man? That's not possible. Do I want to change society? Well, I can try to help it along a bit. Or do I just want to have a nicer life, a wider sort of life, free of all this?' She gestured around her.

'But you love – all this,' Edith said.

'Yes. That's the trouble. Perhaps we are just set for good along a certain path because of our family and rank. I hate to think that could be true.'

'You can react against it.'

'But then it's still *because* of it. Don't you see, Edith? I'm caught either way.'

'I should just forget all that and be yourself,' said Edith. She was not used to analysing other people's feelings, but felt she ought to try with Sophie. What good was it being able to invent monsters of the deep and maidens in distress if you could not understand your own friends? There always seemed to be a glass wall between herself and others. Sophie was the nearest she had ever come to having a friend who made the wall seem to change from glass to water, so that it was quite easy to swim through it and join another mind on the other side. Her own problems were so different from her friend's. 'Psychological' was the new word, whilst Sophie's dilemmas arose from some social constraint.

'This is a strange conversation,' said Sophie, jumping up. 'Tomorrow we must gather mushrooms and see if the water rats are down in the reeds in the meadow. Would you like that? I must show you the Owlet tree now, and then we can go indoors.'

They walked into the orchard, to the end, where there was a clearing. The moon's rays were silvering the trunks of ancient apple trees and plum trees and a medlar tree which Edith recognized from her studies.

'Look across the wall,' whispered Sophie, 'and wish as you do. The tree just opposite is the one where my grandfather once shot an owl by mistake and thought a curse would come upon him. Then another family of owls came to it, when father was little, and he used to imitate their cries. Don't mind the bats if they come out – they're harmless. But look at the tree. That's it – the Owlet tree – I think it's folk magic. Wish now and I will too.'

Edith obediently wished something for Sophie, a rather inchoate wish, but it would have to do. The tree was silent and she could see no owl for the moment. She shivered a little.

They went out together the next morning, swinging their hats by the elastic. Sophie broke into Edith's thoughts. 'Let's smoke a gasper in the woods. I'm dying for one. Mother'd have a fit if she saw me!' She had a small box in her pocket and, when they were out of sight of the farmhouse, she lit up ostentatiously. Edith did not enjoy smoking, so whilst Sophie sat with her back to a tree and her legs in the bracken, Edith went in search of mushrooms.

Sophie thought about Clement when Edith disappeared. She wished Something would Happen, but did not clearly know what. She reviewed possibilities: the present of a bicycle from an admirer, a sudden legacy, a prize for her eloquence, fame as a rebel. She had not known what to wish, that night under the Owlet Tree, and had settled for Alice to get married, if that was what she wanted. It had struck her as being a very unselfish wish and then she had felt ashamed for being proud of her altruism. Was there no way out? Her thoughts reverted to Clem. Clem was what she wished would happen! She was just beginning to find dreaming of him no longer enough. Living in the delicious anticipation of his presence had been fine for the past eight or nine months, and then he had gone away and she had come back north. Clem was known to like walking in the country, but she did not think he would get as far as Thirksay. If he loved her, if he were ever in love with her, he would. But that, though not impossible, was unlikely. She thought, it was not the sort of thing that happened to her; saw herself, rather, tracking him, and coming across him with an old lady in a cottage garden . . . .

Sophie finished her gasper and stood up slowly. She had better find Edith and the mushrooms. Thinking about Clem Bartholomew must not become a way of life. She would take Edith down to the brook to see if they could find the water rat. *The Wind in the Willows* was a book she knew Edith loved. She came upon her in a clearing under some elm trees where grew thick clumps of mushrooms as large as fists and of a peculiar yellowy white.

'Are you *sure* they are edible?' asked Edith. 'I've never seen any as large as this – so chunky.'

'Oh, we gather them every year. I'll be your slave taster, if you like.'

'Seeing them here is different from seeing them illustrated,' said Edith ruefully. 'Look – a whole hat full. Give me yours, too, and I'll fill that. If you're sure?'

Sophie laughed and swung her hat over to Edith. She leaned against the elm trunk, still feeling lazy. Edith did everything so deftly, even stooping and gently plucking the stubby excrescences, and yet she was also vague and short-sighted. Sophie laughed as the spectacles slid down Edith's nose.

'Water rats or cricket next?'

'Water rats, I think. But they'll probably still be playing cricket this evening, so we can go and watch them.'

'Market day in Sowerby tomorrow. I wonder if we shall see Sarah?'

'Did you have your smoke, naughty Sophie?'

'Yes. Give me the hat. Now, follow me to the brook and we'll see if we can find Ethel.'

'Ethel?'

'I call the friendly one Ethel.'

'I didn't know water rats – voles? – could be *friendly*.'

'Ah, but you need imagination, Edith.'

They came out of the wood and crossed a field, putting their hats, filled with mushrooms, on a stile and went down a slope to where lay coiled a brown, deep, but scarcely moving, stream. There were holes pocked in the mud of the bank, overhung by several willow trees.

'She, Ethel, is probably at home.'

Edith doubted it and there were several false alarms and plops in the water before Sophie finally gave up. But just as they were turning to go, Sophie put her finger to her lips and pointed with the other hand and Edith followed her eyes. A small, furry face was poking out of one of the holes in the bank for a moment, looking at them, and then it vanished.

'Ethel?' breathed Edith.

'Ethel it was,' stated Sophie. 'She saw you, too.'

Then they retraced their steps and picked up the mushrooms and they walked slowly back to Church Farm.

On their way back they met villagers at the little station who had come with their coal carts, in the intervals of waiting to harvest their final oat fields; villagers who discussed their earlier harvest of barley in slow and measured tones; they inspected the greengages, which were now ready for picking, and ate one or two which had fallen to the soft ground in their impatience; they discussed the agricultural show as though it were a great event in London, to which all would contribute and about which all would have an opinion; they listened to the sounds of the fields, to the cock crowing, the ring doves moaning and the men shouting in the green and gold distance. Edith was introduced to other relatives and friends by Sophie, who seemed to have softened a little towards them now that she was sure of a return to London. For her parents were now resigned and she felt obscurely guilty because she had got her own way!

Mrs Ridsdale talked to Edith about her parents and Edith invited the Ridsdales to visit Leeds and meet her mother and father if they ever had time to visit the great Yorkshire city to the south. They finished the clover cutting and the thistle cutting with no worse than a cut on Jerome's hand from an injudicious swipe by his brother; the rabbits were shot and hung in the outer kitchen and Sophie averted her eyes. Edith took her sketch pad and drew them. The last field was almost harvested and Sophie's Uncle Arthur was to give a family celebration after they had gone, with plenty of food and drink contributed by Mr Ridsdale and the third partner in the triumvirate, an in-law called Mr Coulson, who was said to be about to acquire more land from Lord Dawne. Mr Ridsdale pooh-poohed the idea and said that, sooner or later, the whole village would be sold off. They had only to wait. Edith dreamed of woods and water rats and owls, but forgot her dreams on waking. Sophie helped her mother make mushroom pie and gathered the wind-falls in the orchard and mulberries from the old tree. Alice came home with her young man, Ben Tollerton, on his first official visit to the Ridsdale home and they all sat in the parlour making conversation. Edith finished her 'confession' for Alice and went with Sophie to watch the lads play cricket, which she could not see, and had never understood anyway, even at school. But they accepted her presence and Sophie was pleased that everyone seemed to like her.

On their last evening, before the journey to York, which they were to make early on Sunday morning in order to see the Minster before their London train, Sophie and Edith went in to say goodbye to Aunt Rose-Ann and were given strong elderberry wine, which loosened all their tongues.

It somehow put their lives into perspective to know that soon they would be away and gone – in twenty-four hours – and would probably never see Aunt Rose-Ann again, though they would remember her and her wine. The old lady was a spry thing and not at all simple. She had her own decided opinions on everything and wanted to talk about the past. Sophie had heard the anecdotes before, but they were new and fresh to Edith and she was able to memorize many of the old words which the survival from the 1820's used to salt her speech, with no self-consciousness.

'You're a Mother Shipton,' teased Sophie, when Aunt Rose-Ann prophesied doom, with some satisfaction, for she would not be there to see it. But she was fond of her great niece and the conversation even turned to love, a topic that was hardly discussable at the farm.

'Never mind the books,' said the old woman. 'Do what you feel like, my dear. I did, and I'm still here. Your mother's family were too strong on the Good Book. Not but what there's every kind of sin and evil written there. But what I always say is, follow your own nose. Did you know I had a letter yesterday from Boy John? He taught me to read,' she went on proudly. 'And now he's got his own fisher fleet. Aye, money's a good thing, but don't let it spoil you.'

Back at the farm they gathered up their books and tidied the sitting room for Mrs Ridsdale, who spoke of sewing a nightdress for her daughter in the winter months. Edith was shown a complicated knitting pattern by Alice and then was asked for a little music. So they had a sing-song round the piano and the boys came in and the two women helpers.

'Better than whist at the village hall,' said Sophie's father contentedly, and his wife sang a ballad for them, accompanied by Edith. Then Sophie asked for 'that sad song', which turned out to be 'Once In The Dear, Dead Days Beyond Recall', and Edith noticed Sophie had tears in her eyes. Then they sang 'Believe Me, If All Those Endearing Young Charms', and 'Will Ye No Come Back Again', and Mr Ridsdale, when pressed, sang 'The Last Rose of Summer' and looked as mournful as

Sophie. Harry asked for something more cheerful so they sang 'John Peel', and it seemed as if they would be there, singing, for ever. But the time came for packing away the holiday and putting all the little presents of food they had been given into a special wicker container, for London.

Edith thought, as she fell asleep, that it had been an idyll and that she would like nothing better than to come again. Even Sophie's goodnights to her mother that night were gentle and grateful.

In the morning, Edith gave Mrs Ridsdale the present she had at first been too shy to give – a handsome tray-cloth that she had brought from home originally, but which did not seem to assort with Bloomsbury furnishings. Harry accepted the cricket bat with joy. They were both delighted, but the goodbyes to the girls on Sunday morning were brisk. Only Mr Ridsdale was to accompany them to York, as he loved to see the Minster whenever he had a chance. Harry and Jerome ran with the cart to Sowerby station, through the same leafy lanes only a fortnight older than on the day of their arrival, and as they got in the first train it was as though time, which had stopped, began again. The later visit to the Minster was brief, and proprietorial on the Ridsdales' part. Edith, comparing it mentally with other cathedrals she had known, had not been able to help agreeing it was the most magnificent. Sophie was thinking of the last sight of her mother and then of Aunt Rose-Ann standing at the bottom of her garden with the gosling. She wanted to get the farewells at the station over with quickly, and by common consent her father did not wait till the train left, but departed with a hug for his daughter and a suppressed emotion in his voice.

'Goodbye, Dad. I'll write every week, and you must come to London – promise?'

He gave a sad little gesture and then shook Edith by the hand. The holiday was over.

In the train, Sophie remarked suddenly, 'We never went minnow-catching,' and then relapsed into silence for quite twenty minutes.

Then she said, 'Narrow-mindedness is what I detest most,' and was silent again.

Edith was thinking about the Minster.

Looking up at the traceries and the honey coloured stone, she had almost sensed the pressure of the past on her back, weighing her down. She would like to go there alone one day to analyse more clearly the impression of light and dark, peace and timelessness. The places which meant most to her were always better experienced alone.

Then Sophie said, 'It won't stay the same for ever – nothing does.'

'You don't want it to,' said Edith, rather sharply for her. Sophie laughed and shrugged her shoulders.

As the train gathered speed, they began slowly to talk of London and London friends again. Even for Sophie, the thoughts of love and excitement had faded a little during the past weeks. Was it her real self which was coming back again? She felt curiously frightened to return, to put all her feelings once more to the test. Yet she had escaped the chains of home and she exulted in that. It was a challenge to stop being someone's daughter, to live through yourself. In Thirksay you could not even *begin* to think about anything important. Thirksay was good for memories, she felt. But she was treated still as a child at home.

Edith, too, was storing up the holiday in her mind and letting it drop deep down inside her, knowing it would surface when it was needed.

They idly discussed Kitty and Frank and Clement and Seb and all their other new friends and acquaintances, throwing their names like coins to each other and catching them.

'Do you think Harry's photographs will come out well? It will be something tangible to remember the holiday by,' said Edith, and then they both fell silent again.

Then Sophie said, 'It was good of you to come, Edith.'

Edith murmured again how she had loved it all and then seemed to fall asleep. In fact, she was thinking that she was lucky, but that life ought to present greater challenges to the lucky. She must not become indolent.

Sophie was thinking how objectively Edith saw the world and wishing that, for herself, it was not all tangled up in subjective emotions. She had a greater distance to traverse towards freedom and was too aware of herself. She must try and be more like Edith. And Edith was thinking: 'I wish I were

106

lively and amusing like Sophie. She never seems to question the reality of other people.'

But none of this was spoken, and slowly the tentacles of London closed in upon them and both their lives there were waiting to be taken up again.

3

Love in London

The fight that was no fight is over,
The uncontested victory won;
The conqueror, sleeping by her side,
Forgets already what is done.

But she, a pulse of deeper being,
Death's wakeful fire from age to age,
In the great army of creation
Enrols and takes her heritage.

L.A.G. Strong: *The Bride*

Sophie greeted London with rapture and relief. She had done her best to reassure her parents about her new life and now she was a free woman again. Both she and Edith had immediately written long thank you letters to Thirksay, but as the weeks passed Thirksay seemed to slide back into a dream. Life went on its usual busy but interesting course at Miller and Penn's. Both young women had been refreshed by the change. In Sophie's case she positively glowed. The sun had caught her face and neck and flattered her rather sallow complexion, cleared it, and brought into prominence her fine, long-lashed eyes. Grant tried not to stare at her. He had had a fairly wretched summer supposedly enjoying himself in Switzerland, but had been glad to return to London. His work was, of course, never far away from his thoughts. Even on his bedside table the books about to come out and ideas for the books he might bring out, piled up. In the office he was his usual ironic self.

Nothing was seen for some time of the travellers, Kitty and Frank. They were to return in October to London from prolonged visits to cottages deep in Hampshire and Berkshire and Sussex where their friends rented accommodation and dealt with sulky fires and even sulkier servants. Clement had gone underground but was said to have written a manifesto for 'Poets of the New Age'. Austin did pay a visit to Toby to announce this news.

'Only hope he doesn't go to the *New Review*,' grumbled the latter.

'Have no fear, our Clement is out of tune with Hueffer and his crew. He's got ideas of his own, but don't ask me what they are. I wouldn't understand anyway. Are you invited to the weekend at Kingston Manor, by the way?'

'I believe Miller has been, but he gets so many invitations I'd be surprised if he accepted.'

'Queer cove, isn't he? Does he spend all his spare time with that odd wife of his down at Chimneys?'

'I expect so. But clear waters run deep, I always think, with my sainted employer. He never speaks of his domestic arrangements to me.'

In fact, Grant had received a whole fistful of invitations for the autumn and was wondering how he could somehow wangle an invitation for Sophie Ridsdale. Then he berated himself for having the presumption to think she might ever want to be seen with him and roundly turned on himself for not being able to get her out of his head. There was something about his little office clerk that stirred his heart as well as his loins, and he wondered what it was. He supposed he would never know. It had not escaped him that she coloured up when Clement Bartholomew's name happened to be mentioned. Youth, he supposed. But a man like Clement would not be a good proposition for a woman. Too wrapped up in himself.

Violet, Grant's wife, was a little older than he, and when he married her she had just been widowed and he had been recovering from a miserable affair that had left his confidence shaken. He supposed they had given each other security. Now he did not want to be secure any more. But he was a gentleman and gentlemen conducted their love lives in a gentlemanly, debonair and worldly fashion. Something, though, was changing in him and he had disagreeable sensations of disloyalty to Violet when he thought about her. His marriage was one thing. Love was now another. And Sophie Ridsdale was a girl he could love, really love. He wanted to introduce her to the world and tenderly protect her from it at the same time. He wanted to make love to her and receive back the passion he knew was in her. But he *ought* to remain a kind fatherly figure. No, it was no use trying to hide from himself his deepest feelings. Yet Violet often said his real love was his work and anything else would be temporary. Perhaps he had some fatal flaw, what the new writers from Vienna (whom he read with a view to publication) were always calling unconscious drives and unconscious memories and repressions. He had begun to wonder whether the expensive education purchased for him by his father had suited his true self. 'Jumped up in two generations,' people probably thought. And the Clements of the world would think he was a privileged person, a Parlour Pink, with no knowledge of how the other half lived.

He was unused to this sort of introspection and shook his head and returned to his typescripts with attempted vigour. But the face and body of Sophie were present at inopportune moments. He was nearly twenty years older than Sophie and ought to know better. And she was an employee, a nobody. No, she was not a nobody, any more than her friend, Miss Broughton. Edith Broughton frightened Grant Miller a little. He could never decide what she was thinking.

In the meantime, they, with others of his staff, might like to go with him to one of those 'Bohemian' evenings which were all the vogue in the literary world. Sometimes they were overnight stays, but he was not really thinking ahead as far as that.

Edith, for her part, was more and more conscious of her own feelings of not-belongingness. She had been happy in Thirksay, and at home the Christmas before that. She loved working in the British Museum on Saturday mornings and did not mind her typewriter occupation either. Other people were the problem. Sophie was fine – Sophie was too caught up with her own reactions to bother about hers. And Sophie would not understand that, for Edith, there was a wall of glass between herself and others. She tried to deny her own feelings of unreality. If she were alone she would do certain actions automatically, but would then suddenly 'come to herself' and be aware of the solidity of her own body and wonder who or what she was to be cut off from others in this strange way.

110

She preserved an inviolable exterior, was always polite, gentle, amused and popular, yet she knew her real self was far away and perhaps only to be encountered when she could write. Nobody, she felt, would ever be able to share the feelings she had when alone, except perhaps some farmer, some toiler, who did not need the words which Edith could supply so easily. Words, in the end, though, were self-defeating, Edith knew, for they approached only distantly the truth of the world and man's relation to it. They were an escape. She wondered idly whether they were an escape for Clement, too, and others like him.

One Saturday afternoon, when Sophie had gone to the free library to bring back her consignment of novels, Edith was sitting alone in the eyrie thinking now and again and dreaming a little and then plunging once more into her research which she had written out neatly in one of her notebooks, where she tried to put both discoveries about herself and about the world. Then Mrs Macalister was heard to climb the stairs rather heavily. Edith wondered whether the rent was due, but decided not.

After a knock and a sudden opening of the door, the lady said: 'It's none of my business, but there's a young man who wants to see you. I wasn't sure if you'd want to see him or even if you know him, miss. Says he's Mr Bartholomew and would you care to accompany him to tea?'

'To tea! But I'm not dressed – I was busy – oh, tell him to come back in ten minutes. Yes, I do know – how strange – '

Edith knew that it was not done to entertain young men in your room unchaperoned, but thought that was all nonsense. However, she had better try to appear as through she understood the ways of the world. What on earth did Clement Bartholomew want? She stuck a few hairpins at random in her coils, washed her hands, grabbed a book, put on a coat and then wondered whether she ought to see him. She wished Sophie were there. He would return in a few moments, had probably gone for a walk round the square. Perhaps Mrs M would think she was courting? How ridiculous! If only they had a little more privacy. Just then she heard Sophie's feet on the top stairs and opened the door as Sophie came up.

'Sophie, it's Clement. He's apparently called and wants to take us out to tea.' She unconsciously changed 'me' to 'us' – that would solve the problem nicely.

111

Sophie went pale, put down her books and gasped, 'Why didn't he write? Nobody knew where he was. Is he with Seb?'

'Mrs M said just Mr Bartholomew. Look, come with me, will you? Or could we entertain him here together? I don't really want to go out.'

Sophie thought rapidly. Perhaps Clem had only come for Edith and Edith was being kind. But she could not miss the opportunity of seeing him, so she said, 'I'll tell Mrs M to send him up as we're both here. It's beginning to rain. What extraordinary manners, I must say,' she said, mimicking Theo Carmichael's voice.

So it came about that the young man was sent up five minutes later to be greeted by Edith, who had taken off her coat.

'Mr Bartholomew, I wasn't really prepared for going out, so we invite you to tea.'

'Oh! It's very kind of you. Hello, Miss Ridsdale.' Clem was a little confused. 'I came back only yesterday and asked Seb for your address,' he said, turning to Edith. 'I, er, wanted to talk about your article on the Norse myths, Miss Broughton.'

'Do call us Edith and Sophie,' interjected Sophie. 'And we shall call you Clem.'

Clem was sunburnt and was wearing a strange cravat and a better pair of shoes than previously. 'Do forgive the presumption,' he said in his best party voice. 'I can never remember whether one is allowed to see ladies alone, these damnable rules of polite society.'

'No, it is not allowed,' said Sophie mischievously, 'but as we are both here you may stay for a cup of tea.'

'Oh, I was just passing,' he said, with an attempt at vagueness. 'I returned to Chelsea only yesterday and am meeting Seb for a meal in Soho.'

Edith was silent, so he went on, 'I wondered how the writing was going on, Miss Broughton – I mean, Edith.'

'Oh, it is quite well, thank you,' said Edith. 'But I need time to produce something worth reading and I don't know enough about folk beliefs to parallel what I think I've discovered underlying my Norse researches, to try and draw some sort of conclusions about what people lived by, or died by.' This was an unusual speech and Sophie was curious.

'I did not know you had these great thoughts, Edith,' she teased. She was going to mention monsters of the deep, but thought she had better not.

Clem was looking very attentive. Had he really come to see how Edith's writing was progressing? 'Have you heard from Kitty and Frank?' she asked, pouring Clem a cup of tea, as Edith seemed not about to do it.

'I hear they are expected back from Oxfordshire, according to Sebastian, who seems to know about most of his friends' movements.'

'And your book?' pursued Sophie. 'When will it be out?'

'I had a letter waiting from Miller: he hopes for spring.'

'And will it be just you, just *your* work, nothing of Frank's?'

'Apparently. Has nothing been said at the office?' He looked suddenly younger, more vulnerable, as he balanced the cup of tea on a chair-arm and tried to take sips and talk at the same time.

Edith roused herself and rose and put it on a table. 'There, you will be more comfortable. I believe Mr Miller did say something to Theo about it,' she said.

Clement looked grateful and took in Edith's long, slim hands and her golden hair and wished he knew her better.

Sophie went on chattering to cover her nervousness and Clem found her easy to talk to. But he did not really want to talk, apart from discovering what the girls knew of his publisher's plans. He could not quite remember why he had come. It was obviously impossible to talk to a woman alone. And why should Edith, the reserved and modest Edith, want to talk to *him*? But Sophie was now on the subject of an invitation to Eltham, to a weekend party at the Blands, which Grant had mentioned casually on the Friday. 'And he is inviting us all – Theo and Edith and me – and I'm sure there will be an invitation for you, too. They like meeting young people and it will be fun, won't it?'

'Are *you* going, Edith?' asked Clement with interest.

'I suppose so, it is almost part of the job,' answered Edith, with a glint of amusement.

'You are not a very sociable person?' said Clement, deciding to plunge. She did not answer, so he went on, 'Like me. I never know where to put my hands and feet with all these smart people.'

'Oh, the Blands are not smart,' said Sophie, with her new-found wisdom.

After this the ice was broken a little and they both talked to Clem as though he were a brother rather than an unknown quantity, never before having been alone with him.

Sophie realized that he looked at her and talked to her as though he were a sort of relation who had been away and was filling up on family gossip. In spite of his lack of social skill he was a confident person underneath and she felt he thought she was rather silly and light-natured and indulged her in conversation. The way he looked covertly at Edith was quite different. Oh, well, if it were Edith he were interested in! But Sophie could not help wishing, when he left, that he had come to see her; oh, how she wished it! It was the only great disappointment of her London life. Nothing she could do would alter the situation. Edith had some sort of mythical quality about her, which Sophie herself recognized, and she tried hard to reconcile herself to it. What use was an easy manner and an attractive face if the man you adored wanted nothing of it? She would try and devote herself to his literary interests, that was what she would do. Edith was a mystery and she dared not ask whether Edith were flattered or annoyed or a little frightened by his attentions.

She went into her room and started on one of the library books. The world was large and there must surely be other men in it who would not spurn her. For a moment, she fell out of love with him.

Edith, for her part, was sorry that Sophie was to be disappointed, and a little angry that the man had, in a way, taken for granted that she might want to see him. Yet it was just a little breaking of the strange glass of isolation that she feared round herself. Perhaps Clem understood that too, and she was a little comforted that he would, perhaps, lead her to a truer estimate of herself. If only that man-woman thing would not always come in between.

Sophie was not reading with any attention. After a few minutes she was gazing vacantly at the ceiling, her thoughts half on Clement. It was hard not to hanker after him. Perhaps if she never saw him again he would disappear eventually from her mind, like the other young men she had briefly fancied, or like a poet whose work she had loved when she was younger, but whose verse she had grown out of.

She realized that she was a little lonely.

Clement was a rebel, too, more like her than like Edith. Most people did not fall in love with people who were like them. But *she* did, loved people with whom she could feel in tune, agree with, like. She believed herself to be a Feminist, in revolt against the degraded position of all women who were expected to subjugate themselves to men. Women were regarded as not only different from the superior species, but as permanent underlings. She felt about the way women were treated as she felt about the way Oscar Wilde had been treated years ago. People still spoke in whispers about the case, but she had made it her business to find out about him. Not that Garnett Edwards was a particularly good advertisement for buggery! She said the word to herself self-consciously.

She was aware, even so, that her indignation about women's endless childbearing did not somehow fit in with her ideals of love. If you were in love you would want what your partner wanted, want to give him something, perhaps a child. And that seemed to involve marriage, an institution ostensibly for the protection of women, but in fact a way of keeping them in the home and deprived of liberty. Liberty was what she put first; free love, and the freedom to love whom you wanted, if he wanted you, of course. There was the rub. She might as well rejoice that she was free, that Clement was not interested in her. Otherwise there might have been conflict between her head and her heart. Was it only feminine to love, and suffer from rejection? Did men not suffer that too? But if you loved no one, you were free. She could not help suspecting that free love, too, might not really be 'free'. What about Kitty and Frank? Was Kitty as 'free' as Frank? If she had a certain liberty it was because she had a little money of her own. It was hard to be a woman *and* poor, whether you were married or not. Polite society ran on money. And most of the writers who espoused the ideal of freedom in matters of love were male! Then she thought, I *am* free! I am alive. I can do what I want. Never mind if Clement Bartholomew will never love me, I shall put my energies into suffrage, the fight for suffrage. That will do to be going on with. But she was conscious of an absence in

115

herself, of a refusal to confront her true nature, overlaid as it was by her violent emotional reactions to the way things were. She would not mind suffering for love, would not mind bearing an illegitimate child, would not mind never marrying, would not mind being spat at for her principles, would not mind even dying, if it were not for the ties that still bound her to home. She did not want to hurt those she loved and perhaps that was her real problem. As she had loved her mother and father, something in her that had been implanted early would make her so guilty, that life and freedom would be impossible. That was it, then; a possible guilt. She went back to her book with a sigh.

She peered through the door later at Edith, who was bent once more over her notebook, and then she boiled the kettle and took her a cup of tea. Women were more restful than men and the best relationship was one of friendship. Even with Clem she would have liked that.

'Do you think I am a negative person?' she suddenly asked Edith as they drank their tea, each lost in thought. 'I seem to hate more than I love,' she added, knowing it sounded rather affected.

'Goodness me!' said Edith, sufficiently surprised to put down her teacup. 'Why, Sophie, you are the most positive person I know! I should like to be like you. I feel that everything takes place apart from me and away from me, as though I were a spectator.'

Then Edith said nothing more, so Sophie was at least comforted that she saw her as a positive person. 'But that means I hate strongly, too,' she thought in bed, later that night. Then she added to herself, 'I shall go where life carries me,' and fell asleep.

For his part, Grant Miller took the surface Sophie to be the true one; which other did he know? He was too old to wonder about hidden depths, saw her generosity and sparkle and smiled at her puzzlements and her vehemences when he heard of them. As time went on and he saw more of her at work he wished there was some person in whom he could confide. This was unusual for hm, as he had always kept his feelings to himself. He hoped she would stay with the firm and perhaps eventually rise in it, sure as he was that she had a natural curiosity and appetite for understanding. He began to be extremely sentimental about her in private moments and startled himself. He remembered even the date they had first met in the ABC and marked it with a little circle in his diary.

Eventually, as another autumn changed the trees in Russell Square to yellow and ochre, and the mist came in the early morning, he took to walking round Bloomsbury and musing in his own lunch hour, enjoying the tinge of melancholy in the air as though he had already had an affair with Sophie and it was over. When an invitation had came from the Blands he had accepted for several of his staff. Usually, people went down to Eltham on the spur of the moment, but it was rumoured that Mrs Bland had been finding it harder to get up to London since her husband had been ill and would welcome a party like the ones they used to give years before. There were, of course, other invitations, too: many small gatherings in London itself, and he imagined that he went to them with Sophie and somehow managed to speak to her, not as an employer but as a lover.

Grant never now stayed at Chimneys through the week, but kept his small *pied à terre* off the Tottenham Court Road, so his wife did not usually accompany him to parties on weekdays. But the Blands wanted them to go down on Friday night and Violet might have wanted to come, too. For the first time in his marriage he consciously decided not to tell her of this invitation. He would speak to Sophie somehow; there was much wandering in the grounds of Well Hall which boasted a moat and a drawbridge and many secret places. He had no plans to seduce her, only wanted to say something of what she had come to mean to him, yet his blood almost ran cold at the thought. He must not drive her from the office or frighten her, but the burden of his feelings and unspoken desires was becoming too great to carry any longer. He ought to dismiss her, find her a better job in another firm. He saw all that and knew his duty, but decided not to follow the promptings of his conscience.

Sophie was excited at the thought of a weekend party where so many of her new friends might also be invited. Clement was going and Toby, of course, and Sebastian, who was a friend of one of the Blands' daughters.

Austin pleaded work and Theo said she had a meeting to attend. Edith was persuaded to go down on the Friday night with Sophie on the train from Charing Cross to Blackheath, where they could change to the Eltham line.

'They say Mr Shaw may be there! Isn't it exciting, Edith?'

Sophie decided to buy a velvet jacket at Debenhams with the money promised by Uncle John for her birthday, and added beads and a blue silk scarf.

'Are Kitty and Frank going?' asked Edith, to whom the prospect of a party was not enticing.

'Of course. They say this may help to add an injection of cash for the printing of *Counterpoint*.' replied Sophie.

'I thought the Blands were not very well off?'

'Well, they are not, but they know everybody and I'm sure Kitty will find backers there.' Sophie added as an afterthought, 'You are not to worry, Edith, it is not smart, just fun. They say all sorts of games are played and people act charades and do pencil and paper games and stay up till all hours!'

When Edith and Sophie, who had travelled with Toby, arrived at the little station after the interminable journey to the suburbs, it was quite dark. They walked down to an ill-lit road from the station, having been given their instructions from Grant, and saw, standing away from the road, the tall house built of brick; an eighteenth-century house, smothered in ivy. The drive led down past a moat and they saw a boat under the willows, the water winding past some ancient stables. When they reached the enormous front door they found a notice under a lantern with the words: 'The front door is at the back', a pleasing conceit. They walked round to the back of the house, which had long windows like the front, and found the 'back' door open and leading directly up to a large central staircase which wound up from the ground floor and seemed to reach the top of the house.

At the top of the staircase on the first floor there was an enormous reception room, with its windows at the back leading on to a large verandah, and steps leading down outside to the bushy garden and lawn, where the moat reappeared under ivied walls. The great room was lit by gas but there were candles in brackets on the stairs and there was the sound of a piano and many voices. A tall, pretty middle-aged woman came to them as they stood blinking in the candlelight at the top of the staircase. She was dressed in a long, green Liberty dress with a velvet jacket and many strings of big beads. She looked tired, but stately, and led them up another inner stair where they deposited their coats and were shown a room for the men and one for the girls.

'No standing on ceremony,' said the woman. 'Enjoy yourselves. Mr Miller is already here. Soup and cheese and apples at midnight.' Then she disappeared and left them in front of a large, spotted pierglass.

'What a strange house,' said Edith. 'You go down first, Sophie.'

Toby joined them at the bottom of the stairs and took both their arms. A portly man with white hair and an eye-glass shouted, 'Welcome to Bohemia!' and ogled Sophie through his monocle. He was dressed neatly in spats and spotted bow tie and turned out to be their host. Sophie felt there would be ways of behaving here, rules for it even, which one would have to pick up as one went along. About twenty young and middle-aged people were lolling in front of an enormous fire at the far end of the big room, which was indeed more like a banqueting chamber than a dining room or drawing room. Flagons of beer and cider were placed at each end of a long table with beakers and glasses and bowls of nuts. Festooned in garlands on the wall were branches of holly and ivy and a large jar of foliage. The piano was behind a screen and several chairs were grouped round it. The evening's festivities seemed already to have begun, though most people had come from London. Grant saw Sophie arrive and then waited for her to come into the inner room. He emerged from a knot of older people and came up to her.

'Like it?' he said.

'I've never seen anything like this! It's like a medieval banqueting hall,' she replied.

He poured her a glass of cider. 'Mind, it's very potent. Our hostess lives on air, you know, so is not aware of the effects of home-brewed cider.'

Sophie had seen Clement detach himself from Seb and move in Edith's direction.

'Almost Saturnalia,' said Grant. He looked round and saw a middle-aged man engaged in dalliance behind a screen with a young woman. The parallel in his own case was too apt. He wanted only to talk to Sophie and led her to a sofa. Sophie looked round as though someone else should be there for Grant to talk to, but there was no one.

'It's you I want to talk to,' Grant said. 'And for a beginning, tonight, at least, my name is not "Mr Miller" but "Grant", Sophie.'

He drank to her and she sipped her own drink. My, it was powerful stuff and reminded her of a harvest supper.

'They'll soon start playing their games and putting on their masks,' said Grant. 'You look very pretty, Sophie Ridsdale.' Sophie felt suddenly nervous and he saw it. 'Can't we be friends this evening? Forget you work for me,' he said, and then, unable to stop himself, having at last got Sophie sitting next to him with the candlelight and the flames from the fire playing on her face, he was unable to say any more.

'What sort of games?' asked Sophie. 'Is it a den of vice?'

'My dear girl! Very unsophisticated games! Acting your favourite heroine, declaiming verse – if you prefer it. This is Liberty Hall. You may do nothing if you would rather.'

He continued to stare at her, till Sophie asked, emboldened: 'Mr Miller – Grant – why do you stare at me?' She said it half-teasing. 'Have I a smut on my nose or is my jacket too outré?'

The crimson velvet jacket was indeed beautiful and set her off like a picture of Gainsborough, he thought. 'You look charming. I like the colour and there is no smut on your nose. I wanted to ask, only, before we all join in the fun and games – are you happy, Sophie Ridsdale? Are you enjoying London? Do you like your work?'

His manner was a little strange, but she was used to him, so answered: 'I am happy, Grant Miller, and I like my work and I am enjoying London. I feel a Londoner myself, now.'

'I want to say – ' he began again, and could not go on. What was the matter with him? 'Never mind, perhaps later. Look, some of your friends and mine are coming to talk to us.'

Kitty Moray was suddenly there, with Frank at her side and Clement. She looked around for Edith.

'Edith is playing chess with Ford,' a voice said. It was Toby.

'Do you know everyone here?' asked Sophie. 'It's wonderful, isn't it?'

'So long as you don't drink more than three glasses at most of that stuff,' replied Toby.

Grant Miller seemed to have melted away for a moment and their host and hostess were distributing masks to all their guests.

'Don't tell Bland you're a suffragist,' whispered Toby in her ear. 'He's an old reactionary.'

'I like Mrs Bland,' whispered Sophie, 'she's beautiful.'

'Ah, yes,' said Toby.

'And Mr Miller has been saying such strange things to me. Do you think he's been drinking?'

'Not he! What sort of strange things?'

'Asking me if I was happy, things like that . . .'

'Aha – don't you know, Sophie? You've made a conquest there. Look out, if you don't want to be caught.' Sophie looked at him, at first uncomprehendingly and then incredulously. 'Didn't you know? Well, I suppose I notice more than most. He's in love with you, Sophie.' Toby twirled his glass between his fingers.

'Oh, Toby, don't say such things, even in jest. He's married!' Her amazement was genuine.

'I believe you don't know the impression you make, my dear. Remember, this is not Society, nor a rural retreat. People come here to be themselves. The place has a magic.'

'Toby – I – '

'Say no more, Sophie, *ma chérie*,' said Toby and grabbed a mask from the tray a young girl was handing around. 'Who shall you be? I think I shall be the inventor of logarithms.'

'Doesn't it have to be your favourite writer or something?'

'Wait, and our host will enlighten us.'

'Bland had clapped his hands and a silence fell, broken only by little crackling noises from the logs on the fire. 'Please act your favourite character from history or literature, and if anyone guesses who you are the mask comes off. Remember – questions only to be answered "Yes" or "No".'

Mrs Bland had joined them and put on a mask. Most of the guests seemed resigned, or perhaps they were used to this unorthodox method of getting to know your party acquaintances.

It was almost like a children's party. Sophie remembered that Mrs Bland was a famous writer for children under the name of E. Nesbit. Who could she pretend to be now? She would be a man! There was no rule against that, was there? Should she be Robin Hood, then or Lord Nelson? No, she would be the poet Shelley.

'Edith,' she whispered, 'will you be Mary Shelley? Then we can go around together. You know more about Frankenstein than I do.'

Edith put the mask on gingerly and then took if off again and said, 'Why not be Byron, Sophie?'

'Then who could *you* be?'

'Oh, I'll think of something. I want to finish my chess game with that dear old man.'

'Edith, you should be the goddess of wisdom – Athene, Minerva.'

'But what happens?'

'You move around asking people questions and when they've guessed you, you take off the mask.'

Someone was now playing the piano and Edith crept nearer the screen to be out of the way of questioners. Then Sophie saw Clement approach her with a mask on. She wondered whom he would have chosen to be. It ought to be the poet John Clare. Grant was suddenly beside her and broke into her thoughts.

'Ask me a question,' he said. 'If I have to be ridiculous I might as well start with you.'

'Are you male or female?' asked Sophie promptly.

'Male!'

'Are you a writer?'

'Yes, of course. But you should have said, are you male, and I should have answered, "Yes" or "No".'

'Are you respectable?'

'No.'

'Are you Oscar Wilde?'

'How did you know?' He tore off the mask, smiling. 'Now it only remains for me to ask you and we can sit down again and chat.'

Couples were already sitting in the low chairs which ran round the walls of the enormous room and late arrivals were heard in the hall.

'It's all very innocent, isn't it?' he said. 'Well, Sophie, are you female?'

'No.'

'My goodness, that's a facer! Oh, put me out of my agony. I hate to see a mask on your face.'

'No, you must ask me.'

Grant rapidly surveyed mentally those whom he would regard as Sophie's favourite authors. 'Shakespeare?' he asked hopefully.

'No.'

'Dickens? Lord Byron?'

'No, No.'

'Shelley!' he said triumphantly, and Sophie, who had decided at the last minute to revert to her former choice, said, 'Yes.'

'Thank God! Let me.' He carefully slipped the mask over her hair and his touch made Sophie start a little. 'Would you care for a walk round the grounds?'

'Well, I'd like another drink,' said Sophie.

She went up to Edith by the large refectory table. Clem was standing near her and Edith was looking a little distrait. 'Nobody's guessed me yet,' she said gloomily. 'Do you think I should cheat and pretend?'

'Who are you?' whispered Sophie.

'I'm Sir Thomas Browne,' replied Edith. 'Do you think it rather recondite?'

'Come on, Clement, I'll give you a clue,' said Sophie to him. He smiled. His mask was off and he looked faintly bored. 'She's a seventeenth-century writer who liked urns,' said Sophie, showing off slightly.

'Oh – Edith – Browne,' said Clement. He seemed transfixed whenever he looked at Edith, but she smiled and said with relief: 'Thank goodness! Sophie, I hate cider; is there any lemonade?'

'I'll get you some,' offered Clem.

The party was now in full swing and two people, still masked, were pushed into the middle of the floor. It was Mrs Bland and a young man whom Sophie did not recognize. The Master of Ceremonies clapped his hands again.

'Come now; the audience may now guess the identity of this fair lady and this esquire.'

Edith whispered, 'She's a Baconian – that's who she'll be.'

'Say so, then!'

'No, I couldn't. Say it for me.'

There was a silence whilst someone guessed the young man was, in turn, Sir Walter Raleigh, Thomas Campion, and the poet Swinburne.

The man tore off his mask. 'You owe me a magnum for this, Bland,' he said. 'I'm here already,' and he pointed at a young man who was sitting fiddling with a box of bricks.

'What, Oswald?' they all shouted.

The young man bowed. 'The very same.'

Oswald looked up and said in a finicky voice: 'A compliment, young man.' Sophie thought he must be a writer too, but she had never heard of him.

There was still Mrs Bland in the centre of the room. Evidently she liked to tease. Grant came up behind Sophie.

'Edith knows who she is,' whispered Sophie in his ear. He seemed no longer strange, but an equal.

'Tell it, then.'

'The lady is Sir Francis Bacon,' said Sophie in a loud voice.

'Edith Nesbit tore off her mask. 'Unmasked,' she said melodiously and bowed to Sophie who winked at the other Edith.

Grant began clapping and then the couples and groups moved round. The game had done its trick and all were ready now to make new friends and gossip with old ones.

'Come out for a walk,' said Grant.

Sophie hesitated. He eyes were bright and her profile almost pert. She looked once more at Clement who was in a corner now with his friend Sebastian and glowering at Edith, who was talking earnestly to Mrs Bland. Even Edith seemed out of her usual body. It was a magic evening, and even more so when the autumn mists swirled round Sophie and Grant in the garden. Someone had lit candles over the stables. 'They used to have fairy lights,' said he. 'She's a genius for friendship, you know. Writes terrible adult novels, though.'

'You've read some of her books for children, I suppose?'

'The rector's daughter lent me one or two; I thought they were marvellous.'

'Isn't it all rather childish?' asked Sophie. 'Lovely, but not grown-up.'

They had gone down some stone stairs to the moat and the moon had come out. He thought of little Sophie reading away on her distant farm. Then: 'Are you cold, Sophie?'

'A little.'

'They stood together, looking at the water. Sophie was expecting him to say something gossipy or cynical, but instead he took her hand and all he said was, 'Oh, Sophie, I do love you so.'

At the words, Sophie looked up at him. 'Please!' she said. 'I don't know you well enough, that's what you're going to say. You are my employer and married men must not say such things . . .'

'Oh, no,' said Sophie. 'I'm against marriage. How can you bear to lose your freedom?' She wished she had not said what had slipped out of her lips before she knew, because it was not quite true. There was Clem, talking to a young woman in the corner of the vast room, and she was visited with a sensation of despair. He would never love her, never want her. And Grant was just flirting with her, surely? Grant Miller was her employer, old enough, at a pinch, to be her father. Yet he was looking at her with a truly sad expression. Did she look like that when she talked to Clem?

She gathered herself together. 'I meant, how can men bear to lose their freedom. It's easy to see why *women* marry.'

He smiled at this and looked away for a moment. Then he said in a rather abstract way, 'I am fond of my wife.' So perhaps he was still not taking his feelings seriously, or hers.

She wanted to say, then why did you say such a thing to me? but that might mean that she was believing what he had said. Should she be amazed or shocked? To have mentioned his wife at all seemed tasteless, wrong. How could you 'love' two people at once? What did he mean? Again he said, this time in a whisper and looking at her once more, 'I have dreamed about you, Sophie, for a long time. And I could love you.'

She had meant to sound sophisticated with her words about marriage and freedom and it had only served to push him further along into what sounded like a confession. She was a little horrified, but fascinated, never having expected anyone to love her seriously, unless she started it off herself. Her employer looked serious. Was he the unknown person who would claim her after she had had her fill of romance? How could he be, since he was married himself? She had been brought up to connect the idea of life-long love with marriage, an idea which she had rejected. And now Grant Miller was upsetting all other people's theories. Should she be angry, insulted even? She did not feel insulted at all. Here, by her side, was a live man, an experienced man, a famous man in his way, saying things to her which she was surprised to hear and yet words which part of her thrilled to in an unexpected way. One little bit of her asked how he dared; another was amused; another flattered; another excited; another frightened.

He did not touch her again or attempt to appear as though anything but an ordinary conversation was taking place, but when she turned to look at him again he went on, 'I don't expect you to say anything, feel anything or do anything. I had to say it to you for it drives me mad. Don't be angry: I won't refer to it again if you don't want me to.'

Sophie was silent. How differently she had imagined a scene of love; some mutual passion instigated by herself; or Clement arriving at the flat with a bunch of roses; or a long letter which she read joyfully . . . . With a shake of her head she recognized her own fantasies. But had not this man his fantasies, too?

'Please – ' she said, swallowing, her throat dry. 'Let's just be ordinary, and friends. I work for you. How can I believe what you are saying?'

'All right, Sophie,' he said with a change of mood. 'We won't refer to it.' But she saw that he was nervous. 'It won't make any difference,' he added.

'A secret?' she asked.

'I suppose it had better be that. Forgive me, Sophie Ridsdale.'

'He was thinking what a fool he was and how he could have managed it all better. He would like to write a long letter to her. Perhaps one day he would.

Sophie was silent, but then he smiled at her, a sad sort of smile, and she smiled back. 'Let's go back and talk to someone, shall we?' he suggested.

Perhaps he was going to suggest Clement as a conversationalist. The mood of the whole party was altered for her. She had only to smile at Grant and he would come to her! He had placed himself in her power. She shivered slightly. She had a secret. He

126

had behaved just as she would like to have done with Clem. But women could not declare themselves, could they? She looked round the vast room again at the knots of people, and heard the roars of laughter and the underlying murmur of friends talking to friends and saw Edith sitting by the fire playing chess with an unknown man. And there were Horatia and Chloë chatting with Seb. For a moment it seemed like a tableau.

'I'll get you 'a drink,' said Grant, who looked more in need of one than she was. Several people stopped him on his way to the long refectory table and there were women among them who seemed, to Sophie, to know him well. She leaned against the window-frame feeling rather peculiar, the thought having just occurred to her that perhaps *he* was her destiny, and not Clement. But, oh, she did love Clement! Why could it not be Clement who spoke such words to her and looked at her with such ill-disguised yearning? Grant was like her; he wore his heart on his sleeve. He wanted a love affair with her, or perhaps she had got it all wrong? She was not sure enough of herself, sure enough of being able to distinguish flirtation from passion. Was there a difference in this strange new world where people did not behave as they did in novels? A little voice inside her was saying, 'He can be your Experience. He will look after you. You are young – take what is offered you, whatever it is. Don't be a coward, let him be your lover, don't think ahead, any further . . .'

And the reply came: 'I don't love him, I don't love him, I love someone else, don't I? And why should I suddenly want to be looked after, why should I commit myself?'

Grant came back. 'I thought, not beer,' he said. 'Mrs Hunt has brought some wine with her. I expect the Blands' cellar was empty. I brought you a glass – here.' He raised his own glass and said, 'I drink to Sophie.'

She accepted the wine and said, 'Can we sit down?'

'Of course.'

She thought perhaps he would not want to be 'seen' talking to her in a special way if they moved their chairs together, but he did not seem to care and found a tattered sofa by the screen near the fire. Edith looked up and Sophie smiled at her. Probably Edith would not remark anything odd and she had bent down once more to her chess game which, by the look of the venerable, white-haired gentleman with whom she was playing, she was winning.

Sophie took a gulp from the wine glass and looked around with interest. 'Do you know everyone here?' she asked Grant, who was eyeing her a little quizzically, she thought.

'Pretty well everyone,' he answered.

There seemed to be many 'Progressives' at the party. The women like Mrs Bland were wearing rather out-of-date Liberty dresses. Various young men were talking in a lively way to these ladies who looked almost as stately as their hostess. Other, younger, women were standing in earnest conversation with older men. Perhaps in Bohemia the customs were all reversed and the young of one sex went with the middle-aged of the other?

'Do you think they are speaking of women's suffrage?' she asked Grant, pointing to a lively group, with 'Oswald' at its centre. She nearly said, 'Or of free love,' but bit her tongue back.

'If they are, it will be out of the earshot of Bland,' replied Grant. 'Mrs Bland would not mind, but he is anti-Feminist.'

'Yes, Seb Harman said so. Yet Mrs Bland looks very emancipated.'

'People do not always do what their convictions tell them to,' replied Grant. 'At least, if society were just, it would be Mrs Bland who owned this house, as it's all paid for by her literary earnings. *He's* a womanizer of the first order,' he added, not quite irrelevantly.

'It's certainly a nice atmosphere,' she ventured, rather shyly.

'Bonhomous is the word,' agreed Grant.

She wondered whether it was perhaps a little bogus, too, if the host did not like the expression of opinion and, in fact, upheld the status quo in his own house.

'These people have nothing really to worry about,' she said next.

'No, so they enjoy themselves. Are you being a little Puritan, Sophie, because private incomes, however paltry, are necessary for fun?'

She smiled. 'I suppose so, a bit, but I'll try not to be.' Good heavens, was she actually flirting with him now?

'It is quite easy to be a success,' said Grant. 'You, particularly, would not find it difficult once you were launched.'

128

'I don't know what sort of success you mean.'

'Ah – conversationally and with the opposite sex. A young man over there has been looking at you with great interest.' Sophie looked across at Austin, who was, in fact, looking at her and who, when he saw her glance, waved rather self-consciously. 'Everyone could be in love with you tonight,' said Grant. 'I know, you see. Young men are my speciality, since I was young once.'

'Must one choose between being a success, as you call it, and being oneself?' she asked him boldly.

'If you ask the question you will never be a *succès fou* and that would be a pity,' he replied.

'But how can anyone be themselves – be natural – when all is chosen for effect?' She stopped, aware that she was sounding like a preacher. Yet it was a problem. The part of yourself you found easy to display was not always the part you felt was the real you.

'You are young enough to worry about your effect on others,' he said. 'Rest assured, you have no need. I, of course, should like to know the real Sophie.'

'Sometimes I feel ashamed when I talk too much,' she said. 'It's too easy. Edith finds it difficult but that is because she is very deep and very true to herself.'

'To thine own self, and all that. But it's a gift to be able to be sociable.'

More of a gift to attract those you want to love you,' said Sophie, throwing caution away.

'Don't, Sophie, don't be sorry for me or tease me.'

She saw he was in earnest. 'Ah, no, I was thinking of myself,' she said. She wondered whether he was jealous of young men, but she was not jealous of other young women – not jealous. Envious, perhaps. So why should Grant Miller feel unsure of himself? Anyway, she did not like 'young men'. It was only Clement she liked and that was doomed in any case, she quite saw that.

'Now I shall introduce you to some young men and so that you are not bored with me, I shall go and talk to Mrs Bland. Come!' he said, and took her arm and piloted her across the room. His touch was firm but gentle and she liked feeling his hand on her elbow. Was all that he had said before just a game? She was still not sure and tried to concentrate on the young men who were all, it seemed, journalists or painters, friends of Mrs Bland's daughters. But Grant did not disappear from her thoughts.

She could see the young men liked her and so she slightly exaggerated her ability to be 'flashy', and was direct in conversation, even slightly forward. She was enjoying herself. It was so easy to talk to the men. They guffawed a lot at everything she said but she thought their eyes were not on her soul but on a small outer case of hers that could be readily summoned when necessary and as easily cast off.

Grant Miller was also, in his inmost soul, a romantic like Sophie. He had always tried to bring together love and desire but had never quite met before the feelings Sophie inspired in him. He was amazed at himself and not a little proud. This special sort of idealized yearning had not before played such a large a part in his life. It hurt him physically to contemplate her. He needed her, wanted her, yet was frightened to think about possessing her. He certainly wanted to put the sparkle in Sophie's eyes, but it left him aching and tender and melancholy to contemplate how he might do it. He asked himself whether he was bad or sad or out of his mind, or plainly foolish. She was not the sort of girl most men would be ruined for, had nothing of the seductress, only a little of the flirt or the tease. He was old enough not to hurt her, he was sure, and old enough to balance his public and private life and only add to hers, not take away anything essential. Yet he felt his worldliness had deserted him in part. Perhaps worldliness was only a shell that enclosed him.

Unlike some of Bland's friends, he was not a philanderer, and therefore, perhaps, even more dangerous to Sophie? But how could Sophie ever feel the same for him? It had not always been his experience that love called out love. She was, after all, a beginner in the stakes of love, a mere child, and that was partly why she so attracted him. And yet he thought she was the eternal Eve, too, and would not be ashamed either of nakedness or passion. Sophie was the world before the serpent, he thought. Right at the beginning he had had faith in her. She was wonderful, beautiful, young, unspoilt. He did not want to spoil her, but he did not know what to do. He would wait and see.

That party at Well Hall was the turning point of many lives. Edith, too, had realized someone was watching her when she was talking to others, when she was playing chess with Garnett Edwards's friend Sylvester, and when she moved across the room and went out for a moment with Sophie and Seb and some other young men, at one point, to look at the stars. It was Clement, of course, and finally he was beside her, saying nothing, but metaphorically hurling himself from a great height and trying to break down the barriers Edith felt were always round her. He was not a man to pay court in a conventional way and certainly she had no desire to encourage him, but felt a little besieged and then wondered if she were imagining things. Sophie had been strange, too. As they went out into the grounds she had seemed even more Sophie-like, excited and a little intoxicated. Edith had seen her in earnest conversation with their employer, but shortly afterwards Grant had disappeared and Sophie was the centre of a crowd of young men. Other young men had accompanied several girls to 'have a look at the moon' and someone had said that there used to be 'moon parties' to observe the moon and the conversation had become rather boring to Edith.

Sophie, too, said little, once they were out in the grounds, until she came up to Edith and said, 'Where are we all going to sleep? Did they tell you?'

'Yes. You and I and one or two other girls who don't live locally or who haven't carriages have been given that room next to the one where we did our hair. Provided we go away before breakfast; there's an early train.'

It was now one o'clock and the cheese and apples and soup had been distributed when they went in and some of the older people were already in their coats and hats. It seemed, however, that the party would go on as long as the hosts were prepared to stay up, and the Blands were still lively, though the chairs had been drawn up to the fireplace and Mrs Bland was telling what appeared to be a ghost story. Grant was sitting in an armchair reading a book when Sophie came in again and she went up to him without thinking. Suddenly he seemed safe and known and someone she did not have to put on her party voice for.

131

She drew a chair up next to him and he put down his book and contemplated her. 'One day,' he said, as their voices were for a moment drowned by appreciative oohs and ahhs from the audience round Mrs Bland, 'I shall go away from a party with you, Sophie, and I shall watch you sleeping and in the morning I shall get you breakfast and wrap you in my dressing-gown.'

She looked steadily at him again, certain, now, how much he had meant of his earlier avowals.

'You have strange hands,' he said. 'Older than your years, and brown, like gypsy's hands.' He took her left hand from the arm of the chair and held it for a moment. Then he kissed it and let it fall back in her lap. She was trembling. 'And you have a terrible mouth,' he added. She did not know what he meant and put up her finger to it, looking upset. 'I mean, terrible that it is too full and wicked,' he added. He must be flirting now, she decided, and said nothing but just looked at him. 'One day,' he said, 'One day.' And then he got up and she got up, too. 'Don't forget, I love you,' he said and then he was over at the side of his host, bidding him farewell. When he had gone she sat on, and then beckoned Edith to sit by her.

Another girl came up and said she was sleepy and the party seemed to be evaporating. A Bland daughter showed them up to the room at the top and, without undressing beyond their camisoles, they were soon in the little beds that had been left ready for them. Edith was asleep quite quickly and the sounds from downstairs faded away. Sophie got up and looked out at the garden in the moonlight and her feelings were in such a confusion and turmoil that she wished for a moment she was back in Thirksay in her own little bed and that Alice was sleeping near her and that life had perhaps not yet begun.

It was later that Sophie learned that one of the ladies who had been present at the Well Hall party had been of those whom the world castigated as being of 'ill repute' because she lived with a man as his wife but was not married to him. He had another, earlier wife tucked away somewhere, but it did not matter that *she* had no interest in the mutual 'husband'; it was enough that out of spite she would not divorce him. Most women took the side of the first lady: why should she divorce a man to please him and allow him to make her rival respectable? Sophie thought the trouble lay in people considering divorce as so terrible. Yet, on the other hand, as she did not really care for the idea of marriage, divorce reform was not high on her list of priorities. *She* did not really want to live with anyone as a wife; it was bad enough, she was sure, being a real wife without being a pretend one!

Mr Miller had been away abroad on some work for the firm the week after the party and Sophie was half-glad, half-disappointed. She had said to Edith, almost jokingly, 'I think he may "fancy" me,' when Edith had asked idly what she had been talking about with their employer at the party.

'And we talked about the position of women,' she had added as an afterthought. It sounded rather solemn and silly.

On the Friday of Grant's absence, however, a letter arrived for Sophie with a French postmark. She found it at the bottom of the stairs on the small table where tenants' mail was placed by Mrs Macalister. Fortunately, Edith was not yet home, having stayed behind at work to finish some typing for Garnett Edwards. At first Sophie did not recognize the handwriting, though it seemed familiar from work. Then, a moment after, as she was mounting the stairs, she realized whose it was. Was he going to say he had been teasing her, that he had been a little tipsy? Fright rather than excitement was her first reaction. She forced herself to make a pot of tea first, before opening the letter in her own room, sitting on the bed.

'My dear Sophie,' it ran.

'I have concluded my business in Paris and will probably be home by the time you read this. I have been walking along the *grands boulevards* and sitting at a pavement café and now I am back in my hotel on the Left Bank. I could not resist writing to you; indeed, I feel a compulsion to write to you which I have resisted until today. Wherever I have been I seem to see your face, Sophie. I have seen no one half as pretty as you, and no one I wished to talk to more than you. Perhaps you thought I was not serious last week? Surely you must realize that I was? When I said I could love you, Sophie, I meant more than that. I *do* love you, dear girl. I had forgotten what it is to love – to be full of the vision of one person, to hear her voice wherever you go. To awake in the night with but one thought: "The world contains Sophie so it cannot be entirely a bad place." You will have to forgive me. I said I would not speak of it again. Perhaps your heart is already filled with similar feelings for another – I don't know, nor do I believe that anyone knowing you could not be in love with you. But for the present I want only to say that I shall behave myself with the utmost propriety on my return. Perhaps we may go the theatre together or take a walk in Chelsea? I want only to be with you, at present, nothing more. There is no one in the world I would rather be in Paris with than you. You would make my favourite city a paradise. I imagine taking you to a little restaurant and walking round the old streets here with you and all the world would know you were my love. I send you my love and my hopes that one day you might, indeed, allow me to know a little more of you, though I cannot imagine I do not already know you almost through and through. With love from GM.'

Well! It was true, then. She had not imagined it all. It was exciting, but alarming. It seemed he would be loving her whatever she did. Should she encourage such feelings? No, she would not exactly encourage him. But she could not find it in herself to discourage him either. She suspected he was the sort of person who would not take no for an answer, even if it took him a year of more. She wondered why he should assume she would not repulse him, that she would receive an 'illicit' love affair with enthusiasm? Yet men, who could always make their desires known, were always at an advantage. That women should express their feelings too, however, was the principle in which she believed. If she, then, applauded feeling and its expression, why should she not be pleased to be the object of it? Why, though, had she not been able to get anywhere with Clem? Was it because she was not the sort of person Clem could love? Would Grant Miller want her to return his love, or did he only require acquiescence in his own emotions? How did mutual love begin? Of course, it was love's physical expression that bound people together and she was not so naïve as to think that Grant would be content to worship a distant ideal for ever. But then, people said that if a woman 'gave in' to this sort of importunity she was doomed. That was absurd too. There was nothing wicked in falling in love with people. Why should there be anything wicked in the physical expression of that love outside marriage, apart from the risk all women ran?

Yet she did not want to 'will' a feeling and, also, did not feel comfortable as the object of a passion. If she analysed it, though, she did want experience. Who better to give it to her than an older, attractive man who seemed to adore her? Could she be like a man and risk an adventure in order to launch herself into adulthood? What had she to lose that a man did not? She felt, too, a certain pride that such a man should want her and was left with the feeling that, in the end, she could not deny herself this opportunity, even if it was because she had a childish desire not to miss anything. So she would give herself up to his love and see where it led her.

When Edith came in she said nothing, having tucked the letter away in her private box of treasures that she had brought back from Thirksay. It held the photograph of a teacher she had loved – it seemed long ago – the programme of a concert heard in Leeds, a photograph of her father in youth, her teaching certificate and some dried roses from the bower at home.

Edith did not remark upon Sophie's unaccustomed silence, for Edith herself was tired and went to an early bed. Sophie lay staring at the ceiling, feeling that destiny had taken a hand, even from that moment in the ABC teashop. She must be brave and confront it. At least it was better than nothing happening.

Each morning after this private decision, Sophie awoke with the feeling that Something *was* going to Happen. She wondered how Grant would speak to her when he returned to work. Would he blush or grow pale or stammer? Would she go pale and confused in his presence? She envisaged their meeting again so many times in fancy, that when he did return and actually came down to the basement to ask her to find something for him, she forgot that he had ever said anything at all and sorted through the letter she wanted with composure. The office was so far removed from the idea of passion – except in the case of Clement, and he was a visitor not a habitué – that she felt the Grant who had spoken to her in the moonlight was unreal. Only when he had stood waiting for the letters, still saying nothing more than a 'thank you' did she venture a glance and found he was looking at her with a smile on his face.

'I got your letter,' she blurted out.

'And I am happy to be back,' he replied and then looked away. 'Shall you like to go for a walk on Saturday afternoon by the river?' he asked then. 'There are some pictures in a gallery I'd like to show you, and we could have tea in Chelsea.'

Just then Mrs Smeaton came in and so he said, 'Let me know, will you?' and had gone.

Sophie bent down to her work and avoided Mrs Smeaton's eyes, but could not help saying, 'There is a lot of work to catch up with since Mr Miller was away.'

The lady said something about never having ever known the place up to date with its work.

Sophie knew she had come over the first hurdle. Everything could stay the same on the surface. She was never going to let anyone know about her private life, whatever she decided to do.

Should she go and walk with him? She wanted to! Apart from anything else she liked walking in London and enjoyed picture galleries, and how could she refuse a treat? Grant Miller would stir her up, he was bound to, she was not a statue.

'Dear Grant,' she wrote, 'I should enjoy a walk in Chelsea. There is no time to answer the rest of your letter. My presence will have to do instead – Sophie.'

She was returning from the post-box when she met Edith coming home. It was dusk earlier now, but a mellow autumn was again rescuing the year from a too early descent into winter and cold. She scuffed the leaves on the pavement with pleasure and at last, having made her decision, which was more than a decision to have tea with her employer, she went in again with Edith and talked of a book she was reading and the pleasures of toasting muffins.

What was so comforting about Grant Miller, Sophie was thinking as she strolled on Chelsea Embankment with him that Saturday afternoon, was that she was not frightened of him. He had been rather silent, a little pale, and she guessed he too was fearful of spoiling things. How different from the grasping men who had so far been her experience of the male sex. Men were always presented to girls as an unknown quantity, as the enemy to be placated. Their bodies were strange; they could give girls babies, were unpredictable. In spite of, or perhaps because of, being brought up on a farm, Sophie had had a good deal of fear of sex, instilled into her. 'People are not animals.' The flaunting males and rutting females were the natural order – poor, witless things to be tolerated as a source of profit, and matter-of-factly slaughtered. It was quite other with humans. *They* must live in the mind, attempting minute by minute to wrench an order from natural chaos. That chaos arose mostly from lust, was mainly sexual, and fear was its watchword and a talisman against anarchy. And, besides, men were unaccountable and often beasts themselves when their bodily lusts blossomed to some wife or woman in close proximity. A man was taken over, possessed by the very devil. The means God had chosen for him to procreate depended upon mindlessness. He became something else till he got what he wanted. Man's double nature had apparently been necessary; it was the sin which Christ came to redeem.

Early on, Sophie had realized this was what the church meant. Lust transformed a male, but was endorsed by a female, descendant of Eve, who must allay his torment. For Woman had tempted Man – she had had to, in order for Christ to come on the scene later. Sophie felt the injustice: blaming it all on 'the Woman' who could not help what God made her do. And anyway, the serpent was there before Eve!

At first all this made her uneasy, then disbelieving, then angry. She knew it was not true, had been invented by men long ago who feared the power of women over them. How it had got mixed up with Christianity, she was not sure, but would make it her business to find out.

Sophie wanted to understand sex, but it must be with a man who shared her ideas about the non-sinfulness of sin, who did not think that love was mindless and whom she could trust to see her through the experience, purge her for ever of conventional morality and reconcile her own nature. She did not want to be loved and worshipped so much as inducted by a man she could both admire and learn from. Since Clement Bartholomew would never want all that love she could have poured on him, her first feelings must go underground. Her fate must rest, for a time at least, with the sophisticated Miller. He at least knew what he wanted. Her charm for him was

137

precisely that she was unformed still, with an enthusiastic zest for living. Even Sophie herself realized that she must possess an unconscious 'innocence'. Yet she could not stop thinking about her feelings, which was not an innocent occupation.

An unremarkable dialogue was taking place betweeen herself and Grant. They were leaning on the parapet of the Embankment looking across to Battersea and the sun was shining on the water.

'Have you ever been in the gardens of the Royal Hospital?' he was asking.

'No. Is that the place we passed with the wrought-iron doors and the lawns behind?'

'Yes. It's one of my favourite spots, but it isn't always open to the public.'

'Here is very nice,' ventured Sophie. 'Perhaps we could see the pictures and then have a cup of tea?'

He smiled. 'London is all very well, but I'd like to take you walking the Surrey hills or on the Weald. One can have too much of other people here.' He looked at her profile as she leaned her chin on her hands and stared over to Battersea. 'You're not wearing your red cap,' he said softly.

She turned towards him. 'I thought the sun should get to my hair and it's warm today; I didn't even want to put on my coat.' She put her hands on to the stone wall as she turned and spoke to him and, after a moment, he took up one thin, brown hand. A complicated mixture of feelings came over her when he held the hand and then brought it softly to his lips and kissed it.

'Oh, Sophie, you are a picture yourself. I don't need art today.'

Sophie half turned towards him. A geranium-seller passed on her way back from Sloane Square. The old woman pushed her little barrow, looking ahead fixedly, not even trying to sell them any flowers.

Sophie was thinking, Clem must live near here. I hope he doesn't see me. Grant had put her hand down. 'I am not very beautiful,' Sophie was saying, 'I'd much rather you thought I was clever.' She smiled.

'You are clever,' he said. 'But more pretty than clever.'

Sophie thought that was not a compliment and was not sure whether, in Grant's scheme of things, he had meant it as one.

'You are the New Age,' he said then.

'Girls of the New Age do not care whether they are pretty,' replied Sophie solemnly.

'How bad for them.' He was thinking, I should like to dress her in a nice dress from an expensive shop and buy her a black velvet toque. Her face is perfect: she does not even use powder. And a parasol, he thought confusedly, with a tortoiseshell handle set with precious stones.

Sophie guessed the direction of his thoughts. 'You will never make me into a fashion plate,' she said.

'I don't want to. You are perfect. And perfection is even more perfect when it is – not fashionable, but . . .'

'I really don't care a lot about clothes,' she said, breaking in.

'My dear Sophie, I did not bring you here to discuss your wardrobe. I wanted to tell you I love you.' He thought, I wish I could see her naked. 'If we are not feeling like looking at pictures, let us go and find something to eat and drink. I know a pretty little tea-room over there where we can talk.'

'One day I'd like to go the Café Royal,' she replied. 'Is it still the place to go? I always thought it would be the place where I should find the meaning of life.'

'More sightseers than Bohemians now,' he said. 'You can go wherever you want, Sophie, just so long as you will go with me. I don't expect you to feel for me what I do for you – why should you? But I'd like to make your life more fun.'

'Fun?' she echoed. 'Oh, Grant, I'd like to fall in love with you; it would be such a waste otherwise.'

He laughed then and she took his hand this time and held it. She was not going to pretend she wanted to change herself into some other creature. He seemed to like her mostly as she was. 'I know you are a good girl,' he said.

'Oh, no, I'm not good – Edith is good. But she is much more unconventional than I am, you know.'

Perhaps he had been thinking she was conventionally 'proper', but he did not seem to mean that, for his next words were, 'I mean, you are serious. Sometimes you frighten me when you look so intense and earnest. I want you to smile and be happy and stop worrying about the world.'

'How can anyone stop worrying about everything that is wrong with us all?' she said.

'I suppose that is part of your charm for me,' he answered, bending his head and kissing her hand again.

Really, she could not convince him, she thought, that she was not the Sophie he loved. And how could she know, really know that, unless she gave in to him? For there might be another Sophie, some worldly creature of pleasure lurking underneath the self she presented to the world.

'I always think love makes you see yourself in a new light,' he went on, determined to try to convey to her the thoughts that had been obsessing him for so long.

'It makes the person who loves see himself differently. Does it make the person who is loved feel different, too?' she asked, keeping her end up. 'You see,' she went on, not waiting for an answer, 'I am not an experienced woman of the world and I don't think I ever shall be, but you make me feel safe.'

'Sophie, that is the nicest thing you have ever said to me,' he said.

She swept on: 'I don't know whether I'm a coward or not – I don't even know whether I am foolish in wanting to love you – but I don't know how to feel loved.'

He put his arm round her as two seagulls circled them for a moment and there was the sound of a tug chugging below them and then a lighter came into sight and there came the mournful cry of another boat's siren in the distance.

'Will you trust me? Will you let me, one day, be your lover, Sophie Ridsdale?' he murmered, his face in her brown hair. 'Forget who I am, forget I am married, forget I'm your employer, forget everything but I love you. Let me love you, Sophie – darling?'

She sighed a great sigh and it seemed to her that this moment was her destiny beckoning. This moment would seal her future. Whatever she did in that future. But how to explain to him that she wanted to know love and yet wanted, in the end, to be free. Was that fair? She did not want just to use him to grow up. But she wanted him to see that, whatever happened, she could not promise away the future. A moment like this, with his arms round her, might carry her into the unknown and take her away from her nature, whatever her true nature was. Young men did not, in her experience, make avowals of love to girls like her. Either they wanted to seduce them or they wanted to worship from afar. And Grant wanted her to choose him freely and did not want a distant worship either. How could she say no, when she saw his eyes as they now bent over her? She closed her own and he kissed her softly on the mouth, on each eyelid, and stayed holding her, stroking her neck and sending pleasurable ripples down her spine.

'There is nothing sordid about it,' he said, looking up and releasing her. 'It is how things are meant to be between men and women. Will you risk yourself one day with me, Sophie? Will you let me open the doors of love to you?'

'If you will take me by the hand and lead me in, but let me go when I have learned,' she wanted to say, but did not.

'I would like to take you away: Paris, or the country. I want to "commit" myself to you. Forgive me, that I cannot go about this in a proper way. Believe me, Sophie, I want you for ever.'

For answer, she looked into his eyes and then, shyly, put her arms round him and smelt the unfamiliar smell of a clean-shaven, well-groomed man and kissed him on the mouth.

'Now I would like a cup of tea,' she said.

He drank her in, the fresh smell of young skin and the soft touch of her cheek and wanted, there and then, to take the pins out of her hair and let it fall down behind her and bury himself in her and wind her hair round his hand and lie for ever by her side. But there was in his desire a strong element of tenderness. Lust was there, but it was not the chief sensation. That was an almost unbearable wish to protect her, rock her, pour love over her and by doing so, renew the wells of tenderness in himself and replenish her, too.

They walked slowly away to the teashop, hand in hand at first, and he did not seem remote any more. The kisses had changed everything between them. Embarrassment, shyness, awkwardness, the peep into the unfamiliar, all had gone and she felt no longer even excited and certainly not apprehensive, but calm and happy. This was to be her life then. She was loved and she would return some of that love; for it was easy, when a man held you in his arms, to love him. She would confront issues of freedom later.

Grant loved that slim brown girl with her Cadogan unpinned and the glorious thick hair falling down her back. He brushed the skin of her neck with his lips as he stood behind her in the Bloomsbury Hotel, for Sophie's initiation was not to be in Paris or Surrey, but in a quiet hotel off another square, some weeks after their walk in Chelsea. He had waited for her to tell him, somehow, that she wanted it, that she was ready. But Sophie had not wanted to wait too long. Instead, she had shut her eyes and jumped and now the bridge between childhood and womanhood was almost crossed with this familiar, yet unfamiliar, man who never so far had hinted at work in the office that she and he were about to embark together on their adventure. So he stood behind her, his face now buried in her hair, in the half-light of a Bloomsbury apartment, with the blinds drawn against the weak sunlight of a November afternoon, and he had his arms round her waist and his head on her shoulder.

Love, she thought. This is love. She wanted finally to be wanted, and wanted she knew she was. She turned round to embrace him. There was no guilt, no fear, no coyness. In Grant's world, people slept together because they wanted to — it was civilized and it was 'fun', too. But more than that, he loved her; and she was safe with him. He had told her not to worry about babies, there were ways of avoiding them, and this did not, in fact, worry her, though it always had before. He had explained there would be small inconveniences but now she had forgotten about them.

'The colour of your eyes today is like the leaves in an autumn forest,' he was saying, and, 'Sophie, you are a stunner. Let's just lie with our arms about each other. I don't seem to want anything else, just at present.'

It was true. He felt almost unmanned by the depth of his love. He knew passion would come in its own time. If they had months together he need not, and indeed would not, want to spend his fortune in a rush of desire, but would want to make it last a slow surrender. But here, there was an afternoon and there would be other afternoons snatched from life and even so, he wanted to lie quietly with her, caress her shoulder, gather her hair into his hands like a harvest and await the tide coming back over the shore.

They lay on the large double bed under a counterpane at first, because it was not a warm day, but when Sophie, in her camisole, tucked her bare legs around him he felt the stirrings of a tender lust.

Sophie had not known that she would know what to do, but she did. 'Tell me you love me,' she demanded, and kissed his ear lobes, with her hands clasped round his neck. How nice it was, how right it was, to lie closely wound together. She must once have lain like this as a child in her parents' bed, long, long ago. What a distance, how many years to traverse before she could be close to someone again. But now Grant was murmuring and groaning and kissing her shoulders and unbuttoning the clothes that remained. She helped him and at last they both lay naked and trembling a little with their exertions.

For a time there were no words; caresses and kisses took their place and the caresses never became wild, but were seductive and slow, and there was hardly a moment when she knew she was no longer a virgin, for they seemed to slip together like two parts that had been once separated and Grant, with the experience of maturity, was gentle and careful. They moved together and she looked up now at the body that was above her and felt his excitement which was gradually growing. Still he looked at her, and she saw his eyes were moist. There had been a little stab and she quivered when she knew he was completely inside her, but he continued to kiss her all over and she returned the kisses and moved under him. 'Bliss,' she said and then he moved more quickly still, looking in her eyes and seemingly unaware of anything but her, not attending to himself but to her. The tide rose and then went back slowly and he closed his eyes as she felt a rhythmic tremble release itself in her body for a long, long time, as though it would never end. Not then did she attain the heights of passionate release, but it was more than enough to feel his own pleasure as it ebbed away, to take his head on her breast and fall into a comfortable slumber.

When she awoke he was looking at her as she lay sideways in his arms and he murmered, 'Oh, my darling,' and, 'Thank you.'

'Are you always so polite?' she teased.

'Did you feel anything, Sophie, Tell me.'

'I felt you, that was enough, and I felt happy and *am* so happy.'

'And you will feel more than happiness, I promise,' he said and put his head back on her breast. She was so young, so soft, so slim and brown. 'Elf,' he said.

They lay together talking a little, until his desire rose again, and this time she was ready and guided him back to where he belonged. A strange thought came to her, that Clement would not make love like this, that Grant, this man in her arms, was not a usual lover.

'I am lucky,' she said.

'No, I am lucky. But I don't want to feel too lustful today, I just want you to want me.'

'I do,' she cried and he gathered her to him once more and this time again there was no storm, but the waves were shared ripples on a summer sea. Sophie saw the sea and the shore and drifted away into a dream, so that she was quite surprised to find that when she woke up it was time for dinner.

'I don't want to get up. Why can't we stay here for ever? I don't want you to go away and back to the world.'

But they had to go back into the world, of course. Their first time together was repeated about once every two or three weeks on Friday and Saturday evenings.

Sophie told Edith she was with Mr Miller and that she was all right and Edith must please not say anything to anyone else. When she returned on the Saturday or Sunday she was always perfectly as usual. Edith knew that they were staying not far away, on the borders of Holborn, and inquired no further. 'I'm happy, Edith,' Sophie said.

Once or twice Grant took Sophie to his *pied à terre* off the Tottenham Court Road, but he was worried that someone might see them – not for his reputation, but for Sophie's. At first, each time they met on the Friday or Saturday evening, if he were too occupied with work on the Friday, it was like an odyssey. Sophie would throw down her cares with her little attaché case which accompanied her and contained a toothbrush, a hairbrush, some French perfume he had given her and a book, in case Grant had to disappear for a time on business or telephone a client from the office. Once, even, they were in the office together on a Saturday afternoon, with the house all silent except for their footsteps. She had wanted to be with him there, for sometimes her existence seemed unreal when she returned to work on a Monday. To see him in his room and to be kissed in the same room she usually saw him working in was strange. But the odyssey continued all that winter in the hotel where, of course, Grant registered her as his wife.

Even so, there were many weekends when he was at home in Surrey and he told her he felt uneasy there, in spite of the certainty that his wife did not know of Sophie's existence, and would probably not have worried if she did. Violet had married him for security and a home for her son, whose father had been a friend of Grant's. Sophie felt uneasy, too, but only when she was not with her lover. When, as winter drew on, the gas was turned low and the curtains drawn she would think that nowhere else and with no one else could she feel so secure and away from the prying eyes of the rest of humanity. Yet it was because of him that she needed protection from the rest of the world, and the paradox was not lost on him or on her. But Grant took her attitudes and feelings to be natural and normal and was at pains to soothe any guilt she might feel. Her worst guilt was that she was, or might be, hurting another woman. How would she herself feel if she were married to him? But she was ruthless, too, and knew that Violet had received far more in a worldly sense from Grant than she was ever likely to.

The odyssey was what mattered and, as they began to know each other's bodies better, she began to sense the depth of his need and to compare it with hers. She began to miss what she had never had, whilst she enjoyed what she had never imagined she needed. Grant bought her little things; she would never accept money from him for, as she said, he paid her a wage in any case and that was for work not love.

She continued to work hard and to learn more about the business when she was with him on those Fridays and Saturdays than she would ever have learned during the week. But Grant did not want her to be concerned with that sort of thing when they were together; only from the conversations they had over a bottle of wine after their lovemaking, when a tray would be sent for and they would dine in front of the fire, did she absorb his interests and his knowledge. Grant learned about his young mistress, too, about her life, her thoughts, her opinions and her soul. He had been right – she was exactly the right woman for him! He seemed to sink further and further in love with her, even whilst retaining the ability to forget 'all that' when he was busy at Miller and Penn. So much was he able to do so, that sometimes Sophie was frightened. She did not resent his work, but worried that she was distracting him, that he would, one day, forget what he should be doing. Yet he did not and seemed able to balance the two parts of his existence tolerably well. Sophie was particularly careful lest Theo Carmichael should ever suspect what was going on, for she sensed the older girl was, or had been, more than a little in love with Grant herself.

She 'had it all out' with Edith one Friday evening in December, when Grant was at home coping with a domestic emergency. Edith had always appeared incurious and was certainly discreet, but Sophie felt she must talk to someone about him for she was beginning to see everything, even herself, though his eyes. 'He is a romantic, Edith,' she said, as they sat by the gas-fire with a teapot on a tray and some rather expensive biscuits in a lacquer box which Sophie had given Edith on her birthday. Edith had given Sophie a hot-water bottle, remembering her remark in the summer, and Sophie was wearing the brooch which her parents had sent her for the same birthday.

'I mean, he falls in love the way I do – I've never met that before. It makes him so vulnerable.'

'You too,' said Edith, stirring her tea, seemingly lost in thought.

'Yes, but I don't mind. I want to be so. It makes me happy to be wanted, Edith.'

'Is he, do you think, a *happy* man?' asked Edith at last, looking up at Sophie.

'I think he is a man capable of great joy in life, but something has prevented him being himself. He says he is happy with me,' said Sophie.

Edith wondered if Sophie was as happy with him, but said instead, 'I expect he knows he is very lucky to have you.'

'I'm lucky, too, Edith. Just think, I might have spent my whole life wishing Clement would love me ...' Even as she said these words, she realized that, in spite of Grant, she still wished it.

146

'He is reasonably worldly, I suppose – Mr Miller?' Edith ventured.

'Yes, of course, and he knows what the world would say and probably will. But I *know* he loves me, Edith, you can't mistake feelings like his – '

'And that makes you love him,' said Edith, looking down at her teacup.

'At first,' said Sophie, with an attempt at the truth, 'I didn't. I wasn't "in love" with him – I never thought of him like that. It was a complete surprise. I never, never would have dreamed ... But I did *choose* to let him love me. I suppose that must be how most women are – they let themselves ... Sometimes I feel I am in two parts and one part is only there when we're alone together. But I still have my other self when I'm alone. I can manage the world better because I know he loves me, but I could live in a different way now, a way I couldn't have done before, even this last summer. It feels as though someone was looking for me, yet now I've been "found" I could be perfectly all right by myself. It's the times between, the times when he's just gone away or we've said goodbye and before I go back to work or come back here to you, when I seem to be in a limbo. I miss him dreadfully, miss someone I never even knew I could love. Isn't it strange? ... Then, afterwards, I'm myself again and can manage perfectly well and feel quite independent. Do I ever give anything away at work?'

Sophie thought that Edith did not always notice things, might not register any difference in her voice or manner, but as Edith knew her better than anyone in other ways, that would make up for her absentmindedness and render her reactions about those of the average person.

'I've never noticed a thing. If you hadn't told me all about it, I don't think I ever would. But, of course, *he* may one day let something slip ....'

'But he's the one with the power, isn't he, Edith? Grant can choose to do what he wants, though I think he's always spent the greater part of his time at work. But it doesn't worry him the way it does me – the separation between the two worlds, I mean.'

'I think men can live in spurts and dashes,' replied Edith. 'They're very single-minded creatures, but only for short periods. Look at Edwards. Who would believe what I'm told he gets up to! Yet in the office he's all of a piece, never gives himself away.'

Edith *was* beginning to notice more, Sophie thought. 'How is Clem?' she asked, for Edith had been to Doughty Street the day before to discuss her little piece on the Norse legends with him and Kitty. Since his sudden appearance early that autumn at their eyrie he had met Edith only in company. She had listened to him and occasionally ventured an opinion.

Clement had said no more than, 'I respect your judgment, Edith,' and Edith still felt obscurely uneasy in his presence. If he had been like Grant she would have felt even more uneasy, but Clement was not one to throw his heart away. He would watch and bide his time with a woman like Edith, of whom, truth to tell, he was a little afraid.

'Why don't you ever ask Mr Miller up here? It would be perfectly respectable if I were here – please don't feel you must keep your worlds apart – and I could always go out,' said Edith.

'Think of what Mrs Macalister would say! No, Grant doesn't belong here, Edith. I want somewhere which can be mine, where he is not, like he has at home,' Sophie replied.

They never spoke of intimate details of physical love when they were together, Sophie and Edith, for each was instinctively discreet and each guessed what was not said. Edith would always be there to help if help were ever needed. Sophie knew, but she did not wish to inflict too many conversations of this sort upon her friend, unless Edith asked directly, which she was not likely to do.

Grant was more disturbed than his competent self would acknowledge. After he had known Sophie for a few months he was in even further than he had ever thought possible. He began to need her, want her, at inopportune moments and for the first time wondered whether it would be better if she worked elsewhere. To possess her had seemed enough, but each possession hinted at further enslavements and from the original tenderness of his lovemaking, which was still always there at the heart, there came also deeper, more anguished feelings. He dreamt of his mother, of whom he had not thought for years, for she had died when he was in his teens. If he had to be away from London, and there were times when this was necessary, he would write vast letters to Sophie and sometimes give her them when they met. Sophie did not feel the same need to write to him, for to see him eventually was, at first, enough, though the pain of parting grew worse as time went on. He could write that he knew he fitted into her life somewhere, that their love was not a mere episode. She had been 'prepared' for him, as he had been 'prepared' for her. He was very romantic.

'I want to make you happy,' he said one day, when Sophie had looked sad before one of their usual partings; he was going to Victoria Station to go home until the Tuesday and she was returning to her flat.

'Oh, Grant, darling. I *am* happy,' Sophie cried and flung her arms round him.

'Don't ever leave me, never leave me,' Grant whispered. 'Sometimes you look so sad.'

'Only because you are going away. I'm all right once you have gone, I get over things quickly,' she replied, smiling.

'I don't want you to get over me.'

'Nor I you – '

'Sometimes, at work, I see your eyes shining and I think, I put that sparkle there, and then I think, what am I doing, why am I not with her always? It is not fair on you, my little love, I know. Forgive me.'

'Do you want me when I am not there?' she whispered.

'Do I! Sophie, you are like a magic drink. When you – give yourself to me, I want you more and more – ' He had never felt this before. Usually desire satiated itself, but not with her. They were meant for each other. Yet it was wrong that physical love should be the first priority when they could be together. 'You know that I love you for all time, whatever you may do, whatever may arrive,' he wrote.

Sophie wished that she did not have this effect upon him, for she had not intended it to be like that. He had what seemed an immeasurable need of her, and though she always wanted to give him all she could of both her body and her spirit, she wished that physical relations could, occasionally, be simpler. She, too, was in deeper than she had ever thought she would be.

There was something in him which would never dry up in his need of her, some wound that she would always set bleeding again. He said, 'Sophie, when you are older you will leave me and get married. Indeed, I know you should; but don't speak of it, I shall die.'

'But *you* are married,' she wanted to cry out, 'it should be me feeling this.'

Grant thought he must be making up for lost time, but only because it was Sophie who had introduced him to a new world of feeling, an uncomfortable world, in many ways, and one he could not help wishing he had entered earlier in life. She was the one and only, the Sophie of Sophies. The worm at the heart of this great and grand passion was the knowledge that Sophie, however much she abandoned herself to him, however much she was his equal in lust and love, in tenderness and in passion, did not love him in the exclusive way he loved her. How could she? She could be greedy, wanted everything of him when he was there, even the parts of himself which he thought unimportant, like his past. She would want marriage with him, if she ever wanted marriage with anyone, he thought. Before she was thirty – a handful of years, he forced himself to think of it – she would want a home of her own. However could that be brought about? Violet would not wish to divorce him, he was sure, and why should she? What he had thought of as a passionate affair could very easily turn into a debâcle. Sophie would be content for a time with a passionate affair, but not for ever. And the only way it could be resolved with the least hurt to her, would be marriage to someone else of her own age. Sophie had told him she had been cast in a rôle that did not truly suit her. After all, she was only twenty-one. He knew she had been in love with Clement Bartholomew, for she had told him of her feelings for the poet. And because Clement had never requited this infatuation, he would always be a threat.

'Good God!' he said one day. 'In four years you will only be twenty-five and I shall be forty-three. How lucky you are, Sophie, to be so young.'

He did not often speak of the difference of their ages except to grumble that young men did not seem to know how to treat girls. 'Will you love me when *you* are forty-three?' he asked mournfully, and shuddered. He wanted it to last for ever and the surest way for that to be impossible was to talk about it, so usually he tried to hold his tongue. And then, after a week or two, they would come together again and he would wonder if what kept them going was the grain of salt in the sweetness, the fact that they could not be together always, were forced to remain romantic lovers. Sophie would like that, even prefer it for a few years, but in the end? Sophie was romance incarnate for him and the 'situation' held its own romance for her too; but she would not want to play that part for ever. What could he do?

Clement had taken Edith to Roches on Old Compton Street to celebrate his book of poems coming out, in the spring of 1912. Their *table d'hôte* was one shilling and sixpence and he intended to have a good bottle of claret with it. It had been on the spur of the moment and Edith had found it impossible to refuse and was sitting miserably at the small table with him, wondering what to talk about. Perhaps they could discuss Santayana's *Life of Reason* which Edith had just finished and was interested in. But that might be rude. She had better discuss Clem's poems. Clement, however, did not seem to want to discuss anything of this sort and Edith was feeling even more walled in by the invisible glass that separated her from others. She tried to talk about some of the books they were bringing out this season, but Clement only gave a quick smile and attacked his sole. Could she perhaps try architecture? She began on York Minster and Clement appeared to be listening, but when she asked him about Salisbury he said, 'I'll send you a poem about that.' What on earth did he want from her? How could she possibly feel easier with him? What did he want to say to her? Why should he choose *her* as a companion for celebration? He was obviously enjoying his dinner and that was a good thing.

She returned to her own fish and it was certainly good. Having despatched his *Sole Véronique* and laid the skeleton tidily on the side-place he looked up and gave an an amused smile.

'How is your friend Miss Ridsdale?' he asked. 'I haven't seen her for months.'

'Oh, Sophie's well – very busy,' Edith replied. She hated gossip.

'Flies off in all directions, doesn't she? Not like you. You are so restful, Edith,' he said and blushed slightly. 'Have another glass. How are the Norsemen?'

'A problem,' admitted Edith. 'I need far more time to understand the detail of the settlements. There are very large gaps in our knowledge, you know.' ('Restful?' Good Heavens! That could only mean he found her a good listener.) So far she had said nothing he had followed up with any interest.

Clement was thinking that Edith did not take herself seriously, only her work.

Edith was thinking she had no 'outer' self and was therefore flummoxed when she had to present one.

'Sophie Ridsdale is a bit of a climber, I've heard,' said Clem, reverting to his earlier topic.

'Oh, no,' cried Edith, distressed. 'Sophie is very genuine and very generous.'

'You are always very loyal, Edith,' he said. 'I admire you, you know.' Edith said nothing. 'I saw her in the Bedford one evening,' he said casually.

'Yes, I believe she does go there.'

'Would you like to go there, Edith? I could take you.'

'I'm always so busy,' said Edith truthfully. 'But, of course, that would be very nice.'

'You are very handsome, Edith,' he said after a pause. Edith struggled to take this in. 'And modest,' he added. Did Edith not know he was besotted with her? What did you do with a woman like this? He had thought that, by alluding to Sophie, she would have picked up that he had a feeling Sophie was leading some sort of secret life and if Sophie had one, why not Edith?

But Edith was feeling a mixture of embarrassment and distance and a little maternal urge towards Clem, who seemed so determined to probe her real self with either insinuations about her friend or weird compliments. She gulped again from her glass and wondered whether wine made things easier or worse. Why should she be so hopeless with people? She was surely not modest, for if she were, she would be thinking about him not about her own difficulties. She liked Clem, but she certainly did not love him. Perhaps it would be better not to go on seeing him, not that she had been out with him alone more than twice.

'You are very secretive, Edith,' he said.

She looked up in amazement. She had, in fact, been thinking how the pattern of the bottle and the vase of chrysanthemums and the silver and glasses on each table would look from a distance above the room, so that people themselves were only part of the general arrangement of things. Looked at from above with a god's-eye-view all that happened down below could be reduced to movement, even birth and death, and one person loving another, and getting closer and merging . . . Perhaps it was the wine that was making her think such strange things, which were certainly not appropriate to an evening out with a young man.

Clement would, in fact, have understood, but did not want these sorts of thoughts from Edith. Edith just had to 'be' and be beautiful – it was not necessary for her to think too much. Why did she always look as though something exciting were happening in her mind? It made a chap feel redundant. Clement was unused to women who were his equal in mind and imagination, but was slowly learning to realize they existed, after his year or so in London. It was clear that Edith had Sensibility. How could he, Clement, profit from that?

Edith made another attempt. 'Did you see the latest exhibition at the Grafton Galleries?' she asked stiffly. She had, in fact, been twice to the exhibition and was deeply interested in the modern movement in art but Clement was not to know this.

Another intellectual, he thought. Why could she not just be herself without involving him in the sort of talk he kept for his male friends?

'Seb liked it,' she said shyly.

'Oh, Seb.'

'He's a nice man.'

'Yes. What will you have now – the chicken croquette?'

'That would be lovely,' said Edith meekly.

'Do you like London?' he asked suddenly, when the order was taken.

'Not very much,' she answered honestly. 'Except for the British Museum and my work. All these people – ' she gestured vaguely. 'I'd like to live in a little market town, in Yorkshire,' she said, with more animation than he had yet heard in her voice. Perhaps her unconscious mind was taking over, for she had never put that into words before.

'You know Wiltshire?'

'Not at all. But from your poems I can imagine it.' He said nothing, so she ventured: 'Do you want to go back there?'

153

'I suppose I belong there,' said Clement gloomily.

'But you have to be in London, don't you, if you want to get on? Though I could write anywhere, I suppose. Perhaps your inspiration would go away if you were too long here,' she offered.

'Yes. Fitzrovia and Chelsea and Bloomsbury are all very well but they're not real,' he answered.

'Not real,' she echoed. 'But I feel nothing is real,' she wanted to say.

They ate their chicken and he finished up the bottle and after some fresh fruit they had a cup of coffee and the conversation languished again.

Sophie began to know her lover very, very well. She heard stories from his past which to her seemed to speak of an age beyond time, though it was only eighteen years ago that he had married Violet Trevelyan, the widow of his best friend Hugh who had been killed in a climbing accident at the age of only twenty-one. The pregnant Violet was only too glad to have her problem solved by the quixotic offer from the young and idealistic Grant that she should marry him and they would bring up Hugh's child together. The only problem had been that Grant, who had envied Hugh his pretty wife, did not love her, although he was fond of her; she was grateful to him, though for some curious reason he could not find her sexually attractive. It was a devastating mistake, but apparently Violet had not minded the deprivation, being devoted to her son, Fabian. She had tacitly allowed her new husband to have his lady friends, the last of whom had been Paulina Scott, a thirty-year-old descendant of some minor aristocratic family who was separated from her husband. Eventually she had tired of the liaison and married again. This was the 'lady' Grant had used to see in Fulham. He had been fond of her, he said, but had borne no grudge when, some time before he met Sophie, she had put an end to their being lovers.

Grant was not a truly promiscuous man, had made a mistake out of idealism in extreme youth and devoted himself to his work rather than to women, though he loved the company of women. Sophie saw that they liked him too. His stepson, Fabian, had taken his name to make things easier, but although he had always been the only father the child had known, they had never hit it off together.

Sophie had an idea that if married couples did not sleep together they could eventually divorce, but was unsure which member of the couple had become bored with that aspect of the marriage. She suspected it was Violet. Grant's wife lived down at Chimneys, but was often with her real in-laws, Hugh Trevelyan's mother and father, in Wales. It seemed a rum sort of set up, but she saw how it could have attracted a young man whose own mother had died when he was at a vulnerable age. Grant felt a duty towards Fabian, and Violet was a splendid housekeeper, and until he met Sophie – he said – he had not wanted to complicate his life with a love that might drag him from his moorings. All this came out bit by bit and she pieced it together as well as she could. Fabian was to follow his stepfather into the firm, as Grant had no children of his own.

'Didn't you want your own children?' she asked once, and a cloud seemed to settle over his forehead.

'Is life such a blessing?' he asked. 'It never happened. Some men don't worry about children, you know.'

'But wouldn't you like *my* children?' she asked.

'I would have liked a daughter like you,' he answered. 'But I'm glad I didn't have her, for then I should not have you, Sophie.'

Sophie could not yet see herself as a mother, either – she was reserving that until she was older. Would she like Grant's children, or anyone's? How could she ever have a child whose father would belong legally to someone else? Was that the objection? She puzzled over it and decided she might one day want a child of her own, but could not imagine who would give her that child.

'I don't feel fatherly to you, you know,' he said.

'And I don't feel motherly towards you,' she answered jokingly, which was not quite true for, in spite of his eighteen years head start, she often felt, in some mysterious way, older than he. She saw clearly that a child would wreck the relationship they had. One day . . . but how could that happen if she were still with him? She pushed the thought away from her as unworthy.

Later that year Grant took her to visit Chimneys when his wife and her household were away. It was the first of several visits.

She found the house overpowering in its size and its evidence of money well spent in the past. It had, as its name suggested, large chimneys at each end of the medieval-looking gables, and in the middle, and was modelled on the last century's idea of a country house which should be up-to-date and yet redolent of an English past.

It was in woodland country with a view to the South Downs and Sussex, and stood in a large, sloping meadow that was full of wild flowers. A copse of beech trees sheltered one side of the meadow. The building itself was unusual with its red-brick floors and great fireplace and inglenook in the entrance hall which opened on to a deep porch leading to the large front garden. There was a minstrel's gallery above the hall, and everywhere there were deep window seats. It also had an extremely modern bathroom and water closets. The rooms above were light and airy, each with a large fireplace and doors of carved oak with shields set in the centre of their panelling. It breathed Rossetti and Morris and aspirations towards both beauty and utility and was certainly handsomer inside than any really ancient house. There were many rooms on the ground floor, opening out of the hall: a morning room, breakfast room, sitting rooms, a study, a large dining room and enormous kitchens at the back. Yet it gave her a feeling neither of the real past nor of the present, but of some attempt, not long ago to combine the two. It was not spurious or 'mock', and was well built, and when the wood fires were all lit, warm, but it was not the sort of house she would wish to live in.

She explored the bedrooms and Grant's dressing room and Fabian's room, where one whole wall was covered in books. Fishing-rods cluttered the 'den' downstairs, a concession to the man of the house, whilst denying him a gun room, for Grant's father's tastes had not lain in slaughtering wild birds and animals. In short, it was a monument to progressive thought and, as a monument, it had grown old-fashioned in nearly thirty years.

Grant did not belong there either, though he must earn part of the money to pay for its upkeep. His father had entailed the rest and Fabian would inherit the lot eventually, by the terms of Grant's will.

'But that won't be for about fifty years!' she cried when she heard this.

They were sitting in the small sitting room that looked out of the side of the house, by a lawn of daffodils.

'You have to make provision for the future, Sophie darling.'

For the first time she felt, rather than knew, that her future and his might not be the same. It was only a fleeting apprehension, and she would not want that great house nor to be its mistress or keeper in any case. But he was committed to it in some strange way to do with his father and marriage and his stepson. She could not help, even so, the moment afterwards, seeing her children and his, darting past the windows and playing on the lawns. She brushed the vision aside as being unworthy. Where would poor Violet fit into that scene?

He had an idea of what she was thinking, for he said, 'Really, it doesn't mean anything to me here.' He put his hand where his heart was. 'It is nothing to do with you and me – we exist in a different dimension, Sophie. Don't look sad; you wouldn't want to be a hausfrau, would you, or a cook or a hostess? The house is taken care of when I'm not there. Sometimes I think my father is watching over it. It will be Fabian's and his children's. By then, who knows? I may be gone away, if not perished.'

She wanted to ask, 'Where will you go and will you take me with you?'

He answered her unspoken question. 'You and I can live anywhere. I don't feel I exist without you – houses have nothing to do with it.'

'Why did you want me to come here?' she asked then in a small voice.

'To see where I am when you are not with me, to show you it is not the true part of me. You have that.'

She knew it was true and yet some awful jealousy, some need to establish, one day, a future for herself, however far away in time, kept poking into her mind and disturbing her.

In bed that night as the spring gales howled down the chimneys of Chimneys and Grant slept, his arm round her neck, she woke, and the thoughts were once more in her head. What was the good of thinking about a future when the present was happy? For it *was* happy. She was loved. She was needed. She loved this unusual man who seemed both to have laid claim to her and placed his own happiness

157

in her lap. She wondered whether she were strong enough to carry him through the years they would spend together. And a little feeling of rebellion, of desire for freedom, for experiment, did insinuate itself into her heart. She had once, in an infantile way, she thought, pretended that Clement, or someone like him, would share her life. Not in a great house built by money, but in a small cottage with a bright, wild garden where she could be mistress and, one day, mother.

But Grant was surely too old to make a start in that kind of existence. He was not, in spite of his air of competence and faint irony, and even at the times when he gave himself up to Sophie, an easy person. He withdrew often into himself – he called it Charging his Batteries – and Sophie knew he wanted to write a history of the ideas which had powered English literature, those concepts which writers only unconsciously expressed as the spirit of the age. He had read widely and, what was more, he had a scholar's mind. In this he was like Edith who having struggled with her Norsemen and produced an article full of questions to be answered by future scholars, was back finishing a book for Garnett Edwards.

Sophie and Edith spent more time together than either spent with a lover or a book. They shared a home, if one could dignify the eyrie with that appellation, and they were constantly seeing each other at work. She was happy with Edith, an easy sort of happiness, though she was aware that Clement was, in some peculiar way, paying court to her friend. She doubted he would have much success. Edith was not the sort of person to burden her friends with her problems and Sophie did not like to ask what might be happening. They acted to each other rather like sisters who knew each other too well to bother going into the kind of detail of their lives that each could guess at, and there was no sense of rivalry which sisters might have had. Now and again they went over to Doughty Street where the usual crowd sat at the feet of Kitty and Frank. Clement's poems had been extremely well received and no one had been more pleased than Frank, whose own new novel came out later that spring. Sophie noticed that if, at one of their gatherings, Edith talked to Seb, Clem would look sulky. Men always saw each other as rivals. Edith, of course, did not notice.

158

Kitty Moray, had noted the expression on Clem's face too, for one evening she said to Sophie, 'Does Edith know what an effect she has on our poet?'

'I don't know. She's so shy, and Clement doesn't know how to talk to women'.

'I think he's crazy about her,' Kitty went on. There was nothing she liked better than a good gossip.

'He's too presumptuous,' said Sophie quickly. Then, 'Of course, Edith is a special sort of person. I don't mean that Clem ought not to appreciate her'.

'She has a good friend in you,' said Kitty, narrowing her eyes, perfectly well aware what Sophie Ridsdale felt for the poet.

It would be easier for Edith if she were not so shy, Sophie thought. She wished, too, that Grant might appreciate Edith better; she was so competent that he took her for granted. Then she thought, 'taken for Granted', and giggled at her own pun. She wished she could be more like Edith. Even Edith's puns were better than hers. Edith might be shy but she had a sense of humour and hardly ever appeared cross. She did not find even the frosty Theo Carmichael annoying.

Should she say something about Clem to Edith? Edith was quite capable of mistaking Clem's interest in her for a desire to discuss literature and would politely discuss his own work with him. Which would please Clem, of course, who, like all young men, Sophie thought, was usually thinking of himself when he was supposed to be in love. At least Grant was not like that.

One day Edith said suddenly, 'Clement seems to want to know me better, but I don't know what to talk to him about.'

'You're very restful to be with, Edith. I'm sure Clem just likes to feel you are there listening to him.'

'He talks about you sometimes,' said Edith.

'Oh, does he then?'

'The trouble is, I like being alone and, yet, I like – would like, to feel part of a family or a place. London is too big. I can manage it but I still don't feel I belong,' said Edith in a rush.

'I like being alone, more than you suspect,' replied Sophie, 'it's just that I hardly ever am.'

'People can be very tiring. I think I could be happy with just one person, but I've no idea whom. I quite enjoy physical work; you know, scrubbing floors and gardening. It's a relief.'

'You don't like people in groups, Edith, and I don't blame you. We live a funny sort of life, don't we?'

'Oh, I'm quite happy, Sophie, but I feel I shouldn't be. My ideas come best when I can be alone.'

'Perhaps it's your remoteness which attracts a man like Clem?' Sophie suggested.

'Would he be surprised if he knew the stuff I write for Garnett?' Edith laughed.

'The trouble with you, Edith,' said Sophie severely, 'is that you don't want power over other people. You're quite in harmony with yourself, so why bother about other people. And anyway, it's just the way you are.' Sophie paused a moment at the door into her inner room and sniffed the late hyacinths which she had bought the week before. She could never assimilate the beauty of flowers. These were heavy and dark blue and their scent, still fresh, promised something she could not imagine, some unearthly beauty far away from these considerations of people and their strange quirks and desires. Yet she had not been moved by Grant's daffodils and wondered why.

The year 1912 changed nothing of importance for Sophie Ridsdale, except that she received another increase in salary and adjusted herself to the absence and presence of Grant in her life. She was still longing to go to Paris, still a little intrigued by Clement and his friends, felt she was seeing life more steadily now and seeing it whole. But just occasionally she would catch sight of herself in a long mirror in the bedroom of the White House Hotel where she met her lover to make love; Grant used to carry her to the bed and the first time she saw herself, dishevelled in his arms, she was startled. That was how people would see her – the young object of middle-aged lust. They were used to each other, of course, but his ardour never abated and she was still proud to receive it, assuage it and return it. She had thought, confusedly, that she was in control of herself, but seeing her own naked body in his arms made her wonder how long she could continue like this. Grant was contented, and she was happy that he was happy and her slave as far as the sensual and emotional side of life was concerned, but she began to wish that she had something in her life that was not work or love. She wished that she could write the sort of nonsense Edith seemed so effortlessly to produce. Of course, it was not effortless. Sophie had tried and had found that her own feelings came in the way of her characters' reactions and actions. She felt herself to be hollow, just a vessel for Grant to pour himself into. People said that this sort of passion did not last.

He said he would release her the moment she asked him to, but he thought she would never ask him. She would not be able to find such a lover easily again. And yet, and yet, he was not her Ideal. She responded to him, but she was not fierce for him.

She was invited to parties where he went and there was always the unspoken knowledge that afterwards, sooner or later, she would be back in his arms. Yet often she wished she could have gone alone to these gatherings to test out her new-found self and see what effect it had on others. Other men did find her attractive, she knew, but she did not want to be unfaithful to the man who loved her, even in small ways. Grant did not enjoy these parties and went out of a sense of duty. They were good for business and he could be safe in the knowledge that usually Sophie was there, brought by him. He longed for the party to be over, for them to be alone together. Sophie was curious to see what other people thought of him. 'A cold fish' was what she surmised and it made her laugh. There were rich women sometimes at these parties, whom she observed with interest, wondering how they spent their lives.

When the lease of his small flat expired, Grant offered to buy another in a district where he was not known, a place where they could both live during the week as though they were married. She felt instinctively that it was not a good idea. How could she work for someone she lived with as a wife, with no one at Miller and Penn's, as far as she knew, any the wiser? And she did not want to leave her work there. It was a dilemma and Grant solved it at first by not buying anything else in London, but going home occasionally in the week and spending more Fridays and Saturdays with Sophie. She had still not met Violet Miller.

'I wish you would tell her, dearest,' she would say.

'But it is none of Violet's business,' he would reply in astonishment.

They began to try other hotels in Bloomsbury, all of which seemed to have been named after the titles of novels by Sir Walter Scott, and riverside hotels in Chelsea, and their love-making became more recherché. Sophie discovered a talent for the acting out of various fantasies and enjoyed amazing him. But he did not really like her efforts, preferred her 'just as she was'.

'I *am* like that,' she would answer.

They never argued or quarrelled except over Sophie's strongly held opinions about Society. Grant professed to scorn it, but earned money from pleasing the consumers of his list and was divided and rather touchy about it.

'If I were a bad girl,' she said once, 'I would demand a share in your business. You could make me a director of the firm.'

He looked at her, slightly puzzled and a little discomfited. But he thought he knew her too well to take her seriously.

'It would be no worse than my living with you,' she said. '*Then* I should have all the disadvantages of marriage with none of its advantages.'

For, by 1913, she was beginning to imagine their child, in some dim featureless future. She never said much about that to her lover, for she knew he would wonder why his love was not enough. She was growing and changing, whereas he, after the first revolution of his feelings when he had found her and made her his, had no more room for change. She knew that a child was a symbol for a different sort of life. She had somehow come to a full-stop in her feelings for him. But when she was with him again and used her uncertainties by converting them into passion, she was, for a moment, satisfied. Perhaps there would come a time when even Grant would realize she was growing away from the something that had been between them. Until then she determined not to think about it.

As nothing can change the past except remembrances of it, nothing can sway the direction of future lives but imagination. Edith Broughton was at heart a fatalist, so did not waste time imagining the next few years of her life. Life was too complex, too *un*imaginable, to be moulded by the will. Chance played too large a part. The inner movements of the psyche did not

162

correspond with the dates in her diary. Night and day were all part of some eternally moving pageant where she appeared to play her part, having had no initial choice in the matter. As she saw her friend appear to grow a little cynical, Edith still envied her plunge into experience.

Edith looked round at her other friends and acquaintances: Cicely Emery, a librarian whom Sophie knew only as a suffragist: Theo Carmichael, who always spoke to her with some reservation in her voice and manner and whom Sophie did not like; Sophie herself, flushed and talkative from a visit to the theatre, or the discovery of a hidden garden square, or sucking a toffee-apple by the fire like a child; Clement Bartholomew, whom everyone thought so handsome and who *was* handsome, she supposed; Cora Benson, a woman given over to an ideal, with her solid frame, gruff tones and cravats; Sebastian Harman, whose paintings opened up the world of his mind to her and who seemed to create from a world she could never ever really enter, in spite of his kind heart; Kitty Moray, whose cough worried her; Frank Laurence, scribbling away and collecting debts by the same post as cheques, and forgetting about them both for months; Garnett Edwards, who had come to rely upon her in a childish way and who had asked her how you washed clothes, since his landlady refused to tell him; Austin Speight, the intellectual whose processes of thought thrilled her, but who had hardly ever said anything to her; Toby Watson, always so cheery and kind and for whom Edith often brewed tea, listening to his comments on the world as he drank it. She looked at them and thought how they were all proceeding on the paths their natures and their contingent circumstances had set out for them, all walking along parallel lines which never met. And she walked behind, watching them, observing them with her writer's eye and wishing she could save them from themselves as they walked through the pages of their lives.

It was November 1913 and Sophie had, unusually, gone home for her birthday. Grant had said she looked peaky and needed some fresh farm air and she had said, 'I'd like to see Father – he hasn't been well. Could I go, do you think?' She had never before asked for any special consideration but Grant was immediately eager to agree she must go home for a few days. Off she had gone, unafraid this time that she would be

163

'reclaimed', and Edith had sent her love to them all in Thirksay. Over two years it was since Sophie had gone home, preferring to spend the time with Grant on the coast, always hoping Paris would be the next holiday.

Edith was sitting sewing and musing. Practical activities like sewing and darning and ironing always set her mind free to roam and she would find hours had passed with sometimes no immediate recollection of what had been the essence of her thinking.

There was the sound of footsteps on the stair and she came slowly out of her dream and stood up. Then a knock. She knew who it would be. Since the summer she had received countless letters from Clement Bartholomew, who had been to stay in Cornwall with Frank and Kitty and then with his mother in Wiltshire. He would not know Sophie was away. His last letter, unanswered by Edith, had been the week before and in it he had spoken of his return. She stood up and went to the door. Mrs Mac must have left the downstairs door open for she had heard no bell ring, but perhaps she had been too wrapped up in her thoughts.

He stood on the threshold, a bottle under his arm and a bunch of roses in the other hand.

'Oh, Clem, you're back.'

For answer he offered her the flowers and put the bottle on the table where lay Edith's work. She wished he had let her know he was coming, for she felt especially distanced from life today. Before she started the sewing, she had been working on the revision of a story for Garnett. She placed her sewing over it. This time she would try to connect with him, to give him a little attention.

'No, don't make tea,' he said and sat down in Sophie's chair. 'I brought us some brandy. I had to see you, Edith. Did you get my letters?'

'Why, yes. Your last one only a few days ago.' She strove to remember what he had been writing to her in that, but could only remember it had been about her.

He caught hold of her hand and she let it lie in his, standing awkwardly in front of him like a penitent. 'Let me,' he said as she fumbled for her glasses which she had not needed for the sewing.

164

'I'll get us two glasses, then,' he offered.

When she brought them from the cupboard under the sink he had already unbottled the brandy. 'Drink, Edith,' he said and handed her a glass. She seemed to be under some sort of spell, for she took it obediently and drank. Perhaps it would make things easier. 'I don't suppose you will listen to me,' he began crossly. 'But I've come to ask you to marry me.'

Edith sat, stunned. This was, indeed, awful. However would she get out of it? She recognized the white-hot willpower under Clement's sardonic exterior and the bitter critical quality which would destroy him rather than let him go. 'I have loved you for two years, Edith, and I want the truth. Do you care for me at all?'

Since he had already asked her to marry him, Edith thought the truth of *her* feelings must be a secondary consideration! Yet he looked so miserable, so pale, that she must take pity on him. He must not make himself a martyr on the altar of herself. It was all wrong and the misunderstanding derived from the person she was, not from any particular disinclination to listen to him or even try to be fond of him.

'I thought about it all summer,' he was continuing and he poured them both another drink.

Edith clutched her glass as though she were drowning. It never occurred to her to tell him to go away. He deserved her time, since he had spent so long in trying to get some response out of her.

'I decided you must marry me – I must marry you – then I can work. Edith, I know you are a flesh and blood woman like your friend Sophie. You are not ordinary, Edith. I adore you, Edith! I've never felt this before – we could live simply – I would work for you – I need you – please answer me.'

Surely this was not happening. Edith felt the wall of glass close in upon her. Why, just a few moments ago she had been sitting calmly and peacefully! If she did not make one final effort to convert herself she might remain behind that wall for ever. But she could not marry him. No. She was sorry for him, almost as sorry as she was for herself, but she was not going to share her life with him. She knew that in her bones. She drank her brandy.

'Don't look so bloody polite,' he shouted.

She gulped again at the drink. What could she give him, or do for herself? It was a dream and the glass walls were pressing against her. She imagined she was putting her hand through the glass and found she had taken his hand. He came and knelt at her feet, his eyes burning.

Weakly, she said, 'I can't marry you, Clem. I don't think I can marry anybody.' But the glass had dissolved a little, like water in her fingers, cold and running fast away. 'I like you,' she whispered. 'Perhaps you just need loving, but I can't do that.' But he had put his head on her lap and she found she was stroking his hair. How odd. A strange recklessness seemed to possess her, for she said, 'You are real, I suppose, Clem, but how can I know whether I am?'

He looked up then, and drew down her head, removed her spectacles and then put her back against her chair and began to kiss her. It still did not seem real and so she made another gigantic effort to emerge from the water she was drowning in and then he released her and asked for another drink. That would help. He poured them both one.

'I know you want me, Edith, I can feel it, but I want you as a wife – you are more real to me than myself. Who do you think those last poems were for?'

Some strange stirring seemed to be taking place in her body, some shifting of perspective. Perhaps if she let herself go along with it everything would become real and the glass and the water would go away for ever?

'Of course I want your body,' he said, 'but because it houses your soul.'

'Clement, how old are you? I am twenty-six and I have never been made love to – '

'I am thirty,' he said. 'And I've never wanted anyone as much as this.'

If she gave in to him perhaps he would let her go, she thought, confused. He came up to her again and pulled her to her feet. She felt giddy with the brandy and wished she had not drunk it, but it made things easier now. But what on earth was she doing? There was some reason for it but she had forgotten. He placed his hand confidently on her breast. She shivered. Then he took her in his arms again and she gave herself up to peculiar swooning feelings. She could feel him hard against her, an alien creature, and she leaned against him. She felt she would either burst into tears or tear her clothes off. Let my mind go, she pleaded with herself. It could all be so easy. She looked up again. 'Clement, I won't marry you,' she whispered. This time he was too far out of his own mind to do anything but groan, and they stood swaying. She heard the gas-fire making little plopping noises and felt it warm against her ankles.

'The bed would be better,' she murmured.

He looked at her for a moment, aghast, and then the other look came into his eyes. 'You are like a gazelle and I shall tame you,' he murmured.

He was certainly very strong, for he carried her to her own bed and joined her on it, tugging at his clothes and hers.

'Is that better? she murmured, as he disposed of various garments, and saw that he was beyond any of her ministrations except the fundamental one of allowing him to possess her.

For a moment everything became clear and she smiled and went on smiling as he plunged into her, even though it was a sensation like nothing she had ever imagined. I am out of myself, was her last thought before he began a rhythmic pushing and pulling. Was he about to murder her? All the time gasping, 'I love you, I love you.' Then he could speak no more and there was only his creaking of the bedsprings and then a cry which seemed to be torn out of him as he came triumphantly inside her. For that moment she saw a whole future, like a long pathway stretching out before her, and heard herself groaning, too. He had been sucking at her breasts, and they felt as though she had suckled a lion cub. Then he collapsed on to her and lay for a moment, still. She covered her breasts again as the room seemed to return and the walls rear up and the familiar furniture swam into her vision. She tried to pull her clothes down over her limbs, but it was impossible. She lay with the whole weight of the world upon her until he lifted his face from hers. He was weeping.

'Forgive me, Edith. Forgive me. You were driving me mad.'

'I'm sorry,' she said. 'Do you think I could have another glass of brandy?'

He got up slowly and brought it to her and when she sat up and pulled herself together she felt a warm trickle where he had been. At least, now, she was a member of the human race. But she would not marry him! She was sorry for him, felt she would like to rock him to sleep, but he was still alien, the rampant male, now cowering and trembling. She stroked his hair.

'I'm glad it was with you,' she said. 'But I can't do that again.'

'You will never forgive me?' he muttered, abashed.

'There's no question of forgiveness. I wanted you to, Clem.'

She wished she had the gestures of a woman who was used to pulling straight a cravat, smoothing down hair, holding a man's hand to the side of her face; but if she had, she would feel he would regard her as showing an affection she did not feel.

'Please, Clement, go now and let me be. Don't come back, please!'

He shook his head in disbelief. But after looking at her with a strange expression of mingled sorrow and bafflement and yet with a sort of adoration, he did go away. She sat in the same chair she had sat in before, doing her sewing, and wondered that the world was back to its usual self. She sat on, looking at the roses he had brought her and thinking that perhaps the glass walls had moved a little further away, only to return. Then she stood up and poured herself another drink and went to bed, where she slept like a child who has endured a temper tantrum.

4

Love and War.

'Arma virumque cano . . .'

Virgil

Sophie had lived for three years in a dilemma. She was now beginning to feel she must assert herself over her nature and what might be her destiny, was formulating questions about her own future. She was impatient for another part of life to begin. She was still proud to be wanted and possessed by a man like Grant Miller, but had begun to acknowledge other feelings, other desires. If *he* could love her, who might also not love her? Clement existed in the shadows, where he had been relegated after her decision to take what was offered her and try to grow up a little. As she did grow up she felt an equivalent uneasiness about whether any woman, the lover of a man, could be really independent. She upbraided herself: she had a job, a room, money for necessities if not luxuries, a man who loved her and a relation with him that could, as far as she could see, go on for ever. Did she truly love him? Now that she had learned the secrets of a man's body and her own responses, what else was there?

She liked to be admired, but the world still made her angry. 'Supreme self-sacrifice' was expected of women, it seemed to her, and she wondered whether she, too, was sacrificing herself for a man. She had not engineered his love for her, but neither was she going to try and keep him for ever. There was no one from whom she could ask advice, and anyway, the heart must be the supreme adviser in these matters. But when she consulted her heart it gave ambiguous answers. Might Grant not, one day, be able to to give her her heart's desire? Because he could not at present, she felt the need for more experience.

169

She was, too, a little horrified to find herself wanting a plausibly conventional marriage in some not-too-far-away future, feeling at the same time a need to round off her life, or at least allow herself, just once, to be the prime mover in the life of passion. Sheer egoism might one day lead her to take risks. She could not remain 'protected' for ever. Her going with Grant had set the seal on her way of life. She had always fallen in love easily as a girl, but now she had come to a full-stop. What if she told Grant that she wanted to be his wife or nothing? He must know that was what she wanted.

It was whilst going through one of these periods of doubt, after her November visit home, that she found herself one evening at a gathering of young poets on Berners Street. Grant had not been able to accompany her and Sophie saw Clement Bartholomew standing at the far end of the room listening to a tall, red-haired girl who seemed to be embarrassing him, for he kept looking away from her rather desperately. Eventually the red-haired girl gave up and went to talk to someone else.

The poetry-reading was over and Sophie went up to Clem before he could escape and said, without much thought, 'Are you looking for Edith? She's not here.'

A moment later she wished she had not said that, for he had gone so pale she thought he was about to faint. 'Is she – is she – busy as usual?' he asked, partially recovering himself, but unable to hide from the experienced Sophie that something was gnawing away at him.

'Of course. Edith is always busy,' she replied. 'But I am not. Why not talk to *me*, Clement?'

Clement rallied a little and Sophie noticed that he had become more socially adept, for he said, 'Can I take you to a pub or something? I'll die if I have to answer any more questions from these harpies.' Sophie was flattered, but his next remark shattered her poise. 'Where is your Keeper?' he asked.

'What do you mean?' She looked fierce, so fierce that he quailed.

'I only meant – people say, that you are always with Mr Miller.'

'Oh, they do, do they? Well, I am free and white and over twenty-one, Clement, and I don't think I have to account for my movements.'

'Forget I asked. You are looking very fashionable,' he said.

'She was wearing her mauve tailor-made suit with its purple velvet collar and cuffs and its long coat reaching almost to her knees. She had owned it for a year now and tried to take good care of it, since she certainly could not afford another for some time and would not allow Grant to pay for her clothes. The jacket sleeves were puffed at the shoulder which gave her rather a military look and set off her face and neck. She was rather pleased with it herself, but said, 'Is that a compliment?'

'I meant it as one,' he replied and they went out together down the stairs into Oxford Street.

It was a cold, foggy evening and Sophie wished momentarily that she was snug at home, or with Grant. They walked up and down side streets looking for a pub where he could take her.

'Nice girls don't go to pubs,' she offered.

'But you are not a nice girl, are you, Sophie?'

She resented that and was silent. If it were to be a battle of wits she would win on points. And she had been crazy about this young man, still could be, she realized, knowing that she had caught his interest. He loved Edith though.

Finally they found a small coffee-house in Soho and Clement sat down and unwrapped the long scarf which he had wound himself into on leaving the poetry reading. He did not help her to a chair nor ask if she wanted to take off her coat. Those were things she noticed now, for Grant was always most solicitous. Well, she could look after herself. If she had come upon Clement like this two years ago, she would have been in seventh heaven. She realized he was a pugnacious man and rather liked the sound of his own voice. The contrast with his written words, now that she had got him to herself for a few moments, startled her. He was a mystery.

'When is the next book?' she began, knowing that writers were always willing to discuss their work once it had arrived at the publishers.

'You ought to know,' he said irritably. 'You work there.'

'I don't know all the details of production. I read most of it, though. As a matter of fact, I asked to see it.'

'So I suppose He gave it to you.'

171

'Grant wasn't in charge of it. Theo was doing all the letters to printers. Surely you've heard from her? She must have asked you about the layout? Not that they take any notice, but they like to tell authors how they feel they should appear, especially Theo. She doesn't like me, so I asked Grant to get it me for an evening. I hadn't much time, but I liked what I read, though some of the poems puzzled me. They're different from your earlier ones, aren't they?'

'Are you really interested?'

'I've always been interested in your work – and in you,' she answered boldly.

He looked a little uncertainly at her, as though this sort of reply was outside the range of his experience and he would not like it even if it were not. She looked down at his thin hands. 'I know you are crazy for Edith, and I thought the poem on the swan was about her – am I right?'

Now he did not grow pale, but blushed. 'It's not your business.'

'No, but I live with Edith and I know her very well.'

He tried to change the subject. He was very handsome and she wished he were in love with her. Greedy Sophie, she thought.

He almost caught her thoughts, for next he said, inconsequently, 'You are a greedy sort of person, like me – ' Then he cleared his throat and, just as she was about to rebut his uncharitable, though true, accusation, he added, 'Has she – has Edith said anything about me recently?'

Oh dear. They were back to Edith again. 'No. I think Edith is a rather discreet sort of person, Clement.'

'She is a strange woman. I think she is frightened of herself,' he said surprisingly.

'She is clever and deep, and she doesn't love anyone as far as I know. I'm sorry,' Sophie said humbly.

'No, she will not want to see me again,' he said. 'Do you want another cup of coffee? I'm thirsty.'

Sophie was intrigued. She was almost sorry for him. 'In my experience,' she said, feeling rather vulgar but sincere, 'people don't love people because they are loved – not always – not Edith, anyway. She has her own work, you know.'

172

'But you,' he said, turning his grey eyes upon her. '*You* accept love, don't you? Yet you are a free woman, not like Edith.'

'That's not true. Edith is a free *spirit*. There's a difference. You forget *I* love Edith too!'

'Oh, women; always loving and giving. What do you know?'

'Edith is concerned with literary creation,' replied Sophie grandly.

'And you?' he pursued.

'You don't want to know about me, only because I live with Edith. But I, well, I liked you the moment I saw you, ages ago, and what good did that do me? You never knew, and now it doesn't matter.'

He looked genuinely surprised.

'Don't mind, I'm not going to pursue you,' she added.

'Tell Edith the question is the same,' he said after a silence.

Sophie stared at him. He really was very attractive. Why did the gods arrange things all the wrong way round?

'So I suppose if Edith won't have me, you would?' he said facetiously.

It was her turn to blush and she felt her eyes filling with tears and turned away to hide them. It was only for a second and then she regained control.

'You know I am not "free",' she said. It was somehow a betrayal of Grant even to mention his name again. And what was she doing here with Clem, who had never wanted and never would want her? She would have wished, except for the fact of his loving her friend, that she were free to be herself with him.

'Theo Carmichael told me you believed in the doctrines of Free Love,' he said.

So there *had* been gossip about Grant and her, Sophie thought. And since when had Clement taken to discussing things with Theo? But she determined not to sound personally acrimonious and replied, 'Perhaps the doctrines of "free love" don't apply very well to women.'

He searched her face. Edith might have said something to her, but he decided to brave it out and said dismissively, 'Oh, "love"! Isn't what you mean, "passion", not love? The urges of Mother Nature and all that?'

173

'Surely, that is something different?' As soon as she said it, she knew it was not; that romantic feelings certainly led to desire in her case. On the other hand, how could you feel 'romantic' about someone who desired you first? She was thinking of Grant, of course.

'I believe in marriage,' he replied, looking steadily at her. He meant with Edith, she knew.

After that there was not much she could say,; and it was a pity. But he was saying, 'At least you don't tell me to cheer up.'

'Artists are not meant to be happy, are they?' she asked, with only apparent guilelessness. Just for a moment she had felt there was a rapport between them, but now it was gone. He only echoed back her own words. How different from Grant, who thought of her all the time.

'You should marry your man, then,' he added, drawing patterns in the salt on the table.

'I can't.'

'At least he "loves" you.'

'Yes,' she said sorrowfully.

There was no more to say then and Clem did not offer to see her home but set off, his muffler bunched around his neck, for Chelsea. She boarded a late omnibus and when she arrived home, found Edith asleep.

Edith looked rather anxiously at Sophie when the latter finally reported her conversation with Clement, but said nothing. It was a dark December evening and Sophie sat deep in her borrowed copy of the *Cornhill* magazine, wishing she, too, could write. Conversations, partly imaginary but based on those she had had with Clement, were continually going through her head, as though she were the privileged spectator and audience at a play. She wished she could write it down, dramatize it. The trouble was, she needed a theme – something to tack all her random observations to, and the only theme that obsessed her at present was the age-old one of the wrongs committed in the name of love. She glanced through the door at Edith, sitting in the other room. It was all right for her, for she had original ideas and seemed to exist in a world of her own. She sometimes thought Edith was more like a man, but that was absurd, for Edith was perfectly womanly. Yet she did not seem to have any problems over love, or anything else. Edith would have been just as at home in one of those fine houses in Hampstead or Kensington with their marble chimney-pieces and bright fires and white curtains and vases of bronze chrysanthemums, or in houses in the country like Chimneys, places which made Sophie feel rather uneasy.

Perhaps Beatrice her new friend was right and it was all to do with class. If that were so, she could not see the rich relinquishing their wealth so easily. Not unless they were forced to, and revolutions always hurt everyone in the end. She had once said something of the sort to Grant, whom she thought would agree with her (since he was rich), but he had frowned and said, 'You are a little Tory, Sophie.' Yet he seemed to like her so, did not take that part of her seriously. And who was *he* to call her that!

She turned up the gas bracket in her room and looked dreamily into her mirror, a dim, brown, tarnished silver one that she had rescued from a junk shop. Downstairs, outside, she could hear the strains of the piano organ; she left the mirror and sat down in the old carpet chair which Mrs M had finally provided and took up her *Cornhill* once more. But she was still restless – 'blue', they called it, down in the dumps, with nothing to account for it, torn between her feelings of injustice and shame that she had not yet made more of her life. It was all very well, indulging in long talks with the likes of Clement but she wanted to count for more in the world. Her own children must, one day, do more than she could, yet she had, as yet, no children and it did not seem likely she would ever have any.

She decided she really needed a religion or something more 'spiritual' in which to believe, but what? Women filled the churches, but they were run by men. The only thing she could think of was to write her own conflicts down privately in an attempt to understand them, but now she was too sleepy and must go to bed if she were to be up in time for work tomorrow.

'Good night,' she called to Edith, who was sitting, writing still, and who replied softly, 'Night, Sophie. I just have to finish this for Garnett.'

Sophie's last thought as she fell asleep was that she could be practically anybody or anything – it depended on whom she was with. And as she was with Edith, she would try to take a leaf out of her book and work harder, think harder . . . And then she was asleep and dreaming of a large house in a forest, filled with the portraits of children whose faces seemed vaguely familiar.

The day after Sophie's reading of the *Cornhill*, she and Edith sat together in Edith's room toasting bread at the gas-fire and having one of their conversations which usually ranged from God to politics in a few seconds and returned, via discussion of happiness, to love.

'Sometimes I feel that I can't act any differently, I mean with Grant,' Sophie said. 'He chose me. Was it fate, do you think? Why did I accept him?'

'Because you wanted Something to Happen,' said Edith. 'And anyway,' she went on, nibbling at her own toast and leaning back in her chair, 'if you believe in equality, you can't be a romantic – and you *are* a romantic, Sophie; romantics believe in power and mystery, they don't want equality and justice and new laws.'

'But that's romantic *men*,' cried Sophie. 'What about romantic women? None of this has ever applied to them, has it? Men don't have to choose.'

'No, I suppose not.'

'But, Edith, you're not romantic, I don't think. So perhaps you don't feel there is any difficulty?'

'I am not in love with anyone, Sophie.'

'I wish I were not. I wish I could be like a man and just enjoy myself, some men anyway, and not get involved; enjoy pleasure and being alive and perhaps one day be a father, without all the messy business of bearing children.'

'"Things are in the saddle, and ride mankind",' Edith quoted and then added, '*I* should like to love someone and feel I really existed as a person and a body, not just a mind.'

'Oh, Edith – of course you exist! And Clem loves you.'

'Yes, he wants to marry me.'

So that was, in fact, the question he said he still wanted an answer to. Sophie put down her plate and cup. 'You're not going to, are you? He's not strong enough for you – he's just not good enough!'

'I thought you loved him once?'

'Oh, love – that's nothing to do with it, is it? You must stay independent, Edith, not like me.'

'He ought to marry *you*,' said Edith. 'I don't think *I* shall ever marry – like your old aunt said, didn't she? Yet, Sophie – ' she hesitated and then looked up, slowly brushing her hand across her forehead, 'I let him seduce me, Sophie, and now I think I'm going to have a baby.'

Sophie was thunderstruck and stood up in shock, 'Edith – what do you mean? Have you gone mad?'

'No, sit down. I'm not mad. I couldn't seem to be able to tell you. It was in November when you were away. He came here and I felt – I don't know – he loves me, or thinks he does, and I was so tired of never seeming to be able to connect with other people. And he brought some brandy; I'm sure he intended nothing but a solemn declaration, a little scene. But I knew what would happen, I just knew, and I let it happen, and it did, and, well, it's clear to me; I'm pregnant. Don't be horrified. I shall manage. I shall go home at Christmas and give my notice. Father will help me.'

'Edith, you don't *have* to have a baby. There are ways. And anyway, you could marry him . . .'

'Now *you're* being conventional. What good would I be to him, once he's fallen out of love with me? He was hungry and now he's fed, and I must take the consequences.'

All Sophie's rebellious instincts rose to the surface. 'But, Edith, you don't have to "pay" for it. It's madness! It was an accident. He was wrong and wicked to lead you on.'

'No, he still wants to marry me.'

'Does he know, then?'

'Oh, no. I shall tell him sometime soon, I suppose. I'll write to him. But I shan't marry him, Sophie. It would only make a wrong act worse.'

Sophie sat down again, marvelling at Edith's stance, but tried again. 'It will ruin your life, Edith. If you have enough money, doctors can safely get rid of babies I know – Grant told me.' And as she said that she thought, I wish it were me and yet, I don't want Grant's child unless he marries me.' Indeed, she was more conventional than she had supposed. 'I'll do anything I can to help you,' she said. 'Oh, Edith!' Tears pricked her eyes and she contemplated her friend who was just sitting there as though she had said nothing remarkable.

'You see, it's as you said. This was meant to happen to me – I can't go against it. I suppose I was foolish, but it was as though I were in the grip of something strange, some mystery. I don't mean passion, Sophie, or pleasure. But I know I must have this child and I shall be selfish and not marry and bring it up myself. I don't like London the way you do, and I shan't live at home and shame mother, but I'm sure my father will help me.'

'They'll want you to marry,' whispered Sophie.

'Mother will, but I don't want to and no one can make me, unless I choose.'

'When will it be?'

'I believe in July. Gestation is apparently forty weeks,' said Edith, with a curious mingling of dryness and amusement.

'You're not even afraid – or sorry – or worried?' Sophie marvelled.

'Oh, yes; I'm afraid of pain and of hurting my parents and of something going wrong, but I do want the baby, Sophie. I've thought about it for a long time. I can't pretend I'm surprised, or even angry, or sorry.'

'But, Edith, dear, babies should come when people are ready, when they want a child with a man they love, surely? You are only twenty-six, all your life before you . . .'

'Twenty-six is quite old and I don't think I shall ever love anyone in a married way. And, Sophie, babies don't come when people are ready, but when *they* are ready to be born!'

'Yes, I know, and in a way it thrills me. But what will Clem say? He will try again and again to marry you, Edith. And, anyway, it's his fault.'

'No, it's my fault, too. He can see his son or daughter and the child will know who his father is. It's just – I want to do this alone. I know I'm right. Don't say any more! I shall go away and write to him later.'

Nothing Sophie could say would alter Edith's firm decision and Sophie was more upset about it all than her friend. She insisted that Edith see a doctor, for she still only half believed the facts and thought Edith, in her unworldly way, might have mistaken what she had done. She did not like to ask for more details and it was true Edith was not a fool, but somehow she could not imagine her friend engaging in such physical things.

178

It made her, for a time, cold towards Grant. Edith was never sick in the mornings and her physical appearance had not yet changed, although her skin and hair looked glossier and more golden. Sophie cried into her pillow more than once and realized that one of her emotions was envy. And she did not want Edith to change.

The doctor, whose name Sophie had had from Grant and who had a practice on Wimpole Street, confirmed that Edith was, indeed about two months pregnant. Sophie went with her and waited in the ante room, and was sure he thought Grant was the baby's father. Edith had refused to wear a wedding ring. Sophie never mentioned the idea of abortion after that, for Edith was implacable.

Edith went on working, just as usual. In the evenings Sophie hovered around telling her to lie down and rest, but Edith just smiled.

'When are you going to tell Clem?' she asked one evening. He had, not surprisingly, not come to see either of them, nor had he written again to Edith. Sophie gathered from Kitty, to whom she had said nothing of Edith's plight, that he was away again.

'I shall write to father soon and go home soon, and not come back,' said Edith firmly, but not answering the question. 'I shall write a letter to Mr Miller saying I relinquish my post; I know he knows, but I must make everything plain.'

Indeed, Grant had received the news of Edith's pregnancy with amazement. Sophie had not told him who the father was. No one else at Miller and Penn's seemed to have guessed anything and Edith appeared so much more 'in touch' with life now that even Theo had said how well she looked.

'What on earth will your father say?' enquired Sophie.

'I expect he'll be upset, but I know he'll help me.' Edith repeated. 'I'm going on with "Bevis Constantine", you know. Mr Edwards asked me if I would, and I can write that rubbish anywhere.'

'But you must get better terms from him!' exclaimed Sophie. 'Babies cost money, Edith.'

'I know. I've asked for a proper contract, a ghost writer's reward, and he says he'll think it over. Then I shall go home with all my things. You can keep my little table and the bookcase.'

'But, Edith, I shall have to find someone to share the eyrie with me: I can't afford it by myself.'

'Wouldn't Grant help?' asked Edith.

'No, No! I might ask Beatrice. She's working for the *Dreadnought*, but I believe she has some money from her grandmother.'

'I'm sorry, Sophie, I hadn't thought of you. It was very selfish of me. Of course you must go on living here.'

'I want to have my own little place,' said Sophie, turning her head and looking at Edith in the mirror. 'I don't want to be a kept woman any more than you do.'

If no one at Miller's had noticed anything untoward about Edith, it was a different matter as far as Sophie and her lover were concerned. After so long an intimacy with Grant it seemed to have been accepted that she knew him rather better than most young women knew their employers. Nothing was actually said, but Sophie imagined a slight coldness between herself and Mrs Smeaton and, of course, with Theo, who had never liked her. There would not have been much mercy for her if *she* had found herself expecting a baby. Not for the first time she marvelled at Edith, who seemed to find it easier to depart, pregnant by a man she had only slept with once, than Sophie would have done with her long love affair. Edith was, she supposed, a 'victim', but she herself was not. She had freely chosen her life, whereas Edith seemed to have had hers thrust upon her. But which of the two was the more free? Edith. Sophie shuddered to think what would have been her own parents' reaction if she had gone home, jobless and expecting.

'Mother would never get over it,' she said to Edith. 'I couldn't do it – I'm too much of a coward.'

'But if you feel like that, you should break it off with him. One day you'll want a baby, Sophie. I'm sure you will.'

'I don't know what I'd do, but I shouldn't be as brave as you. I suppose if my parents had more money – but that's not it, really. It would hurt them more than you think it will hurt your father and mother.'

'I shan't stay at home, I shall ask father to help me find a place on the coast. I told you he has some old female relatives in Bridlington. I've been thinking about it: I could go away before anything shows, and the neighbours and acquaintances of my mother will just think I've gone back to London. Then, when the baby's born, I intend to find somewhere cheap to live. I could use father's money for that to begin with, and pay him back with the money I can earn from Bevis.'

'You've thought it all out, Edith!'

'No, not really. It just seems obvious. I told you I had a few savings of my own, too; not much.'

'Money makes all the difference,' said Sophie sadly. 'But I still don't see why you can't marry Clem.' She had changed her mind about that!

'He can come and see me once I'm settled. I don't really want him meeting mother.'

'Edith, you are extraordinary! Most women would just collapse in panic or anger.'

'Well, I'm not proposing to tell anyone. I'm not exactly proud of it, Sophie. It was my own fault. Clem hasn't enough money to support a wife and *I* don't want to support *him* – he'd hate that.'

'Yes, you're right. But the baby, he'll love the baby.'

'Father will believe I was raped,' said Edith. 'I wasn't, though.'

'Have you already written to him, then?'

'Yes, I wrote yesterday.'

If it had been Sophie awaiting the arrival of a reply from an enraged parent she would have felt sick every morning awaiting the postman, but Edith did not appear to worry. She went about packing her things and finishing off her work and when the answer did come, she read it calmly.

He's not told Mother yet – no mention of horsewhipping,' she said drily.

'Doesn't he want to take you home? I thought he might come for you.'

'No. I said I was perfectly all right and he's to meet me in Leeds and we'll have a family reunion before I do any explaining. I've asked him to write to his old Aunt Saranna in Bridlington. There are three old ladies there, actually, and I could board with them. One of them was a midwife. He says he will.'

Edith made it known at work that she was leaving.

'Have you got anything out of Garnett Edwards yet?' asked Sophie.

'He's promised me fifty pounds a year! I can live on that, if he keeps his word.'

'I shall try to see that he does,' said Sophie. 'Isn't there anything Grant could do?'

'No. He doesn't know all I've done for Garnett; not in the firm's time, mind you, but it's better he doesn't.'

'It all seems like a dream,' said Sophie. 'I still can't believe it. What shall I say to Clem if he turns up after you've gone?'

'I've written him a letter,' said Edith, nodding towards her mother-of-pearl writing case. 'I didn't know where to send it. If he comes here you can give it to him, if you will, Sophie. That's the only part I'm dreading. Try to stop him coming after me till I'm settled in Bridlington.'

'Why don't you write to his mother's address? I can find it in the files – he first wrote to the firm from there.'

'I don't want his poor mother worried. Don't, Sophie.'

'She might welcome a grandchild,' said Sophie thoughtfully. 'I think women usually come round to babies. But she might think you wanted money, I suppose.'

'It's between Clem and me. If Clem had written or come round, I'd say all this to him.' Edith sat down.

'I expect he's too ashamed,' said Sophie. 'But he said the question was the same – I'm sure he will ask you again.'

'He needn't feel ashamed,' said Edith, pursuing that line of thought. 'I'm not a child – it is both our "faults".'

'I wish it were me,' cried Sophie, unable to restrain herself any longer. 'Before I met Grant *I* would have had Clem's baby, if he loved me, even if it meant never seeing my parents again. I wish you loved him, Edith!'

Edith found herself in the position of comforting Sophie. 'Hush, Sophie, you have someone who loves you, too.'

'Clem loves *you*,' repeated Sophie. 'He will insist on marrying you, Edith, I know he will.'

Edith was silent.

Garnett Edwards could not do without Edith and had reluctantly agreed to pay a retrospective sum to her yearly, when he had sold her stuff under his own pseudonym. At least she did not ask for her own name to be recognized, and that would have to do. His accounting was chaotic, but the Moon series and the Monsters were still selling well and the *Mysteries of the Moor and Fen* bode well to outdo them. He knew that Sophie's sharp eyes were often upon him and so he realized he would have to fulfil his part of the unofficial contract.

Sophie went alone one day to an exhibition of post-impressionist painting, in order to contemplate someone else's imagination. She was tired of her own. She stood before pictures of apples and flowers, of ballet dancers and clowns, looked at landscapes and music hall scenes, and she wondered where she fitted in all this. She tried to empty her mind of anything but the objects before her, looked at the streaks of paint or the lines of charcoal and thought what a strange world it was. But there would be no paintings without people to paint them. And Edith was to add to the people, so that, one day, another person would stand before a picture or read a book or drink a cup of tea, and so life would go on.

Edith left London calmly on Christmas Eve, with her boxes sent on ahead of her. She did not seem to regret anything and promised to write to Sophie with all details of her future and her probable address for the late spring and summer.

At the last minute Sophie embraced her and they kissed goodbye, with Edith murmuring, 'Don't worry,' and Sophie trying not to show she was worried to death.

Christmas Day found Sophie just as desolate ... If only she could use the telephone in the office to ring Edith, for she knew they had one of those newfangled instruments in Roundhay. But what could she say? Edith would want to be left alone to tackle her maternal parent after Christmas and needed peace and quiet, not Sophie's agitated questions. The letter for Clement was on the table in case he returned to London. She glanced again at its envelope – 'Clem Bartholomew' in Edie's small writing; so innocuous. Perhaps Clem would see it as a death sentence.

She went out and down the stairs rapidly and walked in the almost-empty streets, seeing families behind the long windows of the houses in the squares and little Christmas trees on balconies. She would like to walk alone in the country; she thought of arriving, unannounced, at Chimneys. She went into a church but the service was over and evensong would not be for another hour or two. Then she could not resist walking by Miller and Penn's. A dark clean-shaven young man was coming out of the big door, which he closed carefully behind him, and for a moment she thought it was Clem. Who could it be? A relative of the deceased Mr Penn perhaps? He looked at her as he passed, but then turned away. She walked round the square in the opposite direction and then slowly back to the eyrie. She had eaten some cold chicken in the morning without much appetite and had opened her presents: a muff from Grant and cards from the family in Thirksay. She should have gone home. Her new friend, Beatrice, had, however, invited her to Hampstead on Boxing Day and that would be pleasant, for Beatrice came from a lively family of lawyers and doctors.

When she returned to the flat it was to find Mrs Mac looking unusually flushed as she peeped round the door of her own dining room on the ground floor of the tall house. 'A gentleman came,' she said, 'for Miss Broughton, but I told him she'd gone home. Said he'd try again. I told him you'd be back, miss – as it's Christmas. No harm, I don't suppose?'

She withdrew once more and Sophie heard loud Scots voices behind the plush handing curtain on its brass rail.

She went slowly upstairs. Clement. It must be. And what had she to do but hand him Edith's letter? Only a day late he was, but too late. At least, though, it was a visitor, and she did her hair and pinched her cheeks to make them pink and poured herself a glass of the bottle of wine Edith had given her to enjoy Christmas with. Better not brandy, she thought confusedly; that was what he and Edith had drunk.

She sat there with her glass, taking small sips and looking across at the letter lying on Edith's table, feeling both a little frightened and a little excited. Should she just give him the letter and close the door or would he want more from her?

About half-an-hour passed before she heard his step on the stair and then a knock, hesitating but then rapid. 'Come in.' She stood up.

He was there before her, the seducer, the about-to-be-father, in all his ignorance.

'Edith is away,' she began. 'But come in. Mrs Mac said you'd been.'

'I got back only yesterday – a visit home and to Frank Laurence's home up north. Why haven't you gone home, then?'

'Didn't you expect to see me?'

'I thought you'd both go away or both stay, I suppose.' He seemed perkier and his manner was pleasant for once. Oh dear, she would have to deflate it. A great weariness came over her.

'You'd better know,' she said. 'There – it's a letter for you from Edith.'

'From Edith! Oh?'

He took it up and she said, 'I think you'd better open it, Clem. She thought you might come sometime and didn't know your address. She's not coming back to London.'

He looked up enquiringly. All in a rush, Sophie went on. 'Read it, read it.' She poured a glass of wine for him, her hand shaking. After all, what was this to do with her? She motioned him to sit and handed him the glass.

He took a drink and put the glass down and then opened the envelope carefully. Sophie was not exactly sure what Edith had written and she waited, turning her head aside, not daring to look at him. Then she lit the gas, all the time avoiding his face. When she finally looked up he was sitting there staring at her.

'Is this true – that Edith is expecting a child? My child?' His voice was hoarse, excited.

'Oh yes.'

'I must go to her straight away. My God, why didn't she let me know before?' His voice thickened and he cleared his throat.

'Drink your wine,' she said, and then, 'Edith doesn't want to see anyone.'

'I shall make her marry me,' he said, ignoring her remark.

'Clem, she won't marry you – or anyone. It's your baby, but she won't. I've tried to get her to accept when you asked her before, but she won't.'

'Edith is going to have my child?' he repeated slowly.

'In late July,' Sophie added.

'Then I must marry her first. What is she thinking of?'

'What were either of you thinking of?' said Sophie. Then added hurriedly, 'Not that it's anything to do with me – '

'You knew, that time we met at the poetry reading, when you talked with me afterwards?'

'No, I didn't, not then. But it is true, and Edith has gone back to Yorkshire for good.'

185

'Why won't she marry me? What did she say to you?'
He read the letter again, slowly.

'She doesn't want to marry, but she does want the baby.'

'Then any man would do to marry, I suppose, so why not me? I was crazy, Sophie. I did wrong, it wasn't her fault. I've been so upset. I couldn't see her. I wrote to her – thought she knew what I felt . . .'

'She does know, Clem. But she doesn't love you.'

Like I could have loved you, she thought. He sat there, so young and so mysterious, with his dark grey eyes and his wavy hair and his thin hands and she was almost faint with desire for him; a sudden airy feeling that swept right through her and made her want to gaze at him for ever. But none of that could be said. 'She thinks it is best to do what she is doing. Her father will help her,' she said, more softly.

'*My* child,' he cried out, and Sophie said, 'Hush, Mrs Mac will hear. I'm sorry, Clement.'

'I thought Edith was different from the rest,' he muttered.

Sophie did not understand what he meant, but replied, 'Edith *is* different, but she is a woman, and you took advantage I expect.'

'I swear,' he replied, staring at her, 'she wanted me to . . . I know she did. But afterwards I felt angry with her, frightened of her . . . Can't you persuade her, Sophie?' His voice sounded a little more normal.

'She doesn't want money or marriage – or anything else. She knows she wants the child.'

'My mother would bring it up for her,' he said.

'You don't understand. She wants a child to bring up herself, however hard it will be – '

'But you know our society. An unmarried mother . . . And Edith is a lady. I loved her the moment I set eyes on her. I didn't want this. But she wouldn't let me talk to her, tell her. She wouldn't let me get near her, not in spirit.'

'She was shy, and she liked you, I'm sure. But not enough to spend her life with you, Clem.'

'Enough to get a child and then deny me fatherhood!' he exclaimed angrily. Then, 'Tell me, do *you* understand her? You'd marry me, wouldn't you, Sophie, if you were in that position?'

'That's absurd, Clem. You'd never love *me* – '

'And what about your man? Are you gong to be like Edith and ride roughshod over men to get your own way? That's what she's doing! Getting her own way! Women!' He looked absurd, and his anger was absurd.

'Edith didn't want to get pregnant, Clem, but now she is, she's doing what she thinks is right. I don't pretend to understand her. Edith isn't a Feminist . . .'

'No, she's a female,' he answered and strode to the window where he looked out unseeingly.

'Clem, you write to her and try once more. Wait a little before seeing her, let her settle into this place she's going to – somewhere on the coast. I'm sure she'll see you then, and you can try again . . .'

'Thank you, Sophie,' he said, turning towards her. 'My child! What a mess, what an unholy mess. And what if her people won't let me see her?'

'Oh, I'm sure her father will want to see you. But Edith is very stubborn, you know. She should know what she wants.'

'And it isn't me she wants. Then who?'

'No one, I don't believe anyone. She's working something out, Clem. I'm sure it will be all right in the end.'

'And in the meantime, my child is to be a bastard.'

'You should have thought of that before,' she said boldly.

'I know, I know. Perhaps it was the only way to get near her . . .'

She was sorry for him then, and her desire had evaporated. 'Clem, I'll talk to her, write to her for you,' she offered. 'But you must see; you don't really want to marry, do you?'

'It's wicked,' was all the answer she got. Then after a silence, 'Do you know what she says here? Did you see her letter?'

'No, Clem, I didn't.'

He read from the letter. 'I can't belong to anyone, please forgive me. You should marry someone who loves you. Please believe it is for the best.'

'You can't make people love you,' said Sophie in a small voice.

'Oh, women usually return love,' he said carelessly.

'Because we can't get to know men properly,' she said, 'in this ridiculous society. Clem, if you could have known Edith

187

for a little while, you might not have gone on loving her. It might all have been in your mind.' Was she being disloyal? She hardly knew.

'So that is your experience, is it?' he countered, and she was silent. 'She keeps saying it's her fault,' he said, looking up again from the letter.

'Fault is nothing to do with it; women always pay,' said Sophie sententiously.

'Don't say that. *I'm* paying, am I not? In anguish, Sophie Ridsdale. You say you can't make people return love, but neither can you marry them against their will.'

'Perhaps if you ask her again, but not just yet. Does she give you her address?'

'Yes. She says letters will be forwarded later, when she goes away.'

'She didn't know where you were, or even that you would come back.'

He looked mortified; angry and yet helpless.

'Edith is a strong sort of person, she doesn't pretend,' Sophie said at last. 'I think it would suit her, living alone with a child, and you can see the child. It's just that she doesn't want to be with you always, you see. She doesn't want to hurt you, Clem, I'm sure. She thinks you will be a great writer,' she improvised, 'but she, too, wants to write. She doesn't have men friends the way I do, or Kitty.'

'I know,' he said at last.

'Promise you won't try to see her until you've heard from her? I said I'd do my best to explain,' she said. 'She need not have told you, you know.'

'I should have minded that. But to know that a piece of my flesh will – ach!' He gave a gesture of disgust. 'I think I shall go out and get drunk,' he said.

'What good will that do? But have another glass of wine – this is *my* Christmas.' She poured him a glass and offered him a Bath Oliver, which he ate absentmindedly.

'This is what happens when women get ideas of freedom,' he said finally, after a pause. Sophie said nothing, but sipped her drink, feeling light-headed. 'I must go, Sophie.' He stuffed the letter in his overcoat pocket.

'I'll see you at Kitty's, then, on Saturday?' she said.

188

'God knows. I must go and think about all this. You must think I'm a cad, Sophie.'

'No, of course not. It could happen, even to a good man, with a good woman like Edie.' Rapidly he took up her hand for a moment and then let it drop, and the door closed behind him.

She tried to read a book, but fell asleep, and woke cold and miserable.

Grant had meanwhile decided that Sophie needed a 'second honeymoon'. Their attachment was subtly changing its nature, but he was still just as much in love with her, if not more. Yet he assumed a pulling away from him, a dissatisfaction whose nature he could not pinpoint. To counteract the 'epiphany feeling', he came over to Bloomsbury on Boxing Day evening, a Friday. The firm was due to re-open on the Monday, but he had tickets for them both to cross to Paris instead, for a long weekend.

'I give you leave,' he stated, smiling.

'But what shall I do if there's a letter from Edith? I'm waiting to hear what happened in Leeds. How can I go away? I keep thinking about her.'

'It's only for two or three days, my dear. Send her a note. There'll be a letter waiting for you on your return. And there's nothing you can do for her now.'

'But I shall miss Kitty's party,' grumbled Sophie.

She was in a bad mood and it would do Grant good to know that she would not just drop everything to be with him. She wanted to be alone for a little longer, and there was Beatrice to settle into the eyrie, and Clem to see. But Grant's pleading prevailed, as it always did. She found herself, next morning, on the boat-train with him and a little later on the Dover crossing. At any other time Sophie would have been entranced to stay in Paris at last, even if only for two days, but she was, at first, still with Edith in spirit.

Grant had business on the Boulevard St Germain and Sophie was, therefore, to amuse herself during the day. She soon found everything delightful, from the croissants and coffee brought up to their room, on the first floor of an old hotel near St Sulpice, to the pungent smell of Caporal tobacco and garlic and the strong scent the women used; from the ring of iron-shod wheels on the cobbles and the sight of the long, white-aproned waiters, the sound of French itself, the chestnut sellers outside the Luxembourg Gardens with their charcoal fires, and the book stalls under the Colonnades at the Odéon. Men looked at her with approbation and even ventured remarks whose meaning was unambiguous. And she was not even annoyed. She sat in a large café, whose tables spread out in summer under chestnut and plane trees, but which was now comfortably sealed off indoors, with its zinc counter and round tables and wrought-iron chairs. This was the life! She was glad she had agreed to come. Never mind Clem and Kitty and Beatrice – they could wait for two days.

She wrote a card to Edith with a picture of Notre Dame on the back, sending only her love from her unexpected holiday and hoping there would be a letter on her return to London. England, and especially London, seemed a childish, overgrown place when compared with Paris, and she sustained her initial mood of pleasure all through the day.

Grant was even more ardent at night, but when he had made love to her, he said, 'We must really talk about "us", Sophie,' and her heart sank.

A meal was to come first, however, in a small restaurant on the Place de l'Odéon and, as the wines were delicious and the service attentive, she was light-hearted again. One man had even come up to their table and bowed to Grant and said, '*Félicitations, monsieur*,' and bowed then in the direction of Sophie. She could not imagine this happening in London. Grant was amused and tender and cast many melting looks at her. She told him, eventually, under the influence of the wine, whose child Edith was expecting and he looked grave. On the way back, taking her arm, he said awkwardly, 'I sometimes have the feeling, darling, that you won't want to be with me for ever. Am I right?'

She was astonished, for she believed such thoughts had been hidden from him. Before she could think, she said, 'I want a baby, too, one day. I want to feel that it's for ever – and how else do people stay together?'

'Then I am not enough for you?'

'It isn't that. But can we never marry, never? Only so you will know I am "for ever".'

He said nothing, so she went on, 'If I were to have a child now, what would you do? What could you do? I'm not like Edith. I don't want to bear a child alone. It's not that I have strong feelings about marriage, but how else can I have security when one day you no longer love me? I haven't any money, either, unless I work for it – and children need fathers.'

'But you know I shall always love you, Sophie. Isn't that enough?'

'So much happened to you, years ago, when you never knew me. How can I catch up with you? And then there's the office, and my parents, and the future: it all seems so uncertain. I don't mean I want a child *now*; but someday, before I am too old.'

They were walking along now on the grey pavement near their hotel, with the night air frostier and drier than the London air, sharpening their senses.

'You mean you cannot leave me and yet you cannot see yourself being with me for ever?' he asked sadly.

'I don't know whether I want to be free, but I think sometimes I must be free for a little time before I "settle down". You caught me so young.' she said.

'You're not in love with anyone else, are you?' he asked, turning to look at her.

'Of course not,' she replied, thinking of Clem.'Perhaps Grant was a little jealous of young men, not just regretful at growing older himself. For her own part she did not like the idea of most young men as lovers. She liked Toby and Frank as people, but felt they would not treat her as well as Grant undoubtedly did. They would be more violent in their love-making perhaps, and that might be exciting, but did it mean it would be eventually satisfying? She saw, looking at him, that he did not quite believe her, that she had a certain power over him that she did not wish to use, because she did not love him enough.

She tried again. 'If we could marry and have a child one day and please my parents and society by doing so and grow old together and be happy then I wouldn't want anything else, but I hate the idea people may have of me – that I am the mistress of an older man, a sort of object to them, in a category. I don't belong to that category. I feel I'm under false pretences.'

'Sophie, you are very silly, my little love. Who thinks such things of you? No one can touch us. You earn your living, you are often alone, you are an independent girl. Why should you care for the opinions of others? Why not be more like Edith in that?'

'But what would you do,' she replied, 'if I were going to have your baby? Is there no way of persuading Violet to give you a divorce?'

'I suppose it could be arranged. But surely, darling, that is not what is the essential thing about us? Do we need to have the imprimatur of society, and my family, and yours?'

'But you are not a "Bohemian",' she cried. 'You are less so than I am. It's true, I feel safe with you in one way – I know you will never do anything to hurt me – but . . .'

By now they were back in their room and he drew her towards him. 'That's what I mean,' she cried. 'I can never deny you and so I can never have one thing or the other.' And she had thought she was strong-minded!

'We must start again and think it out,' he said to her, after he had made love to her more fiercely than usual. 'I'm sure we could arrange things better. For one thing we might live abroad – America or here. I'm thinking of establishing an office in New York and extending our contacts in Paris. I *love* you, Sophie – is not that enough?' He even had tears in his eyes.

She could not, then, be completely honest with him, for she knew that he did love her; and also understood the depth of his need for her. But she did, one day, want to seal his love with a child. Was it a substitute for something else?

'It is the eternal feminine trap,' he said, guessing the direction of her thoughts. 'Anyone can have a baby, even the lowest street drab or the silliest girl.'

She was silent.

'If I were ever to become a father, which God forbid, I'd like you to be the child's mother. Is that good enough?'

It was not good enough for Sophie, in her heart of hearts, but it had to suffice. She pledged herself anew to him that night and returned in a half-pacified mood to London.

Emma, Susan and Saranna Mumby, with whom Edith had gone to stay, were half-sisters of Edith's paternal grandmother and had been a great help to her father in his young days. They had left the industrial parts of Yorkshire for a return, in their old age, to the calmer and cleaner landscape of the East Riding some years before, and they were themselves survivals from another time. Saranna had been born before Victoria ascended the throne, and her sisters not much later, and had practised as 'wise woman' and local midwife. They all doted on Edith, whom they regarded as the victim of a vile seducer, however much she denied it. All were competent women and kindly.

'I am spoilt,' she wrote to Sophie in March. 'I can't believe July will ever come. I pass my time writing and sewing and going for little walks; I believe the good ladies have put it round that I am a widow. I should love to visit Thirksay, but cannot in this condition for I fear it would shock your mother. *My* mother is in the picture. She will never forgive me, I fear. No one else at home knows, except Father and Mother and Edward. Father arranged it all. He was shattered but, as I expected, he did not blame *me*. Ted is less friendly. He is courting the daughter of a local magnate and is worried her family will get to hear of it. But I am safely out of sight and have asked to return in the autumn to a place I knew as a child in the Calder Valley, if I can persuade Father. I could rear chickens and continue my own work. So, all in all, I am very lucky.

'I did manage to visit York Minster again,' she wrote later, in another letter. 'This time I had a longer time to spend than that Sunday morning: do you remember? I felt at peace there and made a prayer to whoever is in charge of things that my child should be born healthy . . .' She went on: 'I'm sorry that I did not succeed in explaining, to you above all, what led me to let, or even, I suspect, encourage Clem to make love to me. It's on my conscience, Sophie, for I know you are still fond of him. It was partly the brandy, I suppose, but I allowed myself to drink it. He was terribly urgent. I suppose you know all about these things, very importunate, but again, it was not his fault that I didn't stop him. I could have done – I've gone over and over it in my mind. I think I wanted to break the glass that is the division between the self and another person. I wanted to feel "real". Does that make sense? Sometimes, often, when I was alone, I used to feel unreal. I'd look at my hands and touch my skin and wonder who I was, what I was doing in the world. Writing was – is – one way of making things real, and I thought that sort of intimacy might deliver me from myself. And, too, I had the feeling of a destiny ("Stupid," you will say, and rightly) that this was meant to happen. Mother Nature did the rest, as I suppose she does with every young woman who wants to feel, or does feel. I can't explain it any more than that. It isn't an explanation, I suppose, more an excuse. It didn't work, for, as soon as it was over, I was back in myself again, and when I sat alone afterwards I was quite calm but in despair. I don't expect even Father understands; he always had too high an opinion of me. Now that I can feel the child moving inside me, a most extraordinary sensation, nothing else seem to matter as far as my body is concerned and I feel quite "real". I only hope I shall go on doing so when I have to care for him or her. But other people, grown-up people, are still distant to me and I'm on the other side of the glass from them. Even with you sometimes, who have been such a good friend to me: I know we are all really alone, some perhaps feeling it more than others. It would be the height of selfishness to make poor Clem "pay" for what he did by forcing marriage and a family on him when he is poor and has so much to do in the world. I wouldn't make him happy, Sophie. He thinks I would, but he doesn't know me very well. He needs a lively, kind young woman to be his companion, someone to forgive him when he is unfaithful, for I know he would be if he married. Then three people would be miserable. He is a romantic, like you, but those sorts of feelings fade in the light of common day. I can't say all that to him, of course . . . It is not durable, Sophie, whatever he thinks. It sounds unkind and is an over-simplification, but I suppose what I have always been looking for is spiritual experience, and, above all, to find it in the ordinary. I felt it a little in the Minster the other day – I suppose because there is a holiness about the place. It was built by ordinary people so long ago and is part of our history, but despite its being so solid and "there" and real, in a way I do not feel myself to be, it also works upon another part of me so that I feel carried up by great pillars, yet knowing I'm bound to earth through time. I felt almost dissolved in that honey-coloured light and that great high silence. It reconciled me to death, to know it was there for a time and will be there after I have gone . . . .'

Sophie read and reread such letters and understood a little more about her friend. She was sure Edith had never written like this to anyone before. Clement, though, would understand her, Sophie was sure. And even if Edith would not marry him – and why ever should she if she did not want to? – he might help her by acknowledging similar feelings, which he expressed in his own verse.

She replied to Edith, for she did not want to lose touch with her friend, and mentioned what she thought of as her own humble experiences of beauty and peace. They had that in common, she and Edith. She might be greedy and seduced by the snares of worldliness and the mystery of personality, but she did understand Edith intuitively, despite the great differences between them.

Edith, meanwhile, went for walks in the cold spring and felt happy to be cut off from everything and everyone. The place she was in was undistinguished in itself and therefore safe. Nothing ever seemed to happen there; you could hardly find a copy of a newspaper and there was no bookshop. She might have been living in the Dane Law except she felt safe, – uninvaded.

At the end of the road was a Dame school for the sons of tradesmen and she went for walks and listened to the children as they came out at four o'clock in the afternoon. She even began to recognize some of the little faces. Children had never worried her; she did not feel 'behind the glass' with them, but talked to them easily and naturally, as though she were one of them. The winds from the sea howled down the roads and she welcomed them and took deep breaths and felt, for a time, that her own storms had passed. She would stop at the end of the road to the beach, as yet unmade-up, and pick little snails off the railings and place them on the wet grass and then sit on the one bench that had been placed on the 'promenade', where no one promenaded except in summer, and gaze out to sea over the wet, brown sands and feel inexplicably happy. It was like living in No Man's Land and she smiled at the pun. After the sixth month she grew larger and the walks were a little more tiring, but she still felt well. Saranna, or one of the others, would be waiting with a hot drink of milk when she returned from her walk, and the talk would be of old days. They never asked any questions of her except once, when the youngest of the three old ladies, in a downright but delicate way, tried to find out whether Edith knew the processes of birth. Edith replied that she was well aware of the way a child was born and had no particular fear of birth. Saranna paused a moment and then, her bright, beady eyes upon her guest and pupil, began to explain the procedures – how there would be pain but they would give her raspberry tea to hurry the child on, and a sheet would be tied to the bedpost for Edith to hold when she strained to push out the bairn, but that nature would do most of the work for her if she would let it.

Edith wondered whether any one of these spinster sisters had ever had a child of her own.

'Just do as we say, my dear,' said Susan, the middle sister, 'and don't fret.'

Saranna was the eldest and the dominant one and she had an abrupt manner of speech and capable-looking hands. They all regaled her with tales of the many births they had witnessed, the many 'childer' they had brought into the world, and Edith was humble and grateful. She did not neglect her writing and every evening, in the light of the oil lamp, sat by the fire in the little parlour and continued her latest Gothic mystery for Garnett. It was incongruous, but life was incongruous.

Her father came over once a fortnight to see that all was well and she wrote to both her parents regularly. Truly, she was the luckiest woman in the world to be so cosseted. The sisters were being paid, of course, by Mr Broughton, but this was never referred to and they did not talk to her as through they were servants or menials, but as equals. They were quite remarkable and Edith wondered how many other women as remarkable and as old, lived quiet lives like these and kept the skills of their generations in their heads and hands and speech. Did they, too, have intimations of Something Other? she wondered. Or was she, alone, a prey to illusions and semi-mystical experiences which were as out of touch with 'reality' as her problems with other people? Sophie, at least, had moments of peace and happiness, for she had said so. But with Sophie they had seemed more akin to half-memories or moods or to the presence of sun or the plethora of beautiful things she envied and was dazzled by. At Thirksay, which Edith was beginning to think of as a past glimpse of paradise, Sophie had been restless. Perhaps, though, one day, she too would make of that lost paradise a whole.

Meanwhile, Edith had plenty of opportunity to observe the three old women and stowed away their 'essence' in her head. Otherwise, she restricted herself to enjoying the place and preparing for the coming child. It should really be Sophie who was having this baby, she thought, more than once.

She seemed able to concentrate better than when she was in London, in spite of the lack of intellectual stimulus. All she needed was in her head, she thought, as she sat in the evening, scribbling, or observing Susan darning and Saranna doing her accounts and Emma trimming a hat for her. The old ladies liked finery on others and were skilful with their treadle sewing-machine. They were constantly reminding Edith she would need new clothes after the baby was born and planned a cream-coloured linen dress with a rose at the waist.

'You'll get your figure back, my dear,' said Susan as she threaded her needle against the light that came in from the window at the back of the house where their 'parlour' was. Obviously, they were thinking that she would eventually marry, even though none of the three had; it seemed they could not imagine a *young* person who would not wish to. A large-brimmed straw hat was brought out and re-trimmed 'for early autumn', but the principal sewing and knitting was, of course, the layette of baby clothes which were wrapped in tissue and the pile of which grew, it seemed, daily. Edith plied her needle, too, and soon there was a box of finished garments. Her father wrote to her regularly but all her mother ever added was, 'I hope you are well.' Poor Mother! Edith wished she could do something to cheer her up, but her mother had said nothing when Edith had arrived at Christmas, beyond, 'Your father has told me of your trouble,' and was no letter-writer. Sophie was another matter. Her long letters arrived weekly. She had not changed and spoke the truth when she said that one of her reasons for writing was to receive replies. Edith always smiled over Sophie's letters.

Sophie in person would be even better than her letters and Edith urged her to spend some time in Bridlington when she visited Thirksay in the summer. 'It would be so pleasant to have you here for a few days in July before the infant arrives,' she wrote. 'The doctor thinks the date of birth will be at the end of that month, but warns me that babies can be either early or late. If you came in mid-July I'm sure I should still be "expecting". Do try! The three "aunts" would be pleased to have any visitors – they are hospitable souls. I feel the place is a real haven and would not mind never seeing London again. A backwater suits me, and there is beautiful country around. I can see the twinkling of Flamborough Head Lighthouse from my bedroom and everywhere you smell the sea and hear it. I often stand just gazing at it, at the horizon and the grey waves, which I hope will have changed their colour when you come here. There are always small boats bobbing up and down in the bay. There is a little fishing harbour, as you probably know, and then, in summer, the boarding houses open for the folk from Yorkshire towns. As yet, though, we have no visitors but gulls. I love the North Sea. I expect you do, too. And I'm sure there could not be a better place to have a baby than within the sound of it. There is something eternal about the sea which cuts one down to size and lets one drift along . . . Did I tell you that Clem has written to me again? He asked me once more to marry him and said he might write to Father to "bring me round". He sounded rather aggrieved, but I can't think about it. It seems long ago and nothing to do with me. That may sound strange but it's true. The "three witches" would not let him see me if I did not want to, I know. I can do nothing but wait – I'm like a ship waiting to land. Or more like a beached whale waiting for the next tide!'

Sophie did go up to Thirksay towards the end of July. She had said nothing to her parents about Edith's plight but intimated Edith was staying with relatives in Bridlington and would be pleased to see her for a few days. They raised no objection and so, after a day or two on the farm, she set off across the East Riding to the coast.

The summer of 1914 was a beautiful one, hotter even that the summer of three years before when Edith had stayed in Thirksay, but with a slight breeze which carried the smell of late stacked hayfields over the Riding.

Sophie arrived in the town of Bridlington in the early afternoon and wasted no time looking at the harbour but walked slowly in the sun along a path that wound round at the top of the cliffs and led to the northern part of the little town, where new villas were in evidence, set back a little from the sea. Butterflies were hovering over the path and the sun's light was refracted by the sea's mirror into thousands of glancing lights and shimmerings. The water that day was blue and swept in a glittering arc across the whole of the bay. Families were already sitting on the sands in little groups and, for a moment, she wondered about families. The faint clamour of children rose up from the beach and it was almost reluctantly that she turned down the sandy lane on her left and found a wider avenue, parallel to the west, where stood the sisters' 'villa', built before the place became popular for holidaymakers. There were roses in the tidy front garden and a honeysuckle climbing over the red-brick walls. All was peaceful. It looked a comfortable sort of house.

Before she could ring the bell she heard a 'Sophie!' and there was the larger, almost Junoesque figure of Edith coming from the path that led to the back garden. She came up slowly, like a ship in full sail, and Sophie could not help staring; after they had kissed each other shyly on the cheek, Edith led the way indoors through a porch and a cool hall filled with the scent of roses, and into a little room at the back. It had a verandah and the garden beyond was shady and cool.

'Saranna, here is Sophie,' said Edith, as a small, neat-looking white-haired woman rose from a rustic seat and put her spectacles and her sewing down carefully before walking up to them. Sophie took the outstretched hand.

'My sisters are in the garden,' said the old lady. 'We shall all make you very welcome. It has been lonely for Edith with only ourselves for company.'

'But Sophie makes it perfect,' said Edith, smiling.

The old lady held on to Sophie's hand and pressed it slightly. 'Edith should be resting, but she was excited when she knew you were coming. There'll be a pot of tea for you in the parlour here in two ticks and you can take up your bag – it's the room on the right, at the top, and there's a basin if you want to wash your hands. My, but it's hot now! Better when the evening breeze comes over from the sea.' She went off quite quickly for such an old woman and Sophie did as she was bid, took up her baggage, washed her hot hands and combed her damp hair. She must offer to help. How pleasant it was here, as though there were no big world outside.

Edith said almost the same when Sophie rejoined her and they sat with a china teapot painted with violets and a plate of home-baked scones, the blinds half-drawn against the sun.

'Saranna likes the sun; they all wear their mother's old straw hats that must have seen Queen Victoria's wedding day,' Edith laughed. 'But they are a wonderful trio. Tell me everything, Sophie. How are London and Grant and Thirksay and your parents?'

Sophie had the impression Edith was not just being polite, but she looked rather sleepy.

'It is the weight of it all,' Edith said, divining her thoughts and pointing to her stomach. 'I've been reading a little about confinements – not encouraging!' But she seemed to be as calm as usual and almost laughing behind her pebble glasses when she took them off and opened her eyes wide. Pregnancy certainly suited her. Sophie had never seen her look so well.

'I'm trying to save up all my strength,' said Edith. 'I can't imagine what it will be like, but if millions of women have done it, I don't see why I can't. And the ladies have been so kind – Saranna in particular – she's brought scores of babies into the world.'

Sophie thought that, if she were in Edith's position, she would be far more nervous; but Edith had never been of a nervous disposition. 'I brought you a little present. Or, at least, for the baby,' she said, rummaging in her linen bag which accompanied her everywhere. She had found the tiny jacket in an old London shop. It was of quilted blue silk and was beautiful.

'This must have cost you a fortune,' said Edith practically. 'But it's lovely! About six months, I'd say – I mean the size. They're very, very small to begin with, babies, although mine feels enormous! It keeps me awake at night now, turning somersaults. I see you think I am going to have a son?'

'I suppose I do,' replied Sophie. 'I can imagine you with a son, Edie. What will you call him?'

Edith seemed to consider the matter. 'I don't know. Fred or Jack or something simple – I thought Mary for a girl.' They were silent for a moment. 'Clem is coming to see me before the end of the month,' Edith said briskly. 'He still hopes to persuade me.'

'I haven't seen him at all. He's been in France, I think' said Sophie. 'I wish you could love him, Edith.' Surely one sort of love could come after the experience, not before?

'I just don't want to live with him, Sophie. And if I gave in and married him, to "give the baby a name" as they say, he wouldn't be happy living with me. He can see the baby as often as he wants, if that is what's worrying him. I don't want to make things worse for him, or for me. I told him again it was my fault. I even told Father that – he didn't believe me, of course. I shall live alone and I shall manage. I suppose it will be hard to go on writing – for Edwards, I mean, – but I intend to go on. I finished something for him last week. Since then, I've not felt inclined. But I know I shall be able to go back to it when everything is settled. It's the waiting that is so long.'

'I think your father must be marvellous. I can just imagine what *my* family would say and do!'

'Father is used to having his own way. He wants to settle some money on me, but I'd prefer to see what I can do by myself. Mother has not come round and will hardly communicate with me. She's very upset. She won't really want me at home with the baby, to shock her friends and neighbours.'

'My mother would have torn me to pieces. I suppose you can't blame mothers. Perhaps yours will come round?'

'She blames Father as much as me. She's never stood up to him before. Now she says his "ideas" unsettled me. I shall go back to the West Riding, though. Father's promised to look for a little place. I thought over how I could keep chickens, and look after Mary/Jack and write. After all, I'm not poor. I'm fortunate, really.'

Edith *was* fortunate, Sophie went on to agree; lucky to be having Clem's baby, for one thing, in spite of everything, and lucky in her father, though she uttered only the latter opinion.

'I shan't mind being a hermit,' Edith added, and took up some knitting, having perched her spectacles once more on her nose.

Sophie felt useless, young, envious, all at sea in the emotions which Edith's advanced pregnancy aroused in her.

More than anything, though, she worried for her friend. What if things did not go well? Edith might die, or the baby might.

'You're not to worry, Sophie. I shall rely on you to keep me in touch with the big world.'

'Grant thinks there might be a war after Sarajevo,' said Sophie.

Edith looked up sharply. 'So does Father. I just can't think about it – it seems inconceivable.'

The two sat, and Edith knitted and Sophie tried to think of interesting topics of conversation, perhaps to tell her about her time in Paris or even to discuss the 'problem' of Grant, but the old days were gone and she felt Edith was being carried away and might disappear for ever. Even telling her of Beatrice's move to share the eyrie made her feel disloyal. There she was, still with the same problem. No dramatic event was to happen to her. Not even a baby. But she tried to be cheerful, though she felt excluded.

Edith went to bed early and Sophie sat in the garden with one of the sisters and then went to bed herself and watched the light from Flamborough sweep round the wall at intervals, inexorable in their regularity. Edith had seemed friendly enough but somewhat detached, and no wonder. How on earth was she going to endure the stigma of unmarried motherhood, even if she were a hermit selling eggs and writing best-sellers for Garnett Edwards? Yet Edith usually did what she had set herself to do and her father was on her side. Sophie fell asleep thinking of her own father and how he would have been just as kind and understanding, she was sure, if he followed his own feelings and not the superlatively censorious ones of his own wife and family and immediate neighbours.

She had three days with Edith; hot, heavy, slow days, in the house on the edge of the seaside town. It felt detached from the world, and Edith said she was reminded again of their holiday in Thirksay. 'Sometimes I feel only the sea can really touch me,' Edith said once as they sat together in the arbour in the garden. 'It was even better in early spring,' she went on. 'Out of season there's something very satisfying about watering places – sad, yet safe.'

'That sadness sounds like happiness to me,' replied Sophie.

Edith was talking more than usual now and Sophie wondered if having a baby would, in the end, change even her.

'The three sisters are like the place,' Edith went on, stitching away, whilst Sophie, for whom needlework was not a pleasure, lay in a hammock and contemplated the foliage of the trees which canopied the garden.

'*They're* out of season, too, a bit like me. They belong to the last century. I feel it's so sad that they won't live for ever, that the world will change. I hate change,' she added complacently.

'But you're going to have the biggest change of your life,' Sophie murmured.

'Yes. This is just a time in No Man's Land. That's how I think of it.'

'No *Man's* Land!' laughed Sophie. 'That must be a rather peaceful country, I think.'

Another time, Edith said, 'Do you think it makes a pattern, all of it, our lives, and the baby? The sisters are happy about the baby. I know they are; they like new life. Perhaps because their lives are nearly over, though I expect they'll live on to their nineties at least.'

'Babies disrupt patterns, I suppose,' replied Sophie. 'But I agree, if life has to go on, how better than choosing to do something happily, not worrying about conventions and marriage and all that. I shouldn't be brave enough, I know.'

'Oh, I'm not very brave; I'm a fool,' said Edith, 'but I try not to think about it. I want only good thoughts going round my bloodstream from my brain to that little thing in here.'

'We didn't make the rules, anyway,' said Sophie suddenly.

'No – I suppose I shall be an honorary Feminist,' said Edith patting her stomach.

'No, Feminists cannot be fatalists, Edith!'

'But at least I shall feel connected to the world.'

Was this what they had all lived for, loved for, been prepared for since childhood? They sat on in the garden and felt time had come to a full stop, a deceptive impression, of course.

'I feel happy because something good is about to happen. Something terrifying and probably painful, but good, Sophie.'

Sophie felt a lump in her throat. 'You are so brave. Will you send me a telegram straight away? I shall go straight back to London – there's a panic on about the Autumn List.' And I might see Clem, she thought.

Sophie left the next day. 'Next time it will be both of you,' she said.

The last sight of Edith was of her standing at the gate with Saranna. That morning Sophie had helped to check the innumerable garments and paraphernalia a baby apparently needed and tied yellow ribbons she had bought in the town on the wickerwork cradle. 'That way it won't matter whether it's Jack or Mary,' she said and Edith had laughed.

Then, 'I wish you could stay with me here,' she said.

Sophie thought, she is belonging more to the world already. Please, God, let her come safely through it all.

On the way back to London, Sophie noticed a stir in all the railway stations and wondered what was afoot. There seemed to be the khaki figures of territorials everywhere and she thought she had come back to earth with a vengeance.

On arrival at Miller and Penn's she heard that Austin Speight had gone to a territorial camp. The papers were full of rumours; Grant looked stony-faced and said little. Clem was not in London and neither was Toby Watson. Sophie could concentrate on nothing except a letter to Edith, begging for her news as soon as anything happened. London went on as usual, seemingly unaffected by the rumours of war, the populace bent on late summer pleasures.

In the event, the birth of Edith's baby was delayed. The sisters said first babies were often late and 'better late than never' and laughed. They did not seem worried, so Edith relaxed. Everything was ready when, on a Friday, the last day of July, a telegram arrived at the Bridlington house.

Edith took the telegram expecting it to be from her father, for his stay with them had been put off; apparently the business community was in disarray and he was worried about some of his European investments.

The telegram was addressed to her and, as the boy waited to see if it needed a reply, Edith read the words, 'Arriving six pm: coming to marry you. Clem.'

She put it down on the hall table and sat down herself. 'No reply,' she said. Saranna took the paper from Edith and read it. She looked up enquiringly. Edith explained.

'Am I to let him in?' asked Saranna.

'Yes – we must. I can't turn him away if he's come so far to see me.'

Edith went back to the sitting room and lay on the Chesterfield. Surely the baby would hurry up now. She was neither surprised nor angry. This period of 'peace' could not have lasted for ever. Peace for her with the unborn child and peace for England, perhaps, too.

She said faintly to Emma, 'I shall have to listen to him. I do wish Sophie were here. He won't still want to marry me when he sees me. I should be like one of those funny sketches in the music hall. Why won't he take "No" for an answer?' Emma said nothing.

At six o'clock precisely there was the jangle of the bell in the hall. The sisters' old servant, Addy, went to open it and Saranna went out to look. Shortly afterwards, with a bland look, she motioned Clement, who was bearing a bunch of flowers, into the sitting room and left him there with the injunction 'Not to tire Miss Broughton'.

Edith lay back and they both looked at each other and then away. 'Don't be cross, Edith,' he said in a gentle voice, unlike his usual ironic one. 'I had .to ask you again. I wrote to your father to see if you'd had the child. I'm on my way to camp.'

'To camp?' she echoed, astonished.

'Yes. There's no doubt that we'll be at war next week – believe me. I've volunteered for training. I was an engineer once, you know; they might make use of me.'

Edith said nothing, but lay staring at him nervously.

He sat down opposite her on one of Saranna's hard-backed chairs. 'I don't ask you to love me, Edith,' he said. 'I don't even ask you to live with me if you don't want to. I know I can be devilishly difficult. But I couldn't just leave everything as it is without trying once more to persuade you to marry me. It all seemed to burst in my head after Austin told me what the high-ups were thinking – we can't avoid war now. Stupid, isn't it?'

She said nothing but breathed a little more easily and folded her hands.

'After all, it is my baby as well as yours – our baby. I've asked about a Special Registrar's Licence, in case of emergency. I suppose "imminent birth" is an emergency? If you will agree, I can take a firm application down to the town hall and we could be married in forty-eight hours as you are at present a resident of Bridlington.'

She stirred as if to remonstrate.

'No – don't say anything yet. Just hear me out.' He got up and walked to the window that overlooked the neat garden and seemed to consider the sight and sound and scent of summer, for when he turned round he looked dazed. 'I know I can't make everything right for you. I've no claims upon you. But I can try to make amends to the child. I want him to have my name. Marry me, Edith. We could be married on the fourth or fifth.' She cleared her throat. When he had mentioned the baby her hand had involuntarily moved to stroke her stomach in a protective gesture. 'It *is* going to be war, Edith,' he repeated.

'Love is a kind of war,' said Edith, her face turned away. 'Who said that?' Then she rubbed her eyes and stared at him. Somehow, decisiveness seemed to have made him appear older and invested him with a certain authority. She saw how he might look when he was fifty and perhaps Poet Laureate. Nevertheless, in certain aspects, she felt him still a total stranger.

'I came either to see the child – but your father said he hadn't arrived yet – or to marry you. Or both, if you want. I shall have to go away on the sixth – I have to report at a camp in Malvern for initial training – but I can come back, I'm sure, soon, to see him. Please marry me, Edith, for the baby's sake.'

'Sit down, Clem,' she ordered. 'Ask Saranna to put the roses in water – no, I'll ask.' She rose clumsily and he looked at her swollen belly and put out his hand to her hand. She let it rest for a moment in his and then gathered herself up and went into the hall. Saranna was waiting outside, sitting on a chair like a small, fierce wardress. 'Please, can you ask Addy to put the flowers in a vase – and make up a bed for Mr Bartholomew – and perhaps a cup of tea for him now?'

She came into the room again and walked carefully to a chair. 'Am I being selfish? I wanted the baby for myself, Clem. It seemed to have nothing to do with you. I didn't want to lay a claim on you when there was none; only my own foolishness made this happen, and perhaps you were a little headstrong, too – '

'I didn't come to ask for forgiveness or to apologize,' he said, and she was rather touched that he was trying to be honest. 'I love you, of course, I think even your friend Sophie believes that, but that's not what I came to say. Only, that you can have my name or not as you will, but that I want my child recognized for what he is: flesh of my flesh, as well as yours. You don't know what it's like to have no father, you, with your kind father. Yes, I could tell he was kind when I got his reply to my letter. You have a happy family and a secure home. You see, Edith, I am illegitimate. My mother was seduced by the man she worked for. I don't want that happening all over again, a child with no real father. I want my mother to have a real grandchild, too, someone she knows I'm responsible for. Please, Edith, marry me; you may only take what help you need from me. I won't force myself on you. I have a sort of duty, so I've come. Say you will – say something . . .'

'You know that it won't make any difference – between you and me?' Edith said awkwardly, feeling the disadvantage of her bulk and her unmarried state and aware that most women would have swooned with gratitude to be made respectable at the last moment. Yet how could she now refuse? She was tired, vulnerable, wanting only for the birth to be over. She knew Clement had a certain power of argument and that if she opposed him now she would be seen as denying her child a father. In spite of everything, Edith looked dignified and Clement truly admired her.

Edith felt there was nothing to be lost in adding a few home truths. She did it in her calm, gentle way, taking off her spectacles and sitting on the old Chesterfield with Clement facing her in an armchair. Saranna had squeezed her hand in the hall, as if to say, 'You can rely on us – don't be bullied, my dear.'

Edith knew that his intention was not to bully her, but, like her, to do the right thing in strange circumstances. So she said, looking him full in the face, 'If it is only to give our child a name, so that you can see him . . .'

'That would be the reason,' said Clem.

'But you could see him – or her – whenever you wanted, Clement. And if you're worrying about money, I shall manage. I have a little income,' she replied, looking down at the carpet.

'I didn't come before, because I felt a certain amount of right was on your side,' he said reluctantly. 'But there isn't going to be time, soon, to discuss these finer points. Edith, if there *is* going to be a war, I am going to fight in it.'

Edith buried her head in her long hands and then looked up. 'Does that make all the difference?' she asked.

'I think it does,' he replied.

She gave a long sigh. She looked up after a minute or two. He said nothing, leaned towards her. 'Then go and settle it – I'll agree,' she said in a firm voice.

He was overjoyed, got up, was about to embrace her or somehow try to convey his feeling, but she only took his hand and said, 'As soon as we can – it can't be long now.'

He looked at her, leaning back in her chair, and felt a surge of sympathy. 'Thank you,' he said.

Edith was thinking, what will Sophie say? She'll believe I'm in his power now! And she felt a queer conviction that the baby was now no longer her exclusive property. There would be a father with a father's rights. She would deal with that when it came. She did not love Clement. She had compromised and the world would applaud. She felt suddenly weary.

'I shall go straight away,' he said. 'I'll try to get it for the fourth – they need forty-eight hours at least, I believe not counting Sunday and the Bank Holiday – I've got the money.'

'Is it expensive?'

'Rather. But that's my business.'

He went out and Edith finally got up from her sofa and went into the garden. She found she had tears running down her cheeks. But she calmed herself and said to the baby, 'It doesn't matter, you're going to be all right. And perhaps you'll want a father – perhaps I was wrong.'

She was sitting in the garden when Clement returned and the smile on his face showed her he had arranged things to his satisfaction.

It was in this way that Edith Broughton applied with Clement Bartholomew for a Special Registrar's Licence on compassionate grounds, as she was expecting his child.

208

The weekend passed, sultry and still, with the sea under a mist of heat and the sun like a spot of light behind a burning glass. The wedding was to be on the Tuesday afternoon, the fourth of August, after the Monday Bank Holiday. All over England people were basking in their gardens, if they had them, or on the sands, and Bridlington was no exception.

Edith examined her face, and her swollen hands. A ring would hardly fit on these fingers, she thought. They would go back to their normal size once the baby was born. Then the wedding ring would fit. There was no time to ask her family to come over and she did not really wish them to be there, so the three sisters agreed to act as her witnesses. The ceremony would be simple and as short as possible. 'I shall tell my mother when it's all over,' Clement had said. She glanced out of the window at Clem in the garden. What a strange man he was, full of surprises. She rather liked him, and smiled to herself. Why should he, of all people, volunteer for the army in the event of war? She had not thought him particularly patriotic. True, he loved England, rural England and all her history, but he was not a man one could imagine as a soldier. Perhaps he felt he needed a change in his life. Or perhaps, she wondered guiltily, he thought she would marry him if he did something quixotic like join the army. Surely, if that were true, he must love her, or was he a little mad too? Well, her boats were burned now and she did not really care. She had held out long enough and he had made her agree, in spite of everything. Edith was not fool enough to think that a man would go on treating his wife with the same caution and reserve as formerly, but she would cross that bridge when she came to it.

She scribbled a short letter to Sophie and gave it to Susan to put in the post-box, for, now, a walk to the end of the road was an effort. Surely it could not be long now? Provided she did not give birth in some dramatic fashion in the town hall. Clem was to leave on the day after to go to his camp. Everything seemed to be happening with indecent haste: after a long period of freedom she was going to be a 'respectable' woman! And it seemed that old England was to go to war if Clem could be believed. She was so out of touch that she hardly knew why.

They waited for news all through the day of the Bank Holiday and on the morning of the 4th. The newspapers were sold out.

Sara said a neighbour had seen a newspaper that said war could no longer be avoided. Edith was to be married in the afternoon. She was taken with Clem in one of the town's new cabs not long before the hour arranged to the town hall where the office of the registrar was. Crowds had been milling round the post office all day waiting for a notice to be fixed about the war news. As Edith and Clem drove by they seemed not to be disappointed. There were shouts and someone held up a Union Jack. Clem looked grim. To Edith, events seemed to have disappeared once more behind glass. On arrival, the registrar glanced at her once and then seemed to avoid looking at her in his embarrassment.

The ceremony was soon over and there were even more crowds on the way back. When they got home they had a glass of Saranna's elderberry wine and toasted each other. Clem was silent. He was shown baby clothes and tried to smile. His confession of illegitimacy had touched Edith and she determined to be as understanding as possible with him before he left the next day. As the telegraph machines tapped out all afternoon to far corners of the world, the news of the great world, that England was at war, Edith's small piece of news was also tapped out to her father in Leeds.

'To England,' Clem said, as he drained his glass. They could hear shouting in the distance mingled with the sound of the sea. It was all almost too much for them. They went up to the room which Edith had slept in since the spring in the Safe House and she went to bed. Clem sat up with her and they talked of war and of themselves, desultorily, as though they had all the time in the world to continue a leisurely conversation.

Edith slept fitfully. Clem was in an armchair and had drawn the curtains back and the early light woke her as it came streaking through the panes. A strange wedding night indeed; she almost ready to give birth; Clem, silent, with his mind half on his future and the war and the world outside waiting for one knew not what. Not for forty-four years had Prussia roused the sleeping giant of Europe, and England hardly knew how to feel or what to do. But the earth was still the same. The sun still rose and babies were still born. That was the only sort of news that would matter to Edith at present.

'You promise – they will send me a telegram as soon as he is born?'

Edith smiled, 'You seem sure it will be a boy.'

She pointed to the crib with Sophie's yellow ribbons still festooning the top and sides.

'Sophie put them there,' she said with a little smile.

'That is just the sort of thing Sophie would do. Does she think you are going to give birth to a hermaphrodite?'

'Oh, I would not mind a daughter,' said Edith carelessly.

'You promise you will get them to telegraph to Malvern, not just about the baby, but about you – that you are all right?'

Edith promised and was touched that he really cared.

Clement dressed and was off, with a squeeze of the hand and a worried look and a brush of his lips on her cheek. Edith had gone downstairs and stood at the front door to say farewell. He came back to kiss her again and to murmur, 'Thank you. Wish me well, and I do wish *you* well, dear Edith.'

She kissed his forehead then, trying to avoid the great bulk of her from brushing against him, for the emotion she felt for him was nothing to do with the reason for the marriage. Once he had gone she drank a cup of tea slowly and then went out into the garden and walked there, sitting down eventually on the rustic seat where, an hour or two later, as she had expected, a twinge of dull pain, which turned into not quite a stab, but definitely slightly unpleasant, came and went, came again, faded away, was forgotten, then reappeared. Edith was, at last, in labour.

Babies are not born in minutes, but in hours, and Edith had plenty of time to think about Clement as she walked up and down during the afternoon. It was slow; sensations came and went, painful, but separated by long periods of nothing much happening, till the next tightening, sharpening, edgy misery began again. She should have kissed Clem goodbye with more conviction, she thought. The world was at war. But the only war she could concentrate on was within herself.

In the evening, as the labour progressed, Edith did not think about Clement at all. At first she was reluctant to lie down, but when the pains came more frequently and stayed longer with her, she was persuaded by Saranna to go upstairs and lie down on the bed they had prepared. Susan was despatched to send a telegram to both Clement and Edith's father to say the baby was on the way, and Emma and her other sister took turns to sit

211

by Edith, occasionally examining her. If things went too slowly they would get a doctor who was an old friend of theirs, but otherwise the baby would be born as a result of the combined labours of Edith and the trio.

Edith was not a groaner or moaner and found it suited her to lie breathing quietly until the next pain should arrive. She had sipped the raspberry tea they had brought her and got up again for a time to prowl round the room, but finally she was forced to the bed again. The curtains were undrawn and she could see the light of Flamborough Head twinkling regularly across the bay. She found she was unconsciously timing her breathing with the light, waiting for it, and when the worst and longest, sharpest pains arrived and her body said, 'No, no,' she firmly said, 'Yes,' with her mind. The light was saying, 'Yes, yes,' too, and for a while it was a struggle between the three of them. She accepted her body's pains, but rose above them each time the light swept over the ceiling.

'Is it bothering you?' asked Emma, whose turn it was to sit with her.

'No, it's helping,' said Edith cheerfully, in the interval between two enormously long pains which made her gasp. She had found that the gasping could help; it seemed to make her breathing rise to a crescendo with the pain and surmount it, fading away at last for a time. I must remember the light says 'Yes' she thought.

After an hour or two the sensations slowly seemed to change; the pain was less, but the urge to do something about it more imperative.

'Not long now,' said Saranna, who had come in when Edith was far away, riding the storm. The old woman looked at her watch which she wore on a long ribbon pinned to her lacy blouse.

'I want to push it out,' gasped Edith.

'Just take some ordinary breaths, my dear. There, let it push you, soon you can help it.' She busied herself examining her with practised hands. Clean towels and linen had been laid out and jugs of hot water and scissors were brought in by Emma.

They placed high pillows now behind Edith and she struggled up to a sitting position. There was still time to reflect, for the new sensations, although powerful, were not exactly painful. They came slowly, and each time, Edith held on to the long sheets that had been twisted and tied to the bedposts at the bottom of the bed and given her to pull when the urge to push overwhelmed her.

'Ah!' said Saranna, 'You're nearly there. Now you can push, my love, next time – '

Edith held on to the sheets and they urged her on with all her powers, once, twice, three times. It was an overwhelming sensation. She could hardly believe what was happening. A flooding in of fullness, of power filled her, and with her eyes fixed steadily ahead, she did as nature bid her and felt a gigantic opening filled with a solid band of flesh, as though a door was slowly widening.

'A big breath, now,' cried Saranna.

Emma was standing at the foot of the bed and Susan was busy with the bowls and the scissors. There was a sound like a plug being pulled and then Saranna was deftly turning the head of Edith's baby round and easing out the little shoulders, one by one. Then, as Edith waited on her command, she was finally allowed to give one last effort and there slithered out, among blood and wet and hair, the form of a child with a large head and a puckered face. Edith saw the child emerge just after midnight struck, and Saranna cried, 'A boy!'

Susan took him quickly, wiped the mucus from his face, cut the cord deftly, wrapped the child in a large towel and gave him to Edith.

'Give him a cuddle,' she said. 'Time for a good clean up in a minute.'

Edith lay back and grasped the solid little mass. He cried again, this time lustily, and then seemed to fall asleep. 'Jack,' she said, and laughed aloud, peering into his face.

They took the child then, and cleaned him up more efficiently whilst Edith gave a final, unexpected, push and the afterbirth slid out, all gleaming, but with little whitish marks.

'That shows he's late,' said Saranna sagely, and Emma put the liver-like mass into a bowl and disappeared with it.

Soon the child was back in Edith's arms. She did not even feel tired. Just terribly happy. And real. This was real. The baby was real now, part of the world, not just part of her. She felt not relief but amazement.

213

'Shall we say he was born on the sixth?' asked Emma. 'It was just after midnight when I cut the cord.'

'The sixth of August, nineteen fourteen,' said Edith, dreamily, and smiled whilst it was her turn to be cleaned and bathed and finally tucked up. They brought Jack to her once more and she examined him. Now he was all red-skinned with little patches of vernix on his body and tiny, delicate fists and feet. His eyes opened again and she looked into them.

'I hope you won't be short-sighted,' she said. 'Thank you, Saranna and Susan and Emma, it was marvellous. Let Clement know, will you, and Father.' She, herself, would write to Sophie. She felt powerful.

'Shall we put him in the cradle or will you hold him? You can feed him when he wakes, they like it; not that there'll be any milk for two or three days, but they like it.'

The three women were all standing round her now and Edith felt like a queen. Nobody had ever told her it would be like this.

'I'll hold him and try,' she said, 'when he wakes up again.'

Then try to rest after that,' said Saranna. 'Keep your strength up, you'll need it. Harder work ahead.'

Edith laughed.

Later she was always to remember the way dawn came that first day of Jack's life and how the whole world was transformed. She felt not just a great surge of love for this little creature, but a great sense of awe. She had done it, she, Edith, whom everyone thought so unworldly. And before they put him in the cradle again and she lay watching the weak, streaky light of dawn, she remembered, too, how, just for a flash of time, there had seemed to be the imprint of Clem's features on that little face. Clem would be glad, war or not. She had done the right thing. Her war was over, whatever happened to the world.

In the morning they all came to her room again and Edith was wide awake and sore. 'Shouldn't he be crying?' she asked anxiously. Jack was in the cradle, quiet, and soon Edith was eating a hearty breakfast.

'He's a good baby, I think,' said Emma. 'Some cry more than others. I shouldn't worry if he's quiet, there'll be plenty

214

of noise later.'

Edith thought, it must be a struggle to be born. 'He's tired, perhaps tireder than I am,' she said.

'Susan went down to the post office with the telegrams,' said Emma. 'I expect your parents will be coming to see you soon. My, but there's a great to do down in the town. It seems everybody wants to be fighting this war. They say everybody under sixty-five has to register for national service. Mrs Earby at number seven is going to help out at the town hall.'

'Don't worry Edith with all that,' said Saranna. 'She won't be required to do war work, she's the next five years nicely mapped out till he goes to school.'

Edith was waiting for a reply to her telegram from Clem and wondering whether he would be given leave to see his child. Clement seemed to have been with her years and years ago; was it only Tuesday they were married? Really, she thought, what had marriage to do with it? Birth was a physical thing; the decencies came later. But she felt a little guilty that things had gone so well. Jack's coming had hurt but not ever quite unbearably. She thought of the sweeping arc of the lighthouse which had seemed to guard over her. She was more worried that now was the time for reckoning with her parents and with Clem. The two of them had sent a telegram to Leeds after the wedding, saying only that the marriage had taken place. It would be up to her parents to tell their relatives and friends and neighbours if they wished. Edith had done her best, in accepting Clem's offer.

At noon she lay cleaned and tidied once more, with only the trickle of the remains of giving birth between her legs and a heaviness beginning in her breasts.

Emma brought up the telegram. It was from Clem, who had received the news at ten o'clock and lost no time in replying. At first Edith did not know to whom it was addressed. 'Mrs C. Bartholomew'; who could that be? Then she realized that was now her name. 'Jack Bartholomew,' she said aloud and wondered whether Clem had told his mother the news. 'So happy – ' read the short message – 'Very busy here. Will try come Brid. Soon. All love to you and the boy. Clem.'

'Saranna, buy me a newspaper please, will you?' asked Edith when they came up with her luncheon. 'I want to get up,' she said. 'I don't see why I should be treated as an invalid. If Father telegraphs to come I want to be up.'

'Nay,' said Saranna, 'rest while you can, love. There'll be time to stir yourself soon enough.'

'I can't let you go on doing all the work, you've looked after me so well.'

'We're that proud,' replied the old lady. 'And so will your man be. He's a grand little lad.' She peered over the sleeping Jack.

'Shouldn't he be given water or something?' asked Edith, anxiously.

'Well, you can, but I reckon nature didn't intend it. Put him to the breast whenever you want – it makes the milk come sooner. They all lose a little weight in their first three days on earth.'

Jack was now resplendent in a white lace cotton nightdress threaded with blue ribbons. The cradle still carried the yellow ribbons Sophie had tied on.

'I feel so lazy,' said Edith.

On the ninth day of August the promised milk came in and Edith felt like a churn, with large buttery breasts which she regarded with astonishment. She fed Jack whenever he seemed to want it, which was quite often. The papers were full of reports, rumours, solemn admonitions and, for the first time, she felt uneasy. What was Clem doing? Why had he taken that sudden decision? She still would not have thought he was the sort of man to offer himself for his country.

A letter arrived from her father, full of relief and good wishes. He had toasted his grandchild in champagne and wanted Edith home as soon as possible. They had not been able to get out of Leeds because all the trains were filled with troops. 'The Germans in Bradford have only just realized they will be treated as the enemy,' wrote Mr Broughton. 'Poor things; it seems war fever is taking over.' He, himself, being under sixty-five, had had to register, but he imagined his factories would soon be switched to making articles for the troops. 'Mother has offered to help in the town clerk's office where your Aunt Ellen is supervising the issue of food cards. I have helped to start a fund for hospital equipment. It is all very terrible. Ted came back from his holiday in Scotland determined to volunteer. Mother wants him to wait for the call-up – no one knows if and when that will happen,' he wrote.

Edith began to feel left out of it all. Whilst men and armies gathered and people joined in the common cause, all she had thought about was the baby. It was true she had been reading Caroline Spurgeon's book on mysticism just before Clem arrived, but that, too, seemed an indulgence. One could not be mystical about childbirth. Could one be mystical about war? Had her new husband some idea of sacrifice, of immolation for a cause? Surely not; Clem was a cynic. Why had he joined up? Had it been, after all, to force her own hand? No, she was not *so* important to him, she thought. His name would go forward not just through Jack, but through his poetry. Clem was in a state of change, of growth, and had chosen to join his country to see what it did to him, she decided.

Then came a letter from Sophie, wild with excitement, thrilled at Edith's news, and only mentioning as a postscript that she had offered her services as a clerk at the Ministry of Defence. They all thought the war would be over by Christmas, and she could go back to Miller and Penn whenever the Ministry released her.

Edith remembered that Clem had told her that Austin had joined up too. She must ask Sophie about Toby and the others.

Edith searched the letter again for Sophie's reaction to her marriage and found it on the back as another postscript: 'I suppose you thought it the right thing to do. I hope you and he will be happy.' Underneath, a row of kisses, 'For Jack.'

Edith pondered this, but scarcely had time to reply as she would have wished, for now it seemed her father wanted her home. And before September arrived, he came in his new car to fetch her and Jack. But where was 'home' now? Edith was sad to leave the seaside and the kind old ladies.

Her mother said nothing, did not even kiss her when she arrived in Roundhay. They had never been close, but Edith felt she might at least have shown some interest in her grandson. As far as her mother was concerned she was on sufferance, even though she was married.

Yet, when Clement was finally given a week's leave, she was quite polite to *him*.

217

Edith told them all of her plans for living some twelve miles away from Leeds, in a cottage next to a small farm, a place a business acquaintance of her father's had once rented, and where she had visited as a child, loving the small village. Her father was reluctant, but Mrs Broughton looked rather relieved.

'You can't manage a baby alone, Edie,' her father said, and it was true that, without the support of Saranna and her sisters, who had themselves seen Edith go with great reluctance, but had preferred to stay on the coast, her time would be fully taken up with the needs of the infant. He was growing, it seemed, before her eyes, and required a good deal of her energies, in spite of being, still, a 'good' baby.

Finally, Edith asked her father to persuade her mother to hint to neighbours that she had married secretly in London the year before, but that her husband, now in training to be an officer, had only now been able to attend to her. Edith hated the deception, but it might cheer her mother up. Now that the country was at war, surely people would have less time to wonder at the sudden birth of a child to a woman they had had no inkling was even married. Mrs Broughton decided to take her husband's advice.

'His family is poor,' she explained, 'but we are reconciled to the marriage. Such a lovely baby.'

Edith felt that Clem would be an ally when he came, as far as her moving away was concerned. 'You must persuade them; tell them you want me to be in the country. Perhaps once Jack is three months old – ' she said when they were left alone together on his short leave.

Clement, though, who was utterly thrilled by his small son, tried to argue with her, and Edith felt trapped.

'I need a little place of my own, Clem. I have to go on writing – I told you I wouldn't take money from you.'

'But now you are my wife!' he said in astonishment. 'I'm training to be an officer – you forget I was once an engineer – they need me, and will pay an officer's pay.'

'It would pay for a girl to help with Jack, I suppose. Father owns the cottage now. It's near a small farm and is not too isolated; the farm's at the bottom of the lane. Please, Clem, persuade them.'

He seemed like a stranger, tall in his uniform. She could not imagine how she had ever allowed him to make love to her. That all seemed to have happened in another age. But now she had Jack and Jack needed a contented mother and country air.

They sat together in the large Roundhay drawing room. All Clem's callowness seemed to have been pared away from him, like the waxy fat round a kidney, to leave only this spare, slim, male creature who was acting like a husband. 'They won't want me for war work with a small baby,' she said. 'Did you know that Sophie is working for the Ministry of Defence in London? I could grow cabbages and feed us, they say there'll be shortages of food, and I could have chickens and sell eggs. I've always wanted to live in the country.'

'You could go and stay with my mother,' he offered.

'I will go to see her,' promised Edith. 'But I don't think it would be fair to stay with her for long. I intend to go to Far Ox Heys, Clem, sooner or later.'

'Is that what it's called? You'll get an allowance from me for Jack, you know, it's all arranged. Now, shouldn't we have him christened?'

'Are you a believer?'

'No, but our mothers might expect it.' He was finding out more and more about his wife and discovering she was not exactly what he had imagined in those distant days when he had worshipped ineffectually at her shrine. But there was no time for reminiscence. Edith had not said she would not share his bed, but Clem found his desire for her had evaporated. Jack absorbed all her physical energies: feeding, cleaning, washing and caring for him in a hundred little ways. He observed her with him and knew the child would be safe with her, for she was wrapped up in him. She was a woman of great feeling, who had never been in love before. He was not jealous, for he had other things to think about. After a business talk with Edith's father and a promise from Edith to write to him regularly about the child, he departed, full of conflicting feelings, sure that once the war was over they would make an effort to be a family. He had not given up his writing either and showed Edith a notebook which he was to carry round with him, along with his pocket Shakespeare sonnets and a lock of Jack's first hair.

Edith was relieved rather than upset when he went. Clement had much to do in the world and she must get on with her own task of keeping his son alive and healthy. She began to write too, about her own feelings, and to record Jack's progress. The routine took up most of her time but she did not neglect her other writing either and was pleased to find, when Jack was about three months old, that she could invent a Bevis Constantine story quite well with one part of her brain, whilst the other was calculating how much longer Jack needed at one breast before switching him to the other. And she knitted for the troops and was able to think out stories as she did so. In spite of her mother's continuing coldness, she felt she had come through. One day soon she was determined to move to Far Ox Heys and begin a new life. Meanwhile, the war must be won and, in common with most of her countrymen and women, Edith was sure that it would soon be over, though the bombardment of the coast in December, when the Grand Hotel at Scarborough was wrecked, and people killed, was a terrible shock. Whitby Abbey, too, already a ruin, was further ruined from shelling at sea. Saranna and her sisters still refused, however, to leave Bridlington.

She wrote regularly to her husband, who was moving from place to place, and received from him a poem for Jack which he had composed in camp. In the New Year, when Jack was already nearly four months old, he had another week's leave before he left, along with most of his regiment, for France. He went to see his mother and then spent a few days with Edith and Jack. He looked older and browner, spoke mostly of his training; the route marches and the physical jerks, the bayonet practice, the firing and the bombing and the drilling. But none of this was what the army now needed from him. As an engineer, they had realized tardily, he could be useful to them in other ways.

Edith felt he had become even more of a stranger. He told her he had got on quite well with the rough and ready type of lads he had met during these months, but she guessed his reasons for joining up now seemed lost in a haze. It had been to do with her and misery and wanting to forget himself, and perhaps a feeling of fate. His predominant emotion, now, was one of love of his country, whichever swine were ruling it, and he was forceful in his expression of these new feelings to his wife. The war was being fought for the wrong reasons, but once you were in it and bearing it, like the rest of your countrymen, you began to care more about staying alive. When it was over you could return to a home of your own; everything would be different then. She knew he was thinking that then she would be a 'proper' wife. He seemed immeasurably glad that he had a son and often spoke of all he would teach him as he grew up. They would live in the country and he would go on writing. Now he had both a wife and a child and a job to do, everything would be all right once the war was over.

This leave was hardly real to either of them. The presence of her parents and of Jack apparently inhibited him from wanting to make love to her. She was relieved, but it did not seem to auger well for the future.

When he left they kissed each other 'goodbye' and he kissed Jack, and held him, and for a moment they were together as a family and Wilfred Broughton took a photograph.

Sophie had started her work with enthusiasm. It was strange at first not being at Miller and Penn's, but, along with most publishers, trade was low and Grant had contracted with the government to publish several little patriotic leaflets whilst paper was still in good supply. She was often alone in the eyrie, for Beatrice Osborn, her political friend, had decided to enrol as a VAD and was away at St Thomas's Hospital doing her training, except when she had her scarce days off duty, when she flopped wearily into bed and stayed there.

'Those sisters are horrors,' she said often to Sophie. 'You'd think they'd be glad that some of us have volunteered to help, but no. They take a sadistic pleasure in ticking us off, and about the most absurd things – bandage-rolling and bedpans. I can't see that the war will be won by folding linen in a special way or scouring out bed pans with Lysol! Really, it makes me despair about women. They are just as bad as men when they have power, especially over other women, but you ought to see the way they kow-tow to the doctors! Men, of course.' Beatrice was red-haired and very downright and sure of herself. She seemed older – they all did.

'You're not losing your convictions, then?' asked Sophie.

221

'No, no. We need a new society, not just votes for women. Sweep it all away, the hypocrisy and the class system and, above all, use a new broom in the corridors of power. I've more sympathy for the ordinary Germans. I expect they're bullied and powerless just as the ordinary British people are.'

The war was not going well. The struggle, which people had thought would be over by Christmas, was dragging on interminably and in 1915 the first Zeppelin raids began. Volunteers in great numbers were sent out to France. Edith wrote to Sophie that Clement had not been able to spend any more leave in Leeds and his letters from France had seemed solemn and troubled. She was to stay at home for the present, but arrangements were being made for her to move one day to the farm cottage on the lower slopes of the Pennines, to the west of Leeds, after the war, if not before. Edith had even volunteered for war work of her own, as she was able to leave Jack with her mother at times. Maud had accepted Jack, but was chilly to Edith still. Two days a week Edith was able, now Jack was weaned, to help out at one of the convalescent hospitals, where casualties had already arrived from the first battle of Ypres.

'I'd rather be a lady postman,' she wrote. 'I've always thought that job would be ideal: long walks and everyone pleased to see you. But they told me I was too old. They can get younger women for less money.'

Sophie longed to see Jack, but could not get away from London, and gradually she slipped into that frame of mind when 'after the war' everything would be possible. She and Grant, who was too old to volunteer, could see each other only now and then, and they would go out into the country when they could. He had offered Chimneys as a convalescent home for the wounded, of whom more and more were arriving from the trenches. Sophie was still restless. The war seemd to have put everything into either cold storage or under a question mark and, at first she clung on to Grant as the one constant factor in her life.

In 1916, London was full of troops and meetings and partings, of Zeppelin attacks and rumour; of WAACS in their khaki caps, women motor drivers and women window cleaners in their trousers, dubbed 'rationals', women tram conductors – though not inspectors, for they were not popular with the conductresses themselves; Special Constables and National Salvage Collections; of suburban allotments where older men grew food, and of 'queues' for shop food from seven in the morning. There was a new Daylight Saving Bill and a great shortage of food, even of potatoes. At whist drives there were prizes of potatoes and of little lumps of sugar in bags which you could then take with you if you went to a friend's for a cup of tea. London, in short, was transformed, and, in Sophie's view, rather exciting.

Sophie was finally beginning to admit to herself that she and Grant would not be together after the war. For a time they did nothing and did not allude to it, though both realized it. But in January 1917 an experience, freely chosen by her, was a turning point in her life. It was then, in the depths of war, that she found she was pregnant. Consulting Grant, who looked upset, pale and worried, for he had been on fire-duty the night before, she was told that she must do what she thought best.

'If you want me to have it, I will,' she said repeatedly. But he only looked at her fearfully and repeated, 'You must decide, my darling. It's your life that would be changed.'

For five days, in the midst of a rush at the Ministry where she was dealing with casualty figures and getting home late and tired, she 'considered'. She knew he would stand by her whatever she did, but marriage was out of the question. Even if she finally married Grant, the child would be illegitimate. That did not worry her. But when she thought of spending the rest of her life as an outcast from her family, unless she could hide the child from them, and that would be absurd; when she considered the war, and even the possibility of defeat; when she finally approached the greatest question of all, which was, did she love Grant enough for their love to continue in spite of a child, she realized that a child would change not only her present life, but would mortgage her future to his. She brushed aside considerations of money and lodging – they were irrelevant – realizing that her freedom mattered more. And yet ... She wanted a baby, she wanted to be as brave as Edith had been. If she could have gone home to affection and comfort in her difficulties and received a welcome, even if her parents had been, initially, upset, she would have had the child. But she knew that once back, she would not be able to escape again, knew that Grant was terrified of confronting her family, and she did not think the beginnings of such a new life auspicious.

She told him of her thoughts one February morning, after sitting up all night with them. Beatrice Osborn had advised her that she could have an abortion. It could be reasonably safely carried out, and she knew doctors who would do it for a fee, had done it for their own girlfriends. Apparently, if they were careful to use sterile instruments to empty the womb completely, it was perfectly feasible.

'If you can pay,' Sophie said nervously to Grant, 'we can have it aborted, but we must be quick. It's much more dangerous later.' She veered from one emotion to another. If only she could have this child and settle down with Grant and be accepted by his family as his wife. But she had no hopes of his really wanting that, and when he replied, 'If you are sure,' she felt the die was cast. It was to be *her* decision.

'But what about you?' she cried. 'Wouldn't you want my child, Grant? Couldn't you go north with me and speak for me to my family? Couldn't you divorce Violet one day, even if we couldn't get married at first?'

'It's you I want, not a baby,' he said heavily.

'If I get rid of it, I shall get rid of any other child of ours. You know what that will mean?' she cried, hoping against hope that he would decide for her, one way or the other.

'What a world to bring a child into,' was all he said then. 'I wish with all my heart that it had not happened. I don't want you to dwindle into a wife and mother.' He loved her because she was young and free and untrammelled.

She thought, it would have happened sooner or later. Their affair was not five years old and she was surprised it had not happened before. After all, that was what sexual love led to. 'I do want a baby, one day,' she said slowly. 'But not if you feel like this. It must be ours, chosen freely, because you want it too. If Violet would divorce you we could get married and live together for ever.' In her heart of hearts she did not want to blackmail him into marriage. And neither did she want to return home as a repentant outcast. If Grant would show any enthusiasm at all she would have the child, even without a wedding ring. He did not. And if he had really envisaged a divorce, he would have

224

left Violet already. At some level, abortion was to do with the failure of love: Grant's selfish love for her and her own fear of hurting her own parents who, if they truly loved her, ought to welcome a grandchild. But they would not. They would be shocked and angry and ashamed. She caught herself imagining what the child would be like, but firmly turned her mind away from such luxuries and arranged to see the doctor friend of Beatrice's. He examined her in a dingy room in a dingy flat off the Earls Court Road and pronounced her pregnant.

'Fifty pounds in cash, Friday evening, and don't mention it to anyone else,' were his terms. 'Except your man, of course,' he said. 'Will he find the cash?'

'Oh yes,' said Sophie. Money was no problem to Grant, even a lot of money, which fifty pounds was; nearly six months salary for her, in fact, if she had been working for him. She shut her mind to any further implications.

Grant insisted on taking her to the place and returning for her three hours later. He looked, in fact, more scared than she felt, but he said nothing else and produced the money.

Sophie would always remember the doctor, who was not Beatrice's friend, but an Irishman, whom she only hoped had a steady hand. There was a woman friend of his there too, a nurse. She was given ether, after being strapped up as though in a hospital, and woke feeling sick.

'All over,' said the man, quite pleasantly. 'A curettage. You "caught" it in good time.'

Her head swam a little, but he said that it was the effect of the anaesthetic. 'You've a jolly good heart and a powerful pair of lungs,' he said, pocketing the cash which she had put on a table on arrival.

Sophie made a speech about him being a benefactor of mankind and he looked rather sheepish. It was true that she felt inexpressibly relieved.

'You may feel sick, but go to bed anyway; it will just be like an ordinary period,' he said, and led her downstairs to where Grant was waiting in the hall, with a hansom cab outside.

They said little as they drove to the eyrie, and Sophie got upstairs before she was actually sick. 'Rest for forty-eight hours,' had been the doctor's last words and, as it was a weekend, she did. She went to work as usual on Monday, amazed that it had been so simple, expecting something would go wrong.

'Medically, it need not be difficult,' Beatrice said. 'You run more risk from the anaesthetic. Did he have a nurse with him?'

'Yes, there was a middle-aged woman there who helped me dress.'

'Women do it with knitting needles and bleed to death,' said Beatrice. 'They don't clear it out properly, you see – goes septic. And most doctors won't do 'em.'

Sophie was glad that she had not known about the dangers of anaesthetics or septic conditions. She had had a lucky escape, perhaps too lucky. She continued to feel nothing but relief, decided she would help other women if they ever needed it and grumbled as to why women had no contraceptives available.

'Because women are not free,' said Beatrice, who had an answer for everything.

But Sophie's feelings, as time went on, were not so clear-cut. She found an initial squeamishness about continuing to sleep with Grant change into a desire to know other men, a need to experience freedom, to choose for herself. It was, in fact, a presaging of the end of their mutual love, although their affair stumbled on for a time. Other considerations paradoxically entered her life: a revulsion against the killing, not of embryos, but of live young men who were being slaughtered daily on the battlefields of France, in their hundreds and thousands, at all the battles of the Great War. It was shared by growing numbers of her acquaintances who were both socialists and pacifists. Whilst not actually sharing either of these beliefs, she agreed that this war seemed pointless, the reasons for it not justifiable, and that a negotiated peace was urgently necessary. The war seemed, too, to provide a context of meaninglessness, against which she should strive to impose meaning in the pattern of her own life.

She felt reckless, dissatisfied, and had time in the spring of 1917 to take stock of that life. What if she were to die in a Zeppelin attack on London? What would she leave on earth? Less than many of those young men who were dying over in France. Not even a child of her own.

Grant had had to go down to Chimneys, which was now commandeered as a convalescent home. Sophie had told him just before he went, not for the first time, that she could not see a future for them together. By chance, at a gathering at Kitty Moray's, she met Austin Speight, who was on a short leave before returning to France. Kitty had just returned from France herself – civilians were still allowed in the south – and was back alone. Frank was working on a farm in Berkshire as a conscientious objector. It had been a hushed, strange evening and Austin had been sombre. He had been sure that Toby was on leave too, but could not find him at his usual haunts. Garnett Edwards had been there with a young subaltern and they had drunk coffee made from chicory and discussed the various war horror stories that were coming through from the front about the incompetence of the British High Command. On an impulse she had invited Austin back with her and, immediately they found themselves at the eyrie, without further conversation, they had made love. Something had seemed to snap in Sophie. For half an hour she enjoyed a physical passion, afterwards feeling no regret, no compunction. She had always liked Austin and found him intriguing, though she imagined he thought she was attractive but ignorant, and knew nothing of his real interests. She was surprised to find herself responding quite simply as a young woman to a young man. Austin was not simple and neither did she love him. She sensed depths and ambiguities even through his initially tentative and then greedy love-making and was not surprised when, afterwards, he had sobbed in her arms before falling asleep.

When at midnight the front door-bell was rung, she had woken him and they had both gone down to see. Mrs Mac was away. Sophie could not make out the figure behind the door from the blacked-out porch, and for a terrible moment thought it might be Grant. The square was shrouded and still, with no moon and no wind, dead. When they unbolted the door it was to confront a telegraph boy.

'It's from Edith,' she said, puzzled, as they moved together under the hall light, having carefully shut the door in case a chink of light should escape outside.

'From Edith Bartholomew' was written at the top of the telegram and then the message: 'To Sophie. Clem was killed on Tuesday 13th at Arras. Jack and I send our love. Edith.'

Austin took it from her and they leaned together, stunned and trembling. She could still feel the soreness on her neck where Austin had rubbed his badly-shaven face and she put up her hand to it and it was as if Clem had kissed her there at last.

Sophie went on with her War Office work, knowing she was still vulnerable in London, for there had been more aeroplane bombardments with civilian casualties. Something new was in the air, even so. Women were much freer than before the war and could even walk alone in the streets at night without being taken for prostitutes or risking their reputations. She often thought of Clem as she walked home alone, though he belonged now to another time, another world. Austin had rejoined his unit in France and had not written to her. She had written a very long letter herself to Edith.

One evening she took a tram up Southampton Row and recognized in one of the women conductresses the figure of small Chlöe from the Doughty Street days. Chlöe recognized Sophie, too, and for a moment they exchanged quick questions and answers.

'I'm married now, to a chap from the art school,' said Chlöe cheerfully. 'He's got TB. We've a little place in Balham. What happened to that poetic fellow you liked, the good-looking one?' she asked, as Sophie was just about to get off.

'He married Edith – they had a little boy – but Clem was killed at Arras,' Sophie stammered and saw Chlöe's shocked face recede as she stood on the platform of the tram with her little tickets. *She* looked happy, anyway.

The last year of the war was always a confusion in Sophie's mind, but the brief and briefly consummated relationship with Austin left her feeling only relief. For so long she had been accustomed to consider Grant in relation to everything she did or thought or planned, and the new freedom, although it brought with it sadness, was a little intoxicating. She found herself wondering what sort of a person she would have been if she had never become his lover, whilst at the same time honestly recognizing that she was more interesting to others because she had been. He should not have made her become what he had wanted to be for him. Yet without that experience, or with another man less worldly, less intellectual than he, she could have foundered into unsatisfied longings or unrequited love. She thought always of Clem, whom she had desired because of his youth and arrogance and his physical charisma. But Clem could have destroyed her, whilst Grant, in spite of his selfishness, had only added to her life and was preparing to do without her for the rest of his.

Neither Clem nor Grant, and certainly not Austin, was the ideal person of whom she had dreamed ever since adolescence. She knew now that such a person did not exist. She might as well create him for herself in her own mind and take what the world of other men offered. So for a time, whilst Grant was still away, she gave herself up to two or three flirtations, and more than flirtations, not because she was unhappy, but to test herself and to exploit for her own self the power she had to arouse men. She was not ashamed of it, but worried that her too soon 'recovery' from Grant meant that she was essentially a light person, a ball that bounced up and away after hurtling to the ground. And the tears for Clem still would not come; they seem locked away in a younger part of herself, though she wept for Edith and Jack. What, now, was there for her to lose when she had lost the child she should have had, if not from Grant, from someone?

Yet even at the time of her promiscuity, a period which lasted only a few months, she savoured more the times when she could be alone to look and consider and think, to read and weigh up the world. In the end she decided that freedom meant nothing if it led to her feeling that her own inner space was being encroached upon. What she needed was a steady love, for she would miss from Grant not his love, but the sharing times, reinforced by habit. What she wanted, selfishly, was someone who would provide her with children in exchange for loyalty and trust. How boring. She was surprised at herself.

When the printing works in Long Acre used by Miller and Penn were destroyed, Grant came back to London and, for a time, she drifted back to him. He always seemed to be grim-faced. He had offered to go and fight in France himself, but he was too old, and was rejected, though the call-up age was, in fact, to go up to fifty later that year. He was forty-seven. He became a Special Constable so that, when there were more air raids over London that summer, he had the opportunity to show great bravery in the rescue of several people trapped under rubble.

By the early autumn of 1918 they had got together again twice after intending to part for good, and twice she had returned to him. He knew of her occasional infidelities, but preferred not to think of them. The third time they parted she made the final break. He said his heart was broken and she had no reason to disbelieve him. But the memory of the child they had never had the courage to have, and also the conviction that her life must now be her own, gave her the courage to part from him. Just before the Armistice he made a sudden decision to go away with his wife to America. From there, he wrote that he had resolved to settle over there, to extend the business in New York. It was to be a new life, a life that would for ever exclude Sophie Ridsdale. She was stunned when it finally came over her that she had, in fact, lost him for good, but she was also relieved that he had been able to go, and wished him nothing but good. It was her failure, she decided. She had forced his hand and he had made the final decision for her.

Sophie was now nearly twenty-nine. The news of the extended franchise for women over thirty raised a faint feeling of pleasure in her, but not as intense as the pleasure of seeing the photograph of Edith's little son. Edith had already begun her hermit-like life at Far Ox Heys and was settled with Jack in a small farm cottage with a piece of land, where she was keeping hens and selling the eggs. Jack was now four, fair, and tall for his age. Edith kept a benevolent eye upon him, but had already begun a novel about an imaginary war between the forces of good and evil, set in the real landscape she saw around her every morning from her window. She was too busy to be unhappy and though she mourned Clement deeply and sincerely, Sophie thought she discerned in her letters, which were not introspective, a feeling of guilt that her independence had been preserved. She had kept only half of Clem's officer's pension and had given the rest to his mother in Wiltshire, whom she had finally met only after Clem's death.

Sophie wrote to Edith: 'How could I not adore your little boy, child of two people I loved; for I did love Clem, though I knew nothing would ever come of it. It seems tasteless and wrong to say that now, after all that has happened, but I had to say it. Clem loved you and he loved his country, but perhaps he was, too, a little in love with death. And he was quixotic. He once said to Austin (Austin told me) that if he were ever killed in the war you would get an officer's widow's pension. If he hadn't married you, you would have been entitled to nothing, nor Jack either. He had you for a little time, and Jack, and a brave death. And he was a good, perhaps a great, poet. What a terrible waste. There was I thinking only of love, and of the consequences of love for women, and Clem had no future at all. I can't bear it. Kiss Jack for me, Edie, and come to see me one day from your northern heights, for I don't know what is going to happen to me.'

It was Sophie now who was finding life unreal. Her adventurous brother, Harry, who had served in the Mercantile Marine, did not come back from the war. She was able to talk a little about him and about Clem to Sebastian Harman, who had returned safely from his work as a war artist. Austin did not come back either. He had survived Paschendaele, had gone down to Trouville and thence to Étaples just before the end of the war during the German bombardment of civilians, which he had also survived. There, he succumbed to the dreaded Spanish influenza a month or two later.

Willy, the office boy, called up in 1915, had seen the slaughter of most of his officers and mates on the Somme, had been gassed, but had clung on to life and was actually at Chimneys when the place was still a convalescent home after the Armistice.

It was a long time before the confirmation of 'missing' was attached to the name of Toby Watson, who had led his men over the top at the third battle of Ypres. He had disappeared after dragging a comrade back into a shell-hole for safety. This death, because it had happened to someone whom she liked, but not loved, who had seemed so solid and kind and sensible, who had joked and looked at her quizzically, shattered Sophie's old convictions that somehow, somewhere, she could find a meaning in existence. By 1919 the password was 'survival'. The world had become a different place, a place of danger and fear and of suffering to her. And Sophie Ridsdale; she, too, was a different person.

Sophie was in Trafalgar Square on Armistice Day 1919 when the processions were passing under Admiralty Arch. It was a rainy, cold, windy day and the quiet crowds, all dressed in black, many clutching their handkerchiefs, their faces tearful, partook in a funeral rite, not a day for the celebration of victory. She had already returned to the office a few weeks before. What else could she do?

Theodora Carmichael was there in the square, for she was a chauffeuse and was driving an admiral up to Buckingham Palace. Solemn music was being played. Theo looked smart in her WRNS costume of sailor collar and black buttons which she was wearing specially for the occasion. She had heard, that morning, that Miller and Penn's had offered her her job back.

Beatrice Osborn was in the square too, in VAD uniform, and Cicely Emery was marching past in the uniform of the nursing yeomary. Each was thinking of all the work needing to be done on behalf of women, now the war was over. Beatrice wished to help a friend in the founding of an association that would help women to plan their families; Cicely was going to write of her experiences in France. War was the fault of men, and only a radical alteration in society would avoid future wars. She had rejoiced in the opportunities for women that war had brought about, but was sad that it had needed a war for them to do it, and sadder still at all she had seen of man's inhumanity to his own species. Now, if women were in charge . . .

Sophie was remembering her dull, but necessary, job in wartime London that had ended six months before and wishing she had taken her courage in both hands and gone to France. It was Grant who had kept her in London just when she could have gone away to do her bit. And Grant was now thousands of miles away.

Next to her on the pavement was a young man who looked vaguely familiar, but she could not at first place him. Was it perhaps one Christmas morning long ago when she had glimpsed a dark, clean-shaven young man coming out of Miller and Penn's; a man who had looked at her for a moment? Was not this the same face? Then, on his other side, she recognized Grant's stepson, Fabian, who had now reverted to his father's name of Trevelyan. Fabian, recognizing his father's old mistress, bowed politely and introduced her to the dark young man. They got into conversation, Sophie and the two men, and went for a drink afterwards on St Martin's Lane. It seemed that the young man, whose name was Michael Carr, was to join Fabian at the firm, which was now to be called Miller, Carr and Trevelyan. Fabian appeared to know that Sophie was working for them, though she had not seen him recently. He intended, he told her, to rejoin his stepfather in New York. He had not been in the war in France because of a 'heart', though she thought he looked quite healthy.

'America's the only place to be now,' he said as they walked towards Bloomsbury in the thinning crowds. Michael Carr paid her attention when Fabian went off on his own devices and continued to do so over the next few months, when they would meet at work and after work.

He proposed marriage to her in December 1920 and she accepted him.

two

CONTINUINGS

1

Far Ox Heys

'The soul's dark cottage, batter'd and decay'd,
Lets in new light through chinks that time has made.'

Edmund Waller: Last Verses

Edith Bartholomew looked up from her noisy little typewriter
when she heard the postman's tramp up to the back door of
her stone cottage at Far Ox Heys. Perhaps today would bring a
letter from Sophie Carr, dear Sophie, who was always, according
to herself, frantically busy, but always had time to write long
letters, at least to Edith. The postman, old Holmes, liked to
stop for a chat, but today she was busy with the re-writing of a
boring tale and could not really spare the time. She waved to him
instead and he waved a letter back at her before putting it on the
window-sill outside, and stomping back to his walk. 'Busy with
her machine,' he said to the dog, who always accompanied him
on this part of his travels. Mrs Bartholomew was well-known
in the district, though she would have been surprised to know
how well, and that some called her the lady hermit. They said
it quite kindly, of course. Her son, Jack, they knew better; a
nice lad with no side to him. They often saw him, out with his
paints, which he carried in the basket of his bicycle. When Jack
was little his school-friends had said his mother was a witch, till
he had punched them and they had stopped.

Edith decided to finish her page before retrieving the letter.
If it were from Sophie she would read it in the afternoon when
she had tidied up a bit and decided what she would give Jack
for his tea. She sighed, but persisted with her typing, and soon
the page was done. She flexed her wrists. Often her hands were
very stiff when she had typed for several hours. A good thing she
had other duties to keep her fit. Yes, the letter *was* from Surrey,

in Sophie's inimitable hand. She put it by the old clock over the range and savoured it in anticipation.

As she got out the ironing board, having decided that Jack's grammar school shirt must be pressed, she was musing, letting thoughts come into her head without prompting. She found ironing, along with most practical tasks, very restful to the brain and some of her best ideas arrived when she was sweeping or feeding the hens or scrubbing the floor. Today, though, she took some time to rid her mind of the Constantine mystery, the next blank page of which was already fixed in her little Remington. That sort of writing ought to be done in a trance in the middle of the night, or if possible, whilst asleep. Edith had had some of her best Bevis Constantine notions arrive in this way.

She looked critically at the shirt. Jack would soon need some new ones. He was growing so fast, had, at fifteen, not yet achieved his full height, but already overtopped his mother. She wished she could see Sophie's children whom she had so far looked at only on snapshots, but she had the fixed disinclination to leave Far Ox Heys. She would go one day, would know when she was ready, but it was not yet. She often worried about her friend who seemed sometimes rather fed up with her domestic existence, though Edith suspected that most of the annoyances were compensated for by her obvious pride in her girls. Three of them now; the youngest, little Clementine Edith, three years old. Sophie liked to pour out her problems to Edith and once they were on the page probably forgot about them. There didn't seem to be anything wrong with her children, they were all remarkably clever and remarkably pretty, but Sophie was a worrier. Edith had had only Jack to worry about, but an only child might be even more precious. One could not, of course, say one loved him three times more than if he were one of three.

Sophie and she had written to each other ever since Sophie's marriage to Michael Carr; she was her link with the big world outside, though Sophie protested she hardly ever saw much of London now, so caught up was she in domestic life. That Michael should have insisted on renting Chimneys from Fabian Trevelyan, who was now in the States with his stepfather, was perhaps not odd. She wondered if Sophie had ever objected. The firm was doing reasonably well now that the war had been over for ten years, though the slump in most businesses precluded large profits. Bevis Constantine went on merrily and even Michael did not know that Edith wrote most of it. She had managed with this money and with part of Clem's pension (she had insisted that the other half still went to Clem's mother in Wiltshire) and a little from the sale of eggs, plus an occasional helping hand from her father, the latter only for Jack's sake, not her own.

Sophie, on the other hand, was quite well off, though she insisted on bringing up her children without a nurse or nanny and with only the help of a girl from the village. Edith gathered that the large garden of Chimneys preyed on her friend's mind, so that Michael had decided to employ a gardener full-time. The Carr children were having a very different childhood from the one Jack had had in their village on its Pennine slope that overlooked a tributary stream of the River Calder. Sophie said she envied her, but Edith could not see Sophie restricted to a small northern village and with no one with whom to have a proper conversation.

Edith did not mind. At first she had found the lack of congenial company rather soothing. It meant she could concentrate on what was in her head. Recently, she had begun to feel that perhaps she ought to make the effort to go to Leeds and mix a little more with her own kind. But she was not sure who her own kind were. The prospect of having to explain herself to strangers filled her with horror, though the 'behind glass' feeling seemed to have gone, had begun to melt away when she had Jack. Having Jack had made her feel an ordinary member of the human race. Jack's early years had been happy ones for Edith and she had never regretted coming to Far Ox Heys. Jack, too, seemed to take it for granted. Why should he not? He had been to the elementary school in the village, where at least the foundations of literacy had been quite successfully laid, and had made friends with the other children at the Calderbrigg National School before going at ten to the little Elizabethan grammar school at the top of the hill, to which he had won a scholarship without undue effort. Painting, though, was what he was really good at, and had been ever since at the age of three when she had found him drawing patterns with his Christmas chalks, patterns which seemed to Edith rather wonderful.

Those early days had been what Sophie called 'gossamer days'. Each day a fragile new web to be spun, always slightly different from the web of the day before, but connected to it by the strong threads of habit and loving parents. Well, Edith had had to be the only parent, and Jack's gossamer days were over now. She smiled as she finished the shirt and put away the board. She reached up for the letter and placed it on her kitchen table along with two eggs on a plate, a loaf of bread and a bowl of apples. She filled the heavy black kettle at the tap and put it on the fire of the range that heated the room and also served to heat the oven where she baked her own bread. Edith boiled herself the eggs and sat down to read the latest instalment of Sophie's life.

Sophie had promised again and again to come north, but something had always prevented her: a childish illness, repairs to the house, Michael away in Europe. But as Edith read on, she discovered that Sophie intended, at last, to visit. The letter was shorter than usual and Edith discovered why. Mr Ridsdale had died and Sophie and Michael were to come north for the funeral. Michael insisted that she come over from Thirksay to see her old friend in the West Riding. He would manage the household in her absence with the help of Joyce, the mother's help, and the cleaning lady, and so on. And Sophie was to take her time. They were just off for the funeral. Edith looked at the date and discovered that Sophie might be arriving in a day or two; would Edith please telegraph Thirksay if it were not convenient, but Sophie did so hope it would be. She longed to see her. How had she managed without her? What a long talk they would have! And she wanted to see Jack. Her children were not to accompany her this time, too much of an upheaval. Phoebe was only seven and Rosamund five, but they were at school, while Clemmie loved being with Joyce and there would be no problem there. Edith finished her boiled eggs, chewed on her apple and mentally went over the preparations necessary for Sophie's visit. Jack would be pleased. Sophie had always sent him such lovely presents: an easel last birthday and oil paints (chosen, she said, by Seb, whom she still saw from time to time on her infrequent visits to town).

Edith read the letter again. How old would Sophie's father have been? She remembered him so well from that idyllic holiday before the war, before everything, she supposed. Before Jack. Before Clem. Edith remained for several minutes staring into the fire which she had banked up and which was so enticingly hot that she knew that if she remained by it she would fall asleep. With a slow gesture she pushed wisps of hair behind her ear and twisted it into a fair bun at the nape of her neck. The hair was a little faded from its pale gold now, but her face was unlined as yet. What would Sophie look like now? In the snapshots she appeared to have lost none of her vivacity, though Edith, when she looked closely, could see that the eyes looked more tired than she remembered. She would be forty at the end of the year. Edith never thought of herself as being of any particular age, but suspected that forty would be, to Sophie, some great bridge to be crossed. Somehow, one could not think of Sophie as approaching middle-age. Sophie should always be young. Edith was filled with a rush of tenderness for her old friend. Dear Sophie. She did so hope she was happy on the whole, though she seemed to have given herself an overdose of duty. Edith was the only person who suspected that, for Sophie, marriage had been a lottery, but one where at least she expected the winning numbers of her lot to be children.

Jack was on his way home. Some of the others were staying behind for rugger practice, but he was not wanted. He had used to play wing, but found the game tedious. He often wondered what his father had been like physically. Everyone always said he looked like his mother, but now he was almost grown up he had begun to think more about the physical reality of the dead father he had never known. He was going to be taller than his father, Edith said, and had always been fairer. Had his father played football? Edith would not know. Jack always sensed some reticence in her descriptions of him. Granny Tolley, his father's mother, had known a quite different Clement Bartholomew, about whom she spoke when Jack went on his annual holiday to visit her in Wiltshire. He liked Wiltshire and its very different countryside, but his first allegiance was to Yorkshire. He loved Ox Heys and the moors. If his father had lived he might never have known Calderbrigg.

Jack was not a particularly shy person, but he was, like his mother, very self-sufficient. His mother had always been different from the mothers of the other boys and he had always accepted that. They had not much money, though Grandpa Broughton was rather rich, he suspected, with his maid and his Morris motor and the gardener who tended his privet hedges. He liked Grandpa Broughton. Grandma, he was less sure about. She used to give him books at Christmas and for his birthday, but never books which showed she really knew the sort of person he was. Last birthday his grandfather had given him a book about scientific experiments and she had said, 'He gets enough of that at School, Wilf.' He and his grandfather had long conversations about science and geography and history and religion and got on very well together. But when Wilfred Broughton realized that Jack was set on being a painter he had looked rather worried. Jack knew that he would have liked him to join the firm, but that was not likely. As far as he remembered he had only wanted to draw and paint. School work ws boring; not difficult, just boring. He learned far more from his talks with his grandfather than from school, where science was not 'real' science, history, not 'real' history, but just something you mugged up for School Cert.

Jack had, in his time, been a champion player of marbles, a bird-watcher, and an explorer, but now he felt he wanted to concentrate on reading and painting. He was torn between his own observations and what was written about in books. Edith had rather a lot of books, mostly picked up second-hand from Fred Power's shop in Bradford market, and there were surely enough there at home without bothering with school. Oh well, once he had got the School Cert, he would see. He planned already to go to the art school in Leeds. His way home this afternoon was rather circuitous. He liked walking, could think as he walked, and came round now, down near the Syke Wells, by the rhubarb fields where he used to paint marsh marigolds in summer. None there yet, though spring had come. He had always been the one with the 'first finds' at his other school; coltsfoot and shepherds' purse in February and later the blue-bells and vetch. His picture of the blue bugle – found on the railway embankment at the other end of the village – still hung, framed by Edith, on his bedroom wall, over the carved angel which his Granny Tolley, as he called her, had given him. It had been sculpted by his father when he was only eight. Jack had tried wood-carving, but the wood in Far Ox Hey's woods was not suitable. His dad had been a writer – he had a book of his poems. There was a poem about an otter and he wanted to see if there were any otters when he went walking with his mother in another, further valley. His mother said she had once seen one in Thirksay, where Aunt Sophie had lived. His father had never been there, she said. He wondered, as he neared home now, whether Edith would be out feeding the hens in her old coat or cooking their tea or at her typewriter. Mother and the typewriter were almost one, a sort of composite figure. As for the hens – one winter his mother had even taken the weakest into her back kitchen!

He quickened his footsteps. 'Hello, Jack,' said an old acquaintance from his national school days and he said, "'lo Roy,' and went on his way. Roy's dad was unemployed. There were many like him now in the village. The farms were small and depended on selling milk, and the textile factories in the neighbouring towns were cutting back. He remembered the General Strike, he had not understood it, when he was only twelve. Now it was a 'Depression', and he imagined a heavy pall of smoke hanging over the towns. Except that in a Depression the towns were freer from smoke and that was bad because it meant there was no work.

When he arrived at the top of the hill, which he could perfectly well have reached a much shorter way, the rag rugs from the kitchen were hanging on a line in the yard. He took up the carpet-beater that Edith had left on the flags and gave the rugs a few hearty thwacks. Edith was in the kitchen and the table was laid for two. He was always hungry these days and this was the best meal of the day.

'Maths homework,' he said as he finished the gammon and eggs and the fresh bread and home-made crab-apple jelly and washed it down with a mug of tea. 'Quadratics – did you ever do them, Mum?'

'I think so,' said Edith. 'I heard from Aunt Sophie, Jack. She's coming on a visit!'

'Coming here? When?'

'Oh, Thursday, I think, though she'll probably telegraph the time. She's in Thirksay – her father's died. She's so looking forward to seeing you. Do you remember when you were little and I took you to Thirksay? You were about seven and she'd just got married.'

'I remember the pig on the farm,' said Jack. 'And a nice dark man. Was he her husband?'

'Yes, that was Michael Carr. I think he *is* nice.'

'Is he coming too?'

'No, she's coming on alone from the funeral. I'll bake some fresh bread and get the little room ready. Perhaps you'll be able to visit her soon, one day. I wonder what she'll think of Far Ox Heys.'

Jack considered his mother dispassionately. He had heard such a lot about Aunt Sophie and thought of her as a mixture of Sleeping Beauty and the English teacher's wife at school. His mother said that Sophie always dressed in bright colours and smoked black cigarettes and she was the best friend Edith had ever had.

'She knew Dad, didn't she?' asked Jack.

'Oh, yes, she did.' Edith thought, I wish I could tell him that she loved his father, but that was a private thing. Still, one day she was sure that Sophie would talk to him about his father if he asked.

Later, when Jack had done his quadratic equations and was sitting reading an adventure story by the fire – he seemed to need something undemanding at the end of the long day, – Edith found her thoughts turning to the past, the unimaginable past, when the Jack, who now sat solid and absorbed by her fire, was not even conceived. How far away it all seemed! Did Sophie, too, think of it as the Time Before, as she did?

Sophie Carr, a day or two later, on the trains to Bradford and thence to Calderbrigg, trains which she had taken after one journey to Harrogate and then another to Leeds, was feeling equally dislocated. There had been all the worry of leaving her children, though she was sure Joyce would cope, and a friend from the village near Chimneys was to drop in daily. Then there had been the funeral, when she had tried to remember her father as he had been, and tried to have the appropriate thoughts for a funeral, and failed. Then Michael had rushed off in Leeds on to the London train and here she was now, alone. How black the town buildings were, she thought; but when the next train pulled

244

out from Bradford and she had despaired of seeing anything but mill dams or derelict yards, suddenly the landscape changed and she saw high hills in the distance and a church on a ridge, and a wonderful sunset over that, and her heart gave a lift. She was nervous though. Silly to be nervous when she was at last to see Edith. Edith knew more about her from her letters than anyone who saw her every day.

The train suddenly stopped on a viaduct and Sophie, tired of looking at a sepia scene of Llandudno and a faded one of Ullswater, took out her mirror and lipstick and touched up her face. She wondered if Edith wore lipstick. It was not the sort of thing you wrote about. Absurd, that they should not have met for so long. Things would be easier when her children were a little older. Michael did not want *her* to be a hermit. That was all right for a woman like Edith who had other compensations, though she chuckled when she thought that even her husband knew nothing of Edith's part in his best-selling Constantine. Michael was a kind husband and she half wished he were here now, except you could not talk properly to your best friend with your husband there. Women acted differently when men accompanied them, and Edith had no husband. It would not be fair. She had told Edith, of course, all about Michael; the important bits, anyway, and she had met him once, of course, in Thirksay, after their marriage. But she thought Edith would not be used to married life, never having had any to speak of, would not be used to having to think of another adult all the time. She powdered her nose, licked her finger and curled her eyelashes up and lit a cigarette, still thinking about Edith. Thoughts of Edith led naturally to memories of Clem. Would Jack now resemble him more? If Clem had lived, would he still be with Edith? Unfair to give an imaginary future to a man who had been killed, but she had often wondered. Edith would have stayed with him, but she would not have been able to write so much or to be so independent. Edith had once confessed as much in a letter to her. Clem's death had released her, she said, into the selfishness a writer needed. It was true she had Jack to look after, but children got used to your ways.

Why did Edith not write about the countryside around here? wondered Sophie, looking out of the window again. The moors were not far away and there were hills and sloping fields and dry-stone walls on every side. Perhaps Edith did and had said nothing about it to her. She had been very occupied writing Bevis Constantine's potboilers for him, but Sophie was sure that Edith must have other writings tucked away. The Moon series and the *Mysteries of Moor and Fen* were not ill-written, Edith could not write badly if she tried, but the subject matter was hardly what Edith wanted to write about.

Sophie brought her mind back from speculation over Edith's writings to speculation about Edith's intimate life. Edith had never said, but Sophie assumed that she led a celibate life up here in the wilds. There would scarcely be the opportunity for anything else, though possibly in Leeds she might find a kindred spirit or two. But perhaps she did not want to. She had always been so reserved. How would Edith cope with Sophie's own life, with a businessman for a husband? For, after all, publishers were businessmen or they went out of business. She could not imagine Edith marrying a man like Michael. The son of a Viennese woman and a British businessman who had made a fortune manufacturing 'Lucky Dips' – children's toys and sweets in mysterious brown paper bags – he had proceeded to other innovations, including little stories for children given away with the brown bags, and as a result his money had gone to making an Englishman out of Michael, who had been packed off to boarding school to learn manners and social etiquette. That was where he had met Fabian Trevelyan of course.

Sophie's first child, Phoebe, had inherited much of her father's family's dark, dapper looks and also the family talent for languages. Sophie checked that she had brought the latest photographs of her three children for Edith to see. There was Rosamund, so much more a Ridsdale with her navy blue eyes and brown hair, and little Clemmie, the sturdiest of the three, a child who preferred digging in the garden and making houses to acting stories as Rosamund did, or reading as Phoebe had done when she was only three.

Now that Michael was pretty much in charge at Gower Place he had started a new series of *Facts for the Layman*. Perhaps Edith might contribute something on English history; those Norsemen she had once been so interested in? She must be careful, though, not to overwhelm her with suggestions. Michael believed the

246

public should be educated as well as entertained; there was enough of the foreigner in him for him to have a touching belief in education. Sophie was not so sure. Michael, though, did not read much fiction – he left that to her. She had even brought some novels with her in her case. Perhaps there was something indecent about that, going to your father's funeral with a bag of books? Her mind still leapt off in all directions once she was released from the burden of domesticity. She hoped she was a good mother, thought she was, but it was an effort. Michael was a good father – when he was at home. Of course, men could always escape the home and go to work. She could not do that; the responsibility of three children did not allow for it.

She 'read' a little for Michael and offered suggestions for reprints now and then, but she could not concentrate long enough to have a proper job. One day, perhaps, she might; though there was not much for women nowadays to do, in a slump, when so many men were out of work. And they did not really need any money she might earn. She had enough to do educating her children, for that was where children did their learning – at home. The children were, she thought, happy; certainly they were always busy, seemed to have inherited their father's energies. Life at Chimneys suited children.

If, fifteen years ago, someone had told her that she would have lost Grant but gained his house, and that it would be filled with children of hers who were not Grant's, would she have believed them? She had tried to put the stamp of her own personality on the place; bright cushions and draped scarves and jugs of wild flowers, and herbs in the garden, though she was not a good gardener. Edith would doubtless be a good gardener. Edith would hate the other aspects of life at Chimneys: the entertaining and the noise.

Even Bea Osborne, who came occasionally for dinner, found it noisy. Bea had never married and was too busy with her birth-control work to spare much time for the idea of children. Sophie's own three she seemed quite to like, though she always had a cynical look in her eyes, Sophie thought, when she talked to her about them. Sophie thought Bea did not take her seriously, was sceptical of her protestations of interest in the wider world. Sophie had 'settled down' and that was that. Married women were another species. Would Edith appear 'married', or more like Bea? She must not talk too much about her children to Edith and bore her. The trouble was that, spending all your time with them, you could not help doing so, even though you sometimes felt dissatisfied with your life. But, after all, what could be more important than bringing up the next generation? How shocked she would have been twenty years ago to overhear herself thinking that! She loved small doses of playing in the garden with Clemmie and even large ones reading stories aloud to them all. That was the pleasant part of life with children. She would be sorry when she could no longer buy toys or games for them. All the teething and toddling and infectious diseases and chaos would one day slide back into perspective, she supposed, and what would be left would be the time she had played with them, talked to them, read to them, answered their questions. At least, she hoped so. She was a possessive mother, but did not truly love all children. Only these three, because they were hers. That was what most people were like, when all was said and done. What would Jack be like? She began again to feel nervous as the train slid through a tunnel and then drew up at the Calderbrigg station, two miles, she gathered, from Edith's cottage. There was an old car in the yard, she saw, but no sign of Edith. She alighted and a man came forward.

'Mrs Carr? I've to take you over yonder to Ox Heys, in the car, Mrs Bartholomew said.'

He took her bags and Sophie thought, at least I shall have a few more minutes to prepare myself. But when she saw Edith waiting at the gate of a little stone house down a rutted lane, over which the car had bumped merrily, she forgot everything except that here was Edie at last. Tall and smiling and not just older, but somehow – she saw straight away – more in charge of herself.

Edith saw a much plumper Sophie, with faint shadows under her eyes and bobbed hair that gave her a youthful appearance in spite of a certain heaviness around the waist. They kissed on the cheek and then drew back for another look. Sophie began immediately to talk about the journey; 'how lovely the skies were up here,' and stopped only when a tall youth came up and whisked away her case, before Edith could say, 'Here's Jack.' He came down soon after and shook hands and smiled.

How like Edith he was, and yet there was a touch of Clem, Sophie thought. Jack was thinking how glamorous the Sophie woman was. Eccentric, too, he guessed, but in a different way from his mother.

Edith said, 'You haven't changed – I would know that scent anywhere!: *Pétales Froissées*! Would you like a cup of tea first?'

Sophie said, 'Neither have you, you look very healthy,' and Edith led the way into the kitchen and put a kettle on the hob and they both sat down at the white wood table. Sophie saw how Edith's hands were roughened with outdoor work, such a contrast to her own which were still ring-encircled, in spite of her domestic duties.

'I expect Jack's changed most,' she said. Perhaps Edith *was* a little thinner; she wished she were herself, and there was more colour in her cheeks; but she was still the same Edith and, after the first few moments, they would be back, Sophie thought, just as they had always been. Edith was thinking, she does not look as dull and dreary as she says she sometimes feels!

'I can't believe it's nine years, it seems like just a few weeks when I really see you – in the flesh,' said Sophie. It was true, letters were wonderful, but they were not real. Here was Edith, real and smiling, and, yes, she *had* changed – and so had Sophie, herself. But their relationship was still going to be the same. When she was with Edith the annoyances of life seemed to fade away. They would come back, but they did not seem to matter. Edith took everything so calmly. Laying a cloth now, and putting some scones on the table that looked home-baked. Now if *she* had had to entertain Edith after such an absence, she would have been nervous and got everything ready for hours before and felt she was acting a part. Edith never acted a part, so you did not need to yourself. Jack was looking covertly at the visitor. She was pretty, seemed younger than Mum. Not a bit like her. He wondered what women talked about when they were together, never having heard his mother have a proper conversation with anyone but Grandpa Broughton.

Edith, however reticent, was mistress of the situation and Sophie relaxed. You did not have to pretend anything to Edith; it was more like being with children who accepted you whatever you said or did. 'How peaceful it is here,' she said as she munched the scones.

'It's noisy in autumn when the gales come,' said Edith. 'We'll show you round tomorrow. Are you tired? I was sorry about your father.'

'It's another world,' said Sophie, thinking things made more sense when she was with Edith. 'I suppose I ought to be tired,' she said. 'Somehow I feel more tired after a day with the children.' I don't get away enough, she thought. 'Yes, I *am* sad about Dad, and I ought to be worrying about the children, but what I feel most is thrilled to see *you*, Edith!'

Afterwards, when Sophie had been shown her tiny room, only big enough to hold a chest of drawers and a single bed, with a little mullioned window looking out over fields, they sat by the fire and Jack melted away. He was a nice boy, attractive too, with none of Clem's surliness.

'How lovely to have a nearly grown up son,' she said. 'I can't believe my children will ever grow up; we've stopped at three, though. Quite enough.'

Edith thought, there is so much to say, but it will get said if we take it slowly. She seems different, but I'm not sure how. Older, of course, and not always talking about herself – '

'Tell me more about your children,' said Edith. 'I'd love to see them, but at present I'm destined to stay here. I will see them one day; you must forgive me for being a bit of a hermit. I'm quite happy, you know.'

'Yes, I can see that.'

So Sophie talked about her children and her husband. And about wanting to do some work that was not just housework and family work, and about her anxieties and boredoms. Edith listened gravely.

'I know I have to go back to my world, but I do envy you your solitude.'

Edith found it difficult to describe her own daily life, as so much of it seemed to go on inside her head, but Sophie was an attentive listener. Edith had forgotten how Sophie listened. Sophie had always been a talker, but a good listener too.

'I don't do much,. I talk to Jack, and people in the village, just to pass the time of day, and I do my bits of work and dig in the garden.'

'And bake bread and keep pullets,' added Sophie.

Edith smiled, 'I'm a hausfrau, you see, like you.'

And then they talked of Jack again. And of her past. Edith brought out a bottle of whisky with great ceremony. 'Father gave it to me at Christmas, but I don't drink much. I'll have a glass with you.'

Sophie lit another cigarette. 'I do wish we could see each other more often. Life is just hurrying by since the end of the war – do you feel that? Things will never be the same again. And children growing up. I can't get used to being the "older generation".'

'Yes, I know,' replied her friend.

How queer life was! As they sat there, the years rolled away in spite of their both feeling that everything was bound to be different; feeling older, and being older, of course. 'It's like casting off a dinghy,' said Edith. 'Having a child, I mean. Once you've left the shore there's no turning back. You just have to go on till you come to another shore – '

'After shipwrecks and buffetings,' said Sophie.

At midnight Sophie said she was not tired, but Edith must be. 'It's such a luxury not to be running a house, even just for a few days. It really is *practical* life I hate, the mechanics of living; they take such a lot out of me.'

Finally Edith gave her a night-light and Sophie went to bed in the tiny room at the top of the twisting stairs. She slept, for once, deeply and dreamlessly and awoke to hear Edith calling to her hens in the yard. She lay for a moment wishing she did not have to go back the next day. Edith always cheered her up. Edith must come and stay with them. Now that she had seen Edith's life she wanted Edith to see hers.

Unusually for her, Edith had not slept very well. She put it down to whisky, which she was unused to drinking and which seemed to start lines of thought in her mind that she knew she must not pursue until she could sit down at her typewriter. She reviewed Sophie's conversation. She had spoken of her husband and of the publishing business, but had grumbled a good deal about Chimneys. It *was* ironic that Sophie should have lost Grant, but acquired a lease of his house. 'No, he'll never come back to England,' was all she had said about him and Edith had not pursued the subject.

Sophie's conversation had stirred up other memories, not so much of Clem, but of those days, years ago, on their holiday in

Thirksay. She remembered little Jerome, who had apparently emigrated to Australia, and Sophie's sister, Alice, who was married to her Ben and already the mother of two large sons. And Aunt Rose-Ann, who was dead, but whom Edith remembered better than anyone else on the farm. Thirksay had been lovely. She would like to run a farm like that. Now, apparently, it was neglected, according to Sophie, though there was an uncle still there farming.

Edith had lain quietly, thinking over all these people and how far away they seemed now, belonging to the life before Jack. But they were far enough away now to be vivid in her remembrance. Was she wrong to have cut herself off from everybody? Probably. It had been partly pride and partly wanting independence and time for her work. But it was true that she was content. Sophie seemed all right really. Perhaps this short visit would have put her day-to-day life in better perspective. There was a rather hectic gaiety sometimes in her manner, but there always had been. She had said she had not, she thought, fundamentally changed and Edith had agreed. But they had both changed in other ways, not too much, but enough. Perhaps Sophie felt more distanced from her old self than she did. Motherhood did change women, as long as they were still growing in themselves. Sophie had spoken, too, of a 'play-acting sort of existence', but Sophie always dramatized herself. She did have an exhausting life – Edith would not have wanted it. But she was amusing, full of anecdotes about her children. Sophie ought to have been a journalist, Edith thought. She, herself, now kept a sort of domestic diary and she might suggest that her friend did too. I always liked the fact that Sophie was open and generous with sharing bits of herself, thought Edith. Sophie asked many questions too, but rather shyly, as if she was not sure whether Edith wanted to go into details about her life. She had answered quite cheerfully, talked about her parents and about Jack, and then Sophie had brought out the photographs and filled in the details. Sophie had asked her if she was writing anything apart from the Constantine stories and she had lain back in her old armchair as Sophie smoked her cigarettes, and replied that, yes, she was writing an 'epic' about war and violence, set in a small village. But it was not publishable yet. The old clock had ticked away over the hearth.

Was she more direct than she had used to be? Perhaps she had a better estimate of herself now. Sophie had made her see that. 'You must send it to Michael when it's done,' Sophie had said. But it was not anything that would please a publisher's heart. People did not want to read about war. Though *her* war was the usual battleground between good and evil. She frowned as she lay awake. She had always hated talking about her writing, but Sophie had the right to know.

Jack had gone off to school by the time Sophie came down to a breakfast of Edith's pullets' eggs and home-baked bread. Then she insisted on helping her with the housework before they went on a little walk round the village. Sophie noticed that Edith seemed well-known there. 'I don't often do much shopping,' she confessed. 'They think of me as a hermit, Jack says. I don't mind that, as you know!'

Sophie wondered where the ideas for *Moon Mysteries* and *Serpents of the Deep* and the new series, *Mysteries of Moor and Fen*, came from. She would not have found much inspiration in Edith's village life, but she supposed that writers found their ideas inside themselves.

'Bevis Constantine, the real man, I mean – or should I say the fake Bevis, since you write his stuff? – has undertaken an interminable novel about Oscar Wilde cavorting in the White Russian cavalry,' said Sophie, as they leaned over a wall on the way back to Far Ox Heys. Edith burst out laughing. 'He's made this faintly disguised Wilde into a twentieth-century figure, but the trouble is, all Garnett's ideas are of the last century. I don't think he'll ever finish it and it will be quite unpublishable.'

'Does he still go for young men?' asked Edith.

'I think he tries, but he's too old for conquests. Sad, when queers get old. Is it sadder than old women, do you think?'

'Old women usually have families to sustain them, I suppose,' Edith replied. 'I wish I was more use to Mother. You know, she's never come round after all these years. Puts up with Jack, but never addresses more than a remark about the weather to me.'

'How ridiculous! I don't know what's to become of *my* mother. I think she'll go to live with Alice. She never got over my elder brother's death in the war.'

253

'Women are usually too busy,' said Edith, reverting to Edwards. 'To keep looking for love affairs, I mean. Or perhaps we make ourselves busy? I sometimes wonder.'

This was the nearest Sophie got, during her visit, to any indication of Edith's wishing to find a man with whom to spend the rest of her life. She did not pursue the subject.

'Tell me about Chimneys, Sophie. I always think you live in a novel, you know, one of the 'new' novels about emancipated women who believe in progressive ideas and keep up with politics and go to galleries and read the latest reviews.'

'Silly Edith! My life is hardly emancipated, you know. Bea's always telling me to get out and go to meetings and look for some work outside what she calls "The Home". *She's* very political, of course. I'd rather read novels, but that's hardly a "modern" hobby, is it?'

'What exactly does Bea do?'

'Oh, she runs a birth-control clinic. I expect I could help out there a day or two a week. I am serious about contraception at least!'

Edith had never met Bea, though Sophie had often mentioned her in letters. 'She says I have too much to do, but not enough to think about,' she added.

Edith did not like to criticize Sophie's friend, so said nothing.

'As she's never had any children she doesn't miss them. Wouldn't it be strange, now, if we had never had ours? What do you think we'd be doing? I expect you'd be writing anyway, and I'd be slaving away at Carr and Penn. I still think of it as Miller's, though, you know. I do think of Grant sometimes. What would he think of me now?'

'I expect he thinks of you too,' said Edith.

By the time they had arrived back for Sophie's second and last night with her friend, Sophie had heard about Edith's plans for another book on the Fabric of Norseland and listened, fascinated, to her descriptions of the research she wanted to do. What a sombre vision her friend had! But Edith insisted on hearing more about Phoebe and Rosamund and Clemmie and listened to Sophie, who poured out more details of her life, stopping occasionally to say she was sure she was boring her. But Edith got a clear picture, for Sophie talked well, of her southern British life: the festivities, the Christmases, the nursery toys, the games, the books the children liked ('You ought to write for children, Edith') the garden, the funny things the children said, the women she met who were married to successful barristers or publishers, the occasional party (she had gone off parties rather), the new slang.

They talked about Theo, who was now a powerful figure in the publishing world. She had never married. Cicely Emery seemed to have disappeared, but Cora Benson was still making speeches in favour of some new westernized Indian religious sect. 'Seb Harman hasn't changed much either,' added Sophie. 'Just a bit fatter. Cheers me up when I moan about the lot of women.' Seb Harman was, indeed, Sophie's present favourite person to talk to in London and a day spent over lunch with him and perhaps a visit to an art exhibition was a great treat if not a very frequent one. He had never married, taught at the Slade, ran a small studio of his own and had a tiny gallery off Cork Street.

'He says I can't still be a Feminist because Feminism presupposes equality,' she said. 'I tell him my Feminism comes more from ideas of justice and freedom, but he says, no, it's about equality and I can't believe in that because I'm a romantic. *You* used to say that!'

'I suppose love *could* be to do with equality?' murmured Edith.

'I suppose it can – for men,' replied Sophie. 'Men are allowed to be "romantic" about women. And they needn't worry about power, as they have it already over women.'

They were both silent for a minute, thinking about Clem.

'Seb always asks after you, you know,' said Sophie. 'He thinks that if I'd wanted freedom I wouldn't have married. I think he thinks I ought to be more like you.'

'Like me!' exclaimed Edith, astonished.

'He thinks you were wonderful; "shy and quiet and such a dear",' she quoted. Edith looked embarrassed. 'Well, you are a dear,' began Sophie.

'It's because he's like Garnett, loves men. I wasn't a threat,' said Edith. How perspicacious she was.

After 'dinner' on Sophie's last day they talked about books, or at least Sophie did and Edith said she supposed that plunging into the world of a novelist was as good a way as any of forgetting yourself.

'Confronting the imminent extinction of strangers,' quoted Sophie. 'Can't remember where I read that. I wish I could forget myself and be a creator, like you.'

'Creators have to have readers,' remarked Edith mildly.

'Oh, it's "Life" I wish to understand,' said Sophie in her grand manner.

Edith laughed. 'Don't we all?'

'But to impose a pattern of your own choosing on the – the flux of existence, that's beyond me.' It was quite like old times when Sophie talked in this way. But now she had learned to laugh at herself a little.

All too soon she had to leave. Edith looked at her affectionately as they said their goodbyes. She would miss her. It was a good thing she did not have much company other than Jack or she might begin to feel just a little lonely when the company departed. Only a little, though. Sophie, in her short dress and her purple scarf and her leather coat and her rather dashing hat, if the present fashion for hats could be said to dash, seemed suddenly small and vulnerable, not like a mother going back to a houseful of responsibilities.

'Thank you, Edith, for having me. Please come to see us soon. Give my love to your handsome Jack, won't you?' And she was gone, in Jim Sutcliffe's old car that waited at the bottom of the lane. Edith turned to go in when the noise of the Morris faded. Sophie always gave her plenty to think about. But she belonged now to another sort of life and one which she still feared a little.

Sophie finally accepted Bea Osborn's offer and helped her out at her clinic in a poor part of London, removed by more than miles from the comfortable Surrey countryside. At the clinic, too, it did not matter that you looked forty.

Once there was the prospect of having a little change once a week, when she was no-one's mother or wife, Sophie began to notice many new things around her: new roads, new 'garden cities', more motor cars, new magazines for women, new implements like the Swan and Waterman pens which were such a pleasure to write with, new distractions like crossword puzzles, and new card games, new dances. Looking around her in Islington though, things had not changed so much in streets which were not so far from those she had known so well in her youth. There were elderly women shopping at different kinds of markets in the open air. They were still wearing their uniforms of long, straggly skirt, cloak and bonnet, and all looked very poor. She enjoyed her first day, as she sat in on the session of callers at the little 'shop' and listened to unbelievable stories of misery from the lips of women younger than herself, who looked thirty years older. Where had she been for the last ten years?

Eventually she was able to spend two afternoons a week in either Islington or Whitechapel working for Bea and her team. She would return tired, but satisfied, from these sorties. The women she saw at the clinic had real problems: husbands who drank and beat them up, too many children, not enough good food or air and too much physical work. She was spoilt in every way compared with them. She was happy doing something for other people, though she often felt inadequate. She felt hollow sometimes, did not understand why. Was it guilt? She had married rather well, was fond of Michael, had three beautiful daughters and led a busy life. Even so, there were bits of herself that did not feel anchored. Parts of herself were still not being used. One could not just live for husband and children and the prospect of a better society.

She wrote to Edith: 'You must never show unhappiness to your children, so that they think your happiness is dependent upon them. That makes children unhappy – and guilty. Put a brave face on things and children will find out soon enough for themselves what the world is like.'

Edith would turn over these words of Sophie's as she scrubbed her scullery floor or ironed Jack's new shorts. She supposed that Sophie would never be completely content; it was the way she was made.

Sophie did not have this sort of conversation with her husband. Rather, she told him of the children's adventures or about some of the women at the clinic. To Edith she would continue her thoughts in letters.

'What do most people live for, apart from their families and their work?' she once asked Bea.

'For pleasure,' replied Bea. 'They fill their lives with sex or food or speed so as not to be bored with themselves.'

'But I'm not bored!' cried Sophie. 'It's just that I wonder what we all live *for*.'

Edith's long 'epic' about the forces of good and evil, set in the north country of her mind, was finished. Sophie was determined that it should see the light of day, for people needed a reminder of what might happen again. She persuaded Michael to consider it and was pleased when he consented and it was eventually published in a limited edition, though little noticed. At least, she thought, she had tried to do something for Edith. It was the only novel of Edith's that was to come out under her own name for many years.

Edith was now engaged one day a week in Leeds on her research into the world of the Norsemen. She had persuaded her old history department, where almost twenty years before she had worked as a secretary, to allow her to use the library. She was also writing poems, which she worked at painfully at night, trying to approach the truth of her life and thoughts in the pattern of words she liked to weave and also remembering clusters of sensations: sounds – baby crying; sights – a man sitting in the drawing room at Roundhay dressed in his officer's uniform; a little boy in wellingtons meeting his Wiltshire grandmother for the first time and not understanding why she was crying, thinking he had done something wrong; words – Jack's first, which had arrived in a rush, at two, after a long silence; smells – the smell of Thirksay beeswax and sun and grass, which she had wished she could recreate here in a wilder part of Yorkshire; the smell of feathers and straw and eggs, the smell of bistort in the valley nearby where she had taken little Jack for 'nature walks' and the smell of conifers planted in that same valley, near a ruined mill, when they had walked in the sun.

But by the summer of 1930, Edith had other preoccupations too. Her concerns did not arise from an overstrained nervous system, nor were they the result of any sense of missing something, or over the passage of time. But she felt, dimly, that she had entered upon a new phase of her life, though the realization had been slow. It had begun the year before when Sophie visited her. Jack was not a source of disquiet to her, even though he had, in some ways become a handsome stranger. They were not essential ways, evinced only the normal development of a young man who had once been a child. It was both a joy and a pain to her. Edith did not worry about his future for she thought he would be able, eventually, to look after himself.

In spite of the Depression and unemployment all around, bringing hopeless misery to many working people, neither was there much real violence in the district of Calderbrigg, unless you went and sought it out, or belonged to some illegal club, like those concerned with cock-fighting or dog-fighting. Unpleasant things had always taken place in the remoter moorlands, where the Chapel spirit had never really penetrated, but these activities were kept secret and not likely to spread into the town streets. Jack's old friends from the elementary school still greeted him. Jack worried about unemployment and wished he understood more about the economies of the capitalist system. Was unemployment inevitable?

He had sat his School Certificate, but was still determined to be a painter. Edith wanted him to stay on at school for a year or two before going to the art school in Leeds. She had hopes that he might eventually go to London where, Sophie assured her in her letters, Seb Harman could have a look at his work and possibly advise him about getting into the Slade if he were good enough. So Jack agreed to go into the tiny sixth form at the old village grammar school for at least a year. He was not in any hurry to leave the north, for he found much inspiration for his painting there. So long as he could paint and walk the moors and perhaps save up for a motor-bike which would get him further afield, he would stay in Far Ox Heys and study art and biology and mathematics. He needed a knowledge of anatomy for his drawings and was still interested in the birds and animals whose skeletons he collected from the fields and woods. He had rigged up a sort of studio in one of the deserted barns of the farm above his mother's cottage, where he kept his paints and canvases. He had made a window in its roof, but was too cold to paint there in winter without a paraffin stove.

Sometimes he walked with Edith for miles on the other side of Calderbrigg, in the deep valleys where they had often been when he was a little boy. He was not averse to his mother's company, for Edith never intruded on his private thoughts and he liked her, as distinct from loving her, which he also did. After one of these walks, Edith wrote to Sophie that the high clouds and the sound of the rushing streams in the valley had reminded her of Thirksay. But the countryside was wilder than the Vale of York – rougher here, even, than Far Ox Heys. Edith felt men were pitted against nature in the South Pennines. She was filled with a sensation she could not define even to herself. It was not nostalgia, for she was not a woman who lived on thoughts of the past. It was something more elemental which lived on those knobbly pastures and hills and moors. Something connected with her Norse studies, which had now blossomed into many notebooks. She had finally finished her short monograph and was still going to Leeds for the one day a week she could spare from the chickens and the other writing, which was more lucrative. Finally she gave up the chickens and the egg collecting. She was not getting weary of physical toil but she was now forty-three and must try to find more time for her other, original writing.

The long years alone with Jack had taught her much; principally, that thoughts could not be wooed, but must arrive and shape themselves in their own good time, and that her patience in teasing out some sort of metaphysic would be rewarded if she would wait. Her acquaintance with nature, if not in the raw, at least not in any very easily manageable aspect on the small farm cottage, and her long-ago acquaintance with death had sharpened her notions of what it was to be alive at all in this new decade of the twentieth century. Solitude only amplified her feelings and she would struggle to express them over many months and finally rescue a few lines from the dross. Although she was often alone, as she always had been, she was never lonely. She was acquainted with the villagers and they with her. She still saw her parents regularly, when her father would send over the motor to bring her and Jack to Roundhay for the day. Edith would not insist that Jack accompany her always, if he had some project of his own to be getting on with, for she knew that Jack was forming his own spirit at this time. The mathematics had led him to look for patterns in his surroundings and his thoughts, and he always had a sketch-book with him wherever he went. He did not mind, however, spending the day with his grandfather, for they still got on well. Broughton, now over seventy, influenced some of his political opinions. He could still not persuade him to go into the business, though Jack often had ideas for the shape and texture of the goods Broughton Ltd produced.

Jack's opinions on politics and religion were, at that time, fierce, if ill-formed. In the sixth form he heard from his mathematics master what was happening over in Europe and Mr Hoskins was sure there would be another war somewhere. But Jack did not discuss these things with Edith, who shrank from talk of another war and had a blind spot for talk about economics. Jack would discuss them with Jim Brook, a friend of his at school, who was destined for university. As far as young women were concerned, Jack liked pretty girls, but was wary of them and scornful of the techniques for attracting them used by most of the sixteen and seventeen-year-old youths of his acquaintance. When he looked into the fire now, or lay in the dark before sleeping, he would see the faces of imaginary girls and dream of a woman who might be an ideal companion one day. He wanted someone he could talk to, as well as desire. The village girls were all right, but he had not yet fallen in love with any of them. They were either given to shrieking and giggling or were extremely respectable, planning their trousseaus and their 'bottom drawers' if given a modicum of encouragement. 'Oh, Jack Bartholomew – he's an artist,' they would say when his name came up for discussion. 'A bit mad, you know, like his mother. Harmless, though.'

Jack was not at all harmless, but they were given no opportunity to find that out. As his school had no girl pupils, he met hardly any daughters of professional men or businessmen. He vaguely dreamed of some magical 'older woman' of about twenty-five who would initiate him into sex.

He was glad when his mother gave up the hens, and encouraged her to spend more time writing. He was helpful in the house, was used to cooking and wood chopping and fire laying, since Edith made no distinction between men's and women's work. But when he was sixteen something happened to his mother that led him to speculate further about the relations between men and women, and to wonder what sort of man his father had been.

It happened like this.

At weekends, there often used to pass Far Ox Heys a group of ramblers or hikers walking in the countryside, who found solace there from hard lives in the industrial towns. Occasionally there would be a solitary walker, but not very often. The people who 'rambled' were not typical of the workers in the towns, nor were they typical of the middle or lower-middle classes. The former now often boasted a motor and the young of the latter prided themselves on their motor-bikes, often with side-cars. Walkers were rarely women, for it was not yet the time for noisy groups of young women with male friends. Sometimes, it was true, there would be perhaps a fellowship from some church of association where women might take part, but the solitary walkers were always men and Jack was used to fetching them a cup of water when asked, before they walked up the hill and went over to the beginning of rougher country and on to the moors which lay to the north and the west of Far Ox Heys.

One Saturday afternoon Jack was out on some business of his own and Edith was sitting by the fire writing, for although it was August it was unseasonable weather and might as well have been February, except that the trees were green, and the wet fields golden. She had not thought anyone would be out walking on a day like this, so when she heard a knock at the kitchen door, thinking it might be a neighbour, she went through with her calm, unhurried gait, to answer it. She opened the door wide and saw a man standing a little away from the door, gazing down the garden as though he had forgotten why he had come. For a moment Edith wondered whether he could be a gipsy, for there were still tinkers and gipsies in the countryside who often came over the Pennines from Lancashire, driving ancient carts pulled by ponies. But the man seemed to have no cart.

'Yes?' she asked and he turned round slowly and seemed to blink.

'I'm sorry,' he said in quiet voice. 'I'm on my way to Denholme and Haworth and wondered if you had such a thing as a piece of sticking-plaster. I called at the farm,' he gestured to the fields below, 'but they had not, and the man there sent me to you.' This seemed to be said with a great deal of difficulty, as though he was not used to speech after long silence or his mouth hurt to move.

'Of course,' said Edith. 'You are very wet; did you fall?'

'No, no, it's the boots. I thought I'd seen to them in Halifax, but they've worn against my skin. I can pay you for a little plaster, if I may?' He made no movement to go inside the house and went on standing there. He was tall and very thin, a bit like a scarecrow who had come to life. His manner was polite, yet not ingratiating, and Edith, who had had her share of beggars and thieves, trusted him.

'Just a moment,' she said. 'I'll cut you a piece. You'd better come into the porch. Would you like a drink? Of water, I mean.'

He swallowed. 'No, no, just a little plaster.'

He came into the porch and put down his knapsack which did not seem very heavy.

'Where've you come from, then?' she asked when she returned with the plaster. He was still standing there, had not moved. 'Do sit down,' she said, pointing to the window seat in the porch. 'You'll have to undo your shoe. Here's some plaster.'

The man's hand movements were deft, in spite of a trembling in one hand. 'Only from over Greetland. I wanted to make Stanbury tonight - I know a barn there – they let me stay there before.' He was taking off his shoe and sock and applying the plaster to his foot as he spoke.

'Good grief, you *will* get wet!' exclaimed Edith in surprise. 'Do you go out in all weathers, then?'

He hesitated before answering. 'Yes. I sometimes work the farms for a bed in the barn and a supper. It's much worse in winter.' He smiled, said, 'Thank you.' and stood up and gave a slight gesture that could have been a bow, before limping calmly off, not looking behind him.

Edith wondered why on earth a man with a cultured voice should spend his time walking in not very hospitable countryside. Certainly not for pleasure, at least it did not appear so; not if he worked for farmers and slept in barns. Yet he had not looked down and out and had refused water. She was puzzled for a moment, but then thought of all the ex-servicemen who were still unplaced in society, twelve years after the war had ended. There was, of course, the unemployment in the district which was steadily getting worse. But he had not looked like a textile worker. Edith sat down to her work again, laughing

263

to herself and wondering what she thought a textile worker should look like. The voice had been educated; northern, but not 'broad'. She thought for a moment about him and then sighed and applied herself, once more, to her notebook. But she felt restless.

Over the hills and moors of the north this solitary walker was seen where others did not often walk. He knew the grasses and the bogs and the hills that would defeat any but the youngest and hardiest. He knew the sheep of the high moors and the cliffs of the east coast and the ruins of monasteries and priories and abbeys whose history he could also know if he were later to read about them in some municipal library. The history of places. That was important to him. He was solitary but he was not savage. He was cushioned, he well knew, by a small amount of money in the bank, which was enough for his needs. And now and again he would walk down into some town or descend to visit some aunt or other relative and be welcomed, if a little guardedly. This life would suffice for a time; the hills gave him the comfort he could not find in a contemplation of people. They would outlast him, and that made him glad. He was doing nothing spectacular; it was ridiculous to think of himself as a sort of outcast.

He could not accept life. That was his trouble. Could not accept anything, really. Not just slaughter and pain and horror and death and fear and terror and dirt and disease and misery, but the world, or what men had made of the earth. He could forget about it, they said, in order to survive, as thousands – probably millions – had done, if he wanted. But he did not want; and that not wanting was not in the control of his will. Nothing had ever really been in the control of his will, he thought. But was he different from others in this? Was he just less deluded? He preferred to believe there was something wrong with him, not with them. Something seemed to have determined his destiny, but the trouble was that he did not believe in that something. Others might. He had once. Some said it was just a trick of the weakened body or some physical depression which had overmastered his mind and his will. But he could not control that physical ailment and therefore, if that were true, had no control over his thoughts either. You could not 'pull yourself together' if you had a broken leg, so why should you be able to if you had a broken soul? He could pretend, of course, but some residue of honesty would not let him. And he was mourning, not just for himself, who was still alive, but for all the others who were not. Sights had burned out his eyes and given him another vision, an inner one that he could not escape even for a moment. Perhaps time would heal, as they said it would. Or he could try to make the effort to forget. If he could only explain what he felt, it would be a burden lifted, but no one wanted to listen. Why should he burden others?

The answer, he knew, was death, a willed and chosen death; and he was not afraid to kill himself. It would be a relief from the pervasive grief and the unpleasant, involuntary states of mind he suffered. But some tiny scrap of 'will', some rebellion in himself, stopped him from taking this easier way. He would tramp the fields and the lanes and live alone and go on trying to sort himself out. Even if there was nothing left to sort.

He would occasionally take on work with a hill farmer who needed help, and in the savage winters of the uplands he had dug out sheep and plodded in the thick snow to shepherds' huts. Once, he had come upon the sea, a steely, vast glittering that had risen out of the mist when he was on the northern moors, uncertain about his exact position. That had been a good day. Some days might have something good about them, if there was a challenge he had taken on and survived. He might even, one day, be ready to return to the valleys, to the towns, to other people. It was only a small possibility, but he knew he might. He was unregenerate, but there still lurked in him that tiny hope of being understood. At least the sheep and the farmers took him for what he was. He did not need to explain himself to them. Perhaps a human being somewhere would understand him without too much explanation. In the meantime, he preferred to walk and to pause, now and again, in some green river valley by some ancient ruined abbey and to let a small orison leap from his throat, out of the circle of crumbling stone where he stood, to reach that emptiness in the sky. He was driven indoors only by continuous rain and then he would smile at his great thoughts and see his achievements for what they were, those of one puny mortal who found cold and rain a trial and longed for fire and warmth and peace. Peace, above all. Peace which, even so, was here in the high moorland and in the hills, where he could forget himself and let the landscape pour into him. Even peace from the rain – a wet benison.

It was October when he came again, and Edith would not have known but she happened to be going to the village cobbler's shop, a small hut by the side of the road that led out of the village, to see if the cobbler had finished mending a pair of Jack's boots. She was unkempt, had hurried out before the old cobbler went home and locked up his shop behind him.

A man had bent down at the door of the hut to tie his bootlaces and when she waited for him to move, so she could take her place at the counter, he stood up and murmured an 'Excuse me'. Then he looked down and smiled at her. 'Did you get to Stanbury, then?' she asked, recognizing him immediately.

'Oh, yes, and much further. But now I'm staying here for a time,' he said.

The cobbler looked up and said, 'Evening, missis,' and turned to look for Jack's boots on the table behind.

The man made as if to go, but something made Edith say, 'Are you going far, then; home?'

The man had very sad eyes, she noticed. He was not dirty nor was his hair uncombed, but he had an air of great weariness, not occasioned so much by walking, she thought. Tinkers or gipsies had brick-like complexions from the constant weathering of their cheeks in the rain and wind. This man seemed to have been drained rather than weathered and she felt there was something wrong, but could not put her finger on it. On impulse she said, 'Why don't you come in for a cup of tea? I only live down there.'

'Yes, I know. The plaster was good, by the way; it lasted till I could get into Keighley.'

The cobbler was peering at Jack's left boot and then said, 'Can you wait five minutes? It needs a stitch or two.'

Jack would be back soon, Edith thought. There was no harm in asking the stranger in for a cup of tea.

'That's very kind. I came round here again because my old aunt lives here. She's away, though.'

'Oh, who is that?' asked Edith politely, but also with some curiosity.

'Mrs Horsfall. Do you know her?'

'No. Everyone knows *of* her, but I don't know her,' she replied.

Mrs Amy Horsfall was, in fact, the elderly widow of the owner of the old quarries which pocked the ground of the whole district like giant footprints. She was the stranger's father's sister, it turned out. He was called Stead, himself, he told Edith over a cup of tea. His left hand trembled when he held it and one of his feet dragged a little and she wondered whether he was a 'nerve case' from the war or from some inherent weakness. Yet he did not seem weak, neither did he appear to have inbibed any alcohol. She said nothing but listened to his halting, quiet sentences about his desire to walk over the Riding, which he had decided to do the year before to try and get himself fit.

For what? she wondered again. But in return for these confidences in the kitchen of Far Ox Heys, she did say that she was a widow and, without meaning to, that her son, Jack, who would be home any minute, had never known his father.

At that, he looked at her and put down his cup and said, turning his face away, 'The war?'

'Yes.' She did not ask, 'Were you in it, too?' but busied herself making another pot of tea.

After a pause he said. 'Many men didn't think there was anything to come home for, after all that. Your husband, if he saw the same sort of things, may have been better dead.' It was said in a flat voice with no emotion. 'My father's a shipbuilder in Middlesbrough,' he told her and, 'it isn't only the physical harm that ruined soldiers, though the poor chaps with mustard gas in their lungs wouldn't thank me for saying so. A blow to the soul, you might say.'

Should she ask him more? No, she thought. It would all come out in its own good time. He thanked her for the tea and went away, but she thought he might come back.

In bed at night she had a rare nightmare that was to do with Clement. It was so unusual for Edith to have dreams or nightmares that she lay awake pondering it. Clement. What would he have done after the war if he had survived? Was it true he was better dead? Surely that was a sort of blasphemy?

Some days later she heard that Hoyle, who still owned the farm at Lower Ox Heys, had taken on a man to help him with the silo and to do a few odd jobs round the place. She saw the new man in the field the next day, mending a fence. It was Stead. He had not yet told her his Christian name. She had listened in the village at the stores to the gossip, which usually passed her by, to see if there were any mention of the new farm-worker. Mrs Horsfall did come up in conversation. 'Oh, they're all snooty, that lot,' some woman said. Was Mr Stead perhaps lodging now with his aunt?

She thought of his pallor and his dark eyes and his trembling hand and the limp. That soft, abrupt voice of his betrayed perhaps the accent of the North Riding. It seemed familiar, pleasant. The next day there was no sign of Stead in the fields and she wondered if he had gone away again, but the farmer came for his rent that day and she summoned up her courage to ask him some silly little question about next year's work and whether Jack might lend a hand. (Jack was determined to earn more money towards his projected purchase of a Raleigh cycle, and that would be one way of doing it. He had given up the idea of a motor-bike.)

'I reckon the chap I've got now won't stay,' confided Hoyle. 'He's a good worker. We need a man we can let get on with it. Said he'd been in the war, he did. He's a nephew of old Mrs Horsfall! I reckon he's spent last ten years recovering from t'war; wandered all over t'place, they say, but he's an educated chap – you can tell that. And Horsfall's rich. I reckon it were shell-shock done for him.'

'He came here in August to ask me for a foot plaster,' said Edith.

'Oh aye? I reckon walking's over for t'winter. He's better off doing a bit of work for me, like.'

Edith recognized that she was unaccountably interested in this Mr Stead. It was unusual for her to feel like that. She had kept out of most folk's way ever since she had come to Ox Heys with Jack, and she could not define what it was that kept her thinking about him. She was not at an age, surely when women started thinking about unattached men? She laughed at herself, but it was true: she *was* interested!

She did not see Stead for some weeks, but then one December afternoon, when the sky looked like a goose's wing and bode snow and Jack was sitting in the kitchen with a book, there was a knock at the door. Jack went to open it and Edith heard the voice she recognized. He looked a little less gaunt this time; perhaps it was his aunt's food doing him good. 'Is your mother in?' she heard him say and then Jack was back in the inner kitchen saying, 'There's a man from the farm. Says he's got a ticket for a concert.' Jack raised his eyebrows at her in mock surprise.

'Come on in.' Edith was at the door herself. He shook the cold from him as though it were really snow and not just a presaging of damp. Edith pulled out a chair for him. Visitors, apart from Hoyle and the vicar, were still an unusual occurrence.

Jack bent his head down to his book and was silent.

'They said, "Mrs Bartholomew might like a ticket",' he stated abruptly. 'It's my aunt. She gets these sent and gave me two, not the sort of thing I go to, but I thought *you* might. Couldn't think of anyone else. Perhaps you and your son?'

'It's very kind of you,' murmured Edith. 'Where, exactly?'

'Hallé in Bradford. Complimentary; no charge.' A ghost of a smile seemed to sketch itself behind his eyes.

'Don't you want to go yourself?'

Jack looked up, observing his mother.

'I don't enjoy good music any more. Do take them.'

'Thank you,' said Edith, looking at the date.

'I'll be off, then,' said Stead. 'Don't worry if you can't go – no one else will. My aunt is not musical.' He drew his greatcoat around him and made his way back to the kitchen door. At the door he said shyly, 'I do go to art exhibitions – somehow they're easier to take. Your son paints, I'm told?'

For a fraction of a second Edith wondered if Stead were a homosexual with designs on Jack, but then he said, 'If you would like to see some paintings one day at the Cartwright, I would ask you to come with me. Not to the concert, though.'

'I'll think about it,' said Edith.

When he had gone she was thoughtful. After all, what did she know about him except that he was a war casualty in some indefinable way, had walked all last summer in search of something, was a good worker, according to Hoyle, and was 'well-connected', if that was the word. That did not cut much ice with Edith.

'We could go to the concert,' said Jack, looking up. 'I wonder why he brought *you* the tickets.'

'Yes. I met him once or twice, but only to exchange commonplaces,' she replied.

Jack thought his mother's commonplaces were other people's intellectual conversation and smiled.

They did go to the Hallé, she and Jack. It was a treat and they enjoyed it and she told Stead so when she saw him in the village a few days afterwards.

'The paintings next?' he enquired. But the snow had fallen by then and Christmas was almost upon them.

Christmas was a time when Edith took Jack to her parents' house in Leeds. She wondered what Stead would be doing. Jack had seen him working over by the old road, doing a bit of dry-stone walling, and reported that he was called Adam. He had shown interest in Jack's painting, but in an impersonal way, she gathered.

Adam Stead, she repeated to herself. No surname could have belonged more to West Yorkshire and yet his mother was perhaps not from there. She thought again of the slightly lilting accent. He had a 'rural' voice, she decided. From Northumberland perhaps. It seemed to come from an earlier time and generation, with a sort of old-fashioned grace. Edith was not given to imagining the real lives of the people she met; it was enough to have to imagine the inner lives of her characters, and she startled herself a little, catching herself doing it. He was certainly attractive, a little gruff, and she wished she knew more of him.

Christmas was rainy and unseasonable and the parents spent it in the usual way. Her father was not a glutton, nor did he drink very much, but there was a circle of neighbours who carried the 'eat, drink and be merry' custom to a rather unjustified extent in those days of penury for so many, and Edith was glad to get back to Far Ox Heys. A few days after Christmas it had begun to snow heavily; Edith and Jack had foreseen that and had been busy hacking logs into manageable pieces. Jack chopped and she used the saw and they sat by their fire on New Year's Eve in their own version of comfort. That morning she had seen Adam and asked him if he would like to see the New Year in with them, surprising herself.

'If I can bring my sledge,' he said. She had laughed.

At nine o'clock she and Jack were sitting cracking nuts. Edith had opened a bottle of brandy which one of her father's business associates had given Mr Broughton and he, in turn had handed over to Edith. The oil lamps were lit and there was a bowl of apples brought down from the loft, where they lay all winter in waxy paper. The fruiterer had been the day before with his cart and she had bought a few tangerines, a great luxury. Usually they grew most of their own vegetables, along with rhubarb, which was a speciality of the district, so Mr Pickles and his cart were not frequent visitors, and she felt she had made a special effort. The mains water had been laid the year before, so there was no danger of the pump freezing up, though there might be some freezing of the pipes that came through into the back kitchen. Still, it looked cosy, even if they were not yet provided with electricity. Edith preferred oil lamps anyway, and they were casting a subdued glow, along with the firelight, when Adam Stead knocked at the back door. Jack let him in and Edith heard the boots being banged against the brick floor. He came in with Jack, bearing a pair of slippers.

'I thought you wouldn't want my farm boots in your sitting room,' he said. Then, fumbling with a parcel, he proffered a book to Edith. 'They told me to read this: "It might do me good",' he said. 'But I thought you must read it first. I'd be better with the story of something a little less close to my own experience.'

'Did they give it to you for Christmas, then?'

'Yes. My aunt bought it for me; it only came out this year.'

Edith took the book and saw it was Sassoon's *Memoirs of an Infantry Officer*. She shuddered. 'More for Jack, I think,' she replied and then, thinking he might feel his gift was rebuffed, 'It was near my husband's experience, too, I think, and Jack is always asking me about the war.'

Jack took the book and was soon deep in it.

Edith poured a brandy for her visitor and one for Jack and a half for herself. As she did so she remembered suddenly,

271

with extreme vividness, the last time she had drunk brandy. That night with Clem when Jack had been conceived. She felt herself blushing inside, but there was nothing on her face to give her away.

Stead said, 'I don't drink much, I'm afraid, but a glass to drink the New Year in, that I will drink.'

This man was not at all like her dead husband; though, if he had lived, Clem would have been much the same age.

I heard them singing "Messiah" in the chapel as I came along,' said Stead. 'Gloomy stuff, except for the Hallelujah at the end. But it fits the place, doesn't it?' He was more talkative tonight. 'By the way,' he said, 'we've never been properly introduced, have we? My mother saw fit to call me Adam, so you must do that too. I know you are Edith,' he added. 'The locals are full of talk about you.'

'What do they say?' asked Edith, emboldened by two sips of brandy.

'Oh, that you are a widow, and used to keep hens, and you're not from these parts.'

'From Leeds. Not far!'

'Another world to them, I suppose.'

'Also full of Sykes's and Sharps and Stocks.'

'And Steads,' he said. 'Though my father went to work on the Tees. Now that *is* a different sort of place.'

'Full of Vikings,' replied Edith.

He laughed. 'Is that what you write about? Vikings?'

'Oh, I've done a little work on the Dane law, nothing much. I write stories for a popular series. I started them long ago.' She stopped, aware that she had never mentioned her pseudonymous writings to another soul in the village.

'You must let me read them. I hope they are an escape; we need one, don't we, with the way things are?'

Jack looked up for a moment and then returned to his book.

Edith's notebooks were on the table behind her and Adam glanced over at them.

'I write about the weather, too, and the things that happen here,' she said. 'Time goes so quickly; there's no other way of recording it. I can tell you what the weather was like on the last day of December for the last ten years, if you want. Jack thinks it pointless to write that down. But, of course, I can't paint, so words have to do.'

'You find you don't remember if you don't write things down? You must want to remember, then?'

'I want to remember the small things; the others can take care of themselves,' she said.

'Oh yes, big things. But one may not want to remember them.'

They were silent for a time, but comfortably. Edith knew that if she did not press him he would talk of himself. Jack was not listening now and she handed over apples and nuts to the visitor and put another log on the fire.

'Was your husband a writer, too, then?'

'Yes. He was a poet.'

He took an apple and bit into it slowly and looked at the fire.

'He died at Arras,' she said.

'I missed that,' said Adam softly after a pause. 'After five months on the Somme I was invalided out.'

'Were you badly wounded?' she asked matter-of-factly.

'No, not badly; in the leg. Bad enough. No good for fighting any more. I've walked many miles on these legs since, but I was invalided for the leg.'

Edith saw he would tell her more in his own good time. His hand was trembling a little again and she wished she could hold it.

'Your husband came worse out of it – or better,' he said.

'Other friends of mine were killed too. It was a lottery, wasn't it?'

'A Devil's lottery, unless you think dying was easier than surviving.'

'No, I don't, though perhaps some do.'

'Yes. But there was no choice. The victory didn't go to the brave, just the lucky.'

'People don't like to talk of it now. It's as if it were something shameful. I even feel guilty myself that I didn't go out as a nurse, but I had Jack to look after.'

'No, I haven't talked to folks seriously about it for years. I did at first. Then they saw it was going to be with me for the rest of my life, and with thousands of others, too. I don't lay claim to any special sensitivity . . .'

'What did you do, before?'

273

'I was going to be a doctor. I'd arranged that rather late, after trying to follow my father in the shipbuilding line. But I was only partially qualified in nineteen fourteen. I offered myself as a medical orderly in a Yorkshire regiment, visions of saving lives, you know. They made me an officer, but after the Somme I couldn't even – ' He stopped.

'What?'

He looked up. 'Save my own, I suppose. Like you, I felt guilty – that I hadn't died – but, well, bitter, that it affected me the way it did. I gave up the medical studies, wandered round, went back to France with the War Graves Commission, but it didn't help. It made it worse. Since then I've been back to help my father, done a spell on the land. But every time I start up again I can't feel it matters. So I walk it out. Do you understand?'

'Oh yes.'

'So last year I thought I'd try again, test myself, live rough, make myself suffer. I suppose Aunt Ada wanted me to stay with her for a bit after her husband died. They thought I might take over the quarrying but the blasting started it up again. I suppose I'm good only for a quiet life; chicken farming or something.'

'You say chicken farming! That's what *I* did for a time! Not any more – it wasn't very profitable – '

'You make more money writing?'

'Just enough to get by, with the pension. We live very simply, but better than most people. I'm lucky.'

She thought he was going to say something about the solitude, almost read his thoughts, and to forestall him said, 'I have to be alone to write.'

'Have you always lived in Yorkshire, then?'

'No. I was in London for four years. I was a passably good typist, you see.'

'You have a lot of talents,' he said.

'Why didn't you want to go to the concert?' she hazarded.

He did not reply for a moment and she thought, I should not have asked him, but eventually he took out a pipe, knocked it on the back of the fireplace and said simply, 'I wasn't hearing the music. Always, before the war, I'd spent a lot of time playing the flute and going to concerts. And that one thing, the best

274

thing in my life, was taken away from me. After the Big Push I found that music changed into – other noises.'

'Always?' She looked at him levelly.

'Usually. And I never knew when. It's a trick of the mind, I suppose. They'd do better to train up doctors for minds, not bodies.'

'Can you separate the two?'

'Ah, that's a question for a philosopher. I don't know. Perhaps not.'

'I shall make some coffee,' said Edith. 'Unless you think it will keep you awake after midnight. What time is it? We must toast the New Year.'

'Nineteen thirty-one,' he said bleakly.

'Mother wrote a book about the future,' said Jack, looking up. 'She thought nineteen thirty-one would be the year for another battle between the forces of good and evil.'

'A novel?'

'Oh, it was a sort of allegory,' said Edith. 'I began it ten years ago when I still felt we could do something about the world, starting with ourselves, I suppose. But time steals up on you. Ten years ago people didn't want to read about battles, did they? Let's hope in another ten years they won't either.'

'May I read it?'

Edith, on her way to the kitchen, paused for a minute. 'It isn't very good. I'm afraid I made it too abstract.' But I shall lend it to him, she thought. I want him to know me. And if I have not already frightened him off, perhaps I can help him too.

She thought of it quite practically. Adam Stead was a man who needed help. And she could no longer, she thought, lose anything by offering a fellow human a helping hand if it were in her power to do so. But in the kitchen, measuring out the coffee, she had to pause for a moment; so strong was the sudden desire to take that hand of his, and stop its trembling and hold him close to her that she held her own wrist hard. No. It was not like that. She admired him. He was so direct in all his complexity. Clem would have liked him, she thought.

When she got back, Adam and Jack were playing chess. Jack was obviously determined to be polite. They were each so lost in the game that she feared to disturb them, but Adam looked

275

up after a moment and then stood up and helped her with the coffee and the parkin which she had baked for the evening.

'We used to eat this on Guy Fawkes night,' he said.

'Do go on playing. I like to watch.'

'Jack, he's quite a good player.'

'Mother taught me,' said Jack. 'She could be good, too, if she wanted.'

The two males were quite happy to munch and sip and concentrate on their game and it was only when Adam caught Jack's queen napping that the game ended rather suddenly, and Adam laughed. She thought, with a start, that she had never heard him laugh before.

'You must come again,' she said quietly when at half past midnight Adam left. It was beginning to snow again on top of the already-hardened snow from the day before.

'I shall sledge down your field into the village lane,' he said, and unhooked his sledge from the hook by the back door where people had always left dogs on leashes. With a wave of the hand he placed the sledge on the path, sat primly upon it and, with a push from a heel, glided down the path to the slope of the field across which ran their little lane, now snow-covered. She smiled. It was unorthodox, but sensible. Oh, yes, he must come again.

Adam Stead had enlisted in 1914 as a member of Kitchener's army, in one of the West Yorkshire regiments. As he was a medical student he was eventually given a commission. His medical studies had started late; his father had wanted him to follow in the business and then there had been a period when he had begun to study theology. Theology had served only to allow him to lose his faith, and at the time war broke out he begun to wonder whether he would even make a decent doctor. He missed the worst of the earlier battles in northern France and his medical knowledge had not been of any use when he found himself, in June 1915, in Montreuil-sur-Mer, attached to the Sixth Battalion of the West Yorkshires, to supervise the digging of graves and other arrangements for a casualty clearing station, in a 'CCS', the 'idea' of which appeared to them all to be distinct from the 'idea' of death. There were many Yorkshiremen there who had enlisted in their home towns and regarded themselves not a part of the battalion, but as a group of 'pals' from the same streets and villages. Some of the 'pals' were just returned from Egypt and were blithe, knowing little or nothing of strategy or tactics, trusting in luck. They were spread about among the regular divisions, or their own sections and platoons were strengthened with more experienced soldiers. Most of the Sixth Battalion were detailed to join the 'Big Push' in the direction of Thiepval, and Adam was sent with them to see to casualties and arrangements for transporting the wounded, should there be any. Behind the 'front', British gunners were already pounding the German defences, but the Germans had been settled in the area for almost two years.

For the whole of the last week of June the bombardment went on and Adam was waiting for the infantry, for when the preliminary bombardments were over the infantry was to follow through. It was all magnificently and meticulously prepared in theory, but wet weather was to arrive and upset all plans and also make it difficult to know what was exactly happening. There was a postponement of the attack for forty-eight hours. Troops had moved up to the assembly trenches, and, behind the lines, every building of every small village was filled to bursting with the young soldiers who had been marched up behind the advance parties.

It was thought that the Germans would be so demoralized by the bombardments that it would be an easy matter to strike through their defences, once the British shellfire had made short shrift of them. In all, along the whole front, two hundred thousand infantry men in their battalions and divisions were on their way to provide the onslaught, each man weighed down with sixty pounds of equipment and sometimes with barbed-wire and pick-axes. Men who were in no way trained soldiers were thinking of fighting as they had fought at home, when perhaps they had come hand-to-hand with a personal enemy or, at worst, fought with knives.

All this Adam sketched out to Edith when he came to see her one day the week after the New Year's Eve party at the cottage. He must have pondered and relived it all many times before, she thought, as almost every survivor had done since the terrible events of each one's private war. Yet he seemed to want to tell her. They were sitting by a bright fire. Jack was at school and Edith had been washing. Items of Jack's clothing were hung over the 'winteredge', the clothes-horse, at one side of the kitchen fire. She had made some tea and had been sitting sipping it for a moment before getting down to the ironing.

Then Adam had arrived, not quite unexpectedly, since she had seen him in the village the morning of the day before and told him to drop in for a chat, any time except the morning which was sacred to her work – except on Mondays when she did the washing.

After he had started to speak of the early preparations for the battle of what was later called the Somme, she had tried to imagine it and wondered whether the things he was telling her had been similar to Clem's experience, later, at Arras. She knew that Adam had not been badly wounded until some months later, at the end of the offensive, but his spirit seemed to have been assaulted earlier than that. He fell silent now and then. She did not try to urge him on, for she had not asked him to talk about the war. It was his decision; up to him. He seemed, at one moment, to wonder himself why he needed to tell Edith all the details which had remained so long in his mind, for he looked at her after a silence and said, 'I don't know why I'm telling you all this.'

Edith thought she knew why. He was sensitive enough to know that she had wondered about him, wondered why an intelligent and educated man should have taken to spending his time rambling on moors without a regular job, or, at least so it seemed. He was not, in fact, attempting some sort of justification, for to a person like Edith, Adam Stead felt, you did not have to justify yourself. She was interested and she was a good listener who did not nod her head or look encouraging or say 'I see,' or 'Really,' or 'How awful.' The hand that did the trembling was laid over his knee and his stiff leg held out before the fire. Nothing else had apparently been affected, but his eyes told a different story, for they seemed to burn as he spoke. She would have said, 'Don't talk if it troubles you,' but that would have been an inadequate response, and perhaps if things troubled him they were better spoken of, though she knew that if it were that simple many men would have been cured.

He knew that she was the right person to talk to. Perhaps there had not been anyone else before to whom he could speak sincerely. 'Oh, July was when I saw the unimagineable first; but the worst was when we were back in Thiepval wood. We were in reserve and I was with the orderlies trying to locate the wounded and sending for stretchers, until there were no more stretchers, with wounded from all over the place – not our own men, even. That was when it was Hell for me. I wasn't wounded then – that came later. It was such confusion in July. Think of Hell's doors opening and hundreds of thousands of men in one week pouring through them all, helter-skelter, in various states of dying and being dead, or half-dead, trying to find a friend or looking for an officer or a sergeant, with an order when the 'final' call came. Then, no more friend, no more order, no more knowing anything. They just fell, and sometimes couldn't be reached for days, even when they were not dead, and were moaning over in No Man's Land. Even the ambulances were shelled. I had to drive a lorry through feet of muddy water to try to reach them. Other men were walking in it up to their thighs.'

'What happened later, then in autumn, when you say you were wounded?' asked Edith.

'Oh, three months later we were at the forefront of the attack when I got my comeuppance. But I was lucky; up till then it had only been my susceptibilities that had been wounded, and the shock doesn't get through to you straight away. I was so busy. But there were worse things to see. The other thousands of devils were exhausted to begin with, for different reasons from me. Some of them had only just come out from home and they'd spent a week without much sleep, carrying ammunition or food and digging new trenches. Our battalion was no longer made up of territorials, or even of people like me with supposedly medical skills, but was a mixture of men from all over the place. No longer the Sixth Battalion but a motley crew; so many dead, so many wounded, so many missing and those left so tired they couldn't even be woken up, asleep on their feet, never mind 'go over the top' when the call came. For it did come and then they did go over even so, feeble and tired to death and wishing they were dead so it would stop and they could go to sleep for ever. And they were stopped in their tracks even when they'd made that last effort. The shelling was so terrible that most of the company

279

commanders were killed outright. Thousands were blasted to death. I saw it. I was there. No one had a clue at HQ what was happening. The ones who'd survived the shells and retreated just refused to go back. It wasn't that they wouldn't; they couldn't – they were physically incapable of moving, and in any case it was impossible. It would have been like killing dead men; what good would that have done except more dead men to write home about? And we were blamed for not continuing the 'advance'. Can you believe it? Blamed. On that one day in September, our lot lost three thousand men, killed or wounded, and just in our little battalion of three hundred and fifty who went over the top, we had two hundred and forty-four killed or wounded; and the bloody general complained later that the men were slack in saluting him! We were only a tiny part of the whole army. All over, scores of battalions like ours for miles and miles and miles, all in the utmost confusion, trying to gain a few yards here or there. Men dying, Edith, *dying*, for an inch of soil. Oh, well,' he said, looking away. 'You'll have heard it all before. I expect. But it doesn't alter the facts.'

'It was madness,' Edith said.

'Even if it hadn't been mad it would have been impossible. No communication at all between the HQ and the front; all those trenches and fields and the liquid mud for miles, all in utter bloody, and I mean bloody, confusion: bits of men, bits of limbs, shreds of puttees, screaming, smoke, mist. I was glad, I can tell you, to get it in the ankle in the end; but it was the sight of the others that just managed to turn my head. I had been going slowly mad, I think. One-and-a-quarter-million casualties on both sides for the whole of the Somme offensive; fifty-seven thousand killed on that first day in July. Can you believe that a year in hospital with a shot through the foot and, after that, ten years of mental hell *still* haven't absolved me? I can't pay back what I saw, and it's obscene even to speak of it. We shouldn't have to talk about things like that. It's an insult to them. Nothing can heal it, you see. Why should I have been spared, among all those hundreds and thousands? Why me? there was no sense to it even when I was doing the things I'd volunteered for, like helping the wounded back over the line.'

Edith had an idea he ought to have been decorated for bravery, but knew that that would have been as meaningless to him as it would have been to her. She poured him another cup of tea. Had he thought he should have advanced and died in that last day's battle?

'Hasn't telling people ever helped to exorcize just a little of it?' she asked timidly.

'The trouble is, you don't want the pain to go away,' he answered her. 'You can't give up your memories. It's not fair to those who died, and it isn't fair to those who listen to you to load them with your own dread and terror. After nineteen sixteen I was good for nothing. That didn't matter so much. I mean, what is one man weighed in the balance and found wanting, because he can't imagine well enough; he can't encompass it; it seems impossible it ever happened? But it's made him see that that is what all life is really like – just a pit of horror. It was what we saw, not just me, all of us; all that pain and agony and misery and death, death, death. And all at the mercy of blind chance. We survived, to remember it for ever. That's far worse than a quick death, I think, having to take others' nausea into yourself, trying to understand. What's a weak leg or a trembling hand? It's the mental pain, and then, at different levels, knowing it and knowing that you know and that it all comes to that in the end. I'm sorry; I shouldn't talk to you like this. You lost your husband.'

Edith was silent.

'It isn't just the sadness and the terror or the fear of death, it's what it does to your idea of *life*, you see. Knowing it happened. It was real – we were there. And there was nothing to save any of us; just the gods sitting above and flicking lives around like swatting flies. Not just the knowing it could be you or ought to have been you, but the denial of everything that you thought life was about. Nobility, sacrifice. Now you see that despair and unpleasantness are never far away. They are in your brain like mental nausea and you can't properly describe them. That's *my* sort of shell-shock, not the trembles. I can't explain it very well, I'm afraid. I should not have started on all that. You must stop me another time, or you won't want another time, will you?'

'Do you think it helped Sassoon and Owen and Graves to write about it?' she asked. 'I mean, would that be to make it just "literature", when really art isn't enough to encompass it? The human condition, I mean.'

'I suppose it might help some people,' he conceded. 'But I was a doctor, or I was almost a doctor, not a writer. I was idealistic, I suppose. I hadn't known of that "condition" before, not really.'

'What I don't understand is why you should feel guilty,' Edith said. 'You were young, they were mostly young; if you had been older, do you think it would have affected you so much?'

He said nothing, pondered her words.

'If it was chance that saved you and killed my husband, why should you feel guilty to be chosen to go on living, especially if life becomes hell? I think you have paid back any guilt by suffering as you have, not that there was any reason for guilt in the first place. There was nothing you could do, as you said.'

'It's not just guilt over being alive. It's guilt over not being able to assimilate all the horrors. You try, but it's just too much . . . To understand the agony of just one man dying in agony is enough. That would take you all your life, unless it were your own death you were reliving and then undergoing. I suppose that is what they say Christ died for. But over a million in five months; a million ways to suffer.'

'Could it ever happen again? Is there nothing we can do to stop it? Surely it couldn't happen like that again? People wouldn't be willing to go through it and to be ordered about and blamed and taken for granted when they'd volunteered in the first place. And for what, anyway?'

'At least we "won",' he said bitterly. 'Though you wouldn't have thought so. And of course it could happen again, though perhaps not for the same idiotic reasons. Ordinary people aren't asked to run the world; and what could they do even if they were given the power? And it rankles still with Jerry, of course. It's the pointlessness that's hardest to bear. What did they die for? Their deaths were so much more important than the causes they fought for. It took away not only my faith in God, which had worn thin by then anyway, but in any sort of order. It was anarchy on the battlefield, and there is anarchy everywhere. Who said, "The centre cannot hold"?'

She noted that he read poetry but said, 'All you could do was to survive and then try and manage your survival, I quite see that.'

'Oh, it wasn't a question of me or the next man, just a question of where will the gods hit next? It wasn't even a question of kill or be killed. Just a mess, a badly organized holocaust. Don't encourage me to say any more. It should be enough to sit here and eat apples. I can't ask for inner peace as well.'

In spite of his saying he must not go on talking about the war to her, Adam did, in fact, speak spasmodically about it again over the next few weeks. Edith was able to piece together the jigsaw of his career in the army and to fit it into the rest of his life which that career so overshadowed. It seemed that, even now, there were things he could not bring himself to say. As an early spring edged into the New Year and very slowly pushed away winter by dissolving it, they would occasionally meet in the village and sometimes he would walk back with her from the village shops, a good two miles away. He was still lodging with his Aunt Horsfall and Edith had the impression he had come to some sort of crossroads in his life. Once or twice she would ask him over for an evening meal, which she would prepare early if Jack were coming home straight from school.

By February, when the snows had gone – though they might always return – she and Adam seemed like old friends. He had read a good deal and took her own writing very seriously, going so far as to take her allegory home and return it with a wad of annotations of his own. And, yet, there was still some constraint between them, which Edith could not quite understand. Of one thing she was sure: he had not talked to anyone for years as he had talked to her. She felt easy with him. Odd, stray memories would come back to him and he would sometimes talk to Jack, too, about such things as the huge cart-horses, the Shires, which had been used in the war to pull guns and ammunition, and also of how he had helped to bury them when they died or were killed or injured, just like the humans who led them. Jack listened carefully and was impressed, and Edith wondered how many bodies of men Adam had helped to bury. He spoke of the mustard gas which had fortunately not affected him permanently, and again of those sounds of the wounded and abandoned wailing in unison like a banshee over No Man's Land; this only to Edith. Edith wondered whether a true account of it all could ever be made, since each man had his separate war, and whether that account were even possible. And also whether his experiences had ruined him for ever.

'Why don't you go back to your medical studies?' she often asked, but he always prevaricated.

'As good as going back to theology,' he would reply. Or, he wanted a simpler life, he was rusty, his knowledge was out-of-date, they would not want him. Obviously he could not be a surgeon, but he was afraid of more than his trembling hand. He seemed to fear something in himself, afraid perhaps of his own weakness, something he could not control, a residue from the mental pain that had afflicted him and still, she saw, afflicted him. Should he try to relive it, or should he try to forget it? She was not sure, compared some of his feelings of numbness in the face of catastrophe with the wall of glass that had used to separate her from the world in the days before Jack.

Adam took an interest in Jack's painting too and Jack asked questions about the battle of Arras where his own father had died.

'Why did Dad have to die?' Jack once asked Edith angrily, after one of their conversations.

All three of them went one afternoon to Bradford to an exhibition of painting and Jack stood for a long time looking at the Clausens and the Rothensteins and newer painters like Matthew Smith and Edward Wadsworth and Nash. 'Great things are still being done in Leeds,' he said.

'That boy of yours will do great things too' said Adam afterwards.

'He's growing up to find the world imperfect,' Edith replied. 'He's a perfectionist, like his father. But I don't think he will be an urban painter. Clem had the same conflict.'

Adam was of use to Jack in his anatomical studies, for he did not seem to have forgotten all he had learnt in Newcastle at the medical school. Never once did Adam suggest that Edith should visit his Aunt Horsfall. He would rather taker her 'out to tea' after an afternoon in one of the smoky towns than suffer the embarrassment of small talk over his aunt's tea-table. But he much preferred to be out in the countryside, even in the cold.

Edith realized how unusual it was for him to have made overtures of friendship and to have actively put himself forward to be her guest, even in the informal atmosphere of Far Ox Heys. He liked also to discuss flora and fauna with Jack and was full of plant lore. Edith found there were gaps in her own knowledge which Adam could fill. She had never seen the twayblade orchid, but Adam brought her one pressed from his wanderings where he had found it growing among the sphagnum moss. It was his ambition to find one of the rare hieracia or hawkweeds. Edith learned that over two hundred plants could be found in the valley where she had sometimes gone with Jack and smelt the pine smell and listened to the rushing beck which flowed past the old, forgotten watermills. She encouraged Adam in all his explorations, for surely nature in the form of plants and birds might heal his memories, if anything could? He had walked great distances in the North Pennines to strengthen his ankle a few years back, and what had started as an exercise had become a love of nature.

Jack was as knowledgeable as Adam when it came to birds, and lost any of his youthful reserve towards his mother's friend when it came to describing the sighting of a pair of ravens on the Pennines to the south of Far Ox Heys. A rare sight indeed, as they were usually found much farther north. Jack was hoping to return later to a craggy outcrop to see whether the pair he had noted had brought forth some fledglings, and planned to see them on the wing by the end of April.

Edith did not have a great deal of time to go for long walks, but loved to take a bus to the nearest stop to real moorland where she could walk for an afternoon. She was not primarily interested in ravens or merlins or in spotting some rare orchid or fern, though she knew the thrill of discovery; she was more inclined to take the landscape as a whole and let it soothe her, to breathe in the sharp air, so fresh in summer and so cleanly cold in winter and spring. She began to look forward to future walks with Adam, even if he or she might pretend that their chief objective was the sight of a bird or the acquisition of some knowledge of geology, or the gathering of bistort for herb pudding at Easter.

It would be quite practicable, from Ox Heys, to go one day into Wharfedale to the north, or on to the moors to the west around Haworth on its high ridge, or even to the Lancashire border. Adam did not seem to want her to go on any walks with him which might necessitate an overnight stay anywhere. He offered to go over one day with her to Haworth, though. She waited for him to suggest it when the milder weather came. There were smaller moors, just as wild, merging into the slopes of their own hills and also woods near Ox Heys itself. They were their first objective, and it happened that they went to one of these woods one afternoon in late March, when spring was still on the way. She hoped it would presage longer, more dramatically remote walks to further places later.

'The snow will still be lying up on the moor,' said Adam as they made their way up a cobbled hill from the village and then turned in past a farm. They walked on down a path that led to a wood that had once been five times larger and where trees, yet ungreen, grew on slopes that were fern-covered in summer, and down to a brown, stony stream.

'I don't feel the cold any more,' said Edith. 'When I came here first I was so cold, and seemed to spend all my time building fires and plugging up draughts.'

'When exactly did you come?' he asked as they stopped for a moment by a dry-stone wall on the edge of the wood.

'After the war. I'd like to have gone somewhere even more remote, but it wasn't practical with Jack. As it turned out, it was a good thing I didn't make myself into too much of a hermit, though I expect folks round here think I am one.'

'Writers are always hermits,' observed Adam, fingering the dark millstone grit that lay under his hand in the irregular stone that made up the wall.

'Yes, there is no time for writing if one is busy with a social life. I've always had plenty to do. I made a bit of a living with the hens and was busy enough bringing up Jack, but after all, I had to put my work first – after Jack, I mean. I suppose round here it is only *half* country, when I think of the places where *you've* been walking, but I don't think I could have managed without a village not too far away. Father wanted us to live in Leeds, of course.'

'And your husband's family?'

'Oh well, there is only Clement's mother left and she is quite old and won't budge from Wiltshire. I send Jack down to see her every year. I don't know her well . . .'

286

'How long were you married, then?' he asked. 'Before he died, I mean?'

Edith wondered how much she could reveal to this Adam Stead, who seemed so interested in her life; but how could you be sure? Still, she was older now and it was all past history. 'I was married only two days before Jack was born,' she said and looked him full in the face.

'Whew!' he said and laughed. 'I should have known not to ask you embarrassing questions, Edith!'

'It doesn't embarrass me, Adam. I didn't want to marry Clement. I did it because he wanted me to. I hadn't ever lived with him and I don't know what would have happened if he'd come back from the war. And, of course, I saw, eventually, that Jack must have a father and a grandmother, I couldn't deprive him of that.'

They began to walk on again into the bare-branched woods with the sound of the brook down below.

'I might as well tell you,' she said and turned back to look at him, for she was walking on ahead, knowing the path well. 'I wasn't in love with him. Jack was what they call an accident.'

'So you determined to be independent; that was why?'

'It was nothing, earning my living. I'd done that before. And I had the pension, and Father was always there to back me up, though I didn't let him much. When I think of what I might have gone through if I were a man, and what Clement must have gone through, my life has not been hard. I didn't care about being "married", that was all.'

Now, she thought she would be happy to be married to a man like Adam who would leave her to wrestle with her own demon as he wrestled with his. And who knew that they might not defeat each other's demons thereby? She tried to brush the thought aside; it was not the first time that she had thought of Adam as someone permanent in her life. Was she thinking of marriage? She had Jack's education to pay for, his long years as a student ahead. And she had no idea whether Adam felt anything more for her than a sort of gratitude for her patient listening to his memories. Yet he did seem to want to go on seeing her. It was nothing like anything she had ever felt for Clement: no compulsion to annihilate herself and let herself be taken where his own passions led. No; in all the workings of her mind she was now mature, even middle-aged, but something which had gone underground before Jack's birth seemed to be struggling to be reborn. Was it love? Or was it a desire, at last, to experience a sensual relation which she had never had, except in the powerful love she had felt for her baby son? Did she have the right to be an ordinary woman? If she did, Adam was no ordinary man. She must not spoil the relationship by expecting too much. But he was speaking again now, as they came out on to a path that led to a stile and then divided. One branch turned down into the wood, the other followed the line of a field and higher ground.

'I didn't think I could ever be happy again, even for a few minutes,' he said. 'And I don't suppose I shall be for long. My leg and my hand remind me, if nothing else does. I wanted to thank you for being such a good friend, Edith. I feel I've known you for so long.'

'Only a few months,' she said steadily.

'I wish I could be more to you,' he said. 'But I'm a wreck: I couldn't ask anyone to share my life with me now.'

He had thought about it, then. 'I'm a solitary person, Adam. My life came rushing at me before I knew what I was doing. I suppose having a baby is a bit like going to war; not that I feel I've come through a battle, but it changed me.'

'He must have loved you very much,' he said wistfully.

They were both leaning against a gnarled tree, a stumpy, thick-trunked oak, whose ancestors had probably been there for over a thousand years. She turned to look at him and took his hand, the one that trembled. 'It was all a terrible mistake. Not Jack of course; I wouldn't be without him. But for me. My friend Sophie, I told you about her, she loved my husband, but she was in a muddle too. It's all so long ago. I lived in a dream, I think. I can remember the feeling, as though everything that took place around me was all unreal, or was I unreal and couldn't connect myself with it? I thought a man's love might bring me through and make me real too. But it didn't. What made me join the human race was having Jack. Perhaps it was all meant to happen like that.'

'Then you didn't know him for very long – I mean, before you – ?'

Edith felt half-ashamed of her reply, absurd though it was. Yet it was easy to talk to Adam.

'I only went to bed with him once, in London; then there was the pregnancy and I went away for that. Then he came to marry me, and in the end I agreed. It was on the day the war broke out, and Jack was born on the sixth of August. It's absurd, isn't it? I can hardly believe it myself. Afterwards, he had not much leave and everything was strange. Clem knew I didn't feel for him as he did for me. He was so proud of Jack though; he would have been a good father, I think, but not an ideal husband. I'm sorry if it shocks you to hear me say that. After all, he died and had nothing. And he gave me his name and a child. I don't think I deserved either.'

'But you had no intimate life with him. Oh, Edith!' He took her hand now and closed it in his larger palm and then covered them with his other hand. 'I'm so glad you told me,' he said. 'Do you still feel isolated and as though you are not "real"?'

'No, but it's too late to pretend I am a young woman.'

'I think you are a young woman in all the things that matter,' he said. 'I wish I were a young man, but I'm not.'

'You missed your youth too,' she replied and put her other hand over his.

'Why, do you think? I can't believe there is any destiny mapped out for us, not after all that happened in the war. If the Supreme Being wanted to give us all a chance to grow up and learn to be ourselves he wouldn't have taken away that chance from your husband or from all those poor wretches I still have nightmares about. It's just chance again, don't you think?'

'I don't know, Adam. Perhaps destiny operates in fits and starts and we've just been offered a respite. God has woken up, or suddenly remembered us.'

'That could be true. But we have to weigh so much in the balance now: Your life. My past.'

'Adam, don't you think that even now you could get over all that? I don't mean forget, but integrate it somehow into the rest of your life? I can't believe you should go on punishing yourself. I know you can't help it but I wish I could help you.'

'It's true, I can't seem to help it. I'd be an awful burden, Edith. You ought to have an easy life now, write what you want, see your boy grow up, have a real man to love you.'

289

'I think you are a real man. You are real to me. There's no glass wall now. If there is, it's made of your experiences, not your real nature.'

'Thank you for telling me your true history,' he said. 'I'd never have believed it, you know. You deserve something better.'

And you, too, she thought. But what was the use? One could not go on proffering a gift if it were not wanted. The trouble was, she was not sure whether he did want it.

'And yours?' she asked boldly. 'Before you went to war, and after?'

'After – nothing. An icicle,' he said. 'Before, a girl I used to love, or thought I did, back home. But she was frightened when I came back from the war, couldn't cope with me, or it. I didn't think I had anything to give her and so she married someone else.'

Edith looked up at him and saw he had found it difficult to say that. He did not want a woman 'poor Adam-ing', but perhaps he would not mind a kiss?

Very gently she squeezed his hand and then kissed him on the cheek. Now he was looking at her gently and with some amazement. I do love him, she thought, if this upsetting lump in my chest is love. He need not ever see me again after today, though.

He put his arms around her for now, and she felt his heart thudding away as though he were nineteen and stealing a forbidden embrace.

'I'm not used to that,' he said. 'You will have to forgive me if I don't know what to do next.'

'What we could do next,' said Edith, and was amazed to find the words coming so easily to her tongue, 'is go away for a week or two when Jack goes to his grandmother's at Easter. You could take me to your moors or your mountains and we could love each other a bit. Or aren't women supposed to say that sort of thing?'

He smiled. 'I don't know what they are supposed to say; it is not "in character", Edith, but, well, why not? I couldn't be a worse companion, I suppose, than I have been this winter with all my glooms.'

'It could be a little holiday for us both; a week away from my next book would be an unexpected luxury.'

'Oh, I think I could spare a week,' he said, and smiled.

He is a good man, she was thinking; and his thoughts were not dissimilar, except that he felt frightened, not that he could not love her, but that it was too late for him.

'I am forty-three,' said Edith. 'I think I deserve a short holiday!'

I shall be a drag, he thought; when she wants to feel happy I shall have a nightmare or be afraid I shall have one, which is worse.

They walked down to the brook at the bottom of the slope and said nothing more till Edith thought he must have decided to change his mind again. But, no; he turned his trouser legs up, stepped across to a boulder in the middle of the quick-flowing stream that was swollen with all the snows of the winter and reached for her hand.

'Your leg?' she asked.

'It's all right. I'd forgotten it for a moment.'

She strode over to him and they both stood in the stream on the boulder together. 'I can't kiss you here,' he said. 'Too risky. Let me reach across to that flat stone there. You'll get a bit wet. There we are – '

He was on the bank and holding out a hand to her, which she took, and they stood together on a pebbly dry piece of earth, looking at each other. She is a good woman, he thought. A very good woman. But it won't work. Never mind.

Aloud, he said, 'I was thinking of staying in a monastery this summer. Do you see how funny that is? And you suggest we go away together!'

'A monastery!'

'Not just figuratively, either. I've been thinking about it all the year. I thought it was that or complete despair, and some despair in any case. Throwing myself on God. And now I shall throw myself on you.'

For a long moment he held her in his arms and kissed her and Edith felt the strangest feeling, as though something she could not give a name to was struggling to live.

After they left each other in the village, for Edith had no wish to force her company and knew he must have some time to think over what had happened, she realized that the chance of happiness for him was slim, whereas for her it was possible.

Was it akin to the sudden urge she had had to give herself up to Clem? She considered this all evening and decided it was not remotely the same. What she had gone without for so many years had not harmed her. A week with Adam could only add a little extra joy to her life. Jack noticed she was quieter than usual and came to his own conclusions about what she had been doing on her long walk with Adam Stead.

At his aunt's that evening Adam finished Edith's allegory for the second time and marvelled that a woman with so little of what the world called experience should have written it. She knew pain, beyond doubt. She was both shy and deep, impulsive and yet restrained, unawakened and yet sensual. And he saw, too, that she had felt guilt over her lack of love for the father of her child. Strange, that it should be an old war-horse like himself who seemed to have aroused some sleeping desire in her to try once more to join herself to another human being. For Edith was not frivolous and she understood his own fears and horrors and that he had never been able to integrate his war experiences. He wished *he* had been born a writer; at least that was one way of reducing oneself to size. But she did not write of herself in her book. It could have been written just as well by a man. He supposed it was what people call poetry.

A different experience would not have altered her very much. And if he found pleasure in her arms, and gave her pleasure, would that alter him? Would it dissolve his own mental anguish? He doubted that, too, but it was worth a try. You could not remake the past, but perhaps Edith was right and you could believe just a little in a free will that allowed you to build on that past. It would not change his despair at the human condition – nothing could do that. But he saw the same stoical recognition in Edith, even if she had not seen men slaughtered all around her.

He would take her to Westmorland or Cumberland. They could at least have a week of 'holiday', and then he would decide whether he ought to, or could offer her more. He wanted to, but was frightened it would not work. Was loving simple? Perhaps it could be part of that stripped-down life he so desired. She had courage and she was certainly unconventional. He allowed himself for half-an-hour, to daydream over a frugal, happy life with Edith, jumping ahead to a time when she could write and he could farm and they could live to a happy old age. He shook his head after all this. Perhaps she just meant a week of love-making. One must not look beyond that, surely?

Adam Stead wanted Edith Bartholomew to be happy. Indeed, he would rather make Edith happy than make himself happy. He had doubted that such a simple thing as a moment's joy should ever be vouchsafed to him again. Edith left him room to breathe. Not many women did that. Apart from what the war had done to him, Adam's nature was reserved. He had always spent long hours alone, even as a boy, amassing what his father had called useless information. Like Edith's, his nature was not a discontinuous one. It was all of a piece and wanted to go out and make wholes. His own inner harmony having been shattered, he felt the world's harmony gone for ever. If Edith could restore that, it would be a miracle. Could love, or even sex, ever do that?

In the middle of the night he decided he must not go away with Edith: it would be unfair to her. For whatever there was between them might be condensed into such feelings as could then melt away under too hot a flame. He must not risk it. At dawn he awoke again and decided it was a love of virtue, or a too insistently important weight lent to the idea of love, that would destroy them both. But she had grown up. She knew the risks. They were both too serious. He would forget his doubts and just take what was offered and hope that she, too, would not be diminished by whatever they could make together.

If Sophie Carr had wished to advise Edith over the next few months of her life she would have counselled that love was a shared illusion, if you were ever lucky enough to find a requited passion, which was unusual in itself. Just as Sophie had been the object of Grant Miller's romantic infatuation for her and as Clement had been the object of her own; love of this kind was a blissful cheat.

But Sophie was not told about Adam at the time. Edith wanted to keep her new feelings to herself. She loved solidly and seriously and did not imagine that friendship or passion or affection or even maternal feelings were separate things. She

293

was poised on the brink of loving Adam and discounted too much introspection about the causes and the possible course of that love.

In her letters Sophie still gave the impression of feeling lonely, wanting to talk to Edith about books and ideas. Her husband was always preoccupied with work, her three children now all at school. 'Don't marry, Edith,' she wrote, with what might have been an intuitive feeling that Edith had some new preoccupation. For her part, Edith resolutely refused to plan ahead, thought only of giving Adam a little happiness and herself a little fresh air and perhaps a little affection in return. Adam was not so deluded. He knew that Edith was not a woman you should enter into a casual relationship with. She was not demanding, but she appeared to him to lift a man up towards the best of himself. She never flattered, never told white lies, but always maintained her clear and gentle gaze and occupied herself with practicalities when necessary.

Jack had gone off to his grandmother's for his promised week and Edith had decided against saying anything to her father about her new friend. She had always discouraged any speculation about her future, the present being enough to be going on with. She mentioned to her parents that she was going walking in the Lake District for a week and left it at that. The most important thing was to get to know Adam better, without the distraction of her work and her daily life and away from Jack's polite gaze. It was not love-making that was her main objective, if, by that, people meant the act of love; that was only part of it, a natural part she had decided, but not essential to her happiness.

Edith was not unduly worried when, after their arrival in the little lakeside village, on an evening when everything was sparkling in a sudden spring sunlight, and after a walk by the side of the lake and a simple meal in a small hotel, they went up to their room and Adam fell immediately asleep. They had each drunk only half-a-pint of bitter, so it could not be that, she thought. She was not tired, so sat on at the uncurtained window, looking out over the lake in the darkness of their room. Adam lay, as if drugged, on the bed that was to have witnessed their coming together. At last she undressed, removed his shoes and loosened his tie and covered him with the bedclothes. Then she sat by the bed and contemplated him in the light of a full moon that had risen above the lake. From time to time he murmured and muttered and she took his hand and held it against her cheek. For another hour she sat there, wishing she could change the images which were undoubtedly going through his head, for the murmuring sometimes changed to a strange groaning.

They had come up at about ten o'clock and Adam had immediately said he was tired and must have a short rest, but they would go out for a walk round the lake when the moon was up. At one o'clock in the morning Edith finally got into the bed beside him and, still holding his hand, drifted off to sleep. She was awakened by a shout, which she thought had come from her own dream, but she knew instantly that Adam was having a nightmare, for his whole body was shuddering and when she put her hand on his forehead it was hot and sweating. She decided to wake him so that he might avoid whatever situation had made him shout aloud and she took him in her arms and kissed him as she might have kissed Jack, woken with a childish nightmare when he was little. Adam suddenly opened his eyes and sat bolt upright. Edith sat up too and spoke quietly to him.

'Oh, God,' he was moaning. 'Oh, God – the ambulance – the blood was all over the floor.'

'Hush, my darling,' she said. 'You are here with me. There is no ambulance. You were dreaming.'

He was awake now and trembling.

'Lie back and I'll bring the Thermos,' said Edith. 'I brought it up from the hotel kitchen for a midnight feast.' The flask was full of hot, sweet tea. He said nothing but sipped it slowly and looked at her pleadingly and almost wonderingly.

'You fell asleep; you were tired and you were having a nightmare. It's all right. It's about three o'clock in the morning.'

'Oh, Edith, I'm so sorry.' He was weeping now. 'It takes me like that sometimes. I can't sleep for days and then I fall asleep and have the most terrible nightmares. And I was going to love you.'

'I've been loving *you*,' said Edith.

She sipped at her own drink, then Adam asked shakily, 'Are you undressed?'

'Yes. I went to sleep. Get undressed yourself.'

He sat up, pulled off his clothes and she made him lie down beside her.

'Forgive me, Edith. You've got a wreck, not a man.'

She knew that, above all, she must not let him give himself up to self-pity, so she said cheerfully, 'I have nightmares too. Are you frightened of going to sleep? Because if you are, we could go for a walk'.

'No, I am not going for a walk,' he replied and seemed to have recovered his spirits.

After that, with infinite care and patience and with apparently no lurking rememberance of his dream, he lay kissing her tenderly; no more. Edith, who had felt she would have to be his guardian angel that night, took some time to forget his moans and murmurs, but eventually she saw that he was, indeed, recovered and enjoyed caressing him.

As they lay in each other's arms, it was very strange to Edith, for it was over seventeen years since she had had any sort of intimacy with a man. The memory returned to her of the night Jack was conceived. She could not believe that she was now over forty. Not that she felt virginal, for now she knew her own body better than years ago, but when Adam said, 'Can we just lie together? I want to save anything else for a time when you haven't had to "nurse" me,' she was a little disappointed. She knew that when it happened, as far as she was concerned, there would be no problems, for she did want him and she would follow the dictates of her physical self. Above and beyond that physical self there was a feeling that she must restore Adam to some semblance of normality and, if that were better done through kisses and words and closeness, she would do it. In some way she felt that she and Adam were the same, that his sufferings had made him hers. They both fell asleep, their arms around each other, and there were no more nightmares that night.

They woke late, to a glorious morning. The hills were guarding the lake and the waters, and in the distance the Langdale Pikes spoke of a whole country waiting to be explored, which would be there when whatever happened to them was long over.

They breakfasted and then went for a long walk round the whole of the lake. Adam wanted to row a boat out to the island in the lake opposite the town on the western shore. By the time they hired the boat, later, Edith had decided that Adam would have been the right person for her if they had met years ago. In spite of his nerves, he was not an uneasy or distracting companion. How she wished she had known him before the war. 'Nature', their natural surroundings, once again played a part in seeming to dissolve any tension or memory of the past. They each took an oar and Edith, who had learned to row with her father as a child, enjoyed the sensation of movement. There was a slight spring breeze, but it was not enough to impede their progress and she rowed with her face dazzled by spring sunlight.

'We are fortunate, said Adam when they had beached the boat. 'It's more like a summer day; but the weather can be very changeable up here.'

'The highest rainfall in the British Isles,' replied Edith. 'I do remember that.'

The island was small and no one else seemed to have the idea of rowing there. They explored it together, for there was a ruined building that looked like a keep, now covered in ivy, and the sound of one or two wader birds. They had sandwiches with them, provided by their hotel, and Edith had her usual Thermos, and a rug which she had thoughtfully brought with her.

'I'm sorry about last night,' Adam began when they had eaten and were once more regaling themselves with tea.

She took his hand. 'We came here to get to know each other. There are lots of ways of doing that, not just one.'

'I'm frightened of the responsibility,' he said at last. 'You haven't had much of what we medical students used to call a "sex" life. Not that they ever thought that was a woman's right.'

Edith picked at the woolly edge of the rug and tried to think how to put her thoughts in order and to say what she wanted to say without making him feel she expected any physical consummation as of right. At the same time she wanted to let him know she would be happy to join herself to him. He was not the sort of man who required wooing, she could see that. Nor was she the sort of woman who would usually initiate intimacies, but something seemed to be called for. Sophie would have known what to do. And he tugged at her heart as he sat there. Was it love he needed or was it a release of the body? Men were all different and Adam had clearly never been a chaser of skirts. He took her work-grimed hand and kissed it.

'Why should it matter so much?' she asked.

'But it does. Maybe it shouldn't. Can we only make love to the people we don't care for, as though it would spoil something else to do it?'

For answer, she took his face between her hands and said, 'Forget I am Edith with my funny life, forget everything except we could make each other happy, even if only for a moment.'

'It would be easier, dear Edith,' he said 'to marry you and live with you and live like brother and sister. Anything else is what I might not be able to provide. Last night I wanted so much to have you and give myself to you, and forget everything, and then I fell asleep. It's absurd, as well as cruel.'

'Don't take it to heart. Let us live from one day to the next. If you had work to do that was more permanent, even if it were to farm or just be a labourer, or if you joined your father at the mill, or took over the quarry; then I think just the daily-ness of it would heal you, if you had someone to come back to who loved you.'

He put his arms round her. 'But it wouldn't be fair, Edith; you have your life, and if you married again, or even if we lived in the same house without that, you would want a *proper* man.'

'You are a "proper" man, and anyway, I can always help you when you have those nightmares, I really can.'

It seemed, though, that physical passion was not yet to be their portion in life. It was more important to get to know each other and wait to see what happened.

'You could live with me. Jack will be going away soon. Let's leave it at that, Adam.'

'It's peculiar enough,' he said, 'that we would be even talking about such things. Most women wouldn't be expected to, or would not say, or would be coy. And why ever should I feel compelled to "prove myself"? I'm not young. I want to learn to love you properly.'

'As far as I am concerned,' said Edith, as coolly as she could, although a tremor in her voice betrayed her feelings, 'I want to love you; I thought about loving you ever since you came back to the village. And I don't care whether what you mean by love is the same. That's my side of the case.'

'It isn't fair, Edith, to be landed with a war veteran, after all you've been through.'

'Fairness has nothing to do with it, my dear. If you want to see the other side of that question, think now, if you married a younger woman, you could have children by her. I don't think it likely I shall have more children and that *is* painful – '

'No, no; I wouldn't want to bring any more children into the world, not after – everything. But if you were pregnant with my child – that is, if we ever – well, then, I should welcome our child. But no other mythical baby, oh no,' he said vehemently.

'Don't you think,' said Edith with a smile this time, 'that considering all our separate difficulties – your war and my enforced celibacy and the state of everything at the moment – that perhaps that is why we found each other; to make a new sort of relationship? Who knows what other people do in their marriages? There must be many strange partnerships. If I were twenty-five again and you were twenty-seven and we were in love and we could marry and there had been no war, just think of how many years we should have needed to understand each other and find out what mattered.'

He buried his face in her shoulder. 'But then we should never have talked like this and we should have replaced the companionship and drinking tea so decorously together with nightly passion, and we should not have known what we were missing.' She said nothing.

'But I know what I am missing,' he shouted, lifting his head. 'I don't want a woman to sacrifice herself for me; think, if I got worse instead of better and you had to be a sort of chaperone to me, or worse still, a doctor.'

'Surely that's very unlikely,' said Edith. 'As a medical man you must know the worst is over?'

'Doctors don't know everything.' Then he calmed down and stood up. 'Let's go back and pretend we've been married since nineteen fourteen. By now, I expect, if most married couples I know are anything to go by, we would have lost interest in each other.'

So there was a sort of easy truce and they stopped talking and gave themselves up to whatever would happen between them. It was a pleasant kind of limbo and in it there came other sensations when they realized that they had similar reactions to the landscapes and to the things they read in the papers which lay in the drawing room of the hotel and to their own memories of childhood. It was a lopped-off perfection, as though a tree had died, but a new shoot had come out from the bole and was growing, at first a little uncertainly, and certainly not when you looked at it; but stealthily.

At the end of the week Edith knew she would marry him if he asked her. He knew her routine, knew she needed long hours alone. But he must find work and stay at Far Ox Heys if that were to come about. She wondered if the idea of the monastery were still in his mind but did not ask. She was not going to play God or be a substitute for Him. To Adam she seemed invulnerable.

Only one thing troubled Edith and that was how Jack might regard a man in the house if Adam decided, in the end, to cast his lot permanently in with hers. She knew her son would never say anything and that he was bound, in the end, to make his own life, perhaps far away; but he was as yet only almost seventeen and there would be several years before he could have a life of his own after the long student days. He had been willing to stay on for another year at the school and then start at the art school in Leeds. Edith hoped that he would then transfer to the Slade for the latter part of his studies. Even then, he would be only twenty-three or four. She would have to earn more money, even if Jack's grandmother died and the pension, such as it was, reverted to her. Edith's father though, had other plans.

'You know, Edie,' said Mr Broughton, some weeks after her return from Windermere, 'if you're worried about paying for Jack, don't be. I know you won't take it from me for yourself and that you've managed wonderfully on your bits and pieces, but Jack will need a proper allowance and you mustn't refuse what I can do for him.'

Jack had come home from his Grandmother Bartholomew's with a portfolio of sketches, mainly of the old lady. Edith marvelled. He had caught the wily, proud quality of Clem's mother, who must have once been a beauty, and Edith saw that now, at over seventy, she had begun to look more like her son as Edith remembered him.

There had always been a reserve between them. The mother blamed Edith for Clem's joining up, thinking that Edith had rejected him and that he had decided to join the army in a fit of pique. This was a little too near the truth for Edith to be comfortable, since Clem's joining up had precipitated her marriage to him. But the proprieties were preserved and, after Jack was old enough to be put on a train to Salisbury and met there, Edith had thought it better for him to go alone and make what he could of his father's mother. It was clear, after a time, that Jack had almost replaced her own son in her heart and so Edith was forgiven, since she had provided her with a grandson.

'She says that if Dad could see me now he'd have a lot to talk to me about,' reported Jack. 'She showed me his certificates; you know, when he was an engineer. It was quite interesting. She doesn't seem to know much about his poems, though.'

Jack did not spend all his time thinking about his father or discussing his grandmother. He was aware that Edith and Adam had some sort of feelings for each other and wrongly assumed it was more on Adam's side. For who would not love Edith? Did his mother really need a husband? She had managed perfectly well without one. He suspected it must be that she was urgently desired by Mr Stead, who had never married, not connecting desires of the flesh with his mother, or preferring not to think about it.

'One day,' said Edith, 'you should go and visit Aunt Sophie. Phoebe must be ten now and by all accounts she's very bright. You draw people so well, love, you might paint or draw Sophie and her children and then one day she could show what you've done to that friend I mentioned, Seb Harman.'

'Mother,' said Jack. 'I'm not good enough yet to paint portraits, the ones of Gran are only sketches. I'd rather draw places than people.'

Edith left it at that, since she knew Jack was a little shy of going to London before he had girded himself with many portfolios of his work. And, in any case, he was due to sit the Higher School Certificate in the summer.

Adam had gone to stay with his own father. 'I don't know how long for,' he said. He wrote to Edith almost every day and she thought she detected a lift in his spirits. There was no more talk of spending another year by himself, tramping round or working for his uncle. He seemed, though, to be nurturing the idea of working permanently for the farmer at Ox Heys. If, when he returned, he decided to do that, then he would have to decide where to live. His aunt had gone away, travelling abroad, they said. Edith waited and was able to write a story for Bevis Constantine by detaching part of herself for the time it needed. It was a relief, in a way. She knew Adam needed more time alone before he decided the direction of his life, and she made it plain in her replies to him that she would take him on his own terms. He stayed away all summer long, but she did not worry.

One day, when Adam was still away, Edith went to Leeds. She had finished her potboiler and was considering starting some more ambitious project. After she had finished her short monograph of the Viking influences in Yorkshire, a work that, if short, was yet concentrated and represented two years of work, she had felt there was more to say in the same field, but this time connected with the language and civilization of Anglo-Saxon England. She was interested, especially, in the history of Yorkshire, and wanted to pursue it back through the Dark Ages. Not only the Viking influence but the Celts and the Anglians and the ancient kingdom of Elmet, on whose borders she lived. The Vikings had made no strong contribution to culture; it was rather in the language they had left behind, particularly in northern England, that Edith was interested. And in their 'heroes of Asgard'.

She decided to go to the public library to see whether any forgotten collection of books was lying dustily unregarded and unread, and when she asked to see the chief librarian was shown, instead, to his assistant. Edith, whose sight had not become less short in the years that had passed since her sojourn in London, was surprised to have the woman, for it was a lady librarian, greet her with, 'Are you not a friend of Miss Ridsdale?' She had been searching for her notebook and looked up. Who could this be?

'Cicely Emery. I used to know Sophie and saw you once or twice before the war,' said the woman. 'Do sit down. What can I do to help you?'

Edith fixed her spectacles more firmly on the bridge of her nose and a rather tall, wide-featured woman swam into view. She had a beaky nose and her hair was still dressed as Edith remembered it when she had first seen her, at the only meeting of the suffragists she had attended with Sophie before deciding that political action was not for her.

'Edith Bartholomew,' she said and put out her hand.

'And how is Sophie? Doesn't it seem years ago?' The voice was gruff. Edith knew that Cicely Emery was an 'outsider'.

'Sophie married after the war,' Edith replied, seating herself gingerly in the chair opposite Miss Emery.

'She should have taken professional qualifications; I always told her that,' said the lady. 'But I suppose she was a romantic. I had the feeling she must have married. At one time I thought she would join the Cause, but she never seemed to have her heart in it.'

'Oh, I think she did,' replied Edith, defending her friend. 'She is still a Feminist. She felt very strongly; but then the war seemed to take away all those preoccupations for a time and, of course, now we have the vote . . .' She trailed off.

'We still have a long way to go. But you didn't come here to talk about Feminism?'

'I came to look for any forgotten-books you might have. I believe not all the nineteenth-century stuff went to the Fotherton Collection at the university. There might just be a chance of Professor Altcombe's monograph on the Vikings turning up here, for example?'

'Yes, that is a neglected field of research. The Germans have done much more than we have on Norse-Anglian relations,' said Miss Emery.

Edith was surprised. Cicely Emery obviously knew her job. 'I wanted, too, to see if there was perhaps something in general about the relations between Celts and Angles in Elmet ... And between Angle and Dane in the Vale of York, for a comparison. Then I want to read up the Norse settlements in the Calder Valley. Strange to think they were the same people who, when they came over from Normandy, found the north such inhospitable terrain later.'

'Are you interested in the Anglian "ministers" too?' asked Cicely.

'Oh, Dewsbury. Yes. And in the Norse crosses . . . '

Edith was always at her best when discussing theories, betraying her enthusiasms, and Miss Emery's manner became quite respectful.

'You may have a look in our archives – a rather grand name for cardboard boxes which no one has yet had time to investigate. The university will want anything of interest, eventually, I suppose, and that will give us a little more room. How strange you should come here! I didn't know you were from the north. What is your work then? Surely you do not make a living from Vikings and Anglians? You must be married?'

'I *was* married,' said Edith. 'But my son's father was killed in the war. I spent the war bringing up my son.'

'So you came from the north, like Sophie? I hadn't realized that.'

'Yes.'

'Oh, those years in London,' said Cicely Emery, who seemed to want to reminisce. 'Will you join me for a sandwich and a cup of tea in my lunch hour? It would be good to talk over old times.'

Edith felt she must agree or she would never get to see the papers – not that she had much hope of finding anything.

'Of course. I come back here at two, and you must get on with your work then.' Cicely Emery took a key from a ring on the desk and added, 'Follow me. I'll show you the store rooms; unfortunately I can't come down with you to help. My duties are somewhat elementary here – to do with the distribution of inferior literature to the populace – or that portion of it that use public libraries.' She smiled and Edith followed her down to a dark cellar, lit with only one bulb and stacked with papers and boxes on tall bookcases. 'I'll leave you here. Try the section marked K. You will come for lunch, won't you?'

Edith assented and began to search the shelves. Her short-sight was now an advantage and she spent a happy morning. In a small box marked 'Archaeological Society Proceedings, 1867' she found what she was looking for: a handwritten set of papers referring, not to archaeology, but to philological researches in Germany and Denmark. It was serendipitious, she was often lucky this way, but at lunch in the covered market (where Cicely said she went to study 'The People') Cicely was impressed. 'My goodness! You had better copy all that; take it home – no one will miss it. They're a lot of stuffed shirts here anyway.' Cicely's relations with her male superiors were obviously not amicable. 'I'm third in command,' she went on, with a rueful smile. She was really quite attractive when she smiled. 'I was a sort of librarian before the war, and before I took up with the suffragists. Then I finished my training after the war.'

'You are, still, then; a Feminist?' asked Edith, chewing her cheese and bread. It was like years ago in London. When had she last had a conversation with a woman about anything but baby clothes or the price of bacon?

'Of course. But there has been a disillusionment. After the war "they" were only too pleased to think that the vote would solve everything; get the women back home ministering to the men and they wouldn't be a worry. Equal pay is, of course, the next objective.'

'I should think so, if the work is equal,' said Edith, surprising herself.

'Ah, the dear, dead days,' said Cicely. 'All that in France changed us all. I belong to the Peace League, of course, and the Co-operative Women's Guild, but the heart has gone out of Feminism. We need a Cause; it will come. I don't rate the prospect for peace very highly.'

Edith was distressed. 'Oh, surely not – not again, after all they went through – ' She thought of Adam and suddenly this talk of political action and even her new ideas of Vikings seemed unreal. Adam was what she wanted. One man who had suffered. Cicely Emery, too, had doubtless suffered.

'I was in the field,' said the latter. 'That's where I met my friend; she's younger than me, but she had a breakdown after it all. We decided to come back north and for me to take a respectable job. Gladys can't work, so she stays at home and looks after me like a wife.'

Edith said nothing, adjusting her ideas of Cicely, who also seemed to place more emphasis on personal relations in the end.

305

'But tell me all about Sophie Ridsdale,' went on Cicely. 'Where does she live and whom did she marry?'

'A publisher – '

'Not Grant Miller!'

'Oh, no, he went to the States. A man who was a friend of his stepson: Michael Carr. He's doing very well, I believe, and they live at Miller's old house. She has three daughters.'

'And she is happy?' pursued Cicely, her hawk eyes piercing Edith. Edith had the sudden idea that this Cicely Emery had perhaps been interested in Sophie in a rather unorthodox way: Sophie, who was certainly no lesbian, but whose charm had obviously made an impression on the older woman.

'She adores her children. She works a little, too. Voluntary work, of course, for Beatrice Osborn's committee for family planning.'

Cicely seemed to approve, for she gave a satisfied murmur. 'She was with Miller for a long time, wasn't she?'

'Yes.' It was none of Cicely Emery's business.

But Cicely pursued the subject. 'These men, they get girls when they don't know their own minds, and I expect she was in love with him. Ah well.'

Edith said nothing.

'You must come over and see my friend and me one evening. We have a nice little flat in Leeds,' Cicely continued.

'My parents still live in Roundhay,' confessed Edith.

'Well, then. We are in Headingley; do say you will come?'

'I may be going away,' said Edith, thinking that Adam must surely return to Ox Heys soon. 'But of course, that is very kind of you and I should love to come. I used to run a little smallholding' she added, to get off the subject of visits. 'Now my son is growing up I don't keep chickens any more, but we live very simply. I had the pension, of course, from the army.'

'Didn't Sophie once say that you wrote novels?' pursued Cicely, looking at her over the rim of her cup.

'Oh, well, I only helped at Miller's; one of the editors – a series,' murmured Edith. What would the fierce Miss Emery think of her potboilers? She did not think she would approve. Edith hardly approved of them herself.

'More money in that than in the Vikings,' observed Cicely.

'A little.'

When they got back to the library, Cicely offered her hand. 'Been most pleasant. Take the papers you want, I'll note it down. So long as you bring them back in a week or two.'

Edith wondered how she was going to avoid her; she would have to see her again when she brought the papers back. She found her rather alarming. But she had had the courage of her convictions, had Cicely Emery. It could not be much fun working here and keeping two people on what was probably a low salary. She wondered what Sophie would say. It would be something to tell her in her next letter. She owed Sophie a letter for, even now, a long missive from her friend was lying in Edith's sitting room.

As Edith copied what she needed and abstracted the short paper from the box and took her leave of the library, she wondered what Cause Cicely Emery would find next and hoped it would not be too unpopular. An anti-military crusade perhaps? But the government was not arming. Where would the danger come from next? She must talk about it to Adam.

All the way back on the little bus Edith wished Adam were with her. She did not want to get sucked into a Leeds intellectual life, had always kept her researches a very private thing. And she certainly did not want Cicely Emery discovering how large a part of 'Bevis Constantine' Edith was.

Edith went on thinking that she did not want to see people unless they were Jack or Adam. Had she really become such a hermit? Cicely, although she had never known her well, seemed to have brought back all the pain and the disruption of her early life. Clement had known of her, spoken to her surely at one of those parties they had all attended? Yet Cicely had never once asked whom Edith had married. That was odd. Perhaps she could not bear to contemplate a woman who had married and lost her husband. Yet she had been very nosey about Sophie. Cicely also brought back memories of Theo Carmichael and Cora Benson. Sophie saw the former, of course, but the latter was now a fat old woman, still stumping around the country preaching the new theosophy. Not that Edith objected to that. The thing was that they had all moved on, those who had been left, except she herself, who was still pretty much thinking and writing the things she had thought about and written about twenty years ago. She must move forward; she must not keep thinking of social obligations as a burden.

Perhaps *she* ought to join the Women's Co-operative Guild? No; on reflection, she was not a joiner of anything. But she would re-read Sophie's letter and tell her about her little visit to Leeds. If only she could tell her about Adam. But she had the truly reserved person's terror of being seen to claim a person or idea and find that it was all a chimera. She thought it was not a good idea to speak of herself, just as she never spoke of her writing when she was in the process of creating. It must remain locked within her or it would vanish like a bubble from a child's pipe, rainbow and perfectly formed but not able to remain perfect, or even real, if the outer atmosphere touched it. Then it disintegrated.

She sat down the next day. Jack was at school and there had been a post-card from Adam, who was up in Grisedale for some unexplained reason, but who sent his love. He was, undoubtedly, using this time away to consider his future, for walking was the one activity which enabled him to sort out his thoughts. Edith took Sophie's long, last letter and read it with some concentration.

'It is such a bore, Edith, playing hostess. Everyone thinks I adore it because I am good at it. I don't. I'd rather be sitting peacefully with you in a garden with no one to cook for or make arrangements for and a good long novel to read. I am really rather lazy, but you know that . . . I thought of you at Ambleside – thanks for the pc. Did you go with Jack? I actually dreamed of the lake, and then of a house in Paris which people were going on to afterwards; it was such a sharp dream! I do long for Paris sometimes, but Michael is too busy and the children not yet old enough to be taken there, for their own good. Perhaps, one day, if we are still at peace, I shall be free to go there and mull over my memories. I never feel nostalgic in London, isn't that odd? After spending all those youthful years there. I liked your description of Jack's painting of the crocuses; "pale mauve and veiny with stiff orange stamens." He must paint Far Ox Heys for me and I will buy it and frame it and let the children see what real landscape looks like, with the light on the snow; or in summer with the shadows of clouds on the hills. Your cottage sounds so comfortable. I often think of you there, and of Thirksay, too, on a frosty winter afternoon, with the big fire in the range. But it must be depressing up north with all the unemployment. It is not quite so bad down here; publishing seems to have picked up and there are even rumours of new houses to be founded.

'Who do you think I saw the other day on my way back from Whitechapel on the underground? Garnett Edwards! He looks most decrepit. His retirement doesn't seem to have done him much good. Michael was glad to be rid of him, though of course that is because we don't have the copyrights of his Moons and Moors etc, etc.

'Michael still doesn't know that you write most of that stuff, but I think you must write to Garnett and make it clear that he leaves you them when half of "Bevis Constantine" pegs out. It seems likely that that might be quite soon, but you never know with old men like him. He's lived in dissolute life for so long he's used to it and his body must have adjusted to whisky or he'd have been dead long ago. I didn't go up to him or anything, but I thought, "I know who you are, you old fraud." *Do* ask him, Edie; he's quite capable of leaving his copyrights to some young fellow or other and then where would *you* be, who have written most of his titles for years? I'm surprised you never did make a proper arrangement, but I remember your saying he's been quite generous in monetary acknowledgement. I shall make it my business to find out how much the series is bringing in to Carr and Penn. Just think, I might be indirectly profiting from what, by rights, should be yours. If he gives you a decent sum each year you can be sure he's getting a good rake-off himself.'

Edith looked up from the letter. She did not want more of Edwards' money, what she had was quite enough, considering the rubbish she wrote. She must tell Sophie so. She returned to the letter. Sophie made a passing mention to Seb Harman, with whom she still liked to talk. 'He's not a marrying man. You liked him once, didn't you?'

Edith had always known that Seb Harman preferred men. That was why she had felt so at ease with him.

'Anyway, Edie, I envy you writing, alone in your wilderness. I mean, alone except for Jack, and he must be away a lot with his pals. Do send a snap of him if you have one. I do wish you would come down and stay with us. The children have heard such a lot about Jack from me and I should like to see him again before he grows to be a man. Rosamund, they say, is like me to look at, but taller, and Phoebe is like Grandmother Carr; at least we think so. Clemmie doesn't look like anybody but herself. I leave you to judge, as I had some photographs taken in the garden the other day which are being developed and I'll send you copies.'

Edith noticed, as she read Sophie's letter, how little she still said about her husband. They were quite a plausible pair, she supposed, in the eyes of the world. but she had the feeling that Sophie sometimes found her husband 'unreal'. She had thrown herself into domestic life for so long, but it still did not seem to satisfy her. And the work for Beatrice Osborn never seemed to give her the feeling that she was actually making some difference to the lot of poor women. 'Only a drop in the ocean,' Sophie would say about her work in Whitechapel and Islington.

Ah, here *was* something about Michael Carr. She read on: 'Michael is always busy. Not that I mind that, as it gives me a little more time to myself. I often think that one can manage a husband and children or a house and children or a husband and a house, but not all three. And just think of working as well, as we used to think we would if we ever married! How did we ever get through all that work at Miller and Penn's and have time to look after ourselves and read and go to parties and flirt? I suppose it is the children that make the difference, or the house, or both. I wish I had not become a bourgeoise, Edie. You will never be one, and you manage to do your own work.'

Edith felt a little worried here. If she and Adam lived together, would she be forced to reduce the amount of her writing? Surely not? She did not have to act as hostess as Sophie did and she had only one child, but perhaps it was a male presence that made for work?

Sophie was now off on another tack. 'When I see the women who come to the clinic, I am ashamed. They have so little, but are always cheerful. What's the good of being a Feminist when only rich women can benefit from Feminism, unless men change? The stories I hear about husbands would make your hair curl, even more than it does already. I often wonder whether marriage is not the reason for women's servitude. I remember I used to think that. But most of the women I talk to in Whitechapel seem to take men for granted. They are much closer to their daughters. The only answer for women would be to deny themselves children, and then where should we be? Even *I* still feel rather guilty when I am away from the brood; it must be Mother's influence – she put such a lot into her family. I must be more like her than I imagined. She is still working away at Alice's – she can't stop. I thought when Father died she would have time to herself, but she doesn't seem to want it or doesn't know what to do with it. And Alice has four children now. Harry was always mother's favourite; she still thinks of him every day, I'm sure. I only realize now how dreadful it must have been for her, and it's too late for us to be nice to each other now. What must it be like to see your children married and with jobs, or "careers" as they call them now?. She's never got over her "baby Jerome" going off to Australia. By the way; Theo Carmichael is apparently still managing everyone. She is said to be a leading light in the Fabians now and also organizes literary luncheons. A Public Person. Bea says she is very efficient; she is on the board of their charity. But Bea is, of course, efficiency personified. She gets more socialist – or communist – every day and is sure that the Soviet Union is the place to go. Crèches for children, equal pay, equal work, and, if the stories are true, everything organized, down to your thoughts themselves. But I have my doubts. I wonder, still, whether a religious solution is not what we all need. But how can we have one if we don't believe in God? The religion of humanity just isn't very credible after what we know people can do to each other. Michael is an uncompromising atheist, with "ethical" values from his Jewish mama. He thinks all women are 'religious'.

' "Well, women *are* the intuitive sex, aren't they?" he says, which is not what I meant. He's not really a "leader", either, but he says that doesn't matter as he has a good idea of the tastes of the Common Man, being one himself! That's why they make profits, I suppose. He is certainly making money; not millions, but quite a respectable little profit.'

Edith saw there was yet more to come, so made a cup of tea and sat by the fire with the rest of the letter. Sophie did pour herself out, to no one else, she supposed, as she did to her. She did not seem to have changed a great deal; was still the same old Sophie. Life might hurtle by her, but it always had done, and there was always something to argue about or plan. Edith was sure that Sophie was a good mother. Yet, she must often think about the past. Grant was a topic that Sophie did not write about in any detail, though she was not chary of mentioning his name. Sophie had always wanted to be 'free' and had then taken great pains never to be able to be so, what with a love affair and a marriage!

Michael Carr did not seem to be the recipient of Sophie's intimate thoughts, but he must have a shrewd idea about them. Her husband was convenient in a way a more demanding man might not have been. Edith's appraisal of her old friend's weaknesses did not, of course, diminish her affection for her, though she would never have poured out her thoughts as Sophie was wont to do.

Dwelling on Sophie's marriage set Edith thinking once more of Adam Stead, of course. Everything seemed to lead back to Adam: Sophie's letters and Cicely Emery's questions and her own feelings of missing him. She wished he would return from his long walking tour.

Sophie had been destined for marriage in a way she herself had not. Why, then, should she, Edith, now feel that she must take the chance of becoming a wife? Was not her life with Jack and with her own thoughts and duties enough? She must have been very unaroused when she was young. It was Sophie who had been far more aware of the power of men to ensnare you, and your own power to respond. Yet Sophie seemed to feel trapped in a relatively happy ménage. Was she, herself, trapped in her own ability to be independent? Up till now, that was. She remembered Clement's urgency and the swooning feeling of being caught up in it, as though she was completely powerless to do otherwise than let him do what he wanted. And that had led to the best thing in her life, which was Jack. She had never grudged him for taking away some of that independence.

Sophie's marriage seemed to have been intended as a sort of sacrifice to the failure of 'love', of her failure to have Grant's child or even to love Grant enough.

Edith turned back to the last page of the letter: the thought that Sophie had 'settled' for something was not far from the

312

back of her head, and her own questions as to whether she, too, was to 'settle' for Adam. Or was that not fair? Sophie had started a new page in different coloured ink.

'I wish I were less neurotic, for I sometimes feel I might go a little bit mad. Nothing specific, just peculiar dreams and occasional nightmares, silly obsessions, anxieties, depressions, that arise out of nothing but my own head. I'm still terrified I might suddenly die whilst the children are young. I wake in the night wondering whether I've ordered enough food for the weekend and what I am going to say to some unimportant neighbour; I feel angry for no reason or I cry and don't know why. I worry about tomorrow and tomorrow, I suppose. I'm too much at home, for when I'm helping Bea I haven't time to worry and always come back tired but strangely refreshed and rather guilty that other people's troubles should leave me cheerful. I know I have to fight my way out of this domestic bog.

'I prefer my own company but sometimes, after a few hours, panic strikes. Do you think I'm going mad, Edie? I've no reason to be really discontented, but I think of Mother and how she was and wonder whether I'm the same. She never enjoyed anything, was always fearful of the future, and I didn't help with my rebellions. I was just not made to be so responsible; that must be it. Michael doesn't worry because I do the worrying for him!

'If you think it's to do with Grant and the past, you are wrong. I don't regret any of that, not even the baby, really, though perhaps it had an effect upon my "unconscious" as the Freudians say. I am not *really* discontented, so forgive me and let us talk of something else. Like a child, I must have something to look forward to, and so let me ask you again when you will come to stay so we can talk like the old days? You could bring Jack; he would have a lovely time painting the woods here, I am sure. It would be good for the girls to have a young man to tell them what's what.' (Edith smiled at this.) 'Chimneys life is fun, or I hope so; the garden is large, and we have a nice car now. "Carr's car," says Rosamund, upholstered in leather, and I need do nothing if I let the "helpers" get on with it. The errand boys deliver if I am lazy; in short, you could have a lovely time.'

The letter ended, 'Your impatient Sophie, who asks you to forgive the length of this letter but looks forward, as usual, to a reply.'

Edith came to the conclusion that Sophie was anxious in order to propitiate the gods. In some illogical way she was punishing herself. If she worried, then nothing dreadful would happen, but that meant always sacrificing the present to the future. Sophie thought that if she relaxed, she would be punished; so she never relaxed. Yet, if she dare relax she could at least be happy in the present. But no, she worried instead, in order not to be happy and therefore not punished! She had never been like this as a young woman; it must have been having the children that had done it, and Edith looked to Sophie's mother for the cause. Now that Sophie was herself a mother, she had taken on the emotional colouring of her own female parent, that being all she knew of mothers. Edith thought of her own mother, to whom she had never been able to speak openly about Clem. She had never forgiven Edith for getting pregnant. She had never understood her daughter and that had been the last straw. She had left her coldly alone, and it was to her father Edith turned, as she always had in childhood. Father took things upon himself. It was what men ought to do; they saved their wives a good deal of trouble. Strong men were what was needed. Strong women too! Perhaps only possible with strong men around? Sophie always *appeared* strong, but it was a strength built upon shifting sands. Edith was sorry for her friend and wished she could do something to help. Perhaps they could go and stay, Jack and she?

She turned over the last page and saw a PS: 'Did you know that Kitty Moray and Frank have gone to Australia? Apparently Kitty is ill, not expected to recover, they say, and Frank wants to found a New Life community out in the Bush. As though that would help poor Kitty to recover.'

How differently life seemed to be treating all the old friends. Edith had heard from Sophie that Frank had come back from his period of conscientious objection after the war more aggressive than he had ever been. The war had changed everyone for ever. Only she, herself, still seemed to be the same.

'Adam, Adam,' she murmured, 'let us make a life together, you and I, never mind "how".' For the moment, she asked Jack

314

when he came in if he would like to visit Sophie at Chimneys at half-term and they considered the plan seriously.

The next week, when Edith had still not yet replied to Sophie, being immersed in the Vikings before she should have to return the papers to Miss Emery, Adam had still not returned. There came, then, on the Tuesday, a sudden wire from a neighbour of old Mrs Bartholomew in Perbury: 'Carrie sinking fast, asking for you both.' They packed a bag immediately.

Jack wrote a note to his teachers to say he had been called to his grandmother's bedside and they were off on the long train journey to Salisbury, with its many changes of station, before a taxi could take them to the village. Before she left, though, Edith sent a note to Adam to tell him she was away. She knew he was trying to decide whether to cast in his lot for good with her and was worried, not on his own, selfish, account but for her, in case he failed her.

But if Granny Bartholomew were to die they must attend the funeral. She could not ask Adam to be there. Mrs Hoyle would keep an eye on the cottage for her.

The neighbour had been right. The old lady had had one heart attack and was soon to have another. She died the day after Edith and Jack arrived, with them both by her bedside. They stayed for the funeral two days later at the village church which was attended by all the old lady's neighbours. Not till they were all back in the little house, only one up and one down, and Edith had given tea and ham sandwiches to the mourners and they had finally gone away, could she sit down and have a moment to herself. Jack had gone out for a walk. The stuffy little parlour appeared crammed with cracked china dogs sitting on mats and faded paper flowers. A calendar was hanging from a nail on the wall and there was a jar of paper spills on the mantelpiece. The china dogs were, though, spotlessly clean and all the embroidered mats washed. The calendar had obviously fulfilled a purpose, for the date of Jack's last holiday with the old lady was ringed.

In the kitchen cupboard everything was cleaned and tidied away and the linoleum was also wiped and the shelves dustless. Edith knew she would have to go through her mother-in-law's effects before she left for home and thought she might as well

315

begin with the drawer of the only table, where she found a bunch of papers tied with string with a label: 'Clement's letters to me in the war'. Underneath were Clem's apprenticeship papers and his diplomas. It seemed to Edith, as she looked at this evidence of the years before he had gone to London and the three years before he was killed in France, which she had never seen before, that she had never really known her husband. She put them all to one side for Jack and then methodically sorted a pile of old postcards before going on to itemize the ornaments.

Carrie Bartholomew had wanted her neighbours to have a memento each of her. The house was only rented; soon another family would move in. There was no will, only the envelope with the money for the funeral. Edith had, herself, paid for that and decided to give the rector five pounds to keep an eye on the grave. Underneath all the other bundles and bits of lace and one or two photographs of Clem as a baby, she found a folded piece of tissue paper. Inside, with a tiny label in Carrie's neatest writing, was a curl of her Clem's baby hair. Edith felt tears rising at the back of her nose as she put it back in its envelope. She got up, then, and washed up the cups and saucers and went upstairs to sort out linen and clothes. There were not many clothes, and when Jack returned she had blown her nose and been round to the nearest neighbour with some crockery and one of the china dogs.

'Ah, Carrie was that proud of her dogs,' said the old woman, a Mrs Vye. 'Are ye sure she meant me to have it?'

She had met Mrs Vye once or twice before on her few visits to Mrs Bartholomew, who was really Miss Bartholomew from the next village, who had come here with her son in the late 1880's, with the rent provided for by her seducer at the Big House. For years the woman had toiled away at sewing and washing for others. She had lived frugally once Clem was grown up. Perhaps she was not all that different from Edith herself. A proud woman and a thrifty one, whose one 'lapse' had been paid for with a life of unremitting labour. Edith made a pile of Clement's school books for Jack to look at and take away if he wanted them, and he looked at them as they sat over another cup of tea.

'I looked at the tablet to Father again,' Jack said.

Clem, who had been buried far away in France, was yet commemorated here, with the handful of other young men from the village who had also died in the war.

It was after six o'clock now and they were to travel back to the north early the next morning. Edith looked out of the door and stood for a moment on the threshold, before an early November dusk fell. The sky was pale blue and smoky grey, with tiny, mapping-pen scratches and blobs of bronze – the few remaining leaves on the thin branches of trees behind the cottages on the other side of the road. She wondered how the boy, Clement, had felt, living in this small place, walking miles over fields, writing his early poems, before he went to Swindon to learn the trade of railway engineering. She remembered the poems that came after that time, poems which Sophie Ridsdale had so admired. She wished Sophie were there with her. She felt she herself did not belong here, that she was an intruder. The funeral of the woman who had given Clem life, to have that life snatched away from her for ever, only underlined the ravages of time. How had she borne it? Yet she had never complained and kept up a brave face to Edith. How could Edith bear it if Jack was snatched away in that manner? The funeral seemed to have underlined her need of a living adult to balance all the sorrow of the world. Jack, though, must not die.

Edith went up to the tiny bedroom where Carrie had slept for over forty years alone. Had she had no man willing to look after her? It was a miracle she had escaped the workhouse after the money from Clem's father had stopped, once the boy had been apprenticed. And Clem's father had died long before Clem had gone to seek his fortune in London. Time seemed to stretch back and back, now that another life was over. Edith could not repress a great feeling of thankfulness that Jack had been born and had given the old lady a little pleasure in her lonely life. Carrie had never been demonstrative, but she had loved the boy.

Oh, she *must* get away, thought Edith. She must find Adam again. He had been away so long. She paused as she passed Jack, who was sitting in one of the fireside chairs by the unlit grate, and took his hand and squeezed it. He looked up at her, his grey eyes for a moment reminding her of her husband's. How strange life was. Because of one evening in 1913 in far away London, she, from even further away, was sitting in the house of a woman who had just died, a woman she had nothing in common with except that they were both mothers and were connected through the young man who had been her son.

'We must be up early,' she said. 'I've left a list of things to be given to the other friends who were at the funeral and I shall ask the rector to dispose of the rest. I've got all the papers and a few letters and these old photographs to take home.' She handed Jack the photographs and went up to the bed, leaving him pondering them.

As they chugged up through the western side of England, northwards, in the first of many trains the next day, Edith's mind was still half on Adam. She did not want, however, to deny her son the opportunity to talk about his father, for the funeral had had an effect upon Jack and he looked thoughtful. He had asked if he might keep for himself the photograph of Clement, which his grandmother had kept for over thirty years, and which neither he nor Edith had seen before. In it, Clem was about the same age Jack was now and it had probably been taken when he left school and started as an apprentice. His eyes seemed to burn out of the photograph at Edith. It was a Clem she had never known except, perhaps, that evening when he had made love to her. How quickly the whirligig of time came round; for now, his son was looking out of the window of the train and with those eyes, less dark, but with a certain unmistakeable resemblance to his father. It was not so much any particular feature, for indeed Jack took after her in nose and mouth and height, but he had Clem's tapering fingers and a way of walking and holding himself, and also, she realized, a certain ruthlessness when it came to doing what he wanted. Jack would not argue, but would proceed to do whatever he had decided to do without fuss. Clem must have had to be more ambitious, more ruthless, to escape from Swindon. Jack would not need to rebel, but he was his own man and would never be deflected from his chosen path, unless, perhaps, a woman would one day steal his heart. He was kinder, too, than his father had been.

318

Just now, as he turned away from the window and looked at her a moment, she decided to ask him what he would think about her taking on Adam Stead. But she could hardly say she wanted to marry him, as Adam had not asked her.

'I wonder when Adam will be back,' was all she said.

They called him Adam to each other; Mr Stead seemed too formal and Jack had been encouraged to talk to him on an equal footing, which Adam, too, seemed to like.

Jack continued to look at her and then, with a slightly embarrassed dip of his head, said, 'I want you to be happy, Mother. You mustn't worry about me.'

His swift reading of her mind startled her, but the awkward emotion touched her too. 'Oh, perhaps he will decide to work for his father now,' was all she said, but their eyes met and Jack read her hopes there. He looked out of the window again. Edith felt she ought to say something more, but did not know what. Was it fair to take on Adam when her son was still in need of her financial and emotional support? Even if her father helped.

'Yes, I think he must work. *You* work hard enough,' said Jack, and she left it at that.

But when, finally, after a whole day and early evening's journey, they arrived at Far Ox Heys, there was a figure sitting on their wall outside the kitchen window.

'You'll catch your death of cold,' said Edith.

Adam Stead stood up.

'I'll go and make something to drink,' said Jack, leading the way indoors.

Adam and Edith stood on the threshold and he took her hand. 'You've come back,' was all she could say.

'For good, I think,' said Adam, and took her bag; no more was said. But Adam returned to his aunt's to sleep.

In the morning Jack was back at school and Edith found it difficult, for once, to concentrate on her work. It was cold, much colder than in Wiltshire, and she was reliving the funeral and idly looking, once more, at the few things they had brought back with them.

She knew Adam would come again and she felt a curious reluctance to clear her thoughts. There was so much between them, so many potentially important things to say. After six months he was almost a stranger again. She looked round her room slowly. Could she give up her quiet life, her solitude and her independence, even for a man whom she undoubtedly loved and whose very life seemed to hang in the balance? Would Adam feel able to offer marriage? Nothing else would seem to do. She wanted to share her life and yet keep part of it to herself. Was she strong enough to give him what he needed? Jack wanted her to be happy. She smiled. Jack obviously thought she would be happy with Adam, otherwise she would not choose him. But happiness was not really the point. Could she and Adam grow together into something more than they could accomplish separately? Was she, perhaps, snatching at a chimera; was she too old to change?

When he knocked at the door she was at her table and rose slowly to open it. For a moment he hesitated and then put his arms round her waist and held her tight.

'Will you have me?' he murmured. 'I wanted to be sure, so I've starved myself of your company.'

'To see if you really wanted me?' she said.

They drew apart and stood looking at each other.

'You know the disadvantages. But I can chop wood, do all the heavy work, light the fires, look after you when you are tired. I can work up at Hoyle's for the time being.'

'Adam, you sound as though you are offering yourself as a servant, or perhaps a tenant. Is it true you've decided to work for Hoyle?'

'Till I get something better. Edith, you haven't answered my question really, have you? I do "really want" you; will you have me?'

'For what?' asked Edith faintly, but smiling.

'For a husband, of course. I wasn't proposing anything else.'

'We must be sensible,' said Edith, feeling far from sensible. 'I've been here alone with Jack for almost twelve years. I have my work to do, I can't offer all the normal comforts of wifehood, however much I could love you, my work must be as important, I mean, as far as time is concerned. I don't need financial support, but would you agree to that? Would it be fair on you?'

'I shall earn something and I shall have times when I must be alone myself,' he answered. 'We need see of each other only what we want. You shall have your room and I

320

shall rig up a little place in the other barn. I don't want you to change at all. You must go on with your writing. I'm quite a good cook.'

'Jack wants me to be happy,' said Edith. 'He told me so yesterday. I know what he meant.'

'I may not be "happy" all the time. Edith, I don't want to take away anything from you, only to add to your life; and if you weren't happy, I swear I'd be off.'

'I want you to be happy, Adam, yet I can't see that "happiness" is what we are really talking about.'

'No. I had a feeling I might complete your life; probably that was vain of me. You would certainly complete mine, if you could bear with me. You know my moods and what you might have to deal with. It would be a risk. But I'm tired of not taking risks. I love you, Edith. *Will* you marry me? I stayed away till I was sure.'

Edith was suddenly back in that room in Bridlington, with Clem demanding marriage. She had said 'yes' then because of Jack. Should she say no, now, to someone so much more finely tuned to her nature?

'I mean, a "proper" wife,' said Adam, suppliant.

'All right,' said Edith, matter-of-factly. 'If you are sure.'

'Yes, I'm sure. When?' pursued Adam, once he had taken the bit between his teeth, was determined to settle this once and for all.

'Couldn't we live together for a bit and then, if it works, marry next year?' It was not intimacy that worried her, not physical intimacy, but her need sometimes to be alone.

'I shall be out all day, and you will work just as you always have. We can share the rest of the chores. And we shall have each other when we feel lonely. But you must consult Jack, too; he is more important than me.'

Edith sat down by the fire and put out her hand to him. He came and sat at her knees and she stroked his hair and they were silent for a time.

'Perhaps we could marry sooner than next year then,' she said.

'Whenever you want, Edith,' he said and buried his face in her lap.

'If you take me on, I don't want you ever to regret it,' he said. He looked up. 'I so love you, Edith. That's why I want

321

to marry you, not just to share your life, or you mine. I really *love* you, darling Edith. And I want to forget part of myself in you. When I was away I thought of you as a "healing herb".'

'I love you, Adam,' she said.

Edith's father was incredulously pleased when she took Adam over to meet her parents the next week. She had explained about his experiences in the war and was worried that when they saw his limp and his occasionally trembling hand they would think her a little mad to believe she could 'rehabilitate' a man who had suffered so much. But Adam was able to present himself in a good light to Wilfred Broughton. He loved their daughter and she loved him and they were surely old enough to know their minds. What was the use of looking for difficulties? They must live from day to day.

'He would like to own a farm eventually,' said Edith when Adam was being shown round the garden by Jack. 'That's what he likes doing best. But for the moment, he's to help at Ox Heys.'

'Why doesn't he follow his father into the business?' asked Maud Broughton.

'He never wanted to, and the war altered him even more. He needs a quiet life – physical labour – to get his nerves back to normal. He's a strong man underneath but he's lucky to be alive at all.'

'And you'll go on with your own work?' asked Wilfred.

'Of course. It's not to make any difference. We shall pool our finances. Adam won't take money from his family. He's managed alone since the war, doing all sorts of things. I suppose one day he will inherit, but we've enough to manage for the present.'

Broughton was not convinced and saw no reason why Edith should continue living in a small cottage, but knew better than to say so.

'Jack is pleased, anyway. I think he was worrying about having to put me first all his life; that wouldn't be right, and in the end he'll have reason to be glad about that. He'll be off eventually, in London, I dare say, after the art school. He'll be relieved to know someone is here with me.'

'Yes; I'm glad, too, Edie – if you're sure?'

'As sure as anyone can be,' she replied.

'Edith is a very private person,' her father said to Adam later, when he joined him in the magnificent garden and Edith was helping her mother to bring in the tea to the smaller of the two drawing rooms, as it was Lizzie's, the parlour maid's, day off.

'Yes, I know. I don't want to take anything away from her, only add to her life, if I can,' said Adam. He was not a man used to being humble, thought the older man. But he was genuine enough. 'She must have her solitude. She has ideas for a new book,' offered Adam.

'Yes, yes. Edith's always been a hard-working person. Like me. But what will you do with yourself? Edith tells me you were going to be a doctor.'

'Oh, that was long ago,' said Adam easily. 'What I'd like to be is a farmer, and perhaps I might do some auxiliary veterinary work. I had plenty of experience with horses in the war. I'd like to earn enough to make things easier for Edith eventually. Perhaps start with a smallholding.'

'Well, you're neither of you young,' said Wilfred briskly. 'Edith will use her war pension. But she will inherit from me one day, after both my wife and I are gone.'

'We think that Jack should be the beneficiary,' said Adam. 'He's the one who will need money for his studies.'

'You think he'll make the grade, then? I had thought he'd make a good engineer, but it seems he's set his heart on painting. I used to paint when I was young, you know.'

They came in then, for it was cold, and tea was welcome. Adam thought he had passed the test, although he knew that the only test of any real concern to him was with Edith.

'So I am going to marry Adam,' wrote Edith to Sophie. 'I know you would like him. I suppose I am rather old to be marrying again, or at all, but it seems I want to. It has surprised me, too. It's not that Jack needs a father; it's a bit late for that. But we think we can do better together than apart. Adam suffered so terribly in the war. Not shell-shock, just despair at what he saw, rather than what he suffered personally; though he did have a wound in the ankle and sometimes cannot stop his hand trembling. I think I can help him over the physical symptoms, not that he's a weakling. He must have tramped thousands of miles since he came back from France, where he worked for the War Graves Commission for a time. He was going to be a doctor before the war, but that's all over. Says he'd rather mend horses than people. For the present he's to take on some work for the farmer up here. He knows about machinery and can turn his hand to lots of things. We'll just have to see how it goes. Don't worry about his "taking away my freedom", for I know you will be thinking, how can I bear to share my life after being so long alone? Adam wants me to go on writing for a living, and knows, also, that I should write in any case. It will be no great hardship to cook for three rather than two!

Wish me luck, dear Sophie; I promise we shall come to see you one day soon. Jack will soon be going off to Leeds and is already amassing a large portfolio of drawings. We're not having a wedding breakfast, by the way, or I should have invited you, of course: just slipping away to the coast for a few days. I wanted, strange to say, to see old Bridlington once more; eighteen years since my stay there. Adam knows all about Clem and the old days, but wants to see for himself where Jack was born. And then we shall call in on his father. His mother is dead and his father is now in Middlesbrough with a flourishing business. Kiss the children for me. I am sending you one little picture I found at Granny Bartholomew's – of Clem as a boy. I thought you might like it.

'As for Garnett, I shall not ask him about the copyrights, but leave it to his own conscience. You did enough, getting my "saga" published, so don't worry. Write and tell me you are glad about the marriage. We shall be back home by the end of January.'

Sophie's answer did not come for a week or two and Edith, reading between the lines, felt a faint disappointment. Under the congratulations. She had let the side down. What did Edith need with marriage? was the unspoken criticism. She would come round eventually, Edith decided.

The wedding took place in the registrar's office in Calderbrigg, one Saturday morning in January 1932. Edith's parents had motored over specially and Jack was 'best man'. Adam's father expressed no interest, but sent a cheque, and his aunt was away once more abroad, so it was a simple and swiftly over affair. They went back to Roundhay for a luncheon prepared by Lizzie, and then Jack stayed on with his grandparents when Edith and Adam took the train from Leeds to the coast.

It seemed to be full of very young bridal couples. Edith had refused a motoring holiday. Adam must have a restful few days, not have to plan journeys and itineraries. She was quite content to stay in a small hotel not far from the part of the town once lived in by Saranna and her sisters. But it had been much built upon since the war, and when she went out that first evening, for a walk by the sea with her new husband, Edith could not help seeing how the very buildings betrayed the passing of time. What had been lanes or tracks were macadamed roads. The once deserted beaches were, even in winter, dotted with visitors. Perhaps even the lighthouse had changed.

They went to bed early, and both slept well and awoke refreshed to walk in the Old Town and then stroll near the harbour.

'I'd like to go over to Flamborough,' said Edith. 'That lighthouse somehow saved my life; and we can walk along the cliffs, too.'

'I thought you'd want to go to Danes' Dyke,' said Adam.

'You think my mind is on Vikings still?'

'But it isn't Vikings, is it? Much, much older.'

'I expect Vikings used it, but it's about three thousand years old. It will cut us down to size. Let's go to Flamborough first.'

So they went to Flamborough village the next day. Their marriage was finally consummated on the second night of their honeymoon, with much mental and physical relief to Adam and emotional relief to Edith. Not yet had they reached the heights of passion, but there seemed to be something more important even than passion: they felt they held each other in trust for the sake of the other, and that their true selves were present, reflected clearly in a glass that was not misted over by lust or illusion. It was, miraculously, a handing over, each to the other, of their separate lives. They were happy and Edith felt particularly full of energy. Adam, too, was relaxed and ready to be impressed. Impressed they both were with the great white cliffs of massive Flamborough Head. They walked on the grassy tops with Bridlington Bay beneath them, the whole sweep of the bay glittering across from east to west and the sound of thousands of sea birds in their ears, making such a din they could not hear each other speak till they moved back a little.

'The last of the chalk,' said Edith. 'This is where it comes out from England into the sea.'

Then they walked over to the North Landing, a mile or two away, and looked at the caves with their special names, as though they were suburban villas, and then on to Thornwick Bay with its rock pools and view to Filey Brigg. It was a clear, calm day; cold, but they had hardly expected it to be warm. Another walk to the coastguard station and then along the headland to the lighthouse, after sitting on a wall and devouring the pork pies they had bought. There was so much to explore that they said they would come back. For the present, they walked to the lighthouse and saw the new building and climbed the spiral staircase to see the hundreds of lenses. A guided tour was available and they walked along behind the guide, hand in hand, asking intelligent questions.

'South Landing and the lifeboat and Danes' Dyke tomorrow,' said Edith, as they spiralled down again. 'Are you tired?'

'No. But I think we should get back.' He smiled and took her arm and tucked it under his.

The brightly painted cobles were pulled up on the North Landing when they returned.

'Look; they'll be crab fishing in summer.' Edith pointed at the boats with their piles of crab pots.

'The boats are like your Viking longships,' said Adam. 'Was it coming here that started your interest in Vikings?'

'No, I've always wanted to know more about them. Let's go and look at the boats.'

Adam found much to interest him in the cobles, and together they spent an half-hour looking and asking questions and watching the fishermen. Adam realized that he and Edith liked doing the same sort of things. Doing them together was fun. They were on their honeymoon, yet they were walking round like some long-married couple.

The rest of the week was spent exploring each other at night and the coast and the villages, the sea and the cliffs and landings during the day. They were continually laughing and continually hungry. Edith thought that her husband already looked years younger. They would never become bored with each other, that was certain. They had so much to talk about, and filled the gaps in each other's information as though they were meant to collaborate in order to get a full picture of the world. Adam thought Edith had rescued him, much as the lifeboats they saw at Flamborough rescued shipwrecked sailors. To her, he was like that lighthouse.

Even Jack thought his mother looked younger when they came back.

The honeymoon had given Edith plenty to think about. It was not the new relationship begun and continued in bed, but the novel sensation of companionship with a like mind. She prayed that, whatever happened to the world, their life would go on as well as it had begun.

New feelings were already sweeping over her and, for a time, she even gave herself a rest from her work, and relaxed. Her greatest joy was that, by the end of their first year of married life, Adam was able once more, occasionally, to listen to the music he had once loved without those other intrusive sounds of war blocking out his pleasure.

2

Closerie des Lilas
1938

The child breathing in the alien air found the place strange. Such a noisy, quarrelsome sort of place it was, but with beautiful wide streets and with so many people who were always thirsty: they must be always thirsty for they sat everywhere, on chairs, on pavements, at tables with glasses in front of them. They did not seem to work like they did in London. They looked different. The young men often slung an arm around the neck of a girlfriend. It was quite embarrassing. The cafés were a bit embarrassing, too; the way these big, grey buildings of a capital city were given over, downstairs, to so many hundreds of cafés, spilling them out into the street. They would not allow people to sit drinking outside the House of Commons or Westminster Abbey! And the smells! Pungent, smelly smells; that garlic they ate and a sort of oily smell from the stuff they put on their hair. And the people washed, not in water, but in eau de Cologne; there were enormous bottles of it in the *Bon Marché* shop. In England, even a little bottle would cost heaps. She knew because she had bought a small phial of lavender water for her mother the Christmas before. It had been unbelievably dear. But scent was nice and the ice-creams were fabulous, wonderful, marvellous. And the ladies walked differently, with a sort of wiggle, and men looked at ladies more than they did at home. They even looked at her mother! There were some shops, too, in another part of the city, where the windows were done like a theatre with gorgeous silks and objects like seashells rising out of dresses.

328

Some windows had only one dress, just one, costing, mother said, 'the earth'.

Mother loved it all, because it was different from home. And perhaps she liked it when men smiled at her in the street. Her sister had even had young men saying things to *her* as they walked along, sometimes making a funny noise like a hen clucking or a sort of hissing or kissing noise, a funny whisper – a long *sssssss*. Still, it was a holiday, and she was enjoying it, though she would also be glad to be home again to see her special garden that needed watering. She did not trust Mrs Copley, who had promised to do it, but the gardener might have done it for her. Abroad was exciting, but home was better, really, thought Clementine Carr.

The young man had been sitting at the pavement café in the shade of the awning for a good two hours. He had drunk a glass of fizzy, yellowish, French beer, and then ordered a cup of bitter black coffee, feeling no inclination to move. It was a hot summer afternoon and this was not a fashionable part of Paris as far as he could guess. Next to the café was a restaurant, now half-empty, where he had gone at noon and partaken of the cheapest menu he could find on the list; some part of a sheep which the English probably never ate. But delicious, simply delicious.

He had bought a French paper, to read the latest news from Spain, and pushed it under his sketch-book. The sight of it seemed to make his insides turn a somersault. Bob and Charlie and Jim would be expecting him in four days at the rendezvous they had arranged when Jack had announced his intention of travelling on from England earlier than they. He had wanted a few days' peace before he made up his mind. And he had done nothing but sit and watch people pass in the streets. The sketch-book on the wrought-iron table before him bore the evidence of time spent watching and recording. He had been down by the river and on to the Ile St Louis and walked for hours, sometimes not caring where he was, except he was in Paris.

The constant procession of men, women and children, all gaily dressed and purposeful looking, passed him in endless hundreds wherever he went on the larger boulevards, and taxis hooted and buses trundled over cobblestones on their way to places with romantic sounding names: Porte la Chapelle, Mairie d'Ivry. And, above all, there was that smell of abroad; of freshly baked bread, the delicious smell of Gauloises, the cologne and perfume used by men as well as women.

He had ridden for pleasure in the métro and come up for air at places where Paris had seemed to peter out, either into grey streets in the north of the city, or into green parks to the south. In the crowded second-class carriages of the métro was the same smell, but intensified: tobacco and perfume mixed with an oily odour, and the ubiquitous garlic. He had swayed along in the carriages, feeling he need never get out. His sketch-book was a passport. He could go where he liked, see what he wanted, so long as his money did not run out, and return at night to that rather dingy hotel on Rue Monsieur le Prince where he would remove the long bolster from the head of the bed and fall asleep immediately, looking forward to his breakfast of coffee and fresh bread.

It was a sybaritic life for one bred in the north of England but he saw no reason to feel guilty about that. He had worked hard for the last five years, not only at his painting, but helping on the farm too. There were museums and churches to visit; he had already been to the Louvre and the Jeu de Paume and the Sainte Chapelle and the Gobelins workshop; there were theatres to patronize, the Comédie Française for one, and a play he wanted to see at the Marigny because the picture outside on the playbill showed a beautiful woman. He had not looked for a girlfriend. Time was too precious for that. Was he not off to Spain next week, with his friends, to offer himself in the struggle against fascism? Was that not the least he could do, he who had had such a good, though hardworking, life?

He stirred the dregs of his coffee cup and tried to assure himself that he was going. It had all seemed quite simple when he talked to his friends in Leeds. He was not a communist, but did he not believe that the struggle in Spain would decide the fate of Europe? Well, he *had* believed that, he supposed – if the great Picasso was on the side of the Republicans, if every thinking person, or almost every intellectual and artist, were right.

The Spanish Civil War had been going on for a long time, yet he could still easily go to fight in it, not that he thought it would make much difference, now, whether he did or not. But his conscience would be satisfied; he would have done his bit, as his father had done, volunteering when there had been no need. A supreme gesture. The trouble was, he was beginning to have his doubts; not about his own courage or whether the Republicans were fundamentally in the right, but about whether it was worth risking your life for another's cause.

Yes, it had all seemed simple in the heady atmosphere of the meetings he had attended. At last, a chance to stop the cancer circulating and perhaps, by doing so, avoid a worse conflict later. At last, a chance to prove yourself and to subsume your own, puny existence in a greater struggle. But he had not really believed the party members, who saw this as an opportunity to bring communism to Europe. Was that all there was to choose between – the right wing against the communists? Along with a few idealists, socialists and anarchists. Soviet Russia, Republican Spain, against Fascist Italy, Franco, and Hitler's Germany? France was foreign enough, he thought, looking across the road at the tall apartment blocks which rose above the shops. What did he know about Spain? He tried to follow the newspaper stories each day and had gone to the Gare de Lyon to see the young men from all over Europe still getting on the southbound trains. But here, when he thought about it alone, it did not seem so simple. And perhaps the International Brigade itself was petering out.

On the day that he had left for France, mentioning only casually that he might go on to Spain, his mother had said nothing, but she had looked very frightened. His stepfather had seemed angry. But Jack was twenty-three, and his life was his own. If he believed in a better world he must take the challenge, realize that one could not live for art alone, that you could not think just of your mother and her fears. He was his own person. His own father had died in the war. The International Brigade casualties had not been anything like those in the war his father had fought, though.

All this tergiverzation was because he was a coward then? His mother would not stop him doing what he thought was right and his stepfather would not interfere. That stepfather had proved himself in the last war. It would be an adventure. He would not be killed. He would sample a little of the struggle and set his mind at rest and return, as so many of the English poets had returned, to write of Spain. But not to cast their lives at her feet. Except for one or two Marxists and intellectuals. But he was not a Marxist, he was an artist. Was it that there was no future for his painting if it did not meet the challenge?

Jack looked up again and thought he would go back to his hotel and sort out his sketch-book. A man who had been looking at him rather pointedly for a long time had finally got up and gone. Jack was used to being followed by men who were attracted to him. He had the looks of a tall, fair Englishman, he supposed, and were not all Englishmen perpetrators of *le vice anglais*? Or was that something else? At any rate, he had had more propositions in the last week in Paris than in five years at home. He did not worry about that. He could deal with them. People in Paris seemed to live at a greater pace and to be more obvious about their inclinations than in England. Paris heightened your reactions, he supposed. It was a relief to throw off English puritanism for a time.

Round the Sorbonne, a lot was going on. No artists there, but plenty of noisy demonstrations in favour of Spain. He had sat at café tables next to Spanish refugees and tried to make out their talk. But he had still not decided what to do. Here he was, in good health, the owner of a diploma and a future student at the Slade (he hoped), wondering whether to risk his life for a cause he only partially understood. And if he did not go, would he feel himself a failure for the rest of his life?

His mother had kissed him goodbye and he had promised to write. She had looked resigned. But she and Adam did not need to worry about him and she would be all right; she had Adam.

He must go into the café for a pee. This beer was a real bladder-wrecker, along with the coffee. He got up and went into the cool hinterland of the café, past the telephone and the zinc bar and the array of bottles of red and green and gold, like an altar behind the counter, and managed to find the lavatory downstairs and relieve himself. Afterwards he looked at himself as he came up, in the long mirror facing the stairs that led to the basement, and wondered whether he looked as 'foreign' as he felt. He would go for a walk in the Luxembourg Gardens, down the *boulevards*, sit by the *bassin* and watch the French children who played under the chestnuts.

God, Paris was beautiful! He would not mind living here for good, though his sort of painting was not fashionable here. He had seen that when he had been to one or two galleries which seemed, to his provincial eyes, to be both more and less sophisticated than a similar gallery in London. But if he lived for too long in a town, even one as lovely as Paris, he would begin to long for more than urban trees, for real fields not parks, for quiet and peace, not eternal bustle and variety. He was thinking that London might be even less to his taste, when he heard English voices at a table on the left which he must pass to achieve the pavement. He looked in their direction and hitched his sketch-book under one arm as he passed. A woman, sitting back, with the sunlight from a tiny hole in the awning scattering a little gold medallion on her hair, and three tall glasses of ice-cream on a table in front of three feminine pairs of lips.

He hesitated for a moment. Surely it was Aunt Sophie and her children? He had last seen them five years ago when he had gone down to Chimneys with Edith and Adam, the year after his mother's remarriage. Would it be rude not to say hello? Yet he felt shy. His mother had not mentioned anything about a holiday in Paris and she usually retailed her friend Sophie's news. Before he could either turn tail or advance to their table, Sophie turned her head and stared at him. He thought she looked strange, as though she had seen a ghost. She half-rose and the girls looked up from their busy lickings. He moved in their direction.

'Jack?' enquired Sophie Carr, sitting down again abruptly.

The girls all stared at him and then smiled. He thought he had better make the best of it. Perhaps they, too, would like a walk in the Luxembourg.

'I thought it was your father,' said Sophie. 'In the half-light, as you came through that door, you looked like Clem. Fancy your being in Paris! Have you time for a drink or something?' She still looked shaken, and one of the girls, the middle one, was looking at her curiously. 'You all know Jack. We were only saying before we came over that we must go north again and see your mother soon; it's been so long! Tell us all your news.'

Jack sat down and ordered another coffee when the long-aproned waiter came up, flourishing his napkin. The girls all shook hands with Jack and he had to bob up again each time.

'Are you all having a holiday, then?' he asked.

'We came yesterday. Mother wanted us to see Paris – she's been talking about it for ages,' said Rosamund, the one who had been looking at her mother.

'Not for long,' said Pheobe. 'I mean, the others. *I'm* going on for a visit to a French family, to improve my French.' She was very composed.

The little one said, 'Hello, Jack' as though he had just dropped in for a cup of tea from a nearby house.

'Well, this is a surprise!' said their mother. 'Do you know, Jack, it's twenty-four years since I've been here. Isn't it absurd? It was before the war – can you imagine?'

'Has it changed much?' asked Jack, disposing of his sketch-book on a nearby vacant seat. Twenty-four years spanned more than his own lifetime.

'No, not really; the feel of it is the same. Have you been drawing, then?'

Jack remembered all the paints and the paper sent over the years to him. She had been very generous. 'Oh, just lightning sketches; there's so much here to draw. I might work up some of them later at home; it's too hot to do anything good.' What am I saying? he thought. I'm off to Spain in a few days. No time for sketching there.

The girls were eyeing him and he looked surreptitiously at them, one by one: Phoebe, the eldest, with her straight, dark hair and serious face, always a book in her pocket, he discovered later. Phoebe did not talk quite as much as the next sister, but no one talked as much as the dramatic Rosamund. She was now about fourteen, he supposed, and looked as though she had no more to grow, only a readjustment of her figure to make it that of a woman. He remembered her long legs and her teasing of him, on his visit five years before. This time, though, she did not tease but looked very openly at him. She had very dark blue eyes and Sophie's nose. She was extremely self-possessed for a fourteen year old, he thought. He saw, with his artist's eye, long, slender hands and trim ankles at the end of brown, smooth, stockingless legs in black sandals.

334

Clemmie, the youngest, was altogether more thick-set than her sisters and she said little, but smiled now and again at him. They were all easy to talk to, easy to feel friendly towards. Their mother looked older. Unlike Edith, she had put on a bit of weight round the neck; her lipstick was rather a bright red, and there were a few silvery streaks in her short hair. But she seemed determined to enjoy herself and had, she said, planned dozens of places to see in the week that was before them. He wondered that she thought he looked like his father. He could not see any resemblance to himself in the one or two photographs he had of his father, Clem Bartholomew.

Sophie, for her part, was thinking that Jack had a little of his father's brusquerie, but in Jack's case it was not meant uncharitably. He was rather reserved. Not shy, just a young man who had not yet quite come to terms with himself, although he had probably almost come to terms with the world. She could not take her eyes off him. He was both Jack and not Jack; Edith's son, now a man; Clement's son, too; and a stranger. Jack, for his part, was thinking how he would like to paint Rosamund Carr sitting at a café table. Rosamund's eyes met his more often than the eyes of her sisters.

'I had thought of taking the girls for a slap-up dinner at the Potée Champenoise,' Sophie was saying. 'Do come too, Jack! It's not far from here. Where are you staying?' Jack told her. 'Of course, you may have planned something else,' added Sophie, recollecting that young men were usually on the look out for young women and that perhaps Jack was not quite alone in Paris. But Jack was free. 'We are in a little hotel near St Sulpice,' continued Sophie. 'I stayed there years and years ago.'

'Yes, twenty-four, you said,' said Rosamund rather unkindly.

'I like this place,' said Phoebe, to cover her sister's rudeness. 'What is it called?'

'Closerie des Lilas,' said Clemmie, looking up and pronouncing the words with a strong English accent. She was twelve, had only studied French for two years, and was no linguist.

It was Rosamund's turn to sound dreamy. 'Can't you just see the artists and their girlfriends here, all dressed in mauve, drinking absinthe?'

Jack laughed. Where on earth had she read all that? Now she was sounding like her mother. Perhaps that was why the two seemed to clash. 'In my experience, artists can't afford absinthe,' he replied.

She smiled.

'And how is your mother?' asked Sophie, looking at him over her glass of tea and lemon. She had not ordered ice-cream, although she would have liked to. Russian tea would be better for her figure. She stirred it and waited for an answer.

'Mother is always the same,' he said. 'She is busy, of course. A new book, I think, but you will know about that?'

'We're all waiting for Garnett Edwards to die,' said Sophie. 'You know about all *that*?'

'Mother doesn't think he will leave her anything.'

'But she has written most of his books since the war – '

'I know – "Bevis Constantine" – I've just read one. Mother didn't want me to read them when I was younger. I don't know why, they're hardly corrupting.'

'She's ashamed of them,' said Sophie. 'Though why she should be I don't understand; for what they are they couldn't be better. I could never believe Edith wrote them, but she did.'

'She says they are out of fashion,' said Jack.

'They'll be in fashion again one day. All people want at the moment are novels about shops or factories, or chronicles of the rich, they don't want Edith's sort of fantasy.'

'Mother writes other things, too,' he ventured. 'Diaries, about the weather, about my stepfather – I don't know. Poetry, too . . .'

'Your father wrote poetry, didn't he?' asked Phoebe.

'Yes. I've only just begun to read it,' admitted Jack. 'I tried when I was little, but it was too complicated for me. Now, I *do* like it. Do you read poetry, then?' he asked Phoebe politely.

'Phoebe reads everything,' said Rosamund. 'We all read masses, except Clemmie who reads the same book over and over!'

'Well, it's very good,' said Clemmie, waking up from a contemplation of Jack. She thought she had perhaps been staring, and blushed.

'It's *White of Selborne*,' said Phoebe. 'Our youngest sister is a country girl.'

'Do you know about otters?' Jack asked Clemmie, who seemed to be rather out of it.

'Otters are almost my favourite creatures,' replied Clemmie.

'Father had a poem about them,' said Jack.

'I once took your mother to see an otter called Ethel,' said Sophie dreamily.

'At Thirksay?' asked Jack.

'Yes. She told you then?

'Oh, Mother is always talking about Thirksay. I think she'd like Adam to farm somewhere like that.'

'That's where Grandma Ridsdale was, wasn't it?' asked Clemmie.

'I'm afraid the farm has been run down,' sighed Sophie. 'Clemmie wants to be a farmer.'

'How strange,' said Rosamund. 'Coming to Paris to talk about otters!'

'But you are a painter, aren't you, Jack?' asked Phoebe.

'I'm still learning.' (But I'd like to paint Rosamund, he thought again.)

'Let's walk back by the Luxembourg and then we can go and get tidied up if we are to meet you tonight, Jack,' said Sophie.

She explained where the restaurant was and they all got up and walked in a bright group down the Boulevard St Michel, past the métro on the other side of the road and a very large café opposite, crammed with students.

'They used to sell chestnuts here,' said Sophie Carr to her old friend's son.

Rosamund was wondering whether her mother had ever come to Paris with Jack's father. She had guessed that her mother had been fond of him, and her romantic imagination supplied the rest of the details. It was odd to think of one's mother being young and in love. But she said to Jack, who was walking by her side, 'They have the best ice-creams in the world on the other side of the street; ones with fruit and lime and cherries. They never make them like that at home.'

It was about five o'clock when they went into the Luxembourg Gardens, down the central sanded path with the fountain in the middle distance.

'Mother, I want to see the goldfish again,' said Clemmie.

'She means the Médici Fountain,' said Phoebe.

337

'Well, I'm going back,' said Sophie. 'Perhaps, Jack, you'd like to show Clemmie the fountain and then come back with the girls. We're at the Sulpice, just out of the gardens at the other end and by the big church and the square.'

'I'll come with you, Ma,' said Phoebe.

Jack hesitated.

'Oh, do come and see the fish,' said Rosamund.

That was enough – he would.

'Look after Jack,' said Sophie with a smile, 'and don't get lost. Of course, Jack, you don't *have* to go with them. They can go again, another day.'

'Oh, Mother!'

'I'd love a walk,' said Jack. 'And I'll bring them back in an hour. What time should I come to the restaurant?'

They arranged eight o'clock and Phoebe went back by her mother's side. 'He's nice, isn't he?' she offered.

'Very. But Edith could not have had a son who was not.'

'It's a pity Father was too busy to come. He would like all this.' She gestured over the paths and borders to the fountain and the trees in the distance and the little children's Guignol theatre. Scores of tidy French toddlers, dressed up to the nines, were out with their mothers or nursemaids, who sat knitting on benches under the shade of the trees. 'It's lovely. I wish *I* could paint,' she went on.

Sophie was thinking of all those years ago, walking here with Grant, she had been only a few years older than Phoebe now. Well, about eight years older and that made a difference.

'I can see why you like it here, Mother,' pursued Phoebe. 'Rosie said, "Oh, Mother will be in her element," and you are.'

'I wish my French were not so rusty. Do you think Jack will bring the girls back safely?'

'Well, he's not going to kidnap them, is he? Clemmie is mad about fish . . .'

Sophie was wondering, as she walked along, how Edith and Adam were getting on together. Surely there might occasionally be difficulties with anyone as solitary as Edith? She had liked what she had seen of Adam, and his feelings for her friend had been clear. But Edith would not say if she were not happy. She probably *was* happy and she had waited long enough.

'It's ages since they came. I wish you could invite Jack to stay; most young men are so boring,' said Phoebe, with all the worldly wisdom of sixteen.

Meanwhile, Jack was strolling along with Rosamund and Clemmie in the direction of the Médici Fountain. Now that Sophie was not there, Rosamund felt less obliged to be abrasive and felt, in truth, a little nervous.

'What have you been drawing?' Clemmie asked. She showed no shyness at all, but was blessed with a direct manner.

'People, Paris, the river, the markets, cafés – everything,' he replied. 'Would you draw us?' she asked.

Jack, who had been hoping he might have Rosamund as a model one day, was delighted. They were quite sophisticated, he thought, at least in comparison with the girls at home at the art school, who, of course, were rather older than these and were alternatively coy or lascivious. 'I would like to,' he said. 'You may sit for me tomorrow, in the Luxembourg or by the river.'

When they arrived at the fountain, Clemmie sat on the sides of the pool, which was more like a large stone swimming bath, and contemplated the large goldfish that lurked in and out of the deep, dark green water. Rosamund, who had no interest in fish, decided to ask to see his sketch-book. They sat down on a seat, having first ascertained it was a free one, and kept Clemmie in sight whilst Rosamund turned the pages of his book. It was indeed full; sketches of walls, roofs, larger ones of streets, women, children, details from Notre Dame, a quick sketch of the *bouquinistes*. He had been busy.

'I wish I could draw,' she sighed. 'But I am going to be an actress, or a film director.'

She is only a child, he thought, but she is very attractive. He felt a little guilty even to have thought that one day soon this girl of fourteen or so would be a young woman, and match him in maturity. She had a sort of challenge about her; she was no ordinary English Miss.

Clemmie called, 'Come and see the grandpa,' and a few people looked up, hearing the clear, English voice.

'I suppose we had better show an interest,' said Rosamund in her best offhand manner and Jack laughed. A girl like this, with something to say for herself, suited him; it was less of an effort to talk himself. In this he was unlike his father.

How remote the idea of going to Spain seemed as he sat there in the gardens with this child, whom he had not seen for five years and whom he had not thought about much since. Was she really the same little girl? Her sister, now gazing raptly into the depths of the fish-pool, *was* the same child as she had been at six. He remembered her showing him her rock garden. They would hardly remember him, he was sure, if their mother had not always kept them up with his doings. Five years, to a baby like Clemmie was ages. To him, the age of eighteen, though a long time ago, was not quite so long.

He got up and said to Rosamund, 'I think we'd better look at the fish,' and they walked over to Clemmie.

'The very old fish is under a plant at the bottom,' she said, not looking up. 'Do you think they have all been here since the pond was made?'

Jack looked at the statue of Marie de Médicis. Seventeenth-century, wasn't she? 'I should think so,' he said. 'I am told there are carp in the Tuileries Garden's ponds!'

'I shall have to see them!' said Clemmie with enthusiasm.

'I suppose we must go,' said Rosamund, bored. 'We must show you our hotel. I went in the church on the square; it was like a theatre, a lovely smell and candles and statues.'

'I shall draw that,' said Jack, impulsively. Wasn't that church also another of these seventeenth-century Parisian remnants?

As they walked slowly back Rosamund was thinking about what she would wear to make Jack look at her. She was a little tired now. They trailed past the *bassin* and along the *allées* to the gate at the end and round to 'their' square. As they passed the Rue de Tournon, she said, 'Mother's friends, Kitty and Frank, once lived here. Did your mother know them?'

'I think I've heard them mentioned,' replied Jack. 'But she died, didn't she, Kitty?'

'Who died?' asked Clemmie, turning round, for she was walking just in front of the other two, not feeling neglected for she had been thinking of making a fish-pond at home.

'Kitty Moray. You wouldn't have heard of her,' said Rosamund.

'They slosh water all down the gutters every morning,' said Clemmie, peering down a drain. 'It runs for ages. That's why it's so clean.'

'They wake me up every morning, doing the dustbins,' grumbled Rosamund. 'But it's fun here, isn't it?'

Some children were running home from school in their *tabliers* and with cases under their arms. 'They start at eight o'clock,' said Clemmie. 'There's a school down Rue Madame.'

'But they break up soon,' said her sister. 'And don't have the same holidays we do.'

'Is this your holiday time, then?' asked Jack. It seemed incredible that Rosamund was still at school.

'No, but Mother says it's "educational" so we have taken a little extra holiday before the real one.'

Jack deposited them at their little hotel which looked clean but unpretentious.

'Eight o'clock,' commanded Rosamund. She had decided to wear her dark pink silk dress in his honour.

Jack sauntered back to his own hotel, considerably less clean than theirs. He stripped and poured a basinful of water, from the sink in his top room, all over his head and shoulders. His head ached rather. But after changing and lying down for a moment he felt better. Mother would be pleased he had met Sophie and her girls. It had been a lucky chance that they had all been sitting in the Closerie des Lilas and that he had stayed there longer than he had intended. The girl, Rosamund, was certainly a beauty. What would she look like when she was eighteen? He thought of painting her in a gipsy dress or with a Spanish mantilla, something romantic which would suit her vivid colouring. Of course, she was still a little girl; well, a girl, anyway, and not the sort of model they would be keen on in Leeds. It was something in her eyes, something both cheeky and yet alluring; perhaps it would be impossible to capture that. And who knew, when she was older she might have lost it?

He had never regarded himself as a portrait painter and was surprised that she had had this effect on him. He must be sex starved, thinking about a girl of fourteen, yet it was not sex that exuded from Rosamund's skin, but life. A Portrait of Life. He smiled to himself as he shaved in the tepid water. Her mother must once have been pretty, too, with that dramatic way of speaking and catching your attention. This daughter would be a match for any mother, but Sophie seemed proud of her. Phoebe, her sister, was a bit frightening, probably very clever.

341

And the little one was sweet in her solemn, decided way; very English-looking, that little one. He wondered if any of them had been to the farm where Edith had told him Sophie was born. Thinking of Sophie and his mother, he supposed they must once have been young like these girls but he could not really imagine it. Funny that Aunt Sophie should call the youngest girl Clementine. Was it after his father?

He realized that, for twenty minutes, the idea of fighting in Spain had gone out of his head. That would never do. He must wake up and stop dreaming about girls and their mothers. But Paris seemed to be the sort of place where those kind of thoughts were fitting. He knew his mother had never been particularly fond of France, indeed she was not fond of anywhere but her home – and of that Thirksay she talked about.

On their way to the restaurant, Clemmie was thinking of becoming a vegetarian; it seemed so unfair to eat lovely animals. But she did enjoy her food. Was it wrong? It was nice to go along with Mother and Ros and Phoebe for once and to be treated as a nearly grown-up girl. Jack was nice, too. He had seemed really interested in the fish. Perhaps it was wrong to eat fish, too? When she grew up she would like to marry a nice man like Jack and have a farm and grow food and look after animals. There was a trout stream at the bottom of Grandpa Carr's garden and sometimes Father fished there, but he never seemed to catch anything. She was sure Jack would be a good fisherman; he looked as though he would be good at doing things, not just talking about them.

Sophie was thinking of Clem and of Jack and of Paris and a shiver went down her back, an unseasonable shiver, before she could think why. Funny how your body sometimes reacted before you knew what you were really thinking about. She had been thinking of Grant Miller, all those years ago in Paris, and the hunger he had had for her, a hunger no one else had ever matched. Not Clem, certainly, though she had had that sort of feeling for him, and not even her husband who had never, as far as she knew, been subject to physical infatuations.

It was such a lovely evening and Paris was at its best. Strange that they should come upon Jack that afternoon. She had been urging Edith to visit for years and bring Jack with her. It must be five years since they had come with Adam to visit Chimneys. Edith did not stir much from home and the next time she had seen her had been without Jack, when Sophie had been to Ox Heys on a detour from Thirksay and the East Riding to see Alice at the time Uncle George was selling up part of the farm. Jack had certainly grown up into a formidable young man. But he did not look in the least like Clement. It was his way of walking and standing that had deceived her eyes that afternoon. She must have been thinking of Clem. She often caught herself thinking of him. He had been dead now for almost as long as Jack had been alive. Thinking more of Clem than Grant, if the truth be told. Stupid. Clem had never liked her, really. She had been too forward for his tastes. A bit like her daughter Rosamund.

Phoebe took her mother's arm. 'I could understand nearly all the paper I bought this morning,' she said. 'I wish I could speak the language better, though. They never speak enough French at school.'

Rosamund heard her and turned. 'Eet is easy to spak *Frr*ench,' she said and proceeded to gabble a language that certainly sounded like French, although not one word was. She shrugged her shoulders and spread out her hands wide.

'Oh, Ros, people passing will think you're mad,' sighed Phoebe. But Sophie laughed. Her second daughter was such a good mimic. A pity she never did any work at school. She would have been a good linguist in a slap-dash way.

'I don't see why we should talk French,' said Clemmie. 'We're not French.'

They had turned down towards the Boulevard St Germain and were almost at the Carrefour de L'Odéon where stood the promised restaurant.

'Champagne and shellfish,' said Rosamund, reading from the menu outside. 'That sounds good.'

'W-ell,' replied Sophie, 'that might be rather indigestible.'

'Oh, Mother!'

'Look, there's *blanquette de veau*, one of my favourite dishes,' Sophie said. How much more careful one was with one's children's digestions than one had been with one's own!

'There's Jack,' shouted Clemmie, as a figure crossed the road and came up to them. He has changed, thought Rosamund, and looked down at her own dark pink silk dress complacently.

A table was found and the party settled themselves comfortably. Rosamund was excited and looked round at the mirrors and the chandeliers and the gleaming glasses and cutlery.

'Much nicer than London,' she said.

'You don't *go* to many restaurants in London,' objected Phoebe.

'Well, you know what I mean.'

'Mummy, there's a tank – of fish,' whispered Clemmie.

'Yes, you can choose one.'

'To *eat*?' she squeaked.

'What else?' said Rosamund. 'They're not for decoration, you know.' Clemmie wrinkled her nose and Sophie tactfully suggested an omelette for the twelve-year-old.

Jack fitted well into the family group. Perhaps people would think he was her son? They were better behaved than most English children, he was thinking; easy and natural. Rosamund looked even more stunning in that dress which went so well with her hair and eyes. Not perhaps a child at all.

Jack noticed that Rosamund had a voice very like her mother's and the same quick gestures.

'You needn't go on calling me "aunt",' Sophie had said, with a laugh. 'Makes me feel old to have a young man calling me that.' She was an interesting person, he thought, though perhaps a bit overwhelming. The French were all rather overwhelming, too. Like them, and unlike his own mother, Sophie articulated her thoughts as they came to her, on the wing, and this necessitated an effort on the part of the listener to keep up with her. He watched her as she talked and gestured with movements which seemed to betray a certain impatience. She had good bone structure too, he noted, must have been pretty once, was even now vivid in colouring. Though some of that may have come from the rouge pot. He almost blushed to have this disloyal thought. But Sophie was now enjoying herself, showing off her French as she ordered the meal and chatted with the waiter. He could tell she was pleased with herself.

Sophie had been thinking much the same thing. Really, her French was quite miraculously restored after only a few days in Paris, and her first sips of champagne made her feel gay and relaxed. They began to discuss where they had been, what they had seen.

'Can we come with you tomorrow if you are going to draw things?' asked Clemmie.

'Jack will be busy, darling. We can't expect him to spend all his time with you three – ' Sophie was beginning, but Jack said, 'I'd love to sketch you *all*. Tomorrow, perhaps? I'm not sure how long I'm staying, though.'

'Oh,' said Clemmie, disappointed.

'Are you going on somewhere else?' asked Phoebe politely.

Should he mention it or not? Jack felt constrained, and he had not decided, had he?

'Some friends of mine are going to Spain,' he said. 'I might join them.'

'But there's a war in Spain,' said Phoebe, who had read her newspaper carefully.

'Yes; some of us felt we should go and join the republicans. Lots of students have gone, you know.'

'To fight?' asked Clemmie, big-eyed.

'Well, it might not come to that. Just to see what we could do to help.'

Sophie wanted to ask, 'Does Edith know?' But Jack was not a child. Instead, 'Are you interested in politics, then? You are not like your mother if you are!'

'No. It seemed the only cause I could believe in. I was too young at the beginning when the International Brigade was formed and it was only this year I really got to thinking about it.'

'Yes, it is the great *cause célèbre*, isn't it. Like the vote was for me. And then I hadn't the courage to go all the way with the militants, and anyway I didn't think their methods were right.'

'And have you regretted that?' asked Jack. The children were listening intently.

'I suppose I have, in a way. I couldn't throw myself absolutely wholeheartedly, even into a cause I believed in. And the war came so soon upon us all, and that was to be won. There was no time during it to think of Votes for Women.'

'But you got them in the end; and now there is another threat. We might still save Europe from another war.'

'I thought that at first,' said Sophie slowly. 'But when those poets died, and when we saw the squabbles between the factions, then I thought; no, it is a matter for the Spaniards,

345

not for the youth of England. However awful things are, let us keep out of it. Of course, it would be different if we were directly threatened. I expect Hitler will have to be dealt with.'

Jack considered this.

'Have you been to see the cemetery at Faubourg d'Amiens?' she went on. When Jack said nothing, she added, 'Where your father was buried.'

'I always think of him being buried in Wiltshire where mother had his name put on the Roll of Honour. But I *had* thought of going, yes.'

She wanted to say so much more; that it was not work risking your young life unless you were forced, and even then, was the pacifist cause not a good one? Opinions were so sharply divided in Spain: even some socialists who were pacifists were not in favour of fighting for the Republic, even now. Was it ignoble to wait until England was directly threatened by a dictator?

'One of mother's friends is active in the Republican Friends' Movement in Leeds. Do you know her – a Miss Emery?'

'What, Cicely? I thought she'd given up her idealism for good. Edith told me she was very depressed, some years ago.'

'Mother says the Spanish war has given her a new lease of life.'

'Some people will always need a Cause,' replied Sophie. 'Let's have a bottle of champagne and the girls can have a glass each,' she said, changing the subject as the wine waiter was approaching them. Edith would be shattered if Jack were to go to Spain. And, knowing Edith, she would have said nothing. But what could *she* say? Jack probably saw it, as his father had done, as a sort of test of manhood.

Clemmie was sitting looking thoughtful. Why were people always fighting?

Jack knew what Sophie was thinking. His father had been only thirty-one when he was killed. And what good had the whole bloody conflict done? Germany was still sulking; the slump had reduced the workers' living standards at home. Then the democratically elected government of Spain had been assaulted in bloody civil war. And what was that to do with him? Had he, in any case, missed the boat for heroics? Born just too late? And he was not a communist or even a socialist or a trades unionist, but a pinkish liberal.

Sophie broke into his thoughts, determined to change the subject, for the three girls were all looking solemn. He wished he had said nothing.

'I'm invited to a *vernissage* tomorrow in the Rue des Saints Pères. Would you like to go instead? Seb gave the invitation to me in London.'

'If I return to England, when I return, I mean, I'm to see Mr Harman,' replied Jack, thankful to have got off the subject. 'About the Slade.'

'Edith mentioned she'd written to him.'

'Yes. I'd like to go to the varnishing.' He thought he had four days in which to decide whether to take that train with Jim and the others.

Sophie wondered whether to mention her friend, Bea Osborn, who was also active in the Friends of the Republicans, but decided not to broach the subject again. Bea was a Marxist and was devoting more time to Spanish refugees than to birth control at present. Another person who had to take up causes. Maybe Jack did too – he could hardly have got that from his mother.

Jack turned to Phoebe, but it was Rosamund he was thinking of. 'I'll sketch you all by the river, and perhaps one day I'll make a painting of it,' he offered.

'You must put Mother in, too,' said Phoebe. 'Dad's always saying she ought to have her portrait painted, but he can never find an artist he likes.'

If he waits too long, I shan't be worth painting, Sophie thought. She remembered the crayon sketches Seb Harman had done of her long ago.

'Oh, Jack, that would be a good idea.'

'I do lightning sketches and then work them up later.'

'Then you must have a good visual memory.'

'Yes,' he said.

'I wish I could remember how things looked,' said Sophie, as they all began on their first course with enthusiasm. 'Like Paris. It looks different and I never realized why. You wouldn't notice the same differences at home, but if you remember how it was – the *people* are part of it – I only realized today that it was the hats and the skirts! It isn't really Paris that has changed, it's the people. All the women with long, trailing skirts when I came here before the war, and their hair up and those hats!'

'Did the children have long skirts?' asked Rosamund.

'No. Well, longer than yours, and frilly white pinafores and ringlets and boots, and of course there were more horses then, and things seemed darker somehow . . .'

'And next time we come,' said Rosamund dreamily,'they'll be different again. I wonder what they'll be like in twenty years?'

'We shall come before then!' said Phoebe.

'Ugh, I'd be over thirty then,' said Clemmie, with surprise.

'How do you like your veal?' asked Sophie.

They all murmured contentedly. The creamy sauce was delicious, like velvet.

'*Crème veloutée*,' said Phoebe, showing off her French for once.

'What are you going to have now, Jack?' asked Sophie, seeing he had demolished his meat course.

He must have been very hungry, did not have much spare cash, she suspected.

'Oh, salad and fruit and cheese. That's what they always have here, isn't it?'

'I shall have an ice-cream bombe with chocolate sauce,' said Clemmie, who shared her mother's sweet tooth.

Sophie and Jack finished the champagne between them and Rosamund gave an imitation of being drunk. How she wished she could grow up quickly and drink more than one glass of champagne.

'Restaurants are one of my very favourite things,' she sighed.

Am I a coward? thought Jack. I don't want to go to Spain. I want to paint this beautiful child and talk to her mother and go back home in August and see about the Slade. He was silent as he drank the black coffee they had ordered and saw Clemmie regarding him seriously. How could he come to a decision?

'There's not much hope now, you know, for the Republic,' said Sophie quietly, trying again, when they were walking back through the warm summer-scented streets. Clemmie was arm in arm with Phoebe and trying to pretend she was not sleepy. Rosamund was certainly not sleepy and was listening to her mother.

'No, I know.'

'Michael says there's no need to be heroic, there'll be plenty of opportunity later,' Sophie continued grimly.

'He really thinks there will be another Great War?'

'Oh yes, if the Germans go on doing what they are doing. And that horrible Mussolini.'

'But the Spanish war is here and now. One must take sides.'

'I take sides, but being no longer young, I counsel against intervention. I had enough even of the Zeppelins in London last time.'

'Do come tomorrow, then,' said Clemmie to Jack, opening her sleepy eyes.

'She has eaten too much,' said Rosamund confidentially to Jack. Her dress looked dark in the night and her face pale and ravishing. Only her eyes seemed to him to glitter.

As he walked back to Rue Monsieur le Prince, Jack was still in two minds. He would go to the gallery with the ticket Sophie had given him and then meet them the day after and draw that lovely girl.

Sophie could not sleep. She kept thinking of Clement and the war and of Paris before the war and its incredible lightness and gaiety. Jack was a nice young man. It would be crazy to sacrifice himself for Spain. She remembered, too, the night she had heard of Clem's death, and remembered Austin. How mad she had been! What if her own daughters behaved as she had! Surely they would not. Rosamund was so attractive, she would be hard to resist in a few years. When you were young you never thought life would not last for ever. Clem had not thought he would be dead in three years when his child was born, surely? Nor Toby, nor her brother Harry ... What a futile gesture. If Jack were to be killed in Spain ... What idealism could prevail against guns? And Jack was not a political person. Even she could see that. Did Ros know that her mother had once loved his father? Perhaps she would tell her one day. Grant would have liked Ros.

Clemmie woke in the night, not with stomach ache, which might have been expected, but out of a nasty dream. She sat for a few minutes thinking about Jack. He was the sort of boy she would like to know better. The thought of him alive was a comfort and she went back to sleep, counting horses which she preferred to sheep.

349

Jack went to the *Vernissage* and enjoyed the hectic atmosphere and the sight of chic women in fancy silk dresses and little hats perched on their curls. There were a few American voices to be heard and paintings which seemed, to him, decadent in a peculiarly modern way. Many imitations of Picasso, but nothing original. He stopped beside one painting of Spain entirely covered in black an[1] red. It made its point, but he was rather depressed when he left.

The next day he met the 'children' and walked down to the Seine with them and on the Île St Louis, where he grouped them at the bottom of a little bridge and executed several rapid sketches. The solidity of the girls against the almost ethereal background of stonework and turrets and house-shutters, was what he wanted to bring out. He drew several of Rosamund leaning back against the stone of the bridge smiling, coiled energy in her arms. And, to be fair, he drew several of Clemmie looking directly at him and some of Phoebe reading. Sophie had gone to a bookshop.

'When are you going to see your friends?' asked Clemmie as they sat at a café table on the right bank, some time later. His spirits sank again.

'I had a dream,' went on the usually stolid and silent Clemmie. Rosamund was staring at a theatre poster behind them and Phoebe was not listening. 'When are you going to Spain?' she repeated.

'I haven't decided.' Clemmie had a curiously compelling look, earnest and pink-cheeked.

'Don't go, Jack. You needn't go, need you? I had a dream; it was horrible – nasty – that there was a war and you were hurt.'

Rosamund stopped looking at the poster to stare at her sister. 'People don't dream the future, Clemmie, you're not a gipsy.'

'Nobody wants me to go, but there are good reasons for going,' said Jack.

'Your father was killed in the last war, wasn't he?' said Rosamund.

'Yes.'

Clemmie continued to look at him earnestly. She was still a child, unlike the other two, and he did not want to upset her.

350

'Sometimes you have to be brave,' said Rosamund.

'Please, Jack, I don't think you should go. After that, I had a nice dream about a farm.'

'You always dream about animals, Clemmie.'

'But it *was* nice. We were all there, and my mother was there and she said "Jack didn't go to Spain." Don't go, please, Jack.' She was most insistent.

'Clemmie, it's not your business,' said Phoebe, looking up from her book. 'Grown-ups have reasons for what they do. Sometimes you have to fight.'

'No you don't, not always,' said Jack. 'Come on. I'm going to take you back to St Sulpice. I'm not going, Clemmie,' he said as he stood up. They were staring at him. 'You're right. It would be silly.' His decision was suddenly made inside his head. He had not known he had made it until he spoke. Was it the child who had made up his mind for him? He never knew.

He was not a hero. He had other things to do. Wait for Rosamund to grow up, for one thing. The smile on Clementine's face was huge, brilliant. She never referred again to the dream she had had during all the time they were in Paris.

When Jack went to the station to see his friends he told them curtly that he had changed his mind. There were more important things to do. He was going to the cemetery near Arras to see where his father was buried and commemorated and then he was going to see Seb Harman in London and to enrol at the Slade. He packed his sketch-books and was seen off by Sophie and her children, who were going to put Phoebe on a train to Tours in a few days and then return, later that week, to England. As the train steamed out of the Gare du Nord he thought he had done the right thing. He could bear Jim's scorn and their anger at his vacillations. They would go without him, that was all. And after settling things in London he was going to walk a bit in the North Riding and hoped to visit that place Sophie Carr had once left, Thirksay farm. Plenty of scope there, he was sure, for a few sketch-books full before starting his new life in London in the autumn.

Clemmie had a satisfied look on her face for the rest of the holiday.

'I think Clemmie's fallen in love,' said Rosamund to Phoebe with a laugh, on Phoebe's last night in Paris. 'She was really upset. It's not like her.'

'I'm glad we can't really dream the future,' said Phoebe. 'Jack was probably not sure, anyway, what to do. Politics are very complicated. Father says there might be a war, in any case.'

'It's a good thing girls don't have to fight, isn't it?'

'It does get you abroad,' said Ros sagely. 'Have you really decided to try for Oxford?'

'In two years, when I'm eighteen. I think my French is improving, you know.'

'I should hate to plan too far ahead. Nice surprises are what I like.'

'Well, you've got two years more than I have to think about it.'

'Mother does love France, doesn't she? Do you think she was once in love with Jack's father?'

Phoebe, who had her own ideas about her mother's past, replied, 'Oh, I think Mother was probably often in love.'

'But she didn't marry the man she loved first, did she? I mean *really* loved, like – oh, I don't know – Tristan and Isolde.'

'I hope *I* shall marry the man I love,' replied Phoebe. 'But not for ages. Jack kept looking at *you*, you know. I'm sure he was smitten.'

'Yes, I know, but he's too young.'

'Too young, you idiot! He's ages older than you – ancient!'

'Oh, I'd fancy someone much older,' said Ros mysteriously. 'Perhaps a Frenchman, or a film director. I shall wait until I'm twenty, though. I've got to be famous first.'

'Good night, Ros. Sleep well,' said Phoebe.

'Night.' Ros fell asleep and for once did not dream of taking the world by storm, somehow, some way.

Jack went to Arras, stopping on his return route to Calais, and spent an afternoon in the cemetery there. He was moved when he saw the rows of graves. How could they not have not affected him, those hundreds of individual headstones looking like empty stamp hinges in their sunny rows! Those dead with names were lucky. His own father's bones were among them, in a marked grave. Edith had told him the row and number and place on a small map. She had never wanted to go herself to see the spot and Jack doubted very much that all the names had been correctly assigned. Clem's name on the Perbury war memorial had always given Jack the impression that he really rested there. He found the grave eventually, with a small cross above it, and just the name and regiment and 'Arras' and the date in March 1917. Clem's son stood there, in the midst of this resting place for dead warriors. He was glad that he had come here and not gone to fight another man's war on a battlefield in Spain. Which causes were worth fighting for? Some, undoubtedly. But which causes were worth losing your life for? Any?

He tried to imagine what lay underneath the greensward. It was no different from what lay under most churchyards or town cemeteries. Except that here, the dead were all young. Young bones. He looked at some of the other names, after standing for a moment beside the war memorial where he also found his father's name; his father who, as the result of a little sensual flurry a quarter of a century before, had given him life. There were names of the British and Canadian young men, Baker and Bates and Bartholomew and Smith, Smith, Smith. If you waited another fifty years or so they would have been dead in any case. It was death he was thinking of, rather than war, when he left. He would remember it well, that place. As he would remember Rosamund.

Seb Harman was away when Jack went to find him in London, but some lady assistant or other, when he asked for him at the Slade, told him that if it were the new entry, she had strict instructions from Mr Harman to take in portfolios, and she promised they would be looked at so long as he had made his formal application from Leeds. Jack was vaguely disappointed. He had arrived in England on a high tide of decision and wanted to get his future settled.

'It *is* the summer vacation, you know,' said the woman, seeing his disappointment and hearing the impatience in his voice.

'I only brought my sketch-books,' he said, and unloaded his haversack.

'You *have* been busy,' she said soothingly.'Make sure each book has your name and address and is signed and then I'll check it with the records of applications.'

Jack was forced to admit that he had not definitely decided to apply earlier on in the summer. He was not going to look a fool and say, 'I thought I might go to Spain.' Neither did he wish to pull any strings by mentioning that his mother knew Mr Harman. It was Sophie who really knew him, in any case.

'I'll stretch a point. Write as soon as you get home, covering letter and letter from your teacher in Leeds, and they must countersign your form of application.'

He did not want, then, to say he had been hoping he might get one of the scholarships, so he took the forms and decided to go north straight away. But he did not want to go home yet. He could fill in the forms on the train and drop them in Leeds on his way back. Before that, though, he was determined to visit Thirksay. One of Sophie's relations might be there, but that would not matter. He wanted, after Paris, to soak himself in some English countryside. Not the landscape of home exactly, but somewhere new, some place he did not know. He was reluctant to go home straight away.

In the train to York he worked out another train journey to Thirksay, after filling in his forms of application. The train was nearly empty and puffed along in a sleepy way, making him doze a little and dream a little; of Sophie's girls and of the cemetery and of a battlefield that he knew was not in Spain. He woke with a start after that, relieved he was back in England. He looked out of the train window at the summer fields, sleeping too in the sun, and suddenly felt happy, despite his tiredness. There would be time to call on Grandpa Broughton in Leeds and then to go home and help his stepfather in his allotment at the bottom of the field near the cottage. He had made his big decision to stay in England and his future was, he felt, mapped out as far as he cared to map it. If the Slade wanted him, he knew his grandfather would help out with his living expenses in London. He did not want to be a financial burden on his mother any longer. And if the Slade did not want him, well then, he would go on painting in any case; perhaps work on farms as Adam had done after his war.

When he got to Thirksay he managed to find Church Farm, but there was only a deaf old man mending some ancient machinery in the yard, who seemed to think he had been sent by some government department to enquire about his pig feed.

The farm was almost derelict; the barn doors were open and there was only dusty harness hanging there. The field nearest to the farm was fallow. Other fields, though, belonging to other farms were being harvested as he walked by them. He crossed another field and passed by an old orchard and a pond. Here, the place seemed more welcoming. It would only need a man or two to get it going again. His painter's eye had taken in the rusty ploughshares and the neglected gates and the beauty of the eighteenth-century farmhouse, however abandoned-looking. Here was his mother's old paradise. He wished it had had some connection with his father too, for curiously enough he had never felt a need to imagine his father in Wiltshire, even after reading poems of his which called up the place of his childhood. He could not see Rosamund Carr here and it was hard to imagine Sophie Carr here either, where she had spent her childhood and youth over thirty years ago. The place seemed more in tune with his own mother somehow, though she would have got it all to rights quickly. It was depressing to see a place so neglected and he felt his earlier mood swing away.

He sat in the sun, ate two tea-cakes purchased on York station, and then went to the village post office to send a telegram home to announce his return. He wondered if the Carrs were back and if Sophie had written to his mother about seeing him in Paris. Well, he had better put Edith's mind to rest, in case she was still imagining him in Spain or on the way there.

After sending his telegram, he bought a bottle of lemonade in the village stores and drank it, lying down in the sun at the edge of a barley field. He could not stay in Thirksay and was rather short of money, so he gathered up the rest of his cash and bought a ticket at the little station halt to Harrogate where he could change for Leeds. There he could settle things with his teachers and send off some of his pictures to the committee, if they were not away on holiday. Stay on a bit in Roundhay then, with his grandparents. They liked having him there. It had been an important holiday one way or another, but he was glad to be back.

A few weeks after Jack finally arrived home at Far Ox Heys, he heard that he had been offered a scholarship at the Slade, not from any influence of Sebastian Harman's, but on the strength of the work he had submitted. And a few weeks later still, Mr Chamberlain descended from his aeroplane at Croydon waving his piece of paper from Herr Hitler to reassure the world at large, and especially England, that there was to be no war. It would certainly have been too late for Jack to have gone to Spain in 1938 as it turned out and, as he soon realized, certainly too late for Spain.

His visits to Paris and to Faubourg d'Amiens and to Thirksay were to become memories of 'before the war', merging into the following year when he found himself in London in a small bed-sitting room in World's End, having enrolled at the college in Gower Street. He had just begun to enjoy his new life when the London parks were being dug up again. The whole sickening business of war was being contemplated once more by a populace half-fearful, half-incredulous, but determined to fight if needs must. By the early autumn of the year Jack was twenty-five, the 'phoney war' had begun. His call-up papers arrived and this time there was no choice and no escape. No volunteering out of youthful idealism, simply a duty. Personal lives were to go once more into cold storage, and he had not yet even seen Sophie's girls again! They had been sent away to school in Wales. Just once, he saw Sophie, when Sebastian Harman took him to tea at Gunther's and the talk was of Edith's decision to help out with the WVS and Sophie's to offer her services as air raid warden in Surrey.

But soon, teas at Gunther's and chat about art receded from Jack's life and the sharp memory of sitting at a café table in Paris receded even further into an even more unimagineable past. Jack was posted abroad, and though he saw no fighting till three years after his call-up, he was often to reflect ruefully that, if he had gone to Barcelona in 1938, he might not have had to fight his country's legitimate battles far away, which on the whole he was glad to do.

Interlude 1940–1945

Edith and Sophie

'It is better to fight for the good, than to rail at the ill . . .'

Tennyson

Phoebe Carr went up in 1940 to a transformed Oxford. Shortened courses were allowed those who might want to join one of the services later, and some of the women took advantage of this, whilst others lasted out their three years before entering upon war work. The atmosphere was that of an emergency: nowhere could you forget the war. Most of the young men had been called up already, or were to be, and there were continual activities that interrupted the pursuit of learning: stirrup pump and trailer pump practices, collecting salvage, Red Cross training courses, fire watching or ARP work, according to taste. You could even test fuses for Morris's munitions factory at Cowley or take part-time work serving in the many canteens of the area, in factories and air force bases. Those less practical members of colleges worked in clubs and hospitals or in the Oxford branch of the WVS, for which Edith was working further north. The lovely college lawns were dug up 'for victory' so that the whole place was transformed physically.

Phoebe found it all rather enjoyable and chose to sort books for the Red Cross on war work afternoons. These were for the prisoners' library and the sorting was done at the New Bodleian. It was more interesting than writing cards at the food office for the Ministry of Food's rationing scheme. Phoebe also found she had quite a talent for taking evening classes, young though she was. Teaching was fun, though she avoided the teaching of games, being one of those girls thankful at last to have escaped compulsory hockey and netball. Later, there were opportunities, which the more sociable girls seized upon, for 'entertaining' Canadians and Americans. Some children, too, had been evacuated to Oxford from the club in the East End which her college had adopted years before.

No longer were the students Lady Bountifuls, working in an alien environment during their vacations; they had to organize activities for transplanted Cockney boys billeted in Oxford. Then there was fruit picking, an activity which got you out of the town, unless you were drafted to pick the principal's redcurrants. Friends spoke of tractor-driving undertaken in their vacations and occasionally on farms in the beautiful countryside all around Oxford, and some active spirits organized harvesting camps. Clemmie would have loved to take part in these, but Phoebe was less interested in aspects rural.

By 1943, when Phoebe had almost finished her degree, Clemmie was seventeen and had left school and been accepted for the land army. 'It's that, or sick nursing, or factory work,' she said to Sophie, 'and I want to farm anyway.'

All the women at home were involved in endless chores 'making mend' and ends meet, cooking egg-less cakes and boiling carrot jam, spinning out their rations and calculating to the last weight of a feather how much they could allow their families to eat. Everything was in short supply.

Michael Carr was at first involved with a Jewish refugee organization, but he still managed to keep up his firm's lists, publishing books for the troops on thin wartime paper 'according to authorized economy standards'. His series of *Facts for the Layman* flowered into an especially popular series for the troops, and he also re-published some of Bevis Constantine's fantasies, which seemed to go down far better now that some escapism was needed. Later, he offered his services to Bletchley Park where, middle-aged though he was, his knowledge of German was of use in helping to crack the enemy ciphers.

Clemmie had chosen her war work voluntarily and had not needed to be conscripted. Sophie was just too old to be conscripted herself, but in the first two years of the war served as an air raid warden in the village. Ambulance-driving was out of the question for her, but her daughter, Clemmie, learned to drive in the land army and managed a tractor. Most of Clemmie's time was spent learning how to plough and harrow,

358

reap and thresh, and she was in her element. She even ploughed on moon lit nights, a tricky rather than romantic job. Tree felling, even, she learned, as well as 'hedging and ditching' and looking after stock. She came to realize the justice of her mother's old talk about equal pay when she found that she was working for only two-thirds of a man's wage. But the friendliness of her mates in the land army made up for her anger at this. She met girls from all over Great Britain whom, as the daughter of a successful London publisher, she would never have met in peace time. Sophie often smiled at this, remembering that Clemmie's own grandmother and great-grandmother would have been at one time among these girls. Clemmie grew strong in the open air life, though she was always hungry. She lost weight, became sunburnt and was extremely happy.

Whilst Clemmie was on the land and Phoebe at Oxford, Rosamund had found work suited to her talents with the Coronet film unit, shooting propaganda films. She started off at eighteen, in 1942, as a general dogsbody, introduced there by the pulling of a few strings by a friend of her father's. The hours were long, but through watching directors and cameramen and seeing the film through, from the genesis in the mind of the writer to the rushes on the cutting-room floor, Rosamund bid fair to become a director herself after the war. That, at least, was her firm intention. She, too, was happy. It was war service just as much as making armaments in a factory, she told herself, and she, too, found friends through her work, male as well as female.

The same year that Rosamund started with the unit as a very junior junior, Jack had gone abroad with the army, and was to find himself eventually chasing Rommel in North Africa. Edith saw him go with some fear but with great pride. She had come round to the idea of this war more than she had ever accepted the first cataclysm in 1914. At heart, she worried as much about Adam, who was still sometimes depressed. It was no surprise to her when, in 1942, after a period as an air raid warden – not that there were many raids in that part of Yorkshire, but there were a few – Adam came home one day with a headache and took to his bed. He recovered from that bout of panic and the headache went, but the next year, when he had joined the

Home Guard and had been given the rank of lieutenant as a recognition of his earlier service in the previous war, he had a more severe breakdown.

Edith understood that it was beyond his control. It was nothing to do with her or their marriage or the eleven happy years they had spent together. It was the war. Adam simply could not stand the war. By volunteering first as an air raid warden and then as a home guardsman, he had thought he might prove to himself that he was recovered, and he obviously was not. The symptoms were not the same as those he had had earlier, before Edith knew him, nor were they connected with his trembling or his old wound in the ankle. Nor was it that nightmares woke him. It was more the physical manifestation of a pervasive anger. Anger over the fact that, for all their sacrifices, war had arrived once more, making the previous bout pointless, and a guilt, too, about the very fact of his weakness. He was letting Edith down; he was no good to her. He was not hungry, but managed to eat his rations, though he was always exhausted. The doctor called it 'nervous depression'.

Edith was sure that that, too, would pass. But before it had passed he was taken ill, physically ill this time, with a sudden loss of weight and a high temperature. This lasted for three months and he was not getting better. Only then, when Edith had decided his mental state must be still reflected in bodily disorder, only then, did the doctor call in a specialist and Adam was moved to a hospital in Bradford. He was given blood transfusions and seemed better for a week or two. Then the symptoms recurred. Edith went every day to see him and talk to him, and was in the middle of telling him, one afternoon, of her plans to buy Thirksay farm for him to work after the war with her profits from Bevis Constantine, which were now coming in, in a steady flow, to the bank, when Adam held up his hand.

'Edie, I shall never farm again. You must listen to me. The doctors don't seem to know what the matter is, but *I* know I'm dying. I was once a medical student you know.'

She was frozen into silence.

Strangely enough, now that he was physically ill, he was much better in spirit and his earlier depression had lifted. She did not believe him, thought that the illness had cured him of his mental agonies and that he was now weak from that recovery. But he continued to lose weight and to feel deathly tired. He came home for a few weeks when she was told there was nothing more the doctors could do. Hospital staff were in short supply, except for emergencies, and Edith was told to take him in again if his temperature began to rise. She confronted the registrar at the infirmary. What was the matter with her husband? Was it a form of growth? Was it his heart? His lungs? They had taken many tests of his blood and never told either of them what they had gathered from this. The young doctor took her into his office. Adam was waiting in the ward to return home.

'It's a disease of the white blood cells. You might call it a cancer of the blood.' He paused, wondering how much she could take.

'Is there no cure?' she asked immediately.

'I'm afraid not. Bring him back in when he feels worse.'

'How long?'

'He could have another few weeks or even six months,' said the registrar, slowly. 'Patients with this disease of the lymphatic system are subject to natural remissions.'

In the end Adam had only just over two months to live. It was autumn again and the Italians had surrendered. Jack was somewhere 'over there'. Edith lived through the worst period of her life and entirely stopped writing; she could not even go on with the journal where she had registered all Adam's symptoms and the progress of his disease and their life and talk together.

It was a gorgeous autumn, an Indian summer, with trees still green and Michaelmas daisies everywhere, like violet stars in the brown, clayey soil and dahlias blazing away in the village gardens. She put a comfortable chair out for him in their back yard, which overlooked her flower garden, and where he could see the plot of land he had tended, further down towards the field which, for three months, he had been too weak to touch. Before that spring, the slogan 'Dig For Victory' had been faithfully followed by them both, and there were potatoes and cabbage to lift and blackberries to gather from the hedges around. It seemed particularly cruel to Edith that the season was so lovely and nature's beauty bursting around them after the heavy summer.

When he was too weak to walk upstairs, she put the old couch from the parlour into the sitting room for the night-time and a comfortable chair for the day into the kitchen, and she brought pot plants and bunches of flowers – chrysanthemums from her neglected garden – and branches of autumn leaves into the kitchen to brighten it up. He watched her as she cooked or mended. They sat there together for long hours and she would read to him from *Parson Woodforde* or *Kilvert's Diary*. The colder weather came and the leaves outside turned yellow and the coal was brought in and logs stacked by the hearth.

Edith grew pale and tired, but continued to offer him hope until such time as he should decide for himself that he must go into hospital. That time came, one day at the end of October, during the week before he went into hospital for the last time. He asked her to accept that he was not going to recover. His mind was just as sharp and his perceptions as clear, but he was very thin and breathless and had terrible sweating episodes at night.

'I don't want you to have false hope, my darling,' he began. 'There is something mortally wrong with me, whatever the doctors say. I feel quite calm about it and I don't want to leave you unhappy on my account. I've had a wonderful eleven years with you.' He paused and she held his hand to her cheek. 'Think of it as eleven years' extra, added to a life that seemed finished. Before I met you I didn't care about living so much.'

She so wanted him to live, had felt that she could save him, if anyone could, from this multiplying cancer in his blood, just as (he said) she had saved his soul before.

'Don't be frightened,' he whispered. 'I love you. I've been so happy. And I know Jack will return, I *know* he will, and that we shall win this war.'

She knew now; that she must tell him what the doctors had told her. It was no time for hiding things. She did so and thought he looked almost satisfied to know. They had been so lucky to find each other, and so happy, she thought. Even if things had not always worked out as she had hoped for him, and his little allotment had not brought in much money, at least they had been together and her life had been completed with him, rounded as it had never been before. Why should Adam die when so many others lived useless, miserable lives? But she tried not to think such thoughts and succeeded in holding back her tears until she was alone in her room upstairs and he was asleep. When she came down again his skin was damp and cold and he could scarcely lift his head when he awoke. He was only fifty-eight and they could have expected at least twenty more years together. She knelt and put her arms around him.

'I'm not in pain, just very tired,' he said and she saw it was an effort for him to speak. He was booked into hospital for the following day. Edith did not want him to go, but the registrar had said they would try one more transfusion.

'Don't talk – there's no need,' she said. 'I wish I could come with you, that's all.' He knew she did not mean, go into hospital with him.

She wept now and he stroked her hair very softly as she put her head on the pillow by him. Then he seemed to fall asleep again.

All that night she sat up with him. There was nothing she could do, but he seemed to want her there. In the morning an ambulance came for them both and took them to the infirmary in Bradford. There, they gave him another hopeless blood transfusion and after it he lay on the high hospital bed, only half-conscious. She wanted him to have no more transfusions. This was the end. Only an oxygen mask and an injection of morphine to help him die.

She was with him when he did. Just before he died he opened his eyes and looked at her and it was a younger Adam, back for a swift moment. Then his breathing stopped quietly, before she had realized what was happening. She took the oxygen mask from his face – the nurse had left them together – and kissed him as he slipped away, and felt as though she was receiving breath from his last breath. She was holding his hand and sitting by him when the doctor came round. One look at Adam and he said only, 'I'm sorry.'

Edith survived the funeral and the emptiness which followed with a stoical disregard for her own feelings, until she was at last forced to her own bed with influenza. It was November now and she had written to Sophie to tell her of what had happened. Scarcely had she been able to put pen to paper as long as Adam was alive, and her typewriter stood shrouded as though in mourning too. She posted the letter and returned to bed. One afternoon a few days later, two weeks after Adam had died, when she lay drained of energy, with the languor of the after-effects of flu, trying to make herself get up and prepare a cup of tea and a boiled egg, Sophie arrived. Edith had never been so glad to see her.

Sophie feared that Edith had lived too long as a hermit till Adam had entered her life and might be set to be one again. She stood in the bedroom door, vivid and solid, and Edith felt that the role of 'mother' suited her, for she took charge, asked no fatuous questions and sat by her side quietly until Edith was well enough to talk. For a few days Edith said little, but slowly she began to describe Adam's death and some of the details of his illness and Sophie listened with patient affection. Edith did not at first cry, but she needed to begin to grieve and she could be completely herself with her friend.

Soon Sophie had her up again and sitting in Adam's old chair. The shopping, such as it was, and the cooking were done by Sophie, and Edith felt spoilt. Occasionally they listened to the news and then put it off to talk a little. But they were never in each other's way. Little by little, Edith grew stronger and began to allow herself to cry, letting the tears run down her face without wiping them away, reconciling herself to her eternal parting from the man she had truly loved. In the evenings they sat together in the old kitchen. Sophie had brought some knitting and was also reading Trollope. Edith would sit looking into the fire.

'One day you must write about him,' Sophie suggested shyly. Sophie had changed; was quieter, seemed to bring more patience to her daily tasks than Edith remembered her as having. They talked during these evenings by the fire, of their children and of the war and their experiences. It was a lot better than letters, Sophie said, and Edith agreed. They seemed to take up their friendship again just as they had left it the last time, not needing to go into long explanations about things. Edith had even managed a smile when she described her own experiences in 1940, finding homes for refugees from the Channel Islands who were billeted in the village and in Calderbrigg, and the times when evacuees from Essex had arrived and soldiers from Dunkirk had passed in lorries along the main road from Leeds and they had gone out with water jugs for the thirsty men. All of these had been found billets at different times. And Sophie told of her relief that the bombing of London seemed to be over and of her time as ARP warden, making herself unpopular. And they also spoke of events further back, of the first war that did not seem to them so very long ago, of their marriages, their fears and of their children again. It always came back to their children.

On they day Sophie left, it was sunny and Edith went out into her garden again to do some tidying up and digging. Adam did not seem so very far away.

The next week she went up on the little maroon bus to Haworth where she had so often walked with him. The desolate moor, and the sight of the Brontë Parsonage, now closed to visitors, and the everlasting wind, were in tune with her mood and were soothing. She sat on a wall, her coat wrapped tightly round her, and thought of Adam and then of Jack, from whom she had heard nothing for months, though she had written to him about Adam's death.

She was to return many times to those moors for consolation. Up there you were alone, so it did not matter that you were alone when you returned, for aloneness was part of living. Adam had made the glass wall dissolve just as Jack had. Now she knew that it would not come back and she tolerated the distance between herself and the rest of humanity. Visits to her mother, even, were less fraught. She tried, once more, to get closer to Maud. It did not work, but she no longer felt it was her fault that she could not.

With Italy defeated and no more air raids in London for some time, the British were beginning to hope, by 1944, that the war might soon be over. But that summer another of Hitler's 'secret weapons' was unleashed, variously called the buzz-bomb, the doodlebug or the V1 'flying bomb'. These pilotless aircraft *Vergeltungswaffen*', or 'reprisal weapons', came over from the French coast and were targeted upon London, where they fell after a long pause when the unpleasant whining of engines stopped. Londoners then waited, and an eternity went by between the ending of the sound and the crash. By the time of the crash, heard in the distance or even quite near, they would know that it had not found them as a target. But the infernal machines were nerve-wracking and most frightening.

Phœbe was now working at another branch of the Ministry of Information from Rosamund's film unit and was in London. She had gained a first class honours degree in modern languages and intended to return to Oxford 'after the war'; Clemmie Carr was in Lincolnshire, working on an arable farm; Michael was still in Bletchley and Sophie was at Chimneys undertaking new ARP duties. It was a cool, poor summer and everyone's nerves were stretched to breaking point.

Chimneys was a little off the path through Kent made by the V1s, but they could be heard in the distance as they winged their way towards London. Sophie was worried for Phœbe; somehow, the concept of London being bombed meant central London, as in the Blitz, nearly four years before. No one, until 1944, had thought the London suburbs would be a prime target and, of course, the enemy had probably not intended that exactly either, but the flying bombs were unpredictable.

Rosamund, now a young woman of twenty, was still working in south east London with her unit, in a suburb in the direct line of bombs. In the last two weeks she had got used to hearing them. They arrived at night and in the daytime, and the sirens or the approaching sound drove most people into their shelters, although, even there, one was not always safe. The sirens were indeed so frequent that people became confused over whether there was an 'alert' or not. 'If it's got your name on it, what can you do?' was the philosophical refrain of the Londoners. Many brought themselves earplugs and tried to ignore the sounds. One morning at the beginning of July, Rosamund was dozing in an armchair in her digs, having been up all the previous night on her shift finishing off an assignment, and did not hear the sound or the sudden silence. She had, in any case, chosen to ignore them, believing that a basement room was as safe as a shelter. She was young and could sleep anywhere, did not hear the dry rat-a-tat-tat of the morning's infernal machines.

A V1 fell directly on the house, completely destroying it. All its occupants were killed. Rosamund passed from sleep into death with no knowledge of what was happening. She was dug out later, still in her chair. If she had gone into the ATS or the WRNS, she would most likely have survived the war. That was all Michael could think, later.

Clemmie had been stacking wood a hundred and fifty miles away at the very moment the bomb fell, and stopped suddenly with a giddy sensation. So sure was she that something terrible had happened that she telephoned her mother, a long and laborious affair. Sophie reassured her, and it was only some hours later that Sophie herself was informed of her second daughter's sudden death.

Michael Carr could not believe that they had just buried his daughter. He clung to Sophie as to a raft, and Sophie, who had hold tightly of his hand and of Phoebe's could not even cry. At last It had happened: what she had feared years and years ago, when the children were little. Clemmie was walking behind them for a moment as they came out of the cemetery in Lewisham. She was too numb to think directly of her sister; her thoughts kept reverting to childhood. In Paris, six years before, she had imagined in a childish way that one day Jack Bartholomew would marry Rosamund when she grew up. She was so much the prettiest of them all. Suddenly, she realised that no one would ever marry Rosamund now. That thought seemed somehow worse than the fact that she was dead. Clemmie had once imagined she might have saved Jack's life by insisting he should not go to fight in Spain that last summer of real peace. Now she was older, she suspected he had decided against it in any case. but it was not Jack Bartholomew, but her sister Rosamund, she should have 'saved', her lovely sister, the sister she had known all her life. They had been together for the first years of the war, at school, and had been close to each other in Wales as they had listened to the news or suffered from chilblains, and felt continually hungry. When Ros had left to work in London, Clemmie had not been able to bear school and had left almost as soon as her sister. The last time she had seen her had been last Christmas, when Mum had come home from staying with Edith, whose husband had died with no Jack to comfort her. Clemmie had been sure that they would all be together one day soon. She knew that Rosamund had had a man friend, for Ros had told her, but sworn her to secrecy. And she thought again, now Jack will never be able

367

to marry her, and Ros will never know when the war is over. Ros will never know. The thought made her realize that her sister was dead.

Sophie knew she would never recover from her daughter's death. She could not, at first, seem to take any notice of anything. It was not even sorrow she was feeling; she was too numb for that and longed to able to feel something, even wild grief. Edith would understand. She had assured Edith, once, that one day *she* would be able to feel again, though she would be changed. But her second daughter had been, she finally acknowledged, more to her than anyone. She got through the days by proceeding from one task to another, like a robot, a robot with drooping shoulders and bent head. Michael, who had now returned to his civilian work, begged her to take a holiday, or abandon herself to her grief, but she could not contemplate the first and was incapable of the second.

Both Clemmie and Phoebe stayed at home for a few days after the funeral and then Clemmie went back to her farm. Sophie clung to her domestic routine with obsessive determination, but had not been able to eat anything.

'Look after yourself, Clemmie. It'll all be over soon,' Phoebe said as she kissed Clemmie goodbye at King's Cross.

'I wish she had not had her eyes closed,' whispered Clemmie. 'I never could think of her asleep.'

For answer, Phoebe only squeezed her sister's hand and went back to her London bed-sitting room to cry alone.

All the way back to the Midlands the train wheel said, 'All over soon, All over soon' in Clemmie's head, and when she tried to stop the refrain it changed to 'Rosamund's gone, Rosamund's gone'.

That had not been her sister lying there in the chapel of rest, not Rosamund. For a moment she was filled with a sudden wild hope that it had been someone else, that Ros would come back home, pushing the door open with one of her swift movements. What would Mother do, who would have willingly died for that daughter? And father, who had had to go back to his work, leaving Mother all alone?

Clemmie was soon so busy being sorry for her mother that it hurt when she started to grieve once more for herself.

Then she mourned on Rosamund's own account and that hurt even more.

Edith was wearily feeding her new chickens when the call came through from the farm that she was wanted on the telephone. She went straight in to the Hoyles'. All Sophie could say was, 'Ros was killed,' and then silence.

'I shall come,' Edith replied and put down the telephone.

Without another thought she packed a case, locked up the cottage, asked Hoyle to see to her hens, and was at the small village station in ten minutes. Sophie must not stay alone to be reminded by every whining aircraft of her poor daughter. They would sit together and she would do for her dear friend what Sophie had done for her last autumn. No good pretending things would ever be normal again. This was the worst thing that could ever happen to Sophie. Edith thought grimly, 'Yes, my journey is really necessary,' as she passed the posters on the wall at Bradford station and made her way through the night in a deep, blacked-out countryside to London, through Doncaster and Wakefield and Peterborough and Grantham, on dull, dirty, shrouded trains.

All the way she kept being reminded, not of Adam's death, nor of Rosamund, nor even of Jack – who might, himself, have died – she had heard nothing now since Christmas when a letter had come from Milan – but of that journey the other way round long, long ago, before there were any wars, when England was a pleasant land, at peace, and they had gone north, full of the excitement and pleasure of youth. They had not been much older than poor Rosamund had been at her death.

One look at Sophie's face, Sophie, who had been sitting huddled on the platform at the small Surrey station waiting for every train from Waterloo all the next morning, told her that she had been right to come. Now it was her turn to comfort and succour.

Jack had been taken prisoner when the Allies pushed up from the south of Italy in 1944. What with all the orders and the waiting about, and the countermanding of orders and the complicated plans always changing, and the lack of news and

369

then too much news, and the slow advance and the lack of water, and no real beds, even for the officers, it was almost a relief to have been taken prisoner. The end of the war was surely not far off, and the Italians he came into contact with were well-disposed. He was put in a farmhouse before they moved him up the boot of Italy with five or six others.

The Germans were edgy and jumpy and the prisoners were a burden. The first lot of Jerries disappeared and eventually a new lot came to the house and marched them to a railway station. All Jack could think of throughout was the sweaty journey north in a goods' wagon was, bloody hell, he had left behind in camp one of the books of drawings he had amused himself doing in North Africa, between battles, so to speak. Egypt had taught him he did not need sun for his sort of painting, and Italy was teaching him that the pictures in his head were more 'there' than the sight of the land he passed: endless parched plains, then endless fields, with one red-roofed house in the distance if you were lucky. There did not seem to be any natives about, just occasionally the sight of a woman stooping over an un-cut harvest field. It was a comfort to think *that* still went on, though they did not appear to get many fruits of the earth in the camp in Milan, where he later arrived.

He composed himself to wait, to do whatever was necessary to keep up morale, and to think about nothing much beyond the next meal. The nights were different though. There was the lack of water which left them all thirsty, and wine was no help, especially the mucky stuff they were given. He lost weight, but thought he would survive. Being thirsty was worse and led to terrible dreams, not of being butchered, but of dying of thirst in a desert and reaching an oasis, only to wake up just as he was about to plunge his head in the blue pool of water he found there.

Then they were moved again, and to a superior camp. The Germans were fewer; they were needed to stem the Allies advance in the south, and those who were left were keen to get the whole thing over. He received, miracle of miracles, a Red Cross parcel from his mother, dated a few months back, and shared it out: some dried banana and some chocolate and cigarettes, but no note. Evidently, all the incoming parcels had been routed to this city. He had written to thank her through the Red Cross but did not expect his letter would arrive.

All you could do was wait, and to pass the time he began to sketch his fellow prisoners and some of the Italians, who were more like Arabs, dark, and speaking what must be a Sicilian dialect.

Soon they were to be taken to a town near the French border in the mountains of Savoy, and in late April 1945, when the Germans who were left were thinking about packing their bags, he was still there. Once the Germans had gone, the Italians rejoiced, and Jack had waited in a faded hotel in Aosta for a week before a few of his fellow ex-prisoners decided to cross the border to ex-occupied France. They had crossed in an old car over the pass of the Little St Bernard, hemmed in by great snow-capped mountains, so that on the day peace was declared, Jack found himself in a tiny ski resort in French Savoy which had itself been occupied by the Italians as well as the Germans. The Italians and the French although originally on different sides, had far more in common with each other than either had with the Germans, and both had heaved a sigh of relief when they went. Nature looked down differently on the two parts of Savoy, caring only for barriers of mountain and snow.

Jack waited for news from England. Miraculously, the Red Cross had seen that he had got late news of his stepfather's death. But since then, nothing, although he suspected Edith would have written regularly. He had no means of knowing whether his letter of condolence had ever reached her, either. Now he was apparently to 'commute' between Aosta and the Isère valley, his grammar school French being deemed useful whilst they waited for the Americans to arrive, along with, he hoped, bits of his old regiment from the south; the bits which had not been taken prisoner earlier, when their advance had not been as far as Jack's. He had begun to manage a smattering of Italian, too, had been painting in his spare time and now was to be put in charge of supplies.

He found the French village a strange mixture of age-old customs of forgotten winters when the rich had come to ski, and modern plans for hydroelectricity, which the Mayor explained to him would be paid for, he hoped, by the Americans. The village seemed dislocated, out of time, like some seaside town in winter. There was a feeling of abandonment, which was illusory, for the peasants and farmers and châlet owners had carried on with their lives under the Occupation much as before, except that food, never very varied, had become scarce. The main thing was, the war was over.

Each day, when he shut up his little office at the *Mairie*, where he was supposed to be in charge of rationing and of petrol allocations, he went back to 'his' châlet for a drink of the Chambéry vermouth which the Germans had laid down in the cellar, and ate his meal of black bread and goat's cheese. He longed for fruit. Perhaps some would come through when the convoys came up from the south. He would sit and draw all he remembered of his past three years in North Africa and Italy and now France, sketching faces and places from memory. But he often felt irritable and jumpy, perhaps because the tension was now relaxed.

On the day that Edith's letter finally reached him, sent on from the Red Cross in Milan, he had thought at first it was a letter from his captain with demob papers. He sat for a long time before opening it. She had typed his name; he knew his mother's machine, and his heart beat fast. He went out of the châlet, up the narrow street by the tiny chapel and on to the road that led up the valley through woods, and then plunged down to the stream below, to a rickety wooden bridge. On the further side of the valley were fields where grew pink and blue and yellow flowers, most of which he had never seen before. Not primroses or harebells, as on his beloved South Pennines, and not even orchids that he might even have seen in his valley at home, but meadow flowers: gentians, great bulbous, yellow trollius, yellow saxifrage, purple and yellow violets, doronicas, and other tiny plants with Latin names which he had to look up in a book he found at the châlet. Evidently, the Germans had had nature lovers among their officers.

The letter smelt of England in some indefinable way and, even more curiously, he was reluctant to open it. Soon he would be back where the letter came from and soon he must reassemble himself there through work.

He sat down on a bank of sparse grass and looked up to the mountains in the distance, on whose tops snow always stayed. There was even snow on the lower slopes of the nearer hills, and further down the hills several cows were scattered, munching, their bells tinkling in the distance. Every morning he would hear the cows going up to pasture. They had probably been going up to pasture in the same way when Hannibal crossed the Alps.

He brought his mind back to his widowed mother, and England, and opened the letter, written, he saw, only three weeks before, on the day the war ended.

'Dearest Jack,

Wherever you are, I feel sure you are safe, although your last letter from the camp in Milan is now six months old. I know I shall soon see you again. You were worried about me now that Adam had gone. Don't worry Jack, you know I shall manage, though life is strange and I am often lonely, a thing I never was before I married A. I have to tell you another sad piece of news: you remember Rosamund, Sophie's second daughter, whom you saw in Paris? She was killed by a flying bomb in June '44, I've written to you about it before, but I have the feeling you may never have received my letter. Her mother is devastated. I was glad to be able to go down to Chimneys for a few weeks last year after it happened. Do write to me, Jack, as soon as you get this letter. And perhaps you could write to Sophie and Michael. Phoebe is working at a ministry in London and has been a tower of strength to her mother and father. The little one, Clemmie, is still in the land army and Sophie says that she wants to stay on a farm now that the war is over. I am well and beginning to write again and to get some work together, perhaps for a new book.

'You may be glad to hear that your grandfather, now eighty-eight, is still alive and reasonably well. Mother, too, is alive, but frail. They are looking forward to your return. Please write and tell us when you are coming back. I look every day now for a letter . . .'

Jack had, in fact, written the week before and presumed that Edith had received this, or soon would; but he was filled with a complicated mixture of sensations when he came to the news

373

about Rosamund Carr. Essentially, they were of disbelief. She, who had been so full of life, to be *dead*. He could not believe it. And she had been dead a year! Edith must have written many letters to him which he had never received. He was suddenly filled with an urgent desire to get home, waste no more time looking at flowers and drinking vermouth. He walked back with a great rage in his throat and went straight up to his room where he wrote a savage letter to Edith and then tore it up. Each time he had become attracted to a woman when he was in Egypt, and even when he had slept with one or two, he had found himself thinking, 'One day I shall see Rosamund Carr again.' And now she was dead.

The war *had* been worth the fight, he supposed. Of course it had. But had she ever thought of him? Probably not.

He wrote a short note to Sophie and Michael, not wishing to intrude upon their grief but trying to express that he knew what they had lost. 'I hope very much to see Phoebe and Clementine when I return home,' he added.

Then he passed several strange days when everything he had had not time to question for so long, seemed to rear up in his mind and even rob him of sleep. In the night the questions seemed deep and original, but when he woke again he could not formulate them even to himself. It was something to do with 'meaning'. Not exactly where could the meaning of living be found when the war was over and survival was no longer the only imperative, but rather, was there any 'meaning' at all?

He wondered whether his mother had had these sorts of questions in her head when she was young. Not that he was any longer really 'young'. He was thirty-one that year. Six years of his life had been spent fighting a war. War was not an abstraction, but what meaning had it? The world of war and news and victory, the world of other people even, was not what tormented him in the night: the outside world seemed unreal. It was a sort of metaphysical dizziness, he recognized, and it would be partially relieved only by being ignored, or by other preoccupations taking him over. And that was not an answer. He wanted to say goodbye to war, to the world of 'news', and get home, think hard, and paint. But if he did that he would certainly not be able to forget the big questions; there might be a temporary relief, but his art would have to address itself to them.

For the first time, he wondered whether he was a true artist. He found solace in the natural world too much to want to create out of his mind a completely new world when he painted. He might be a survivor from another age of painting. Painters were concerned with objects, with light, with surfaces, and with the reality of their paint and what they did with it. Was it just another way of evading the question?

Jack did not realize how like his mother he was. Less interested than she in historical truth or in fantasy, he was as practical as she was, and pursued, just as Edith had been, by the problems of feeling real in an unreal world or feeling unreal in a real one. He still kept thinking of Rosamund when he was out walking or when he sat drinking with two or three fellow officers who had come up from Italy a few days after him. She seemed to have become a symbol of reality. It would be so easy, now, to live on the surface, to enjoy sex, breathe the free, pure air of the mountains, plan for his future in a practical way. But he felt in a hiatus of his life, a sort of limbo, longing to get back home and yet almost frightened of going in case he forgot the questions that now seemed so important.

His companion in the châlet 'Les Pins' was a Scotsman from Glasgow, who had been a student of Spanish before the war, and together they would listen to several scratchy old records on a gramophone left by the Germans. They were of songs Jack remembered hearing in Paris in 1938, though they were older than that. *La Paloma* and *Adios Muchachos* filled the summer evening air and when some businessmen from Chambéry arrived to stay in the village and several bottles of champagne were broached, he found himself remembering the last time he had drunk champagne, in Paris with Sophie and her children, and it filled him with a melancholy that was, he felt, a trap. For one ought to be more than melancholy about a beautiful dead girl. He could not even try to convey his feelings in paint or pencil. He tried to draw her as he had last seen her. Somewhere, there would be those sketches he had made in Paris. What was the use of asking philosophical questions when they were questions with no answers? The life of one girl was a precious thing and to know another human being was one way of getting closer to reality.

In this, he was like his mother. He sensed that not until she met Adam did Edith find her 'reality'. That, too, had been taken away from her. Would his mother need him now?

Instead of dwelling on the sad aspects of the past in the present, he concentrated on drawing objects from his childhood which seemed to have retained immense significance; he drew the old kitchen at Far Ox Heys and the patterns of frost on the panes there on winter mornings, and the garden on winter afternoons. That made him long again to be home. With water-colours he found in a child's trunk in the cellar of the châlet, he painted some of the flowers from the alpine meadows to take home as a memento of the time and place. Those flowers, at least, were 'real'. Some fellow had had sent to him, from the Red Cross library, a book on modern English painting and Jack looked at the familiar paintings, particularly those painted by fellow North Countrymen, Yorkshiremen whose work he had known well, and felt his spirits revive a little. Romantic individualists, most of them were, never staying long with the abstract or the surreal. But he wanted to paint landscape, English landscape, transformed by his own imaginative vision. And he might paint a few people.

He felt nostalgic, patriotic, did not really want to return to the Slade. He wanted to get himself a job, if he could: his Leeds qualifications might be adequate for teaching in a school. He might give London a try, and if it did not work out he would take some ordinary post and try to integrate himself once more into civilian life and see what happened to his painting. Afterwards, perhaps, if he thought he was any good, he might launch out as a full-blown landscape painter, and might do occasional portraits for money, if he could find patrons. He was English and he could not help thinking that the English were always, basically, landscape painters.

The weather for the last week or two of Jack's stay in Savoy was brilliant. The skies were like frozen cream, the air dazzling. Once or twice, when he went back over the frontier into Aosta, he saw on his way the eternal snows high over the pass. But this snow did not give back that white light he remembered from the more domestic snow on the Pennines. It was set and hard, almost inhuman, not belonging to the fields and hedges and lanes or roof-tops, but only to the top of the world. All in all, he was glad when his papers came and, very soon, was speeding through a shabby and run-down France on his way to Boulogne, and eventually home.

Over a year after Rosamund's death, three strange little incidents took place which, in their way, helped Sophie to stop feeling numb.

She had been re-reading the letter that Jack had written to them. Something Jack said about that time in Paris seemed to give her mind a little jig, and it was so painful that she looked up, wondering if she had been stung by a wasp, having forgotten what it was like to feel a stab of sorrow. Then it went again and she went upstairs to bed. Michael was away for the night at a special conference of the committee which intended to form a new Book League. She took a book to bed with her, without noticing or caring what it was, and found she was staring at a book of pre-first war painters: Gore and Sickert and Steer, whom she had always loved. One of the latter's paintings was so like Rosamund that her heart stopped and resumed its beat only with pain. That was the second reminder that she could truly feel again. The third was the greatest and the one that finally threw her back into the land of living. It came with Michael's morning paper when she got to the 'deaths' section, drawn there by some need to convince herself that dying was quite a common occurence. And there it was: 'Aug 9 1946, suddenly in Greenwich, Connecticut, Grant Miller, publisher, aged 75. Sincerely mourned by his wife Violet and stepson Fabian. RIP. Funeral private. No flowers. Donations in lieu to UNRRA. Friends please accept this, the only, intimation.'

It went through her heart, quite literally, like an arrow this time; not a swift stab of some forgotten emotion, but a physical sensation that turned her stomach upside down and made her back bristle and her hair stand on end. And with it there came, in its wake, another emotion that felt as though a very rusty, very heavy door, was being opened at the back of her throat and she found with amazement that she was sobbing with rasping, noisy, tearless sobs. Was it for Grant or for Rosamund? It did not seem to matter. She was crying, swollen tides of despair and grief and pain, like the pain of the return to life of a cramped limb.

It did not, of course, end there. Many months were to pass before Sophie managed to balance her mourning and her sense of anger. If Grant were dead, he who had once meant so much to her, then Ros, too, could be dead, who had meant so much more. She read Jack's letter, and other letters, many times afterwards and looked at the painting that was so like her daughter and, though she was never quite the same Sophie, she ceased to be that stiff and insentient robot and became human again.

4

Clementine

'This was one of my prayers: for a not so very large piece of
land, with a garden and a spring of water near the house, and
a little bit of woodland as well.'

Horace

One day when Jack, now demobbed, had already been home
to Yorkshire and returned to London to try and finish his
studies, there had been a visitor at Far Ox Heys who called on
Edith one Saturday afternoon, a young woman in breeches and
green jacket who looked as though she was used to an open air
life. At first Edith did not recognize her, thought this must be
another rambler come to call for a drink of water, or perhaps
old Hoyle's daughter-in-law, who had been away during the
war, working 'down south'.

'Yes, I'm Clemmie Carr,' said the girl, and smiled. 'Mother
said I must call on you one day, so here I am!'

Edith remembered the solemn, practical little girl she
had met at Chimneys. She was a sturdy-looking girl still, with
a direct manner, and her voice was quiet and pleasant. Edith
was delighted. Apparently Clemmie was on the way from one
job to another, still in the land army. How strange that now
another generation should be wandering around after another
war, possibly uncertain what they were going to do.

'Oh, I want to earn my living on the land,' said Clemmie
when she had been offered tea and was walking round Edith's
garden of lupins and rambler roses and late peonies. 'It's a
question of where and how. I know almost enough now to run

a small farm of my own, you see.' Edith was sure she did. She had an air of competence.

They discussed Sophie, who, Edith was told, was still very depressed, and Phoebe, who was to return as soon as possible to Oxford to work for a B. Litt. Then Clemmie asked about Jack, and Edith had to confess that he was not enjoying London. Clemmie intimated she would study for an agricultural diploma. She, too, did not like cities.

Edith thought Clemmie was an easy person to talk to. Her interests were practical and she was obviously level-headed and gave an impression of solidarity. Whose face did she remind Edith of? It was not her mother or her father, but it was someone she had once known. It was when Clemmie was bending to stroke Edith's new cat, Asgard, that Edith suddenly realized who it was. Aunt Rose-Ann, of course! A younger version of that shrewd old lady.

'I was sorry about your husband's death,' said Clemmie. She looked directly at Edith, as though to challenge some conventional expression of grief in her face, some polite mourning. But Edith was not given to immediate conventional expression of the inexpressible and said nothing, only reached up to cut a rose. 'Will Jack come back north?' Clemmie asked. 'Or will he stay at the Slade?'

'I don't know,' Edith answered, smiling.

'When I was a little girl and he drew us all in Paris I was frightened he would be killed in that war in Spain,' said Clemmie.

'And I was frightened he wouldn't come back from *this* war,' replied Edith. 'But it was your sister who didn't come back.' Clemmie looked glad that Edith had spoken those words.

'Do you ever stop missing people?' asked Clemmie, impulsively.

'No, I think not.'

Edith gave Clemmie the rose, and Clemmie offered after a silence, 'I should have prayed for Ros, not for Jack, I suppose. I feel better doing something active. I like your north. I feel I belong up here. I liked Lincolnshire too.'

'What about your mother's old home?' asked Edith.

'Thirksay? My mother's uncle has died – you know that? Mother was only talking about it in her last letter. The ministry

380

ran the farm in the war with the help of one of my cousins – Aunt Alice's eldest son. It had gone to pot before the war.'

'The land is very good there,' offered Edith. 'Here, it's very clayey and the slopes make it difficult to farm much arable. The farmers have a few sheep and there are one or two little dairy farms in the village. It's a hard life. But the Vale of York has the best soil in England.'

They went indoors. Clemmie said no more about her immediate plans.

'They'll want to give the men the jobs,' said Edith. 'All the returning warriors.'

'Oh, well, I might find something else. I suppose I could go to the North Riding and see if there's anything there for me. Or to Aunt Alice's in the East. Mother wants me to have a rest first. But I *must* do that agricultural diploma. They've shortened it for ex-land girls.'

Edith cut a large piece of the parkin which she still baked every week. 'You will be able to feed Jack up when he's here,' said Clemmie. 'Do give him my best wishes when he comes home.'

She was off soon afterwards and Edith sat alone, thinking of Sophie's children. Sophie had told her, during that awful time last year after Rosamund had died that she had had the feeling in Paris that Jack was rather taken with her second daughter, although of course she had only been a girl of fourteen. Jack had never said anything to Edith about her, or about any of them, except to say that they were all nice girls and it had been a stroke of luck meeting them like that in Paris. It was a long time ago – longer than the eight years of conventional calculation. Clemmie seemed older than her years now. Twenty: what one lived through at that age! Clemmie was very English, thought Edith, appeared breezy and practical, but there were hidden depths, she was sure. How long had she been praying for Jack?

Christmas 1946 was cold, although not so cold as that of 1944, the coldest for fifty years. There was a great shortage of coal. Jack, after attempting to take up his studies again at the Slade, had felt frustrated, not knowing how he really wanted to paint. The New Romantics were in vogue and that went well with his own inclinations, but he had needed the stimulus of other buildings, other landscapes. He was now back at Far Ox Heys trying to decide what to do, spending a good deal of time gathering sticks and chopping logs for Edith's fires. He would try to find some work locally. It would have been quite easy to have gone on in London, but at the age of thirty-two, he had finally known his student days were over. He would paint in his own way, wait for things to come back to him. But he must first find paid employment and have the satisfaction of normal life: money in his pocket and a routine.

He felt life had been too quick for him, grabbing him up from his studies, depositing him in the army, dropping him down in the fighting in North Africa and then Italy, shoving him into the German lines and into the prison camp and letting him make his way at the tail end of the war into those mountains and home across France. He felt he had been spewed out hardly knowing his own mind any more. He needed to get his bearings, to learn to live in an ordinary way, see familiar things freshly. He had been disorientated, dislocated. The answer was to do a job of work. Then he could readjust himself to civilian life. He had also discovered in himself a great desire to stay in the north. His mother was pleased. They did not always need to voice their thoughts to each other, although there was plenty to say when they did, about themselves and the world. Like all sensitive people they were both trying to assimilate the knowledge of concentration camps, and of the atom bomb, and it was part of a wider knowledge of death, both personal and impersonal.

Once Edith said, 'If you had not come back, if you had been killed, what should I have done?' He had never seen her face so sad. What an irony that had been; that he should be alive and that lovely little girl, whom he remembered so well, dead.

Clemmie was apparently now at an agricultural college in East Anglia finishing a truncated course, and Phoebe was back at Oxford. The great news, though, was that Chimneys was to be leased to an American friend of Fabian Trevelyan's, for Michael and Sophie had decided to leave Surrey for good and to live in Hampstead, where memories of Rosamund would not meet them at every turn.

Sophie had written to tell Edith that a picture had arrived from New York which at first she had thought was a painting of her daughter, Rosamund. But it had turned out to be a 'Portrait of Sophie Ridsdale', painted before the first war by Seb Harman, worked up from a pastel drawing. Even Seb had forgotten it. Grant had taken it to America and kept it for over thirty years. Edith remembered Sophie's sitting for Seb and was not surprised when she read on to learn that, according to Fabian Trevelyan, Grant had hung it in the inner sanctum of his office where Violet never apparently penetrated.

This set Edith thinking that Jack might still have the drawings of Sophie's three girls that he had painted in Paris. Wouldn't it be a good idea, she thought suddenly, if Jack were to work them up into a painting for Sophie. She went to his 'studio', the barn at the bottom of the garden, and asked him.

'I never threw away the sketches I did. They'll be somewhere around,' he replied. 'Rosamund was a beautiful child. I often used to think of her. Your Sophie must have been pretty too, when she was young,' he added.

Jack did not forget and went, one day after Christmas, to his old trunk which had been sent back from London in 1939 when he joined up. He was hours looking through the many, many drawings and notebooks. He had meant to look at them anyway. Perhaps he *would* try to paint a picture for Sophie and her husband. He found the sketches amongst a bundle of papers at the bottom of the trunk, detached from the others of the same year, slightly damp and musty, but covered in tissue paper. They were all there. The Seine and a café awning and the three of them. Phoebe reading, Clemmie staring solemnly at him and finally Rosamund, leaning against the bridge, one of her full face, another in profile. There was yet another of her, too, this time leaning back in a chair. He had coloured in her pink dress. It was only eight or nine years ago, but, God, it seemed eighty or ninety.

He would paint all three of them again from his sketches. It would be something to solve technically before he started on landscapes again. He remembered Rosamund's young face well, having that sort of visual memory which he supposed Seb Harman also possessed. It would probably not be a great work of art, but it would be an offering, something only *he* could do.

A painting was more alive than a photograph. Rosamund would live again, as she had once been.

A week or two later Jack was taken on as teacher of art (for the time being) 'on supply' at the Rydings Grammar School, in a small town to the east of Calderbrigg. The school had a good art department, held together during the war by a married woman teacher who, now the war was over and her husband returned, had decided to stay at home to start the family she had had to postpone. She had left the school at Christmas; Jack heard of the unexpected vacancy, immediately applied for the post and was told, by the end of the first week of January, that he been offered it as a temporary measure, as he had no art teacher's diploma from the Ministry of Education. He thought it would suit him well for a time, until he sorted himself out. He liked children, though he knew nothing of teaching. He was keen to be among new people, people who had not suffered too much in the war, whose lives must now go on into a new world but who might, perhaps, appreciate someone who had had his fill of travel, but who might widen their horizons. These were his vague thoughts, but he did not stop at theory and had immediately sought out his old tutor in Leeds for advice.

'There might be work for you here, Jack, if you can wait a bit; the whole place will be reorganized.'

'No,' Jack said. 'I want to get on with it. If I'm no good as a teacher it's only a temporary job and, who knows, I might learn something myself.'

'Aren't you going on, then, with your own painting?' the other began.

'Of course I am. I just want to work at something different for a bit. I need a change, something fresh, lots of things going round my head. You'll see!'

He got his reference, for de la Sallée was well known in the area and had examined for the board Jack would be teaching for. He went into the school before term began and was shown round by Mrs Harris, who wore a smock which he was not sure denoted pregnancy or the artistic life. He saw what was needed, was given the key to the cupboards in the stock room and a battered old syllabus. He studied various efforts of the children, some of them quite impressive.

He decided to go on living at home. The school was easily reached from Far Ox Heys by bus, or if his mother ever had any petrol available in the future he could use Adam's little old Austin. The maroon single decker buses went up from each smoky little valley 'over the top' and down to the next. The route was interesting and the views magnificent from the crest of each hill. Even though there was still a sort of spiritual greyness hanging over England like a pall, what with rationing and the cold and the dearth of decent housing, the landscape was still the same; no bombs had destroyed this section of the backbone of England, unless you counted a clutch dropped in a ploughed field in 1941. Sunsets were the same, and dawns; the church on the ridge, far away against the sky, still stood as it had for many, many years, marking out distant boundaries of the parish. In the larger towns there were new arts cinemas starting up, and bookshops and concerts were well patronized.

Jack felt that there was, too, a good deal of optimism around, now that Mr Attlee and his friends had been summoned up to usher in the brave new post-war world. Never mind bread rationing and coal shortages, he thought. England was at peace. *He* did not mind the lack of goodies and the children did not miss them, as they had never known them. It was the older adults who longed for a spot of pre-war glamour; for pretty clothes and tropical fruit and chocolate and nylon stockings and whisky. Jack had, himself, been one of those soldiers who had voted Labour, feeling that England was ripe for change. Politics no longer really interested him: he no longer placed his hopes in revolution, if he ever had. He remembered little Clemmie telling him not to go to Spain. Well, he had not gone, but he had done his bit. He was alive. Out on the tops of the moor where he sometimes went to walk, he breathed in the sullen air and knew himself to be lucky.

He had been with Edith to visit Adam's grave and that had been a solemn day for him. His grandmother in Leeds was now not expected to last much longer and there would then be the problem of Grandfather Broughton to sort out. He had seen them both often after his demobilization and appreciated the old man even more than he had done as a boy.

'Grandad is what they call a Grand Old Man, isn't he?' he said to his mother. 'He's an unusual person.'

'He was my salvation before you were born, Jack,' said Edith gravely. Jack and his old grandfather were about as companionable as two men could be, finding either a great deal to say to each other or indulging in friendly silence. Jack visited as often as he could spare the time at weekends, though the two buses required to get to Leeds and then out of it to Roundhay were always full. Workers were going into the factories even on Saturdays and the cry was 'Workers First' when the long queues moved forward. Well, now *he* was a worker.

He felt quite nervous on the first day of term. It had been snowing and the buses were delayed, but he had gone out early, knowing this would happen. But he was free; to earn a living, to paint what he wanted, to be lazy at weekends if it suited him (though he did not think it would). On the bus he thought about his painting, seeing the white hills out of the window and the children in their green uniform running in at each stop, staggering under heavy satchels. For the present, he was safe. By the end of the day he would be Mr Bartholomew, the new art master. He was not too worried about what the children would think of him. Men who had been in the army started off with an advantage.

The bus stopped at the bottom of yet another hill and the children pushed out of it. He followed them, safe still, for an hour, in his anonymity. He supposed the male staff would be old codgers, too old for the war, and was rather dreading having to be matey, but he intended to spend most of the breaks away in his own sanctum. He must have a look in the school library for art books and start his own course on art appreciation. There were no end of things he could do. Ideas kept going through his head and jostling others out. He must not move too quickly; he had seen that Mrs Harris preferred the decorative side of painting, and lessons in perspective. Well, they would have those, too. There was no more time for thinking what he would do and could do, as by this time, he was entering the school and following another male member of staff, who seemed to know where he was going, along a corridor and up some stairs at the other end and then along a top corridor, where the man paused, adjusted his tie, and then strode into an open doorway. The masters' room was full of cigarette smoke and Jack discerned several tobacco-wraithed figures moving about by some lockers at the end or sitting in leather armchairs that had seen better days. He knocked at the half-open door and a little tubby man with a moustache and a black gown, carefully pleated at the front but rather long for him, bounced forward as though he had been waiting behind it.

'I'm Bartholomew, replacing Mrs Harris,' offered Jack. He did not feel at all nervous; more intrigued to see what life was like behind the barricades.

'Come in, come in,' said the tubby man quite genially. 'Have you seen the secretary?'

'Not this morning,' replied Jack, 'I did last week.'

'Oh, you'd better pop in there at break and go down with the rest to assembly in a moment. We start at nine fifteen. You won't have a class – a form, you know – if it's art you've come for, lucky chap.'

A taller, older man materialized at this point. He, too, was wearing a gown. Jack thought perhaps he could wear a smock like Mrs Harris to distinguish himself as a non-degreed 'artist'.

There was a rushing hither and thither for a few moments in the room, but then one by one the men left, looking pre-occupied. A bell went and there was only Jack and the older man, Binks apparently, the second master, who took him into the morning assembly.

The Rydings Grammar School was a thirties building with an impressive porch in the middle and staircases at each end, one for girls, one for boys. Jack thought, that first morning, that he had never seen so many girls together, unless in some NAAFI canteen; and these wore uniform, too. Bottle green pinafore dresses or skirts, fawn blouses and green blazers. He was visited by a sense of incongruity. All this had been going on whilst he had been mopping up blood and sand in North Africa or opening his Red Cross parcel in Milan. This was civilian life with a vengeance, with its sets of rules and other sets of unwritten rules. Some of the older girls looked quite attractive, though there were a lot of spotty faces and rather greasy permed hair. The boys were grubbier looking and some had outgrown their blazers. Their long arms poked through the sleeves, leaving an expanse of hairy wrist. Adolescence in full flower. Oh, well, perhaps art would do them good.

He wished he had had more time to prepare for the twenty or so fifteen-year-olds who were waiting in a straggly queue outside the room for his first lesson. Quickly he established his priorities – this was not all that different from the army – and soon each of the bodies was sitting on a chair behind a desk that could be raised into an easel, and water was poured into twenty pots. A girl put up her hand and said she was paints' monitor and Mrs Harris had said she could go on with this task. After about fifteen minutes they were all sorted out. They were quiet, appraising him. After all, he thought, these people had chosen to study art beyond the call of duty, so he assumed they were keen. He sat down and, for the first time since he had been in the bus that morning, recollected his thoughts on teaching painting. Was all teaching to be like this? He would be lucky if he could rescue an hour or two a day from the marching and praying and 'duties', whatever they were, and all the tedious details of administration, registers and so on.

But he was calm, did not allow himself to start worrying, and said, 'Well, after all this business I suppose you might like to get on with some painting. We've got an hour left before break, I think. Right, I'm giving you a choice and I want to see what you can do with it, OK? Choose a person in this room or an object, or imagine or remember a place – I don't care what you paint so long as you really *look* at what you are seeing – or imagining. It's up to you.'

There was a silence and then another girl put up her hand. 'Please, sir, Mrs Harris usually gave us old papers. And how can we paint a place if it's not here?'

He realized she meant exam papers; their exams were to be in the summer. 'Yes, I know,' he lied, 'But I don't know you yet and I must learn your strengths and weaknesses first before I can advise you about your School Certificate exam.'

A few looked gratified: a few sighed and looked out of the window.

'I shall be busy sorting myself out,' he said. 'A lot to do. Try looking in your mind's eye for a landscape. We'll go out sketching later.'

'Please, sir, can we talk?'

'So long as you're not stopping each other working; I suppose at your age you can get on with it without my breathing down your necks,' he answered breezily. 'I shall shut you up if necessary,' he continued. 'Get on with it now. After half an hour, I come round.' The monitor was called Janet, so he said, 'Janet, any queries are referred to you and you let me know later. Right?' He saw some people arranging objects; an apple, a jar of water; others were ruling out squares for patterns. Janet looked self-consciously prim and important, but was probably better at sorting out the detail than he was.

Really, he would have liked to sit down and paint a picture of his own, but he had better get on with checking his registers and stock-room and keeping an eye on the 'children'. He began to arrange the pastels for the lesson after break which was to be the first form, group A. 'Free Expression', it said on the syllabus Mrs Harris had left him. He took a piece of paper and wrote down a list of essentials for this lot, who were sitting, getting on with their work in a most gratifying way. He referred to the dog-eared 'syllabus' that dated from 1938. 'Perspective/Line drawing/Colour balance/Each candidate to draw one of the following from memory . . . Each candidate to draw and paint one of the following . . . Still-life subjects . . . *NB* the materials must be assembled and locked up ready for the examination the day before . . . Bulrushes, vases, animal bones, flowers . . . Each candidate to present a portfolio of the three best pieces of work done during the year . . ..' He wondered who marked this. He would bring an assortment of objects from home and ask them to do the same for next week. He should have thought of that.

The time went by quickly, to audible sighs, and he went round to look at their interpretations. Several girls had drawn each other, a boy had drawn a desert landscape with a plane turning tail and cowering children lying flat on the ground – not bad. 'Do we need to paint?' a boy asked. 'I'd rather draw cartoons, sir.'

'Just what you like today,' replied Jack.

A girl with plaits was busy on a landscape of cypress trees and Mediterranean blue; another had drawn the contents of her satchel – books and an orange.

The bell startled them all. 'Leave your work to dry if you've been painting, you can finish on Thursday,' Jack said, with a glance at the timetable.

They smiled at him as they went out and he sat there for a moment before gathering up his notebooks and making his way back to the masters' room where the hubbub was indescribable. He signed himself on for a school dinner, mentally resolving that if it were dreadful he would go to the nearest pub or bring a sandwich. There was probably some regulation which kept teachers in the school, though.

Later he looked through the work they had done in class, some of it not bad. He *should* have brought things with him.

Jack was to find that teaching was more like a mixture of drilling a platoon, checking a quarter master's stores and being a padre than he had supposed. He would get them through their exams, though. He had no doubt of that. The younger children were more imaginative than the older, even if their technical mastery was minimal. Where could you start? He re-read his Herbert Read and concluded there was a vast gap between theory and practice. Twenty adolescents in one room, with all the attendant logistics required, did not leave much room for the encouragement of imagination. But he was determined to win through. What he had not realized was how tiring teaching was. Not the walking round the perimeter of the school field on 'break duty'; that was quite pleasant if you could think as you walked. Nor even the actual teaching. But the adjustment to the other adults in the school who seemed to regard art as a frill, far from the real nitty gritty of existence; the constant burden of administration; registers, equipment lost, pencils, paper not arriving, homework to mark, apart from getting to know each individual. He decided he would give a twenty minute lecture on his Mondays with the fifth form and would take pictures of his own to discuss. So might their horizons be widened, and his own.

He made a collection of objects: feathers, old birds' eggs he had collected, some books, some dried honesty from Edith, some birds' bones, again from his own long ago collection, and some scissors, spoons and playing cards, a vase or two – objects both natural and man-made – and lugged them all to school, where they joined some dusty plaster casts. He also brought his large post-card selection from galleries and museums: Viking brooches, Constable landscapes. Later, he would take them out in the school field and the park to study roofs and perspective. At present, it was still snowing, the snow making graceful and magical the dark landscape. That was what *he* wanted to paint.

390

That same January saw Jack's mother putting together her new book, '*The Hermit of the Hey*'. It had nothing in common with her Bevis Constantine efforts, except that it was typed on the same old typewriter, and little in common, either, with her epic of good and evil, first written twenty years before, which Edith now felt like disowning. Still, she could not pretend it had not meant something to her when she wrote it, in the years after Clem's death. Edith was now fifty-nine and she little expected to make any sort of splash in the literary world. She had been taken by surprise by the reception of her very first Constantine, when it was reissued, but had little hope of *The Hermit*. That was a mingling of matter-of-fact observation, in the form of a diary kept over many seasons of many years; of poems, dreams, meticulous descriptions of the weather, and longer pieces describing places and experiences, a gathering and weaving together of Edith's 'epiphanies' in which she tried to give a coherent form to the shape of life. No opinions. No remarks about her reading. One section described Adam's death and she had written it clearly and simply and with apparent understatement. Would it be worthy of him?

She had wanted, throughout this new book, to sustain various levels of understanding and of metaphor, to distill the essence of her last thirty years as a private person reacting to both private and public events, without appearing chatty or self-important. It was, in one sense, a 'personal' book, but it gave nothing away, would not appeal to readers who wished for biographical detail, although she was using her own name for it. No one knew that the other new book she was to publish that year was to be the last of the Bevis Constantine's. She had finished it in the autumn of '46 and it was to be the first of his works to be given the name of 'science-fiction'. She had drawn on her knowledge of the Vikings and Anglians, for it concerned a war-like tribe who invaded a peaceful land and who could be opposed only by the use of a certain type of magic. These tribes were finally banished to outer space, despatched there in long planes with prows, to remain there for good. But the magic which the invaded had used began to turn them, too, into 'Vikings'.

'You'll make money with that, Mother,' Jack had said when she showed it to him.

'It's only a re-working of the book I was writing in 1940. I don't know enough about atom bombs or I'd have had them take one into space with them.'

'Well, you won't need to write any more, will you? You can do what you want now.'

It was true, for the copyrights left to Edith by Garnett Edwards, which covered the reissue of the work of the last thirty years, were beginning to prove phenomenally lucrative. The second and then the third books were going into new editions and, quickly, new printings. Michael Carr was delighted, since he published them all. These older, 'forgotten books' were a bonus. Bevis Constantine could now keep Edith Stead, and the latter, with her *Hermit*, could write as she wished. Edith was far more apprehensive about this work under her own name. Perhaps she was on the wrong track completely. She wondered who would want her lucubrations, which were neither the chronicle of a farming year or the thoughts of a lady gardener or exactly an autobiography.

'Spiritual autobiography, Mother,' said Jack.

She was to dedicate the book to Adam, in memory.

She was confined to the cottage for weeks, for the end of January saw immense snowfalls which lasted well into March. By the end of the second week of February there were power cuts, followed by cold intenser than any they had known. The huge snowfalls wrought havoc on the hill farms and Edith wondered how Clemmie was coping and was glad she was not at present on a farm full-time. Jack read to her from the newspaper that four million sheep had been lost. 'The planting season will be very late if it goes on like this,' she said. 'Just the wrong year for low crop yields.'

'Perhaps summer will make up for it,' Jack consoled her. He knew how closely she followed events on the land.

When spring finally came she went over on a visit to the North Riding, and returned with a happy look on her face, but a great sadness, too, that Adam, for whom she had planned, was no longer there to see the possible fruits of her literary career.

'Look who's written to us,' said Edith one Saturday morning. Jack had eaten a quick breakfast and was off to his barn with a great sense of relief that today he could paint for himself and need not worry about his pupils until the Monday. He paused for a moment at the kitchen door. The letter had been addressed to 'Mrs E. Stead and Mr J. Bartholomew' and so Edith had opened it, a little puzzled.

'Who?' asked Jack, looking out of the window at the rain which had been falling all night and seemed set to fall for ever.

'Read it – it's Clementine – I told you she came over last year and Sophie said she might write to us, remember?'

Jack took the letter, came back to the table and poured himself another cup of Nescafé, a great luxury in civilian life. The handwriting was large, well-formed, plain, but pleasant to read. It was unusual for him to receive letters. He had not yet re-established himself as a correspondent; so many of his old friends had gone away; one or two were still unaccounted for, 'Missing', and those who had returned, as he had, to Calderbrigg did not need to write him letters. Women were always better correspondents, he was thinking as he began to read it. The letter was to tell him and Edith her news. She seemed a downright character from what he could gather from her style and handwriting. He could scarcely envisage how she must look now, though. His mother had said she looked like some old lady she had once met long ago on her visit to Thirksay.

'My course is nearly over; not that I've really learned very much. I think you can learn only by doing, on the land anyway, and perhaps it's the same with art? I am going to stay with my Aunt Alice whom Aunt Edith knows, I believe. They have a farm on the Wolds and it will be a different sort of work. Perhaps I could come over one day if you are not too busy? Mother said you might be; you must tell me if you are. How do you like being a teacher, Jack? I'm afraid I never learnt a lot at school; they never taught me anything I wanted to know! I'm not a great letter writer, so you must excuse me – keeping accounts is bad enough! I passed my written exams, but you would have to be a half-wit not to. Love, Clemmie.'

'How old is she now?' asked Jack.

'Nearly twenty-one, I think. She likes the north; I don't know how Michael and Sophie produced her. But she's a nice girl. She must still be very cut up over her sister.'

393

'Yes, I remember in Paris when they thought I might go to fight in Spain, she was the one who tried to dissuade me. Of course, I'd really already decided not – or something in me had decided for me. Rosamund was the beautiful one. Even when she was still not grown-up.'

'I'd always thought Sophie rather underrated Clemmie and Phoebe,' said Edith. 'Phoebe must be a clever girl – looks like her father. This youngest one is quite a character, too. Have you done anything about those sketches you did?'

'I haven't forgotten – I've been so busy.'

'Sophie knows that any of her family are welcome here, but they very rarely come north now. Mrs Ridsdale died two or three years ago and Sophie's never really had much in common with her sister Alice. I wonder how Alice will get on with Clemmie? She has three grown-up sons, two of them needed for their own farm; Clemmie's cousins,' mused Edith. She seemed to know a lot about Sophie's relations, Jack thought.

He rather looked forward to seeing this grown-up Clementine, curious to see how she had turned out, but he had not much time for thinking about anything but his work at the school, for teaching was proving not only tiring, but quite interesting. He still looked forward to the weekends and did not consider himself a 'real' teacher. In any case, as soon as other better qualified teachers than himself were released from the Japanese POW camps or the colleges of art, they would not want him to stay, he was sure; and if he were serious about teaching he would have to go off to Leeds for a year to work for the teaching qualifications.

Jack found, to his surprise, that he was quite enjoying himself. The school had the feeling of a close-knit community, and was a happy place on the whole. During the war, art had flourished in the little town. Pupils still spoke of the wartime national poster competitions, of their own and their parents' amazement and puzzlement over 'modern' art when London had sent them travelling exhibitions. The fifth and sixth formers were quite capable of discussing what they thought art was about.

He canvassed for support among his pupils and enlisted their help in starting up an art club after school, once a week. He took his pupils to Leeds and Manchester to see the municipal collections there and refreshed his own knowledge of nineteenth-century English painting. There were plenty of volunteers from the boys to work at design and from the girls to paint flowers and landscapes. He started portrait painting off and was quite pleased with the results. The boys were interested in the architectural models for which he solicited the help of the maths teacher and an old friend from Calderbrigg. There was little time for him to take them out to paint in the countryside around, but several keen spirits undertook solitary or group expeditions to paint in Wharfedale, and by the beginning of spring he felt that he had covered all he should and that a basis had at least been laid down for those who were to specialize, with enough of interest for the others to carry them through life as amateur painters or 'appreciators'.

Clemmie had still not made an appearance and Edith hoped her letter had not gone astray. Edith had been reading up more about farming once she had packed up her last manuscript and sent it off to Michael Carr. To Sophie, she had written a short letter asking her to read the book first and tell her truthfully whether she was barking up the wrong tree. Now that she was lucky enough to be earning sums of money that made an appreciable difference to her standard of living, no longer dependent on weather or on her pension, Edith felt she had forgotten what a gamble farming was. Farming profits had apparently been worse last year than the year before; they must recover. The land had to be re-equipped and methods devised to bring it up to date, but most farmers had no profits to plough back. She talked long with old Hoyle who was still working his little mixed farm next to the cottage, but he was gloomy and felt that agriculture would be allowed once more to slip backwards now that the war was over. Like most farmers he had been overworked during the war and felt his efforts had not been appreciated by the Powers that Be. 'They'll be wanting to return to importing food again, mark my words,' he said to Edith. 'They won't spend a bloody penny on development and we've the best farmers in the world – but we can't make food from nowt.'

Electricity had been scheduled for his farm. It had already arrived at others in the district, along with mains water. But what was the good of that, with no men to work on the farms? 'Bloody Germans were t' best,' went on Hoyle. 'Who'll gather t' spuds now Germans have gone?' Edith gathered that the 'Bloody Huns' had actually *liked* work. What was needed was capital, and then willing labour.

The conditions for farm-workers must, of course, be improved; so many farm cottages had not been re-conditioned and there were no grants towards the cost of improvements. Edith often talked to Jack about this. He was not surprised that his mother was such an enthusiast. She was a remarkable woman. Not content with writing readable stories, she had done research on medieval charters, and Vikings, and created a garden, and now she had written a book which he suspected would be her best. And she never seemed to tire, even though she had lost her beloved Adam. They often spoke of Adam. Now that Jack was more experienced he began to understand why Adam had been so ill after that first war. It was not, as he had sometimes rather disloyally suspected when he was a lad, that Adam had been afraid. Rather the reverse. It was that his body had let him down after the war as a result of his own horror at what he had been forced to see. He had been a brave man – perhaps braver than many who were not so sensitive and whose memories had not acted upon their bodies.

Jack dug out a sketch of Adam he had done before the war and decided to work on that, too, as well as the projected picture for Sophie. Years ago it had been an effort on his part, at first, not to resent Adam a little and he was thinking about him when Edith, who had just had the telephone installed, came back from it to say that Clemmie had rung from the farm on the Wolds and was to come over to see them the next weekend. Now that her visit was really to take place, Jack felt a little cross. He had been so busy at school, and then at home in his painting barn, that he rather resented having to do the honours in his precious free time. He had also been asked by the English master to help with the forthcoming school play, to be produced at the beginning of the next term, and was much exercised by the problem of stage scenery. Truly, English schools needed Jacks of all trades. He hoped it would all repay the effort.

Other jobs were also looming. He was requested to take a party of pupils to York, too, for a day to 'observe' the Minster. Someone else had murmured that a new member of staff was needed to collect National Savings and Jack had hoped they were not looking at him.

The next Saturday morning Edith was called by her father to say he was worried about her mother. Edith had been planning to go over to Leeds the following week to see her and decide whether she should go into hospital for observation, but thought she had perhaps better go straight away. Jack offered to meet Clemmie off the bus to allow Edith to fulfil her filial obligations.

Edith went off to her parents in Roundhay in her little car with just enough petrol, and Jack tidied himself and the cottage up and went out to the village where stopped the bus from Bradford. He wondered whether he would recognize Clemmie. Would she have grown tall? Would *she* recognize *him*? Should he say something about Rosamund or let it lie? He was still thinking of this, and also of his painting, as he walked along. He had started to use all three of his old Paris sketches to make a new picture of them and wanted to hold the picture of Sophie's youngest daughter in his mind before he met her in the flesh nearly nine years older. He rounded the corner where the buses stopped and saw a young woman standing there looking up at the sky. She transferred her gaze when she heard his footsteps on the pavement. It must be her. Yes, it was.

'The bus was early,' she said as he came up. 'I'm sorry if I didn't give you all much notice. I thought it better to come now or I should never get away.'

She had a green canvas bag with her. They shook hands rather solemnly.

'I would have recognized you anywhere,' she said.

Jack glanced at her briefly before taking her bag. She had grown taller and slimmer, but that was to be expected, though she had curves in the right places. Her face was browner than he remembered. Must be all that fresh air.

'Do you remember the way? Mother told me all about your last visit.'

'Past the library, up to the right. Then the hill and the field with a bull on the left and then, I think to the right at the top and down that little lane with the oak copse?' she answered.

He whistled. 'Who's got a photographic memory, then?'

'I always notice places,' she replied, swinging along with him. 'And it was a nice bull.'

He laughed. They slowed down a bit up the hill, leaving the village behind them. Of course, he had forgotten, she had a southern accent. He was so used to the Calderbrigg variety of English that he almost forgotten that young people could speak any differently. 'How is your aunt – Alice, is it?' he asked politely.

'Oh, busy. She always is. The farm's very big. My cousin who's come back from the war will help to pull it back into shape.'

'Mother has had to go to Leeds; her mother's not too well.'

'Oh, I'm sorry; I must be a nuisance, but it was now or never,' she said. 'I've to go back for a month on a farm in Norfolk to finish the practical part of my diploma. Beans and beet.'

'But you won't stay there?'

'I thought of going to Canada to farm, but then I knew Mother would be miserable if I did, so I thought I'd look around, try another sort of farm after that. I'd like to do a bit more with sheep.'

'You used to like pigs,' he offered.

'Fancy you remembering! Yes, I still like pigs. How is *your* work?' she asked.

'You mean how do I like being a teacher?'

She looked up at him as they paused for a moment on the brow of the hill and looked over the green landscape with its woods and fields and the higher, browner hills enfolded in the distance.

'It's right enough.' Jack answered the question with a parody of broad Yorkshire. Clemmie laughed.

Over lunch, which they both prepared, she was quiet. He wondered why, as she had been so chatty before. Then he saw that she was not used to speaking over meals. But she did not seem to mind silences. Afterwards they washed up and Jack wondered whether to mention the picture. He looked at her, sitting comfortably over a mug of tea. She had strong-looking hands, nails cut short but neatly, medium brown curly hair brushed away from her face, brown cheeks with the faintest rose tinge, sturdy-looking wrists, a little lipstick – was that usual for an ex-land girl? She put down her mug.

398

'How are your parents?' asked Jack. They had better get over the mention of her sister, he thought.

'Mother is well, but a lot more subdued than she used to be. Do you remember when we met in Paris? Mother did a lot of talking then, I remember. She was like Rosie, in that.'

He looked at her swiftly. 'I *was* sorry – about your sister – it was terrible–'

'Yes, it was. Rosie and I were great friends, you know. We quarrelled sometimes, I suppose sisters always do a bit, and Phoebe didn't like arguments, so Rosie and I were closer at school together and everything. I like talking about her, Jack, don't worry. I have to get over it. You liked her in Paris, didn't you? I mean you were grown-up and we were only little girls really, except for Phoebe. But I remember you liked looking at her; I *do* remember that.'

'Yes, I did.' How very easy it was to talk to Clemmie, once you began.

'Everybody liked looking at her,' went on Clemmie. 'She was so pretty.'

He wondered whether she had been jealous of this sister. He waited, but she said no more and they found themselves talking of Clemmie's work in the war and then of his own time in the army, so that the conversation passed from the hay harvest and crop rotation to the Italian Front and camp life.

'I wonder what we'd all have been like without a war,' she mused. 'Do you remember you were going to Spain? I remember that; and I made a nuisance of myself, begging you not to go?'

Yes, he remembered. What she did not tell him was her romantic childish dream that Jack must be saved for Rosamund to marry one day.

'I found my sketches, the ones I did in Paris. Would you like to see them? Mother thought I might paint something for your parents with all three of you as you used to be; or do you think that would be morbid, or upset them?'

'I think it would be a lovely idea and I'm sure Papa and Mother would love it,' she answered. 'And I would, too. Where do you paint?'

He decided to show her the barn and they spent the rest of the afternoon looking at his more recent pictures, before going out for a walk. When they returned, the car was back in the yard and Edith with it. Jack looked encouragingly at his mother.

'Crisis over for the present,' said Edith. 'She's to go into a nursing home for observation next week.'

Clemmie looked suddenly a little shy. 'I'm sorry to come at a difficult time for you, Aunt Edith,' she said. 'You must let me cook for you; I like cooking.'

'Mother likes it, too; you'll be lucky to be allowed in her kitchen,' said Jack, laughing.

Edith embraced this youngest child of Sophie and told her to sit down and rest and Jack would bring them all a drink.

Clemmie had nice manners, Jack noticed. She was not awkward, though in a way he could not define she looked younger than her age. She had a level, honest gaze that slightly disconcerted him. Edith was obviously enjoying the presence of another woman and, unusually for her, began a long conversation in the kitchen with her guest, who was given potatoes to peel. Jack was amused. Edith usually liked to be left alone with her thoughts when she cooked. He guessed they were talking about Sophie and so went up to his room after laying the table and did a bit of work on his marking scheme for school on the Monday.

'I'm afraid it's very dull,' he ventured, when they were all sitting down to a delicious Yorkshire pudding and Clemmie was describing the delights of the coast.

'Aunt Alice's farm is by the sea,' she explained. 'It's beautiful. If I hadn't wanted to be a farmer, I'd have liked to be a sailor.'

'Like your Uncle Harry,' said Edith.

'Oh, did you know him?'

They talked about Thirksay then.

'*You* ought to have been a farmer, Aunt Edith,' said Clemmie. 'You seem to know a lot about it.'

'I take an interest,' said Edith. 'I only ever kept hens, though my second husband started a little market garden here in the thirties. We sold peas and beans and rhubarb; I'm afraid potatoes and rhubarb are not very interesting. I prefer stock to crops. Though, of course, I love my flower garden.'

'I'd like to run both,' said Clemmie.

400

'Do you actually enjoy the labour?' asked Jack. 'I mean, it's rather different running a farm, I should have thought to *working* on it.'

'I found it terribly hard at first. In the war we never stopped – sometimes sixteen hours a day. But I got used to it. And farm work is so varied. Not that I wouldn't enjoy making money!'

No, she is her father's daughter, too, thought Edith. She has that air of success.

Clemmie changed the subject to her sister Phoebe who was back in her Oxford element. 'I've been to see her only once since she went back. It's a nice quiet life, I suppose, and she loves her research work. But all day in libraries – ugh!'

After supper they talked around the fire and Jack taught Clemmie to play chess. Then Jack brought in his old portfolio of drawings, persuaded by Clemmie, who wanted to see her sisters as Jack had seen them.

'I'd only just started using the sketches for a big oil painting,' Jack explained. 'I don't get much time at the moment, but I shall have it done in time for your mother's birthday.'

'How do you know her birthday?'

'Well, it's the same day as *my* mother's.'

'Of course! I'd forgotten.'

Clemmie took the sketches and looked at them a long time without saying anything. Jack thought at first she was disappointed, but when she looked up she had tears in her eyes.

'That is exactly what Rosie used to look like,' she said. 'I don't know about me. You've caught Phoebe reading. And Mother, too. I'd forgotten how she's changed. They *are* different from photographs. You've put a little colour in, though. I remember that dress of Rosamund's. She used to love it. She wanted to impress you with her best dress.' She was thinking, we all thought you were marvellous; a handsome young man. It's not true that little girls don't notice young men. Phoebe had been quite impressed with Jack too. Of course, she had been a bit older. Jack was thinking, I like her; she's almost the same person as she was at twelve. Then he looked at her more closely as she sat in an easy way in an old armchair, her trousered legs crossed at the ankles and her head against the back of the chair. She had no more than a fleeting resemblance to her sister Rosamund, perhaps more of a likeness to her mother, whom he remembered well. But she was larger, sturdier, and her hair was curlier, her eyes grey. Not a cold grey, more like the grey of a misty morning. Her cheeks were rosy, and he noticed, too, that her nails were cut short, and her hands looked capable. She was a larger, calmer, version of her mother in a manner, but the figure was different, fuller. You would not call her 'pretty', more 'handsome' if that did not make you think of someone much older. And Clemmie was young, so young.

Edith had gone out of the room to make some coffee and Clemmie said, 'I like it here; so cosy. It must be a very old house.'

'Oh, Mother has made a few improvements, but it was here to begin with in the seventeenth century. It's older than the farm.'

'I love old things; things that go on and on. I suppose that's why I like farming. If someone doesn't go on with *that*, there's no future either. There's no point enjoying the past if it's not going on somehow into the future, is there?'

He considered. Was that why he wanted to record things and people and places and ideas in paint? Growing things out of hard labour and skill was perhaps not very different from creating pictures.

'A friend told me of some swans that come to England every year from Siberia; they've been coming for hundreds of years probably. Isn't that wonderful? Even in the war they came, unless guns stopped them, and the swallows came back every year to that farm I was on in Lincolnshire, even to the same shed; from North Africa, I expect. Don't you think that's comforting? Have you read your mother's latest book?' she asked, when Jack had agreed about the swans and the swallows.

'Yes – the serious one? I've read all the others too; the Constantines.'

'Papa loves them. He thinks your mother is a genius,' she replied. 'But Mother did say something about a different sort of book. I don't know how people can write books; it takes me all my time keeping up with living. How can you spend your life writing or painting? You live for it, I suppose?' Clemmie's questions were always direct and to the point.

She seemed to have a lot of self-confidence for such a young person.

'Edith – Mother – is naturally talented,' he replied. 'Some people have a gift for shapes and colours and lines and others for words. It's not really to do with how you live. I suppose *you* have green fingers; perhaps it was something you inherited?'

'Mother thinks I got it from her parents and grandparents, though it passed her by, she says. I know she envies your mother, I mean in a nice way; she's awfully fond of her. Wasn't it sad about your stepfather? Poor Aunt Edith.' She cupped her chin on her hand and spoke with real sympathy.

'Yes, he was a good man. But he'd had an awful time after the first war.'

'And your own father being killed in that war, too. Our families have suffered quite a lot, haven't they?' She thought, but did not say, I'm glad *you* weren't killed.

'Your mother knew my father too, Mother says,' said Jack, getting up to poke the fire, for it was still a cold spring.

'You know I was called after him? Mother liked the name anyway, but *I* think it was a case of unrequited love! Did you know that? Of course, I'm called Edith too, after your mother.' She was very open and ingenuous.

'Yes, I know.'

She was looking very earnest. She went on after a pause, 'I'm glad she married Papa, he is a very steady sort of person; you would like him. Do you ever illustrate books?'

Jack explained that that was not his sort of thing and they went back to discussing the instinct for making patterns and shapes out of life or organizing clods of soil into ploughed fields when Edith returned.

'I can't draw at all,' Clemmie was saying. 'I once tried to draw my favourite dog, but he looked like an animated hearthrug when I'd finished!'

'What sort of dog was that?' asked Edith.

'Oh, a mongrel. I reserve my pedigree interests for cattle and horses, but sheepdogs are my favourite, I think.'

'Breathing life into pictures is very difficult, pursued Jack.

Clemmie was a refreshing conversationalist and it was a relief not to be responsible for *her* education. He wondered if she had ever been in love, or slept with a man. She did not have

403

a trace of the silliness he still found in his girl pupils, or most of them, and remembered thinking that very thought about the three of them before the war. He and Clemmie seemed to have quite a lot in common, too. He could not quite put his finger on it, they were so different in their interests, but there was an indefinable feeling of restfulness about Clemmie. He wondered whether Phoebe had it too. It was an attractive quality. He was sure the dead sister had not been restful, would have had the men running after her. Clemmie seemed unaware of her own qualities. He felt she was talking to him as if to a brother she had never had.

Clemmie was feeling happy – happier than for a long time, for she had not seen quite eye-to-eye with her Aunt Alice and Alice's family. She had suspected they thought she was 'forward' and they had seemed amazed that she should want to work a farm for her living. That was *their* province, who had worked the land all their lives. It was strange, Clemmie thought, as she undressed for bed in the little room over the kitchen that night; she had met Jack only twice and the first time she had been a child, but she felt she knew him. She had been very bold, writing to him as she had done, even if in a joint letter to his mother. What she did not know about him she would like to discover. Of course, Mother had always talked a lot about Edith and her son and they were, she supposed, predisposed to like her, or at least Aunt Edith was; but she remembered that feeling in Paris she had had and that dream, whose content she had forgotten, but whose atmosphere had made her determined to beg him not to go away and fight. Ever since then he had been somewhere in her mind as a man she liked. She had had a short and not un-sweet flirtation with an Italian prisoner of war when she was eighteen, working on a farm, who had, to her amazement, offered marriage. Her physical passions had been aroused then and it had been revealed to her that she had better be careful if she were not to fall into a trap that would prevent her doing what she most wanted. 'Playing with fire', they called it; she preferred to think of it as a natural, but slightly dangerous pastime which could not be indulged in in the way her animal charges indulged themselves – briefly, but satisfactorily. Male animals did, anyway, she thought sleepily. Strong young females had to be a little more careful. But Jack might be the man she wanted; not that she supposed he would ever realize it.

Maud Broughton died a few weeks later, not unexpectedly, and Edith mourned her as a woman she had never been able to get to know or to understand. It was her great failure in life. Not that her mother had wanted any intimacy with her, even before she had disgraced herself by getting herself pregnant before marriage. Edith remembered her father forcing her mother to receive her at home after Jack was born. She had been married by then, of course, but Maud had not seemed able to forgive her. Her father had been a ruthless man in his own way. Her mother might have been happier with a more ordinary business man. But it was too late to change her now.

Maud was old and ready to go, but still conventional to the end. She preferred her old maid, Lizzie, to tend her rather than Edith, but accepted her husband's decision that she should go and stay at a small private nursing home where she could be better looked after. Edith had offered to stay in Roundhay, but Wilfred replied that Mother would prefer a little comfort and the ministrations of Lizzie, who was herself in her late seventies. Lizzie was then allowed to accompany her mistress to the nursing home. Edith tried again and again to talk to her mother before she died, wanting to say that she had always understood how she felt over Jack's birth, but all Maud would say was, 'I wish you would get Edward to come.' Edward was telegraphed in Canada and did return, but only the day before his mother died. Edith and he were strangers, though he was impressed by being told more about her writing from his father.

After the funeral the problem was what to do about Wilfred. But he insisted there was no problem; he would go on exactly as he had done. If Lizzie wanted to come back and help with the house, she could; but for himself, he would be staying in his study where there was a fire and he could manage for himself. He was genuinely grieving over Maud, in a puzzled way, with regret that he had never really been a companion to her because she had not been able to be one to him. He feared he had been rather a managing husband, but that was what she had seemed to want. She had been a good wife to him. In his rather naïve

405

way he wondered now whether she had been jealous of his love for Edith.

Edward stayed on for a bit and they talked business, and when Edith came over they discussed the short holiday which Edith wanted her father to have. He was so frail looking, but his mind was as sharp as ever. She would take him in her little car to Silverdale on the Lancashire coast for a short holiday. He was finally persuaded to agree, but stipulated a week was long enough. Edith thought that, by providing a break from routine, his new, future time alone would seem less terrible, for she realized that many things had been done for him in the past by way of creature comforts which he would miss if he insisted on living alone. She even offered him a room at Far Ox Heys for the rest of his life, but he said, 'What are you thinking of, Edie? I must be near the firm.'

He had effectively been retired for twenty years, but still kept an eye on the place, now run by two young brothers. Edward had shown no interest in ceramics, but was prospering in 'real estate' in Ontario, whither he soon returned.

So Edith took her father off to Silverdale; she needed a break herself and was still waiting for Carr's reaction to her *Spots of Time*. It would do her good to look after her father. No one would believe it when they heard him speak, but he was ninety. He had taken pains to preserve his erect carriage, though he now needed a stick. They sat in the sun and enjoyed slow walks in the woods and watched sunsets over Morecambe Bay, but she worried whenever she looked at him. She knew she had always truly loved her father. What would she ever have done without his firm moral support? Not that she had ever accepted any of his money for herself once she had settled in Far Ox Heys. Only for Jack. Jack was her father's pride and joy and he still hoped, against all counter indications, that he would go into the business, where a partnership awaited him. Jack had it in his power to please the old man, Edith thought. But he would not become a businessman. She and Wilfred sat together and discussed the works of Samuel Butler, whom he was re-reading. His eyesight was still good, though like his daughter, he had been short-sighted when he was young.

Whilst Edith was away Jack was busy. The school summer term had begun. He had had a letter from Clemmie and written back to her. She was constantly in his mind and he wondered what was the matter with him. He worked on the painting and slowly it took shape. Strangely enough, when he considered it, he saw that the figure of Rosamund, which had occupied the centre of his sketches, had seemed to recede – or was that only his imagination? Sophie looked directly at the painter and the viewer, but Rosamund was looking into the far distance and, try as he might, he could not alter her expression. Surprisingly, it was Clemmie who dominated the picture. Was it because he had seen her recently? He tried to judge whether he had imported a new look to her face, a look that had not been there in 1938, but could not see that he had. What, then, had crept into the painting? The Clemmie of the Paris picture was a child, there was no mistaking that; but she had an interesting face, a face he had never really noticed then. How should he have done, since she was a mere child? Did she shine now because Rosamund was dimmed? He was completely baffled by the change. It must be in himself. He looked again at his picture of Clemmie and saw in it unusually strong features which he had never consciously noticed. He wondered if his mother had a photograph of that old aunt they said she was like. Probably not, but he would ask her. Perhaps Sophie had one. Of course, Michael Carr's mother was Jewish – perhaps that was it. Clemmie, though, was very English-looking too.

He tried again, painted her alone from his original sketch, in an effort to forget her present face, and succeeded a little better. He would have to start again with the big painting; it was unbalanced. Just for interest, he painted the Clemmie he had seen a few weeks ago by herself and again the strange, dominating look reappeared. Perhaps he was never meant to be a portrait painter and had better stick to landscapes. He would go walking in the summer and do some sketches.

Clemmie decided, for her part, that she wanted to see Jack again. She was stuck in the last week of her final 'practice' and could not keep inviting herself to Far Ox Heys. How could she get to see him? Then she had an inspiration. She could apply to do a bit of mixed farming in the West Riding, where he could be reached. She consulted the 'situations vacant' in the *Farmers' Weekly* and filled in an application for work on a hill farm: location – the Pennines. Object – learning about sheep. Then she posted it and waited. She would not write to Jack again, had a horror of appearing to pester him, although his letter in reply to hers, thanking him and his mother for the weekend had seemed to show a surprising eagerness to see her again.

Clementine was a very loyal girl with a tenacious memory. As she had never forgotten Jack, the young man who had materialized during that Paris holiday, neither had she ever forgotten the way Jack looked at her sister, Rosamund. Never once had she been remotely jealous of her. Rosamund had always been accepted by Clemmie as somebody special and beautiful, who deserved the best in life. Now that she was dead Clemmie had felt for a time cut off from her own feelings, bereaved in the true sense, for there was no one left on earth like Rosamund, no one to look forward to seeing and to want to please in quite that same way. Rosie had always put herself out for Clemmie too, in spite of the youthful quarrels; had confided in her and even depended a little on her in less obvious ways than Clemmie had drawn sustenance from her. Only the war and their being apart had allowed Clemmie to grow up. She did not deny that, in the last few weeks, her feelings for Jack had developed. Jack was a link with her sister, even though her earlier daydreams about him had been a child's fantasies. She was not, on the whole, a daydreamer, for her energy was usually turned outwards; she was not too introspective. People said of her that she was 'down to earth' without meaning any criticism. She was certainly open in manner and her little experience with the Italian had not changed that. She did not take herself too seriously, so was surprised to find herself thinking about Jack in what was not a 'Clemmie' way. It amazed her more than a little. Writing to him, meeting him, and then his letter had raised him from that old figure of daydream, already unusual, to a real person who seemed interested in her. What could he find of interest there? But there was no denying that new feelings were stirring in her.

Meanwhile, there was the job to plan. It was poorly paid, but she would learn about sheep even if she did not see Jack. She could hardly wait to hear whether she had got it. She found herself wondering how she would tell him if she did get it; he would think something was up! Still, she had already told him and Edith that she wanted to do a bit of sheep-farming, hadn't she? What would Aunt Edith think of her if she found out? She felt restless and put it down to unsatisfied desire, for Clemmie was completely aware that these sorts of feelings usually arose from sex. The war had accentuated the importance of sex, what with parted lovers and snatched affairs and general excitement and uncertainty. She knew Rosie had had some sort of love affair for she had been told; not much, but enough for Clemmie to feel a little shut out from her sister's life. There had always been the feeling that the affair Rosie was having or had had, would not last the war. She knew her sister well enough.

She felt gloomy after her initial restlessness. Jack was, after all, twelve years older than her and had probably had many girlfriends and even, perhaps, had one that very minute. She was sure there would be some scheming schoolmistress making a dead set for him, and what could an ordinary girl, who wanted to be a farmer, give a clever person like Jack, a painter? Then she roundly turned on herself. 'You make me sick,' she told herself in the mirror of her stuffy farm bedroom, the week she was due to leave, her future still not decided. Nothing had yet arrived from the Pennine farm. 'I love Jack,' she said aloud, experimentally. It sounded rather silly. The trouble was that everyone must, surely, find him attractive, making her problem worse. She vowed to tell no one about these feelings, but to be as cool as possible if she saw him again. She did *like* him, anyway, and she was not a completely ignorant person. She was good at her job. Neither was she really ugly, she thought, looking once again in the glass. It would be up to him. She would not betray herself. Men did not like girls who threw themselves at men. It seemed unfair, though. Men could pursue women, couldn't they, as much as they wanted. Mother had always said that.

Clemmie had discounted the very quality which Jack saw in her– her youth. He thought of her as an unspoilt creature, rather shy underneath her insouciant exterior. She kept coming into his head all that week. She was not like anyone he had ever met before, but his life for the last six years had been odd. She was *sui generis*, existed entirely separately from his memory of Rosamund or from his memories of girls with whom he had had short affairs, and even now from his memory of her as a twelve-year-old child. He had had a few affairs and none had lasted. He felt restless listening to the other male staff talking about marriage in that jokey way Englishmen have who see themselves as unwilling victims of women. Feeling restless led to 'settling down' he realized.

On the Friday afternoon, three weeks after Clemmie's visit, he was waiting for a woman to come out of the mistresses' staff room and thinking what a silly name a 'mistress' was. It seemed to be the first day of real summer and the sun was beating through the long windows of the landing over the girls' staircase at the other end of the school's top corridor. Miss Jessop had a list for him of girls who were to be excused art because of some 'outing' or other and he had sent a child to knock and ask for it. The men and women staff never mixed at break, though they ate together at dinner-time. The women's room was said to be much more comfortable than the men's and he could hear a few peals of laughter coming out of it. He was standing near some lockers; there was a general lack of space for the sixth form, who had to leave their possessions all over the place, and this was one of them.

He stared vaguely out of the window and for a moment felt purely happy and wondered why. The sky was blue; it was warm; he could see two pairs of girls playing tennis on the school courts beyond the playground and there was the sound of some bus going down the hill. Things seemed to stop for a moment, though he could see motes swirling in sunbeams in the dusty air. Then, with an inner eye, he 'saw' Clementine Carr, as though she was hovering over the stairs, larger than life. Curious . . . He shut his eyes and she was still there. Clemmie, with a face different from the one he had painted long ago and also indefinably different from the one he had seen three weeks before in reality. He felt, after the joy, a sort of yearning, an almost physical tremor, so that he blinked and then shook his head. Clemmie disappeared, to be replaced once more by the sunbeams, which had never really gone away, and the sounds from the staff room returned. Had he had a vision? He blinked again, thought about her again experimentally and found he wished she was truly there. Just then the child who had been sent with the message emerged with a piece of paper and he smiled at her.

'Mr Bartholomew is ever so nice,' this child confided to her friend that afternoon. 'He has a lovely smile.'

410

'Are you sweet on him, then?' the friend enquired.

'No; I only noticed it today. Teachers are human, you know.' The child's father was a teacher, so she should know, her friend thought.

All through that afternoon Jack seemed to be in a slight dream – not unpleasant, but as if his vision were faintly impaired or he had a slight temperature. It was only when he arrived home, after a bath and a quiet supper, that he realized he must be in love.

In the middle of the night he woke and thought, no, it must be sex starvation. Then he fell asleep and in the morning thought again, what is wrong with love and sex starvation coming together? Clemmie's 'presence' on the stairs for that brief second had felt 'physical'. He was attracted to her, to her solidity, her strong, open face and her nice, plenteously endowed body, the legs rather muscular from all the hard work she had been doing for the past three years. He groaned and jumped out of bed and thought, what can I do? I must see her! He was filled with an excess of physical energy, unusual for a Saturday morning. The day outside was sparkling, sky already periwinkle blue, with the woods to the north, where once Edith had walked with Adam, a brilliant green. A day for walking and painting if he could not see Clemmie.

But the post, which had so often brought him the paints for his boyhood attempts at landscape, was to bring a short letter from Sophie's child. He took the mail from the peak-hatted figure of the postman, who was on his way to the back door. Jack was out sniffing the warmth like a cat. He could not believe it: a letter from the person he had most hoped to hear from, at the time he most wanted to hear from her; and for a moment he turned it over in his hands recognizing her script-like hand and the Norfolk postmark. He read it as he leaned against the wall of the enclosed garden at the back of the house. Brief, but satisfying. Could she read his mind?

'Dear Jack, I thought you would be interested to hear that I have been offered a job sheep farming in the Calder Valley – a few miles to the west of Ox Heys, as far as I can see on the map. Thought you would like to know. Tell Aunt Edith I'd love to come and sample her scones, having just sampled her last Bevis book which Pa sent on to me.'

She added the address and said she would be there next week and perhaps, if she had little to do and could get away at the weekend, Jack might like to come over to see her.

Jack could not see that there would be much to do with sheep at the present season, but doubtless there would be other jobs for her. The girl seemed to like work. He was filled with an elation; at least they could probably have her back over in Ox Heys, now and then. He might even offer to take her to art galleries!

When Clemmie had sent off her letter she had been filled with a sort of shame at her daringness. But she hoped it had appeared, as it partly was, a family letter. And Jack could take it from there.

Edith had said, 'Of course she must come over, but I don't expect she'll have much time off. It's not far from where we used to walk when you were little; remember the valley with the bistort, and you sketched one of the deserted mills and the waterwheel?'

Jack did remember it and wrote immediately to the farm with an invitation for her first free day. Still under a sort of apprenticeship, she would be given time off. He suggested he came over and they could spend an afternoon in the valley, as the weather was still so good. But of course, if she preferred, she would be more than welcome at Far Ox Heys any weekend. Her telephone call came about ten days after her settling in. She would have to be back at the farm for her late milking shift; there were a few cows, milked by the farmer's wife, who liked her Sundays and late Saturdays off. It might be possible to get a whole weekend later.

Jack was to meet her after the midday meal at the farm – she enclosed a bus timetable. She would be ready, wanted to explore the country round the farm which she had so far not had time to do.

When she saw him coming across the level field, having toiled up from the bus-stop – the farm was on the top of a hill, not far from a high village – Clemmie's heart gave a little jump. She had changed from her muck-raking clothes and put on a pair of green slacks and a kerchief in her hair. Jack thought she looked like a partisan when he saw her. They looked at each other a little warily as he came up, and Clemmie thought how in place Jack looked. Not like a townie or even an artist, but a man who knew places like this and appreciated them.

'I'm sorry if I smell of manure,' she said with a sly smile. 'They have no proper bath and I've been busy all morning with it.'

'I thought we could have tea over the valley. I've brought Mother's coffee Thermos and some of her scones; how do they feed you here?' said Jack.

'Like all farms nowadays, they seem to exist on curd tart and cups of tea. I'd be glad of a change.'

They turned together and walked back over to the road that wound up from the bus route. It was a very clear day and the valley was hidden below them. Over to the north were some of the same hills that ended up near Haworth in moorland, sketched in distant brown.

'Are you sure you'd rather not have a rest. It seems like a busman's holiday to make you walk.'

'No, I need to wind down, even from physical work. People forget that to walk for pleasure is quite a different activity. But don't let's hurry – I needn't be in till dusk.'

She told him about her new work as they walked along and Jack gave her the news from the art room and his attempts to make the children really look at things.

'They could try drawing sheep,' she suggested. 'A ram would be a lovely subject; they're very handsome creatures, rams.'

Neither said anything more personal and each was feeling, perhaps I made a mistake and this is just a friendly call. For it *was* friendly. They seemed to have a lot to say to each other, but perhaps when they endured a silence it was more in the nature of a pregnant pause than formerly. The path led down to the wooded valley and they heard other 'hikers' in the still distance. The sun was kind and, once they were in the woods with the new sound of water from the stream below, the green-ness of the leaves and the pungent scent of ferns seemed to enclose a magic paradise, with the colours almost enamelled, like a medieval painting. Jack cast surreptitious glances at her when she was by his side, but when the path narrowed he went on in front and Clemmie looked at his shoulders as they swung along in a nice rhythm, and at his hair, still like his mother's, quite fair and thick. It was hard to believe that he had been in

413

combat, that he must have things in that head that she could not guess at. When they came level again and began the descent to the brook, they gave each other a cautious smile and Clemmie's heart beat strongly again.

'It was nice of you to give up a free afternoon,' she tried.

'Don't be silly, Clemmie. I wanted to see you again: I thought you'd be off again and I wouldn't for months. It was a piece of luck for me that you found a job near. I thought you'd prefer the south or Wales for a change.'

'No, I love Yorkshire – ' She did not say that there had been other, better paid and more interesting jobs advertised.

'We could go up the other side and even get on to the moor,' he said. 'Mother and I used to walk near here when I was a lad.'

'A lad,' she echoed. 'Jack the lad.'

He laughed.

The stream was a rushing, boulder-strewn affair, dark, the colour of stout, with the same peaty foam. Clemmie sat on a boulder by it and he came to join her.

Experimentally, as though (he thought) he was seventeen and out with his first girlfriend, he put down the small haversack he was carrying and, as they looked at the waters, took one of her brown hands and covered it with his own. She shivered. He was closer to her than he had ever been.

'You look like a fawn or a mountain sprite,' he said. 'I'd like to paint you.'

'I thought you took your sketch-book everywhere,' she said in a small voice.

'No, not when I need a hand to hold yours.'

She said nothing to this, but did not withdraw her hand.

'I'm thirsty. Couldn't we have some of Edith's coffee?'

He withdrew his hand and took out the Thermos which he unscrewed carefully and poured out into the top for her.

'I'm sorry, I forgot another cup. You drink first and then I'll get your germs and you won't get mine.'

She drank slowly, her eyes on the stream. 'Just think, all that water was hurtling along all the time I was a child, all through the war when you were away, and just going on the same when Ros died, *all the time*.' As she mentioned her sister's name she felt a weight lift from her back.

414

'But not the same water,' he said gently.

Without thinking, she went on, 'You would have loved her – Rosamund – everybody did. Even that time in Paris I could see you thought she was beautiful. I thought she was beautiful, too. I plotted in my mind that one day you would fall in love with her properly. I felt I had to save you for Rosie; I was just a little girl, but I can remember thinking that.'

'So you didn't want me to be killed in Spain so I could be with your sister?' he asked incredulously, following her train of thought and thinking something was coming out of Clemmie that he had better encourage if he were ever to hold her hand with the grasp of a lover, rather than a friend or 'cousin'.

Clemmie took a breath, put down her cup and said, 'I truly loved her, Jack; I can't believe she's not *here* any more. I still think of things to tell her. I know it's worse for Mother and Father, but I feel as though I'd been cut off from something and sometimes that it's me who is dead.'

'Oh, Clemmie! Rosamund was only a child when I saw her that time. It's true, I did think she was beautiful and I did remember her, and thought and wondered what she would be like when she grew up, but I remembered you all; it was one of the nice things to think about in the war.'

'You had no father and lost your stepfather, and had to go and fight, whilst I've done nothing. But Rosamund would have been famous; she was very talented, you know. She was beginning to learn to direct films, even though she was so young. They all said at the funeral – the crew and the director and the other film people – that she would have been a really great person.'

'I expect she had people who loved her there, too, I mean, apart from her family. I wonder whether she would have gone on to be famous as you say, or whether she would have got married. It's hard for a beautiful woman. I mean, I can go on with my work and ...' (he thought better of saying 'get married' as it seemed this was not quite the moment, though Clemmie seemed in confessional mood), so added, 'and have a private life. But for women it's harder.'

'Oh, that's what Mother is always saying. But Rosie was tougher than my mother. Your mother has managed though, hasn't she? My father thinks the world of her writing – that new book – he's always going on about her. And Mother still envies her, I think.'

'She had to work. *I* was there and my father, Clement, your name-sake, was dead. She didn't marry Adam till years after.'

'And then, I suppose, she was lucky and he let her get on with her work?'

'My stepfather really appreciated her; and she has a domestic side, too, you know. They made each other happy, though I sometimes wonder whether it was not too late for Adam. Her marriage may not have turned out quite as she'd imagined; he was perhaps too 'wounded'. But I'm sure she has no regrets.'

How had they got on to his mother? He tried to turn the conversation back to Clemmie. 'Clemmie, *you* are not dead or wounded, however unfair you may think that is. And you have work you want to do. I've thought far more of you than of anyone else in the past few weeks, more about you, I think, than I've ever thought of any girl.'

She looked at him, paused a moment and then said lightly, 'I've thought about you, too, Jack, but it's still a bit mixed up with childhood and the shock of Rosie dying. It's still a shock. I haven't any special talents, except for hard work, and it's not going to be easy for a woman now the war is over, especially in farming where there are plenty of men to do the job. Have you done any more to that picture of us?'

'Yes, it's nearly finished. I've been working on it at weekends, and the most surprising thing has happened – ' How could he put it to her, that her face stood out and that it had been a little to do with the picture when he had suddenly found himself thinking about her physical presence and then falling in love. For he was sure, now, that it was love. She touched him deeply with her modesty and her slight earthiness.

Clemmie was feeling, oh, he is so near, I want him far more than I ever wanted Giovanni . . .

'The picture made me see you differently, I suppose,' Jack said.

'How?' she almost whispered.

'Well, your face began to stand out. Not your sister Rosamund's, not your mother's even, and *she* has a most interesting face for an artist. Your eldest sister seemed vaguer, I suppose.'

416

'Yes, Phoebe is quieter and makes more impression when you know her well.'

'*Your* face; let me look at it again. Now, that's not a very artistic feeling I have when you're sitting near me, but it is a face that I thought I might know better. No, not to paint it, but to know it. I began to wonder whether one could ever paint the portrait of anyone one did not know well. It's a common problem, I suppose, for painters. But that wasn't my problem. I wanted to make it a good picture, but even more I wanted to know you. So, you see, there are problems for men too!'

'Beware of artists!' replied Clemmie with a shaky laugh.

'I do so like you, Clemmie,' Jack said. How could he say 'love' when he had just said he did not know her well enough?

'I like *you*, Jack.'

He was thinking, I could not love anybody more than this. It was a live woman he desired. Did she feel it was a sort of disloyalty to her sister that she should be loved?

'I'm sure that if there had been no war, I should have ended up feeling as I do about you – *you* are the one I'm talking about, Clementine Carr.' He looked at her as she emptied the dregs of her coffee over the glass, and waited for a reply. He could not go on without some sort of positive reaction. But she had said she liked him. That was all he had said to her. Who would be the first to say more?

He saw a small tear on Clemmie's cheek and felt indescribably tender towards her.

'Why are you crying, Clemmie? Is it for your sister?'

'No – not – ' she struggled to regain composure. She cleared her throat and then said in a rush, 'There was an Italian prisoner of war, on a farm in the war. I let him make love to me once or twice. I was angry with myself afterwards, as though I might have put Rosie in jeopardy, and *you* were fighting them. It was because *I* wanted him to, it wasn't just him. I'm sorry, Jack.'

'Clemmie, why be sorry? You're only human, and anyway, I thought girls spent a lot of time in the war having flings, did you think I'd be shocked?'

'Yes.' She paused a moment and then went on, 'I thought you might be shocked that I had those sort of feelings. I've

417

never thought them *wrong*, but it wasn't just an animal thing –
not that there's anything wrong with animals. I didn't love him,
I suppose; I was curious, and I wanted a man. You see, Rosie
had a lover, too – an older man. She told me, and somehow I
felt that she would have had a lot of men, but it would not have
stopped her ambitions. And Rosie told me, one time in London
when I was on leave and she was talking about him, she said,
"Be careful, Clemmie, you have strong passions." I asked her,
do you have them, too? And she said something strange about
love not really being important to her. It was fun and she liked
to have people admire her and he was "besotted" – her words.
And I was envious, you know, not jealous, of my own sister.
And so I thought, I shall do what I want if a man show's he's
attracted to me. Of course I wasn't pretty like her. So I did.
And afterwards I felt quite relieved that it was all right and
that I was quite normal, but I didn't seem to have all those
romantic feelings about him that we are supposed to have. He
was just a body, but bodies are nice.'

'Yes,' said Jack. 'And there's nothing terribly wrong in
enjoying them; it's just whether that is satisfactory in the
long run.'

'I thought most men thought that was . . .'

'I don't know about "most men", but I think we are
as capable of love as women, Clemmie.'

Clemmie had been struggling to keep her dignity, but
his last words went straight to the right spot. Never mind
'being in love'. Jack and she understood each other and
that was marvellous. The mixture of feelings wound round
the memories of her sister began to unwind themselves a
little, and she realized that what she needed was a friend
who understood them and yet did not reproach her and
who would also accept her physically, without thinking she
was forward or lewd or lacking in self-respect. Silly words,
because people were silly about sex and women. Still, she did
not want to say it first, whatever it was, and waited for Jack to
say something more.

'I think we've talked enough, except for one thing, Clemmie,
before we get up and walk to the top of that wood up there. I
think you are the most desirable woman I've ever met and I
also think I'm falling in love with you.'

418

There was a silence and he was just about to get up, thinking, now I've ruined everything, when Clemmie gave a gasp and turned her face to his. 'Oh, Jack, I love you, too, I really do! I thought I mustn't say it, but now you have – I *do* love you, Jack!'

He put his arms round her and they nestled close together, savouring the moment. He was incredulous, but ready to be convinced; and before a moment had passed, he was sure, when she said, 'I applied specially to come here so I could be near you. I had a feeling about you, and it grew and grew when I went away, and I thought I was being silly – we hardly knew each other really – but we *do* know each other, don't we? I feel we do.'

'Yes, we do.' Then he kissed her and they began to laugh, not out of embarrassment, but because everything suddenly seemed simple. It would not be, of course, but it seemed so and the moment was magical.

After that, they seemed to fly to the top of the hill opposite, though they must have toiled up it in reality, and once at the top and looking once more at the moorland and the blue sky, they walked along holding hands, happier than either had ever been before.

Even the mutual declaration did not stop them discussing other things, in a similar mutual, unspoken agreement that now they were to 'get to know each other'. They talked of Clemmie's war and her work and they talked of Jack's adventures and he told her of one or two of his affairs and described the boredom and fear of both fighting behind the lines and being prisoner; they talked of Jack's teaching and they talked of things they saw on their walk which, again by mutual consent, was not to be too far, as the sun was warm and they could sit overlooking the next green valley before eating Edith's drop scones and discussing how they were to see each other more often. Weekend walks on moors and in valleys would not always be enough, but for the moment they would have to suffice, and anyway, they both enjoyed walking, thought Jack. He was worried that Clemmie was already tired enough from her sheep-checking and her finishing off the last hay ricks. When they laughingly measured their arm muscles in an attempt of Clemmie's to prove she had muscles as hard and strong as a man, and when they stood at the end of that afternoon, their arms round each other, they both knew that this was only the beginning of an exploration, again mutual, but more intimate.

Jack finished his picture the same week that Clemmie's farmer, a dour man, as harsh as his land, decided that a nephew of his wife's was the more deserving of a job and gave her notice. But Jack had a plan. Clemmie must go home for a week or two (for she felt she had rather neglected her parents and also wanted to see what they had made of their new home), and Jack would come to London at the end of this summer term. They had still not become physical lovers, but knew that would be inevitable, and Jack decided that this was to be no hole–and–corner affair, but could be pursued on a proper holiday – a holiday such as neither had had for some time. Clemmie must, and would, find another post, she was determined, and he wanted her to do what she wanted. And he must save money. But there was nothing to stop them going to Paris later in the summer, was there? He felt that in Paris the ghost of Rosamund would be fully exorcized, and now that travel was once more possible they could afford two weeks away.

They both thought of it as a 'honeymoon' and looked forward to it in August. Jack was first to stay in Hampstead. Sophie was a little intrigued by this 'new' daughter who announced she was going on holiday with Jack, but made no objection. When at last the time came for him to visit, the picture carefully framed and wrapped under his arm, Edith saw him go with a sort of regret. Letters had, of course, passed between her and Sophie, but nothing had been said about the two 'children'. Edith thought it premature and referred only to Clementine's convenient work near Ox Heys and what a pity it had had to end.

Sophie, when Jack arrived and had been shown the new guest room, did not think of him as anything other than first of all and always Edith's and Clem's son, and secondly as a painter. Jack, however, observed Clemmie's mother closely, though she was unaware of his scrutiny. She had taken to wearing horn–rimmed glasses and had her greying hair now pulled back in a French pleat. Her skin was still dark and unwrinkled. It was Michael who seemed more personally aware of him. Jack never felt he had properly appreciated Clemmie's father till then. He turned out to be down-to-earth about painting and about his youngest daughter.

Jack had arrived at four o'clock, met by Clemmie at King's Cross. After three days they were to go off to France. The 'surprise', the nature of which Sophie had not guessed, was unveiled after tea. Jack had worried lest it might be a shock or that he might have been thought presumptuous, but Clemmie prepared the ground be taking them all to see Sophie's portrait first, which was now in the pleasant dining room of the house, on a Georgian terrace in the heart of the village.

'I'd have known a Seb Harman anywhere,' Jack said. 'He puts his paints on like cream; smooths it on.'

'Do you think we ought to have it cleaned?' asked Sophie. 'Michael thought not.'

'No, it's been well looked after,' answered Jack, with a feeling that here was a story of whose details he was ignorant.

Clemmie had said, 'Oh, an old flame of Mother's had drawings done years and years ago, when your mother and mine were in London, and then they were worked up to an oil.'

Now Jack said, 'He's caught something – I don't know exactly what, but there's a tension there; youthful energy, perhaps.'

Sophie looked gratified to hear this from a young man.

'Now for *your* present, Jack,' said Clemmie, wanting to take his hand, but feeling shy; though her parents must surely know she was not going to Paris with him just to look at pictures, or even for a well-earned rest.

Jack brought it into the room and prepared Sophie by saying, 'I wish I could have put you all on, but Mr Carr was not there when I did the sketches.'

Michael undid the string slowly and eased the canvas from the covering. 'The frame isn't very good; I can get you a better one in London,' murmured Jack.

Sophie's hand flew to her throat. 'It's Rosie,' she said huskily.

'We thought you'd like to have all three of us,' said Clemmie gently, taking her mother's arm. 'And Jack was doing it for months; it's his present to us all.'

They were all looking at it and, for a moment, he felt excluded, though it was his work, his offering. He had finally made all three children look out of the canvas as though they were looking out at life; they seemed to be looking at something in the street, their heads slightly turned, and the mother was looking at them – Sophie as he had seen her then, just embarked upon middle–age, streaks of silver in her short hair. Rosamund was in the centre of the painting, as she had been the day he saw her, the brilliant face looking away with a slight smile curving round her lips. But eyes were drawn, then, to the other two. Phoebe looked as though she were about to look up from her book and Clemmie, alone in full face, was smiling.

Sophie gazed and gazed at it. 'Oh, Jack,' she said, 'that's how you saw us. Oh, Michael.' Her husband put his arm round her and they all stood and seemed to be drawn into the picture themselves for several minutes.

'You've got Rosamund just right,' Sophie said after a pause. 'That's how I – we – remember her. And Clemmie; you were a funny little girl! it's almost as though he guessed all our thoughts, isn't it?'

'I don't want to look at it too long,' she said then. 'I shall look at it every day for a little and look forward to seeing it; it's beautiful – I mean as a painting, not just because it's us.'

'I think we should all have a drink,' said Michael, breaking the spell. 'Jack, you're a genius, like your mother!'

Sophie sat down and smiled at him. 'He used to paint crocuses and animals, didn't you, Jack? But this is the best I've ever seen of your work. Edith never said. Did she like it too?'

'Aunt Edith thought you'd be pleased,' said Clemmie.

'I am. It's a happy painting, full of promise,' said Sophie. 'It's how I want to remember Rosie. Phoebe must see it soon; she's coming for a few days when you go off on your French trip.'

'I'm looking forward to seeing Paris again,' said Clemmie, looking at Jack. Sophie was thinking; it hurts less, just a bit, to see Rosie like that. Different from photographs.

'She certainly had a look of you when she was fourteen,' said Michael quietly to her as he poured a glass of wine for his wife.

Jack was looking again at the portrait of Sophie by Sebastian Harman. It made him want to paint Clemmie alone. Michael was asking whether he was going to specialize in portraits, and the conversation turned then to other painters. Sophie spoke of her old favourites; Sickert and Steer and Whistler, and Jack went on to consider whether he, too, might do his own 'Little White Girl'? Whilst Michael was comparing Seb's picture of his wife with Jack's and saying she ought to have one of her as she was now, to complete the progression, at which she grimaced and sighed, Jack was thinking of this new idea for a picture of her daughter.

They sat on in the London summer dusk whilst Jack pondered painting northern snow in that white light he had always wanted to catch. A white girl in a white landscape . . .

'You must paint your own mother,' said Michael, breaking into his thoughts. 'We ought to have the picture of the writer of our runaway best sellers in our main office!'

'I do wish Edith would come to stay,' said Sophie. 'Couldn't you persuade her now, Jack? It's three years since she came to me. I miss her.'

'I think she might,' replied Jack. 'She's still reluctant to join the literary world, though. When exactly is *The Hermit* out?'

'On our Autumn List. We could have a party for her; I'm sure it's going to do well,' said Michael. 'But does she still insist on no one's knowing about the Constantines?'

'Surely it wouldn't matter now,' said Sophie. 'Edith has never had her due.'

'Financially, she is having it,' said Jack. 'I think she's still a bit ashamed!'

Before they left for Paris on the boat from Newhaven, Clemmie and Jack went across to South London and visited Rosamund's grave and stood silently there, apart and thoughtful, until Clemmie took Jack's hand and he knew that she had drawn him into her own grief, and felt the better for it.

When the young couple had gone to France, Sophie had too much time to think. She looked at Jack's painting and sadly remembered the past. It seemed, now, to belong to the same world as the earlier one, of Grant and London and the days of her youth. If only time would stop; but she needed time, too. To be alone was also necessary sometimes. She would write to Edith again. Michael had, it was true, grown closer to her since the girls had gone away, and that helped, but only a little. She had married because she wanted children and now one of them had gone for ever, cancelling out part of the meaning of her life, and the others were no longer children.

She had finally registered the joyful look Clemmie wore whenever she looked at Jack and hoped that he returned whatever it was that her youngest daughter was feeling for him. They would find out, she supposed, on holiday. She felt more protective of Clemmie than she had ever felt of herself, though Clemmie was independent and had managed her life well so far. She was so young – yet she was the age Sophie had been when Grant Miller had claimed her. If only Jack could love that secret part of Clemmie which was the essence of her being, as she herself had loved his father in vain. Grant had loved her like that. He had wanted a picture of her, perhaps because he feared she would not always be his. And Clem Bartholomew had had that strange passion for Edith. Did Jack feel like that for her youngest daughter? She did not know him well enough to decide. He was a bit like his mother. You could say that she had loved Adam Stead wisely, and that must eventually have had a good effect on Jack. But she did not want Clemmie to marry yet! She wanted her to be independent and strong.

She herself had wanted, at Clemmie's age, to marry Grant, but it would not have worked. He had had his own illusions about her, had worshipped a Sophie who did not exist. He must have been shocked to realize that she was quite different from his ideal, though she could not even now, over thirty years later, blame him for having seduced her. She was glad that she had had his love, when she was slim and young, not the conventional idea of Woman, not passive, nor dimpled, nor gentle, but rather fierce and independent. But her female–ness had cheated her. Grant had imagined things in her that were not there and ignored aspects of herself that were: all in all, it had been *une grande illusion*. That sort of passionate love was always an illusion. It was not needed to carry the race forwards, must be an oversight of nature or a little trimming added in an absentminded moment by the Creator. All that lust and romance and passion might not, in the end, be as strong as love for children.. It was a trick of nature that one led to the other, for lust alone would have done quite well.

She brought her thoughts round to Clemmie again. Clemmie did not have illusions and might, therefore, be a more contented person than her mother. She was certainly a sensual girl; Sophie knew her own children well enough. More sensual than Phoebe, or even than herself, and perhaps even more than Rosamund might have been. She must try not to feel possessive over Clemmie. You did not, however, want your fledglings to fly away even if you knew that they must, that they were separate people.

She tried to analyse her love for her children. A loved person was not just the cluster of feelings you felt for them. Not even the proud, but anxious, feeling she had had for her small children could be called pure, and disentangled from selfishness and possessiveness; and the yearning to have things stay the same for ever. She wondered what Edith had really felt for Adam. She had, as yet, read only the first part of the manuscript that had arrived at the newly reconstituted Carr and Penn's and was sure that Edith would have something to say about married love. For Edith was truly unselfish, though others might think of her lonely life up in the north as a selfish one. Edith had always been different. She thought she had uncovered a sort of reserve in Edith's son that was part of Edith too, but it might only have been the slight constraint young men feel towards their elders and particularly towards the parents of a young woman in whom he was obviously interested in a rather grave way. He was, even so, Clem Bartholomew's son. A nicer man than Clem, though. Clem had been exactly Jack's age when he died. She shuddered, turned her thoughts deliberately away from death.

She looked at a blackbird who was standing some way away in the grass, looking at her. The blackbird's destiny was pretty well fixed and predictable. He had never decided to behave as blackbirds do, just followed his nature, was not in charge of himself. Nobody was, really. That was another disturbing thought. She went back to musing over her youngest daughter. Clemmie seemed all right. She trusted life. Sophie hoped it would never disappoint her. Clemmie's hopes were not higher than her talents, and she had always been a rather happy girl. Sophie looked at the blackbird and smiled. She got up from her garden chair and went into the drawing room, blinds down against the sun, and was visited with a sudden stab of memory: Thirksay on a hot day and the sounds filtering through the window of the parlour and the sound of bees in the honeysuckle. That had been real. That had meant something. And she had left that place without a thought.

Jack and Clemmie woke to a mutual embrace, on their first morning in Paris. They had arrived late, at a small hotel in a city still shabby from wars, though every street had its awninged cafés, and the *boulevards* were as crowded as ever. They had washed, gone out for a meal, strolled back as though they had all the time in the world; but the moment came nearer and nearer when they knew they would finally lie together and begin that process of sensual knowing which can go on between lovers for months and even years. They had undressed calmly, lain together on the enormous bed that seemed too big for the hotel room and finally Jack had asked in a rather teasing way if she would like to go to sleep. What with the voyage and the eating and the unaccustomed feeling of being, now, for whole days and nights together, he had thought perhaps she would like to sleep; and if so, they would. 'No,' Clemmie had said, 'not yet,' and proceeded to embrace him in ways that did not betray any lack of expertize, but seemed to flow out of a superabundance of energy.

She lay against him, measuring her body against his, and was finally still whilst he kissed her all over, marvelling at the smoothness and softness of a woman's body, even of a tanned and apparently tough young body like Clemmie's.

He retraced her spine and caressed her limbs and kissed her neck, his tongue delicately exploring her ears and then resting on her lips, before licking them softly as though he were exploring and pointing a brush, she thought; then insinuating it into her mouth and darting little kisses there on the inside of her cheeks. He licked her eyelashes and curled them up, and then held her breasts with a feeling of delight and thus advanced on places no one had ever been, not even the ardent Giovanni, whose love–making, though pleasurable, had been of the briefest.

Clemmie tugged him down to lie on her stomach and felt there were certain other procedures which might now take place. She was smiling, and continued to smile whilst Jack slid himself into her as though he owned a silken divining rod and she was earth, being at first gently tapped and measured and explored for water. Then she felt an enormous feeling of liquidity, as

426

though she were a cup of sweet, moist, sugar being stirred, with crepitations and bubbles. The rod became more insistent, more rhythmic, and the comfortable waves raised themselves to a little peak. Was it desire or was it the result of desire? She could hardly tell that first time, but lay open and felt a surge of pleasure which emanated from Jack and spread all over her. She neither moaned nor gasped, but lay looking into his eyes.

He kissed those eyes shut and murmured, 'Darling Clemmie . . .' and fell asleep. She was happy; glad that they were finally together and fell asleep herself with the rod, now a snub-nosed crumpled little morsel of flesh, nestling inside her.

When they awoke it was dark still and another metamorphosis had taken place and this time it was Clemmie who began to kiss him languorously, making him groan and begin once more to stab inside her, to their mutual excitement, once more to fall asleep and to awaken when the sun was high in the sky. Then Jack said he was to pay attention to a neglected part of her anatomy, which made her giggle and then gasp and give herself up to sensations whose exquisiteness she remembered from early dreams, long ago, when sex was an unknown word, though not an unknown feeling.

'I'm hungry,' she said after this, and, 'I do love you.'

'I'm hungry, too, but I'd rather have *you* for breakfast.'

'If you don't eat you'll die of starvation and I shan't have my rights,' she said.

So they got up and passed the morning eating croissants and drinking coffee and looking around them, merging this into lunch at a tiny restaurant in a side street where everyone seemed to smile upon them benevolently.

'Blissful,' said Clemmie, in what Jack called her posh voice. 'But I want to walk a bit this afternoon or I shall forget the use of my legs; take me to a gallery and tell me about pictures.'

'A glutton for punishment,' he replied. 'All right.'

They enjoyed walking round the Jeu de Paume, which had just come out of its wartime wraps, and Renoir's paintings seemed to be in tune with their mood. In the evening they sat by the river and held hands and talked about anything which came into their heads, until they both felt so sleepy that they went back and made love in a hazy way and fell immediately, this time, into two dreamless sleeps.

'I can't remember what it was like really. I can remember you, and sitting here. It must be the same place – I remember the name,' said Clemmie the next day when they sat at the Closerie des Lilas and looked out at the crowds. The coffee they were drinking was a mixture of chicory and coffee beans.

'They had acorns in Savoy,' said Jack, and then, 'it's the same place; I expect German officers sat here.'

'The bread,' said Clemmie, after considering this. 'I rather like that yellowy, maizey stuff; do you suppose there is no real bread yet?'

'I have the impression the poor probably don't have much choice, but the black market is obviously operating for the rich.'

The people in the streets were shabby and there were many memorials to fallen members of the resistance from three years before, flowers kept alive in little vases and often added to by passers–by. The houses were the same as before, still tall and grey. The people were just as voluble, in spite of bread rationing and chicory and constant political upheaval.

'Glad you came?' he asked, taking her hand. He could not seem to stop touching her. 'I'm afraid you'll vanish,' he said.

They walked arm–in–arm, went to the theatre and listened to the same play that had been on in '38, strolled round the *bouquinistes* and the bird market and the flower market; approached and went into innumerable churches, pungent with incense and candle grease; walked in narrow, forgotten streets in Montparnasse; went to the top of the Eiffel Tower and were not displeased to descend; meandered round bookshops and picture galleries; were importuned by Arab carpet sellers; sat in the Luxembourg by the fountain and went to see Clemmie's fish, which had been replaced after the war; counted their money, carefully limited themselves, after the first two days, to one good dinner a day and a lot of maize bread and wine and cheese for lunch; wandered over the whole of the Left Bank, preferring it to the other, though there were few tourists there either except for some English schoolchildren; looked at the high, secret walls of schools shut up against the return, in autumn, of those Parisians' children lucky enough to spend their holidays on *colonies de vacances*; went to the Alliance

Française where newly–discovered film stars were glimpsed signing autographs; went to the best film of the last two years, *Les Enfants du Paradis*, and were entranced; smelled the same garlic and gauloises and perfume of pre–war days and listened to the clatter of the dustbins in the early mornings and the rush of water in the gutters. They went to a *bôite de nuit* on their last night, where they shuffled along together until Clemmie said it was only an excuse for kissing and they could do that better in their hotel; bought presents of perfume and cigarettes for their respective relations and friends and existed in a timeless, but vivid, paradise where it was hard to tell whether the pleasure came from each other's company or also from the place.

'The old clichés are true,' said Jack. 'Paris hasn't changed.'

'I could live here for a time,' said Clemmie. 'But I'd want to go to the country, I think, in the end. I'd love to see the rest of France if it's anything like this.'

'Another time,' he said, and she knew there would be another time.

Jack had also managed a few sketches, in charcoal, and meant to put them together into a book to remember the place and the time. They 'snapped' each other in their favourite places and altogether behaved as lovers always do in Paris. And, like holidays for all lovers who are also hard–working members of society, the holiday came to an end and they were back, too soon, on the Newhaven boat, clutching their passports and feeling they had been away from England for years.

Jack stayed over in London for one night, but Clemmie was going for an interview to a farm in Oxfordshire – another temporary post – so there was no point in his staying longer. They were both sure of each other and, although a parting seemed inconceivable, it must, for the moment, be endured. She saw him off at the sooty, steam–laden terminus.

'Whatever else, I shall come to London before Christmas. Try to arrange a bit of time off to see Phoebe,' he counselled, 'and if you can't manage, you are to come up north and stay with us before that.'

He admired her insistence on getting on with her work, would not have wanted a woman who had nothing else to do but sigh after him, however much he, too, would miss their being together.

429

'Anyway,' he went on, 'I shan't be teaching for ever; I have to decide by next spring whether to take the diploma or not. And we can see each other at Christmas.'

'I just wish I was settled and could stay in the same place, that's all,' replied Clemmie. 'I don't want to ask Father to buy me into anything – they're not too well off at present with all the expense of moving – in spite of your mother's providing the firm with a little gold mine.'

It all seemed banal, tedious, after the joys of Paris; but they both knew that life was like that and both were practical enough and steady enough to take what they could from the moment and believe firmly in the future.

But when the moment came for the train to go, Clemmie felt a lump in her throat. Jack squeezed her hand over the window of the train and said only, 'Wait for me, and expect a letter as soon as you arrive down in the country.'

'Or a sketch,' said Clemmie with a little smile, and the train moved away slowly.

Sophie said nothing as Clemmie packed to go down to Charlbury the morning of the next day. She thought her daughter looked extremely happy and that was good. Clemmie *was* happy, but wanted the progress of her love to be uninterrupted and found it rather an effort to get herself off again. It was worse at night, in bed. Before, she had not missed Jack physically; she had longed for him, which was not the same.

'Jack and Clemmie do seem to get on well,' offered Michael to Sophie that night in their own bed, as they lay reading.

'I suppose they've quite a lot in common; both rather self–sufficient,' replied Sophie. 'And both like work.'

'We must have a party for Edith at Christmas. Do you think Jack'll be able to persuade her to come down for one?' asked Michael, putting a marker firmly in his *Parson Woodforde*, which he was re-reading with great pleasure.

'I'm sure *Clemmie* could persuade her,' said Sophie.

It was over three months before Jack and Clemmie could once more be together again. The farmer in Charlbury was a new man and not used to the women he found on the farm when he returned from the army. Clemmie worked extremely hard and even offered to help him with his accounts, which she saw were in a muddle, but he obviously intended to replace her with a young man who was decanted on him for six months to learn the ropes. She stuck it out, for he was rude and a tyrant to his poor wife as well, but when he gave her her notice in November, she decided not to demur. Let him discover how useful a young man might be who had had no experience whatever of farming. The labourers were not happy there either, and several had applied for work in the car factory at Cowley. He would find out soon enough that you could no longer expect to treat people like dirt and have them stay, if there were better paid work elsewhere. Phoebe asked her to stay in college for a few days in Oxford.

Many letters had passed between Clemmie and Jack and, as Clemmie had surmised, many sketches. She wished Jack could get away to stay with her in Oxford, but that was impossible. He would come down to Hampstead before Christmas with his mother, who had agreed to the party in her honour.

Clemmie said to her sister, 'I never thought she would, but Jack said it was time she enjoyed a bit of company. I don't know how I managed to persuade her.'

'What's she really like?' asked Phoebe. 'I always thought it strange that she and mother were such close friends.'

'Oh she's unusual, you know, but very kind; and she's awfully fond of Mother, too, so that is all right!' Quite what was all right Phoebe could guess.

Clemmie had written to Edith begging her to attend the party, saying how much Sophie wanted it. Perhaps that had done the trick.

It was December and the unusual had happened – there was snow lightly powdering the ground. Nothing heavy yet, or disagreeable, but that might happen any time. Jack had been busy with his own school tests and his pupils were ready for a break after a long autumn term. He was finding the work easier as he grew more used to it, and no longer prepared too much nor expected too much. He had discovered some older pupils who had real talent, tried not to concentrate too much on them, for it was among the younger and more naïve children that he found the sort of magical work he looked for, still from

431

the province of childhood though, even here, the influence of the cinema and the war was strong.

'If I am to go down to Sophie's before Christmas for this party,' Edith had said, 'I hope you will have broken up and can be there too.'

'Of course; I shall be away the minute school breaks up, and the party's not till the twentieth. Most of the sixth formers are being postmen and the younger children never do any work after their exam, so they could have broken up earlier. I wish I could have gone to see Clemmie in Oxford; she's glad to get out of that place where she was working. I think she ought to take a rest. Couldn't she come here afterwards?'

'I expect she'll want to be home for Christmas, dear.'

'Yes, I suppose so.' When were they to be together again as they had been in Paris? One could not spend one's time having holidays. Or meeting in snatches. Perhaps there might be work for her at Hoyle's farm. He resolved to ask the farmer.

It was suddenly brought home to him why people got married. To be together always. They could live together of course, but what would be the point? They might as well be married. Of course, she was very young. And she wanted to work. She might not find the situation as much of a nuisance as he was beginning to do. He was surprised at himself. He had thought a month or two, or at most three, would go by quickly, but it was harder than he had expected. He missed her body, of course, but more than that he missed her companionship. Their budding love must not wither in the frosts of absence. It was not being tended and watered enough, he decided.

The snow had reached Oxford, too. Clemmie wandered around the place and even found herself studying the Faculty of Agriculture papers she found in a specimen book.

'Do many girls read agriculture?' she asked her sister.

'Not many. I expect *you* could have done instead of going into the land army – if there hadn't been a war.'

'But how can you learn a thing like farming unless you *do* it?' protested Clemmie.

'Oh, it's a pleasant way of spending the time between eighteen and twenty–one,' replied Phoebe, somewhat cross from reading so many stupid entrance papers in her own subject.

'I think I'd rather save up for a farm of my own,'

dreamed Clemmie, 'now I've got all the diplomas and things from the college.'

'And as much, or more experience as most people of your age,' added Phoebe. She was finding her young sister newly interesting.

So Clemmie wandered round colleges and bookshops and ate a lot of toast and drank many cups of tea and wondered what Jack was doing. What a difference three years made to young women. The college was quiet, apart from the shyly drifting figures of eighteen–year–olds hoping that this would not be their last visit, as well as the first, to the temple of Academe. A few nonchalant undergraduates who had stayed up to work, since the term was so short, could be glimpsed on bicycles, till more snow fell and they stayed in college rooms. Clemmie bought a bottle of perfume, as her Paris purchase was at home and there had been no occasion for perfume on the farm. She felt idle, glad to be shot of the bad–tempered, ex–major Greene, but a little uncertain what to do next.

A letter from Jack arrived, care of Phoebe, with a picture of a student postman staggering under a large bag. She supposed she could always be a postman, but it was too late to apply now for Christmas. Her 'career' was just not taking off. Jack and Edith would be arriving in Hampstead very soon and so she would go home for Edith's party. Phoebe was to come home for a few days, later. A mysterious 'friend' was abroad, but Clemmie gathered he would be returning in the New Year.

'I shall paint *you* this time,' Jack had written. 'That will be an occupation for us both. Do come and stay after Christmas up north. I still have hopes of finding you a job on Hoyle's farm.'

Soon Jack would be with her again! How had she ever let him go away without her? She would muck out Hoyle's byres for him or help with the early lambing, if only she and Jack could be near each other.

The party to launch Edith's book was to be a small one: Edith would not consent to anything too pretentious. The book had been held up because of the paper shortage. The bookshops were full of the Constantines which had been rushed off the presses during the last year, on rather inferior paper. Edith had seen she would soon be a household word and had determined no one should connect her with the author of the other book. It was to be in vain. Some enterprising journalist had twigged that at least one half of Bevis Constantine was still around and a few reviewers had asked questions of Theo Carmichael, still ensconced in the top room of the old house on Gower Place. She had seen it as a matter of pride that a woman could write a Constantine; she had not told them that the book scheduled for the New Year was a Constantine, though she hinted it was by the same author; a pseudonym, a book of reflections and memories, their new season's *bonne bouche*.

'Edith Bartholomew – who *is* she? Has she written before?' had been the question of the enterprising literary editor of *Views and Reviews*, and Theo had let slip that the writer had written before; some epic in the twenties. Michael had been cross when the same editor telephoned him for more information. He would have to come to some arrangement with Edith. She would have to declare herself one day, and it would certainly help her sales.

'It's been thirty–five years since she first began with Garnett,' said Sophie. ' She's kept the secret a long time.'

'It's bound to come out,' said Michael. 'What can I do about it? Why is she being difficult?'

'Edith doesn't see it as being difficult; she always said the stories were a joke. But I think she enjoyed writing them as time went by and was a bit astonished at herself.'

'There's no need for that. I shall have to explain to her that it's for the good of the firm; she won't mind doing something for *us* if we put it like that.'

So he staved off the questions and they arranged the party for the day after Edith and Jack's arrival.

Clemmie came home first, in a taxi from Paddington, in the afternoon.

'How nice you smell!' said Sophie. 'Is it something new?'

'Bond Street,' answered Clemmie.

Sophie noticed that Clemmie was looking quite smart in a new tweed suit and green blouse. 'I bought them at Ellistons, do you like them?' asked her daughter.

'Cousin Janet at Woldby would call them wizard,' replied Sophie.

434

'I bought a dress, too,' said Clemmie. 'White silk!'

'Edith and Jack will be here in time for supper; there's enough hot water for a bath. *I* found a dress for you too, that used to be mine years ago,' said her mother.

Phoebe would come along later in the week, but Sophie thought that it would be the first time for many, many years that she and Edith and Michael would be together with Jack and at least one daughter. The party on the morrow was to be held in their newly–painted drawing room and she had been busy putting up a Christmas tree.

Edith intended to return north before Christmas – wild horses would not keep her in London – but Clemmie was not sure whether Jack would return with his mother or stay in London. If only she and Jack could go away somewhere without the parents and their friends. But Christmas was Christmas and she supposed that Jack would return to Yorkshire so as not to leave Edith alone. If Farmer Hoyle were willing, she would go north in the New Year.

Snow had fallen again by the time the two northerners arrived and there was a white afternoon light before sunset that set Jack dreaming. He kissed Clemmie in private and said, 'My 'little white girl'. I wish Mother would stay here a bit and I could paint you; it would only take a few days. By the way, Hoyle agreed – you can be of use. So you *can* come and stay with us.'

They stood with their arms round each other in the small room next to the drawing room until they thought they had better join the others. Edith had been greeted by Sophie with great joy and been taken up to her room. Michael came into the small room.

'Have you asked her yet – about revealing her pseudonym?' asked Clemmie. 'They're all keen on telling the world tomorrow that Edith is Constantine,' she explained to Jack. 'Perhaps you can bring her round. But be tactful.'

Copies of the *Hermit of the Hey* were on the table in the hall. Edith, of course, already had her copies. Michael had had a special binding made for the last four Constantines and was to present it to her at supper.

Edith washed and dressed rather nervously. She knew,

without being told, what they were going to ask and had been thinking it over. Why had she always been insistent that her hack work should never be attributed to her? Was it just pride? If so, Jack had said she should be proud of that, too; it had helped them to get by, even during her marriage, for Adam had never earned very much. But she dreaded publicity of the 'Hermit–turns–out–to–be–Manufacturer–of–Monsters variety. She had agreed to this party idea of Sophie's because it was important to the firm. But she had made up her mind. She hoped nothing would be said at the party, but once she was back home they might not contradict reports of her own writing. Please, God, they would not find her 'Hermitage'.

Jack came down to supper to a room filled with firelight, rosy against the white landscape outside. Sophie was already in the room, putting a few final touches to her table decorations: holly and ivy from her new little garden. She leaned against the door surveying her room and suddenly thought, I must have chosen Hampstead because all those years ago, when I went to the suffragist meetings, it was to rooms like this one: white paint and bronze chrysanthemums and firelight and elegant chairs. She had managed to find six chairs in an old junk shop in Camden Town and to strip them down and polish them and, although they needed new seats, for the original tapestry was worn, they would do. I've come to this! she thought; it looks fairly prosperous and it's certainly more homely and comfortable than Chimneys ever was, whatever efforts I made to make it so. I'm a hostess, giving a party tomorrow to a 'literary celebrity' as they have begun to call them. Dear Edith! After supper they would look again at Jack's picture of Paris and her children. Automatically, the thought of Rosamund was there behind every other thought. She knew, now, that you never got over the death of a child. She might not cry so much as time went on, but the remembrance would shape every other thought she had. How empty and pointless it sometimes seemed to be furnishing a house and making a good meal and thinking about clothes and polishing old silver and buying books, when the bottom had fallen out of your life. But life had to go on, was what they always said, though Sophie often wondered why. It was true that any occupation was better than none and she had tried, by throwing herself into domestic tasks and by concentrating on the matter in hand, to forget, for a moment at a time, that still empty space in her heart.

The room looked pleasant: there were vases of mimosa bought at great expense from the florists, imported from the South of France, and there were the old candlesticks which had been a wedding present from Michael's parents, polished and shining. Michael's vast collection of Penguin first editions was in a special bookcase and the firm's own books in another, and Sophie's own books scattered everywhere. However much she tried to be tidy there were always more possessions all over the place than in anyone else's house.

Sophie still suffered from a guilty feeling that only by tackling more than one thing at once would things ever be done, and the same applied to her reading and her domestic work. Still, Edith would not notice. She suspected that the room, however pleasant, was a bit of a jumble of styles and certainly not fashionable, nor really elegant. But it was like nowhere else and that had to be a consolation. Michael was obsessively tidy with his own things and did not seem to mind what the other rooms were like, so long as he could keep his 'office' the way he wanted it. Sophie had her own style, he knew, just as she had her own way of dressing; never up–to–the–minute, but always a collection of clothes that she liked and would wear out rather than discard. Today she was wearing a red pre–war paisley dress and blue shawl, long silver earrings and a pair of fairly in fashion 'ballet shoes' that were comfortable. She wore waistcoats and ties of silk, and wool berets and cossack boots when she went out, all items which she had kept for years. The room smelt good; a mixture of wood smoke and mimosa and the scent which Sophie always wore and which Clemmie had brought her back from Paris at great expense, since it was pre-war stock.

After a quick look round the room and a stroke of the current cat, who refused to budge from the fire, Sophie decided she had done all she could and went into the kitchen where the trolley of soup plates and glasses was waiting to be wheeled in. Clemmie came downstairs, she had apparently been chatting to Edith, and helped her mother in the kitchen. Michael had been sent a plucked goose and a small turkey from the country, where one of the firm's printers lived. The turkey had been cooking all afternoon.

'Don't worry, Mother, your meals are always fine,' said Clemmie. For Sophie, always feeling herself hopelessly impractical, made such efforts to plan her domestic tasks that there was more likelihood of food being over rather than under–cooked. 'Father's brought up some of the pre–war claret,' said Clemmie, helpfully sorting out plates to warm without being asked.

'Yes, he kept a lot in the cellar at Chimneys; there was some new sherry, too, and we shall keep most of that for tomorrow, but you might just check that he's giving Jack and Edith a drink – and bring me one, too.'

Michael was doing all that his wife had hoped he was, and was entertaining Jack and Edith with a description of the special exchange he had had with a French publisher. 'He resorted to bribery in the end,' he was saying. 'Twelve dozen bottles of claret and burgundy in advance of the money on translation rights of the first three 'Moon' mysteries. So you see, Edith, you have earned your drink,' he concluded.

Jack thought, they have made a great effort. He was unused to seeing food and wine in such abundance in post–war England.

'I shall send you back with a few bottles of sherry for yourself, if you can carry them,' Michael said to Edith as she drank her sherry.

The dinner was delicious. The turkey was neatly carved by Michael, who left nothing to be desired in the direction of culinary accomplishments except that he always refused to wash up. Sophie had got hold of some chestnuts for the stuffing and there were plenty of baked potatoes and sprouts, and bread sauce with onion and continental tasty sausages from the new grocer's in the village.

'I haven't had a really good meal for ages,' sighed Clementine. 'The farm was dreadful – worse than those curd tarts. Mrs Greene had never cooked before the war, and in Oxford they are still at the plain but wholesome stage. I bet the men's colleges eat better.'

As the first claret was poured from the decanter, Sophie said boldly, 'To Bevis Constantine and to Edith.' Edith lifted her glass as they toasted her. Jack thought his mother and Sophie both looked like young girls in their excitement. They were enjoying a good pre-war sort of meal.

Edith cleared her throat. 'As to that, Sophie – and congratulations on your excellent cook – keep it a secret till we get back home, but I've decided I mustn't stand in the firm's light any longer.'

'You mean you'll let it be known?' asked Sophie, holding her breath.

'Amen,' said Jack and felt a good mouthful of claret irradiate his stomach and send happy messages along his veins. He looked at Clemmie who had had a chat with his mother.

'Yes, you may say so if anyone asks; but I do hope they won't.'

'Toasts ought to be at the end, not during,' said Michael. 'But as Sophie has begun: here's to today's cook and to *Hermit of the Hey*.'

'And to peace,' said Edith dreamily.

'And good will to all men – and women,' said Jack. He felt he and Clemmie were the adults here; the three members of the older generation seemed unaccustomedly young, and for a moment he wondered what his mother and Sophie had really been like in their youth. The food was delicious and Sophie was flushed and pleased. The main course was followed by a Christmas pudding which Edith had made and actually posted in order for it to arrive in time. It was duly set alight, and brandy butter, this time from America, was also passed around.

After nuts and brandy and coffee, Michael said, 'Here is a little present for you, Edith.'

Edith blinked rather nervously. The wine was good – she had forgotten how good it could be. But presents always made her shy. The parcel was brought from the old oak dresser which Sophie had put in the dining room rather than the kitchen, and was wrapped in heavy-duty brown paper. The others watched her anxiously. But she laughed when she saw the bound volume. 'Did I write all that nonsense? How kind of you!'

'It's a rarity,' said her host. 'Look at the last few pages.'

Edith looked. Her short-sightedness was now proving a boon; her eyes had caught up with her age and surpassed it, and without her spectacles her eyes gave a completely different aspect to her face. Large and almost green, they made her face look younger. Bound with the three first Constantines was Edith's article on Norsemen from 1909. 'Where on earth did you find it?' she asked in surprise. 'I lost it long ago.'

'Frank Moray sent it back to the firm, after Kitty's death. He was going through all their old stuff in a fit of efficiency and somehow it had got lost again. The invaluable Theo rediscovered it a few months ago and brought it to me.'

'Well, well,' said Edith, 'though of course, I've changed my view–point a little since the later work I did; still, I never thought I'd see it again. Thank you, Michael; you are all being too kind.'

The conversation became more relaxed and even Edith became voluble. Much gossip about old friends, news of Fabian Trevelyan's new wife, a dissection of Theo Carmichael's character, Michael's new list; and then about the portrait of Sophie, which they had moved, and which now hung opposite Jack's picture in the drawing room. They went to look at both pictures. 'One day I hope the house will be worthy of its pictures,' said Sophie.

Edith put her glasses back on to look at the picture from afar. Jack's painting was, of course, known to her, as she had seen him working on it, but the one of Sophie made her catch her breath.

'I wish someone had done one of you, too; they were happy times, weren't they, on the whole?' said Sophie.

'Yes. I remember you just like that. It's remarkable how much of you is there in it. And that velvet jacket! I remember that too! Will Sebastian be coming tomorrow?'

'Yes, he's looking forward to seeing you.'

Jack was also examining the portrait, in his case the painterly qualities rather than the personal ones.

He and Clemmie sat on the window–seat together, with their coffee, only half listening to their parents' conversation. Clemmie had changed again before dinner. 'I like what you've got on,' he whispered. 'Surely you didn't buy *that* in Oxford?'

Clemmie laughed. 'No, it was mother's years ago. She had to let it out as I'm rather bigger.'

It was a low–waisted dress of flame–coloured taffeta and Clemmie had put on an equally old brown velvet jacket over the strappy shoulders. Jack could not take his eyes off her.

'Let's offer to wash up,' she murmured. 'All this talk of their old friends makes me nervous, and I'm sure they'd rather do it without us.'

In the kitchen, free at last, they embraced slowly and he took her hand and held it to his cheek. 'Don't go away again. There's a room for you at home, for propriety's sake. And I'm sure Hoyle can find plenty for you to do at the moment.'

'Yes, I'm coming. But I shall stay here till Christmas is over.'

'We might get away now and then at weekends,' he went on.

'Have you decided about the school, then. Will you go on?'

'I just don't know; it's a regular income, but if I'm going on with it, I must take the diploma in September and then I can't get on with my own painting. Clemmie, if we got married we could manage, I'm sure –'

'What?'

'I said, if we got married. Don't look so surprised; you didn't think I was going to lose you, did you? I wanted to wait before saying it, but I could decide better, I think, if we married; perhaps in the summer, when you've done a bit more work on the farm and I've saved a bit more.'

'But where could we live, darling Jack?'

'We could afford one of those old weaver's cottages: the rents are low – people do manage. You haven't said yet if you *will* marry me.'

'I shan't marry anyone else,' said Clemmie. 'But I must find a farm. I really do want to go on working, Jack, but could I work and be married? All the girls I know are just giving up on their own work when they get married. Let's not say anything yet, but see how it goes up in Yorkshire.'

She kissed him. 'I do love you, Jack, but I'm not sure about marriage. Let's keep it a secret for the moment.'

She leaned against him feeling the rough tweed of his jacket with the patches at the elbows. 'I like your new corduroy trousers; you look very handsome,' she said.

Marriage! It was rather a sudden shock. But what else had she thought might happen with a man like Jack? He was ready to settle down after the war. Was she? So long as she could do her work, it would be all right. If only Jack could paint for his livelihood. She felt guilty that her mother would not want her to marry so young.

They washed up together so that when Michael came in to offer them another brandy and to listen to the carol singers who were at the front door, they were discussing the possibility of his getting commissions to paint portraits.

'You two look solemn,' said Clemmie's father, quite aware of the undercurrents of intimacy which formed the bond between his youngest daughter and Edith's son.

'Yes. Jack wants to stop teaching and paint, but he says he's too old to take up another grant.'

'I want to paint Clemmie,' Jack said. 'I think if I could get together a few paintings, the one in the drawing room and some others I have at home – Clemmie thought that Seb might help – I might manage an exhibition.'

'Well, he'll be here tomorrow, so why not ask him? I wish you *would* paint Clementine; I'd commission it myself if I could afford it,' said her father.

'Oh, I wouldn't want to be paid for that,' said Jack as they moved into the hall. 'That would be a labour of love.'

'Yes, indeed,' replied Michael, surprised.

If we got married, it would please Edith, I know, thought Clemmie. But Mother might be furious! She's always gone on about not wasting yourself and getting involved too early in having children and so on; *she* didn't get wed all that young, though, did she? I wonder why? And *I* want to have a job. I want to work a farm. I've always wanted to; Jack wants me to as well, doesn't he? He doesn't want to lose me, I know. Oh, I wish I could just say yes and forget all my ambitions, but I can't . . .

Clemmie would have been quite happy to creep into Jack's room, or he into hers, that night, but Jack felt it would be rather 'off'; not that his mother would be shocked, but he had a curiously old–fashioned idea of propriety and you did not sleep with another man's unmarried daughter in his house, even a man who belonged to so-called 'progressive' society. So they bade each other goodnight and exchanged a chaste kiss. Clemmie's mind was still in a whirl, but the brandy and the excitement and having to get up early on the morrow to help with Edith's sherry party, got her to sleep at last.

Jack lay at the top of the house, turning over all possibilities of employment and mentally going through his pictures for an exhibition. It would have to be local, he supposed. Perhaps Seb knew people at the Arts Council who might help. Or perhaps his painting was no good and he needed years more apprenticeship before he could be accorded a one–man exhibition. He was only an unknown, if no longer young, serviceman. But he would cast aside any pride or false modesty and approach Sebastian Harman the next day.

Edith went to sleep quickly, as she usually did. They had all been so kind. And Sophie looked a little less ghost–like. Michael Carr had been kind, too; she was lucky in her publisher. But she must get back, soon after the party. Work called and London would be giving her a headache if she stayed too long.

'Jack seems serious about Clementine,' said Michael to Sophie when their light was put out.

'She's only twenty–one, darling – all her life ahead of her.'

'He's a good man, though. I wish we could settle her with a little capital so she could start something up of her own.'

'Perhaps next year; you're doing quite well.'

'No one's making a fortune in publishing at present,' answered her husband. He, too, wanted his youngest daughter to be happy, and the look Jack had given her in the kitchen had made him feel old.

Sophie lay awake a long time. She knew that Edith's son was not one of the jokers who don't fit into the Happy Families pack of cards.

Edith went to few parties and had never had one given in her honour. But she found, half way through the crowded six o'clock gathering in Sophie's double room (the dividing doors had been opened making the room's proportions quite grand), that she was rather enjoying herself. Of course, nothing had been said about Bevis Constantine, although Edith fancied Theo Carmichael had looked at her in a rather peculiar way; but that might have been because she had put her glasses on again for self–protection, in spite of Sophie's protests, and faces had become a little vague again. They were all so friendly, she thought. They were all successful people, enjoying expanding their egos in an atmosphere of achievement and flowing drink.

There was old Seb, and Sophie's friend, Bea Osborne, whom Edith had never met in all these years; and there was Gideon Carr, Clemmie's grandfather, sublimely unaware of the reception he was getting to his bluff talk about business. And there were many other publishers and writers of literary gossip, and one or two artists, and even some neighbours. There were a few young people, too, as well as Clemmie, and Phoebe, who had come home specially for the party and who seemed a most intelligent girl. And there was a woman poet and one or two other writers on the firm's list.

Edith was passed from mouth to mouth and did not really have to say anything except: 'How kind' and 'Yes I prefer the country'. By mistake, she said to one of the authors, 'Yes, I prefer obscurity,' and he repeated this to everyone. Several rather frighteningly intelligent young men spoke to her. They had read the book, had received early copies and were enthusiastic.

One of them said, 'I can't understand how this can be your *first* book.'

Edith recollected herself and replied, 'I wrote a long novel, many years ago, about war and peace, and I've studied Anglo Saxon history, you know.'

He looked a little mystified, but another young man overheard her remark.

'Hugo is very ignorant, Mrs Bartholomew. The conflict between aggression and appeasement runs through all your work, I feel.'

The first young man looked furious. Edith felt things had not changed much over the years and tried to believe this party was because of her, that she was no longer the publisher's assistant, but The Writer. She got into conversation with the woman poet, and enjoyed that.

Michael made an announcement half way through. That was a surprise. Another! They seemed never–ending. This time, no one else but Theo and Sophie had known about it. He held up a book and the voices were, for a moment, stilled.

'I'd like to present a little book to Edith's son, Jack. Some of you will have read the poems of Clement Bartholomew. After tonight, all of you will. We have just reprinted a small book which came out before the first war. My wife drew my attention to it, but wanted it to be a surprise for Edith and her son. I hope you will accept this little book with pleasure, Jack, and I hope it will go into many, many reprints.' He came up to Jack, shook him by the hand and handed over a small, dark blue volume. It was Clem's second book, that had been mostly forgotten about, swallowed up in the great morass of war and sunk without trace.

Jack took it, with a glance at his mother, and murmured his thanks.

Edith and Clemmie came up to him and Sophie, too. 'I wanted it to be a real surprise. We only found one copy left, but Michael insisted it was a real discovery.'

Edith took the book and opened it at a poem she well remembered, and so did Sophie.

'The first famous Bartholomew,' said Clemmie. 'And your mother, the second. And you'll be the third, Jack. Seb wants to talk to you.'

Other people came up, then, to look at the book of poems. Seb came up to Jack. He looked, at first sight, raffish and Bohemian, but his paunch was now pronounced, under a well-cut brown corduroy suit that a Bohemian could certainly not afford.

'Jack, why didn't you get in touch earlier? Burying yourself in Yorkshire!' He touched his nose with the tip of his little finger and fixed Jack with his sharp, worldly eyes.

Jack had no time to reply, for then another man came up, resplendent in a plum-coloured velvet waistcoat, and pumped his hand. 'The picture, my dear! It's wonderful, isn't it?' The newcomer, who might be a gallery owner, turned to Seb, whom he seemed to know. Jack thought at first, he must mean the picture of Sophie, by Seb. But no, he meant the mother and daughters in Paris.

'And Clemmie tells me you are still painting better and better and you are going to paint *her*,' said Seb. 'What bone structure she has! We must talk – have another drink – I've got a bit of a pull, you know, now; Arts Council, in the provinces *and* my little gallery we're starting up again. Why, Edith!' The other man melted away and Seb enfolded Edith in his velvet embrace. She started back rather nervously, but then smiled. 'My dear, I can't believe it. *Your* book – Michael tells me it's wonderful – and Clem's, too, and your son! Well, well . . .'

Seb, she saw, was plumper and certainly 'successful', but she remembered his eyes, which were still as twinkling and piercing as they had always been. Clemmie came up and winked at Jack and he felt pleased as punch.

'You must meet me in Leeds next week. I'm arranging an exhibition of post–war northern painters,' said Seb.

'I haven't started the one of Clemmie, though I've been meaning to for months; I'm teaching, you see,' he explained.

'My dear chap; what about a little exhibition of "Carrs", with my old portrait of Sophie, too? I'd almost forgotten about that, you know. Imagine! I haven't painted for years – too busy – but it would be a link. What do you think, eh?'

Good heavens! Seb must think he was some good if he thought his own painting would get a lift from Jack's. This made Jack feel gratified, but thoughtful. Edith overheard and remembered the plans for her first husband's first book; hadn't Frank Laurence been going to join him in it? But Seb really did seem pleased to see her, Edith thought, and if it would help Jack . . .

She was glad she had consented to this socializing after all; *she* had never thought of reprinting Clem's poems nor of pushing Jack a little to get his work exhibited. She was lazy, she decided. Her life had been sunk in her work, and then in Adam, and then in her work again. How trying it was talking to people, though quite pleasant. Someone had even asked her her opinion of the Labour government. She saw Sophie looking at her and smiling.

'I expect it makes you glad to be out of it most of the time,' she whispered. 'Some of them are Old Pretenders, but some are nice. Are you pleased about Clem's book? Is Jack?'

'I'm *so* pleased, and so is Jack. It's all rather overwhelming! And Seb is talking to Jack about an exhibition . . .'

'He'll launch him, you know; and as Jack is good it will be a success . . . I wanted to talk to you about Jack,' said Sophie. 'You know Clemmie is very fond of him. I get the impression

446

he's rather smitten with her; has he said anything?'

'He doesn't need to. He couldn't like her more than I do,' said Edith. 'Don't worry; she can have a go at Hoyle's and stay with us and see how it goes.'

'You will look after her? She's so young; I mean, I know they had to grow up quickly in the war, but – '

'I know. Don't worry, Sophie: his intentions are honourable.'

'I didn't mean that! I know they are. Here am I, talking like my own mother; it must be the drink! It's just that she is really keen on her work and if she settled down too soon she might regret it.'

Edith was thinking of how she had been 'settled down' by the birth of Jack. She was holding the book with the very poem Jack's father had quoted when he came to see her that night in 1913. Life went on, but was not so very different really. Clemmie was more self-assured than she had been, or even than her own mother.

'I expect they'll get up to mischief, but I have my own ideas about their future,' she said mysteriously. Sophie gave a puzzled smile and drifted off to join her other guests.

Later, when everyone had gone, she crept quietly into the drawing room again, with it's smell of cigars, and remained there looking at the picture of her daughters, wondering how a world could contain both parties and wars. Michael found her there, and took her hand. He liked her better now than she had been when Seb painted her. That was another Sophie; the one Miller had known.

Later, he had the satisfaction of seeing his best author, his two daughters, his wife and the young man whom he felt sure Clemmie loved, together round the fire with mince pies and coffee. There was a lot to be said for family life, he thought, thinking of Seb and his successful but rather lonely career.

Edith left the next day and Jack accompanied her, whilst the two girls loyally stayed to make a family Christmas.

Clemmie arrived north on New Year's Day. Edith was out and the two lovers could not help being glad that for one afternoon they would be undisturbed.

'I've started to plan for my painting of you,' Jack said. 'I'd like to do a nude. Perhaps I will one day, but for the present

447

I shall remain conventionally ignorant of your charms.'

He took her into the old barn, which had, for so long, been his 'studio'. There was a stove there, fed by wood, and a large skylight, closed now, various shelves and an easel.

'Surely the light is not good enough?' she asked.

'I used the place mainly to get away by myself when I was a boy and, of course, when I was in Leeds I didn't really need a place to paint here. So now I sit and think and, in summer, I paint outside. I don't need a special light for the sort of painting I want to do of you. Except the light from snow and there will be that soon, I'm sure.'

The painting was to be called 'The White Girl, 1948', and his intention was to experiment with all shades of white, making the dress a white with faintest pink, a window looking out on to the bluish white of snow and other objects, partaking of a parchment white with slight yellow colouring. Only Clemmie's face and hair would not be white, and there would be, somewhere, a touch of green betokening spring.

'A ribbon in your hair, perhaps?'

'I want you, Jack,' Clemmie said softly. 'Let's make love and then you will paint even better.'

For answer he buried his face in her hair. He could not say anything light–hearted, as he would have wished, for he felt the strong urging of his body; not because he must have a woman, but because he wanted this one. He closed the barn door and they made love on the old rug that Jack had brought in from the house. The rough floor underneath dug into their hip bones, but they only noticed that afterwards.

Clemmie rubbed her spine ruefully. She looked round the barn again in a daze. There was a smell of paint and even, she thought, of grain from long–ago autumns. It was entirely appropriate that their passion should have the farm and the easel for accompaniment.

'Do you realize, it's the first time in England?' she said. 'How ever did I do without you?'

'I know, my darling. But Mother wouldn't mind if we slept together; she's not a conventional person.'

'Somehow, I don't want to make Aunt Edith feel responsible for me – it might worry her. I know she wouldn't object or be embarrassed. It was obvious last week, wasn't it? I'm sure Father knew.'

'Why shouldn't they know? I want to marry you, Clemmie – '

'What, marry a cow girl?' she said. 'I've come here to work, too. I do wish everything could be settled, though. It's stupid.'

She saw that, sooner or later, she would have to decide – but when? Was Jack preparing to go on teaching? She did not want to be 'kept'; wanted both Jack and work.

'Would your mother want a big wedding?' he asked.

'Oh, Jack! You make it sound so settled. Mother's not all that keen on weddings.'

'But it *is*, isn't it?' he asked, ignoring the last remark.

'I don't know,' she answered, kissing him. 'I could go on working here if Hoyle likes me and I'm of use, but you don't really want to teach for ever, do you?'

'We could live on a grant if I did that teaching course.'

'Jack, darling, I don't want you to sacrifice anything for me. We must both work, you know.'

The light from the enormous skylight in the roof, which had been put in for Jack when the barn fell into disuse, was now fading, so they went back, rather reluctantly, into the house.

Clemmie was to go the next morning, a Saturday, to discuss with Hoyle how she might be of use to him.

Edith returned about seven o'clock and was obviously very pleased to see her. Clemmie was given the small room which had once been an attic. Jack had offered to give her his own room, but Edith had looked rather quizzically at him, as though to say that Clemmie would be spending some time with her son, but might like to have a small space by herself, where she could sleep whenever she was tired, out of the way of the others. She would be getting up early and going to bed early. Fortunately, the farm was only five hundred yards away and Clemmie was given a key to Far Ox Heys.

'I must do some cooking and cleaning for you,' she insisted. 'I just want to be one of the family, not a special guest.' Then she blushed.

Things were sorted out in the end and, after a talk to Hoyle, who needed help with his cows and cabbages as well as with his accounts for the Milk Marketing Board. She felt she would do quite well. Jack would be busy at the school, but they could spend the evenings after supper together, when she had done the milking.

She began a new way of living and found there was more to time spent with Jack than sensual bliss. On the evenings when she was free, she sat by the fire, physically tired, but glowing with the satisfaction of work done; and sometimes, though Jack was supposed to be preparing work for school or making comments on his pupils' efforts, he would be drawing her, filling page after page with ideas for his picture. The actual painting could only be done at weekends and he longed to begin it. He had set so much store by the picture he could already see in his mind, that he was also half–fearful of actually beginning to paint.

As he had said he it would, it began to snow again in mid–January, and he took his easel into the back parlour where the light from the snowy windows was just right for his purposes. The parlour was seldom used in winter, Edith preferring to type in the kitchen at her old table, as she had always done from the earliest time that he could remember. One Sunday he started to paint and, as he painted, he felt that the tension in him from wanting Clemmie and yet needing to school himself to wait for her, was enabling him to produce a magical quality of expectancy in this picture of a girl who was Clemmie and not Clemmie, the picture of a physical presence, but also an inner picture of his idea of her.

He experimented, at first, with blocks of white, with a view of snow through a round window. He seemed to be working both from a mental image and also from his direct experience of her, trying to express what he saw in her. As he painted, intellectual concepts, such as the knowledge that what he saw depended upon his own experience, too, and on his own personality, refused entirely to go away. Yet what he loved in her was also what he 'saw'; painting, being in this way, like love. He loved Clemmie, he supposed, because of what he was himself; something in him responded to something in her. He could not have painted this picture without loving the sitter, though other pictures might be different. At the same time, of course, he could not put the whole of Clementine into the picture, only those aspects which were significant to him and served to emphasize, and even create, the vision of his inner

450

eye. Yet his inner eye had already selected for him, so the argument was circular.

When he was not painting he would sometimes try to explain this to her and also to explain what conclusions he had come to about his work with the children. Clemmie listened with unfeigned interest; not having any preconceived notions, she was open to all his suggestions and he made life seem richer and more mysterious for her. It was as important to Jack that he should paint, as it was for him to love her; that was why he understood that she, too, wanted to work.

'I'm not there at school to make the younger ones draw, but to try to teach them how to "see",' he said.

'Or, perhaps, how to look?' she offered, having begun to learn from him in this direction.

'One day you ought to draw me at work,' she said, thinking that a picture of herself in a white dress, though possibly also a 'technical' exercise, was also the picture of an idealized Clemmie, the real one spending most of her days in a duffel coat and boots.

Indoors, she wore some red stockings that had been Rosamund's sent from America probably.

'Now you look like an art student,' he said.

She knitted him a pair of yellow socks which he wore with touching pride. Edith was amused, thinking of her friend Sophie and her attempts at knitting and sewing. Clemmie was much more practical.

As Jack painted away, slowly and carefully, a balance seemed to appear on the canvas, a balance of colour and line and solidity. And yet, there was something ethereal about it. What Clemmie called 'idealizing' her, he supposed. What he chose to paint was akin to the unconscious selection of a lover, who sees certain facets of the beloved which no one else has ever seen before.

When the picture was finished to his satisfaction, he thought, he would make love to her again. She had a vague idea that that was his intention, as though he were like a monk, putting away all thoughts of satisfaction of the flesh in order the better to worship. At other times, when they were in the room together before the fire, as she sat reading or knitting, listening to the wireless or talking to Edith, it seemed to her that they had been 'married' for years.

Edith neither avoided their company nor sought it. Her own domestic routine kept her busy and also her idea for her new book. She had always been able to think best when occupied with some manual task and did not need company – at times, positively spurned it. She would listen to Jack sometimes and think about what he said and think that her son was not all that different from herself, though how she would teach others to write was something she could not imagine.

Jack said he was no psychologist, just wanted his pupils to enjoy making things and painting things, whether they got their ideas from the world they lived in or from their own heads. Edith said that colours and shapes were in one way like words: even writers were possessed of a 'vision'!

'I have to teach them to give themselves a chance to feel, to enjoy life, so as to want to make something for themselves. Technique comes later,' Jack said magisterially.

'So we are all embryo artists?' asked Edith sceptically. 'What about the children who have a talent for drawing? Isn't it because they "see" differently?'

Jack considered this, as he considered all his mother's ideas. 'Anyone of normal intelligence can learn some technique,' he replied. 'It *is* important, but it's no good having it if you have no imagination.'

'Perhaps the ones with the artistic gift also have that,' she replied.

'And you enjoy what you're good at,' offered Clemmie. '*I* started by wanting to farm, being interested in it for its own sake, then I had to learn *how* to farm – like milking cows. It's no good just liking cows!'

'But if you don't like cows you'll never be a good milker,' said Edith.

'The problem is, how to get people to like cows, I suppose.'

These conversations usually ended in laughter, but also made Clemmie thoughtful. How different people were! Her sister Phoebe had never shown the slightest interest in farming; her gift lay with languages and she gobbled them up for pleasure. But Edith seemed to have many interests.

Jack taught Clemmie how to make patterns. He said she

was a good student guinea pig, and she did some appliqué work with coloured shapes and rather enjoyed herself. Lino cutting was also now on Jack's school syllabus and so she tried that, too.

'Easier than potatoes,' said Jack. 'Where our interests meet – potatoes – you grow them and I cut them up to make patterns from them!'

'It's more like playing than working,' said Clemmie.

'Ah, well, many people would say that that is what art is: ineffable play.'

'Without the gardener or the farmer, you'd have no potato prints,' she objected, and stuck to her guns. She delighted him by her matter–of–fact attitudes, yet she had quite a good imagination herself and was subtle, too, in her judgment of people.

Edith found her company more and more agreeable. It was so pleasant to have another woman in the house. At her 'real' work, Clemmie was now cutting cabbages from frosty ground. They had had several snowfalls and the last one stayed on the ground for days. The cabbages were frozen stiff and Clemmie's hands were like lumps of ice themselves. Some women from the village came in to help, for there was only old man Hoyle and his son-in-law and no remaining German prisoner-of-war. Clemmie became friendly with the three women. It was like old land girl days. Thank goodness this winter was not as harsh as the previous one had been.

Edith resolved to be Clemmie's ally, as unobtrusively as possible. It was not just that she hoped the girl would marry her son: parents were often blind to their own children's needs, not imagining, in the bottom of their hearts, that they could be different from themselves. Perhaps it was easier, too, for a woman to have a son, so that she was never tempted to project her own past feelings upon him, as though he were a surrogate for the continuation of feelings. She had seen Cicely Emery again that week, who was intrigued that Sophie's daughter had come to stay with her. Cicely looked more elongated, more intimidating, with her mop of curly hair now white. She still lived with her friend, Gladys, and had retired from the library service with half–pension. Politically, she was still optimistic and worked now for the Labour Party. She knew Jim, the friend of Jack who had gone to Spain and been wounded later in the

Second World War.

Cicely being so unchanging in all her changes, Edith began to wonder if she had changed much herself. This sort of introspection was foreign to her and she tried to shake it off. She was too old, anyway, to be bothered.

She decided, on a day that was windless, to go up to Haworth again, her sure remedy against feeling out of touch with herself. The snows had melted away and underneath the wet, recently white, ground she thought she could smell the spring, although it would be some time before it actually arrived. As she had not enough petrol, she took the little long–distance bus.

She stood on the path that wound over the field from the parsonage and looked over the moors which, in autumn, would have been covered in ling. The wind here was never far away, although the weather today was superficially sunny and calm, if chilly. The nearer expanse was broken by outcrops of boulders of millstone grit and the land itself was uneven, tussocky, a broken down dry–stone wall petering out on the right by the path that led over to the next moor. There was a wooded valley deep in a cleft on the right, going up to the bleak farmland and crowned by the ruined farm, Top Withens. On one side there leaned a cluster of thorn trees. On the distant horizon beyond the 'V' of the valley, there stretched further hills, greyish brown, in the distance, and shadowed by the immense clouds that swept over the edge of the county. She gulped in several deep breaths of the sharp air. There was not a sound here except the occasional wuther of the wind; no sheep, no curlew, no farmer's growl or dog barking. Over to the right, near the old farm, a mile or two away above the valley trees, further dry–stone walls snaked down from the top like black ribbons. The land must have looked very much the same, over a thousand years ago; hardly cultivatable, save on the lower slopes, once the 'intake' of the farm but now abandoned.

She walked across to a broken–down wall and leaned against it and thought of Adam, who had once so often accompanied her on walks like this one. Walking 'where her own nature led' was, to Edith, profoundly satisfying, but she did not agree that death was preferable to life, as the same poet had seemed to say with her 'nothing lovely here'. This harsh earth was beautiful – it was all they had, and Adam would never share it again. But, for the moment, he seemed to be back with her as she looked up again at the sky and the hills. Time slipped briefly and she felt disembodied, as though she, too, were dead.

Then the sound of the wind came back again, the prehistoric wind that could be heard only by sentient creatures; the invisible but powerful wind, and Edith came back to herself, releasing thoughts of Adam to it. He was gone, but she would remain for a little time before she, too, was gathered to that wind as thousands upon thousands of invisible dead had been gathered in, in Elmet: Briton, Angle, Norseman, bounded by their own times, released, at last, to that natural eternity. Even so, she wished that, alive, she could stay there on the moor with dead Adam; but the present time must claim her. Ordinary life went on away from the 'Heights', Edith was thinking as she walked back to the nearest village, from where a two–hourly bus service would take her home. Sophie knew that, too, but must still always be hoping for the sound of Rosamund's voice in the hall or her footsteps on the gravel, coming home. Both of them would often be called back to the past, but they could not stay there.

While Edith was at Haworth and Jack was finishing his picture, Clemmie had an extra Saturday afternoon's work. She had fed the calves and the poultry, which Hoyle had belatedly decided to keep now that eggs were at a premium, and even spared a moment to talk to the tame rabbits, who, alas, would be on someone's table before long, and she had written one or two orders for fertilizer. The farm was 'mixed', but mainly they grew oats, cabbages and rhubarb, with a small dairy herd and a few sheep grazing in the fields on higher ground, on a piece of land that had once been moorland. It had been used again for sheep in the war, when every available piece of land had come into use. All the land above a certain height at Ox Heys was really moorland, but the valleys occasionally spread out a little, before the valley proper was reached where now were the towns. There were, here, miles of country with older centres of population; villages that had been taken over by far younger towns. Clemmie liked this countryside, though it was true, no farmer would make a fortune from it.

She had been up quite early and seen that Jack had a letter waiting for him from London. 'Seb Harman', she guessed. He might be coming to Leeds and had promised to look at Jack's work. She was hopeful of an exhibition, here in the north where Jack belonged, rather than in Cork Street. Even the small towns were still aware of the 'culture' that had been encouraged in the war, and they had not slipped back into philistinism as yet. And there had always been businessmen like Edith's father who had interested themselves in things other than making 'brass'. Oh, she liked this North Country.

She came back to the cottage at about three o'clock. Jack was nowhere to be found: he was probably putting the finishing touches to the picture, which she was to see as soon as he pronounced it done. She went to the kitchen to wash her hands and heard a whistling noise. He must have put the kettle on and forgotten, so she made a pot of tea for them both. She stretched out near the fire and waited for him come in. She had almost dozed off, tired from her early rising, when she heard the latch click at the door and there was Jack. 'Have you been for a walk? You were nowhere to be seen; I didn't look in the parlour,' she said.

'No – good girl. It's finished. I went for a walk.'

He looked excited, but strained.

'And Seb Harman wrote; he's coming up next week and I'm to bring him round to have a look at all I have here. It'll be half–term, so I'll have to sort things out a bit.'

He sat sipping his mug of tea and she saw his hands had not yet been cleaned and the smell of paint thinner wafted over from them.

'When can I look at it, then?'

'When it's dark. I want to see the effect in candlelight. I *think* it's all right. I hardly dare look again at it myself.'

At dusk he went into the parlour and lit some candles and then called her in. She stood at the door. 'Come in. Close your eyes first.'

She obeyed. 'Now stand there,' he commanded.

She stood, waiting.

'Now you can open them. Funny – a portrait you didn't 'sit' for!'

She knew he was talking only to cover his fear that she would not like it. At first she could see nothing but the haloes of the candles, but then she made out Jack, who moved away

456

from the picture on the easel to reveal his work, and she saw the culmination of his endeavours: a girl in a white dress, pale white with the faintest tinge of pink. A girl looking like a bride, the slight pink suffusing the silk skirt as if from underneath, from the skin. Blocks of other whites might have detracted from the white of the dress without that pink glow, but were, in any case, so arranged that the girl and the dress seemed to be of a different colour. The only other colours were the grey of the eyes and the brown of the hair, with a green ribbon threaded through it.

It was both her and not her. It was beautiful, Jack's idea of her; but also a painting that was beautiful in itself. She did not know what to say, except that she could see that he had succeeded in what he wanted to do. So different from the picture of the three girls in Paris. This picture was more solid, the paint put on more thickly, and yet, at the same time, more airy. The whites dazzled and held the eye, the dress swirled motionlessly and the snow took the eye out of the window reluctantly, as though warmth and love were inside, radiating from the dress. She went up to it to look more closely. The paint was still wet. Close to, she saw that white was not really a colour at all, but all colours.

'It's simply beautiful,' she said. 'Not me; more an idea of whiteness around me.'

He had made her glance slightly downwards in the picture and she could not guess what he had thought she would be thinking.

'It's me, but it's better than me – more romantic – I don't know, Jack. I think it's the best picture you've ever done, not because it's me.'

She wanted to touch the girl, to understand her. Then she tried to look at it as though it were just a pattern, as Jack had often told her to.

'Girl in White, 1948?' she queried. 'Clementine at the Window? Study of a Girl? Study in White?'

'Let's leave it to Mother to give it a title,' he said.

She went up to him and laid her hand on his shoulder. 'You think of me as a bride; but it's a solid girl, all right. I could almost be jealous of her,' she said.

He laughed and drew her face down to his and suddenly

they were kissing each other passionately.

'Mother never comes in here, and she's probably going to be late – there isn't much transport from Haworth!'

'Thank you for the picture,' she managed to say, before all his pent–up longing beat over her and more than anything she wanted to be wanted – by Jack and by the man who had painted her. The candles bloomed against their skin and then he blew them out and they fell together on Adam's old sofa, which had not been manufactured for lovers but had to suffice. She was always to remember the smell of paint on his skin and the smell of candle wax, as though this was their real marriage. She was fierce and he was even fiercer.

They lay for a moment afterwards, drowsily laughing and murmuring, and time, for once, seemed to have come to a stop.

In the morning, the picture looked different in the colder light and the snow seemed to have become bluer, but the girl had a new secret smile fixed for ever.

Edith was thinking of Sophie, who needed some aim, something beyond the happiness of her children or the success of her husband so that she could feel regarded for herself. She had always been a fighter and Edith felt she had not carried the fight through. She remembered the Sophie of some fifteen or twenty years before, when her children were little, and the anxiety she had felt then. Well, she had done a good job on her children, if Clemmie was anything to go by, and need have no worries about *her*. Sophie would not want Clemmie to marry young. Yet, wouldn't *she* have been happier, in the end, to marry at twenty–one if Clem Bartholomew had loved her? Clem's namesake loved Jack, she was sure, and was not afflicted with her mother's doubts and agonizings.

She had once heard Clemmie say to Jack, 'Mother thinks women have children only when they have given up on their own lives, as a sort of consolation prize.' The girl had not said it bitterly, but as a statement of fact. 'I think she must have married on the rebound.'

'But marrying isn't an end – it's only a beginning,' Jack had replied.

Of course, it was easy for a man to say that. Edith could not see Clementine giving up her own work.

It was no use worrying about it: they would find their own way. Edith thought of her own inner life, the thoughts and dreams that still came to her and did not disturb her as they would have done Sophie. She accepted them for what they were – primitive images. But the psyche, or soul, which sounded better in English, in its 'dark cottage', was a poetic conceit. She had once had a dream that her own soul was turned into a little, leathery, dachshund–type dog, which itself turned into a leather pouch and was thrown around and caught by strange shapes; shadowy people in the corners of a dimly–lit room. Why her unconscious mind should see itself as a piece of leather, was funny as well as mysterious. Edith thought there must be some buried memory there. Her inner and outer worlds irradiated each other. Sophie's trouble, she thought, was that there was sometimes a dissonance between the inner and the outer, as there had once been, long ago, for her. The dark cottage did not only reflect the outer world of sensation, a world which had begun to be known at birth, but belonged, too, to an inner truth, formed by, and through, memory. Here, the world of the philosophers might hold a key; but the philosophers did not agree about the answer, and it was unlikely there was one. *She* preferred to believe that there was some core of being that was not just formed by social and personal circumstances. Let Sophie make more of the *outer* world; it might suit her better. She remembered discussing much the same problem, over thirty–five years ago with her friend. People did not change in essentials, even though the world of other people was for herself no longer behind a glass wall.

The next afternoon she wrote to Michael Carr. 'It occurred to me that Sophie might very well return to the work she did before the first war. She was a good critic and immediately recognized the worth of my first husband's poems. I'm sure she needs an occupation; you must forgive me for writing to you, but I think you have it in your power to give her a new lease of life. Theo Carmichael was always aware of Sophie's abilities, was even rather jealous of them. Surely it isn't too late to give Sophie a proper job in the office and let her find her feet there again? She's younger than Theo, who is

459

still with you. Sophie has felt much anxiety in the past and I believe you must now give her a chance to prove herself, apart from the domestic round. Forgive me for speaking plainly. You know her better than I, but a friend may sometimes see what a closer relation can not. Ask your wife to return to work: give her the chance to make a life again, now that your children have grown up. Please don't tell her I wrote – let it come from you. Will you do this for Sophie? I think you will be surprised at what she will be able to do for the firm, at a time when everything is changing in the world of publishing. I'm sure you won't regret it if you can persuade her. She has a good deal of energy, many original ideas and much past experience on which to draw. Doing brief reading for the firm is not enough; take her in properly at the office, Michael. Forgive me if I am presuming too much, but I am convinced she needs real occupation away from the home.'

Edith signed and sealed the letter, after adding how very happy Clemmie seemed to be, and posted it with a feeling that she had burned her boats. But he wanted her to stay on his list, she was sure, and she had the right to say what was in her mind. She addressed it to Gower Place and put 'personal' on the envelope.

Then she wrote her letter to Sophie, managing to hint at her feeling that more women ought now to enter the world of publishing and business. Clemmie's generation should not be the only lucky ones with a certain independence of action.

'We are not yet old, Sophie. There are things we can do, now that the war is over, that before all our sadnesses perhaps we could not do. I am writing something new, this time a little attempt at topography and the influence of place. Thank you for sending the other reviews on to me – you can review me yourself next time, if you will!'

She looked up suddenly, remembering the pattern she had seen a few days ago, of two houses' roofs, miles apart against the sky, showing that the same builder had built them both. All the secret lives of people in strange houses . . . She must finish the letter, stop thinking about secret lives.

She signed the letter, and the image of the poor little soul came back: the piece of doggy leather, the word 'dogged' she supposed, and the toughness of leather. That

460

was what the dream had been about Surviving, even if buffeted and thrown around. Rosamund, the prisoners in Buchenwald and Auschwitz, had had no chance to survive, but then neither had Adam. Nor any of them, in the end.

She sealed her envelope and then added a PS on the back: 'Jack has painted the most wonderful picture of your daughter and Seb Harman is to come over next week to look at it and his other work.'

Clemmie and Jack were thinking and talking about quite different things. Jack had told her how he had imagined his father to be and how he could not imagine how his mother, so vague and gentle, had got herself involved with him. As they talked they felt they were getting to know each other better, though there were still many things to discover.

'It's faintly incestuous,' said Clemmie with a grin. 'My mother and yours, your father and my mother. I'm sure she was in love with him. Look how she was over the 'poems'. They were never lovers, I don't think; she had that long affair with the Miller man; did you know about that? Poor Mother, doing all the things she always warns against. Why do people get so frightened for their offspring? She is the same as she says Grandma Ridsdale was – always worrying about her children. I don't believe Mother wants either of us to marry, but perhaps that's not fair; she married Pa, after all.'

'I don't think we have to re–run our parents' or grandparents' lives,' said Jack. 'I often wished I could have talked to my father. Adam talked to me, but he was a different sort of person, strangely innocent in spite of all he went through in the first war.'

'Funny how it's all turned out, isn't it?' remarked Clemmie. 'And *you* are going to have a wonderful exhibition of pictures: I think it will be better doing it up north – you being in Yorkshire.'

'If it doesn't work I can always do the teaching diploma next year in Leeds and find a permanent post, I suppose,' he said.

'Wait and see. I'm sure you're a very good teacher; you've taught me a lot,' she replied, giggling. 'But I'd rather you were a penniless artist, and happy doing what you really want.'

'Artists aren't *always* penniless,' replied Jack.

She put her woolly–mittened hand in his. Jack loved her. Incredibly, he loved her. And she would have him for the rest of her life, whatever else happened in the big world outside. And she would be a success; somehow get hold of a farm, work it and make it a home for them both. She was filled with dreams and plans. Luck might play a part, but Sophie's daughter had a good opinion of herself and nothing was impossible. The world was opening up and she had someone to go through life with.

When Michael Carr approached his wife a few days later with his suggestion that she might like to return full time to the firm, she burst into tears. That Michael should have such faith in her when she had had so little, recently, in herself, was a surprise.

'You mean you will?' he asked. 'I should have thought of it earlier – we need someone to build up the list, especially since our new young man went off to build himself an empire.'

Sophie dried her eyes and said, 'I'm so out of date; you'll have to tell me all about the financial position and the plans. I've been very neglectful. I'm sorry, it was the house and everything; I didn't seem to have any surplus energy to listen to you. But – oh, Michael, I'd like to try to work again!'

'Theo's opened up our European markets again and is in touch with several translators from the German and French and Italian, and now that we don't have any need to share our list in New York, since Fabian has taken over completely and separated us, it's easier, in a way. I can start afresh and not feel I must bend the list to transatlantic preferences. Well, you will see yourself what's needed – apart for a good injection of capital! Young British writers are what we want, in tune with the future, not harking back any more to the thirties, though we might do some *really* old reissues.'

'There's an awful lot of Francophilia around,' said Sophie.

'That will last for a time, but we need to rebuild, now, on our own roots; things that got neglected during the war, and also plans for the next thirty years. We need some good, strong, steady sellers. Edith's work is our best acquisition – even the last book is still doing well; and, of course, the Constantines. People are asking for new titles, but she's refused to write any more.'

Sophie felt excited and apprehensive. What would her work exactly involve? Would she, one day, be able to own some shares of her own in the company? But she wanted an ordinary job, not to be at the office because she was the publisher's wife. He knew this, for he was not impercipient, blamed himself for not suggesting it earlier. Good old Edith. *She* had confidence in Sophie.

'Could I visit the London Library and check through all the ancient fiction lists to see what might be reprinted. You've got Theo to find out what's going on abroad and your fiction editor to see the new British stuff.'

'Yes, the London Library's a good idea. We need a new broom to sweep old dust; but we never get to the bottom of the slush pile! You could call in and make a start on that, as well. After all, you used to read for us. This would be more than that, though.'

'Would you *pay* me, Michael?' she asked, he thought rather pathetically.

'Of course!' Let's say a part–time rate to begin with, and then you organise a plan and present it at the next general meeting; in the meantime you needn't go to the office every day.'

'I'd rather go and work there, if you have a cubby–hole. And I'd like to prepare a working paper of suggestions. Michael, I'm sure I *could* be of some use, and if I am, you can pay me out of any profits I make for you!'

She was enthusiastic and he hoped that it was going to work. In a year or two they might be making a better profit and then she could take a 'title' for herself. After wartime economies and restrictions they were short–staffed.

Sophie, for her part, wondered why she had never thought of doing all this before. Well, of course, there had been the war and before that the bringing up of the children. She wondered how Bea was getting on with her expansion of the family planning clinics; she had not worked for Bea since '39. Bea might begin to treat her as an equal if she had a 'proper' job. She was excited.

One February morning she went into the old office. Of course, she had been there since she left it over thirty years before, but as the wife of the partner, not in her own right.

463

The tall, thin Theo, whose hair was still black, greeted her. She did not look too sour.

'We've found a little cupboard and there is a whole room of junk upstairs nobody's looked at since before the war, as well as the unsolicited stuff which usually comes to me. I'd be glad if you would start by taking some of that home every week and writing a few short reports. I'm off to Paris myself next week, chasing up existentialists. Mr Carr said you wanted to look at our old lists, too, and might have some ideas for a rejigging. Were you pleased when we reprinted Bartholomew's poems in the limited edition?' she asked curiously. She was being much nicer to her than Sophie had expected.

Sophie answered crisply, 'No one could have been more pleased, unless it was Edith.' God, how strange it is to be back, she thought. Theo has not changed in looks – she's had no children; she's rather handsome. She likes being in charge.

What *had* changed was the whole district. There had been bombs in Bloomsbury, but nothing like the quantity that had fallen on the City, and there were new shops springing up all over the place. She had coffee brought in to her instead of going out, and began on the sorting out of manuscripts and typescripts, some of them dated as far back as 1939. When, after lunch, she went up to the junk room, she was dismayed. Piles of cartons, boxes, parcels. Things had changed in that neat top room where the orders used to go out. The men who had worked there long ago were dead or retired and the typists downstairs were new faces. She thought of Willy; where was he now? And Toby, who had been replaced after his death by an older accountant, now himself retired. Michael should have told her more of how he organized things. She had never asked. She must make it her business to find out without appearing intrusive. Some of the staff obviously did not know who she was. Theo could not have told them and that was a relief. But she did not hanker after the old Sophie Ridsdale days. She felt rather confident, in fact, though perhaps it was absurd for a middle–aged woman, so long 'out of work' that was not centred on the home, thinking she could be of use to an outfit which had done without her since 1921. But she would persevere.

She began a list of priorities, which she sent for typing and copying, sorted one of the large boxes at the top, made a pile of twenty manuscripts from the slush pile and went home via the London Library where she went through fiction published by Miller and Penn, beginning with the authors whose names began with an 'A'. Some dated from before she was born. Grant must have read these once.

She then called it a day and arrived back in Hampstead about seven o'clock with two chops and some apples to cook for their dinner. Over them, she told Michael what she had been doing. He had been out in Hertfordshire at the printers, but seemed pleased.

'I shall have to get Mrs Wilson to call three times a week, rather than two, or our house will look a mess,' she said. 'I'll pay it out of my own earnings; I'd like to feel I was doing something for us both.' Her eyes sparkled, in spite of her tiredness.

Michael blessed Edith. He thought his wife looked happier already, and certainly younger that her fifty–eight years. They must not grow into two old fogeys in their empty nest. It would need a good year to see what Sophie's ideas brought forth, but he was confident that some of her suggestions would be followed through. He trusted her taste.

While Sophie was busy with old books and new books and unpackings and readings and reports, Clemmie and Jack were waiting for Seb to pronounce definitively on Jack's work. He had come over in a large car, whisked over from Leeds by an Arts Council minion, and spent a whole afternoon with Jack going through all his paintings and drawings. He had whistled when he had seen 'Clemmie in a white dress' and seemed impressed. And he had spent a lot of time looking at Jack's old landscapes and his newer drawings and his latest painting, done after the portrait; 'A Pennine landscape'. A verdict was awaited.

Meanwhile, Edith's father became ill and Edith had to go to stay with him. Finally, he was taken to a nursing home, still game to the end in spirit, though sadly wasted in body. Edith visited him every day there and he died at the end of March. Edith stayed over in Leeds after the funeral to see a solicitor.

The morning after the funeral Clemmie woke feeling sick. At first she thought she must have eaten something that disagreed with her. She managed to get up and go to the farm, thinking

465

it would pass; but after doing the milking the feeling returned and she had to go back to the cottage, telling Mr Hoyle she had a stomach upset.

Jack was still in the kitchen when she returned. She stood at the door, pale and sweating. He was having his breakfast before dashing down the road to the bus, for Edith had the car with her. He was feeling very upset about his grandfather's death: it was at a great age, of course, and the old man had been very lonely by himself in Roundhay, even though it had been his choice to stay there. Pneumonia, 'the old man's friend', had killed him in the end. They had all gone back to the empty house in Roundhay, with a few elderly relatives of Edith's parents and cousins and their children, and been given tea and buns by Edith and the retired parlour maid who had cried all the time.

'I must have had something to disagree with me,' Clemmie managed to get out, before rushing to the sink under the window. Jack put down his case and sat her down at the table, clearing away the remains of his breakfast.

'Clemmie,' he said in a carefully measured voice. 'Do you think you might be pregnant?'

In spite of working with animals and being aware, daily, of the connection between animal insemination and birth, she was astounded. It really did not seem to have occurred to her.

'Oh – but you – used something – didn't you?'

'Not that time when I'd finished the portrait. Oh, Clemmie, I'd be so pleased. Perhaps I wanted it to happen – '

'Oh, well, that explains it,' said Clemmie matter-of-factly. 'I have missed a period, now I come to think of it.'

'And even then, you didn't think – '

'I was sure you'd used something; not that I bothered to ask, did I? Oh, Christ, Jack, I'm an idiot. What shall we do?'

'You want a baby, Clemmie, don't you? You want to marry me, too?'

'You know I do – marry you, I mean. I hadn't really thought about a baby! I think it would be nice. But, Jack, I can't give up my job; we haven't any money – '

'I earn enough,' he said. 'I can go on teaching when I've got my diploma.'

'Mother will be furious with me if I am pregnant, I know she will! Still, perhaps it's just that I've been overworking or something. I just never thought it could happen to me; not yet, anyway.'

'You'll have to go to the doctor, love; find out for sure.'

'I feel a bit better now. I'll go back to the farm. Funny, I'm sure my mother once told me she was never sick before she had us, and they say girls take after their mothers. Oh, Jack, have we mucked it all up?'

He came and put his arms round her. 'I wanted us to marry soon; perhaps this is just a sign for us to get on with it? So long as you *do* want a baby? I mean, I didn't do it on purpose!'

'I *know*. Of course I'd like a baby; I'd like hundreds, if they were yours. It's just – my work and everything.'

She stood there after he had gone and shook her head and tried to remember dates. Phoebe or her mother would have had everything worked out. What would be the best thing to do? She decided to go back to work and see how she felt and then go, in a day or two, to the doctor in the village who had a surgery on Thursdays. But perhaps by then something would have happened and it would not be necessary. You are a fool, she told herself. Too busy thinking about Jack and about the animals to look after yourself. I should have asked Jack. It was worth it, though. She fell to thinking of that particular love-making in the parlour with a reminiscent smile. Yes, she wanted a baby, but she wanted, also, to go on with her work. Marriage was neither here nor there, was it? Poor Jack would have to teach for the rest of his life, she supposed, if he had to support a child. That was not fair.

When Edith returned that afternoon, she was tired. She thought Clemmie looked tired, too, when she came in. Neither Jack nor Clemmie said anything to her, but next morning when Edith got up at her usual early hour she heard Clemmie being sick in the lavatory downstairs. Jack was hovering on the stairs himself. When Clemmie emerged, looking green, Edith took one look at her and guessed the truth. Not that she had been sick herself; she, too, had been lucky. She said nothing, though, and Clemmie went off to work as usual. When Jack came down for a cup of coffee she was in the kitchen.

'Has she been to a doctor?' she asked.

'No, not yet.'

'Jack, you should have had more sense, unless you both planned it?'

Jack had hardly ever heard his mother sound even a little angry and stopped, his cup half way up to his mouth.

'Yes, I know that her mother would think it a woman's responsibility; but Clemmie's only twenty–one, Jack,' Edith went on.

'She's not sure yet.'

'Oh, *I'm* sure, Jack. If it's what you want and what she wants, it would be a great, great joy to me,' said Edith, and there was almost a break in her voice.

He looked at her in astonishment. To change from anger to joy, from one moment to another, was unusual for Edith. 'But she wants to go on with her work! *I* shall do the teaching diploma in any case; but how can she have a baby and work on a farm?'

'Jack, go with her to Doctor Brown's on Thursday, find out for certain.' Edith was always very direct about physical processes and Jack was not embarrassed. He knew his mother had realized they would sleep together when she made Clemmie welcome at Ox Heys.

'Yes, I will. I'm sorry, it was my fault –'

'Never mind, just find out. Look after her when she comes back today from work. I'll have a talk to her, if she wants. Don't worry. I'm very fond of Clemmie, as you know.'

'Mother, I love her! We wanted to get married soon anyway. At least I did – '

'I know that, and it's time you had a home of your own. But does she want to? Had you decided, in any case, to go on with the teaching?

He hesitated. 'No, to be truthful. But I will now: needs must.'

She saw just a trace of his father in him, then. All men were a little the same if they had got a girl into trouble. Not that she thought, for a moment, that Jack was not fully aware of his future responsibilities. As his father, too, had been aware. But this was a *mutual* love, she was thinking, when he said again, as he turned to go, 'I love her, Mother. I love her.'

It could have been better arranged, thought Edith, as she washed the dishes and then put on her spectacles and sat down again at the table with her account books. She kept thinking of her father, now a handful of ashes, and of a new

468

life that may have begun before that one ended. And of Sophie who might blame *her*. But she had an answer for them all. She was getting ruthless in her old age, she thought. Jack should have been more careful, of course, but he did want to marry Clemmie. It was Clemmie who was the problem. Jack might very well find a permanent post once he was fully qualified – he would have to decide about that in any case. But the girl; had she not thought that love led to babies? And she a farmer! Perhaps it was a false alarm, she thought again. But she was sure it was not.

Thursday came and the two lovers went together to the doctor's surgery. It was all very brisk: an examination and a sample in a bottle to be taken the next morning. Doctor Brown said it was too early for him to be sure, but the bottle would make if fairly certain, one way or the other, and if she missed another period by the end of March, they would be really sure.

'A negative could be positive, but a positive rarely negative,' he announced.

This was a new procedure they had devised at the university medical school which did the testing. Usually, girls had to wait three or four months to be sure, but he had a small private practice in the city.

The bottle was filled, the sample taken by Clemmie to the doctor's again, and then they waited for the verdict. Clemmie felt a little better and Edith hoped she was going to be one of those women who are sick for a little time and then improve once the first three months are over.

The result finally came through in a brown envelope addressed to Mrs C. Carr. Edith left it on the table. Clemmie had gone to the farm and the postman had arrived late that morning. Edith then went out. Jack was already away.

When Clemmie came back there was no one in the kitchen; just the letter on the table. She looked at it a few times before making a cup of tea and then sitting down with it in her lap. If she were *not* pregnant what would she want? I *do* want to marry Jack, I *do*, she thought. Even if we don't have a baby, I do want to. But I want my work too. I've studied hard for it and worked hard for so long. But if I have to choose, I must be brave. If I'm not pregnant I could go on working and we could buy a little house one day and I could go every day to a farm, like a labourer, as I do now, even if I were married. And Jack would have his job at school. And then we could save up and rent a farm somewhere where he could find work too. And then when I was older I could have a baby and go back to work, if we could afford a girl to look after it.

She suddenly felt it was more important to have Jack than a child. But she felt resentful that she might have to choose between marriage and farming. Jack, had, anyway, suggested he went on teaching.

She took a deep breath and opened the brown envelope. 'Your pregnancy test,' it stated, 'is positive'. What had the doctor said? 'A positive is never a negative, though a negative could be wrong?' Then she was pregnant. She was! And she would have to choose Jack. No farm now, Jack the teacher, she the housewife. She had chosen rightly in her heart, but she put her head on her arms and cried. Mother would be furious – throwing everything away for a man.

There Edith found her, half an hour later. Clemmie gestured towards the letter and sat there saying nothing. 'He wanted to be a painter – and now – it's my fault – he'll have to go on teaching,' she sobbed.

'What is this nonsense, Clemmie?' said Edith, filling a kettle for another cup of tea. 'Jack is the responsible one in all this. All men have the power to make girls pregnant, *and* he is a lot older that you. I knew you might run the risk, so blame me. Your parents can blame me, if you like. I should have talked about the immorality of unmarried sex! Come on, now, drink up.'

Clemmie dried her eyes, but looked pale and wretched. 'If I'd not even been pregnant, but *forced* to choose – between my work and Jack – I'd have chosen him. But now I've no real choice, have I? I don't want Jack to have to give up everything and go on earning money teaching, when all he really wants to do is paint. Why should he have to give it all up to look after me and a baby? It's not fair.'

'Just as fair as for *you* to give your work up,' replied Edith. 'And he could go on painting, in any case; whereas you can't run a baby and work, without help.'

470

Clemmie thought 'running a baby' was a funny expression and smiled weakly. 'If only I had some money of my own!' she said. 'But, at present, I know my father is finding it difficult. The new house cost quite a lot of capital as he didn't own the old one.'

'I expect one day that will work out,' said Edith comfortably. 'We can't all have rich fathers.' She stopped, thinking of her own father and how she had refused money for herself from him, long ago.

'When Jack comes in I have something to say to you both,' she said, with a sort of diffident briskness which even Clemmie, in her downcast state, remarked.

They were all sitting at the table. Jack was still fingering the envelope and holding Clemmie's hand.

'Farmers' wives work and have babies,' Clemmie said. 'So why not farmers?'

Jack squeezed her hand. 'Please let's get married, straight away,' he said.

Clemmie smiled, but looked troubled.

'It's a good thing we knew in good time, about the baby,' said Edith. 'I suppose it will only hurry up what you were going to do anyway.' She put her spectacles on. They waited, as she looked about to say something. Jack thought his mother looked rather impressive. He must paint her with her angular face and soft greying hair and her little gold–rimmed spectacles.

'Before you tell your mother and father,' she began, 'I was talking to the solicitor about my father's estate yesterday. Long ago, I asked Father to divide whatever he left between my brother Ted in Canada, and Jack.'

'No – no, Mother,' said Jack, distressed, and genuinely surprised.

'Now, listen; that was all settled long ago and there's no arguing about it. I have quite enough for my needs; there's a separate little legacy for me from my grandfather, which will now come to me. But in your Grandpa's will, Jack, it says specifically that anything he leaves you must be used to further your career. He knew how hard it is; and there isn't as much as there would have been if he had still been a partner. And then there were all the expenses of mother's illness and living so long himself. But it's enough to start, so that you don't need to work full–time. However, that

471

still doesn't solve the problem of Clemmie and her work and your child.' She paused. 'Many years ago I went to stay on your grandparents' farm, Clemmie, and I've never forgotten it. It was before the First War, when your mother and I were both working in London. The farm wasn't very prosperous, although they didn't live badly; later on, as you know, your grandfather died and your grandma went to live with your Aunt Alice. As you know, the farm went on being worked by your great–uncle, until he was too old, and then he left it to Alice. Alice was doing quite well in Woldby, so she leased it to some man in the village who neglected it. That was when you saw it, Jack,' she added, turning to her son. 'Remember, in 'thirty–eight?'

'Yes, I went there after I'd been in Paris. I wanted to see where Aunt Sophie had lived. Adam had given me the idea of being a sort of "gentleman farmer" myself. *I* don't know. It was pretty derelict.'

'In the war,' said Edith, turning to Clemmie, 'your Aunt Alice got a manager in, as there were more profits to make, then, if you could get labour; as you well know. I had had the idea of buying it one day for Adam to work, with any profits I might make, but the war came and my husband died, and the idea had to be shelved. When I started to make a little money, Father invested it for me. So before you came back from Italy, Jack, I began to buy Thirksay from Alice. Her boys were away in the war and her husband had enough to do with Woldby. I've been to see your Aunt Alice once or twice, recently. Your cousins have enough to do with their own farm now and your youngest cousin, Tom, wants to go to university and isn't interested in farming. Alice was willing to sell what was left at Thirksay. I took out a mortgage with the Agricultural Mortgage Company which I've nearly paid off; the profits from Constantine, I'm afraid! All the money from the old copyrights reverted to me in Garnett Edwards's will. So the farm is now mine. It's my wedding present to you, Clemmie. Not to Jack, he's got enough from his grandfather. I was waiting to tell you both about it, but I wasn't sure *when* you would marry, or even if Clemmie wanted to marry. Sophie and Michael might have made some objection to my encouragement, I suppose, but I don't believe they will now. You've rather jumped the gun!'

Jack and Clemmie sat, stunned, scarcely able to believe all this. Clemmie said, 'So I shall be able to farm *my own farm*, and Jack will be able to paint: oh, Aunt Edith, it's wonderful! I can't believe it.'

'There is a slight catch,' said Edith. 'You'll need a manager, and I'm not yet sure whether the old one will stay on. And some labour. But there are two or three women in the village I've spoken to, who want work. It's only a little farm now, but I expect it could be expanded. There'll be headaches with all the problems farmers have at the moment.'

'Mother! To think you've been plotting this for years! How did you know Clemmie would turn up and want to be a farmer?'

'I didn't. At first I wanted it for Adam, and then, when he died in the war, I thought I might stop writing and take it over myself: I've always wanted to try, but now I'm too old to begin. The chickens weren't all that successful, were they? And I have to go on writing – but no more of those Constantines! They've served their purpose.'

'What will you live on yourself? If you only have your little pension, the sort of books you want to write now won't bring in a fortune, even with a legacy.'

Edith said nothing.

'It's what I've always dreamed of; I never thought I'd be able to do it for years and years,' said Clemmie.

'I'm doing it, not just for you two, but for the baby,' said Edith. 'I've *quite* enough to be going on with.'

Clemmie thought she did not deserve all this. Edith must have made good investments, helped by her father. Edith was realistic. Perhaps the world ran on money more than on love.

'When Jack was little and Clement at the war, I was in the same position,' Edith said. 'I wouldn't take money for myself from Father, bless him, but I paid him a very low rent for this cottage, and then I had my own little income from the books. What's money for? I know I haven't expensive tastes and I've seen you both work till you drop; I was only worried that Jack might think it beneath his dignity to have money from his mother, and he isn't going to. All the farm will be yours, Clemmie, in your name. Jack can take a hand, I suppose, if he wants. But I expect he'll be too busy painting landscapes!'

'People will certainly think it odd,' said Clemmie, looking at Jack. 'It should be *me* painting, they will think, and my husband driving the tractor. You won't mind, Jack, will you?'

'Mind!' said Jack, looking at his mother speculatively. 'It's true, we've never been rich, but you've always held everything together. And I shall have a working wife as I had a working mother! I'm bloody spoilt!' He laughed.

'I'm sure Seb will reply soon about the Leeds thing,' said Clemmie, hoping his male dignity was not affronted, though it did not seem to be.

'He *has* replied,' said Jack. 'I was going to tell you. He said he thought I could only paint portraits if I felt for the sitters; he'd seen some of the others I'd done and said they were OK, but not like the one of you, Clemmie, and the Paris one: those were quite different. And he looked at a lot of my landscapes, some painted from memory from France and Italy, and he said my future lay there; so perhaps it will be the right place to live for a painter. I shall enquire about a part–time teaching job as well. There's sure to be something in York – plenty of schools there.'

'So that's all right,' said Edith, taking off her spectacles and regarding them with approval.

'There's still my mother and father to be told about the baby – and everything. Mother always said it would be years before I could afford a farm. I don't think she liked Thirksay, did she, really? the farming bit missed a generation.'

'Your mother *did* like it,' replied Edith. 'But she had to get away; she wasn't like you. I think she'll be pleased when she's got over the shock of being a grandmother and been cross with me for doing what I've done.'

Clemmie got up and kissed Edith, who looked suddenly a little lonely. 'I didn't do it on purpose,' Clemmie murmured, 'but I'm glad I'm going to have your grandchild; everything's suddenly turned bright. I felt so awful a few hours ago. I'll accept being sick for nine months, to show how grateful I am!'

'Don't forget the baby will have two adoring grandmothers, and a grandfather as well,' said Edith. How Adam would have loved a grandchild of hers. How cruel it was that he should have died.

To her father, too, as he lay the last week in hospital

before he lapsed into a coma, she had said that she was sure Jack and Clemmie would marry; and he had smiled and said, 'I shall miss being with you all.'

'After all, it's from your father's firm that I've made my profits,' said Edith.

'I couldn't have a better mother–in–law,' said Clemmie to Jack, later. 'She must be rather good with money, mustn't she? I don't deserve it.'

'She ought to have my grandpa's money,' said Jack. 'But it'll be no good trying to make her change her mind; she's all for women looking after their own lives for themselves. Sometimes I think she's a much stronger Feminist than the people who go on about it. She had a hard time of it when I was little, but she had her independence, I suppose. Circumstances always seem to force her to be alone.'

'She won't be alone; she'll have us and a grandchild. Oh, Jack, I'm so happy. I shall work and work and work – you'll see. I've never even seen Thirksay yet, though she told me about it once. Tell me what it's like.'

They looked at the papers Edith had left for them on the table to go through. There was so much to plan. Jack decided he must first write to Michael and Sophie Carr. Weren't men supposed to ask for the hand of a daughter? And then there was his own resignation to give in, for the summer, and the baby to plan for, and the farm to move to, and all that entailed. And a wedding! He could not escape a wedding.

If Sophie had not spent the whole of the previous day in a highly successful meeting with the fiction editor, who approved all her proposals for reprints and possible discoveries, she might have felt differently about Clemmie's letter. She had opened Jack's first, not recognizing the writing. This was the one morning she stayed at home to sort out her odd household jobs and plan her week. In the afternoon she was due to go back to the office to continue her tidying up of the top rooms, with their dusty files and neglected correspondence.

So, it was all beginning all over again, she thought, and put the letter down. She could not suppress a spasm of irritation at her happy–go–lucky daughter. And dear, clever, devious old Edith. To think she had been planning to buy the farm at Thirksay all these years. Probably also planning for Jack to marry one of her daughters? Edith had a good 'business' head on her shoulders; she got that from her father, whatever they had used to think about her being vague and unmaterialistic. Then the extreme generosity of Edith's offer struck her; a farm, *Church Farm*, to go to her Clemmie, not to Jack. Money for Jack from old Mr Broughton. The couple were to be envied.

She sat down by the window in the kitchen. It was raining steadily and she knew, with certainty, that if she had not spent a good day yesterday feeling that she had had something to contribute to the firm, she would have felt extremely gloomy. That her youngest, little Clemmie, whom she was reluctant to acknowledge was out of childhood, should be expecting a baby; that thought could have precipitated tears, if it had come six months ago. But now, as she read through the letters again and lit a cigarette to accompany her excitement, she felt quite extraordinarily pleased. The little lamb sounded quite sensible in her letter, written in her usual round hand. Determined, too. Michael might perhaps be a bit miffed, but he would not, could not, stand in their way.

And Edith? Her thoughts reverted to Edith, who had wanted this, she was sure, though she would never have said anything about it to anyone. She must write to Alice. Alice would be amazed that a woman was going to run the farm. But Clemmie was qualified, and experienced, too. It would not be easy; she knew enough about farming to know that. But Clemmie would put everything she had into it. Michael would have done something, eventually, for her, she knew, when business recovered. Michael, to be a grandfather! How strange to be married to a grandfather! And, worse, her husband to be married to a grandmother! She sat dreaming, her head cupped in her hand, seeing the farm as it used to be. She had not seen it for years, but Edith had. And the little baby, boy or girl, would have them both as grandmothers. And Clem Bartholomew, lost long ago, would have been the other grandfather.

She roused herself and got ready to go out. Michael should be at Carr and Penn's; she would go and tell him the news herself. And Phoebe in Oxford – she must write. Would they want bridesmaids? Would Clemmie want to be married in white? Lots of 'expecting' brides did. Somehow, though, she did not think so. Should she wait for Michael and then send them a telegram? Yes, she had better.

Sophie went out of the house feeling as excited as though it were her own wedding; more so in fact, for that had been a rather uneasy affair in 1921, when she had finally burned her boats. She went down into the underground to Russell Square, trying to recall what she had been going to do that afternoon and, by the time she got to the office, could hardly wait to speak to her husband. When she did find him alone there, she must have looked so strange that he rose to greet her with an expression of alarm on his face.

'Clemmie's going to marry Jack and she's expecting a baby and Edith has bought Thirksay farm for her,' she got out in a rush and then sat down suddenly. 'I don't mind,' she added hurriedly, looking away.

'Oh my!' said Michael. 'Well, I'm not surprised.'

Later, they went for supper to a little restaurant in Holborn. 'Can you imagine writing to *your* mother like that?' Michael asked with a laugh. He was delighted about the marriage, delighted about the baby, very impressed about Edith's plans for the farm.

'She'd have had a heart attack!' said Sophie. 'Clemmie takes us for granted, I suppose, though I detect a slight anxiety amidst the euphoria.'

'He's an interesting chap, Jack,' said her husband. 'I knew, of course, how he felt about her – it showed at Christmas and before. I wasn't sure about *her*. I think she knows her own mind, that grown–up baby of ours. I expect we shall have to start treating her as a future Mum now, though, not a baby.'

'You know,' said Sophie, later on, as they ate some zabaglione, her favourite dessert. '*We* were treated as 'girls' till we were about twenty–five; it was only the first war that began to change all that. "Girls", of course, could get pregnant, too . . .'

'And the last war took it further. I hope it doesn't all go back again now. I've a suspicion women will, once more, be expected to down tools and take up their toasting forks. Of course, a baby *is* a full–time occupation.'

'Clemmie is going to *work*, Michael,' said Sophie solemnly. 'She won't have time for toasting forks.'

'You regret not working when they were little, then?' he asked, a bit fearfully.

'No, not really. I seem to be able to do only one thing at once, however hard I try. But she's different; more self–confidence, I suppose.'

'Phoebe'll go on working too, I expect,' he said. 'If she marries that chap of hers.'

'One day – when Theo retires – I've been thinking, wouldn't it be a good idea to get Phoebe to join the firm? She'd be wonderful with all the foreign stuff.'

'You're getting as bad as Edith – match–making!'

'Oh, do you think she did?'

'I wouldn't be surprised. Edith is very determined.'

'Yes, Edith's hand is behind the arrangements; but she couldn't make them fall in love!'

'Fancy persuading her father to leave Jack his money, rather than her. She's always refused to have much money, but she was probably richer than any of us, before she bought the farm.'

They sent a telegram: 'Delighted. Do come London ASAP. Sophie and Michael.'

Before the wedding at Thirksay Church in early July, Clemmie and Edith stayed at Church Farm, for there was a lot of work to be done in the farmhouse and the negotiations with Mr Thwaites the agent to be concluded, once the freehold had been handed over by the mortgagers. Painters, plumbers, electricians and joiners were kept busy and Edith showed herself to be no mean hand at plastering and repairing.

Jack planned his exhibition for the autumn, as well as doing a full load of teaching during his last term at the Rydings. Every Friday night he came over to Thirksay and he and Clemmie pored together over agricultural catalogues and decorating schemes. He began to strip and clean out a room where he intended to do his painting and a room for the baby. The country round Thirksay intrigued him. Some of the farms were vast affairs, with fields stretching to the horizon, in comparison with which their own was a tiddler. He began to draw horses again, for they had not yet been entirely supplanted, and he went for moonlit walks round the village, thinking about doing some etchings in the Samuel Palmer tradition. He had found his interest in older North Country landscape painters rekindled; and he had always admired English landscape painting and now wished to carry it on in his own way, for his own times.

'I'm a romantic painter,' he said to his future wife. 'Mother says father had the same tug to the old and traditional in his poetry, but I think he was more of a radical than I am, in practice.'

'Just as Mother is more "Progressive" than I am,' answered Clemmie. 'I feel I've always known this place; have come back home. Why did she ever want to leave it, do you think?'

There had been a second printing of Edith's earlier book and a review in a serious weekly of the Constantine books, amazing her with its analysis of 'the factors of folk memory mixed with Gothic revivalism', and also, apparently, 'existential angst'. That made her laugh.

Aunt Alice was amused that a woman was to take over the Thirksay farm. 'She'll have her work cut out,' she said to her husband. 'But Edith's behind them both. Yon Clemmie, for all she wears trousers, doesn't see herself as boss over her husband. A good thing they've got Thwaites, though. Eh, I never thought anyone to do with our Sophie would want to come back north, but there you are; there's nowt so queer as folk! I will say, she's a good worker,' she added rather grudgingly.

Michael commissioned Jack to paint Edith, and Jack made a few initial sketches. At first, he had thought he would paint her at her writing table, but the result was tame and not the way he saw her. It was Clemmie who suggested he paint her in her old coat and clogs as she looked out from the Far Ox Heys garden over to the hills, her profile rather like that of one of the prows of the Viking ships she had studied so much. That was better. He thought that was the real Edith.

'The richest soil in England,' said the solicitor in the York estate office, when Clemmie signed the freehold contract some weeks later. It was a pity there were no sheep in their part of the Vale, Clemmie was thinking, but one could not have everything.

'Lots of people are diversifying, I'm told, to pigs and chickens,' he had added.

'I want to re–sow what was arable,' Clemmie replied.

The arable land had been neglected since the war had ended and the subsidies had been withdrawn, but with careful management she thought it could be made to pay.

On their way back, Edith pointed out various fields and told Clemmie there had been strip–farming there long before the Conqueror. 'There was ploughing and grazing and hay–making and turf for cutting as well as trees for firewood – all in little strips,' she said.

Clemmie thought what a lot her future mother–in–law knew.

The essentials were planned. Two fields would be ploughed and sown in the autumn. The byre had been cleaned and restocked for the few cows she intended having and there was space for possible pigs and chickens in the very part of the yard where, fifty years before, they had flourished.

On the telephone, telling her mother this, she was surprised to hear Sophie reply, 'Yes, the hens always liked that part of the yard. You'll find they lay down by the old fence, on the bit of yard that looks out over the pond on the other side; I often used to be sent to collect eggs there.'

Clemmie tried to think of her mother as a small girl on a farm long ago. It seemed incredible.

On her wedding day, Clemmie wore her pink silk 'New Look' dress with its swirling long skirt and a frothy pink veil perched on top of her curls. She was carrying the roses which Sophie had picked for her that morning from the old garden – Aunt Rose–Ann's roses, now Clemmie's – and they set off her wonderful complexion. Jack, at the front of the church in an uncomfortable grey suit, breathed a sigh of relief when she came up to him and Michael released her to him. Edith, standing in the front pews with Sophie, looked tall and stately, her hair in its unfashionable bun set off by long earrings.

The front pews were filled: Alice Tollerton in her best costume, her ruddy–faced husband beside her, who knew this village probably better than any of them; their three tall sons, two of them farmers; Phoebe, studying the prayer book and sitting next to her friend Guy, a post–graduate research student, who looked so like her that people took them for brother and sister.

Behind them the pews were filled with a motley collection. Fabian Trevelyan had been invited, on a whim of Sophie's, as he was in England for a few week; a stouter Fabian, now, with an American accent. By his side, Theo Carmichael, in an unseasonable fur, her long feet shod in elegant French shoes; plump Seb, looking cynically upon everyone and wondering when he might have a drink; Cicely Emery, thin and shrivelled, with her wild mop of white hair and her unbending gaze, sitting by little Gladys, her companion and lover these thirty years. Bea Osborn had arrived, in a gaberdine, holding a large bag. She was attending out of her friendship with Sophie but could not restrain an atheistic sniff at the language of the parson. The teachers from the Rydings were sitting stolidly next to Clemmie's friends, several young women with expressions of envy and admiration on their faces when they looked at Jack. Mrs Elsie Wainman was thinking of all the weddings she had seen in this church and how young Clementina, as she called her, brought back the face of old Aunt Rose–Ann. Her husband, Alf, was next to her, uncomfortable in his hired finery, but actually the most formally dressed of all the men. He kept running his finger under his collar in agony.

Other village families were there too, other Ridsdales and Fountains, sitting next to visitors from the West Riding; the Hoyles and Mrs Sutcliffe and Mrs Brooke from the farm. Grandfather Carr had not been well enough to travel, but had sent a telegram, at this moment reposing in the village post office where Alice had used to work There were babies there too in church; the grandchildren of the children who had played in the village fields when Edith had first visited the farm. The church still meant something to the inhabitants of the village.

The sun burst through the side windows. It had rained overnight, but now the weather was clearing. The congregation relaxed and began to enjoy themselves once the service started. Having told them that the honourable estate of holy matrimony had been established by God and was not to be undertaken unadvisedly, lightly or wantonly to satisfy men's carnal lusts and appetites 'like brute beasts' (Clemmie smiled to herself), but reverently, discreetly, advisedly, and soberly, the rector went on to remind them all for what his holy estate had been founded. Jack almost looked at Clemmie's stomach, but remembered just in time. All waited with bated breath when what Sophie always called the Jane Eyre clause arrived on the rector's lips. But that passed without any incident, except the crying of a small baby at the back. Michael gave his daughter to be married, and Jack and Clemmie found their right hands taken firmly by the rector, who now looked stern.

Clemmie wondered who 'I, John Wilfred Broughton Bartholomew' was for a moment, and then recollected. Jack said, 'I do,' in a rather surprised voice, as though of course he took her for his wedded wife; no question about it. And after 'I Clementine Edith' had plighted her troth, the rector changed his expression to a beaming smile and pronounced the Ceremony of the Ring. Prayers followed and then, 'Those whom God had joined together let no man put asunder . . . I pronounce that they be man and wife.'

A few women from the village wiped their eyes before the blessing and the prayers. Then the rector went up into his pulpit, the congregation gratefully sat down, and he gave his address, dwelling upon the virtues of these two young people, much to their embarrassment, and ending with, 'The happy coincidence that they were to take up residence where, for two centuries at least the bride's ancestors had tilled the land and followed the plough.'

Edith, who did attend her own church occasionally to commune with herself and her maker, was wondering what form of 'marriage' had existed in Thirksay in the so called Dark Ages, but brought her wandering thoughts sternly back to the present.

The 'Wedding March' was a triumphant coda to the whole affair. Everyone followed the happy couple out of the church, pausing to greet and chat.

'As weddings go, it was very nice,' said Bea to Sophie. Sophie was aware that a tiny reference to family planning might have been expected from her old friend's lips. But Bea did not seem to have noticed Clemmie's pregnancy.

'What's it feel like to be a mother–in–law?' she asked.

'Somewhat easier than being a mother,' Sophie replied.

The wedding breakfast was waiting at Church Farm, all

arranged by the York caterers under the command of Mrs Thwaites, who had chosen this role. By this time, the sun was high in the sky and the smell of honeysuckle was wafting over the garden. The house had been freshly painted outside and the garden tidied up. Long trestle tables, covered with white cloths and with bowls of roses, awaited the revellers. Jack thought it looked like another Impressionist painting, one of those Monet gardens perhaps.

The rector talked to him about architraves and clerestories, under the impression that Jack was as interested as his mother in Norman architecture. People arrived across the fields from the church and there was a general mingling.

Champagne had been waiting in the farm cellar all week, enough for a regiment. But the older members of the congregation were full of that specially charitable set of feelings towards the human race which weddings arouse in all except the most cynical, even before the champagne did its work.

Jack and Clemmie did their rounds. No marquee, no line of formal handshakes, but hearty groups and many thank yous for the presents, which were even now in the back parlour awaiting the guests' inspection. Clemmie had told everyone exactly what she wanted and the evidence was there in the clock, the coal scuttle, the baking set, the refrigerator from Grandpa Carr, the wireless, the vases, tablecloths, and all the other impedimenta necessary for the setting up of a post-war home. Sophie had given them a cradle and Clemmie insisted on its taking pride of place amongst the presents, in happy disregard for convention.

Phoebe found a great deal to say to Fabian, and Seb to Edith, after pumping Jack's hand and saying, 'If only your dear dad could see you now, old man,' and raising his glass.

This is our real history, Edith was thinking; this is what I wish I could convey to others. The champagne had satisfactorily spumed out in the sun and wetted the grass with its heady bubbles. Chairs had been brought out and the cold chicken and strawberries and cream handed round from the long trestle tables. A Stead cousin and Alice's younger son brought out their cameras; the rector was toasted and, after extremely short speeches from Michael and Jack, received with the usual heavy applause, more champagne was drunk.

'Happy?' said Alice to her sister.

Sophie smiled. 'Yes; and to be here again.'

'Your friend, Edith, is a fairy godmother,' said Alice. 'I always thought she was. Do you remember when she came once on a visit and played the piano to us all? I was courting Ben then, and we went to market. Doesn't it seem a long, long time ago? Who'd have thought we'd have two wars to go through.' She hoped she had not upset her sister. Sophie though, had had her glass refilled and was thinking of Alice and herself; two middle-aged women, most of their lives behind them, once children here. A long, long time ago, indeed.

'I was going to tell you: I heard from Jerome in Australia last week,' said Alice. 'He's a grandad now, so he's beaten the both of us!'

Later, as the sun blazed down upon the party, some of the older people went into the house and Sophie found Edith there. 'To Edith,' she said, raising her glass. 'To Bevis and the Hermit.'

Edith smiled and held up her own glass. 'To Sophie,' she said. 'And to Carr and Penn, of course.'

Jack and Clemmie eventually found each other again and turned, each to the other, faces betraying secrets to which no parents would ever be privy. Coffee was brought out and further photographs were requested of the bride and groom. Clemmie took up her roses again, and Jack and she stood for a picture for the family albums, set apart, now, from the others, who were there because of them. Alice's son mustered all the rest of the guests in small groups and then into one large one, before some of the village guests began to make moves preparatory to leaving. Clemmie was not to 'go away', so did not need to change her dress; but by the time the shadows were lengthening and everyone had seen the presents, they were saying goodbye to the last of them and Clemmie threw her roses from an upstairs window. They were caught by her sister.

Sophie and Michael, with Phoebe and Guy, were to motor to York for the rest of the weekend. The others were to take the London train from York. Edith was to return to Far Ox Heys: she had work to do. The catering men and the helpers were dismantling the trestles. A few stray children were running around among the orchard trees.

'They *are* happy,' murmured Sophie to Michael, as they turned away.

'Happiness – or something like it,' answered Michael, as they stood at the garden gate and waved goodbye.

Soon everyone had gone, the children had been fetched home, and Clemmie came downstairs, still in her pink dress. Jack was making more coffee. 'None for me, thanks,' she said. 'It's supposed to be bad for babies. Let's sit in the parlour and eat up what they left – I'm hungry!'

Jack's exhibition in October was not an unqualified success. Some of the metropolitan critics were a little haughty about the traditional aspects of his work. The Yorkshire ones, however, took him to their hearts.

'Am I going to be that phenomenon, "the popular artist"?' said Jack to his mother.

She laughed, thinking of the Constantines. 'Read what Irving said again,' she said. '"Without a painter like Bartholomew to pace out the field, many of us would be lost . . . His pictures give pleasure, but also make us ask questions about our heritage. We see our landscape and our people as more than configurations, but as solidities which we ignore at our peril . . ."'

'Um,' said Jack.

The portrait, of course, had been much remarked upon too.

'A depth of feeling seldom evidenced nowadays, when to take pleasure in the human form seems somehow old–fashioned.'

'It is easy to see that this painter loves women and girls,' said another.

But it was Clemmie he loved, as much as paint and more than plaudits.

Clemmie had immediately buckled down to work on the farm, trying to establish priorities. She inspected the farm buildings, the dykes and hedges, found a barn needing repair, which had to be seen to without delay, and gaps in the hedges which Mr Thwaites had been too busy to mend all by himself. Hedging and ditching were urgent and Jack took a hand. It was a change from painting and provided a balance.

A cowman and dairy girl were found in the village and a small herd re–started: the work was endless. Clemmie would return to it once her baby was born and could be left with Mrs Wainman's daughter, who was looking forward to the task. There had not been much of a harvest; it would be different next year, she vowed. She was young and strong; outdoor activity would be good for her. Mrs Wainman's other daughter was to come over to help with the housework. Clemmie worried only that they could not afford it, but it was no good trying to do everything herself and knocking herself up. The part of the farmhouse they had made habitable was small. Jack would repair and paint and see to all the rest, bit by bit. They were lucky to have a home; so many young married couples had none. But they certainly worked for it.

After his exhibition, Jack began to change his style. Now that he was seeing so many natural processes more clearly than ever before, this vision seemed to push him to try to understand them from the inside. He experimented with shapes and mass and began a series of interiors and still–lives as autumn set in.

On a day when it was impossible to conceive of summer, when a cold wind had shorn the leaves from the last of the trees and only the holly and ivy were green in the garden, and a few straggling third–time–round roses, on the same birthday as the two grandmothers – the twentieth of November – a child was born to Clemmie and Jack, in the old back bedroom where Ridsdales had been born since the early nineteenth century, and perhaps even earlier. After only eleven hours of labour, from the first twinge to the baby's cry, attended by Jack and a midwife – the doctor arriving just at the last moment to check that all was going well – a seven and a half pound daughter pushed her way into the world. They named her Rosanna Mary Sophia, for her great–great–great aunt and for both grandmothers.

Jack was overcome by the whole thing; more than his wife, who took it all matter–of–factly. The cradle came into use and was put in their bedroom. Clemmie was soon up, sitting in a low nursing chair they had found in the old stable loft. He was reminded again of a painting, this time a Renoir; a good old–fashioned painter, and a lover of women.

Edith and Sophie waited a week or two before coming to see their granddaughter. It seemed to them that only yesterday they had been witnessing their children's marriage and now those 'children' were themselves parents.

'Weddings and baptisms should really go together,' remarked Sophie, rather tartly. 'It's the baby that seals the bond.'

Edith laughed. 'In my case, the interval was even shorter, if you remember!' She thought, but did not say, that she and Adam had needed no offspring to regard themselves as truly married till death them did part.

The early days and nights were hard work, but Clemmie was what Mrs Wainman called the best cow 'a good milker', and also took pleasure in the process. Soon, Rosanna was sleeping most of the night. She was a 'good' baby, though a noisy one, and had a hearty appetite. The midwife recommended a weekly weigh–in, which they did on the kitchen scales. A pound a week, sometimes more, astonished the grandmothers.

'The birth didn't hurt much,' said Clemmie to her mother. 'I suppose I was lucky. and Jack was thrilled to see it all happen. We don't speak of it in the village – they think it's faintly disgusting!'

'I'll be able to be a midwife if I fail at painting,' said Jack. 'Life is full of surprises.' It had been the most fantastic natural process he had ever seen and he was so fond of his baby that Clemmie had to ration his holding her.

'I'd like another baby soon,' said Clemmie. 'And if it's a boy next time, we shall call him Thomas after Grandpa Ridsdale, Michael after Pa, and Adam after Jack's stepfather. That's what we'd decided on as Rosanna was being born: it was so exciting at the very last minute to see she was a girl and we said, "Hullo, Rosanna."'

'Rosanna – Rose–Ann,' said Sophie. 'When are you having her christened? I presume you are?'

'The first weekend of the New Year,' replied Clemmie. 'She has to belong here, you know, and that's the best way.'

Sophie marvelled at her pragmatic daughter. When she thought of the fuss there had been when she was sixteen and had refused to be confirmed, and her agonizing over her beliefs. Still, it was their child, not hers, and Rosanna would have 'benefit of clergy'. Jack, the agnostic, was quite prepared to regard baptism as partaking of some symbolic significance, he said.

Sunday, January the second, nineteen forty-nine, and Rosanna Bartholomew was dressed in the old lace christening gown lent by Alice. All the family had assembled, that winter day.

'Tell me about the books you're intending to reissue,' Clemmie asked her mother, preparing to be instructed, as she was prepared to be instructed by her husband in the mysteries of paint and canvas. They were going over to the church in the afternoon, and were resting after lunch.

Sophie smiled and a different sort of satisfaction appeared on her face from the fond, but rather anxious, look she gave her baby granddaughter. 'Nobody will have read them for years,' she replied. 'I wanted to find old titles by women writers; if possible, ones who earned their living from their pens. Some did, you know, especially in the eighties and nineties. Errant husbands and too many children made it a necessity.'

'It's nice to know there were women before me who ran things,' said Clemmie innocently. 'Sometimes I wonder whether I've bitten off more than I can chew.'

Rosanna was asleep upstairs. 'I'm so thrilled to have her. It's incredible, isn't it? But I do wonder sometimes whether I'm doing the right thing, wanting to carry on my own ambitions . . .' she stopped.

Sophie was surprised. She had never thought such worries afflicted her youngest daughter.

'You will manage, Clemmie. I know you will. And it would be wrong to sacrifice all the other things you can do. Of course, you'll put Rosanna first if she's ill, and you'll never be as light-hearted as you once were; but the baby won't thank you for being possessive – you'd be surprised how quickly they grow up.'

Jack looked leaner, harder, stronger, when he came in to say it was time to go over to the church.

The baby had woken up and Sophie took her on her lap and gazed at her. She had the strong impression that, more than anyone else, Rosanna resembled her grandfather, Clem Bartholomew.

When the ceremony was over Rosanna was hungry, and was taken back straight away to Church Farm. Sophie and

Edith stood together at the back of the church. Edith took Sophie's hand and squeezed it.

'Well, we're still here,' said Sophie. 'Two old dears, I suppose. All those things I used to get so angry about,' she said. 'Here I am, in church again, seeing my granddaughter christened.'

'Perhaps you've changed,' said Edith.

'I suppose the rector thinks we all take belief for granted.'

'Clemmie is very realistic,' murmured Edith.

'Oh, they're doing what they want, those two. And they are both kind people. We should take *some* credit,' said Sophie. They stood there for a moment looking at the churchyard. 'We've come through,' Sophie said finally, and looked at Edith and imagined her as she had used to be, as the rays of winter afternoon sun came through thick branches on to her once golden hair, now grey.

They went towards the lych gate and stood and looked at the sky, all pink and crimson and gold bars and lakes and pure, small patches of pale green and violet. Michael was standing there, waiting for them.

'I was thinking; when Rosanna's our age it will already be the next century.' said Sophie to him.

'I was remembering that bit of Lucretius,' said Edith. 'The fire of life going on like a torch, handed from one runner to another in a relay race.'

They were all silent, then: 'Come along,' said Michael. 'We can go and drink to our mutual descendant. I expect you want some tea, Edith?'

Sophie paused for a moment, looking at a tombstone which bore the legend: 'The Lord giveth and the Lord taketh away'. 'I must tidy up Father's grave again tomorrow,' she said.

The three of them walked back together across the field path to the farm, Michael between his wife and most successful author. They all came up to the lighted farmhouse to join the others, and to contemplate the precious Rosanna. Their own immortality lay in the body of that tiny creature who had taken blood and bone from all three of them – and from Clement Bartholomew.

Later, Edith and Sophie, who had once walked these fields and gone out from them into the world and their own different futures, looked down silently at the now sleeping child, who

489

would one day choose her own path. Then they tiptoed out of the room to continue their own lives.